François Mauriac

A MAURIAC READER

TRANSLATED BY

GERARD HOPKINS

INTRODUCTION BY

WALLACE FOWLIE

NEW YORK
Farrar, Straus and Giroux

Originally published in French under the titles *La Pharisienne*, 1941; *Le Baiser au Lépreux*, 1922; *Génitrex*, 1923; *Le Desert de l'Amour*, 1925; *Le Noeud de Vipères*, 1932.

These translations by Gerard Hopkins first published in 1946, 1950, 1950, 1949, 1951. *Le Noeud de Vipères* in a different translation is published by Sheed and Ward under the title *Vipers' Tangle*.

Printed in the United States of America

Designed by Herb Johnson

A Kiss for the Leper

Genetrix

The Desert of Love

The Knot of Vipers

Woman of the Pharisees

Contents

The Art of
François Mauriac
by WALLACE FOWLIE

FRANÇOIS MAURIAC is the novelist of his province, of which
Bordeaux is the center. Only one river goes through it—
the Garonne—and only one social class of the province is described in the novels—the bourgeoisie, which is Mauriac's own
class. Nature in this province seems to be limited to two characteristics: the pine trees of Les Landes (a region near Bordeaux)
and the slopes cultivated by the vinegrowers. Such is the im-
mutable natural setting of the novels. The houses and the gardens around the houses are very much the same because they
belong to the vinegrowers or to the owners of the pine forests.
The silence inside the houses and outside is broken from time
to time by storms and by the sound of the ocean waves, at a
distance, as they crash against the sand of the beaches. A sudden hailstorm can demolish an entire vineyard. The fires that
so easily break out in the pine forests represent a constant
threat to the families that live in the large houses, almost as if
they were animals in their dens, at the edge of the *landes* (which
correspond almost to a waste land and often appear to be the
end of the earth, their roads lined with ferns as tall as a man
and with half-burned tree trunks.)

Because the bourgeoisie, with its fixed institutions and habits,
is the social world of Mauriac's novels, we are constantly aware
of the bourgeois dreams of money and legacies, of family rank
and prestige, of the divisioning of property, of family jealousies that
can be as momentous as revolutions in the province of Mauriac.

It has often been pointed out that Mauriac's world is as closed
and unchanging as the world in Racine's tragedies. It is a world
of three major characteristics: provincial, bourgeois and Christian. The key to Mauriac's art is his fidelity to this tripartite
world from which he never tried to escape, and which he continued to describe during all of his Paris years.

François Mauriac was born in Bordeaux, on October 11, 1885.
The following year his father died. He, his sister and three
brothers were carefully brought up by their mother, a very
pious woman who appears as a character in Mauriac's novel,
Le mystère Frontenac. The boy began his formal studies with
the Marianite fathers in a suburb of Bordeaux where he read
Pascal and Racine with special devotion. He prepared a *licence
ès lettres* at the Faculté des lettres in Bordeaux, where he
studied under Fortunat Strowski. In 1906, he went to Paris in
order to seek admission to the Ecole des Chartes. He was admitted, but decided not to attend. He had begun publishing
poems at this time, some of which appeared in *La Revue du
Temps Présent* and in *La Revue des Jeunes*. His first volume
of poems, *Les Mains Jointes*, appeared in 1909. He married
Jeanne Lafon in 1913. The Mauriacs had four children, two
daughters and two sons. During the war Mauriac served in the
medical division of the army. After the war, his life was divided
between Paris and his estate at Malagar, about fifty kilometers
from Bordeaux. The property has a vineyard overlooking the
Garonne River. It is quite accurately described in *Le Noeud de
Vipères*. In 1925, the Académie Française awarded the *grand
prix du roman* to *Le Désert de l'Amour*, and a few years later,
in 1933, elected Mauriac to the chair (*le fauteuil*) of Eugène
Brieux. A cancerous condition of the throat necessitated an operation on his vocal cords. During the Occupation, he published in the clandestine press under the name of Forez. His first
editorial appeared in *Le Figaro*, on August 24, 1944, and thus
began his career of political writer and commentator. He helped
to found *La Table Ronde* in 1948. On November 6, 1952, he was
given the Nobel Prize in literature, in recognition of his work
as novelist, dramatist, critic and journalist.

The official and auspicious beginning of Mauriac's literary career was the recognition of his first book of poems, by no less a
personage than Maurice Barrès, in *L'Echo de Paris*, March 21,
1910. The article briefly described the kind of poetry *Les Mains*

Jointes represented by saying its father was Verlaine and its grandfather was Sainte-Beuve, and then called upon the young writer to leave the troubled springtime of his life and become a man. Barrès's article was the prediction of a success that was to come twelve years later with *Le Baiser au Lépreux*, Mauriac's fifth novel, published in 1922. It was a short novel, of only one hundred and twenty-six pages, but it was a story of violence of a young man who believed himself ugly and incapable of inspiring love. It was the first victory in a long life of victories which paradoxically came from the creation of an art essentially consecrated to the depiction of personal torments. The early two volumes of verse, of which the second was *L'adieu à l'adolescence* (1911), did not in any way announce the kind of novel that Mauriac was to write. It was the poetry of a placid and wise child, who remembered and rehearsed his earliest religious practices. Nothing in the poems predicted the tragedies of the novels.

In the third novel, of 1920, *La Chair et le Sang*, the Mauriac situations and themes began to appear: in the figure of a young peasant seminarian who is cajoled by two youthful and wealthy aristocrats, in the themes of love and religion joining with class prejudices and an anguish over the emptiness of the world which is partly neurasthenia and partly metaphysical. The two words of the title, *la chair* and *le sang*, "flesh" and "blood," are the keys to all of Mauriac's works. André Gide, much later, will speak of his admiration for this novel.

In *Préséances*, of 1921, the fourth novel, Mauriac gave his first picture of the closed Bordeaux society, of the bourgeoisie controlling the wine industry, and the portrait of that type of youth isolated from the adult world and suffering over passions that are ill-understood. *Préséances* is not yet the Mauriac novel constructed around a "crisis," but it is a telling analysis of provincial snobbishness and of a certain form of human suffering. All the future characteristics of the Mauriac novel are in *Préséances*: the vague sadness of a young man aware of a mysterious and tragic dichotomy between the flesh and the spirit, equally disturbed by the bestiality of his instincts and by the signs of corruption in the society around him.

Mauriac's fear is not of man's instincts, but of sin, because the world he depicts in the province of Les Landes and Bordeaux is organized in accordance with mystical laws. The hero of the fifth novel, Jean Péloueyre (*Le Baiser au Lépreux*), is the subject of Mauriac's first profound study of a human life, of an ugly-looking boy whose existence is barren and solitary, but who, because his family has wealth, is given a beautiful wife, Noémie. Her husband's body is repulsive to her. The tragedy between the two is narrated swiftly and objectively, without digressions. With this novel, Mauriac created the form of fiction he will make his own: a tragedy of lust and love and silence, with no trace of oratory, no trace of eloquence. Success came quickly to *Le Baiser au Lépreux*, whose early printings soon reached the figure of 30,000 copies. It was published in *Les Cahiers Verts* of Bernard Grasset, in 1922.

This was the year of Proust's death. The group of writers associated with *La Nouvelle Revue Française* (which had begun appearing in 1909) were the most important figures at that time in Paris: Gide, Rivière, Suarès, Claudel, Proust. Very little attention had been paid to François Mauriac. But with *Le Baiser au Lépreux*, his name and his art became known, and he took his place that year beside the leading writers of France. The book was translated into English at the end of 1922, and *La Nouvelle Revue Française* began publishing serially *Le Fleuve de Feu*, the seventh novel, which was to appear in book form in 1923.

The title of the latter novel, "river of fire," is a mystical phrase from St. John, which Mauriac had undoubtedly come across in his readings of Pascal and Bossuet. It has to do with that aspiration to holiness, with that Eden-like purity Mauriac sensed in Rimbaud, and with the problem of concupiscence which seems to join the body with the soul. It is the most harassing problem in Mauriac's novels, the one he returns to endlessly in his efforts to understand the difference between a Rimbaud, whom he sees as a poet yearning for the absolute, a figure separated from all others in his life, and that type of young man he had seen in 1922, attached to the surrealist bars, mildly imitating Rimbaud but without the poet's genius. He writes of this problem, in its historical setting of the twenties, in his book *Journal d'un homme de trente ans*.

The study of eroticism, especially as it occurs in the life of a young man, is developed in *Le Fleuve de Feu* and in most of Mauriac's subsequent novels. This study is to become more explicit and more daring in the books of D. H. Lawrence, Henry Miller and Jean Genet, but Mauriac, perhaps more than he realized, asked questions concerning human behavior and proposed explanations that go very far in elucidating the origins and the forcefulness of sexual drives. *Le Fleuve de Feu* as a novel does not bear the formal perfection of *Le Baiser au Lépreux,* but it introduces into Mauriac's work the theme of sin, the theme of the conflict between good and evil, which will continue, with increasing emphasis, in the other novels.

Evil for Mauriac (he will name one of his novels *Le Mal*) is a man's own life, his own solitary existence. It is the closed-in space where his life unfolds, the very climate of the world he inhabits, the network of instincts that attract him and repulse him. Evil is that force that ties him to the rack. Such definitions of evil are not uniquely Mauriac's. They can be found in Bossuet, for example, and in other French writers. But the art into which such definitions are cast is Mauriac's own, and it is this form he perfected that gives him the high place he occupies in the history of the French novel.

For a drama to form in his mind, Mauriac has written (in *Le Romancier et ses personnages*) that he has to see it taking place in a setting where he himself has lived. He needs to be able to follow his characters from room to room. Even if the characters remain somewhat indistinct to him as a novelist, he is reassured if he can smell the mustiness of a corridor they walk down, or hear the sounds they hear in their daily life. As a child, and unknowing of what he was doing, he stored away in his memory scenes and smells and commonplace events, intonations of speech, themes of conversation that later in his life of a novelist he drew upon. The models of his characters were men and women he saw and listened to, but he claimed on many occasions that they became in his novels other kinds of men and women, characters, in a word, created by himself, for whom he alone was responsible.

First, as a boy living in his province and observing all of its customs, and later as the novelist of that province, Mauriac knew that such things as stables, laundry rooms, vegetable gardens, farmyards were integral parts of a family. Characters cannot be separated from their setting. A family is the atmosphere it creates and its setting is formed by small bits put together, whereby the present is explained by the past, and where one begins to see in venerable houses men and women living and suffering from monstrous desires and obsessions.

Genitrix, Mauriac's eighth novel, also published in 1923,

marks an advance in the novelist's skill in concreteness. For the first time he uses a device which he will develop and perfect in future writings: a device called in the art of film-making a "flashback," whereby the past is inserted into the present, and whereby the chronological sequence of the narrative is broken up. The title of the novel announces the drama between mother and son, the drama of a possessive maternal love. Félicité Cazenave exploits her triune power of woman, mother and widow. She is the first to be qualified as a "monster" in Mauriac's repertory of characters.

The son, Fernand Cazenave, after his young wife's death, caused to some extent by his neglect, is gradually obsessed by remorse, and a growing horror for his mother's tyranny. She, in her turn, dies, and the son, in total solitude, begins to reconsider the domination, the imposing power of his mother, who in death recaptures her initial role. *Genitrix* is the story of three characters: a young wife who is indirectly assassinated, her husband who is dispossessed of feelings that could have made him into a stronger character, and his mother, a terrifying figure of will power and cruelty.

The reception given to this book was laudatory. With it, Mauriac became a celebrity in French letters.

Le Désert de l'Amour, of 1925, is one of the most accomplished examples of Mauriac's art. The tragic elements of the story and the form in which the story is cast are more skillfully fused than they had been in the earlier novels. André Gide once described classical art as that form which tends toward litotes (*la litote*), namely an art using slight means to express a great deal. Mauriac's art is clearly representative of litotes. It is a sober condensing of very grave psychological problems.

In a Paris bar, Raymond Courrèges, aged thirty-five, recognizes Maria Cross, whom he had once known in Bordeaux and with whom he had fallen in love when he was eighteen and she twenty-seven. Before he speaks to Maria in the bar, his mind goes back to the two years of his youth, between sixteen and eighteen, when he was tormented by this passion. The main part of the novel begins here with a study of adolescent love, with the incommunicability of passionate love, with the strange bewildering law by which men fall in love with beings who do not love them. Mauriac says, as Racine had said in the seventeenth century in his tragedies, that we do not choose those whom we love. They appear in our lives, and we are incapable of not loving them. Hence, the desert of love, the solitude and the barrenness of love.

Between Raymond and his father, Dr. Courrèges, there is no understanding, no communication. There is a similar estrangement between the doctor and his wife. This is the background of family incommunicability against which Mauriac sets the dual passion of father and son for the same woman. The love of the doctor for Maria Cross is far more idealistic and patient than the son's love for her, which is violent and sharp. The personal drama of Maria Cross is more subtle and more complex than that of the two men who pursue her, each according to his own temperament and age. Maria is an indolent woman who arouses sensuality in men and then wishes to treat them as children.

The fact that Maria Cross is ostracized by the society of which his family is a part intensifies Raymond's attraction to her. There is a kinship between Maria's loneliness in Bordeaux, her role of almost a pariah and courtesan, and the insistent sexuality of the adolescent which cuts him off from the world, especially from the family world in which he had lived as a child before his sexual needs were felt.

This theme of the isolating power of sexuality is more overtly developed in *Le Désert de l'Amour* than in the other novels of Mauriac. The story derives its form from the sharpness and the relentlessness of this instinct in Raymond Courrèges. The center of the study is the hero's increasing assurance of his virility and of his indifference to everything in the world that his body was not created to penetrate. After using a tramway as the symbol of the strangeness and the stark anonymity of the first meetings and longings of Maria and Raymond, Mauriac uses an exterior scene of nature as prelude and prediction for the central scene of attempted seduction. A violent rainstorm ravages the garden outside Maria's house. Raymond crosses it to come to her and can hardly contain the pent-up energies and desires that urge him to perform an awkward and frustrating scene. His passion is wasted like the garden itself, and this defeat marks the beginning of his life of hardness, of his desert life in love.

On its publication in 1926, *Le Désert de l'Amour* was awarded a prize by the Académie Française. Before he published his next novel, *Thérèse Desqueyroux*, in 1927, Mauriac wrote several essays all of which were concerned directly or indirectly with the major themes in his novels: provincial life, Bordeaux, adolescence; and essays on a few writers who had influenced Mauriac's thinking about the absolute and about the persistent problems of desire and longing in relationship with the absolute: Pascal, Jacques Rivière, Proust. Of these essays, the one entitled *Le Jeune Homme* (1926) throws considerable light on Mauriac's understanding of adolescence and of the psychological problems obsessing the type of young man who figures in so many of his novels—Raymond of *Le Désert de l'Amour*, Augustin of *Préséances*, Daniel of *Le Fleuve de Feu*.

As a man advances in age, the repetition of his acts, the development of his habits, tends to determine his character and fix his life into something mechanized. It is a resignation to the past, to that slow accumulation of habits that form us and shape our character. The young man is the hero of his freedom, for Mauriac. Only a man of genius maintains this freedom in later life! Narcissicism is a strong ingredient in a young man's character, and this tendency to self-study and self-admiration protects him, according to Mauriac, from dangerous excesses. He must preserve his body and his appearance that give him pleasure. There are many different types of young men in Mauriac's books: refined and brutish, saintly and sinful, outgoing and surly, but they all have in common a nostalgia for childhood, for the purity of childhood. The source of a man's acts and of a woman's is childhood, and often Mauriac compares those acts, committed later in a man's life, to plants whose roots cannot be pulled up.

In the year or two that followed the publication of *Le Désert de l'Amour* and when he was writing *Thérèse Desqueyroux*, Mauriac explored carefully the universe he felt his books were forming, that universe defined by his province, by the habits and traditions of his provincial protagonists, by the young men inhabiting the province whose desires never seemed to be satisfied, who were obsessed by ambition or lust of one kind or another.

In *Thérèse Desqueyroux* Mauriac reached a degree of maturity in his outlook and an admirable control over his craft of a novelist. The character of Thérèse is a summation of his understanding of humanity, a witness to Mauriac's basic belief that a crime does not take place outside of humanity, that criminal monsters are also men and women. Thérèse did poison her husband, but at no point in the story was she criminally and deliberately the poisoner. Nothing is ever made that clear in Mauriac's art. The crimes in his novels are only partially, inadvertently committed. He makes it impossible for us to declare any of his characters fully responsible for a crime.

With *Genitrix*, and markedly with *Thérèse Desqueyroux*, the Mauriac novel became one that was built around a crisis. In the latter novel, Thérèse, after leaving the Palais de Justice in Bordeaux, where she heard the verdict of *non-lieu* (no grounds for prosecution), took the train back to Argelouse, the small town where she lived with Bernard. During the ride back, she recapitulated in her mind the details of her fate, *l'inimaginable destin*.

By brief soundings, by intermittent descents into the heart of his hero or heroine, Mauriac builds a story which, told otherwise, might appear unthinkable, unlikely. He will be accused of seeing only the drab and monstrous aspect of life. In his answers to such complaints (he published some of these in the first volume of his *Journal*, 1934), he has constant recourse to such writers as La Bruyère and Pascal, Montaigne and La Rochefoucauld and Chamfort, who discovered in the noblest acts of man traces of egoism and vanity and profit. Unlike Dostoevsky and Proust, Mauriac is unable to include all human traits in his novels, the good and the bad alike, provincial life and Parisian life, a single character and his complete social-historical situation. He claims he did not choose his characters. They were in him, because they came from his town and province.

When Mauriac wrote that his characters come from the most confused and troubled part of himself (*mes créatures naissent du plus trouble de moi-même*), Gide, in commenting on the text in his *Journal* (4 June 1931), pointed out that if Mauriac had been a more perfect Christian, he would not have had subject matter for his books.

Le Noeud de Vipères, of 1932, is a richer, more fully developed type of novel than the eleven novels Mauriac had published previously. It is the story of a family told by a shrewd avaricious member of the family. It is the journal of a man who despises the others in his family, and who despises himself. The family is called an organized, hierarchical cell which conceals the life of the family: rivalries, hatreds, jealousies, all forms of incompatibility.

The hero of the story, a man of sixty-eight, looks at his past

and tells of the various forms of hatred and revolt and vengeance his life represents. As he writes his journal, the members
of his family are waiting for his death. He tells of his failure
in finding love with his wife and his children. He speaks of the
torture that old age is for him, and the conviction that he has
had nothing from life and that he can expect nothing from
death. One child, Luc, son of his sister-in-law, seemed to like
him, but the boy was killed in war.

The phrase *The Knot of Vipers* is used by this man to describe
his heart. It is the picture of reptiles entangled with one another which only the sword of death can cut off. The journal
describes a heart proliferating with venom. His wife Isa, for
whom he is writing the journal, dies before he is able to give
it to her. God is alluded to at the very end, as if he were someone waiting: *comme si cette paix qui me possédait eût été
quelqu'un.*

The Mauriac heroes dream of sin without committing it.
They are the least free of fictional heroes in the sense that they
are always presented as being directed by and inhabited by
forces they cannot control. In a chapter of *Trois Réformateurs*,
Jacques Maritain accuses Rousseau of corrupting the thought of
modern man, of creating secrets in the heart of man today
that are closed off from the angels. Mauriac, in answering this
accusation, pointed out that Rousseau, if he helped to form
the sensibility of modern man, is not solely responsible for the
ills of the soul. But the subject matter of the novelist is for
Mauriac the passions of the heart and the sins that man is able
to commit. In analyzing these sins, the moralist and the philosopher can remain detached from them. But the novelist, the
man of imagination, cannot describe them without conniving
with them. In this literary-theological dispute, which involved
not only Maritain, but Gide as well, the word *connivence* is
everywhere present. Mauriac is well aware of the fact that
many Christian readers tend to reject him because of what
they find to be a complacent and even compromising picture of
evil in his novels. Agnostics, in their turn, tend to reject him
for limiting the world of his books to one where the doctrines
of sin and belief in God are too blatantly exposed.

La Pharisienne (1941) was the only novel Mauriac published
during the war, and for many years it was believed to be his
last novel, until in 1951 and 1952 he published *Le Sagouin* and

Galigaï. Gide called hypocrisy by various names: fraud, lying, duplicity, *mauvaise foi.* Mauriac called it pharisaism, because it is that turn of mind and that form of human experience where religion and lying meet.

The character Brigitte Pian, whose life story is narrated in *La Pharisienne,* is a hypocritical woman whose religious pride turns her into a monster. She is a type of believer who has never been absent from the history of Christianity. Whereas *Le Noeud de Vipères* is the monologue of a kind of monster, *La Pharisienne* is the story of a character told by a narrator, by the young son-in-law of Brigitte, Louis Pian. He speaks in the first person, and the novel is just as much the story of his own life as it is that of his stepmother. Brigitte Pian's religion is carefully, narrowly codified. Her sense of charity is regulated as if it were a clock. She observes the letter of the law rather than its spirit. The novel is a detailed study of a soul believing itself to be on the way to sanctity, and totally blind to the hypocrisy of its daily existence.

The work of the writer is for Mauriac the justification of his life. He would consider that his novels contain the essential truths about his life and his mind. On every page of his books, the novelist is at the bar defending himself and his ideas and pleading for the justification of his existence. Against the background of decorous conventionality in a Bordeaux household, Mauriac has projected characters of illogicality, of passion and complexity. These are his creatures and his creations. He is concerned with the deepest motivations within them, within their suppressed desires and their unspoken dream fantasies.

If the content of Mauriac's novels is somber and passionate, the form of his style permits him to say anything he wishes about his characters. The disorder of crime and chaotic mental states in the novels of Mauriac is offset by the sense of order which controls his writing. He believes that behind each novel there exists a part of the novelist's own life, a personal drama either directly experienced or imagined. Thus the writing of the books becomes a deliverance of personal suffering, of suppressed anger or desire. And the characters in the books almost resemble scapegoats, mystically loaded with the sins which had been committed or imagined by the novelist. His art is a transposition and not a reproduction of reality.

The major attack on Mauriac's conception of the novel (where

Mauriac believes the novelist has full knowledge of his creatures, although never denies them freedom of will) came from
Jean-Paul Sartre, in an article written before M. Sartre enjoyed
the fame he does today (*La Nouvelle Revue Française*, February 1939). The existentialist philosopher argued that the Christian writer, because of his belief in man's freedom, is admirably
suited to write novels. Dostoevsky would be a leading example.
But Mauriac, according to Sartre, sees the whole of his universe
at all times. His dialogue, like that of a play, is always effica-
cious and moves rapidly ahead, whereas the characters of Dostoevsky and Faulkner do not know what they are to say next.
They are freer than the creatures of Mauriac. And Sartre concluded that God is not an artist and neither is François Mauriac! This criticism of Sartre has, in its turn, been criticized as
greatly limiting the art of the novel. Mauriac is a descendent,
not from the novelists of the nineteenth century, from Balzac,
Flaubert and Zola, but from Pascal and Racine and Baudelaire,
writers whose sense of human tragedy is closely allied with a
religious interpretation of man's fate.

At the beginning of the century, Charles Péguy stressed the
important position which the sinner occupies in Christendom.
Le pécheur est aussi de chrétienté. Mauriac's novels illustrate
this significant and dramatic role of the sinner. It was particularly after the publication of *Les Anges Noirs,* in 1936, that
the criticism of Mauriac's themes grew almost into an organized
protest. His answer to this accusation is always the same. He is
interested in the problem of evil, and finds nothing exceptional
or outrageous in his characters. The newspapers alone furnish
sufficient proof that in every city, every day, crimes are committed that are more strange or more monstrous than those of
his novels. As a novelist, he isolates one of those cases and
analyzes its genesis and its development. A novel is a steady
floodlight focused on one of the lurid stories of passion which
the journalists dispatch with flagrant irony and disinterestedness.
Mauriac has called his novel a matter of "lighting" (*éclairage*).

Mauriac's characters testify to a human nature formed and
conditioned by a long background of orthodox Christianity. In
many of the characters there is only a nominal or hypothetical
adherence to the Catholic faith. And yet, the deepest part of
their nature reacts to the forces in them and around them, as if
the Church, acknowledged or unacknowledged, governed the

beginning and the end of human existence. Mauriac has always claimed that in such natures as these, the struggle between good and evil is clearer and more dramatic than it is in others. He claims that the Catholic, more than other Christians today, feels a more metaphysical or historical terror in the presence of sin and in the memory of sin. Many of Mauriac's characters live within a deep solitude, and this solitude is presided over by an ancient knowledge of sin. They are immobilized, not so much by their own personal experience of sin, as by some ancient sense of responsibility for the sins of mankind. The Mauriac character, even if he performs his religious obligations in the most perfunctory manner, even if he does not perform them at all, ties himself up with the sins of the dead, and fills his solitude with the terror that comes from the sense of solitude created by the alienating force of sin. The bareness of the Mauriac scene is in constant complicity with the bareness of his creatures' hearts. It would be difficult to discover in any literary traditions a more cosmic sense of evil.

The writings of Pascal still remain, especially in France, the chief source of psychological inquiry, in the Christian tradition. According to this tradition, the human heart is the microcosm of the universe, the container of immensity. Mauriac studies in his hero's heart, in Jean Péloueyre of *Le Baiser au Lépreux,* in Fernand Cazenave of *Genitrix,* in Raymond Courrèges of *Le Désert de l'Amour,* its tragic precision and uniqueness. As a novelist, he combines in a subtle and almost indistinguishable way the roles of Freudian analyst, in his study of the secret disorder of sin, and of the theologian, in his study of the origin of sin. Throughout the novel, the deepest part of man is imperiled. It is the dramatic representation in characters, of Pascal's wager passage (*si vous gagnez, vous gagnez tout; si vous perdez, vous ne perdez rien*), and one cannot tell which state will win out: grace or damnation. The typical novels, such as *Le Baiser au Lépreux, Genitrix* and *Le Désert de l'Amour,* are inconclusive in the theological sense, because the novel, as M. Mauriac conceives of it, is the story of the peril or the disorder in which the hero finds himself, and the novel stops at the moment when the peril may come to an end.

Pascal, abstractly as moralist and philosopher, and Mauriac, concretely as psychologist and novelist, depict the mysterious dignity of sin and the blindness of men who do not love what they think they love. If Mauriac appears Jansenistic by inspiration, he is not so doctrinally because of the freedom of his characters. In them he sees the constant unpredictable interplay of nature and grace. The leading trait of Mauriac's hero is perhaps his nostalgia for a lost purity. The novelist is concerned, as Pascal was, with the existential character, with the wretchedness of the soul without God. At one time, Mauriac defined himself as being the metaphysician working with the concrete. His excessive use of the word "drama" is a clue. In his mind, everything becomes a drama: love, passion, family, poverty, nature, evil, religion, grace.

Mauriac's range is not wide, but he has produced, within that range, remarkable books. His characters are authentically human beings. His chances for literary survival seem superior to those of such currently successful writers as Sartre and Camus who are better equipped philosophers than Mauriac. The best effects of Sartre and Camus are those of intellectual abstraction. The effects of Mauriac are those of a creation.

Mauriac's genre is the tragic novel, but a form in which external happenings have little importance. The novel is based upon psychological inquiry and development. On the surface, his characters lead normal lives, but inwardly they are victims of some grave conflict which the novelist projects as a force far more dramatic than any external event could be. This is the basis for Mauriac's succinct delineation of character, for the intensity of his tale, for the vigor of his images. If at times the dénouement appears weak and unprepared, it is because, as Mauriac himself would say, grace is always inexplicable and always fated to appear, in a novel, as a *deus ex machina*.

A Kiss for the Leper

A Kiss for the Leper

❀ I ❀

JEAN PÉLOUEYRE lay stretched upon his bed. He opened his
eyes. The scraping of cicadas sounded from all round the
house. Sunlight oozed between the slats of the Venetian blind
like molten metal. He got up. There was a sour taste in his
mouth. He was so short that the low dressing mirror reflected
his pinched little face, with its hollow cheeks and long, pointed
nose. It was red in colour, and seemed to have been worn away
like a stick of barley-sugar as the result of prolonged sucking.
His cropped hair grew to a point low on his prematurely wrinkled
forehead. When he grinned he showed his gums and a set of
decayed teeth. He was filled with a more intense self-loathing than
usual and addressed his image in words of pitying solicitude. "Go
out, and take a walk, you poor devil," he said, and ran a hand over
his ill-shaven chin. But how could he leave the house without waking his father? Monsieur Jérome Péloueyre had laid it down that
a solemn silence should be observed between the hours of one and
four. Nothing must be allowed to disturb his siesta, which was his
sole guarantee against the ravages of sleepless nights. The whole
house was frozen into immobility. Not a door was allowed to be
opened or shut, not a word or a sneeze must break the overwhelming silence. After ten years spent in begging and complaining he
had finally trained Jean and the servants to observe his instructions, and even occasional passers-by had got into the habit of
lowering their voices as they walked beneath his windows. The
very farm waggons took a roundabout way to avoid creaking past
his door. But in spite of all these careful arrangements for the
preserving of his slumbers, he was no sooner awake than he
began to complain of plates rattling, dogs barking, humans
coughing. Maybe he felt that utter silence might have produced

3

the sleep from which there is no waking, a sleep which empties itself in death as a river is emptied into the ocean. The return to consciousness was always, with him, a painful process. Shivering, even in the dog days, he would sit down with a book close to the kitchen fire. The flames were reflected in the polish of his bald head. Cadette, busy with her cooking, paid no more attention to the master than to the flitches hanging from the beams. He, on the other hand, kept close watch on the old country-woman. He never ceased to find it a matter for wonder that, though she had been born in the reign of Louis-Philippe, and had lived through wars and revolutions, her experience had been limited to the fattening of a succession of pigs whose deaths, each Christmas, drew from her bleary eyes a few poor tears.

The blazing heat of summer always exerted an irresistible attraction on Jean Péloueyre, in spite of his father's siesta. It brought him the assurance of solitude. He could slip down the street, keeping to the thin line of shade cast by the houses, safe from the giggling mockery of young girls seated with their sewing in the open doorways. The sight of him miserably slinking past was sure to provoke an outburst of feminine laughter, but at two o'clock in the afternoon the women were still asleep, sweating with the heat and complaining of the flies. The well-oiled hinges made no noise as he opened the door. He crossed the hall where the big store cupboards gave out a smell of damp and preserves, and the stench of boiling fat came from the kitchen. The flip-flop of his rope-soled shoes seemed but to intensify the silence. From its rack beneath a boar's head, he took down the small-bore rifle which was known to all the magpies for miles around. Jean Péloueyre was the sworn enemy of magpies. The umbrella-stand was filled with the walking-sticks of many generations—his great-uncle's gun-stick, his grandfather Lapeignine's fishing-rod and sword-stick, and sticks with iron ferrules which recalled holidays spent at Bagnères-de-Bigorre. A stuffed heron stood on a dresser.

Jean went out. The heat parted and then closed behind him like the water of a pond. He was bound for the spot where the stream, just before it flows through the village, makes a packed treasure of its icy coolness, rich with the smell of running water, beneath a clump of alders. But he remembered suddenly that on the previous evening he had been plagued by the flies. He

felt an urgent need to talk with some human creature. He
therefore directed his steps towards the house of Dr. Pieuchon,
whose son, Robert, a medical student, had come home for the
vacation that very morning.

There was no life about the place, no sign of life, though the
sun, streaming through the half-closed shutters glinted, now and
again, on a pair of spectacles pushed back on an old woman's
forehead.

He turned off between two blank garden walls. He was particularly fond of this narrow passageway, because there no
prying eyes could lie in wait for him, and he might walk at will
along it, deep in thought. Thinking, with him, was accompanied
always by much frowning, gesticulation, bursts of laughter, odds
and ends of poetry spoken aloud—in short, a complete pantomime productive of constant mirth to the people of the town.
But here the kindly trees drew close about his lonely colloquies.
Yet, how much rather would he have had about him the tangle
of a city's streets, where he could have talked *ad infinitum* to
himself and no one would have turned a head to notice him! Or
that, at least, was the picture he had painted for himself of
what life in the great cities was like. It was based upon what
Daniel Trasis told him in his letters. This friend, much against
his family's wishes, had gone to Paris to "take up literature".
Jean saw him in imagination poised for a leap into the hurly-
burly of the Paris crowds, cleaving them like a diver. By this
time, no doubt, he had learned to swim in that new element,
was already panting his way towards a clearly envisaged goal
—fortune, glory, love, all the rare and refreshing fruits which
hung out of the reach of Jean Péloueyre.

On silent feet he entered the doctor's house. The servant told
him that the gentlemen had lunched out. Jean decided to wait
for young Pieuchon, whose room opened from the entrance hall.
So eloquent was it of its owner that no one, seeing it, would
have felt the need to know more of him. There was a pipe-rack
on the wall, together with a number of posters announcing students' balls. A skull, with a cutty stuck mockingly between its
teeth, stood on a table. There were several books bought for
holiday reading: *Aphrodite*; *l'Orgie Latine*; *Le Jardin des Sup-
plices*; *Le Journal d'une Femme de Chambre*. A volume of
Selections from Nietzsche caught Jean's attention, and he began

to turn the pages. From an open trunk came the stale smell of a young man's summer clothes which have been stuffed away just as he took them off.

This is what Péloueyre read:

"What is the meaning of 'good'?—All that enlarges the sense of power in a man, the will to power, and power itself. What is the meaning of 'bad'?—Whatever is rooted in weakness. Let the weak and the failures perish: it is for us to see that they perish. What is more harmful than any vice?—Active pity for the feeble and the underdog: in fact, Christianity."

Jean Péloueyre put the book down. The words burst in upon him like the blaze of noon when the shutters of a room are thrown open. Instinctively he moved over to the window and let in the fury of the sun. He read the appalling passage through again. He closed his eyes, then opened them and stared at his reflexion in the glass. What a wretched little ferrety face he had, a country face. "Hobbledehoy" was what he had been called at school—and that was what he looked, with a miserable, undeveloped body, untouched by the normal miracle of puberty—a dainty offering, indeed, for the sacred founts of Sparta! He remembered how he had looked when he was only five, at the Convent School, and how, notwithstanding the superior social position of his family, all the prizes and good marks had gone to his pretty, curly-headed companions. He recalled the elocution test, in which, though he had read better than anybody else, he had been placed bottom. He sometimes wondered whether his mother, who had died of consumption, whom he had never known, would have loved him. His father had always made much of him, as of an ailing replica of himself, a feeble shadow which he trailed at his heels, as he shuffled in carpet-slippers through the world, or watched from his bed in the alcove that smelled of valerian and ether. Monsieur Jérome's elder sister, Jean's aunt, would doubtless have detested him—had it not been for the fact that the adoration with which she surrounded her son, Fernand Cazenave, with whom she lived in B——, a man of some importance and President of the Borough Council, so absorbed her energies that she barely noticed the existence of anybody else, could be said scarcely even to see them. There were times, all the same, when, with a smile or a word, she would draw Jean Péloueyre out from the state of nothingness

which was his normal existence, simply because she shrewdly
reckoned that this son of an invalid father, this poor wretch who
was destined for a life of celibacy and an early death, would
canalize the Pèloueyre fortune for the ultimate benefit of Fernand
Cazenave. . . . Jean took in at a glance the arid emptiness of his
life. He had wasted his three years at College in a series of
friendships all jealously guarded from the eyes of the curious.
Neither his boon companion, Daniel Trasis, nor the priest who
had taught rhetoric had ever really understood why he looked
so like a lost dog.

He opened the Nietzsche volume at another page and gulped
down the two hundred and sixtieth aphorism of *Beyond Good
and Evil*, which treats of the two moralities—the Morality of the
Masters and the Morality of the Slaves. He looked at his face,
which no amount of sunburn could make less yellow, repeated
Nietzsche's words, and listened to them moaning about his
brain like an October gale. For an instant he seemed to see
his faith lying like a stricken oak at his feet. Was not what he
saw, lying there on the ground in the sweltering heat, his faith?
No, no—the tree still held him tight with all its myriad roots. The
storm passed, and he found once more within his heart the beloved presence of a mystery under the thick foliage that now
again hung motionless about him. But he had suddenly made
the discovery that Religion, for him, meant refuge. For the ugly
orphan it had opened a way into the night of consolation. Someone upon the altar took the place of the friends he had never
had, and that devotion after the flesh which he would have
given to a mother had become concentrated upon the Virgin.
All the unspoken confidences which stifled him, were poured
out in the Confessional, or in his silent evening prayers, when
the shadow-laden vessel of the church gathered and held the
last remaining dregs of the earth's coolness. Then it was that
his heart broke like a shattered vase before the feet of the Invisible. Had he been curly-headed, like Daniel Trasis, had he
been blessed, like him, with the kind of face that women never
tire of stroking, surely he would not have stayed content with
a crowd of old crones and domestic servants? He was of the
race of slaves denounced by Nietzsche. He could discern in
himself the distinguishing mark of servitude. In his face he
bore the signs of an ineluctable damnation. His whole being was
made to be trampled underfoot. To that extent he resembled his

father—a man no less devout than himself, but with a greater knowledge of theology, who had been used at one time to wade patiently through Augustine and Aquinas. Jean, to whom dogma meant little, whose religion was all emotional outpouring, never ceased to wonder at Monsieur Jérome's more intellectual approach. All the same, he remembered the words which his father was never tired of repeating—'Where should I be now if I had not had Faith?' Not that faith, in his case, was strong enough to send him to Mass when he had a cold. On the major Feast Days, Monsieur Jérome was always accommodated in the overheated Sacristy, where he sat, swathed in mufflers, following the Office.

Jean Péloueyre went out. He walked, as before, between the two blank walls, watched by the silent, kindly trees, gesticulating. Now and again he deliberately pretended that the burden of his faith had fallen from him, that the buoy to which he had clung, which had kept him alive upon the waters of life, had vanished in a flash. It had gone, and nothing remained— nothing at all. He revelled in the sense of utter exposure, rolling it, like a flavour, round his tongue. Words forgotten since his schooldays came to his lips, pressing for utterance: " . . . *My wretchedness doth exceed my hope. . . . I praise thee, O Lord, that thou hast persevered with me. . . ."* A little further on he set himself to prove to an audience consisting of trees, piles of stones and blank walls that there have been Masters even among Christian men, that the Saints, the great Orders, the whole fabric of the Universal Church, have offered a sublime example of the Will to Power.

Wrought to a pitch of high excitement by his thoughts, he was recalled to the present only when he heard the sound of his steps upon the flags of the entrance hall—a sound which, when he reached the first landing, produced from somewhere an ailing murmur. A whining, sleepy voice was calling for Cadette, and was followed at once by the flip-flop of the servant's slippers as she moved across the kitchen floor. The dog barked. Shutters were thrown back. Monsieur Jérome was awake, and the house had cast off its spell of silence.

It was the hour of the day at which the old gentleman, with puffy eyes and a sour taste in his mouth, saw the world in its most sombre colours. Jean Péloueyre sought the refuge of the drawing-room (never used except when there was company),

which was as cool as a cellar. A mouldering wallpaper showed
the underlying plaster in patches. A clock divided up the passing
stream of time, though there was no one to hear its ticking. He
burrowed deeply into a thickly padded chair, bared within
himself the spot where Faith lay agonizing, and drew in deep
draughts of anguish. A fly buzzed and settled. A cock crew. . . .
There was a quick trill of birdsong . . . then another cock . . . a lot
of cocks. . . . He slept until that most delightful of all the hours
of the day when it had been his custom to walk through the
little winding lanes until he reached the church, where, entering by the smallest door, he would let himself drift aimlessly
about the scented darkness. Was all that over? Would he never
again keep that particular tryst? The only one that poor sluglike
Jean Péloueyre had ever known. He did not keep it now, but
went instead into the garden, where the setting sun made him
say: "It's getting less hot." The air was a flutter of white butterflies. Cadette's grandson was watering the lettuces—a good-
looking oaf with bare feet thrust into wooden clogs, and a great
favourite with the girls. Jean Péloueyre always avoided him, feeling ashamed to be the boy's master. Would it not have been
more fitting that he, the weakling, should serve this young and
glorious God of the garden? He dared not even smile at him
from a distance. Whenever he had to deal with country-folk, his
natural shyness almost paralysed him. Many a time he had tried
to help the curé with his parish work, and in Sunday School, but
had always slunk home in the darkness, oppressed by a feeling
of self-contempt, knowing himself to be stupid and an object
of universal mockery.

Meanwhile, Monsieur Jérome was strolling along the garden
path with its border of little bunchy pear-trees, with its heliotrope and mignonette and geraniums whose fragrance he could
not catch, so overwhelming was the scent of the great lime.
Monsieur Jérome dragged his feet. The ends of his trouser-legs
were tightly fastened between ankle and slipper. His battered
old straw hat had a silk band. He wore round his shoulders an
ancient knitted cape discarded by his sister. Jean recognized the
book he was carrying—a volume of *Montaigne*. No doubt, the
Essays, like his religion, served the old gentleman in the guise
of an alibi, made it possible for him to dignify with the name of
wisdom his failure ever to achieve anything. Yes, thought Jean
Péloueyre, his poor parent always gave the name of stoicism or

of Christian resignation, turn and turn about, to the utter use-
lessness of his existence. At that moment, Jean felt very clearheaded. Certainly, he loved his father, and as certainly he
pitied him, but the feeling of which he was most conscious
just now was neither love nor pity, but contempt! The sick man
was full of complaining—he had a pain in his neck, he couldn't
breathe properly, he felt sick. One of the tenant farmers, Du-
berne d'Hourtinat, had come storming into the house saying
that he'd got to have a room added to his cottage, so that he
might house a great clothes-press belonging to his married
daughter! Was there no place where he could suffer undisturbed? Nowhere he could be left to die in peace? And, to top
all, to-morrow was Thursday—which meant public market and
private invasion. His sister, Félicité Cazenave, and his nephew,
would reign supreme in the house. From dawn on there would
be no sleep for the invalid, because the cattle in the market
square would wake him. The din of the Cazenave's car at the
front door would herald the arrival of the weekly scourge. Aunt
Félicité would force her way into the kitchen and upset all his
feeding arrangements in the interest of those of her son. At
nightfall the couple would depart, leaving Cadette in tears and
the master at his last gasp.

Cringing and weak in the face of the enemy, Monsieur Jérome
fed his rancour in secret. He had grumbled so often about getting his own back on the Cazenaves that Jean paid no particular
attention this time when the old man said: "We can cook their
goose, Jean, if only you'll lend a hand—but will you?" Jean,
whose thoughts were a million miles away from the Cazenaves,
merely smiled. But his father was watching him. "You ought to
cut a smarter figure at your age," he went on. "How badly turned
out you are!" Though Monsieur Jérome had never before shown
the slightest interest in his son's appearance, Jean was not unduly perturbed. He had not the faintest premonition of what
was waiting for him at this critical turning-point of his life. He
took the volume of *Montaigne* from his father's hand. "My own
preference", he read, "is for a life that shall be unruffled, dull
and silent. . . ." Well, *their* life was most certainly unruffled, dull
and silent! They watched a puff of wind ripple the surface of
the water in the garden tank, where tadpoles were nibbling at
a dead mole. Monsieur Jérome, convinced that the dew was beginning to fall, hastened towards the house. Jean, with nothing

when the ancient brougham had stood waiting in the rain to take
him across the *Bazardais* to the religious establishment where the
children of the Landes sit poring over their dictionaries while
their thoughts are busy with the shooting season. His trunk,
which had once belonged to a great-uncle, still retained a few
scraps of its flowered paper lining. Monsieur Jérome had always,
on those occasions, broken down and sobbed, pretending that
he was in for one of his attacks—so cowardly had he been when
the terrible moment of parting actually arrived. It was more
than probable that the poor man's rule of silence dated from
that time, but the silence had always been faintly troubled by
the ailing presence of young Jean. And so it came about that
the boy had worked, until he was fifteen, with the curé, and had
never gone away to school at all, except when the time came for
him to take his baccalauréat. . . . What was this sudden whim
about getting him married? He remembered something very
odd that his father had said to him, the evening before in the
garden . . . but what was the use of worrying. He told himself
that people like him didn't get married. . . . The Cazenaves must
be mad to take so ludicrous an idea seriously. They were urging
his father now to tell them the name of the "intended", but the
arrival of siesta-time saved Monsieur Jérome from the necessity
of answering their questions. In spite of the heat, mother and
son went for a stroll in the garden, while Jean, in a perfect
frenzy of uneasiness, watched them from the passage window,
walking up and down, deep in talk.

The sound of the car starting up was a presage of departure.
The old gentleman woke from his slumbers, and Jean, as soon
as he heard the shuffling of paternal slippers, made his way to
the room that reeked of medicines. Within the walls of this evil-
smelling laboratory the truth was revealed to him. All this talk
of marriage was no joke. It was seriously intended that he should
take a wife, and that wife was to be Noémie d'Artiailh. The
long, three-panelled mirror showed Jean his body at full length.
It looked as shrivelled as heather after a heath fire. "But she'll
never have me," he stammered—and trembled as he heard the
unexpected reply: "She has already been sounded and shows
no dislike of the idea. . . ." Her parents were in the seventh
heaven, unable to believe in their good fortune. But Jean shook
his head. With outstretched hands he seemed to be warding off
a mirage. How could any young woman willingly come to his

arms? Noémie, glimpsed at High Mass—Noémie, with eyes like
two black flowers into which he had never dared to look?
When her mysterious body walked past him up the nave he
felt upon his own the little movement of the air set eddying
in her wake. He thought of it as of the only caress that he
had ever known. . . .

But all the while his father was droning on, explaining his
intentions, which were fully shared by the curé. The essential
thing was that there should be Péloueyres to come after them,
and so make it impossible for the property to pass either to
Aunt Félicité or to Fernand Cazenave. Monsieur Jérome added:
"When the curé makes up his mind to get something he usually
gets it, you know." Jean's smile was more like a grimace. The
corners of his mouth trembled, and he said: "She'll regard me
with horror." His father did not so much as dream of protesting. Never having been loved himself, it did not occur to him
that his son might possibly know a happiness which he himself
had missed. But he was perfectly prepared to run over the catalogue of Noémie's virtues. The curé had chosen her after careful
consideration. She was a shining example to the whole parish.
She was one of those who do not seek in marriage the joys of
the body. Gifted with a strong sense of duty, submissive to God's
ordinances and to her husband's will, she would develop into
one of those mothers who are still to be found, women whose
fundamental ignorance of life is proof against any number of
pregnancies.

Monsieur Jérome coughed and grew slightly sentimental. "Comforted by the knowledge that you are happily married and safe
from the Cazenaves," he said, "I shall face death with a mind
at rest. . . ." The curé was anxious that no time should be wasted,
that Jean's fate should be decided at once and his boats burned.
He had better speak to Noémie the very next day. She would be
waiting for him after luncheon at the Presbytery, where Madame
d'Artiailh would find some convenient excuse for leaving the
young people together. Monsieur Jérome's words poured out in a
torrent. Anticipating the inevitable discussion, and aware that
he would have to fight hard in order to overcome his son's un-
willingness, he felt nervously overwrought, and his hands were
trembling.

So complete was Jean's bewilderment that he could find

nothing to say. He was horribly ashamed at feeling so panic-struck. Here, surely, was an opportunity at last to escape from the herd of slave-men, and to act like a Master? This unique moment had been given him that he might break his chains and become a man. To his father's request that he should say something, he replied with a vague nod of assent. Later, when he came to look back on the instant of time in which his destiny had become fixed, he admitted to himself that ten ill-digested pages of Nietzsche had tipped the balance. He ran from the room, leaving Monsieur Jérome amazed at the ease with which he had carried the day, and impatient to let the curé know all that had happened.

By the time he had reached the bottom of the staircase Jean was already growing accustomed to the miracle, and felt him-self to be, in a vague sort of way, less chaste. Though he was still virgin, it had been revealed to him that virginity might not, perhaps, be a permanent state. He actually dared, in the secrecy of his mind, to conjure up a vision, and to gaze at it unflinch-ingly with brooding eyes. His head swam. It was enough to make him feel faint. He was seized by a desire to take a bath. It often happens in that part of France that baths are used for storage purposes, and the one belonging to the Péloueyres was filled with potatoes. These Cadette had to remove before it could be used.

After dinner, Jean Péloueyre took a walk through the little town. He was very careful not to gesticulate or talk to himself. Looking very stiff and official, he raised his hat to each group of persons he passed seated in front of their house doors. At his approach they fell silent, like frogs in a pond, but nobody laughed. Soon he had left the last of the houses behind, and the open road was before him, still white and blinding, stretch-ing between two ranged armies of black pines. The air was as hot as the inside of an oven, and the thousands of little recep-tacles standing by the trunks and filled with resin diffused a smell of incense about this great cathedral of the woods. At last he was free to laugh his fill. His shoulders shook, he cracked his finger-joints, he cried aloud: "I am one of the Master Race, the Master Race, the Master Race!" and repeated, again and again, certain lines of poetry, being careful to mark the caesura: "Par quels secrets ressorts—par quel enchainment—le ciel a-t-il conduit—ce grand événement?"

❊ *III* ❊

JEAN PÉLOUEYRE dreaded lest the conversation should peter out. The fear of silence was so strong in the curé and in Madame d'Artiailh that they felt impelled to touch on every conceivable topic, squandering their available material in a mad profusion. Very soon there would be nothing left to talk about. Noémie's dress overflowed her chair like a magnolia plant in a vase. In this shabby little parlour God was everywhere, on the walls, on the mantelpiece, but it was the smell of her young body that filled it. The sappy, untamed fragrance of July was unescapable, the fragrance of too strongly scented flowers which it is wise to remove from a room at nightfall. Jean turned his eyes, but not his head. Noémie had come down from her pedestal. It was as though, at this short range, he were seeing her through a magnifying-glass. Eagerly he scrutinized her, trying to see her faults, to descry the "flaws" in this quivering, living metal. There were blackheads on her nostrils. The skin at the base of her throat seemed to have been burned by too violent an application of iodine, which ought to have been washed off. At something the curé said she showed, in a sudden smile, a pure white palisade of teeth. They flashed for a moment only, but long enough to give Jean Péloueyre a glimpse of one of the incisors which looked faded and suspect. Embarrassed by his gaze, she kept her large, dark eyes lowered. It may well have been that he was looking hard at her so that she should not look hard at him!

The curé, Heaven be praised, was perfectly capable of carrying on the conversation unaided, and could continue indefinitely with his desultory prosing. It was easy to see, for all his plump body, that he was essentially an austere man. The dwellers in the outlying farms regarded him as something of a mystery, but in the town itself he was much beloved, and many a soul, under his direction, had reached a high degree of sanctity. It sometimes happens that the meek *do* inherit the earth, and his was a case in point. In manner he was quiet and retiring, but he had a will of iron—though he could bend it as circumstances might require. He always kept the prettiest girls away from the weekly dances, and set his face, with professional austerity,

against the amorous propensities of the local lads. That he had
rescued the postmistress from the very brink of adultery was
not generally known. And now, he had come to a definite
decision in his own mind that for Jean Péloueyre to remain single
would do him no sort of good. It was, too, a matter of some
importance to this shepherd of souls that the House of Péloueyre
should not, one day, become the House of the Cazenaves, that
the wolf should not be made free of the fold.

Never, till now, had Jean noticed how deeply women breathe.
Each time that Noémie inhaled, her breast very nearly touched
her chin. . . .

. . . The curé decided to abandon all further pretence. He got
up, saying that doubtless the dear children had a good many
matters to discuss, and invited Madame d'Artiailh to go with
him into the garden and see how the greengages were coming
along.

It was as though the dark room had now become merely the
scene of an entomological experiment, with one little black,
frightened male left confronting the female in her glory. Jean
Péloueyre no longer moved at all, no longer even raised his
eyes. It would have served no purpose to do so. He sat there,
imprisoned in her gaze, while she took the measure of the larva
that was to be her destiny. The beautiful youth with the face
that never remains the same for two moments together, and who
haunts the dreams of all young girls and keeps them tossing
sleepless on their beds, obsessed by the image of his firm, hard
body and the taut pressure of his arms—had melted away in the
shadows of the priest's parlour, had faded so completely that
now there was nothing left of him but a frightened cricket cow-
ering in the darkest corner available. She looked her destiny
straight in the face, knowing that it could not be avoided. The
idea of refusing the son of the Péloueyres was impossible.
Noémie's parents might live in constant fear of the young
man taking to his heels, but that their daughter should raise any
objection would never have occurred to them.

For the last quarter of an hour all that life had to offer her
had been sitting biting his nails and twisting and turning on
his chair. He got up. He looked smaller standing than he had
done seated. He stammered out something, but she seemed
not to hear. He repeated the words: "I know I don't deserve . . ."
At this she protested: "Oh, Monsieur. . . ." He abandoned him-

self to a mad access of humility, said that he fully realized no one could ever love him, and asked only that she might let him love her. He had found his tongue at last, and his sentences began to take shape. It had taken him twenty-three years to reach the point of pouring out his heart to a woman. In an effort to express the beauty of his feelings, he gesticulated as though he had been alone—and that was precisely what he was.

Noémie looked at the door. She felt no surprise. All her life she had heard people say that Jean Péloueyre was a "card", a "bit touched in the upper storey". On and on he talked, and the door stayed fast shut. This fantastic, gesticulating creature was the only living human being in the whole house. She began to feel uncomfortable. There was a lump in her throat. At last Jean stopped, and she felt the same kind of fear as when one knows that a bat has got in through the window and is hiding. When the curé and Madame d'Artiailh returned she flung her arms round her mother's neck, not dreaming that her emotional outburst would be interpreted as an expression of assent. But already the curé had touched Jean's cheek with his own.

The two ladies left the house unaccompanied, so as to avoid rousing curiosity among the neighbours. Jean Péloueyre, peering through the shutters, saw Madame d'Artiailh's brittle, skinny figure moving away down the road, and Noémie trotting behind her like a dog. Was he aware of the slightly rumpled dress that would never again bloom in its pristine glory? did he realize that, in the bent neck, he was seeing the outward sign of a flower that had been cut and was already wilting?

The clumsy youth, accustomed to hiding from the world and determined to pass unnoticed, remained for several days bewildered and stupefied by all the hullabaloo that raged about him. Destiny, like a magic formula, had snatched him from obscurity. Nietzsche's words had tumbled the walls of his cell in ruins. With shoulders hunched, and blinking eyes, he went about like some night-bird blundering at noon. The people about him were changing, too. Monsieur Jérome broke all the rules of his carefully ordered existence, and took to interrupting his siesta in order to accompany the curé on his way to the Sacristy. No longer did the Cazenaves put in an appearance each Thursday. The only sign of life they gave took the form of circulating atrocious stories about Jean Péloueyre's general state of health, with references to certain peculiarities which, so it was said, rendered him highly unsuitable as a subject for matrimony.

Jean, meanwhile, looked out upon the world from the depths of his humility, marvelling to think that the d'Artiailhs should actually be envied on his account. Everyone was saying that Noémie deserved her good fortune—no one more so. Her family was a very old one, but it had come on evil days. Monsieur d'Artiailh, having been fleeced in several business ventures, had quite unashamedly been reduced to filling a minor post at the Mairie. It was no secret that he and his wife had had to give their "general" notice at Easter. Jean Péloueyre, looking at himself in the glass, decided that he was not so ill-favoured after all. Wherever the curé went he made a point of saying that though the Péloueyre boy might not be much to look at, he had a very superior mind. The respectful silence in which Noémie sat each evening while, stretched on the drawing-room sofa, her affianced listened to himself keeping up his end in conversation, led him to conclude that what the curé said was true, and that what a serious-minded young woman really valued in her husband-to-be was intellectual distinction. He was as little constrained in her presence as he had been, formerly, on his lonely tramps. He grimaced, gesticulated, and quoted odds and ends of verse without prefacing them with any comment, while the lovely creature, snuggling in a corner of the same sofa, appeared to lend as willing an ear to his talk as once the trees had done that lined the empty roads.

He observed no reticence in his confidences, and went so far as to tell her all about Nietzsche, whose influence might well force him to alter his whole attitude to the problem of moral obligation. She sat there, wiping her damp hands with a tiny handkerchief rolled into a tight ball, and staring at the door beyond which her parents were busy whispering, though she could not, thank Heaven, make out the sense of what they were saying. The general gossip on the subject of his future son-in-law was beginning to cause Noémie's father a deal of anxiety. At every important moment of his life he had been robbed and cheated, with the result that he could not help feeling that this apparent dawning of good fortune must conceal some threatening disaster. His wife, however, maintained that the only basis for these slanderous tales was deliberate mischief-making on the part of the Cazenaves, and the fact that, hitherto, women, as a result either of religious scruples or natural timidity, had played no part in Jean Péloueyre's life.

As soon as eleven o'clock sounded through the moonlit silence, she would open the door, omitting all preliminary of cough or knock. She had long given up all hope of finding the young people in anything that might even remotely be called a compromising situation. Still, she apologized for interrupting the "turtle-doves", but pointed out that it was well past "curfew" time. Then Jean would bestow a fluttering kiss on Noémie's hair and walk off down the street with only his shadow for company. His triumphal progress wakened the watch-dogs, and the brightness of the moon kept them from going to sleep again. Thus, even at nighttime, his presence filled the village with noise. The curious thing was that he no longer felt the kind of emotional thrill that had come to him when, in church, Noémie, in her freshly ironed dress, had driven ahead through the enclosing air. He shook his head in an endeavour to put from him all thought of that September night when she would be his to do with as he willed. It might never come. A war might break out. Somebody might die. There might be an earthquake. . . .

Noémie d'Artiailh, in her long nightdress, was saying her prayers, watched only by the stars. She loved the feel of the cold tiles beneath her naked feet. Upon her tender breast she felt the cool compassion of the night. A tear slid down her cheek within reach of her tongue. She did not wipe it away, but licked it off. The quivering of the lime-tree and the scent of its blossoms seemed, somehow, to melt into the Milky Way. No longer did her dreams, of fancy bred, wander at will along the highways of Heaven. The crickets scraping away beside the hole in which they lived reminded her of her lord and master. One night, lying outside her sheets, a prey to the hot darkness, she broke into little whimpering sobs, and then groaned deeply, looking at her chaste, her untouched body that burned with all the vigour of young life, yet was fresh as any flower. What would her cricket do with it? She knew that his rights over her would be supreme, that he might caress her as he willed, might perform that fearful act of mystery, after which a child would be born to her, a tiny Péloueyre, black-haired and weakly. . . . Never, for the rest of her life, would she be free from her cricket. He would be with her always, even in her bed. Her mother, who had caught the sound of moaning, came

in to her (all scalloped nightdress and scanty, plaited hair). On
the spur of the moment the girl invented a story to the effect that
the idea of marriage was hateful to her, that she wanted to enter a
Carmelite Convent.

Madame d'Artiailh, without attempting to argue, took her in her
arms and held her close until the intervals between her sobs grew
longer. Then she assured her that, in matters of this kind, one
should always go for advice to one's spiritual director. But had
not that advice been already as good as given? Was it not the
curé himself who had chosen for her the way of marriage? Well-
trained little daughter that she was, all gentleness and piety,
Noémie could make no answer. She never read novels. She was,
as it were, a servant in her parents' house, bred to obedience.
They told her that good looks were not essential in a man, that
marriage produces love as a peach-tree produces peaches. . . . But
all this was unnecessary. In order to convince her it was enough
to repeat the popular saying of that neighbourhood, that *the son
of the Péloueyres is not the sort of man a girl refuses*. No, a son of
the Péloueyres was not the sort of man a girl refused. One didn't
refuse farms—tenant and freehold—flocks of sheep, silver plate,
linen that was ten generations old and lay neatly piled in tall,
deep, sweet-smelling presses—the chance, in short, of marrying
into the best that local society could offer. One didn't refuse the
Péloueyre boy.

❀ IV ❀

THERE was no earthquake, nor were there portents in the heavens. Dawn on that Tuesday in September broke gently over the
earth. Jean Péloueyre had slept so soundly that it was necessary to
wake him. The flags of the entrance hall and the stone threshold
of the front door were almost invisible beneath the spread foliage
of box and laurel and magnolia. The many odours of the house
were drowned in the scent of that trodden scattering of flowers.
The bridesmaids, incapable of sitting down in their long dresses,
stood whispering together. The bar-parlour of the *Cheval-Rouge*
was festooned with paper garlands. The breakfast would arrive,
ready cooked, by the ten-o'clock train from B———. Along all the

roads victorias were bringing in whole families of white-gloved
guests. The sun shone on the badly brushed top-hats of the men
whose "swallow-tails" kept the country-folk agape with admiration.

Monsieur Jérome unmasked his batteries. He had decided to
stay in bed. That was his way of ignoring all such things as fu-
nerals and marriages among his neighbours. In those solemn moments he always swallowed a tablet of chloral and drew his
curtains. It was remembered how, when his wife lay dying, he
had gone to bed on the top floor of the house, lying with his face
turned to the wall, and had refused even to open an eyelid until
he could feel sure that the last spadeful of earth had been shov-
elled on to the coffin, that the last guest had been safely packed
into the train. On this morning of his son's marriage he forbade
Cadette to throw back the shutters when Jean Péloueyre, looking
like a green lad, and lost in the panoply of his wedding garments,
came in to ask his blessing.

It was a terrible day! Shame and timidity flowed back with
sudden force to overwhelm Jean Péloueyre. Though the procession moved through a din of bells, his sense of hearing, sharpened
by long years of shooting trips, enabled him to catch the pitying
comments of the crowd. He heard a man's voice murmur: "What
a dam' shame!" Young girls, perched on their chairs, spluttered
with laughter. Halfway between the blaze of the altar candles and
the muttering congregation, he swayed, and caught at the velvet-
covered prie-dieu for support. He could feel the mystery of a
woman's body trembling at his side, though he did not turn to
look at her. . . . The curé began to read. On and on he went. . . . If
only he would go on for ever! But the sun, scattering confetti on
the old worn stones, would sink at last—and then would start the
reign of the revealing night

The heat had turned the food. One of the crayfish smelled bad.
The ice-pudding was running and had melted to a mess of yellow
cream. The flies preferred to be crushed rather than abandon the
dishes of pastry, and fat women were suffering tortures of constriction in their tight clothes. Patches of sweat remorselessly
stained the fabric of their bodices. Only the children, seated at a
table apart, yelled for joy. Peering from his abyss of misery,
Jean Péloueyre watched the faces around him. What was Fernand
Cazenave whispering to one of Noémie's uncles? Like a deaf-mute
Jean read the meaning of the phrase in the movement of his lips:

"If only they had listened to us, this tragedy might have been avoided. But things being as they are, we couldn't very well interfere."

⚘ V ⚘

THE bedroom of the Family Hotel at Arcachon was furnished in imitation bamboo. There was no curtain to hide the domestic objects ranged beneath the washstand and the wallpaper was stained with the marks of crushed mosquitoes. A mingled smell of fish, seaweed and salt-water drifted in from the harbour. The purring of a motor-boat receded in the direction of the outer channel. Two guardian angels hid their shamed faces in the folds of the cretonne window-curtains. Long was the battle waged by Jean Péloueyre, at first with his own ice-bound senses, and then with the woman who was as one dead. As day was dawning a stifled groan marked the end of a struggle that had lasted six long hours. Soaked with sweat, Jean Péloueyre dared not make a movement. He lay there, looking more hideous than a worm beside the corpse it has at last abandoned.

She looked like a sleeping martyr. Her matted hair clung to her forehead as in the throes of death, accentuating the thinness of a face which might have been that of a beaten child. Her hands, crossed on her innocent breast, clasped a faded scapular and a necklace of sacred medals. Someone should have kissed her feet, lifted her tender body, and run with it, still unwaked, to the open sea, there to leave it to the chaste mercies of the creamy foam.

⚘ VI ⚘

ALTHOUGH their circular ticket was valid for three weeks, they descended upon the Péloueyre home ten days after the wedding. The town was alive with chatter, and the Cazenaves, without waiting for their usual Thursday, hastened round to read the

news in Noémie's face. But the young woman kept the secret of
her heart well hidden. The d'Artiailhs and the curé soon put a
stop to all the talk. The young turtle-doves, they said, had merely
preferred the peace of the family hearth to the noisy bustle of
hotels and railway stations. Emerging from the church, after
High Mass, Noémie in her finery smiled as she shook hands with
all and sundry. If she could laugh it must mean that she was
happy. Her regular attendance at daily Mass caused no astonishment. Several women made a mental note of the fact that, when
she had taken Communion, she remained on her knees with her
thin, sad face hidden in her hands. The conclusion drawn from
her despondent looks was that she was pregnant. Aunt Félicité
turned up one day to gauge with furtive and appraising looks
the size of her waist. But an intimate talk with Cadette—the
ancient Sybil was found presiding over the weekly washing—
reassured her. From then on she thought it politic to stay away,
not wishing, she said, to seem, by her presence, to approve a
monstrous union which had been the work of priests. She planned
to reappear upon the scene at the very first rumblings of a drama
the opening of which could merely be a matter of time.

Meanwhile, Monsieur Jérome was amazed to find that his
daughter-in-law looked after him with all the passion of a Sister
of Saint-Vincent-de-Paul. She brought him his various medicines
at precisely the right times, arranged his meals in accordance
with a strict dietary, and, with gentle authority, enjoined complete silence upon everybody when he was taking his siesta. As
in the old days, so now, Jean Péloueyre made good his escape
from the paternal home, and still crept along the least-frequented
lanes, clinging to the walls of the houses. Hidden behind a pine-
tree on the edge of a field of millet, he would watch for magpies.
He would have liked to hold each passing minute captive, and
so keep off for ever the coming on of night. But with every day
that went by the light began to go earlier. The pines, surrendered
to the fury of the equinoctial gales, gave out a muted echo of
the roaring of the fierce Atlantic storm that reached them from
the sands of Mimizan and Biscarosse. Above the dense bracken
rose the little huts of turf which the people of the Landes use in
October for shooting the wild pigeon. The smell of rye bread
gave a sweetness to the air about the farmsteads. As the sun
sank he would have a few last shots at the homing larks. The
nearer he came to the town the slower he walked. There was

still a little time left, a short while, before Noémie would begin
to suffer from the feeling of his presence in the house. He crossed
the hall on tiptoe. She was always on the look-out for him, a
lamp held high, and went to meet him with a smile of welcome.
She offered her forehead to his kiss, felt the weight of his game-
bag, and went through all the movements of a wife who is made
happy by the return of her best-beloved. But it was only for a
few minutes that she played her part. Not for a moment did she
deceive herself with the thought that she had taken him in. During the evening meal Monsieur Jérome saved them from the embarrassment of silence. Now that a young nurse had charge of
him, he was for ever describing his symptoms. She had taken
upon herself the duty of interviewing the tenants, and had much
estate business to discuss with him. He was filled with an admiring wonder that this young girl should be the only person
in the house capable of checking the agent's accounts and keeping an eye upon the sale of pit-props. He attributed to her, also,
the fact that he had put on well over four pounds since his son's
marriage.

When the meal was over, and Monsieur Jérome sat dozing with
his feet on the fire-dogs, husband and wife would find themselves
at last irremediably alone. Jean Péloueyre settled down as far as
possible from the lamp, scarcely breathed, and did his best to
fade into the surrounding darkness. But nothing could alter the
fact that he was there, and at ten o'clock Cadette brought in the
candles. The journey up the stairs was terrible! The autumn rain
whispered on the roof, a shutter banged, a farm waggon rumbled
into the distance. Noémie, kneeling beside the dreaded bed, repeated in a low voice the words of her evening prayer: "O God,
here on my knees, I thank thee that thou hast given me a heart
capable of knowing and of loving thee. . . ." In the darkness Jean
Péloueyre could feel the adored body shrink away from him. He
put as much space between them as he possibly could. Now and
again Noémie, stretching a hand to touch the face which now,
because she could not see it, seemed less odious, would find it
warm and moist with tears. At such times, filled with remorse
and pity, she would strain the unhappy creature to her, as, in the
Roman amphitheatre, a Christian virgin might, with closed eyes
and teeth fast clenched, have leapt forward to throw herself
before the waiting beast.

❀ *VII* ❀

PIGEON shooting served Jean Péloueyre as a pretext for spending
whole days away from her whom, by the mere fact of his presence, he hourly murdered. So quietly did he get up that Noémie
never waked. By the time she opened her eyes he was already
far away, jolting over the muddy roads in a country cart. He
took out the horses at one of the farms, hid himself close to a
turf hut, and whistled, always on tenterhooks lest a covey might
already have been sighted. Cadette's grandson shouted, in response to his signal, that he could come on, and then the waiting
began—long hours of mist and day-dreaming lulled by the sound
of sheep-bells, the cries of shepherds and the cawing of rooks.
By four o'clock sport was over for the day, but, in order to avoid
reaching home until the last possible moment, Jean would slip
into the church. He said no prayer, but just stood there, a bleeding victim, in Someone's presence. Often the tears would start
to his eyes: often he felt as though his head were resting on invisible knees. . . .

When he got back he pitched on to the kitchen table his "bag"
of slate-coloured birds, the half-swallowed acorns showing as
lumps in their crops. Then he would stretch his feet to the blaze
until his boots began to smoke. He could feel the bitch's tongue
warm on his hand. Cadette would be busy soaking bread in the
soup and he would follow her into the dining-room. Noémie would
say: "I didn't know you had got back"—and then, "Do go and
wash your hands." That would send him upstairs to the bedroom,
where the shutters had not yet been closed. . . . A lamp shone
on the rain-filled ruts of the road. . . . He washed his hands, but
did not bother about cleaning his nails. He was careful to keep
them hidden under the edge of the table so that Noémie should
not notice. He gave her a sidelong look. How white her ears
were! She had no appetite. Clumsily he pressed her to take a
second helping of mutton. "But I'm not hungry, I tell you!" A
faint, submissive little smile, and sometimes the vague pursing of
her lips into the semblance of a kiss, would take the edge off these
short, sharp bursts of impatience. She looked at her husband
with the direct gaze of a woman who, at her last gasp, and

comforted by faith in Heaven, looks straight at death. She continued to smile as one wishing to comfort a sick man who is
near to dying. . . . It was he, Jean Péloueyre, who had brought
those heavy shadows to her eyes, who had drained the colour
from her ears, her lips, her cheeks. The simple fact of his being
there was enough to suck the life from this young body. The
very ruin that he caused made her all the dearer to him. Was
ever a victim more truly loved by her executioner?

Monsieur Jérome was the only one among them all who flourished. The gentle old man was unaware of any suffering but his
own. To the amazement of those about him, he announced with
delight that he felt considerably better. His asthma was less persistent than it had been, and he was managing to doze into the
early hours without the help of any drug. Having to deny himself
Dr. Pieuchon—whose son had had a haemorrhage and was
being treated at home—had brought him luck—or so he said. Fear
of infection had led him to break off all communication with his
old friend. He swore that his daughter-in-law could do all that
was necessary, and that she was more experienced than any
doctor. Nothing disgusted her, not even having to help him
when he visited the lavatory. She had a knack of making the
dreariest diet palatable. Condiments were forbidden so she sub-
stituted lemon and orange juice, and occasionally a drop of old
Armagnac. In this way she roused his appetite, which had been
dormant for fifteen years. She had taken to reading aloud in order
to assist his digestive processes, and, though she was nervous at
first, soon did it well.
  She was quite tireless, and never stopped, pretending not to
notice the old man's regular breathing, which always meant that
he was dropping off. The clock struck. One more hour subtracted
from the shuddering horror of the dark nuptial chamber: one
hour less of having to watch the movements of that horrible
body stretched beside her and pretending, out of pity for her, to
be asleep. Sometimes the feel of his leg would wake her, and
then she would slip into the space between the bedstead and the
wall: or a light touch would set her trembling. He, thinking her
asleep, would venture on a furtive kiss. When that happened it
was her turn to simulate unconsciousness. For she always feared
that, finding her awake, he might be tempted to go further.

❊ *VIII* ❊

THEY never had any of those quarrels that usually flare up between lovers. They knew themselves to be so deeply wounded
that they dared not strike at one another. The tiniest cause of
offence would have carried mortal poison, would have been beyond all hope of cure. Each was scrupulous never to touch the
other's sore spot. Their every gesture was carefully calculated to
spare unnecessary pain. While Noémie undressed he looked the
other way, and never went into the bath-room while she was
washing. He acquired new habits of cleanliness, ordered a quantity of *Eau de Lubin*, with which he drenched himself, and shivered in a cold bath every morning. He held himself to be solely
to blame for what had happened, while she was filled with self-
loathing because she was not a wife pleasing to God. No reproach, even unspoken, ever passed between them. The eyes of
each implored the other's pardon. They decided to say their
prayers side by side. Enemies in the flesh, they found union in
their nightly supplications. Their voices at least could mingle.
Kneeling there together, each in a world apart, they met in
the infinite.

One morning they met, entirely by accident, at the bedside of
a sick old man. They jumped at this new pretext of proximity,
and, therefore, once each month, paid regular visits to all the
sick of the neighbourhood, each giving to the other credit for
this act of charity. On all other occasions Noémie carefully avoided
Jean, or, rather, her body avoided his, while he was for ever in
flight from her disgust of him. She tried, but in vain, to react
against her sense of physical repulsion. One gloomy November
day, though she hated walking, she forced herself to follow him
out upon the heath as far as the deserted marshes, where the
silence is so intense that just before a storm blows up one can
hear the muted thud of the Atlantic surges on the sand of the
seashore. The blue-eyed gentians were no longer in flower. She
strode ahead like someone seeking to escape a danger, and he
followed some way behind. The shepherds of Béarn, from whom
Jean Péloueyre was descended, and who enjoyed rights of pastur-
age on these bare lands, had, many centuries before, dug there

a drinking pool for their herds, and on its muddy brink husband and wife stood for a while together. Jean's thoughts were busy with those long-dead peasants who had fallen victim to that mysterious ailment of the Landes, the "Pellagra", and had invariably been found at the bottom of pools like this one, or with their heads buried in the slime at the edge of a standing water. He, too, longed to clasp between his arms the niggard earth that had moulded him in its own likeness, and to end his life stifled by its kiss.

❀ I X ❀

NOÉMIE'S reading was often interrupted by a visit from the curé. He called her "my child", and accepted her offer of a glass of home-made cordial. But he seemed no longer able, as in the old days, to embark on theological arguments with Monsieur Jérome, or to amuse him with stories of the local clergy. He was a judge in whose presence they all put on their masks. Their eyes were expressionless. They felt that he could read their hearts. The conversation was desultory, and he no longer felt at ease. His every word seemed to point to something which, as yet, could not be clearly seen. He stretched his short, swollen legs to the blaze, and would suddenly, now and again, shoot quick glances at the silent couple, and then turn his eyes away. Less peremptory, less sure of himself, than he had been once, he had for some time given up retailing—as he had loved to do—those passages of words in which he had become involved with some local rationalist, passages always thickly studded with the recurring phrase—"And then I floored him by saying. . . ." Monsieur Jérome remarked that he had never seen the curé so worried since the day when a former Mayor had announced his intention of having the church bells rung for civil burials, and to use the hearse which, by rights, belonged to the ecclesiastical authorities. The curé was anxious that Jean Péloueyre should resume work on a piece of historical research relating to the parish, upon which he had once eagerly embarked, only later to abandon it. The young man gave as his excuse the absence of several essential documents. The truth of the matter was that his enthusiasms were shortlived, and that he never completed anything that he undertook. The first few pages of the books he read were always scribbled over with notes, but the last were left uncut. He could not think properly unless he was walking, with the result that he never settled down for long at his writing-table. One evening, when Monsieur Jérome had gone to bed, the curé insisted on reopening the subject. Jean Péloueyre maintained that it would be quite impossible for him to carry his work further unless he could consult certain specialized books at the Bibliothèque Nationale. A journey to Paris, however, was not to be thought of. . . . "And why not, dear boy?" The curé asked his question in a low voice, playing all the while with the fringe of his sash, and keeping his eyes obstinately fixed upon the fire. A very small murmur made itself heard: "I shouldn't like Jean to leave me." But the curé pressed his point, arguing that it was a sin not to make the most of such talents as we have. Incapable of teaching in Sunday School or of administering works of charity, Jean ought not, any longer, to play the part of an idle workman. The good man warmed to his theme. The sad little voice spoke again, though obviously with an effort: "If Jean goes, I shall go with him." The curé shook his head: Noémie had become indispensable to the dear invalid upstairs; besides, the separation would not be for long—a few weeks, a few months, at most. . . . She could not maintain her opposition. Nothing more was said, and the curé put on his thick coat and his clogs, preparatory to leaving. Jean Péloueyre threw a cape round his shoulders, lit the lantern, and led the way.

The short and rainy December days made it impossible for husband and wife to avoid one another—except when Jean Péloueyre went out after woodcock, and even then, he had to come back at four o'clock, when it began to get dark. A single fire and a single lamp sufficed to bring their estranged bodies into a close intimacy. The whisper of the falling rain around the house made them feel sleepy. As always in winter, Monsieur Jérome had rheumatic pains in his left shoulder, and complained a good deal. But Noémie's health was improving. Every day now she forced herself to dissuade Jean from going away. She had taken a sacred vow to do everything possible to keep him with her. Her pleading made it impossible for the wretched man to remain in a state of indecision. By seeming to hold him back she compelled him to make up his mind. He looked at her with the eyes of a beaten

dog. "I must go, Noémie." She protested, but the moment he
showed any sign of faltering, instead of pressing her advantage,
said no more. Monsieur Jérome, though he was fond of quoting
from *Les Deux Pigeons*: "*l'Absence est le plus grand des maux*",
was secretly delighted at the prospect of being left alone with his
daughter-in-law, and all the time the curé went on nagging at Jean
whenever they met. What could the poor youth do against a plot
so well and cunningly laid? Quite apart from the fact that, in his
heart of hearts, he knew that the verdict of banishment was right
and proper? Save for a single pilgrimage to Lourdes, and his
honeymoon at Arcachon, he had never left his rut. But to plunge
alone into the hurly-burly of Paris was tantamount to drowning
in an ocean of humanity far more terrible than the Atlantic. But
too many people were intent on pushing him over the edge, and
it was finally decided that he should leave during the second
week in February. Long before the appointed day Noémie began
fussing about his luggage and the clothes he should take with
him. Even before he left she had begun to recover her appetite.
There was more colour in her cheeks. One afternoon she had a
snowball fight with Cadette's grandson. Jean Péloueyre watched
them from a window on the first floor. He had no illusions. He
fully realised the significance of this recovery in her spirits. As the
fields free themselves from the grip of winter, so was this
woman freeing herself from him. He was leaving her that she
might once more put forth her flowers.

Jean Péloueyre lowered the dirty window of his carriage, and
watched Noémie's waving handkerchief until the last possible moment. How gaily it fluttered!—a signal of leave-taking and happiness! For the whole of the last week she had intoxicated the man
who was now going from her by an assumption of tenderness, and
the apparent warmth of her response had been so marked that,
one night, deceived into the belief that she was coming to life
beneath the stirring of his breath, he had been tempted into saying: "What if I shouldn't go, after all, Noémie?" Though all this
had passed in the concealing darkness, and though her only reply
had been a stifled exclamation, he had guessed the panic terror in
her heart, and had been unable to keep himself from adding:
"Don't worry; I'm going all right." It was the one sign he gave
that he had not been taken in. She turned her face to the wall,
and he could hear her crying.
    The little train was running through the pine-woods, and

Jean Péloueyre sat watching the familiar trees slip by. He recognized the thicket where once he had missed a woodcock. The line ran parallel with the road along which he had so often driven in a farm cart. He could refer by name to this or that passing farm, swathed in smoke and mist, standing on the edge of a fallow field, with its bakehouse, stables and well, tight held in its embrace. He knew the tenant. . . . He changed trains and was whirled across the great expanse of heath over which he had never shot. At Langon he said good-bye to the last outposts of the pines, parting from them as from friends who had accompanied him on his way as far as they could, and, now that they had come to a halt, stretched out their branches in a final blessing.

❧ X ❧

HE took a room in the first hotel that he encountered on the Quai Voltaire. He spent the morning watching the rain fall upon the river which he had not yet plucked up sufficient courage to cross, and then, at noon, slipped along to the station restaurant at the Gare d'Orléans, where he sat dozing amid the din of trains which were leaving with a load of happy travellers for the south-west. When he had finished his meal he felt that he could not stay on without ordering something more, and drank two glasses of liqueur as a postscript to his bottle of white wine. His spirits soared nimbly into the absolute. The nervous twitching of his face, his broken snatches of speech, brought an occasional smile to the lips of the waiters and of people sitting at the nearby tables, but for most of the time, wedged between the revolving door and one of the pillars, he remained unnoticed. He read the newspapers right through, advertisements and all. Murders, suicides, dramas of jealousy and madness—all were grist to his mill. He stuffed himself full with the world's tragedies.

After dinner he took a platform ticket and hunted for the coach bearing the label "Irun". In twelve hours' time its large windows would be reflecting the monotonous countryside of the Landes. He reckoned that the train would pass less than fifteen miles, as the crow flies, from his home. He put his hand on the side of the carriage. When it jerked into movement it was as though he were watching one half of himself disappearing for ever. He went back to the restaurant. An orchestra was playing and the powerful spell of the music filled him with a sensation of despair. It brought vividly before him the ghost of Noémie, nor could he shake himself free from the obsession of her presence. He let his imagination play over the details of a body at which he had never dared to look save when its owner was asleep. Through the long nights of September, with the moon spilling its light over the bed, the sad young faun had learned to know it better than he could ever have done as a lover happy in the mutual ecstasy of possession. What he had held in his arms had never been more than a corpse, but, with his eyes at least, he had penetrated to its mysteries. Never, perhaps, do we know anybody more completely than the woman who does not love us. At this very moment Noémie would be lying fast asleep in the huge, cold room, happily asleep, freed from a repulsive presence, revelling in the pleasure of an unshared bed. Across the sundering miles he was aware of his loved one's happiness, a happiness that owed its being to his absence from her side.

Holding his head in his hands, he worked himself up into a mood of anger. He would go back to the country, would force himself upon her, would take his joy of her, even if it meant her death! He would make her into the chattel of his pleasure. . . . Then her image came to visible life in his mind, silent, submissive, with the sweet, drooping breast that was like a tree with an offering of fruit. He remembered those moments of acquiescence when, without a cry, and almost dying with the horror of the experience, she had lent herself to his desires. . . .

. . . He settled his bill, walked along the quay to his hotel, and undressed fumblingly in the dark, so that he should not see himself in the glass.

On every third day they brought him with his morning chocolate an envelope which he sometimes left unopened till the evening. He cared nothing for those insincere expressions of impatience for his return! The only comfort he could find was in the thought that Noémie's hand had rested on the paper—that the nail of her little finger had made the tiny scratch beneath each word. Towards the end of March he thought that he detected a note of sincerity in what she wrote: "I know you don't believe me

when I say that I long to see you again, but that's because you
don't really know your wife. . . ." In another letter she said: "I
miss you." He crumpled it up, and turned to another, this time
from his father, which had reached him by the same post. "You
will find Noémie much changed for the better. She looks plumper,
and is really now a fine figure of a woman. She attends to me so
well, and coddles me so sweetly, that I quite forget to thank her.
The Cazenaves never put in an appearance nowadays. I know
they think that you two have quarrelled. Well, let them think. I
am bearing up wonderfully well, but I can't say the same for
young Pieuchon, who never goes out at all now, except driving in
a carriage. His condition is generally thought to be hopeless,
though one of the doctors from B——— says he can cure him with
a tincture of iodine and water. The young 'uns fade away a good
deal quicker than us oldsters. . . ."

With the coming of the first fine weather Jean Péloueyre took
his courage in both hands and crossed the river. He stood looking
down on the Seine in the golden dusk, and his hands on the
warm parapet caressed the stone as though it had been a living
body. He heard a voice behind him murmuring words. It called
him "dearie": it said, "Won't you come home with me?" He saw
a young face close to his own, bloodless beneath its paint. A puffy
hand, devoid of nails, sought his. He took to his heels and did
not stop in his headlong flight until he reached the entrance to the
Louvre. There he halted, panting slightly. Would he ever dare to
listen to the invitation even of such a creature as that? Some
woman who was *not* Noémie? . . . For the first time he wanted to
find pleasure in the thought of an accomplice, of someone who,
though she might find no pleasure in their traffic, would at least
regard him with indifference, and not with disgust. But even
that amount of poor and sordid pleasure was inconceivable. The
bitter knowledge of this ultimate misery swept over him, and his
anger flared anew. Why not seek forgetfulness tonight in acquiescent and submissive arms? Surely it was for men of his sort
that these sellers of endearments existed?

He watched the evening sky reflected in the troubled water
of the Tuileries Gardens. Children crowded about him, made
curious by his gestures. He slouched away with drooping shoulders, made the round of the Place de la Concorde, reached the
rue Royale, and, because it was time for dinner, felt brave
enough to cross the threshold of a famous restaurant. Sitting

close by the door, facing the bar where parrots with aigrettes in
their hair sat perched as though at a mahogany feeding-trough,
he revelled in the knowledge that his appearance caused no surprise to the women customers, nor to the black and greasy
waiters—the sewer-rats of expensive restaurants. This glittering
tunnel attracted too many savages from the Americas, too many
farmers and lawyers from the provinces, to see anything particularly funny about Jean Péloueyre. The Vouvray brought colour
to his cheeks, and he smiled at the herd of animals attracted by
the mahogany trough. A fat blonde slipped off her stool, asked
him for a light, took a sip from his glass, promised him in a low
voice exquisite happiness for five louis, and then hopped back
again, hopefully, on to her perch. Though an old gentleman at the
next table advised him to wait till closing-time, because "the left-
overs reduce their prices", he paid his bill and went out. He was
joined on the pavement by the lady. She hailed a taxi and they
were driven to some place behind the Madeleine. There was no
vestibule to the hotel. The staircase led straight down to the
street like a drainpipe designed to suck up all the filth of the
pavements.

The sound of hairpins on marble woke Jean from his lethargy.
He saw a pair of arms that looked enormous where they joined
the shoulders. Bows of pink ribbon adorned an expanse of quivering flesh. She called him "petit loup", while, with infinite care,
she removed her stockings of artificial silk. This eagerness to give
herself, this acquiescence, this submissiveness to his will, modified
by no trace of disgust, horrified Jean Péloueyre far more violently
than Noémie's shrinking fear had ever done. The woman saw him
fling a note on to the table, and was struck speechless with
amazement. But before she could so much as make a movement,
he was out of the house, slinking along the street like a thief.

In the noisy crowds of the boulevard he knew the beatific sense
of relief that comes when some great danger has been avoided.
The bare branches of the chestnuts drew him to the Champs-
Elysées. He found an empty bench and sat down, out of breath
and coughing a little. The light of a lopsided moon was quite
eclipsed by the glare of the arc-lamps. It must, he thought, be
spreading its calm radiance over the vast stretches of dark tree-
tops that lie between the Ocean and the Pyrenees. He no longer
felt miserable. A sense of purity invaded him. The thought of
his wretched chastity delighted him. A time was coming when

Noémie and Jean would love one another through an endless summer's day. He tasted in anticipation the perfect mingling of their two bodies at last made glorious. In a great splendour of light their immortal, their incorruptible flesh would cry aloud in invitation and response. Aloud he said: "There are no Masters. We are all of us born slaves and we grow into the freedom of the Lord." A policeman approached, gave him one look, then, hunching his shoulders, walked away.

Every afternoon Jean sat outside the Café de la Paix on the brink of a sombre flood of human faces. Secret diseases, drink and drugs had stamped with an indistinguishable and appalling identity thousands of countenances that were, all of them, those of children. He was fascinated by the manoeuvres of the prowling prostitutes, and set himself to classify the herd of famished she-wolves. He played a game with himself which consisted in trying to guess what particular vice was the animating principle of this or that gentleman with the monocle and the slobbering lip. Hungrily he sought one single face that might bear the distinguishing mark of a ruler, of a master of men. Could he have found but one member of that chosen race, he would have followed him, but he saw only vacant looks and trembling hands. Unnatural lusts had set their foul stamp on faces unaware of prying eyes. But even if he had come on some such Master as he sought, would there have been any assurance that he would have been immortal? Jean Péloueyre, sitting at his table on the boulevard, and gesticulating as he might have done between the walls of some village street in his native countryside, quoted to himself Pascal's comment on the ultimate end of even the most brilliant of worldly careers: when the game is done, one is always the loser. Bear witness to that, O Nietzsche of the softened brain—one is always the loser! . . .

Some young people close to him nudged one another. A woman seated with them put a question to Jean. He started, threw some coins on to the table, and took to his heels. Behind him he could hear the woman's voice: "Mad as a hatter!" He slipped away through the crowd, scampering like a rat past the shop fronts, elaborating in his mind the plan of an authoritative essay which should be called: *The Will to Power and the Will to Holiness*. Here and there he saw his face reflected in the glass of a show-case, but did not recognize it as his own. Bad food had left him more emaciated than ever, so that he was little more than skin and bone. The Paris dust irritated his throat. He should, by rights, have given up cigarettes altogether, but, in fact, he was smoking more than ever. He kept on spitting and coughing. Recurrent fits of giddiness forced him to cling for support to the street lamp-posts. He preferred to eat nothing at all rather than endure the agonies of indigestion. Would he be picked up one of these days in the gutter, like a dead cat? Well, if that happened, at least Noémie would be free of him. . . .

Thus did he brood, until at last he ran aground in a cinema, attracted thither less by the promise of the screen than by the prospect of continuous music. . . . Quite often, feverishly wandering, and dropping with fatigue, he would take refuge in a public bath-house, where the light was dimmed by gauze screens, and, to an accompaniment of dripping taps, he could enjoy the illusion of being freed from the burden of his body. He sought these wretched hideouts only because for a long time he knew no church in Paris but the Madeleine—the only one he passed on his walk from his hotel to the Café de la Paix. But it so happened that on one occasion, having changed his route, he came across Saint Roch, and thereafter its shadowy interior became his daily haven. Its smell conjured up the church of his childhood, and he found in it the certainty of a Presence—the same here, at one of the traffic intersections of a vast city, as in a remote country town. Not once did he cross the threshold of a library.

He might have lived on like this until the day of his death, had not a letter reached him one morning from the curé, calling him back to the fold. There was a note of urgency about it, notwithstanding the fact that it brought good news of Noémie and of Monsieur Jérome. In a mood of profound mental distress Jean Péloueyre got into the coach labelled "Irun", which, so often, he had felt sliding away, gently at first, beneath his hand, then gathering speed, towards the south-west.

❀ *XI* ❀

THE curé had had no special reason to send off his letter of recall. He had made up his mind, actually, after hearing one of Noémie's weekly confessions, which had contained nothing but a list of the most ordinary and venial shortcomings. But she had begged her director to give her spiritual assistance and so strengthen her in her fight against certain temptations into the precise nature of which she did not enter.

She had owed no small part of the pleasant languor which accompanied her early days of convalescence to Jean Péloueyre's departure. The mere being left to herself was a continuing delight. She drifted through the days completely happy in her own company. Incapable though she was of self-analysis, she felt, somehow, that she was different. Once more she was living the life of a young girl, but her body told her that she was a young girl no longer. Disgust had made her avert her eyes from the spectacle of her own budding womanhood, but the stranger who lived deep down in her seemed bent on seeking some mysterious satisfaction. Uneasy at finding that she could not now enjoy the peace of mind which she had known before a man had come to possess her, she found it impossible not to notice the state of discord which reigned between her unawakened heart and her partially awakened body. The rending laceration of her whole being had brought nothing but horror, but the body sees to it that nothing of what it has endured shall ever be wholly forgotten. Because she never read anything but her prayer-book, and because, as a well-brought-up young person, she had never had a really intimate friend, neither confidences nor novels had so far enlightened her on the nature of her smouldering desires.

And then, at last, Destiny gave them a local habitation and a name.

The March sun was bringing a flash and glitter to the puddles in the market square. So heavy upon the house was the spell of Jérome Péloueyre's siesta that not so much as a creak was emitted by the furniture. Like all the other women in the town, Noémie was busy with her sewing. She sat in the embrasure of one of the ground-floor windows. The shutters were half closed. The table billowed with linen waiting to be darned. She heard the sound of wheels and saw an English trap draw up a few feet away. A young man was in the driving-seat. He seemed to be looking for somebody of whom he might ask his way. But the square was empty of life. Filled with curiosity, she pushed the shutters back. At that very moment the stranger turned his head, raised his hat, and asked where Dr. Pieuchon lived. She gave him the necessary information. He thanked her for her help, flicked his horse

with his whip, and drove off. Noémie settled down again to her
sewing. All day long she plied her needle, while her thoughts
played truant. She had given no conscious heed to the stranger's
face, but its features were stamped upon her mind.

Next day he drove by again. This time he did not stop, but as
he reached the Péloueyres' house reined in his horse, and scanned
the shuttered windows for a sight of the young woman. At least,
that was what he seemed to be doing, for he bowed. At dinner
that evening, Monsieur Jérome said he had had it from the curé
that young Pieuchon was going from bad to worse, and that his
father had called in a young doctor from the county town who
was very highly thought of. He treated tuberculosis with strong
doses of tincture of iodine, of which medicine the patient had to
take several hundred drops diluted with water. Monsieur Jérome
expressed doubts whether the Pieuchon boy's stomach could toler-
ate such a mixture.

Each day the trap drove past, and each day it slowed down opposite the Péloueyres' house, though Noémie never once opened
the shutters. The young doctor regularly bowed in the direction
of the narrow strip of shadow where youth invisible was drawing
in the breath of life. The townspeople showed much interest in
this iodine treatment. All the consumptives of the district began to
try it. It was confidently asserted that Pieuchon's son was better.

The spring that year was early. A spell of warm weather at the
end of March freed the earth from its winter numbness. One evening, Noémie was able to leave the window open while she undressed. She leaned upon the sill, a prey to mingled sadness and
joy. She felt wakeful. She stayed there, face to face with the darkness which, by some secret process of its own, "revealed" to her
the face whose print she bore within her consciousness. For the
first time she let her mind dwell upon the stranger and deliberately gave free rein to her thoughts. Since he bowed so regularly
every day without so much as setting eyes upon her, would it
not be more polite to open the shutters to-morrow and return his
salutation? Having decided to do this, she was invaded by so
sweet an emotion that she put off the moment of going to bed.
Feature by feature his face took shape in her mind: the black,
curly hair, glimpsed for a moment when he raised his hat—the
deep red of lips beneath a short moustache—the country clothes
with the clasp of a fountain-pen catching the light—no tie, but a
silk shirt open at the neck.

Bundle of instincts though she was, she had been trained to

keep a watchful eye upon her conscience. Consequently, she was
at once on her guard. The first warning came when, as she was
saying her prayers, she realised that she had to start each one of
them over again because a smiling, sunburnt face stood between
her and God. Lying in bed, she was obsessed by the thought of
him, and when she got up next morning, still only half awake and
haunted by the memory of her dreams, she found that her first
thought was that she would soon be seeing him again. During that
morning's Mass she kept her hands over her face. At siesta-time,
when the trap slowed down before the house, all the ground-floor
shutters were hermetically sealed.

It was at this time that the exile began to get the letters which
caused him so much astonishment, the letters in which Noémie
wrote: "I miss you." Through all those days she sat in the dark
room waiting until the trap should have gone by before opening
the shutters and settling down to her work. One afternoon she
told herself that scrupulousness carried to such lengths was, in
itself, a sin. "I'm getting all worked up," she thought. The business
must be settled once and for all. She would lean out of the window and return the stranger's salutation. She caught the sound of
wheels and her hand hesitated at the clasp. But for the first time
in two weeks the trap did not drive past.

When the moment came to give Monsieur Jérome his valerian
she went up to his room and could not resist the temptation to
tell him that the new doctor had not paid his customary visit to
the Pieuchons. This was no news to Monsieur Jérome. Young
Pieuchon had had a relapse on the previous evening and could
no longer absorb the iodine. He had brought up a basinful of
blood, said the curé. The spring is a dangerous season for consumptives. It was a matter of common gossip that Doctor Pieuchon had said some hard things to his colleague. The young practitioner would almost certainly not care to show his face in the
town again.

Noémie interviewed one of the tenant farmers, and helped Cadette to fold the washing. At six o'clock she went to church to
visit the Blessed Sacrament, after which, as usual, she looked in
on her parents. But after dinner she complained of a sick headache and went to her room.

She began to lead a more active life. Her poultry throve.

Dressed in her Sunday finery, she took her share in the social
visits which the ladies of the town exchanged with much solem-
nity each year. She made the round of the farms. She loved driving along the forest roads churned into ruts by the heavy farm
carts. Cadette's grandson was in charge on these occasions, and
she sat beside him. Gorse bushes made splashes of yellow amid
the tangle of dead bracken. Dead leaves trembled on the oaks,
still clinging to the branches in the teeth of a warm breeze from
the south. The neat round mirror of a mere reflected the tall pine
trunks, the greenery of their tops, and the blue sky beyond.
Each one of all the innumerable trees showed a fresh and bleeding wound, and the heat of the day drew out the smell of resin.
The notes of the cuckoo brought earlier Springs to mind. As they
bumped over the uneven surface the boy was constantly flung
against her, and then they laughed like a couple of children.
Next day the young woman complained of stiffness, and the agent
was left to complete the survey of the estate. Except at Mass no
one saw her again until the day of Jean Péloueyre's return.

❧ XII ❧

SHE was waiting for him at the station. Her organdie frock was
like a flower opening in the sun. She was wearing cotton mittens, and on her bare neck a cameo showing two cupids struggling with a goat. Several children were amusing themselves by
walking along one of the rails. The whistle of the little train could
be heard long before it came in sight. Noémie wanted her emotion
to be one of joy. Absence had given a softened outline to her
memory of Jean Péloueyre's features. She had, as it were, fashioned
her husband anew that he might no longer be repulsive to her.
The image she retained of him had been subtly retouched. So
strong was her desire to love him that she felt actually impatient
to clasp the unreal Jean Péloueyre in her arms. If round the budding
softness of her body desire had hovered, lighting upon other faces
than his, she could truly call God to witness that never once had
she permitted so much as one disloyal thought to enter her mind.
She felt, now, quite sure that she would reap her reward, that
the man who got out of the train would be a different husband

from the one she had sent upon his travels with so keen a sense of happy release.

Jean Péloueyre appeared at the door of a second-class carriage. He certainly was different from what he once had been. The weight of his suitcase was almost too much for his weak muscles, though Cadette's grandson took it from him without difficulty. As he leaned on Noémie's arm, he seemed a little unsteady on his feet. "My poor Jean, you're *ill!*" He, too, found it difficult to recognize his wife in this strange young woman, so vastly had his absence improved her. She showed a full-blown brilliance. The contrast between them was even greater than it had been in the priest's parlour, when she had been a woman in her glory, and he a stunted little male. Their appearance evoked a good deal of whispering, and Jean felt ashamed to be seen by the man at the newspaper stall, by the stationmaster and by the local porter. "I ought to have sent the carriage to meet you. Why didn't you write and tell me you were ill?"

Noémie got his bed ready, washed his face and hands, spread a white cloth on the night-table, and put within reach a number of magazines which had accumulated for him during his absence, and which she had not even taken out of their wrappers. Like a poor child surprised by unfamiliar coddling, he looked at her suspiciously with his small, sharp eyes.

Monsieur Jérome was strongly opposed to the idea of calling in Dr. Pieuchon. Kindly and gentle, as a rule, he was exasperated at the thought that anyone else in the house should dare to be ill. No sooner had his son gone to bed than he followed suit, complaining of pains all over his body, and roughly refusing Cadette's offer of assistance. Noémie went in to see him, not so much to find out how he was as to get his consent to the doctor's visit. He gave her a point-blank refusal. Pieuchon never left his son's germ-infected pillow. If she was so set on seeing a sawbones she had better send for the "young iodine fellow". She turned her head away and said that she had no confidence in him. Besides, didn't he go to see all the consumptives for miles round? Monsieur Jérome silenced her angrily. That, he said, was his last word, and he didn't want to be plagued any longer. He turned his face to the wall, as he always did when he was feeling especially bad, heaving at intervals the most heart-rending sighs, and repeatedly muttering those "Oh God's" which in the old days had been wont to awaken Jean in the dead of night.

When Noémie returned to her room she found the servant setting up a camp bed. Nothing of Jean Péloueyre was visible on
the pillow but a pair of gleaming red eyes, two flushed cheeks,
and a sharp nose. He stammered out an explanation: said he
felt cold in the big bed, that he had always preferred a narrow
one, that he thought it unwise for them to sleep together—at
least until a doctor had examined his chest. She would have
liked to protest, to pretend that she was disappointed, but not a
word could she summon up. She kissed his damp forehead, but
he turned away his head, finding the gratitude expressed in that
caress quite intolerable. Quietly, sadly, the hours passed. Stretched
in his world of silence, he slept, and woke only when he heard
the tinkle of a teaspoon against a saucer. Though he was not
seriously ill, Noémie supported his shoulders while he drank,
and he drew out the process so as to feel for as long as possible the
warmth of her arms against his neck.

Twilight fell. The church bell began to ring. From the stable-
yard came the voice of Cadette's grandson crying "Coom oop, old
gel," as he harnessed the horse. The door was pushed open by
Monsieur Jérome. He had slippers on his bare feet and was wearing a dressing-gown covered with medicine stains. Ashamed of
his ill temper, he had come to beg their pardon, though he pretended, as a reason for his visit, to be so anxious that he could not
wait a moment longer without being reassured. At his orders, Cadette's grandson set off to fetch the "young iodine doctor". Jean
Péloueyre protested. He was a bit tired, that was all. A few days'
rest would put him right. The doctor wouldn't understand why he
had been sent for in such haste.

Noémie sat in the shadows. She did not speak a word, but listened to the sound of wheels growing fainter. Without a shudder, without a sob, she wept. An April shower was whipping
the windows, hastening the fall of darkness, but neither husband nor wife called for the lamp. At long last Cadette brought
a light and set the table for their evening meal close by Jean's
bed. While they were eating Noémie asked him whether his historical researches were finished. He shook his head, and she did
not return to the question. The sound of the trap reached them
from the yard. Jean Péloueyre said: "That's the iodine doctor."
Noémie got up and remained standing at some distance from the
lamp. She could hear the murmur of voices and the sound of
footsteps on the stairs, and it was as though she were listening

to an approaching storm. Cadette opened the door and he came
in. He looked fatter than Noémie remembered. He was what was
known locally as a "personable chap", with his black hair and
high colour. He had elongated eyes like an Andalusian mule, and
he turned them boldly on Noémie, tracing the lines of her body
with a lingering thoroughness. His thoughts, too, had been wandering, and very much in her direction! She felt too nervous to
move from her patch of shadow, and was actually shivering.

He, meanwhile, was busy examining his patient. "D'you mind
unbuttoning your shirt?—a handkerchief will do, madame. . . .
Now count thirty-one, thirty-two, thirty-three. . . ." The light from
the lamp fell on collar-bone, shoulder-blades and ribs . . . on all
Jean's pitiful exposure. . . . There was no reason to be alarmed
about Monsieur Péloueyre, but the state of his lungs ought to be
very carefully watched. . . . The doctor prescribed a tonic and
some cacodylate injections. Now and again he glanced at Noémie.
Could he be thinking that she might deliberately have inveigled
him into the house? It was, after all, rather an extraordinary thing
to make a doctor drive six miles on a dark night just to listen to
the chest of an exhausted man! He stayed on some time. Speaking in his rather thick accent, he denied that he had ever claimed
to be able to cure so advanced a case of tuberculosis as young
Pieuchon with iodine treatment. His drawling, rustic voice filled
the room with a sense of something massive, something mascu-
line. Noémie felt herself to be the object of a gaze that, as it
were, dribbled from beneath the man's saffron-coloured lids. The
impression she made on him was that of a silent ghost. He concluded what he had to say by remarking that the best they could
hope to do was to forestall the onset of the disease. Monsieur
Péloueyre, he pointed out, was a rich breeding-ground for bacilli.
"He is not so much tubercular as *potentially* tubercular. . . . The
late Madame Péloueyre died of consumption, did she not?"
. . . The medical talk came strangely from lips better suited
to dispense kisses than scientific comments. He must certainly
keep a very careful watch on the patient. This he said, hoping
that she would ask him to repeat his visit. But Noémie said nothing, and he got up. Without further beating about the bush, he
asked whether Monsieur Péloueyre would like him to come again,
if only for the purpose of giving him his injections. "What do
you say, Noémie?" She made no reply, and he, thinking she had
not heard, repeated the question: "Would it be a good thing,

Noémie, if the doctor came again?" This time she did answer. "It's really quite unnecessary," she said, and so uncompromising was her tone that Jean was afraid that their visitor might feel offended. He declared, therefore, that the decision must rest with the doctor. That fine upstanding young man showed not the slightest sign of embarrassment, but promised to come immediately should they see fit to send for him. Then Noémie took the lamp and led the way out of the room. She went quickly down the stairs, conscious of his warm breath on the back of her neck. The trap was standing in front of the door. The doctor climbed into it without getting so much as a glance from her. Cadette's grandson made a clucking sound with his tongue. The night wind blew out the lamp which the young woman was holding high, and she stood there in the dark, on the threshold of a dead house, listening to the sound of the wheels slowly dying away.

That night she did not sleep at all. Jean Péloueyre, in the camp bed, was restless, muttering broken phrases. She got up to tuck him in, and laid her hand upon his forehead without waking him, as she might have done to the child that she would never bear.

☘ X I I I ☘

Two days later Jean Péloueyre resumed his former habits. He crept out of the house during his father's siesta, kept a watchful eye open for magpies, and came home as late as possible, after paying a brief visit to the church on his way back. Noémie was already losing her gloss. He noticed the dark shadows round her melancholy eyes, and how, when they looked at him, they expressed only a gentle humility. He had hoped that his period of exile from the marriage bed might have had the effect of reconciling her to his proximity, but she continued to fight desperately in an attempt to overcome her sense of disgust, and the effort was wearing her out. Often she would call out in the night, begging him to come to her. When he pretended to be asleep she would get up, go over to his bed, and kiss him—as saints, once upon a time, were in the habit of kissing lepers. No one can tell us whether the stricken wretches rejoiced to feel upon their sores the warm breath of the Blessed. But Jean Péloueyre would wrench himself free from her embraces. It was he, now, who cried aloud in tones of horror: "Leave me alone!"

The high garden walls were half hidden under a dark riot of lilac. The dusk was filled with the scent of syringa. Cock-chafers boomed in the light of the sinking sun. One May evening, after the Litany, the curé made an announcement. "Your prayers are asked," he said, "for the success of a number of young persons in their examinations, for the happiness of several young married couples, for the conversion of the father of a family, and for the recovery of a young man now lying gravely sick. . . ." All knew that he was referring to young Pieuchon, now *in extremis*. The June lilies bloomed. Noémie noticed with surprise that Jean no longer took a gun with him on his walks. He said that the magpies knew him too well, that the sly creatures wouldn't let him come within range. She began to fear that these expeditions took too much out of him. He returned from them, now, no longer with a look of animation on his face, but pale and exhausted. He pretended that his lack of animation was due to the heat. One night she heard him cough repeatedly. In a low voice she said: "Are you asleep, Jean?" He told her that his throat was a bit troublesome, that there was nothing really wrong with him, but she noticed the effort that he made to keep from coughing, and with what little success. She lit a candle, and saw by its light that he was bathed in sweat. She looked at him in an agony of fear. His eyes were closed, and his mind seemed concentrated upon the mysterious working of something deep within him. He smiled at his wife, and she was tormented by the spectacle of so much gentleness and calm. In a low voice he said: "I'm thirsty."

Next morning he had no trace of fever: indeed, his temperature was, if anything, subnormal. She felt reassured. It would have comforted her to know that he wasn't going out after luncheon, but there was nothing she could do to prevent him. Her importunity seemed to get on his nerves, and he kept on looking at his watch, as though anxious not to be late for an appointment. Monsieur Jérome made a joke of the whole business. "You'll get her thinking that you're off to meet somebody!" To this Jean made no reply, and the hall echoed to his quick steps. The sky was tarnished with storm-clouds. It was as though the silence of the birds had struck the trees to stillness.

All that day Noémie sat at one of the ground-floor windows,

nursing her fear. At four o'clock the church bell began to strike a series of single notes, widely spaced. She crossed herself, because the sound meant that somebody was at the point of death. She heard a voice out in the square saying: "It's young Pieuchon they're ringing for. He almost slipped out this morning." Heavy rain-drops were making little holes in the dust, so that it gave off the smell of stormy twilights. Because her father-in-law was still sleeping, she went to the kitchen and chatted to Cadette about Robert Pieuchon. The old woman was deaf and had not heard the passing-bell. She said that the "young master" would be sure to bring the latest news, and when Noémie showed surprise heaved a deep sigh and added tearfully that she was sure the "mistress" didn't know anything about it, because otherwise she would have stopped the "poor young gentleman"—and him so delicate—from spending all his afternoons with the Pieuchon lad, as he'd been doing for more than a month now. He'd forbidden his old Cadette to breathe a word to a soul. Noémie pretended that the news did not surprise her. She went out. It had stopped raining, and a dusty wind was buffeting the heavy clouds.

She walked in the direction of the doctor's house. Death had already closed its shutters. Jean Péloueyre appeared on the threshold. Although there was a sort of a blight over the day, he seemed dazzled, and blinked his eyes. He did not notice his wife. His clay-coloured face gave him the appearance of one not of this world. Instinctively he went towards the church and entered it. Noémie followed him at a distance. The damp chill of the nave caught at her—that earthy chill, as of a newly-dug grave, which envelops the living when they go down the steps into old churches which are slowly settling beneath the heavy hand of time. Once more she heard the cough that had woken her the night before, but now it was echoed and endlessly repeated by the vaulted ceiling.

❀ *XIV* ❀

JEAN PÉLOUEYRE had asked that his bed might be taken to one of the ground-floor rooms opening on to the garden. Whenever he found difficulty in breathing, the iron bedstead was pushed out into the verandah, and there he would lie, watching the patches of blue sky between the leaves contracting or growing larger. An ice-machine had been installed, because, except for plain, cold milk, he could swallow almost nothing but a little sweetened ice. His father came to see him, but would stand all the time at a safe distance, smiling. It may be that Jean would have preferred the darkness of his room, where his sufferings would not have been so plainly visible: but he had chosen to die in the garden, that Noémie might be the less exposed to infection. Morphine made him drowsy. Rest! Rest after those horrible afternoons at young Pieuchon's bedside, listening to the dying man's despairing outbursts as he thought of all that he was leaving—riotous nights in Bordeaux; dancing to a mechanical piano in roadside cabarets; bicycle expeditions, with the dust clinging to his thin, hairy legs, and that feeling of being all-in; above all, the kisses of young women.

The Cazenaves spread a rumour that it was only Monsieur Jérome's meanness that kept from his son the beneficial effects of a warmer climate, or of treatment in a mountain resort. But, quite apart from the fact that Jean was the last man in the world to wish to die away from home, Dr. Pieuchon had given it as his opinion that nothing was so good for consumptives as the forests of the Landes. He went so far as to festoon the sick-room with pine branches, as for some religious Feast, and had bowls filled with resin put round the bed. At last, having come to the end of his own medical knowledge, he called in his young colleague, only to have his view confirmed that Jean Péloueyre's system could no longer stand up to massive dosages of iodine.

Although Noémie received the good-looking young man with an air of complete indifference, she could not but notice how he turned pale whenever he looked at her, or if their hands happened to touch. At each meeting she took a positive delight in the knowledge that nothing in the world had any meaning for her now but the presence of her husband in his sick-bed. But perhaps, deep down in her heart, she was conscious of the young male who had gulped down bait, hook and all, and was unperturbed only because she knew that whenever she had a mind to do so she could lay him on the bank beside her, alive and twitching. . . .

Jean Péloueyre would not let her kiss him, but liked to feel her cool hand on his forehead. Did he believe now that she loved him? Assuredly he did, for he was heard to murmur: "Be thy Name for ever blessed, O Lord, for that thou hast let me know

the love of a woman before I die. . . ." And, as once on his lonely
walks, so now, he pondered endlessly one single line of poetry,
and, weary of saying his Rosary, while Noémie was feeling his
pulse, would mutter over and over again, in a low voice, Pau-
line's outburst: *"Mon Polyeucte touche à son heure dernière—*
and smile. Not that he thought of himself as a martyr. People had
always said of him that he was a "poor creature", nor had he
ever doubted that they were right. Looking back over the grey
waters of his life, he felt strengthened in his self-contempt. What
stagnation! But under that sleeping surface had stirred a life-
giving freshet, and now, having passed through life like a corpse,
he was, on his death-bed, as a man reborn.

One evening, the curé and Doctor Pieuchon stayed so long in
the hall that Noémie went out to them to complain bitterly about
their conspiracy of silence. Why had she and her father-in-law
never been told of Jean's daily visits to the consumptive? The doctor hung his head and pleaded in excuse his ignorance of Jean's
state of health. Himself a man of infinite kindliness, how should he
have felt surprise at a devotion which he would have shown without thinking twice about it, and especially when his own son was
its object? The curé's defence was more aggressive. It was Jean
Péloueyre himself who had enjoined silence, and where a priest's
penitents were concerned the most scrupulous tact was necessary.

"But it was you, Father, who urged him to make that fatal
trip to Paris. . . ."

"Was it only I, Noémie?"

She leaned against the wall, picking at a hole in the plaster—
which was painted to look like marble—and making it larger. The
sound of coughing reached them from the bedroom, and the flip-
flop of Cadette's slippers.

The curé spoke again:

"I did what I did only after a deal of praying. We must
love the ways of the Lord. . . ."

He put on his heavy coat. In his secret heart he was wrestling
with conflicting emotions, and spent sleepless nights shedding
tears over Jean Péloueyre's fate. In vain did he tell himself, over
and over again, that the sick man had made a will in Noémie's
favour, and that it was Monsieur Jérome's intention, once the poor
boy was dead, to give the house and as much of his property as
he could to the young woman—on condition that she never re-
married. The curé was a man of scrupulous conscience, though a

little too much inclined to meddle in the lives of others, and he questioned with relentless rigour the motives which had led him to act as he had done. He had quite sincerely believed that there was every chance of the marriage turning out happily—and, *sub specie aeternitatis*, could anybody doubt that he had been right? After all, what had *he* got out of the business? As a good shepherd should, he had been concerned only for the well-being of his flock. Each time that he thus sat in judgment on himself, he ended by pronouncing absolution, but that did not prevent him from endlessly reopening the enquiry. He dreaded lest he might have lost the power to distinguish between justice and injustice, nor could he help feeling oppressed by a sense of uncertainty when it came to evaluating his own actions. He felt humbled, and less and less, now, did he attempt to assume the airs of priestly infallibility. When celebrating daily Mass he no longer let the train of his cassock hang free, and he had given up wearing the three-cornered biretta which distinguished him from his humbler brethren of the cloth. One by one, all his petty vanities fell from him. He felt no pleasure at the news that, though he was not senior priest, the Bishop had bestowed on him the right to wear a hood over his surplice. How came it that he, a guardian of souls, should ever have cared about such trivialities? The only thing that mattered to him now was to get clear in his mind the part he had played in this drama. Had he really been an obedient servant of the Lord, or was the real truth that a poor parish priest had usurped the functions of the Eternal God?

Meanwhile, every evening a trap rattled over the frosty roads, carrying the young doctor homewards. The moonlight filtered down through the close-set tops of the pines, scarcely impeded by their interlacing branches. The dark and rounded summits of the trees hung in the sky like a flock of birds struck motionless. Every now and again the stocky shadows of wild boars crossed from verge to verge of the road, a few hundred yards in front of his horse's head. The trunks thinned out round a patch of ground mist that shrouded a stretch of open grassland. The road dropped into the ice-cold exhalations of a river-bed. The young man, wrapped in his goatskin and shut away in a small world smelling of fog and tobacco smoke, knew nothing of the stars that twinkled above the tree-tops. He kept his nose to the earth, like a dog on the scent. When he was not thinking of the kitchen fire in

front of which he would soon be drying himself, or of the soup
laced with wine that was awaiting him, his mind was busy with
Noémie. There she was, within reach of his hand, yet he had
never touched her. "All the same," said the sportsman in him,
"I've winged her: she's wounded." He knew instinctively when a
female victim had been brought to bay and was begging for
mercy. He had heard the cry of her young body. He had possessed many women—some, forbidden fruit, some, the wives of
men and not discarded bits of rubbish like that wretched Péloueyre. Winged now, and less capable of resistance than most, was
she to be his only failure? Naturally enough, while her husband
was getting on with his dying she would observe the decencies,
but what was it, before the man had fallen so desperately ill,
that had held back so succulent a partridge whom he had already
half succeeded in hypnotizing? What was the emotional influence
that had kept her lurking in the shadows, out of range of the
lamp? Some different kind of love? He did not believe that she
was particularly religious-minded. He thought he knew her type.
He had already measured swords with the curé when he had been
out after another of his lambs. Religious women were adepts at
the game. They made no bones about the venial sin. They would
flutter about the flame, scorching a foot, and then, at the last
moment, would slip through one's fingers, as though twitched by
an invisible thread to the confessional.

He made his plans for the days ahead when Jean Péloueyre
should have "kicked the bucket". "I'll get her all right," he told
himself. And smiled, for he had the patience of the people of the
Landes, whose method in matters of sport is to lie hidden till
the birds come within range.

❀ X V ❀

FORTUNATELY for Jean Péloueyre, who had to fight for every breath
he drew, the summer's heat grew less intense. The frequent
storms of September turned the leaves red. Cadette's grandson
brought the sick man some early mushrooms smelling of forest
loam, and provided distraction by showing him ortolans snared at
dawn which he would fatten in the dark and serve, later,

drenched in old Armagnac. Coveys of wood-pigeons gave warning of an early winter, and it would soon be time to set decoys
in readiness for the shooting season. Jean Péloueyre had always
loved the autumn, feeling in his heart the call of the harvested
millet-fields and of the wild heathland known only to the lonely
pigeons, the sheep and the winds. When, at dawn, the window
was thrown open to ease the patient's breathing, the smell of the
air brought a reminder of those melancholy homecomings in
the October dusk when he had been out shooting. But he was
not allowed to make his last long journey in peace.

Noémie did not realize that we owe a debt of silence to the
dying. Just as in the old days she had been incapable of concealing her disgust, so now she could not suppress the evidences
of remorse. Insatiable in her desire to be forgiven, she moistened
his hand with her tears. In vain did he say: "I, and I only,
Noémie, chose you out. . . . It was I, and I only, who showed you
no consideration. . . ." She shook her head, blind now to everything but that Jean was dying for her, that he was a great-hearted,
noble-minded man, and that she would love him truly if only he
would get well. She would pay back a hundredfold the tenderness which she had learned to treasure so jealously. How was she
to know that even before he struggled half-way back to health
the new bond between them would have begun to work loose,
that she could love him only so long as he was at death's door—
quand il touchât à son heure dernière?[1] She was very young,
very ignorant, and sensual. She did not know her own heart.
But its feelings were genuine enough, and she had made an offering of them to God. Clumsily, she demanded from the dying
man the word that would have lightened her burden of remorse.
But these scenes sapped his courage, so that he wished, above all
things, not to be left alone with her. This he often would have
been (for Monsieur Jérome was chained to his bed by a conspiracy
of ailments) had it not been for the young doctor's devotion. It
amazed Jean Péloueyre that a stranger should be so attentive.
Though he could not talk, he found comfort in the man's presence.

One afternoon at the end of September he woke from a long
spell of dozing to see Noémie in a chair by the window. She was
asleep. Her head had fallen back, and he could hear her un-

[1] I have repeated the French phrase because it is a deliberate echo
of the line from *Polyeucte* already quoted—TRANSLATOR

troubled breathing, as of a child. He closed his eyes again, only to open them once more at the sound of someone at the door. The doctor came in very quietly. The idea that he might be expected to utter a word of welcome made Jean a coward, and he pretended to be still asleep. The young man's shooting-boots creaked. Then there was silence, a silence so complete that Jean was tempted to steal a look. His friend, the stranger, was standing close to the unconscious woman. He did not at first bend over her, but was almost imperceptibly leaning forward, and his strong, hairy hands were trembling. . . .

Jean Péloueyre closed his eyes. He heard Noémie's deep tones: "You really must forgive me. . . . You took me by surprise, doctor. I think I must have been asleep. . . . Our patient is not so well to-day . . . this weather is so exhausting. Look, not a leaf's stirring. . . ." The doctor replied that a south-westerly breeze was blowing, and Noémie said: "A wind from Spain always means that there's a storm on the way. . . ." But the only storm of which there was a sign was foreshadowed by this pale young man, frenzied with desire, whose eyes seemed to be as heavily overcast as the sky. Noémie got up and went over to Jean, putting the iron bedstead between herself and the man whose brooding gaze was fixed upon her. His voice, when he spoke, was thick: "You must look after yourself, madame . . . if only for his sake." "Oh, I can stand up to anything; I'm as strong as a horse and never have any trouble about eating and sleeping. . . . I just can't understand how people can die of grief. . . ." They sat down, with the width of the room between them. Jean Péloueyre seemed still to be dozing. Without moving his lips, he murmured to himself, stressing the caesura: *"Mon Péloueyre touche à son heure dernière. . . ."*

It was as though he were lying in the arms of Autumn, wrapped about by her veiling mists, and drawing in the fragrance of her tears. He had less difficulty in breathing, and occasionally took a little nourishment. But all through those days he was suffering as he had never suffered before. Still alive, he stood on the very brink of death. Of Noémie he had no doubts, but could not help wondering what weapon she would find to use against the handsome young man when the land of shadows should at last have swallowed her husband up. The sad ghost of a dead man cannot keep apart those who are predestined to love one another. But he showed no sign of the terror that had him in its clutch. He

pressed the doctor's hand with a smile. How dearly he would
have loved to live on, merely to join battle with this rival, to see
himself preferred above him! What dark madness was it that
had bred in him the wish to die? Even without Noémie, without
any woman at all in his life, how sweet it would have been to
drink in the air! How much more delicious is the dawn breeze
than the touch of loving hands! . . . Drenched with sweat, nau-
seated by the smell of his own sick-bed, he looked at Cadette's
grandson standing outside the open window with an offering of
the first woodcock . . . Oh, those shooting mornings! Blest magic
of the pines with their tufted tops of faded grey against the blue
of the sky, with their look of humble folk caught up in glory!
Deep in the forest, a streak of green grass, of mist and alders,
must even now be marking the course of a stream stained yellow
by the sandstone of its bed.

Jean Péloueyre's pines formed the vanguard of that immense
army which bleeds its life away between the Ocean and the
Pyrenees, dominating the acres of Sauterne and the torrid valley
where the sun is a real presence in every shoot of every vine. . . .
With the passing of the years, Jean Péloueyre would have worried
less about the state of his heart, because ugliness, like beauty, is
smothered up by age, and he would at least have had for his
delight the yearly return of the shooting season, the freshly
gathered mushrooms. Past summers glint in bottles of Yquem,
and the sunsets of dead years set red gleams in the Gruau-
Larose. Sitting before the roaring fire in the kitchen, a man can
read, while all around the heath is drowned in rain. . . .

Noémie was saying to the doctor: "There's no point in your com-
ming back to-morrow."

And he replied: "Certainly I shall come. . . ."

Did she understand? How could she not? Had he ever declared
himself? Would Jean Péloueyre die without knowing the issue of
this battle which was being fought out beside his bed? It was as
though someone, realizing that the poor man was slipping away
from the world without suffering overmuch, had hastily contrived
a series of bonds which he could break only at the cost of prodi-
gious efforts. But break they did, one by one, until at last he was
ready for the final plunge. His passions died first, and a day came
when he could give to all the selfsame smile, the selfsame tribute
of gratitude, undimmed, unqualified. Not now was it lines of poetry that he repeated, but: "It is I: be not afraid . . ."

The rains at the end of winter drew a curtain about the shad-

owy room. Why should anyone worry whether Jean Péloueyre
were suffering, since, for him, suffering was a joy? The only signs
of life that reached him now were the crowing of cocks, the
jolting of waggon wheels, the summons of the church bell, the
vague rustle of rain upon the roof, and, at night, the hoarse cries
of preying birds, the screams of murdered animals. The last dawn
of his life showed at the window. Cadette lit the fire and the
room was filled with its resinous smoke. It seemed the very life-
breath of the blazing pines which, so often, on torrid summer days,
had been blown into his face from off his native heaths. It touched
his dying body. The d'Artiailhs insisted that though he could
still hear, he could not see. Monsieur Jérome, in his dressing-gown,
all marked with medicine stains, stood by the door, a handkerchief pressed to his lips. He was crying. Cadette and her grandson were kneeling in the half-light. The voice of the priest seemed
to be forcing open invisible doors with the pressure of propitia-
tory words: *"Go forth, Christian soul, into life everlasting, in the
name of the Father who made thee, in the name of the Son who
redeemed thee, and of the Holy Ghost who sanctified thee, and in
the name of Angels and Archangels, of Thrones and Dominations,
of Principalities and Powers. . . ."*

Noémie fixed on him her ardent gaze, saying to herself: "He
was beautiful. . . ."

The townspeople confused his passing-bell with the ringing of the
morning Angelus.

❀ XVI ❀

MONSIEUR JÉROME took to his bed. The mirrors in which Jean
Péloueyre had so often seen his own wizened face reflected were
masked with sheets. They dressed his body as though for High
Mass. Cadette even put a felt hat on his head and a prayer-book
between his hands. The kitchen was filled with the sounds of
preparation, because forty people would be sitting down to dinner.
Several farmers were keening round the hearse like the professional mourners of ancient days. It was the first time that the
curé had ever officiated at a really grand funeral. A pair of gloves
and a penny wrapped in paper were given to each guest. It
rained during the service, but later the sky cleared, and it was

fine until they all got back from the cemetery. Deep in the earth
Jean Péloueyre lay waiting for the resurrection of the dead, in the
dry, sandy soil which mummifies and embalms its corpses.

Noémie Péloueyre smothered herself in crape for the space of
three years. Her great sorrow made her, quite literally, invisible.
She went out not at all except to Mass, and never crossed the
square until she had made sure that nobody was about. Even
when the first hot weather came she wore about her neck a tight
collar edged with white, and fear of gossiping tongues kept her
from buying a black dress of too glossy a silk.

About this time word went round that the young doctor had
been converted. He was seen at Mass on a weekday, having
looked into the church between two professional visits. Whenever
the curé was asked to make some comment on this event, which
must have been highly gratifying to a parish priest, a smile
showed on the thin-lipped mouth, with its look of having been
buttoned up, but he said nothing. Perhaps his authority and power
of persuasion had grown less, because he utterly failed to get
Monsieur Jérome to alter the clause in his last Will and Testament
which laid it down that Noémie must not marry again. Similarly
he failed in his efforts to modify the rigours of a mourning which
he held to be excessive. Monsieur Jérome took much pride in the
knowledge that he belonged to a family whose widows never left
off black, and the d'Artiailhs showed much zeal in their endeav-
ours to keep Noémie swathed and swaddled. That was why, on
winter dawns, when it is very dark in the church, the young doctor could no more pick out the widow in her sable draperies than
she could see her husband through the obliterating stone on which
she kneeled each day. He saw no more, at most, than the radiance
of a young face sparkling with youth, in spite of fasting Communion mornings, and the trials of a cloistered existence. The day
after the Anniversary Mass, when it became known through the
length and breadth of the little town that Noémie Péloueyre was
determined never to lay aside her mourning, the doctor's Christian feelings broke down. He avoided not only the church but his
patients as well. Old Dr. Pieuchon heard a rumour that his young
colleague was drinking heavily, and that he even got up during
the night to take a swig at the bottle.

Monsieur Jérome had never been so well, and his daughter-in-
law had a good deal of leisure on her hands. She gave a considerable amount of attention to the estate, but the pines needed
very little watching. The sensible, repetitive nature of her re-

ligion did not take up much of her time and was nourished on a
minimum of devotional reading. Scarcely capable of genuine med-
itation, she entertained a faith that was largely a matter of formulae. Since there is scarcely any poverty in the resin country,
and since the duty of marshalling once a week the squalling
Children of Mary round the harmonium, made but a limited in-
road on her days, what else was there for her to do than to
conform to local custom, and find amusement in a moderate preoccupation with questions of food? In the third year of her
widowhood she began to grow fat, and Dr. Pieuchon found it
advisable to prescribe an hour's walking exercise each day.

One afternoon, when the weather was beginning to get hot,
she went as far as the farm known as Tartehume. Feeling rather
tired, she rested for a while on the grass bank at the side of
the road. All about her the gorse was humming with bees. Horse-
flies and other noxious insects which swarmed in the heather bit
her ankles. Though she was a strong young woman, she was
conscious of a feeling of oppression round her thudding heart,
and the thought that there lay almost two miles of a hot, dusty
road through a recent clearing in the woods between her and
home obsessed her to the exclusion of all other thoughts. She had
a feeling that the endless miles of pine-trees with the resin oozing
from gashes in their red trunks, and the vast stretches of sand and
burned-up heath, would hold her prisoner for ever. In her unedu-
cated and ignorant mind something that resembled Jean Péloueyre's tormented questionings took shape. What more natural
than that a poor woman dying of thirst in this world of smouldering ash, in this life of utter solitude, should raise her eyes and
stretch her hands to the cool waters of Eternal Life?

She wiped her damp hands with her black-edged handkerchief,
and kept her gaze fixed on her dusty shoes and the ditch where
young bracken fronds looked like opening fingers. But at last she
did look up, and caught full in her face that whiff of rye-bread
which she had come to regard as the very life-breath of the farms.
At once she was on her feet, trembling. A tilbury, which she recognized at once, was standing in front of the house. How often,
peering through the closed shutters of a window, had she not
stared, with more of love than any sight of the stars would have
woken in her, at those gleaming axle-caps! She shook the sand
out of her dress: some farm waggons jolted past her: she heard
the cry of a jay. In a cloud of horse-flies she stood there motionless, her eyes fixed upon the door which, in a few moments, a

young man would open. With parted lips, and a feeling of tightness in her breast, she waited—like some humble and submissive animal. When, at last, the farmhouse door was pushed ajar her eyes searched the deep patch of shadow in which someone was moving. A familiar voice, speaking patois, was prescribing enormous doses of iodine. . . . He appeared. The sun set every button of his shooting-jacket aglow. The farmer was holding his horse by the bridle. He was saying that this was the worst season of the whole year for heath fires, because everything was already dried up, there were no green growths in the underbrush, and the absence of rain meant that the heather was never damp. . . . The young man gathered up the reins. Why did Noémie retreat? Some power kept her from running to meet the man who was coming in her direction, and dragged her backwards. She plunged into the heather that met above her head. The brambles tore at her hands. For a moment she paused, listening to the sound of wheels upon the road she could not see.

Fleeing thus, she was thinking, no doubt, that the town would never accept in silence the prospect of her abandoning the respectable status of widowhood, that there existed in Monsieur Jérome's will a clause which would always keep the d'Artiailhs from consenting to what Madame d'Artiailh referred to as a "crazy match". But would not Noémie's instinct have swept away such obstacles if a law higher than any instinct had not caught it by the throat and strangled it? Small she might be as a human being, but she was condemned to greatness. Born a slave, she had been called to a throne and must exercise regal powers. Do what she might, this rather fat, middle-class woman could not avoid a destiny that had made her greater than herself. Every path but the path of renunciation was closed to her. At that moment, standing in a cloud of flies among the pine-trees, she knew that loyalty to the dead would be her humble glory, that it was no longer possible for her to turn her back on Fate. Across the dry heath she ran, until, at last, worn out, her shoes filled with sand, she flung her arms about a stunted oak whose brown leaves were still unshed, and quivered in the hot breeze—a black oak which had about it something of the look of Jean Péloueyre.

La Motte, Vémars, July:
Johannet, Saint-Symphorien

September 1921.

Genetrix

I

S HE's asleep."
"Come away—she's only pretending."
In this wise, at the bedside of Mathilde Cazenave, did her husband and her mother-in-law whisper together. She could see, through her lashes, on the wall their huge commingled shadows. Walking on tiptoe, they made a creaking progress to the door. She heard their footsteps on the echoing stairs, followed by the sound of their two voices, one shrill, the other hoarse, filling the length of the downstairs passage. Now they were hurrying across the icy waste of the entrance hall which separated the wing where Mathilde lived from its twin, where mother and son occupied adjoining rooms. A door slammed in the distance. The young woman drew a breath of relief and opened her eyes. Above her head was the rod, shaped like an arrow, from which depended, round the mahogany bed, curtains of white calico. The nightlight revealed a few bunches of the blue flowers with which the wallpaper was spotted. On the table a green tumbler of water edged with gold began to shake in response to the shunting of a locomotive in the nearby station. The shunting stopped, and she could catch the murmurs of the late spring night (as, when a train comes to a halt in open country, the traveller becomes aware of the chirping of crickets in a strange land). The 10 p.m. express roared by and the old house shuddered. The ceiling trembled, and somewhere, in the loft or in one of the empty rooms, a door must have blown open. Then the train rumbled across the iron bridge spanning the Garonne. Mathilde, all ears, played a game with herself, which consisted in listening to the metallic din until the very last moment before it died away. Very soon it was drowned in the whisper of the rustling trees.

63

She dozed off, then started wide awake. Once more her bed was trembling, not the rest of the house this time, but only her bed. Only after a few seconds had passed did she realize that body and bed were shaking. Her teeth were chattering, though already she felt hot. The thermometer lying by her pillow was just out of reach.

The movement ceased, but the sensation of heat mounted within her like a lava flood. She felt as though she were on fire. The night-wind bellied the curtains and filled the room with the mingled smells of syringa and coal-smoke. She remembered how, two days before, as she lay drenched in the blood of her miscarriage, she had dreaded the quick exploratory touch of the midwife's hands upon her body.

'I must be over 104. . . . They wouldn't hear of anybody sitting up with me. . . .'

She stared with dilated eyes at the flicker of light upon the ceiling, and lay there cupping her unformed breasts in her two hands. She cried out in a loud voice:

"Marie! . . . Marie de Lados! . . . Marie!"

But how could the old servant, Marie—known as "de Lados" because she came from the market-town of Lados—who slept in one of the attics, possibly hear her? What was that black mass near the window, that crouching animal, seemingly gorged and somnolent, but perhaps waiting to spring? A moment later she realized that it was nothing but a raised wooden dais. Her mother-in-law had had one put up, years ago, in every room of the house, so as to make it easy for her to follow the movements of her son when he was out, whether making the "round" on the north side, pacing the path that ran along the southern boundary of the garden, or expected back by the east gate. It was on one of these contraptions, in the small drawing-room, that Mathilde one day during her engagement had seen the old woman's huge body rise in a sudden fury; had watched the feet stamping with rage and had heard the voice crying:

"You shan't have my son! You shan't take him from me!"

The mounting lava in her body grew chill. She sagged beneath a weight of infinite weariness. She felt bruised and beaten all over, incapable of stirring a finger, unable even to unbutton the neck of her nightgown and so give air to her sweating body. She heard the squeal of the door that opened on to the front steps. This was the hour at which Madame Cazenave and her son, armed with a

lantern, were in the habit of crossing the garden on their way to
visit the secret room which had been built close to the labourer's
cottage, and the key to which never left their keeping. She could
imagine the nightly scene—each of them waiting for the other,
and the talk going on behind the door with the heart-shaped
aperture cut in the wood. Another cold fit seized her. Her teeth
chattered. The bed shook.

She groped with her hand for the bell-pull—an ancient contri-
vance which had long been out of working order. She tugged at
it and heard the scraping of the wire along the cornice. But no
bell sounded in the depths of the darkened house. Once again
she felt burning hot. The dog in its kennel underneath the steps
started to growl. Then it broke into furious barking because somebody was walking along the narrow lane which ran between the
garden and the station. She said to herself: 'How terrified I should
have been if this had happened yesterday!' In this rambling house
that was always trembling, the French windows of which were not
even protected by shutters to the ground, she had known long
nights of lunatic terror. Many were the times she had started up
in bed crying: "Who's there!" But she was not frightened now.
It was as though no one in the world could reach through the
blazing furnace to touch her. The dog was still growling though
the sound of footsteps had ceased. She could hear the voice of
Marie de Lados: "Quès aquo, Péliou!" followed by the noise made
by Péliou as he thumped the steps with his tail in high good
humour and Marie tried to quieten him in patois: "Là! là! tuchaou!"
Once again the flame withdrew from her burned-up body. Her
sense of overwhelming fatigue drifted into a state of peacefulness.
The illusion came to her that she was stretching her bruised and
battered limbs on the sand of the seashore. The idea of praying
never entered her mind.

⋛ II ⋚

FAR from where she was lying, in the small drawing-room next
to the kitchen, beyond the entrance hall, mother and son sat,
though it was June, watching the flames of a log fire flicker and

fall. A half-knitted stocking lay on Madame Cazenave's lap. With one of the long needles she was scratching her head, which showed patches of bald scalp between the strands of dyed hair. From time to time Fernand paused in his occupation of cutting aphorisms from a popular edition of Epictetus with his mother's scissors. This former high-school boy had decided that a book which should contain the sum of all the wisdom taught to man since man had begun to live upon the earth must be capable of revealing to him with mathematical certainty the hidden truths of life and death. Strong in this conviction, he was making a methodical collection of didactic sayings on every conceivable subject. Only in this occupation of "cutting out" could he recover that sense of tranquillity which he had known as a child. But on this particular evening neither mother nor son could rid themselves of their secret thoughts.

Fernand Cazenave jumped up and stood there on his long legs, listening.

"I think I hear her calling."

He shuffled in his slippered feet to the door. But his mother was at pains to call him back:

"Surely you're not going out into the hall again? I heard you cough three times this evening."

"She's all alone."

What, she asked, did he think could happen to her? Such a lot of fuss about an "accident"!

He gripped the old woman's arm and told her to listen. They could hear nothing but the noise made by a locomotive, the song of a nightingale in the darkness, and the creaking of the old house in response to the rattle of shunting trains in the nearby station. It would not begin trembling again until the passing of the early-morning express. But sometimes, in addition to the regularly scheduled movements of traffic, long lines of freight-trucks would set the earth shaking. Each time that happened the two Cazenaves would start awake, light a candle, and look at the time.

They sat down again, and Félicité, hoping to divert her son's attention, said:

"You were going to cut out the reflection you read to me this evening: don't you remember?"

He did remember. It had been from Spinoza, and ran roughly: "Wisdom lies in meditating not on death but on life."

"It's good, isn't it?"

Because he had a weak heart, the terror of dying dictated his choice of maxims. Instinctively, too, his mind, more used to dealing with figures than with ideas, picked out such as it could grasp with the minimum of effort. He began to walk up and down. Several relief maps hung against the green wallpaper. A sofa and a number of chairs upholstered in black leather gave the general impression of a waiting-room. The windows were festooned with long narrow strips of wine-coloured material. The lamp on the top of the desk illuminated an open ledger and a wooden bowl containing pens, a magnet and a stump of black sealing-wax. Monsieur Thiers smiled from the interior of a crystal paperweight. When Fernand turned and came back towards his mother he noticed on her pallid, puffy face the hint of a strangled smile. He threw her a questioning glance.

She said: "It wouldn't even have been a boy."

He protested that Mathilde couldn't be blamed for that. But the old woman merely wagged her head and, without raising her eyes from her knitting, announced that she had "taken the measure of" that little school-marm from the very first. Fernand, who had resumed his seat beside the small table on which a pair of scissors gleamed among a litter of clipped sentences, took his courage in both hands.

"What woman *would* you have approved of?" The angry glee of the old woman broke into words: "Certainly not of her!"

She had made up her mind on that point from the moment of their second meeting, when the feather-brained little bit of trash had actually dared to interrupt Fernand with a "You've told us that already"—just as he was beginning on his favourite story about the only time he'd come a cropper at school, when he had walked straight into a trap laid by the examiner without so much as seeing it, and how he had carried off the whole affair that evening with a magnificent gesture by going to the Opera in a white tie and tails to hear *Les Huguenots*. . . .

"And a lot more which I won't bore you with."

But the little nitwit had soon met her Waterloo. Only two months after his marriage the dear boy had gone back to the little room, next to his mother's, which he had occupied as a child, and the interloper had been left almost entirely to herself in the other wing. She had been of no more importance in the house than Marie de Lados until the day came when she'd shown cunning

enough to take a leaf from the book of those women who, during
the Terror, had escaped the scaffold at the last moment by declaring themselves to be with child.

At first the slut had won hands down. She had become sacro-
sanct in Fernand's eyes. He had been almost bursting with pride
to think that one Cazenave the more was about to be ushered into
the world. He thought as much of his "name" as any lord could
have done—a fact which caused constant exasperation to Félicité,
who had been born a Péloueyre—"one of the best families in the
Landes"—and hated to think that when she had become a Cazenave in 1850 her husband's grandmother was still going about
with her head tied up in a handkerchief. For the first five months
of the girl's pregnancy she had just had to put up with the situation—though she'd been busy enough on the sly! The enemy
might have produced a living man-child. . . . Thank the Lord,
though, the midwife had said from the very first that the prospec-
tive mother was physically malformed and would almost certainly
have an "accident".

"I know you so well, darling. A daughter would have meant
nothing to you. The very sight of her would have plunged you
in gloom. She would have been just as much worry and just as
much expense as a boy. In the first place you'd have had to
have a nurse, because Mathilde could never have fed the child
herself. She's useless for anything like that. *I* was up and about
a week after you were born, and didn't wean you until you
were eighteen months old. Then I began all over again with your
poor brother Henri . . ."

He got up, kissed her on the forehead and said with a solemn
air:

"You were made to be the mother of heroes!"

Then he went back to his chair, and a few seconds later the
snip-snip of the scissors began all over again.

"Tell me, Fernand, what would you have done with a little girl?"

The old woman pressed her point hard, not sparing herself to
make the most of her triumph:

"Can't you see now that she would have brought up a daughter
to hate us?"

He sat staring into nothingness with his round, prominent eyes,
as though trying to focus the image of that tiny ghost, of that
tenuous bugbear existing in his mother's ingenious mind. But, not
being gifted with imagination, he could see nothing.

He could not see the little child whom, at that very moment, his wife was conjuring into a fancied existence to console her for having to die in a lonely room. The tiny bloodstained bundle that her elderly attendant had whisked away might have grown to be the living, breathing creature whose lips she thought she could feel at her breast. What would it have looked like? Lying there, racked with fever, she saw in her heart a baby face unlike any she had ever known—a face of no great beauty, an ailing little face with the same birthmark at the left corner of the mouth that she herself had had. 'I would have sat beside his bed always until the express had gone by, for it would often have frightened him.' She would have shut herself and the child within the borders of a kingdom not of this world, and those who hated her would have been unable to cross the frontier. Her sick brain in which the blood pulsed was obsessed by a question to which there could be no answer: Does God know what sort of tree would have grown from seed that has died? Does God know how those eyes would have looked in which the flame of life has never flickered? Surely, surely, one would meet in the world of the dead all those thousands of pre-existing beings, would know what the little bundle of flesh might have become, what it had the potentiality to become? . . .

But here Mathilde's thought could go no further. The fiery tide was ebbing, the fever making pretence to drain away from the shivering body drenched with a sticky sweat, a prey to that nothingness which is the ante-room to death. She felt as though she had been shouldered aside by some savage beast. Ah! perhaps at any moment now it might return! . . . Stretched on her back, she waited for the shivering fit to begin again, watched for the signs of its approach. But it did not come. She gazed into the depths of her being as into a tell-tale sky when one hopes, yet hardly dares to hope, that the storm is moving away. Perhaps she was going to live after all! Hot, sluggish tears wetted her cheeks. She clasped and kneaded her sweating hands: "Remember, O most gracious Virgin Mary, that never was it known that anyone who fled to thy protection sought thy help in vain. . . ."

She was cast upon life's foreshore and could hear once again the night sounds of the world of men. The breath of darkness was stirring among the leaves. Great trees were murmuring beneath the moon, but no bird waked. A huge wave of fresh, pure wind, born of the ocean and roaring its way above innumerable

trees, and then across the stunted grape-shoots, had taken a final
sweetness from the garden's scented limes, and, dying, now broke
at last upon the drained, exhausted face.

⊷§ *III* ß⊷

GREAT though her weakness was, it held a sense of sweetness.
The only hint of violence came from the beating of her heart,
though its mad racing brought her no pain. She was *not* going
to die. Restored once more to life, never again would she let
her enemy strike her down. As long as another pregnancy
was possible she could force her enemy to lay down her arms.
To get the better of her mother-in-law, *that* was the only thing
that mattered! It would be mere child's play to bring Fernand
to heel. Where she had made her mistake was in thinking that
once married she could abandon all self-discipline. And so she had
too soon given rein to that spirit of ironic mockery which she had
been careful to restrain during the period of their engagement.
She had thought the battle won before it had been joined. It
had been easy enough, she reflected, to stir the embers of desire
in a timid man of fifty by exercising her charms across the privet
hedge which separated the Cazenave house from the garden belonging to the Lachassaignes, whose governess she was—all the
easier because the plump fish had been more than ready to swim
into the net. What she ought to have realized, as she followed
with a watchful eye, from behind the barrier of leaves, the constant tussle between mother and son, was that the man meant
to use her as ammunition for his own purposes, that, once safely
in his power, she would be no more than a weapon in the daily
struggle in which they were engaged, a struggle in which, up to
date, the mother had always come out on top. Lying, this evening,
in a deep well of exhaustion, she made up her mind that from
now on she would control her fits of mocking laughter, would
blunt the point of the goad with which she had driven to frenzy
a man who had grown used to being adored. She forgot that
she was the product of a wretched and penurious past, that she
had deliberately grown a tough skin against adversity, had fash-

ioned for her use a sword of irony, had built a wall of mockery between herself and the world.

   As a small girl, living in a humble house on the Boulevard de
Caudéran—the kind of house known in Bordeaux as a "lean-to"—
she and her young brother, Jean, had indulged, even in those
far-off days, in secret jokes at the expense of their schoolmaster
father when he looked up with a fixed and faraway gaze from the
pile of exercises which he was busy correcting. The shaded lamp
cast its restricted beams on his thin hands and on the sheets of
paper covered with childish scribbles that lay beneath them, shining with a strange and greenish radiance on the bent face, and
making it look as though it had been carved in stone. It was only
later that Mathilde and Jean came by the knowledge that their
mother had not died in Bordeaux, as they had been told, but in
a distant land where she had been living with a husband who
was not their father. Their laughter had been innocent of malice,
because no groan from the man beside them—fate's victim, cornered and at bay—had reached their ears.
   It had been a glory fraught with danger that had come the
way of the "intellectual" with a beard as neat and cared-for as
his style, when, in the course of a series of ten lectures on "The
Sufferings of René", given to a class of young Bordeaux ladies, he
had won the heart of a certain Mademoiselle Coustous (the niece
of a shipowner whose father had been ruined on the turf). But it
had been beyond his powers to protect her from the renewed
offensive of a young man from her own social world. So completely innocent had the professor been in the whole affair that
several members of the Coustous family—though they had all refused to be present at the wedding—showed a willingness, after
his betrayal, to return his greeting when they happened to meet
him in the street. Later, as the result of mental strain brought
on by a succession of worries, trivial in themselves but cumulative
in their effect, he had become so run down that even the correcting of school exercises had been too much for him to cope with
unaided. It was then that Mathilde, herself a student, had begun
to help him; she, too, who had supported him each morning
as he climbed into the tram at the Croix-Blanche terminus, and
had gone with him as far as a side-street behind the school buildings which he took in preference to the main approach to the
front entrance, because there was less danger of his meeting the

morning procession of day-boys. Motionless on the kerb, she would watch him walk away unsteadily towards the class-room where, in all likelihood, he would have to start the day's work by quelling some juvenile uproar. It had been an agonizing time, but her distress had not kept her from laughing when the Lachassaigne cousin—their "good angel"—said that he could not imagine why the professor had not sent in his resignation, or when Madame Lachassaigne (who, before her marriage, had been a Mademoiselle Coustous) announced that if *she* had been in their position she would most certainly have cut down household expenses and done without a maid.

Mathilde found it no less comic that both her father and their cousins should show such a marked preference for Jean, who had the face of a baby angel, curly hair the colour of molten gold, and small pointed teeth which he displayed every time that he indulged in a burst of childish laughter. He might *look* innocent enough, but it was his habit to leave the house after dark by the drawing-room window, and it was she, on those occasions, who sat up to unlock the front door when he came home in the early hours with a look of obscene secrets in the frank gaze of his eyes enlarged to more than their normal size by the physical exhaustion of his pleasures, dirty hands, shirt unbuttoned, and the mark of passionate bites on the girlish whiteness of his neck. She would let the tousled angel of the dawn into the house with never a word of reproach, though an expression of caustic mockery would show upon her lips.

When, once, during an intrigue which he was conducting with a lady of the vaudeville stage, he slunk off to the pawnbroker with several pieces from the household's modest store of table silver, she said not a word either to her father or to the Lachassaignes. Everything, she thought, was all right when he redeemed his pledges and put them back into the sideboard drawer with an air of such sweet repentance that, stranger though she was to all manifestations of demonstrative affection, she could not refrain from kissing the dear, angelic brow—though it was somewhat less unsullied now than it had been in April, and showed a number of pimples. Repentant or not, the angel continued to slip out of the house every night all through that fatal spring, and because he was not sufficiently immaterial to pass through stone walls Mathilde still sat up to let him in. Sometimes, with a furtive look in his eyes, the angel would refuse to go to bed, but would stand jingling a number of gold coins in his trouser pocket and then suddenly spill them in a shower on the table, remarking that there was plenty more where they came from, though there most certainly was not. He smelt, in those days, of tobacco, cheap scent and the frowstiness of unmade beds. He took to humming to himself:

> I'm here at your feet,
> But you don't know, my sweet,
> Whether I love you or hate you.

She would beg him not to wake their father, and then he would make her go into the kitchen and hunt around for what food she could lay her hands on. Rather to her surprise, she derived a kind of bitter pleasure from these midnight feasts. She understood very little of what he told her. Temperamentally opposed to all this purulence of wasted youth, she remained impervious to his charm, but sat listening to his wild talk until the sound of the first tram reached their ears in the shivering dawn.

Finally, a scandal blazed up, though it was quickly smothered, thanks to the headmaster, to the Lachassaignes and to the Coustous. Mathilde never knew what it was all about though she realized that the police were involved, and that a deal of gratitude was owing to the Lachassaignes for shipping Jean off to Senegal, where there was a branch of the Coustous business. Her father lingered on for several months in a state of semi-consciousness. The Lachassaignes said that for his sake, as well as for that of everybody else, one could only hope that the end would not be long delayed. When at last he did die they all declared that it was a blessed release. Madame Lachassaigne gave it as her opinion that in Mathilde's place *she* would not have insisted on so much mourning, seeing that, as always, the family would have to foot the bill.

This they did, and more, for they took the orphaned girl with them to their country house near Langon, where they always spent the hottest months of the summer. It became Mathilde's job to see that their gawky and rather backward daughter did not get overtired. They said of their destitute cousin that she was "really very tactful and knew how to keep herself in the background". Certainly, no sooner was dinner over than she seemed to melt into thin air, and even during the meal was remarkable, if at all, for her colourless hair, her unseeing eyes and her drab clothes. Every description of dirty linen was washed in her presence, her host and hostess seeming to ignore the mild-mannered stranger who pretended to be blind (though she saw) and deaf (though she heard).

In their house Mathilde indulged to the full, though secretly, that taste for ironic mockery which, later, with the Cazenaves, was to be the cause of her undoing. At that time she was all aridity, all dryness, a wasteland without water. She thought that she could judge a gentleman by the standard of her father, who had been betrayed by his wife, mocked by fate, and less well rewarded for his services than a taxi-driver (he had actually hoarded cigarette-ends in a tobacco jar). She was quite sure that love was merely what she had seen embodied in the person of that brother with the look of a bedraggled angel whom she had been used to find at night cast up high and dry outside the peeling front door of the family "lean-to".

Her attitude to the Lachassaignes was one of repressed and concentrated cruelty. Their sole preoccupation, she decided, was food, and succulent food at that. Husband and wife were embedded in succulence. They might have been taken for brother and sister so alike were their fat faces and their greasy chaps for ever running with rich juices. She compared them to two jellyfish whose expanding tentacles could reach no further than their daughter Hortense who, already "has enough pearls"—as she confided to her diary—"to conceal the scrofulous rash upon her neck." She was filled with contempt for them at mealtimes, as she sat there listening to their slow talk interspersed with the rumination of large mouthfuls of rich food. "Only after they have swallowed do they resume the thread of their conversation. They are the kind of persons who never sacrifice nourishment to words." She devised an epitaph for them: "They ate and put a bit aside."

But on the other side of the privet hedge the gambollings of quite another couple had already begun to divert her mind from the bitter amusement which she found in contemplating the Lachassaignes. This particular hedge bounded the south path which was Fernand Cazenave's favourite refuge from the maternal eye. Glancing nervously to right and left, the fifty-year-old mother's darling would saunter along it, puffing, like a guilty schoolboy, at a surreptitious cigarette. If Félicité happened to catch sight of him from one of the wooden daises which she used for the purpose of spying on his movements, he did not always have time to get rid of the butt in one of the shrubberies. There had been an occasion when Mathilde saw him secretly devouring a melon—forbidden food because of its heating properties—and received full in her face the segments of rind which he flung over the hedge. She wrapped the tell-tale objects in a newspaper, hurried round to the Cazenaves, told Marie de Lados that someone had been robbing her kitchen garden, and then hastened back to her point of vantage behind the privet, whence the distant rumblings of the breaking storm were already audible.

But quite often it was she who was spied upon. She pretended not to see Cazenave's stocky head and shoulders showing like the stone bust of some pagan god between the branches of the medlars, the nut trees and the privet. Not that she was tempted to build castles in Spain on the strength of the hot eyes that brooded upon her with such maniac fixity. Young women in the Garonne valley grow used to being stared at with hungry lechery. But Monsieur Lachassaigne seized the opportunity to be heavily jocose at her expense. He made up a story to the effect that Fernand Cazenave had been asking him about the young woman, about her tastes and her character, that he wanted to know whether it were true that her mother had been a Coustous. . . .

It was only natural, therefore, that Mathilde, in the light of these revelations, should call to mind the odds and ends of talk which had reached her from across the hedge (for mother and son, in close escort, like two ancient frigates, would constantly walk together along the south path, vanishing from view at its further end, to reappear when they had completed their round).

To-night, lying in the darkness, feeling so weak that it was beyond her strength even to stretch her hand to the eiderdown, she could still, in memory, recapture the sound of their voices. The shivering fit had not begun again, but she felt that her limbs would never emerge from the depths of fatigue in which they lay submerged. Quite possibly she would not recover from this condition of bruised and battered exhaustion. Her body had been broken, she thought, not by illness, but by the blows rained upon it by the man and his old mother, who at this very moment, probably, were sitting in the study which had been for her the scene of so many depressing evenings: 'She's taking the logs off the fire, pushing the chairs away from the hearth, putting the wire screen on the grate. She's saying to her son: "I won't kiss you now: I'll come and tuck you up when you're in bed." . . .'

She remembered how her heart had started beating one day

when, crouching behind the privet, she had awaited the gathering
storm already announced by the confused sound of their two
voices. At last the pair had come into view at the far end of the
path. It was he, at first, who had talked the louder, accusing
Madame Cazenave of having made him decline an offer made
him by the local Radical Association at the time of the last elections. She had not even allowed him to retain his seat on the
General Council. . . .

They had stopped a few paces from Mathilde's hiding-place.
The old woman said: "All I cared about was that your life
shouldn't be cut short . . . d'you understand that . . . cut short?"

"What nonsense! I saw Duluc yesterday, and he assured me
that I am as strong as a horse, said I should live to bury the
lot of you. What you mean is that you want me to live for ever
tied to your apron-strings. That's about the size of it!"

"You, as strong as a horse! Duluc was making up to you. Why,
ever since you had scarlet fever when you were ten there's
been every kind of thing wrong with you, and half the time the
doctors didn't know what the trouble was. What about the chronic
bronchitis you developed when you were doing your volunteer
service . . . to say nothing of the ailments you've brought on
yourself since?"

"You've always been against my marrying, because you don't
want to lose your hold on me. . . . You've never had but one idea
in your head, to plan a nice solitary life for me."

"You married? . . . That would be a sight for sore eyes!"

"It's no use your trying to get out of it. . . ."

The old woman shrugged her shoulders. She was out of
breath and was mopping her red face with a pocket-handker-
chief. Mathilde knew now, though she hadn't known then,
what it was that had made his mother feel so safe. Often, after a
day spent in bickering, it had been Fernand's custom, armed
with a suitcase, from which all the necessaries would be missing,
to catch the evening train into Bordeaux, there to meet the woman
to whom Madame Cazenave always referred as his "hobby":

"I'm sorry to say that Fernand's got a hobby in the rue Huguerie," she would say, adding: "But he has her well taped. I
don't need to worry about him. He'll never let her make ducks
and drakes with his money."

But the "hobby" never succeeded in keeping Fernand with her
for more than a few days. He would come back shivering—be-

cause he had forgotten his flannel undervest—dropping with sleep because he could never get any rest in a double bed—furious to think how much he had had to spend on tips and restaurants— worn out and depressed because that particular form of exercise was thoroughly bad for his nerves.

"I'm catching the ten-o'clock train to-morrow morning."
"Well, have a good time and enjoy yourself."
Mathilde could remember the tone in which this exchange of threat and reply (so rich in consequences for her) had been barked out. Scarcely had she heard them than she made a secret resolve that she, too, would take the ten-o'clock train.

No use deceiving herself now. So far the shivering fit had not returned, but the sensation of cold was so intense that she half believed it to be the effect of the night-wind and of the icy chill produced by her sweat-soaked limbs. She, and no one else, had been responsible for the wretchedness that had come to her. She had had no feeling of tenderness for this middle-aged man. A sort of mole-like instinct had set her burrowing blindly for a way of escape from her life of dependence. The worst of a humble situation is that it compels us to see everyone with whom one comes in contact solely in terms of their usefulness, to demand only that they shall serve *our* needs. That one preoccupation had dictated her attitude to those about her, to every incident with which she was confronted. She had picked them up like cards and turned them over, always hoping that a trump had been dealt her. Whenever she had found a door ajar she had pushed it open, careless, in her feeling of captivity, whether it would prove to lead into open country or to the edge of an abyss. But on that morning when, saying that she was going to the dentist, she had taken a second-class ticket to Bordeaux, and sat down opposite Fernand Cazenave, she had never really imagined that her manoeuvre would actually succeed....

There was no room, now, for doubt. Once again the mortal storm swirled down, shaking and racking her, driving deep into her very being as though intent on tearing this young and living tree from its roots. She remembered how, when as a small girl she was feverish, she had thought it fun to feel her teeth chattering. Now she could enjoy the sensation to her heart's content. How the bed was shaking! It hadn't shaken like that when the fit came on her for the first time. From the heart of her cyclone she was aware, with curious lucidity, of the peaceful darkness that lay about her possessed and tormented body. She could hear in the withdrawn and sleeping world the flutter of birds awakened by the moon. So faint was the breeze that it scarcely swayed the topmost branches. She was overcome by a feeling of utter loneliness. Why was her father not here, sitting, as he had always done in the days of her childish ailments, beside the bed, pushing back her damp hair with a clumsy hand? She could remember how he used to sit, correcting exercises by the faint glimmer of the nightlight until it was time to give her her medicine. The dead cannot stretch a helping hand from the tomb to those they have loved in life. She cried aloud the name of her brother Jean, who, maybe, was still alive somewhere. She should have been at greater pains to keep in touch with him, even though he did leave her letters unanswered. . . . In what sea had that poor, leaky vessel foundered? . . . She had stopped shivering, and was now in the burning fiery furnace of a terrible onset of fever, blazing from head to foot like a young pine-tree. She could see upon a barren stretch of shore, beneath a burning sky, a heap of rotting matter, now covered by the spume of an incoming wave, now left bare by the ebb, only to be covered once again by the rushing waters. The face was horribly decomposed, but she could see that it was her brother Jean's. On no other man's name, but only on his, did she cry in her delirium. She had loved nobody and been loved by none. Her body that had never been consumed by love would now soon be devoured by death. The rending annihilation of passion had not been for her a foretaste of the last utter dissolution of mortality. Her body would die without ever having known its own secrets.

❧ *IV* ☙

ONE hour later old Madame Cazenave struck a match and looked at the time. For a few moments she lay listening intently, not to the dark intensity of the waning night, but to the breathing of her beloved son on the other side of the wall. After a brief and silent debate she got out of bed, slid her swollen feet into a pair of old slippers, and, wrapped in a purple dressing-gown, left the room, carrying a candle, went downstairs, walked along a passage and crossed the empty spaces of the hall. She was now in enemy territory. As softly as she could she climbed the stairs, but even so the treads creaked under her feet. Once she stopped and listened; then moved on. Outside the door she extinguished the candle which had now become useless, and strained her ears to catch sounds coming from within. The staircase was filled with the grey light of early dawn. Not a cry, not a groan reached her, but only a noise that was like the muted rattle of castanets. She knew that what she was hearing was the chattering of teeth. The noise continued for a while. Then came a cry on a rising note. . . . Only God could read the expression on the face of this listening Medusa whose rival was lying, behind the door, at her last gasp. She was sorely tempted not to enter, to let the inevitable take its course. . . . She hesitated and moved away; then changing her mind, turned the handle.

"Who is it?"

"Only I, my dear."

The room lay now revealed not by the nightlight, but in a pure and icy radiance filtering through the Venetian blinds. Mathilde watched her nightmare moving towards the bed. Through the chattering of her teeth she cried:

"Let me alone! I don't want anything! It's just a touch of fever!"

The old woman asked whether she would like some quinine.

"No, nothing—nothing at all—only to be left alone, to turn my face to the wall. Go away!"

"As you will, my dear."

She had no more to say. She had done her duty. There was nothing with which she need reproach herself. What must be must be.

Mathilde, who had raised her two hands in a gesture of execration even after the enemy had fled, held them still for a moment in front of her eyes, appalled to see how purple and congested they had become. Her heart was beating wildly, like a strangled bird whose wings move in a rapidly weakening flutter. She tried to look more closely, but could not see that already her nails had turned blue. Even in this final moment of her agony she did not believe that the night upon whose threshold she was standing would be with her now for all eternity. Because she was utterly alone, she did not know that she had reached life's ultimate

limit. Had she ever been loved, the clasp of arms would have
made her realize that she must tear herself from the close embraces of this world. No need for her to break free who never had
been held. No solemn voice whispered in her ear the name of a
Father who might, perhaps, be terrible, nor threatened her with
a mercy that might, perhaps, be inexorable. There was no tear-
stained face for her to leave behind, nothing to mark for her
this slipping into the shadows. She died quietly, as those die
who are unloved.

✌❧ V ❧✌

"You hear what Duluc says?"

The banisters shook under the doctor's weight.

The door of the dead woman's room had been left ajar. Marie
de Lados could be heard blowing her nose. After thirty years in
practice Dr. Duluc knew all about puerperal fever. Was Cazenave
proposing to teach him his business? Useless to get a nurse in
forty-eight hours after a miscarriage had occurred.

"Besides, a nurse couldn't have done anything. It wasn't puerperal fever that had carried the poor thing off. It was her heart
let her down. If *that* had been all right she could have struggled
on for three days at least. I've known cases who put up a good
fight for more than a month. Don't you remember that when I
tested her heart—that time when she was down with influenza—
I told you the aorta was affected?"

The big staircase window made a dirty smudge on the blue of
the sky. Fernand Cazenave shook his mother's hand from his arm.

"You hear what Duluc says, darling?" she said again.

For the third time, like a man talking in his sleep, he repeated:

"I ought to have had a nurse."

He held out his hand to Duluc without looking at him, then
slipped into the dark, elongated shadow made by the crack of
the half-opened door, and saw Marie de Lados bending over the
bed. Sitting down a little way off, by the table, he realized
that she was busy plaiting the still living hair. The shunting
of a locomotive set the glass of water trembling. Out on the land-

ing Madame Cazenave and Duluc had raised their voices and
Fernand occupied his mind by trying to hear what they were
saying. . . . Had he ever seen a dead body before? Yes, his
father's, thirty-seven years ago, in the ground-floor room which
had later been turned into the study. How calm his mother had
been! He remembered how she had kept on saying while she
kissed him: "This is the beginning of a new life for you. . . ."

She came back into the room, holding a number of telegrams
in her hand, and saw her son sitting there motionless. There was a
sound of voices in the garden. The Sisters had come from the Convent, several of them. Would Fernand like to have them brought
up? He made a negative movement with his head. She touched
his arm.

"Come, darling. Don't stay here; it's bad for you. You know
how impressionable you are."

He shook her off without even turning his head. She went
downstairs to send the visitors away, and then returned. She
begged him to get some rest, employing all the usual arguments.

"What's the point in wearing yourself out? . . . That won't do
any good. A fine thing it'll be if *you* get ill. . . ."

He spoke at last, still keeping his eyes averted:

"What time was it when you came and listened at her door?"
She said she thought it had been about four.

"You told the doctor that you heard her teeth chattering."

"What I meant was that on thinking things over afterwards I
came to the conclusion that what I had heard *might* have been
the chattering of her teeth."

"Why didn't you go back?"

"She had said that she wasn't in any pain, that she only felt
rather hot. . . . I offered her quinine, but she refused it. I left
her with my mind quite easy."

"In that case, why did you pay her a second visit at six to see
what was happening?"

She made no reply. She felt upset, not because her darling son
was questioning her like a judge, but because there was a note
of anguish in his voice. She found comfort in the thought: 'He's
not really unhappy. . . .' But what terror there was in the suspicion
that he might be! Had Mathilde been alive at that moment she
could not have endured the burning, brooding look with which
the old woman fixed the mortal remains that never more would be
conscious of any feeling at all. . . .

She must go downstairs and see to the sending out of formal announcements to friends and relatives. Time was pressing, but she could not bring herself to leave the two alone. There was nothing in the world she would not do to break that final *tête-à-tête.* . . .

. . . And then, suddenly, she felt ashamed of her emotion. A picture from an illustrated edition of Michelet flashed vividly before her mind's eye: the picture of one of the Popes who had had the body of his predecessor exhumed, had sat in judgment on him, had passed sentence upon him, and then flung himself in a frenzy of hatred upon the corpse. . . .

Only one night, one short night, and then the undertakers would have done their work. By to-morrow the body would be encased in lead, and Fernand's gaze would beat in vain against a sealed and triple sheath. Never again, after that, would he look upon her face. But with what fervour was he looking now! Never had he gazed on anybody with so sad and silent a concentration. Once more she approached him, took his hand, and in words that were half prayer, half command, said:

"Come!"

He pushed her from him. She went to the door. How peaceful the sleeping face looked, how freed from strain and happy, as though strong in the assurance of being loved! As she went down the stairs she was in torment. But once out of the dead woman's presence, once she had begun to address the envelopes, she quickly recovered her poise of mind. Why worry? Wouldn't Fernand, from now on, belong to her and to no one else? Marie de Lados came with a message from her son not to wait luncheon for him. She smiled, reassured by the very extravagance of the gesture. Not for long would the dead keep him from her. He was not the man to let himself be put out for a corpse. But he knew no greater happiness than to make his mother suffer. She had been wrong to try to get him away by force. Had she pretended not to care, he would already have had more than enough of gloom. . . . Putting things at their very worst, he would come down to dinner that evening, sure enough.

She had to spend the whole day in the drawing-room, where the shutters had been closed, the mirror covered, and the furniture wrapped in dust-sheets, receiving relays of women all dressed in black and all whispering behind their veils. Without exception they praised Madame Cazenave for bearing up so well.

Without exception they silently hoped that at about four o'clock they would be offered *something*—if only a biscuit—either because they wanted to feel that the day had not been altogether wasted, or because the presence of death awoke in them an instinctive longing for the rites sanctified by centuries of tradition, a confused desire for those libations which serve to appease the spirits of the departed. But they had to raise the siege with their fast still unbroken.

As soon as Félicité had speeded the last of her parting guests, she asked Marie de Lados whether the master had come down yet. The servant replied that he was still upstairs, and had given instructions that a poached egg and some broth should be taken to him at seven, together with his dressing-gown, his slippers and the bottle of Armagnac. She'd always said, she had, that the master wasn't a Péloueyre for nothing. He might pretend to lose his temper at times, but when you came down to it, there wasn't nobody better'n him nowhere. . . . So said Marie de Lados, and had had a strong feeling that she had better leave it at that, though there was nothing to be seen in the dark hall but the vague bulk of her mistress standing motionless.

"Get back to your kitchen, you old fool! . . ."

The tone in which Madame Cazenave issued this order was the same as that in which, forty years before, when Marie, at the end of her strength, had collapsed into a chair, old Péloueyre had exclaimed: "Get up at once and stop pretending!" He could not bear to see a servant sitting down. In those days Marie de Lados had even taken her meals standing, snatching what food she could get in the intervals of serving her employers. She had no right to a chair, except in the evenings, and only then on condition that she occupied herself with spinning. . . .

. . . Upstairs, they were wrapping the body of the woman whose sufferings were ended in a rough homespun sheet which other servants, long dead, had woven. . . .

Madame Cazenave dined alone. All the while she ate she was listening intently, convinced that at any moment now she would catch the sound of a creaking stair announcing the arrival of her exhausted son. Just as she was leaving the table she fancied that at last she could hear the expected noise, and at once assumed an expression of elaborate indifference. But it was only the 8 p.m. express which had made the door of the loft fly open.

"He'll have come to his senses by to-morrow evening. . . ."

She threw a shawl round her shoulders and went down into the garden. The east wind had filled it with smoke from the station, but the smell of limes and syringa was stronger than the stench of coal. The tree-tops were filled with birds settling down for the night with a whirring of wings. The old woman looked up at the Venetian blinds from behind which glimmered a funereal radiance. She muttered to herself: "There'll be nothing very fresh and sweet about you to-morrow morning, my fine lady!" As she passed the magnolia bush a nightingale took fright. The crickets fell silent in the dry and dusty paddock grass as she passed. She saw in imagination her son shivering in the dawn light beside a woman who had died the previous evening. He had always been so terrified of death. How odd he must be looking!

∽§ V I §∾

HE CERTAINLY was looking odd. Wrapped in a dark-coloured dressing-gown, his head resting against the back of the large wing-chair, he sat gazing fixedly at Mathilde. He had already filled and emptied one glass of Armagnac, and a second stood on the small table at his elbow. Moths were fluttering round the two candles, and it was as though their shadows bumped against the ceiling. Once he spoke Mathilde's name in a voice that his mother would not have recognized. He got up, went across to the bed, chased away a fly, and stood looking down at the spectacle of a face made beautiful by eternity. Again and again he murmured to himself in words that no ears but his could have heard: "Blind! . . . blind!" . . . not realizing that, in fact, he was seeing her for the first time now that death had wiped out all imperfections. There was nothing in the expression of her features to tell of the greed, the hardness or the strained attention of a penniless girl, for ever calculating, mistrustful and seeking shelter behind a mask of mocking irony; nothing of the hunted animal at bay, nothing that spoke any longer of grinding toil and the relentless bars of the prison-house. Had Mathilde, in her lifetime, been happy and adored, she might, perhaps, have looked as she looked now, her face submerged beneath a tide of peace, made free and at rest.

"Blind! . . . blind!" . . . In his slightly fuddled state, Fernand

could hear within his heart the uprush of his anguish. In a fervour
of intoxication he took this stranger to himself. The suddenly
released waters of his spirit crashed through the ice of a winter
that had been abnormally prolonged. Now, for the first time,
when he was already in his fifties, he experienced the pain that
can be inflicted by another. What most men discover while still
young, he, at last, had found to-night! A bitter sorcery bound him
tightly to a corpse. Again he drew close and touched her cheek
with his finger. Long after he had withdrawn he could feel
upon it the lingering sensation of eternal chill.

Something, he knew not what, was vanishing from the face
before him. The terrible moment had come when, looking at the
dead, we say: "there's a change. . . ." He left the room and leaned
over the banisters. Only the night sky lit the scene. The same train
which, twenty-four hours earlier, Mathilde had heard in her last
agonised struggle for life, now thundered by. The fabric of the
great house trembled as it had done in those long hours of her
terrified wakefulness. He remembered that he had promised her
to have full-length shutters fitted to the downstairs windows. He
dwelt upon the thought, finding comfort in the knowledge that
he had shown her at least some kindness in those months of pregnancy. Then he went back into the room. Was he only imagining
a smell, or was there, indeed, some subtle emanation from the object in its clinging shroud of sheets, that now repelled him? He
threw the window wide open and pushed back the blind. He was
not of those who are wont to gaze upon the stars instead of
sleeping. Faced by the slow revolution of a galaxy of worlds, he
had a feeling that he had been brought suddenly into the presence
of a miracle—that he stood upon the brink of mystery. The restlessness that once had led him to cut sentences from printed
books grew large within him. Between the window and the bed,
between a universe of dead worlds and one dead thing of flesh,
he stood, a lonely, living creature.

Not daring to approach the corpse again, he stayed by the window, breathing in the damp night air. The scent of growing things,
the rustle of shadowy presences, woke in him the idea of a happiness he might have had, but which would remain, now, for
ever unknown. He clenched his fists. He could not accept the
thought of Mathilde's nothingness. Had his mother entered the
room at that moment, he would have cried aloud: "I don't want

Mathilde to be dead!" in the same tone as, when a child, he had
wanted everyone to take to their beds if he were ill, had begged
for one of the horses from the merry-go-round at holiday festivities, had demanded strawberries in December or begged to be
allowed to play with a real gun which could really *kill* something.

Remembering one of the sayings he had cut out which had referred to the immortality of the soul, he shrugged his shoulders.
Mathilde's soul! What did he care about the soul! Were there
people so idiotic as to find comfort in such fairy-tales? What he
craved was the gift of her living body. What he longed for was
to see upon the fearful and suspicious face that had been hers in
life the sudden flicker of happiness. He, who had always been incapable of escaping from himself, even in the frenzy of physical
satisfaction, realized now, too late, that what the body blindly
seeks is a pleasure that lies concealed outside itself, that only by
mingling its delight with the delight of another body not itself
can it find assuagement. He felt upon his forehead the imprint
of his nails. The sobbing cry of some creature of the night sounded
so close to the house that he started back, his heart thumping.
"Perhaps," he said to himself, "it is the *frégasse.* . . ." (that mysterious bird of the Landes which is attracted to houses not where
death has struck, but whither it is on its way).

The night was at its peak. There would be no train now till
five o'clock. No breeze would stir the deadweight of the leaves.
Even from the meadows nothing came except the sleepy murmur
of vegetable dreams. He went across to the wardrobe, but started
back because the horror of his own face peered at him from the
mirror. It was as though already in himself the same corruption
lurked as was at work already in Mathilde's body three yards
away.

Again the sobbing night-cry sounded—so close that it might
have been in the room with him. The creature must have settled
on the chimney, perhaps even in the flue! He stared at the black
iron plate which closed the hearth. Had he not heard the beat of
sinister wings? He shrank back towards the door, defeated. He
would return to his mother. Not for nothing had the old woman in
the other wing remained seated on her bed; had kept herself
from running to the help of her ungrateful son. She, too, had
caught the night-bird's note, and thought contentedly: 'He won't
be long now: I know him!'

Fernand, in a panic, ran out on to the landing. A light was

moving, filling the staircase well. Marie de Lados appeared, holding a lamp. She was wearing her Sunday best. Round her head was a black silk scarf, from beneath which protruded the elongated lobes of her ancient ears. It had occurred to her that the master must be feeling sleepy. He took the lamp from her hand and went downstairs so quickly that the flame blew out. He reached his room, undressed in the dark, and fell asleep. At almost the same moment his mother, hearing his quiet breathing from behind the wall, resigned herself to the thought that she would not be able to give him a good-night kiss.

At the other end of the house Marie de Lados was sitting upright in her chair, not leaning her head against its back, and casting a strange shadow on the wall. Her toothless mouth moved rapidly. The beads of her rosary lay in the hollow of her apron like grains of corn and barley.

⤳ VII ⤲

HEAVILY veiled in spite of the heat of the morning, which was already considerable, Félicité Cazenave emerged from the garden's easternmost wicket and reached the road that ran parallel with the main line from Bordeaux to Cette. She strode ahead with her bust thrown prominently forward, her two hands crossed on her stomach, her skirt dragging in the dirt and dust. For a while she kept to the highway, then turned right towards the cemetery. She did not cross the threshold of the city of the dead, but tapped with her finger on the glass door of the keeper's lodge. A sullen voice—the voice of a man who had long ago given up all hope of a tip—answered her question before she asked it—and announced that Monsieur Cazenave had not been seen there for close on six days. She set off again, breathing heavily, but with a sense of relief, feeling that she had scored a point in her battle with the woman who was dead. During the week following the funeral (at which he had appeared like a man in a trance, with so deep a look of anguish on his face that the neighbours had been quite nonplussed), Fernand had visited his wife's grave each morning without fail, taking with him a bunch of ill-assorted and short-stemmed flowers, such as might have been plucked and bundled

together by a not very skilful child. But now, at last, his devotion
was showing signs of weakening. A change was coming, thought
Félicité to herself. She needed in some sort to be reassured, but
deep down she was oppressed by a feeling of lassitude. By nature positive, she had found that her accustomed weapons were
of no avail against a ghost. To produce any effect she must have
living flesh on which to work. The tactics of her vanished rival,
crouching, as it were, in Fernand's vital centre, and in possession
of him as of some captured fortress, disconcerted her. Not that she
hadn't foreseen the rancour and the hate with which this adored
son would pursue her, hadn't realized that his craving to inflict
a hurt on her would be tenfold magnified (even as, when a child,
sitting on her lap, he had been in the habit of butting her with
his knee till she cried for mercy). But nothing of the sort had
occurred. Instead, he had behaved with an indifference, a spiritual
absentmindedness, which put her off her game, and kept her
from developing any freedom of manoeuvre.

As she pushed open the garden gate she felt tired. She was
sweating beneath the heavy panoply of her mourning. Entering
the garden, she was met by the strong scent given off by the
old box-hedge which surrounded the pumping contraption where
Grisette, the donkey, stood dozing on the pathway of trodden
dung. She jabbed, as she always did, at the animal's tough hide
with her umbrella. It jerked awake and into sudden movement.
'What does it matter,' she thought, 'whether he goes to the cemetery or into the fields to dream, since his mind is always dwelling
on *her.*' This morning, as on other mornings, with one shoulder
slightly higher than the other, and wearing on his head a three-
year-old straw hat which he had had dyed, he had left the house,
dressed in a strong-smelling alpaca coat. But it was at noon,
especially, when he came home and sat down opposite his mother,
that his mind seemed furthest away. Nothing seemed to "take"
with him. He no longer reacted to words which formerly would
have put him beside himself with fury.

She settled down on the little dais behind the study window,
whence she could watch his every movement, like an ancient
queen dethroned. With her knitting lying untouched upon her
lap, she stayed there, looking out, never for a single moment
taking her eyes from the garden gate. The passing of the 11 a.m.
train announced his impending return. Each day she waited for
her adored son to come in, as though with his appearance the

hideous spell would be broken. 'He'll come back to me all right,' thought the mother to herself: 'Men don't change after they've turned fifty.' It did not occur to her that he could have changed. He was the same small boy, prone to fits of temper, whom she had dandled on her knee. He resented the fact that Mathilde was dead. Even death could not baffle the violence of his desires.

When it became clear that he was late she stepped down from the dais and began to pace the room, saying to herself, for the hundredth time: "I must get it clear in my mind: I *did* go up: I *did* knock at her door: I *did* ask whether she was in pain, and she *did* reply that she didn't want anything. . . . Yes, but when I went into his room he was looking up the word *infection* in the medical dictionary. . . ."

So deep was she in thought that the sound of Fernand's steps in the hall took her by surprise. She heard him ask Marie de Lados whether luncheon was ready. There being a quarter of an hour to wait, he went into the garden. Félicité watched him from behind the curtain. He was standing quite still in the middle of the path. At what was he looking? She could not know that with his mind's eye he was seeing the room in the rue Huguerie where once every month his "hobby" used to wait for him. There was always a number of small Turkish towels hanging on a line in the window. She called him her old skinflint, because, do what she might, she could never get a penny more out of him than her fixed fee. Such had been Fernand's history in matters of love. . . .

He raised his eyes to the windows of Mathilde's room. 'All the same,' he thought, 'she must have known, during all those months of pregnancy, that I loved her, that I was taking her part against my mother. But she probably decided that it was because of the child. . . .'

He tried to remember the occasions on which he had treated her with gentleness; but in vain. The only thing that came back to him—and it came with the force of an obsession—was the recollection of that last trip they had made together to Bordeaux, and how ill-tempered he had been because he thought she was spending too much on things for the baby. "In my young days," he had grumbled, "a mother wouldn't have dreamed of *buying* baby clothes. She would have made it a point of honour to knit every stitch herself." Mathilde, silent and weighed down by the load she was carrying, had dragged along at his side. They had gone into a rather better-class restaurant than those he usually frequented when she was with him. There were flowers on the table. She had unfolded her napkin and smiled, happy and re-laxed at last. "We serve *à la carte* only, sir," the waiter had said in reply to his enquiry about the price of the dinner. With a furious glance at the menu he had got up and asked for his hat and coat. They had had to walk right down the whole length of the room again, past the whispering diners and the sniggering waiters. Then they had set off again along the blazing hot pave-ment of the Allées de Tourny. Fernand had pretended not to notice that she was crying.

He went back into the house. Madame Cazenave hoisted her-self to her swollen feet and moved to meet him. "How hot you are, you poor old thing."

She tried to wipe his streaming face with her pocket-handker-chief, but he turned away.

"You're positively soaking: run away and change, or you'll catch cold."

He made no reply, and she added:

"I've laid out a change on your bed."

Moving clumsily she followed him into the study. A sudden wave of anger swept away her control:

"If you get ill, who'll have to look after you, I should like to know? I, of course!"

At this he swung round on her:

"Or, alternatively, you could leave me alone to die—too!"

She staggered under the blow and could find no answer. They crossed the kitchen, omitting their usual routine of lifting the cov-ers from the saucepans and peering inside, and entered the shut-tered, stuffy dining-room.

"You're eating nothing."

Really worried this time, she repeated the phrase. Not to want to eat is regarded in the Landes as the sure preliminary of sick-ness and death. Loss of appetite is equivalent to the loss of taste for all the best that life can offer. There is only one thing left for the sufferer to do—take to his bed and wait for the end.

Marie de Lados broke in with:

"You beaint eating nothing either, ma'am."

Such failure to enjoy their food was quite different from the pretended distaste in which mother and son had indulged when

Mathilde had been running the house, turning up their noses in mute agreement at everything set before them, in the hope of forcing the younger woman to surrender the reins of government. When Félicité returned to the study she found that she was alone. The dear boy had not followed her. This had always been the time when, after coffee was served, they had sat side by side on the black leather sofa, her head on his shoulder, sharing the same newspaper, giggling like a couple of schoolchildren, starting guiltily apart when Mathilde opened the door, like two people who have been interrupted in the middle of a private conversation. She could still hear in imagination the offended voice of the little schoolmistress, their enemy, saying: "Am I disturbing you?" —and her own replying: "Oh no, we've said everything we had to say."

Such skirmishes had been the good lady's dearest delight, the very substance of her day-to-day existence. . . . Where had her darling gone to earth this time? It had been obvious, that he was at the end of his tether, and he was probably lying down. His aimless wanderings exhausted him. If he insisted on overtaxing his lungs and his heart he must take the consequences. . . . Unoccupied and miserable, she would have liked to seek him out. But what good would it do? He had got into the habit, latterly, of bolting his door against her, as though she had been Mathilde.

A beam of sunlight, slipping between the half-closed shutters, drew a bright sparkle from the frame of a photograph standing on the mantelpiece. It was a picture for which Félicité had an especial weakness. A month after the marriage, mother, son and daughter-in-law had "sat" for a perambulating artist. But just before the shutter had clicked, Fernand had dropped his wife's arm and taken his mother's. Ever since that day Félicité and her son had beamed into the room from the cabinet-size group, while the young woman, standing behind, showed an unsmiling presence and dangling arms.

Madame Cazenave could not resist the temptation to take another look at this reminder of their happy times. She went over to where the picture stood, but came to a sudden, sickening standstill when she saw that the frame was empty. Her eyes sought the table, caught by the glitter of the scissors which Fernand used for cutting out his "sayings". They shifted to the wastepaper basket. Heavens! wasn't that *her* smile, *her* thrust-

ing nose, *her* spreading front, showing through the woven wicker-
work? She flung herself upon the photograph which had been so
foully destined for the garbage can. The wretched creature had
carefully cut out Mathilde's face. Doubtless he was carrying it
about with him now in his notecase, against his heart. Probably
it was his delight, in moments of solitude, to take it out and kiss
it ardently. . . .

. . . For the past two weeks the old woman had endured everything without a murmur, but this tangible evidence of her banishment broke down her resistance. A wave of maniac fury swept
everything before it, so that her gnarled and swollen fingers began
to tremble. She stamped her foot just as she had done, on that
day long ago, when she had cried out to Mathilde: "You shan't
have my son—never!" She went to the door. Her face showed
the tense, mindless expression of a woman carrying a loaded revolver or a bottle of vitriol under her cloak. Perhaps there are
not different kinds of love, but one kind only. This ageing woman,
deprived of the son whom once she had wholly possessed, had
been dealt a mortal blow. The craving to own, to dominate,
spiritually is more bitterly tenacious than the desire which urges
young bodies to couple in an ecstasy of mutual ravishment and
hunger.

She felt stifled, and threw the shutters open. The midday sun
lay with a molten heat upon the burned-up garden. Between
the dusty squares of grass the gravelled path had the colour of
ashes. The puffing of a train pulling out of the station reminded
her of the struggle of congested lungs for air. Blind with anger,
swaying on her feet, she went out on to the landing. At each
upward step she had to pause for breath, but she forced herself to
climb the stairs until, at last, she reached the room of her ungrateful child. It was empty. There was a litter of medicine bottles
and a smell of urine. The sight, in the mirror, of her purple cheeks
filled her with terror. Where should she run the traitorous wretch
to earth if not in her enemy's lair? She went downstairs again
(her ailing legs trembling beneath her), hurried along the corridor, crossed the shadowed hall, turned into another corridor, and
reached at last the stairs leading to the stronghold of the all-
powerful dead. For some seconds, all strength gone from her,
she stood motionless outside the door, as she had done on the
fatal night, and listened. But not as on that night did now the
eye of God see in the expression of her old, expectant face the

chasing shadows of surprise and hope. This time she stood shaking and alert, all ears for the faint sound of snoring, broken now and again by a hiccup—for the stifled breathing that she knew so well—delicious music made familiar by those many nights when, from the other side of a dividing wall, it had brought assurance of the loved one's presence. In that happy past she had been wont to lie awake, her mind and faculties so centred on the sound that insomnia became for her the sweetest of all fortune's gifts. . . . But now the power of someone dead lay like a barrier between her and her darling's slumbers. A fresh surge of anger lifted her. Blind to all else, she turned the handle.

She had to screw up her eyes. The two windows were wide open, and through them struck the savage glare of June. Some lilies, set in two vases on the table, filled the room to suffocation, as though it had been fast sealed. Between them, in a frame adorned with seashells ("A Present from Arcachon") which was too large for it, stood Mathilde's photograph, cut with pious care from the group at which she had been looking a few minutes before. Laid out in front of it were the girl's tiny engagement ring, her wedding ring, and a pair of soiled white gloves. To complete the scene, Fernand lay slumped in the great wing-chair, his head fallen forward, struck down by sudden sleep. A bumble-bee was banging against the ceiling and the mirrors, seeking the open window. That found, its heavy drone was lost in the blazing inferno of the sky.

Félicité's boots creaked. Fernand shifted his position. She paused, then took a step towards the table, her hands outstretched in the gesture of a Polyeucte, destroyer of images. She longed to spit upon the pictured face, to tear it to shreds, to trample it underfoot . . . but dared not. Fernand's head had fallen on his arm, which lay sprawled upon the table. All of him that his mother could see was an untidy tangle of grey hair. Her face was pouring with sweat, but it felt cold. Her sight was clouded. The blood throbbed in her ears, so that she seemed to be listening to the sea's sound in a shell. She wanted to speak, because her tongue felt heavy. She could not tell whether the sounds she heard were caused by crickets or by flies or by the throbbing of her own arteries. An invisible hand pushed her towards the bed, forced her down upon the couch where Mathilde had suffered and had died. She lay cringing there like an animal,

waiting. At last the sense of heaviness lifted from her eyes, the
constriction vanished from her throat. The dark bird of evil omen
took wing and flew away. She breathed again. Her son was still
sleeping to an accompaniment of little choking sounds. Danger
was still close at hand, and the sense of it made her sweat and
tremble. But the look with which she now brooded upon the
altar standing between the outspread arms of her unconscious
son had less in it of hatred than of fear.

✑ *VIII* ✎

THE ATMOSPHERE which hung about the evening meal was not
that to which Fernand had grown accustomed during the periods
of their mutual hostility. His mother's very look surprised him. As
a rule she sat straight-backed and majestic, a symbol of domination. This evening, she seemed to have collapsed, and her colourless cheeks sagged. What he felt now was not pity so much as a
bored irritation at the thought of the blow with which he was
about to fell her. He was afraid that she would not take it without
a strident protest. Her attitude, when at last it came, was more
coldly detached than he had dared to hope. What she had seen
that day had, in some sort, prepared her. Consequently, she did
not tremble when Marie de Lados came to ask her for a pair of
clean sheets so that she could make up the master's bed in the
poor dead lady's room. She handed over the key of the linen-
cupboard to the servant, touched her son's forehead with her
lips, and took her candle. Fernand suspected her of playing
some deep game. But no such idea was in her mind. Aware that
she had already suffered betrayal in her son's heart, she felt no
surprise that he could pass over to the enemy bag and baggage.

Once in her own room, however, she felt frightened by the
unaccustomed silence. She seemed for the first time to be aware
of the trembling of the house which, for the convenience of his
business (*Northern and Local Timber Ltd.*), her husband, Numa
Cazenave, had built facing the station. Left a widow, she had
found comfort in the sound of her darling's noisy slumbers on the
other side of the wall. They had served as a barrier between her
and the perils of the darkness. Not furtive footsteps, nor the iron

resonance of the great bridge across the river, nor the fury of the equinoctial gales, nor the singing of nightingales in the lilacs, had ever prevailed against the sleeper's breathing. The few hours that he needs must pass in Mathilde's room had but made sweeter the triumph of his resumed presence there next door to her. But how strange now seemed the darkness as she lay in the room where, for fifty years, she had spent her every night! The last train before the early-morning express set the windows shaking. There would be nothing more except endless lines of freight waggons, the noise of which, since the engines never whistled, sank into the substance of her dreams. Useless any longer to sleep with her lips pressed to the wall beyond which her son no longer choked and snored. Better to turn upon her other side, to close her eyes, to empty her mind of all thought. . . .

. . . Suddenly she started up. 'Somebody's walking in the garden!' Had she really heard somebody walking? At times the breeze rustled the leaves so gently that she could swear it was the sound of footsteps. Félicité struck a match, heard no repetition of the noise, and blew it out again. But in her mind's eye she held a clear vision of the rambling house standing all exposed in the darkness with its defenceless windows. In imagination she could see a furtive face pressed to the glass, a hand, armed with a diamond, silently cutting a hole in the pane. How could she prevail upon Fernand to fit the shutters which he had refused to order when Mathilde asked him? The best thing would be to remind him of the dead woman's wish. In an access of devotion he might carry it out.

It was borne in upon her that this momentary terror had been the young woman's companion night after night. Coincidence? . . . Chance? . . . The old woman shrugged her shoulders and told herself not to be a fool. But memories of servants' stories, deep buried in her mind, rose now to the surface, and older memories still, of things that had frightened her as a child. No, no, it was not true that the dead seek vengeance. Moment by moment corruption was eating ever more deeply into what remained of Mathilde as she lay in the third grave to the left against the end wall of the cemetery. Nevertheless, Félicité explored the darkness with her eyes, as though she could sense a swarm of unknown presences behind the seeming reality of things. She forced a laugh. She believed in nothing that she could not touch. She had been born in the days when only a few sandy tracks linked the

Landes with the outside world. The "Terror" had driven the priests
away. Her own mother had not made her First Communion until
the day she was married. At the beginning of the previous century
the children of the Landes had had but one religion, that of the
implacable and fiery sun; had known but one Almighty, the
blaze that burned the pines—a swift-moving, unapproachable
God who left in the wake of his progress a host of smoking
torches.

Coming downstairs rather later than usual, because she had not
slept until the early hours, she saw Fernand's hat and stick lying
on the log-box in the hall. How was it that he had not gone out?
Marie de Lados assured her that he was still sleeping. She could
see for herself, the woman said, that the Venetian blinds were
lowered. With her eyes fixed upon the windows, Félicité suffered
as many agonies as though her rival were clasping Fernand in
her arms. "I'm going mad," she said to herself. Had she ever
known worse torture when Mathilde was alive? Again she formed
her silent words: "You know perfectly well that she is no longer
there. . . ." That might be true, yet as surely as though she were
present in the body, she was holding prisoner in her bed the man
who, while she lived, had fled from her. Félicité could not remember ever to have suffered such sordid misery even in the
days that had immediately followed the marriage. It was then,
during those weeks, that she had felt convinced of her eventual
victory. A week after the wedding, while the young couple were
still at Biarritz, Fernand had written her a letter which had filled
her with such joy that, from having read it again and again, she
could repeat its sweetest passages by heart:
        . . . You were right. Only a mother is capable of understanding
a man like me. All other women are as strangers. They believe
they love, when, actually, their thoughts are concentrated on
themselves. The man's health has to take second place to their
pleasure. They think it right and proper that he should spend
money like water to satisfy their most trivial whims. Women who,
before they were married, never knew where to look for their
next meal are always the most insatiable. You remember that
hotel close to the station at Bayonne—not a very luxurious sort of
place, perhaps, though you and I found it perfectly all right—well,
Mathilde refused to stay there, because she said she'd seen a
squashed bug, and because there was a smell of slops. We had to
move into one of those places I loathe, where there's a crowd of

servants who do nothing for one and then look daggers when one
tips them a shilling. Mathilde thinks I'm mean, and talks about
nothing but herself. She's not the slightest bit interested in anything that concerns me. And to think I used to grumble because
you were always fussing! She merely laughs if I so much as
mention my health. If I'm still well it's certainly no thanks to her!
In the train she had a draught roaring through the carriage. She
gets up at night when I've gone to sleep and opens the window.
I needn't tell you that the pain in my left shoulder has started
up again. She's for ever sneering at something or other, criticizing
the way our family behaves, and saying that it's perfectly disgusting not to wash before going to bed—which is ridiculous,
seeing that one's got to go through the whole business again in
the morning! I can't tell you more than a tiny part of what I have
to put up with. But don't worry, mother dear; your son will do his
duty to the bitter end.

It had been a summer's morning just like this one. The arrival
of his letter had filled the old she-wolf with mingled happiness
and anxiety. How sweet her memories were of the ensuing
weeks! Signs of a growing disharmony had accumulated, until a
day had come when, after a night the vicissitudes of which remained wrapped in mystery, he had come to her with a face as
white as a sheet, and had said: "Please have the bed made up
again in my old room. . . ." She had been waiting for that moment
of ecstasy, not daring to hope that it would come so soon. She
could see herself again as she had been that day, seated by the
narrow child's bed in the carefully aired room, the bed on which
Marie de Lados had piled the sheets smelling of mint and running
water. . . . But now, alas! . . . The sun was burning through the
mist. The birds had stopped singing, though she could hear the
scrape of a cicada. The shutters rattled as Marie de Lados closed
them in front of the windows. The south wind felt hot on her skin,
and smelled of burning pine. Over above the Landes the sky must
be overcast with smoke touched to crimson by the flames. From
moment to moment the thirst of the tormented earth grew fiercer.
Péliou was scraping a hole with paws and muzzle to make himself
a cool shelter in which to sleep. Félicité could hear, as she had
heard the day before, the throbbing of her arteries. She stood
perfectly still fearing that the slightest movement might make a
beckoning sign to death. She uttered a few words as a mad
woman might have done, and Péliou pricked his ears, thinking

them addressed to him. On the bed where Mathilde's body had lain she saw, in imagination, her son's. Seized by a sudden panic, she pulled herself together and walked towards the sun-drenched terrace steps. The lizards' throats were pulsing and the air was filled with the scent of geranium. Just as she reached the first step one of the French windows was pushed open and Fernand Cazenave appeared. He said: "Breakfast's ready, mother."

He was alive. He stood there before her in the merciless sunlight. His straw hat was tilted over his eyes and hid his face. Her heavy old body felt light as air as she mounted the steps to her darling, standing motionless above her. But her joy was short-lived. Seeing him at close range when he took off his hat to kiss her, she had to keep herself from crying out, so ravaged did he look. The dead woman had done this to him! His lips were drained of colour as though he had been drinking vinegar: his eyes were bloodshot like those of an old dog. . . .

. . . As he took his place at table, he, in his turn, gave his mother a long look. Throughout the meal it was clear that each was made nervous by the other's presence, but while she never took her eyes from his face, he soon became absorbed in his own thoughts, drawn by some inner vision from which nothing, ever more, would turn his gaze. It was all very well for Marie de Lados to bewail the fire which was blazing over towards Landiras, saying that the tocsin had not been sounded because the blaze was too far away from the village—what tocsin that ever rang could have startled Fernand from that memory of the first night he had spent in the room where Mathilde had died?

IX

AT FIRST he had almost enjoyed stretching at full length beneath the vaporous white wings of the bed-curtains that hung from a rod in the shape of an arrow. The windows were open and beyond them the night was breathing like some familiar presence. There was nothing to remind him of his vigil by the dead, nor yet of the bird of death. Quite the contrary, in fact, and he lay there on his back, his hands clasped beneath the sheet, his legs straight and rigid—for all the world like Mathilde as he had seen her last. He could feel himself drifting between gentle tides into the depths of an infinite repose. She was there with him, not so much as a separate entity, but within him, her body made one with his. He felt a tingling responsiveness which brought back to his consciousness their bridal nights. Slowly his thoughts took form, gathering about the hours when he had felt her frightened presence at his side. The picture thus presented to his mind's eye was at once so pitiful and so grotesque that he shook his head and groaned aloud. Like all the men of his race, and like the majority of all mankind, he should by rights have died without ever knowing the pangs of love.

Fate had played a sorry trick on him by troubling in an ageing body waters that lay deep hidden. The muddy stream had cut a sluggish channel, nor had he fully realized what was happening. His forebears had been jealous lovers of trees and vines. Numa Cazenave had wished only that his folk should pile upon his grave the greasy clay of a land which had been his solitary passion. When he had taken a wife he had had to ask a friend "how one behaved" with a woman. To all the vanished fathers of his line marriage had meant but one single thing—an increase in worldly possessions, an assurance of the continuity of property. The certainty of the family's survival had been their challenge flung in the teeth of mortality. In almost every case one son had been enough to perpetuate the fragile chain of life which, till the world's end, would bear the burden of a patrimony endlessly enlarged by bridal doweries and testamentary bequests. Never had love come to change the course of that single, powerful stream. Their wives, whether Péloueyres or Cazenaves, had always been the kind of women who murmur in the nuptial bed: "Hurry up now, and let's get it over." But inevitably a day would come when on one link in the chain of life a spot of rust would appear and begin to eat into the precious metal. For those who came after, for those as yet unborn, there would be but a heritage of misery.

There was horror in the mute enmity that lay between Fernand and his mother. It was from her he had received the legacy of fire, but it was her doting jealousy that had prevented him from keeping the flame alive. That he might not escape from her she had willed that he should be a weakling. Only if he were less than a man could her power remain unquestioned. She had brought him up in a lunatic distrust of women. Ever since his fifteenth year he had divided them into two categories—"the sort who want to trap you" and "the sort who give you a dose". No doubt, if he had been passionate by temperament, obstacles of this kind would not long have kept him from doing as he wanted. But, in the first place, he came of the stock of those peasants, so familiar on the country roads of France, whom one sees walking home of an evening, arms swinging, hands empty, holding the middle of the road like kings, with, trotting behind them, a poor harassed female more loaded with baskets and packages than a donkey.

Further, because all life long his self-confidence had been kept under subjection and control, he had grown into the type of young man who, from sheer terror of not being found attractive by women, maintains that a fellow can always get the wife he wants provided he is willing to pay the price she asks. It was a matter of pride with him to hold that those who boast of getting their women for nothing do, in fact, spend a great deal more in the process than their shrewder fellows. He was fond of saying: "They know exactly where they are with me, and precisely how far in the matter of money I am prepared to go . . . that I'm not one for frills, and that they'll get no flowers and presents out of *me!...*"

But now, lying on Mathilde's bed in the darkness, he remembered how, one fine day when the noon sun was blazing on the garden path, he had seen behind the bee-loud privet a young girl's body. . . . Had it only been a question of taking a stand against his mother's authority, would he really have broken through the hedge and seized that honey-smelling prey of flesh and blood, would he really have thus plunged into a world of dangers? Doubtless the impulse had at first been born of a wish to avenge his thwarted manhood—but behind it there had lain a deeper desire. He realized this now, now when it was too late to satisfy the latent hunger, when that selfsame prey of flesh and blood and intoxicating scent had turned to corruption and become a horrible and nameless thing . . .

He got up and moved on naked feet about the room, stumbling against the furniture. He said out loud: "She *did* love me. If she hadn't loved me she wouldn't have suffered because of me. . . ." He shook his heavy head and groaned. "No, no, love didn't enter into it. . . ." His face puckered into the same ugly grimace as when he had had one of his childish crying fits, and the tears streamed down his cheeks. For a moment he stood still, biting his nails, and said: "Was there another man?" Not until this moment had he ever been jealous, because overweening pride had kept the emotion from him. Another man in Mathilde's life? Anguish was very close to him at that moment, but he remembered something that his mother had said to him time and time again: "At least she's respectable, one must grant her that. Respectability's about the only merit she *has* got", adding, in reference to the Coustous woman who had been Mathilde's mother: "For once in a way it's not true to say like mother like daughter."

What he did not know was that when the old woman had given this grudging praise to her daughter-in-law she was remembering a certain luncheon at the Merlets, a luncheon given in honour of the young couple's return from the honeymoon, at which a master from the local school had been sitting at Mathilde's right. He was popularly credited with being a poet, and was in the habit of giving advice to the Merlet girls who dabbled in verse. Félicité Cazenave had got the impression, while the meal proceeded, that Mathilde was drinking in every word that fell from the lips of this dark and elegant young man. Who but God could know whether the girl hadn't, for a moment, felt a lightness of the spirit, a sense of surrender, the sprouting of some deep and secret bud, a barely perceptible attraction towards this neighbour who dropped his voice to quote a line of poetry in the hubbub of the meal's end? Laughter was creasing the country faces around the table, and he, no doubt, was dreaming of a romantic love that he had learned from books. But at that moment coffee had been brought in, and Félicité had rather crudely urged him to recite something. He had refused, and she had begged him at least to write a few lines in the album in which her daughter-in-law was in the habit of copying her favourite extracts. From then on Mathilde had been on her guard. Félicité was quite incapable of concealing her wiles, and her daughter-in-law liked to think that she could "always hear the clump of her boots a mile off". The schoolmaster had not got so much as a glance out of her, and when, later, he paid a visit to the Cazenaves, the young woman had refused to come down to the drawing-room. Fernand could sleep in peace. He had never been betrayed, even in thought, by the poor creature whose sole preoccupation had been to keep the tally of their uneasy relationship, and avoid trouble.

He dismissed the subject from his mind. He saw his whole life stretch before him arid, melancholy. How had he been able to cross such wastes of sand without dying of thirst? For years he had not been conscious of its emptiness. Only now did he feel the torment. Mathilde had died without even knowing that he *was* thirsty, and now she was dead and he lived on. If one stream had dried up, he thought, a thousand others would quickly bubble into view. What easier than to replace Mathilde? Loving now, for the first time in his life, he resented the mirage which plunged the whole world in darkness, leaving one single image only bathed in light. Corrupted from his earliest youth, he had never really grown up.

Accustomed to use all things for his pleasure, to turn everything to his own advantage, he tried to reassure himself with the thought that Mathilde had been but the occasion of his discovering a universe of delights which he could now profitably explore with another. . . . But what other? A vision formed in his mind's eye of towels hanging out to dry in a window of the rue Huguerie. . . . What others? In the contracted world of his dishonour, in the tangled strands of the sticky web which his mother, for his protection, had set about him for half a century, he struggled now, a great fat fly held captive. He struck a match and, holding the candle high, looked at himself in the glass. The cult creates the idol. Mathilde, perhaps, and Mathilde alone, might have been able to attach herself to this ageing and irritable god whom forty years of maternal adoration had formed and conditioned. Too late! He went to the window. A few drops of rain must have fallen, for he could smell the scent of the ravished earth. He lay down on the floor, flat on his stomach, his face resting on his folded arms, and there he would have stayed, had not the stiffness in his joints sent him back to the bed. At length sleep put an end to his troubles. The first birds woke, but him they could not wake. He might have been the lifeless simulacrum of a human body.

❦ X ❧

It was during luncheon on the following day that Félicité Cazenave, facing across the table the middle-aged man who was her son, found that, for the first time, she was no longer thinking of him as a piece of property snatched from her by another's

hand and which she must recapture by violence. At that moment
her love began to resemble the love of other mothers who demand nothing in return for what they give. Within the silent old
woman, sitting there and making an effort to eat, a tumult of the
soul was taking place. Possessive love had been trampled underfoot, had actually recognized the need to abandon its most sacred
privileges. The only thing that mattered was that he should be
happy! Had it been in her power to call Mathilde back from the
country of the dead, she would have done so. The heady fumes
of renunciation opened to the eyes of her devotion a perspective
of blinding radiance. So strong is the instinct of self-preservation in the emotion of love when faced by the threat of complete
destruction, when the earth beneath its feet trembles and the
heavens above its head are rent, that it sets itself the task of creating a new heaven and a new earth. That is the moment when
she who is no longer loved murmurs to him who loves no longer:
"You shall not be tormented by the sight of me. I will not be
exigent. I will make my home in the shadow of your presence.
I will surround you with a protection which you shall not even
notice." In such a way did Félicité Cazenave, drinking defeat like
wine, cast the food of renunciation to her famished passion.

She broke the silence, and in tones of supplication said:
"You're eating nothing, dearest: you must eat."
Without raising his head, he replied: "You're not eating, either."
True to his habit as a spoilt child, he added: "I've never been
able to eat alone, with somebody opposite watching me the whole
time."
"But I'm really very hungry, dear."
She tried to swallow a mouthful, though the effort caused a
muscular contraction in her throat.
When they left the table Fernand at once moved off in the
direction of the enemy wing. She called him back.
"There's something I want to say to you, my boy."
For a moment he hesitated, then, with a bad grace, followed
her into the study.
"What is it you want?"
She had gone straight to the window and half opened the shut-
ters. She turned around now, but, at sight of her son, lost her
self-assurance.
"I'm worried about you. The kind of life you are leading will
do you no good. You are eating your heart out, as Marie de Lados

would say. You *must* find something with which to occupy your mind. . . . Go and see the members of that Committee again. You are in the prime of life. The municipal elections will be coming along in a few months' time."

He growled out that he had given up thinking about all that for a long time past, just as she had wished. To this she made no reply, and he asked whether that was all she had to say. She took his arm, and when next she spoke there was a note of intensity in her voice:

"I can't stand by and see you just fade away. I'm not going to let you die."

"As you let her?"

She cried out that she had had nothing to do with his wife's death. How could she have foreseen that poisoning would set in? Why wouldn't he believe Duluc? There had been no reason to have a nurse.

"Besides, I *did* go to see her that night."

"Oh, I know. . . . I know . . ."

"I knocked at her door. I asked whether she was in pain. She answered that there was nothing she needed. It wouldn't have been too late, even then, to have pulled her through if her heart hadn't failed. Duluc's told you that a hundred times. 'Neither you nor I could have done anything,' he said. 'That sort of poisoning is never immediately fatal. It may go on for days. But your wife had a weak heart.' . . ."

She walked up and down the room, talking as much to convince herself as her son. She raised her voice as though wishing to be overheard by someone invisible yet within earshot. He, meanwhile, had moved away from the door, and all the time that his mother was speaking covered his face with his hands. At last he broke out with:

"It was you who killed her . . . killed her a little more with each day that passed."

She protested in a burst of anger: "That's not true! I merely defended myself, as I had every right to do. If it comes to that, we are both of us involved."

"What, precisely, do you mean by that?"

"Which of us, you or I, dealt her the shrewdest blows? Answer me!"

Fury swept through her like a fire, burning up her will to renunciation even before it had come fully to birth. It was no longer a question of sacrificing herself, but of overcoming a rebel son, of proving herself to be the stronger of the two, as she always had been.

She was shouting now.

"Take a look at yourself! No one but your mother could have put up with you for a moment! I've fought you tooth and nail for fifty years—I, your mother—and it amazes me that I am still alive to tell the tale! When *she* came on the scene, poor little wretch, I knew she wouldn't last long. It didn't take you more than a year——"

"Shut up! . . . Don't say another word!"

She recoiled at sight of his ashen face, at sight of her son's hands raised and trembling. As he came towards her she leaned against the wall. She met him in his wildness with a smile. Her whole attitude was a challenge. It was as though she were casting in his teeth those words addressed by another mother to another son: "Strike me . . . strike my womb!"

Terrified because he realized what he had been on the brink of doing, he stopped dead. Suddenly sobered, he stared at the old woman who had borne him, on whom he had been about to lay violent hands. He saw the poor, breathless body standing there at his mercy—and all the secret tenderness of childhood burst suddenly through the hard rind of his spirit in an anguished cry:

"Mother!"

She had fallen exhausted on the sofa, and he leaned his head against her shoulder. He had run for shelter to this sanctuary of living flesh, because for him there existed no other refuge in the world. Like one in the last stages of despair, who would say good-bye for ever to the earth, yet flings himself upon her as upon the breast of a harsh stepmother and draws her scent deep into his darkened spirit, so now this man, forced to his last gasp, clung to the old woman who had given him life. And she, nerveless and crushed, tasted happiness for one brief moment with closed eyes. Only too soon he would recover his self-possession; only too soon the realization of his passing weakness would be an added grievance between them. How she wished that this moment might be eternal! Her arm was growing numb beneath the burden of his heavy head, but she knew only that she was a mother who, through winter nights, stays awake because her child cannot sleep unless it holds her hand, who remains in one position for hours together, her arm stretched over the bed's edge, suffering agonies

of pain, surrendering her frozen fingers to the will of a baby
executioner. For a long time, as in the days when, a young woman
conscious only of the animal instincts of maternity, she had nuz-
zled avidly the new born child, so now, her lips remained pressed
to the forehead of her ageing son. Never again would she provoke him, never again make demands on him. Instead, she would
give him back the will to live, would bear him a second time.
She surrendered to the illusion that the well-beloved, in his turn,
would seek, would welcome rebirth. She did not realize that,
while for her the object of so much passion was there, heavy
against her knees, and that his presence was all the weapon she
needed to confront the assaults of destiny, he, bred up in spiritual
corruption, he who for half a century had broken every toy he
had been given, had just lost the last of them at the very moment of discovering its incalculable value. Well might she look at
him, poor woman. Already he was getting to his feet, wiping
the sweat from his forehead with the back of his hand. Well
might she look—and listen, too, to the sound of his footsteps dying
away in the house of death.

◄§ XI §►

SEVERAL days of released tension followed, because the sky, too,
had lost something of its blazing ardour. For a whole week storms
wandered backwards and forwards over a countryside that was
almost emptied of human life (for it was that time of the year
when there is nothing to be done but to leave grapes and sun in
silent communion). Even the trains seemed to be finding it difficult to drive a passage through the dog days. Word went round
that between La Réole and Tonniens the heat had expanded the
rails. At last a night came when a gentle susurration woke both
son and mother. With such eagerness were the leaves drinking in
the first drops of falling moisture that it was almost an hour before
the rain succeeded in forcing its way through to the crust of the
burned-up world, before the earth could be transpierced and left
to liberate its scents—scents that told of a desire not yet assuaged
though already transmuted into joy. In that torrid land men's passions echo back the violence of the heavens, and, sometimes, too,
share in its waning. At mealtimes Fernand no longer maintained

a malignant silence. Not that all constraint had been lifted from the relationship of mother and son, but he did, at least, show her deference, did treat her with a deliberate solicitude, did pay her those little attentions due to an old woman. He never left her now until they had had their coffee. But she was cautious and took care not to exploit her advantage. To herself she said: "I will save him. . . ." But, alas! though he no longer treated her with cruelty, he was still bleeding because of what the enemy had done to him.

Around this scene of drama in suspense, the great trees—planes and golden poplars, oaks and tulip-trees—waved their rain-drenched leaves beneath a kindlier sky, hiding from stranger eyes the mother and her son. What is commonly said about provincial life and provincial gossip is true only of those humble folk who are forced to live cheek by jowl. Nothing is less penetrable by human eyes, nothing so breathes an air of mystery, than the walled estates so closely hedged by trees that those who live in them seem only to be in touch with one another and with heaven. It was generally agreed in the city that the attitude adopted by the Cazenaves was right and proper. The less deeply we feel the loss of a relative, the more important is it to exaggerate the trappings of our woe, and in some such terms could be interpreted the continued withdrawal of the pair.

Nevertheless, all through that rainy September Fernand went out religiously each morning, wearing an old cape with the hood pulled over his head. His favourite walk was along the lane which separated the garden from the main Bordeaux-Cette railway line. On the freight-waggons in the sidings he would read—without paying much attention to the phrase, and certainly seeing nothing horrible or ominous in it—the label which said "Men 38–40". Then he would turn and go home. His mother waited until he was close to her, and only then tried to read the message of his shut and inexpressive face. Each day the tension in it grew less. It looked almost peaceful: so much so that at first she thought the change must be deliberate. But could he have gone on cheating her for so long? Somewhere he had found a softening influence, a source of consolation that was hidden from her. His health was better—though not because of anything that she had done!

Once, in the old days, she had dismissed a servant for boasting that she had saved Fernand's life when he had the scarlatina. Now it was a dead woman who had saved his life, and she no jealous mother could dismiss. Thus was her last prop knocked away. She was useless to him. Never, since the days of his earliest infancy, when he was already a spoilt and fanciful brat, had she seen upon his face so vague and sweet, so almost childish, a smile. For fifty years her favourite refrain had been: "What would you do without me! It's lucky for you I'm here! If you hadn't got me I don't know what would happen!" Alas! for all the attention he paid her now she might not have existed at all, and yet, without her, in spite of her perhaps, he had once again found peace. The knowledge that they are needed prolongs old women's lives. Many of them die of the despair that assails them when they realize that they can no longer be of use. Some of them, when already at death's door, revive because a widowed daughter or an orphaned child cries to them for help. Félicité could do nothing more for her son. But, if it came to that, had she, in the days when her domination was supreme, used it in such a way as to make him happy?

At night when she could not sleep, when she lay feeling a hostile silence all around her, she would say to herself: "Any other sort of life would have killed him. If he had been left to himself he would have been dead by this time." But what did she really know of him?

The wind, sweeping above the miles of heath, reached at last the indeterminate line where the thinning pines open on to the sacred acres of the Sauterne grapes, and there, blowing aimlessly, uncertain what to grip and tear, suddenly concentrated on the garden trees which, feeling themselves seized in a rushing, wild embrace, start to sway and shudder all together.

One last function, at least, she could perform, and, by so doing, serve her heart's darling. The dead woman might work upon his ailing spirit, but over his sick body she could have no power. It still belonged to the mother from whom it had emerged into the world. Fernand obstinately refused to see Dr. Duluc. Madame Cazenave, therefore, consulted him in secret. It was his view that she must overcome her son's dislike of food. He must be made to eat, and so "enrich his blood". Therefore, she forced herself to eat, so that he might be persuaded to follow her example. Though the state of her arteries made a light diet imperative, she stuffed herself with butcher's meat. Each time they sat down to a meal the same dialogue took place:

"You're not eating anything, darling."

"Nor are you."

"But I am. Look at me. Do have a little more steak."

"I'll have some more if you will."

In all forms of martyrdom there is an element of the sublime. No matter how degrading the manner of the death imposed, it is always life that is sacrificed.

Félicité could no longer bear to be alone. Every afternoon now she betook herself to the kitchen. She could not resist the temptation to confide in Marie de Lados.

"He couldn't stand her while she was alive. He has no cause to regret her now."

"No truer word could you have spoke, ma'am."

"He talks of her as he does only because he knows it gives me pain to hear him. I'm a fool to let him see that it gets on my nerves."

"Maybe so, ma'am."

Marie de Lados was grinding coffee, but all the while her frightened eyes, like those of a cringing dog, never left her mistress's face, so terrified was she of not immediately responding to her moods. A fawning smile had now become a fixture on her humble countenance. Nevertheless, she said nothing when Madame Cazenave added:

"When you're dead it's for a long time. . . . The dead are fast movers, as they say."

Marie de Lados said nothing, because each Sunday, at the seven o'clock Mass, as she went back from the Sacred Table to her seat, her widow's veil drawn over her head, the ghosts of all her sleeping race came regularly to life within her faithful heart, a long and dwindling vista of dead forebears, starting with the woman who, years before, had been left to die, perhaps of hunger; including the mother and the father who had never spoken a kindly word to her; nor omitting that odd sport of nature, Jaouset, who had found her on the heath one summer's evening of '47, and whose beast of burden she had been for thirty years; and ending with the little child whom she had lost when he was only three. All those who once had dragged out existence on an obscure farmstead came back again to life in a heart that was filled with the love of God. Marie de Lados, flinging wide the door, welcomed the crowd of her unknown ancestors, grouping them about that Presence which alone possessed the place.

"I'm not worrying. There's a saying that the absent are always in the wrong."

"True enough, ma'am."

Félicité said no more. Shrugging her shoulders, she left the kitchen. She was beginning to realize that the absent are always in the right, for they are of those who never spoil love's handiwork. If we look back over our lives we see that it is from those we have loved the best that we have always been most separated, the reason being, perhaps, that familiarity breeds contempt. It is those whom we see every day who are in the wrong.

      ❧ *X I I* ☙

THAT season of the year was drawing on when, in spite of the freshness of the early hours, one hesitates to light the first fire of the season as though fearful of the unknown. Before and after each meal the Cazenaves took refuge in the kitchen. This fact alone brought mother and son into a peculiar intimacy. No longer could he rest content with the small change of conversation. Each word he spoke bore witness to a secret travail of the mind, to strange and unexpected accesses of curiosity.

"Were you and papa ever really in love?"

What an odd question for a man to ask who had always thought so much more about the living than the dead! She did not know what to answer, feeling, as she did, that the word "love" on her son's lips had suddenly taken a new and searching significance.

But he would not let the subject drop.

"What I'm getting at is this—did you ever love him as much as you love me?"

The two things, she said, were quite different. It was impossible to compare them. And that was true. What possible connexion could there be between an insatiable craving to dominate, to possess—the sort of craving that was roused in her by the darling being upon whom all her pain and all her happiness depended, to whose life all her life was bound—and that mere habit of affection and companionship which death had so soon cut short, leaving the widow with but small desire to mourn her loss?

Numa Cazenave had had a lonely death, because it so happened that Félicité had taken Fernand to Salies for a course of the waters. She knew that her husband had had a fall just outside the house where the Merlet girls lived, as he was returning from his daily card-game at the Club. But she remembered nothing of what had been told her about his last moments, with only strangers round him; about how, the previous evening, he had made a tour of inspection of what was dearer to him than anything else in the world—the charitable institution which he administered, a tiny piece of "property" which meant so much to him that he had left instructions that some of its heavy clay should be heaped upon his grave; about how his last words had been "in faith is our salvation". She would not let herself remember the secret sense of satisfaction that the end had come without her having to witness it, that the only thing left for her to do, now that he was gone, was to settle his business affairs—an occupation which brought her much pleasure. Never having been in the habit of examining her conscience, she felt no compunction about indulging the heady pleasure which came over her at the realization that now she was free, that now she was alone with the sole object of her passion—whom she immediately removed from the school where his father had insisted on his going as a boarder.

"Did papa really suffer when my brother Henri died?"

This new question set her trembling. A great fire of vine-shoots was throwing a flicker of light upon the faded chequer-board of the tiled kitchen floor. Marie de Lados was busy plucking the first pigeon of the season. Under the lamp, her grandson, his fingers stuck in his ears, was picking an uncertain way through the questions and answers of the Catechism: *"Are there, then, three Gods?"—"Indeed, no, sister, the Three Persons of the Holy Trinity are one and the same God."* The boy, whose name was Raymond, always spent the weeks of the grape harvest with his grandmother, because his parents were away working on the Marquis's estate at Chateau Yquem.

"Both your father and I suffered."

"But you told me yourself that it was papa who insisted on having a photograph taken of Henri on his death-bed . . . and that you'd thought it wasn't worth the trouble."

She saw again, in imagination, the family album, and in it the pale, lifeless, obliterated and terrifying face of the vanished child. How strange it was that Fernand should show this sudden curiosity about things dead and done with! He was like a man who, insufficiently prepared and in a mood of absentmindedness, has been on a trip through beautiful country, and later is miserable when he thinks of all that he has missed, of all that he will never see again. He was laying a compulsion upon his mother to recall her husband's shattering grief, to remember how sickly and weak hers, by comparison, had seemed, when their younger son had died. One thought only had terrified her then—to the exclusion of every other consideration—that Fernand might catch the same disease. She had been afraid, too, that it might be a serious disadvantage to the boy in later life to be known as the brother of someone who had died of meningitis. When she thought to herself 'It might have been Fernand' she felt as though she had been delivered from a great sorrow. Oh, God! why must he stir the dust of these old memories? Forty years had passed since then.

She raised her eyes and looked at him. He was standing with his back to the fire, fidgeting with his left leg as he had a way of doing when he was following out a line of thought. Ah! it was still the hand of the enemy at work! Only she could have awakened in this middle-aged man so desolate a curiosity about what had been, so strange a taste for useless dreaming. But it was not in Félicité's power to imagine the nature of her son's daydreams at this moment, nor to follow their bizarre meanderings. His thoughts were of her, his mother, and of himself, and in the secrecy of his heart he was saying: "I am the more to be pitied of us two, because she has had me, but I have never had anything."

The vine-shoots crumbled to ashes and the kitchen filled with darkness. Marie de Lados lit an oil lamp that stood upon the table. The American-cloth covering was soiled and torn by a succession of knives. The child sat with his elbows propped upon it, busy with his Catechism. His hand, buried in a thatch of hair like a crow's plumage, looked white by contrast. He was still muttering to himself: *"Are there, then, three Gods?"*—as though he did not know that there is but one—one sole and single Love. Now and again he lifted his sleep-laden eyes and gazed upon the sombre presence of his masters seated by the hearth. In the scullery Marie de Lados was washing crockery, as she had done every evening for sixty years. When she came back into the kitchen her grandson was fast asleep, his head on the table, his mouth open. She looked at him and a smile of unutterable sweetness spread a radiance over her face that seemed as though it were carved from a piece of ancient wood. It might have belonged to one of the Black Virgins. She dandled him in her arms, though he was old enough now to take his First Communion. His charming little head lay against her shoulder, his scratched and grubby legs hung

down with the weight of their nailed boots, which looked, for
all the world, like the iron-shod hooves of a small donkey. She
carried him away without stooping her old body. She had become
a farm servant when no more than twelve years old, a maid of
all work, what is called in the Landes a "slavey". In those days, she
had had to move about the house with a child's hand in each of
hers, and carrying on her frail shoulders the youngest of the family. If he cried, it was she who was beaten.

Félicité, feeling the eyes of her beloved son upon her, raised
her own. It was long since he had been so tenderly aware of her.
In a sudden surge of emotion she rose heavily from her seat, put
her arm round his shoulders, drew down his head, and murmured:

"I have found my little boy again: he is sorry for his old
mother."

Could she have known what he would reply she would have
bitten back the words. Scarcely had she uttered them than the
blow fell, full on her heart.

"It is she who wants me to be good to you. . . ."

And he kissed her on the cheek.

She broke from him. A freight-train trundled by into the distance. She could hear the horrible echo of his words in her heart.
It was to the enemy she owed this favour! She must bear the
burden of this worst and final shame. So great was his love for
Mathilde that he had brought her back to life, had convinced
himself of her continuing presence, not only in his mind but in
the room with them. From it he had derived a sense of peace
such as, when his mother reigned supreme, he had never known.

A cataract of water fell from the sky upon the leaf-strewn garden paths. In the darkness a copper pan shone like a glowing
human face.

⇜§ XIII §⇝

NEXT evening mother and son were seated in the same place.
Fernand had said: "Why shouldn't we have lights in the study?"—
but Félicité had answered: "Time enough for that when winter
comes." As a young girl, waiting in the lost loneliness of the Landes

for the coming of a husband, she had been wont to sit, as now, in the kitchen where the air smelled sweet of chestnuts and aniseed. But in those days not a lamp but a resin dip had shed its light upon the recently published *Three Musketeers* lying open on her knees. It was the time of day when in those distant years, Marie de Lados had been allowed to sit down on condition that she would busy herself with spinning. The dogs growled because of the wild boars drawn thither by the smell of pig. The napkins laid across the mouths of the earthenware jugs upon the table showed white. Visiting neighbours left their clogs at the door, and a gust of pine-scented night entered the house with them. A country waggon bumped over the ruts in the sandy lane. To-night it was the whistle of a train that shattered the darkness.

Félicité could hear the blood throbbing in her temples. She told Marie de Lados that she felt as though there was an iron bar in her stomach, and that she ought not to have taken a second helping of eel. She had done so only to tempt her son to follow suit. The shaft that had struck her twenty-four hours earlier was still embedded in her flesh. She said nothing. Not a word would she utter which might call forth a second blow like that.

Marie de Lados was "hearing" Raymond say his Creed. He always came to a dead stop in the same place.

"Again, from the beginning!"

"I believe in the Holy Ghost, the Holy Catholic Church, the Communion of Saints, the Forgiveness of Sins, an' the Life Everlasting——"

"What about the *Resurrection of the Body*? . . . Again."

Glibly he ran through the opening words, then, like a young and frisky donkey, checked at the same turn in the road, a look of stubborn uneasiness upon his face.

"Again, from the beginning."

At once he started off at an easy amble, then broke into a gallop, only to be brought up short, ears well back, before—the *resurrection of the body* . . .

"Where's t'brat's brain a-got to . . . say it, now, twenty times over."

At this, the child, his face wreathed in grins as though he were playing the game which consists in saying Peter Piper Picked a Peck of Pickled Peppers very fast, set about repeating *resurrection of the body, resurrection of the body*, as hard as he could go.

When he had finished the voice of the master made itself heard:
"There are those who believe that the flesh is raised again. . . ."
As always, when matters of religion cropped up in conversation,
Marie de Lados became immediately suspicious, drew herself up
and looked at the master over the top of her spectacles. Seeing
that he was not laughing, she became reassured. Félicité pretended not to understand of whose flesh it was that he was thinking, and grumblingly remarked:
"You know we promised Marie de Lados that we would stop
getting ourselves mixed up in all these stories about the good
God. . . ."
Then, as an afterthought, she added:
"I'm not feeling at all well."
To this he made no reply, but started walking up and down
the kitchen while Marie de Lados lit a candle and led the child
away. At last he came to a halt at the farther end of the room,
as far as possible from the fire, and pressed his forehead to the
black window-pane. His mother, in the grip of deep distress,
spoke his name, but he did not hear her. She saw nothing but the
vague outline of a hulking body looming in the darkness. She
wanted to call him to her, but no sound came. She could not see
him at all now. He was no longer there. It was as though he had
been swallowed up by, lost in, the darkness of the late autumn
evening. At last, with an immense effort, she managed to cry
out:
"Where are you?"
He replied, without turning his head, that he could hear rain,
and pressed his face once more to the window. He stayed like
that for a long time in a sort of relaxed torpor, listening to the
obstinate drip-drip of water on a magnolia leaf which stood just
outside, and then, as a puff of wind came and went, to the brief
flurry of drops from the soaked branches; finally, to the noise
of the last express as it dashed through the station without stopping, a wild dazzle of light and speed and danger in the blackness. Only then did another sound reach his ears which he thought
was familiar. For some weeks now, after dinner, his mother had
taken to dropping asleep with a suddenness, a completeness,
that made it seem as though she had tumbled straight through a
hole. When this happened she gave vent to unpleasing snores
and her head dropped forward, the jaw hanging open. He wanted
to be left alone with his thoughts, but, teased by the sound, no-

ticed that it was more stertorous, more encumbered, than usual.
He turned, took the lamp from the table, and approached the
sleeper. He did not at first realize what had happened. Her face
was the colour of mud, and her wide-open eyes looked lustreless.
Her tongue was projecting slightly from the left-hand corner
of her mouth, and all that side of her face was fixed and rigid.
The other had contracted into an ugly grimace.

⤚§ *X I V* §⤙

"THERE's nothing to be done," said the doctor, amazed to find
that the old woman was still alive. She was completely paralysed
and incapable of speech. She had been moved downstairs into
the study on the ground floor, so as to make it possible for her
to spend the daytime in the kitchen.

"There be allus summut or summ'un for to occupy her mind,
there," said Marie de Lados. "Her can hearken to t'train and look
at t'clock just to see whether't be up t'time or not."

But her life now was nothing but a prolonged waiting for Fernand. He went in to see her at eight o'clock each morning, and
took his breakfast coffee on the corner of her table. He gave her
a kiss on the forehead, and she settled down to watch him eat.
At first the stare of her dimmed and bloodshot eyes had been an
embarrassment to him, but gradually he found that he was paying no attention to it. After the midday meal, which he ate alone,
he sat down for a few moments by the invalid, opened the *Petite
Gironde*, and, though he was by this time accustomed to her
ways, arranged the paper so as to have it between him and that
fixed and hungry stare. "She do reg'lar gobble 'm up with her
eyes," said Marie de Lados. When he had finished reading the
news he went out. His mother sat gazing at the door long after
it had closed behind him. With the only hand that she could still
move she kept on rubbing at her dress, always at the same spot,
which was becoming worn and shiny. Her darling came through
the kitchen again on his way to dinner, after which the evening
proper began. He no longer kept his face hidden, perhaps because he felt partially protected by the darkness, perhaps because he had resigned himself to performing this last act of char-

ity, to sitting there and letting himself be adored. For her the
whole long day was but preliminary to these evening hours. Her
eyes were taking their last fill of him before darkness should overwhelm them. . . .

Only when it was hard upon the third hour was the sponge
offered to the victim. How much more bitter than gall was the
sight, upon that taut and suffering face, of so much love offered
to another! Yet Félicité Cazenave felt dimly that it was a good
thing she should suffer for her son. What she did not know was
that she had been crucified.

She died at the winter's end. The people of Langon still tell how
he hung over her open grave, how he had to be forcibly restrained from jumping into it. Not one of them among all that
crowd of people in the failing light understood that all he wanted
was to catch a glimpse of the coffin in which all that remained
of Mathilde was turning to dust and ashes.

⤃ XV ⤄

FERNAND CAZENAVE at first believed that it was only an importunate solicitor who was keeping him from Mathilde. How could
he concentrate his mind, how plunge to those emotional depths
where the loved one lay in wait, if, at every hour of the day,
a paunchy little man imposed his presence on him, spreading
out an endless array of documents and for ever demanding his
signature? His father, Numa Cazenave, had disinherited his son,
then a minor, in favour of his wife. The will was illegal, but it
would never have occurred to Fernand to dispute it. There are
still many old families whose members take no account of the
law if it happens to conflict with the expressed wishes of the all-
powerful head of the clan. Besides, Fernand, having reached man's
estate, had been only too glad to shift all financial responsibility
on to his mother's shoulders, which could carry the weight with
ease. He had received from her each month all the money he
needed, and this position of dependency—which had so irked
Mathilde—had terminated only when the old woman had had
her stroke.

When Fernand Cazenave finally appended his signature to the last of the documents he felt convinced that what had destroyed his peace of mind, the condition of heavenly apathy, which so far had made possible his moments of communing with Mathilde, had been nothing but the fuss and bother connected with his investments and his rent list. Later, however, he came to realize that it needs very little effort to keep a current account at the Bank, and that pine trees will go on growing with the minimum of attention. He understood now that if, each All Soul's Day, his mother had regularly driven out in her trap on the pretext of keeping an eye on her "acres of treasure", her real reason for doing so was the urgent need she felt to breathe, once every year, the fragrance of her family trees at that period of the equinox when the wind sets their dark tops waving. Though the widow had quickly got rid of the vineyard which had been the delight of her husband's heart, she would never consent to alienate even a square yard of the gloomy forests among which she had been born.

Fernand could clearly remember those endless expeditions of his childhood when he had been taken to pay a visit to his Péloueyre grandfather. The journey had involved a drive, first through the Sauterne country, and then, when the vines and the smiling valley of the Garonne had been left behind, on and on until they reached a lane which had been trodden into holes by passing herds of oxen. His mother, in those days, had worn a bonnet with black ribbons tied under her chin, so that her face had seemed to look out at him from a frame. Bumped by the ancient two-wheeled vehicle, his head thrown back, he had seen the cloud-wrack of an October sky swirling across the space of sky left visible between the buffeted tree-tops, and had cried aloud each time a wedge-shaped flight of birds had crossed from one bank of agitated greenery to another. Sometimes a running freshet would take the road into a hollow where the presence of the stream was betrayed by a sudden chill in the air, and then his mother would wrap her cloak about him like a black wing. She was afraid he might catch cold. If, on the contrary, he complained of feeling too hot, she would thrust an anxious finger between his collar and his neck.

Once, on a day of thunderstorms, gadflies had worried the horse so unmercifully that he had kicked out and broken a shaft. It was at the season of the year when darkness falls with great suddenness. While the country boy who acted as coachman was repairing the damage Fernand and his mother waited by the side of the road. He could still remember how safe and happy he had felt in that deserted lane already brimming with the dusk, just because his mother had been there. Above high banks of blackened grass the short russet fronds of burnt bracken trembled in the breeze. He had heard the animal-like cry of a shepherd calling together his charges who were astray and bewildered in a patch of fog. . . . He had felt safe and happy, just because his mother was there. . . .

He looked about him. This was the very room in which Mathilde had died. There was the shell-encrusted frame from which her unsmiling face looked out. A woodpecker sounded a note of spring. The morning air was full of mist and sunlight. Only when he had managed to climb from the depths of years gone by to the surface of a more immediate past would he once again feel Mathilde as a presence. He wooed soft sentiment, thinking how short a time they had been together. No longer now did death give the daughter-in-law advantage over the mother, for by this time her old enemy had joined her in the third vault on the left against the end wall. Both, from now on, belonged to a world that had vanished, and Fernand was incensed to feel how little of his life had belonged to Mathilde, over what long tale of years brooded the vast shadow of his mother.

He finished dressing and took a turn in the garden, glancing furtively at the study window, where there were no longer old and watchful eyes to exasperate him. Was it because he no longer felt himself spied upon that he was so little moved by any wish to be with Mathilde again? Was it only when his mother's possessive love had hedged him with constricting flames that, oppressed by the sense of pursuit, he had plunged into those regions of himself where his wife waited? The flames had guttered out now, the fire which so often had made him furious was cold, and he was left alone and shivering among the embers. Some men are capable of love only when it is indulged at someone else's expense. What drives them to another is the wailing of the woman left behind.

Fernand, aimlessly sauntering along the south path, stopped to sniff first one rose then another, pouncing upon them like a heavy bumble-bee. But the privet hedge woke in him no memory of a face. Marie de Lados called him in to luncheon, and he ate more plentifully than usual of freshly gathered peas. Sitting alone after the meal in the study where the paralytic's bed still stood, he had a momentary feeling of well-being, and his thoughts turned briefly to his "hobby". He decided to send a telegram to the rue Huguerie, sat down at his desk, and tried to remember (the impulse already weakening) the form of words that once he had been used to write in such a heat of urgency (because the thought of doing a bolt had always come to him after one of his scenes with his mother). It had been all very well for her to mock at him, to exclaim: "You'll be in a fine state when you get back. . . . Three days and you'll come crawling home!" He knew perfectly well that she would worry herself sick, that life would stop for her until she saw him again. But for the anguish that he left behind him, he might never have gone at all. How humiliating, yet how sweet, his return had always been, when, in an atmosphere of happy chiding, of tender ridicule and an infinity of small attentions, he had gradually come back to life.

The thought that now he would return from Bordeaux to an empty house struck a chill to his heart—the thought that he would come back, a bruised and beaten prodigal, and not see her, as he got out of the train, leaning over the balustrade of the terrace, shading her eyes with her hand and trying to pick him out from among the crowd of travellers. He tore the telegram into tiny pieces. There was nothing he could do. It was his mother who had decided that he should live only in terms of herself, only, as it were, drawing in the breath of life through *her* nostrils, who had permitted no competition of work, amusement, hope or love to divide his loyalty. Now, from the depths of the grave, she could triumph in the perfection of her labours. The maternal sun had barely set, but already the man she had borne and shaped was revolving in empty space, a world cut adrift from its orbit.

✺ XVI ✺

THE RARE pedestrians who used the road that skirts the main line from Bordeaux to Cette would frequently stop to eye the silent house among the trees whose threshold, it was said, none

ever crossed. For a few weeks they noticed that the Venetian
blinds were regularly drawn up at the windows of the room where
Fernand Cazenave passed sleepless nights stretched on Mathilde's
bed. But a day came, in the middle of the summer, when they
stayed closed. In what Félicité had always called "the enemy's
wing" all life had been extinguished. From week to week, change
and change about, a brief flicker of life seemed to show, first in
the windows of what had been Madame Cazenave's room, then
of the one where Fernand had hoped to find sleep on his childhood's bed. But wander though he might from bed to bed, on
each he was the wretched victim of insomnia. By the time autumn came, and Michaelmas brought the gypsies in their scarlet
rags to pitch camp against the garden railings, and to light their
reeking fires, Félicité's room and, later, Fernand's remained permanently closed. As in a human body near its end, so in this
house, life withdrew from the extremities and became concentrated in the kitchen. The bed which had been set up for the
paralytic on the ground floor had not been moved. Henceforward
it was used by Fernand. Each morning, after a perfunctory wash,
he went into the kitchen, and sat down in the armchair at the
corner of the hearth whence his mother had been used to devour
him with her eyes while she waited for death.

Upstairs, the dust grew daily thicker in the room where Mathilde had died. It had dulled the glass of the shell-encrusted
frame behind which the unsmiling face of a young woman was
becoming progressively dimmer. Lilies that had been dry and
brittle months ago still stood in the vases which once Fernand
had filled and tended with such fervent care. Marie de Lados
grumbled that she couldn't see to everything.

She found it impossible any longer to be the humble, frightened slave she once had been. She had been forced into too
close a proximity with her ancient idol, saw it now fallen,
knocked from its pedestal and wholly given over to her tender
mercies. Fernand insisted that she should still sleep in a little
black hole adjoining the study, as in the days when she had
nursed her mistress, so that, should he need her in the night, his
slightest whimper might not remain unanswered. She was his final
refuge. She had known his forebears, and her sauces, concocted
in accordance with long-forgotten recipes, filled the most distant
corners of the house with smells that his grandparents had loved.
She had "washed" for three generations of Péloueyres, and her

hands had become worn in the process. But Fate had ordained
that Fernand Cazenave should be pursued into the very fastness
of even this last asylum, should be driven, at last, from his final
line of defence.

With the coming of the wild duck, the wood-pigeons and the
grape harvest, Raymond, Marie's grandson, whose parents were
employed in gathering the Marquis's grapes at Yquem, drifted
back into the kitchen. He had grown into a good-looking, strap-
ping urchin, with large, prominent ears and a chest the colour of
fired earthenware. His bare, clean feet made a flapping sound on
the worn flags of the floor. A look of ill-concealed merriment
gleamed in the eyes that were like two red grapes. At first Marie
de Lados had been afraid that he might tire the master, because
he was for ever in and out, leaving the door open or letting it
slam. But Fernand did not like to hear him scolded. He followed
this little hopping blackbird with the same brooding look with
which, a year before, he had watched his silent mother. He would
have liked to talk to him, but what could he say to a child? Sometimes he would take from his waistcoat pocket a round box of
cough-drops, and when Raymond came within reach would prof-
fer the bait and murmur: "Like a sweetie?" Then the boy would
stop, breathless and blushing, and, while he helped himself, Fernand would catch his arm and hold him prisoner. But Raymond,
turning away his head with its blue-black thatch of hair standing
up like a bird's plumage, and shuffling his feet, would try to
break away.

As soon as Marie de Lados felt sure that the presence of her
grandson was not distasteful to the master, she took steps to keep
him with her all the winter. Fernand failed to scent danger.
Félicité would not have allowed herself even to weigh the merits
of such a request. She knew that "one must never be under an
obligation to people of that sort". She would have sent Marie
de Lados packing to her kitchen range with a warning not to "get
above herself". She would have said to her darling boy: "I don't
know what would happen to you if I weren't here! It's lucky for
you I am! If it wasn't for me, you'd have fallen into the trap. You
can't see farther than your nose, or look after yourself any better
than a baby. If I didn't keep an eye on the grapes, the first person
who liked to try would have them all. . . ." But she was no longer
there to walk ahead and clear a path for him through the bram-

bles. He had no suspicion of the threat hanging over his head, not even when Raymond's parents allowed themselves to be persuaded to leave the boy with Monsieur Cazenave, though they put up a show of making a great favour of their permission.

It was not long before Fernand took a dislike to the young creature with his enormous appetite and chilblainy, ink-stained hands, who took no more notice of the master of the house than he did of the sideboard or the clock. Dislike turned to horror when he noticed that Marie de Lados was growing slack in her duties. She began to neglect her sickly idol of old days in favour of the boy, so brimming with health, who was of her own blood. They had to wait now for him to come home before beginning dinner, and the sound of his clogs on the garden steps soon became the sound that heralded the serving of a meal. A mild cough which Raymond caught in December was enough to make Marie de Lados desert the little room where she slept within her master's call. But there was worse to come. Under pretext of having to nurse the lad, his mother took up her quarters in the house. Marie de Lados went in mortal terror of the young woman, a toothless, sunburned country wench who pecked and glared with the ferocity of a barndoor fowl. The father, who worked in a wine-storage cellar, joined her at nightfall—a great hulking lout of a fellow, bred in the Garonne valley, with a distended stomach bulging over blue trousers which no belt ever managed to keep up,—a ruin of a Hercules with guts rotted by the deadly sweetness of the sugary Sauterne vintages. Even when the boy became convalescent the pair of them sat down every evening in the kitchen, while Fernand Cazenave had to have his dinner brought to him in the dining-room, which was always icy cold in spite of a roaring fire. All the time that he was eating his modest meal he could hear their coarse laughter and loud voices, though whenever Marie de Lados opened the door to attend to his wants, all that reached his ears was a mutter of patois and the rattle of spoons on plates. As soon as it was closed, they resumed their noisy talk.

What they never realized was that, in the cold room with its yellowish panelling of imitation wood which he had always hated, Fernand Cazenave was not alone. Each time that he raised his eyes from his plate he could see, sitting where she had always sat enthroned for half a century, the majestic figure of his dominating mother—more imposing in death than she had ever been in life, whose angry and Godlike countenance caused her feeble son to feel ashamed. Why didn't he chase this pack of vermin from the house, it seemed to say? He would re-create in imagination the awe-inspiring divinity whose merest frown had set the underlings, the courtiers, the farm-hands and servants of every description, tiptoeing about the room. An old Aeneas, tottering to his final fall, he stretched to this all-powerful "genetrix" his suppliant hands. Browbeaten and defeated, he adored the woman who had always been so strong. How admirable his mother had been! It was absurd to think that a little giggling schoolteacher should ever have had the effrontery to cross her path! Mathilde, whose ghost was present, too, but far from the fire and sitting in a draught, as she had always done in life, no longer appeared to him as deified by death. All that he could remember now was the stooping back, the craven air of a beaten animal, the yellow eyes of a tormented cat.

A passing train set the house shaking, but the shrill voices in the kitchen drowned the noise it made as it crossed the bridge over the Garonne. Something of his mother's temper, of that wild fury that had so often set the heavy, haggard woman stamping with rage, took hold of Fernand. He jumped up, and was already half-way to the door when Marie de Lados appeared with a plate of milk pudding. She stared at her master. Experience had taught her to detect the first signs of a gathering storm. There was uneasiness in her voice as she said:

"That girl be disturbing of you. I'll say summat."

Trembling, she returned to the kitchen. "That girl" filled her with the terror that all old people in the Landes feel for their children. (Her daughter and her son-in-law, having screwed her wretched savings out of her, penny by penny, still accused her of having money hidden away.) . . . For a few moments Fernand could hear the old woman's voice uninterruptedly droning on. Then, suddenly, in a horrible hoarse scream, her daughter embarked on a tirade in the local patois. Nothing marked more clearly the curious state of isolation in which Fernand Cazenave's life had been passed than the fact that he was quite incapable of understanding patois. Standing with his ear glued to the door, all that he could make out was that Marie de Lados was standing up to her children. But what was it they were demanding of the old woman? The word "maaster" recurred too often in their talk to leave him in any doubt that he was the cause of this quarrel. But he could hear very little, and left the dining-room by way of the hall. His footsteps woke an echo in the vast space, at the far end of which the shutterless French windows showed two rectangles of frost-bound sky. Passing along a corridor he made a circuit and came back to the kitchen's other door which was immediately facing the main staircase. Shivering in the darkness, he could now hear not only "maaster" but "t'brat" as well. Marie de Lados exclaimed in French: "But a tell thee him's not once asked after t'brat." If *she* didn't know the master, was the burden of her argument, she'd like to know who did. He wasn't the kind of man to bother his head about a brat! The boy had amused him for a while, but now he didn't want to see any more of him. After all, a body couldn't *make* him. . . . But at this her daughter broke in with a screech: "Of course you could: you could make him do anything you wanted. Why, the old rag-bag's lost without you. . . . You've got no feelings for your own flesh and blood, that's about the long and the short of it. . . ." Then they started again, shouting at one another in patois.

Fernand drew himself up to his full height. His mother drove him forward. Her spirit lived in him, possessed him. What was he waiting there for? Why didn't he burst unannounced into the room and kick the table over? . . . His legs refused to obey him, his heart began to thump: "I must sleep on it. . . ." He dropped on to the log-chest the lid of which was half open. It shut down with a bang, and the sharp report produced a pause in the shrill altercation that was going on behind the door. He got up and went into the study, where the fire had not been kept in. When at last he got into bed and blew out his candle he noticed that Marie de Lados had failed to lower the blinds. From where he lay he could see the night sky undefiled. It had been raining all day and the trees were dripping in the midst of a silence which seemed supernatural. The quiet sound of falling tears filled the night to the exclusion of all else. Peace came to him, a feeling of detachment. It was as though he were conscious of some realm of love and silence away beyond his own horrible existence, beyond the aridity of his heart, of a land where his mother lived, but a different mother from the one who, but a moment back, had possessed him like a Maenad, a land where Mathilde turned to him a face no longer tense and tragic, but for ever at peace,— a face that wore a smile of happiness.

At daybreak the rustle of the rain woke him. How he hated

these dark winter mornings! He could not even remember now
that he had felt the promise of a strange beatitude. All the brack-
ish tide of his rancour flowed back with the coming of the
gloomy dawn. He lay curled under the blankets. His old body
was aching. He saw the day ahead of him like a sandy, empty
road, leading across the burnt-up land. He closed his eyes, hoping to doze away the minutes that separated him from the oasis
of breakfast. While Marie de Lados was lighting the fire and setting
the hot coffee and milk beside his bed, he pretended to be asleep
with his face pressed to the wall.

≈§ XVII §≈

FERNAND CAZENAVE sat down, after his midday meal, in front of
the kitchen fire. He would have been terrified could he have
known how closely, in the pouring December darkness, slumped
there in his armchair, he resembled his mother in her last days!
Marie de Lados came in supporting the weak steps of her grandson who had got up that day for the first time. She looked at
the "master" and tried to fathom his thoughts. But he never shifted
his gaze from the flames in the grate. She pushed the frightened
boy towards him, saying:
"Come on now, say summat to the master, can't 'e?"
Fernand Cazenave did not even turn his head. She persisted:
"The mite's in a poor way, thin as a rake—all eyes."
And she pinched his arms. The master had taken up the tongs,
but had to put them down again because his hands were trembling. At last he fixed the urchin with an icy stare. Incapable
though he was of speaking patois, he did remember a few words
which had been constantly in the mouths of his grandfather
Péloueyre and of Félicité, his mother, whenever they had wanted
to be rid of some instrusive man or beast:
"Bey-t-en!" ("Be off with you!")
He had risen from his chair, and still looked like his mother—
but in the days of her awe-inspiring inflexibility. Marie de Lados
retreated with a frightened curtsey, dragging with her towards
the scullery the dishevelled child who hopped behind her like a
sick blackbird.

He settled down for the evening in front of the study hearth. At four o'clock Marie de Lados brought the lamp and closed the blinds. He was left alone until the sound of shrill voices warned him that Raymond's mother was in the kitchen. He crept into the ill-lit hall and sat on the log-chest like an old woman, not making a movement. "Noa, noa," he heard Marie say in a supplicating tone, " 'twill set t'blood a-rushing to's brain . . ." But a moment later the sound of her voice was submerged beneath her daughter's flow of patois. She exclaimed that *she* would see about laying the table, but why did her words sound so menacing? Fernand felt cold and went back to the study, where he sat motionless, staring at the fire. At seven o'clock Marie came in to say that dinner was ready. She took the lamp and held it high, as she did every evening, flattening herself against the wall to let him pass. The light fell full upon her wrinkled old face. He went through the kitchen, pushed open the door of the dining-room—and suddenly the meaning of what he had heard dawned upon him. On the clean cloth, opposite his own place, another had been laid, and, because the table was very high, the young woman had put a pile of books on the chair to enable Raymond to eat his soup more easily.

The boy was snivelling on the other side of the door. He dared not enter the room in spite of being ordered to do so by his mother, whose voice was growing progressively louder. Fernand Cazenave felt a wave of blind anger form within him and swell to a toppling height. It was with a feeling of joy that he let his mother force an entry, invade and possess him. He filled a glass with wine and swallowed it at a gulp, then, with a sweep of his arm sent the plates destined for the child crashing to the tiled floor. When the din had subsided he had the impression that there was but one person left alive in the kitchen. He burst into the room. The first object he saw was the child's mother standing with the look of a frightened hen, and, behind her, Marie de Lados, her clasped hands raised in prayer. He remembered the phrase of patois which his mother had always used when she wanted to shoo away anyone, man or beast:

"Annèt ben!" ("Get out of here!")

The young woman took a few paces forward, and then, suddenly recovering her voice, said it was he who had wanted to have the boy stay in the house, that he had stood in the way of his getting a good job elsewhere, that it had always been under-

stood he would look after him. . . . The child, she shouted, had
grown very much attached to him. . . . Then, intimidated by the
master's silence and by the cold fixity of his glare, she let her
words dribble away into silence.

He said again: "Annèt ben!"

At that, beside herself, she screamed out that if they went it
wouldn't be alone, that they would take the old woman with
them. Did Marie de Lados understand what had been said? She
uttered no protest, but stood there, half turned away, her face
hidden in her gnarled old hands with their prominent veins. The
scullery door was pushed ajar, and the boy peered through, looking like a young fox cornered in his earth. His mother, strong in
the conviction that this final threat had given her a stranglehold
on the enemy, showed her hardened gums and blackened teeth in
a grin of triumph. The sight of it had the effect of handing over
Fernand Cazenave, bound hand and foot, to the maternal demon.
With trembling fingers he fumbled in his wallet for a hundred-
franc note which he flung at Marie de Lados (though it was her
daughter who picked it up). Then, throwing the door open, he
addressed the old servant in a voice from which every vestige of
life seemed to have departed:

"You can come back to-morrow for your trunk."

She stared at him. It was as though not this master only, but
all her many masters, now dead and gone, were turning her out of
the house. She made no move, and he said again in a voice that
sounded to her like old Péloueyre's: "Bey-t-en!"

He flung back his head, and his neck swelled like that of an
outraged Juno. It was as though his mother stood there before
them in the flesh.

⇜§ *XVIII* §⇝

FERNAND CAZENAVE waited until the clip-clop of their clogs
had died away beside the main line. Then he filled his glass
again, emptied it, and left the dining-room. The last train had
rumbled away over the river. The house had stopped trembling.
A few vaporous clouds were drifting across the sky beneath a
hidden moon which thinned the darkness with a diffused radi-

ance. He stood in the middle of the unlit hall, and caught sight of himself in the mirror which hung by the front door.

The silence about him seemed deeper than on ordinary nights. He could not recollect that he had ever been aware of the sound of Marie de Lados's breathing in the course of his lonely evenings. But the breathing of a sleeper, even in a distant room, sets a quiver moving in the air so that, though we know it not, a tiny ripple of human warmth breaks like a wave upon the heart. For the first time in his life Fernand Cazenave knew the meaning of utter silence. Because he could hear, as on the previous evening, the interminable dripping of the trees, because round all that dying house there was no sound but that of gently flowing tears, he was now, perhaps, recapturing his earlier mood, was finding once again the peace that waited for him on the threshold of that kingdom where his mother was his mother still, yet someone else as well, someone who had moved him to turn an old and docile servant out of doors. He had a feeling that there was another presence living and breathing in a world apart, spreading a gentle influence around him, calming his anger, filling him with a loathing of all harshness, imparting to him a sense of mysterious detachment. That, at least, was how he felt. He forgot the wine that he had drunk, forgot that a very slight degree of intoxication is often enough to fill us with premonitions of eternity . . .

The cold roused him from his pleasant torpor. He began to shake all over, and his teeth chattered as Mathilde's had done when she lay dying. Along the passage of the "enemy wing" he went, shivering, from room to room, till he reached one where the moonlight, creeping through Venetian blinds, touched a shell-encrusted frame and threw upon the wall a faint shadow of withered lilies. A door opening on to the landing gave access to the loft which stretched the full width of the house from wing to wing, above the hall. A skylight held the pure radiance of the night like water, and spilled it on a chest adorned with painted tulips. Stumbling against dead objects, he opened the door of the little attic where Marie de Lados had always slept in the days before she was called to watch beside her sick mistress. She had never ceased to make her toilet there each morning, nor to keep, locked in a black wooden trunk, the sum of her worldly possessions.

The cold here was intense and smelled of soap and of that peculiar something that hangs about the clothes of people who work for others. The skylight, narrower than the one in the loft, concentrated the limpid shine of the night sky upon a plaster Virgin with outspread hands, though leaving in darkness the crucifix above the bed with its coverlet of old figured cretonne which made the one splash of colour, struck the one note of richness, in this tiny cell. Marie de Lados would gladly have parted with it had anyone told her that it was "worth money". Upon it Fernand Cazenave sat down. Leaning forward, his elbows on his knees, his face hidden in his hands, he wept. The cold froze the tears upon his cheeks: his body shuddered. He felt suddenly afraid that he might die alone here in the attic, and tiptoed from the loft. He had to cling to the banisters on his way down to bed.

He did not sleep. The weight of all eternity seemed to press upon his limbs, upon his chest. Was he dreaming, or was there someone moving in the garden? It could not be a dream, because Péliou started to bark furiously and then suddenly fell silent. It occurred to him that he had forgotten to shoot the bolts. He heard the front door open, gently pushed from outside, but felt no fear. The sound of footsteps died away in the direction of the kitchen, and a light flickered on the ceiling. He closed his eyes, then opened them again. Marie de Lados was holding a lamp, screening it with one hand, so that the light fell full upon her face, the face that was like that of a black Virgin. She stood quite still, making no movement until he called her name:
"Marie!"
Then, setting down the lamp, she came towards him, and he felt upon his forehead the touch of her toil-worn hand.

                                        Johannet, Saint-Symphorien.
23rd September 1923.

The Desert of Love

⚛ I ⚛

FOR YEARS Raymond Courrèges had been cherishing the hope that one day he might run across Maria Cross, the woman on whom he had so ardently longed to be revenged. Often in the street he would follow some chance passer-by, thinking to have found her. But in the course of time the edge of his resentment had become blunted, so that when, at length, they did come face to face, he felt, at first, none of that joy shot with fury which such a meeting should have stirred in him.

It was only ten o'clock when he entered the bar in the rue Duphot. The coloured jazz-band was playing softly for the delectation of a solitary waiter. Over the tiny floor which, when midnight came, would be crammed with dancing couples, a ventilating fan was making a noise like a gigantic bluebottle. To the doorman, who said, with a look of surprise, "Don't often see you here as early as this, sir," he replied with no more than a wave of the hand, which conveyed a wish that something should be done to stop this intrusive bumbling. The man did his best to explain, confidentially, but without success, that the new system "absorbed the smoke without causing a draft". Courrèges gave him such a look that he beat a hasty retreat to the cloak-room. Up in the ceiling the ventilator droned to silence, as though a bee had suddenly alighted.

The young man sat down at one of the tables, thus breaking the immaculate vista of white cloths. A glance in a mirror showed him that he was not looking his best. What's the matter with me? he wondered. God! How he hated a wasted evening—and all because of that swine Eddy H——. He had had to dig the fellow out and almost drag him to a restaurant. During dinner Eddy had scarcely listened to what he was saying, and had excused his

inattention on the ground of a sick headache. He had sat perched
on the very edge of his chair, impatience in every line of his
body, obviously preoccupied with the thought of some happiness
to come. No sooner had he finished his coffee than he had taken
eagerly to his heels—eyes shining, ears flushed, and nostrils flar-
ing. Raymond had spent the day in delighted anticipation of their
dinner and of the evening that was to follow it. But, no doubt,
Eddy had in prospect pleasures more stimulating than any offered
by a mere exchange of confidences.

Courrèges was amazed to find that he felt not only disappointed
and humiliated, but also sad. The discovery that the companionship of a friend to whom he attached no particular importance
could show as thus precious to him came as a shock. It was something entirely new in his life. Up to the age of thirty, being quite
incapable of the selflessness demanded by true friendship, and
devoting much of his attention to women, he had disregarded
everything that was not an object to be possessed, and, like a
greedy child, would have said, had he put the feeling into words,
"I like only what I can eat." At that period of his life he made
use of his cronies either as witnesses of his conquests or as re-
cipients of his confidences. He looked on a friend as, first and
foremost, a pair of ears. He liked, too, the feeling that he could
dominate them and control their actions. Influencing others had
become a passion with him. He flattered himself that he had reduced the demoralizing of his companions to a fine art.

Raymond Courrèges could have built up a big career for himself, as his grandfather the surgeon had done; his uncle, the
Jesuit, and his father, the doctor, if only he had been capable of
harnessing his appetites to work, if only his natural tastes had
not led him to concentrate all his energies on the achievement of
immediate satisfaction. But by now he was reaching the age at
which only those who address themselves to the soul can set
their dominance on a firm foundation. The best that Courrèges
could do for his disciples was to assure them a quick yield in
terms of pleasure. But the younger men of his acquaintance preferred to share their adventures with others of their own age, and
his circle was growing thin. In the preserves of love there is no
shortage of game, but we soon find that the little group of those in
whose company we set out grows smaller year by year. Those
who had survived the dark violence of the war had either dwin-
dled into husbands or had their natures distorted by the pursuit

of a calling. He noted their graying hair, their protuberant bellies, their bald pates, and hated them because they were the same age as himself. He accused them of having murdered their youth, of having betrayed it even before it had fled from them.

It was a matter of pride with him to be taken for a "post-war product"; and this evening, in the still empty bar, where the only sound was the muted thrumming of a mandolin (the flame of the melody rising, falling, flickering), he studied with fierce attention the image thrown back at him from the mirrors, the image of a face with a thatch of vigorous hair on which his thirty-five years had not yet set their mark. It came to him, as he pondered, that age would lay hands upon his life long before it touched his body. If it bolstered up his self-esteem to hear women say among themselves—"Who's that tall young man?" he knew that the keener eyed twenty-year-olds no longer thought of him as forming one in their ephemeral group. Maybe Eddy had had something better to do than talk about himself to an accompaniment of wailing saxophones; on the other hand, he might be doing just that at this very moment in some other bar, laying bare his heart to some youth born in 1904, who would constantly interrupt the flow of his talk with "me, too", and "that's just what I feel. . . ."

A number of young men began to drift in. They had assumed expressions of self-conscious arrogance preparatory to crossing the floor, and were now, at sight of the empty room, visibly embarrassed. They gathered in a little cluster round the bar. But Courrèges had made it a rule never to let himself suffer because of the behaviour of others—whether mistresses or friends. True, therefore, to this principle, he set himself to stress the lack of proportion existing between the insignificance of Eddy H—— and the feeling of uneasy restlessness which was the legacy left behind after that young man's defection. . . . He was pleased to find that this weed of sentiment, when he tried to pull it out, came away without any difficulty. He wound himself up to the pitch of thinking how little it would mean to him, next day, to show his friend the door. He even contemplated without concern the possibility that he might never set eyes on him again. It was almost with a sense of gaiety that he thought, I'll wash my hands of him once and for all. He sighed with relief, only to find that a sense of unease remained which had nothing whatever to do with Eddy. . . . Ah, yes, of course, that letter! He could feel it in the pocket of his evening-jacket. No point in reading it again. Dr. Courrèges, in communicating with his son, made use of a telegraphic brevity of expression which was easily remembered:

Staying at Grand Hotel duration Medical Congress. Available mornings before nine, evenings after eleven.

Your father,
PAUL COURRÈGES

"Not if I know it!" he murmured, unaware that his face had taken on an expression of defiance. He held it against this father of his that it was less easy to despise him than the other members of the family. On reaching the age of thirty, Raymond had demanded a lump sum down comparable to what his sister had received on her marriage. But in vain. Faced by the parental refusal, he had burned his bridges and taken himself off. But it was Madame Courrèges who held the purse-strings, and he knew perfectly well that his father would have acted generously by him had he been in a legal position to do so, and that money meant nothing to the old man. "Not if I know it!" he said to himself once more, but could not, for all that, help catching the note of appeal which sounded in the dry little message. He was far less blind than was Madame Courrèges, who felt only irritation at her husband's undemonstrative nature and brusque manner. "He may be a good man, and he may have a heart of gold", she was fond of saying, "but what good is that to me if I never get a glimpse of it? Just think what he would be like if he was *bad!*"

Just because it was so difficult to hate his father, Raymond found these claims upon his affection hard to endure. He wasn't going to answer the letter. All the same. . . . Later, when he thought back to the circumstances of this evening, he remembered the bitterness of his mood when he entered the deserted little bar, but forgot what had caused it—the defection of a friend called Eddy, and his father's presence in Paris. He believed that his sour ill-temper had been born of a presentiment, and that a connexion existed between the state of his emotions, on that occasion, and the event which was fast approaching. He always later maintained that neither Eddy nor the doctor was, in himself, capable of getting him worked up like that, but that, from the very moment he had settled down with a cocktail, some inner voice, some clamour of the flesh, had warned him of the imminent appearance of the woman who, at that same moment, in a taxi which had already reached the corner of the rue Duphot, was rummaging in her little bag, and saying to her companion:

"What a bore! I've forgotten my lipstick!"

To which the man replied, "There'll probably be one in the ladies' room."

"What a mad idea! one might catch . . ."

"Well then, get Gladys to lend you hers."

She came into the bar. A cloche hat completely obliterated the top part of her face, leaving visible only her chin, that feature on which time sets the sign-manual of age. Forty years had, here and there, touched this lower segment of her countenance, drawing the skin tight and sketching a hint of sagging flesh. Her body beneath its furs must, one felt, be shrunken. As blind as a bull brought suddenly from its dark pen into the glare of the arena, she stopped short on the threshold of the glittering room. When her companion, who had been delayed by a dispute over the fare, rejoined her, Courrèges, though not at once recognizing him, said to himself: "I've seen that fellow somewhere—bet he comes from Bordeaux"; and then, suddenly, as he looked at the face of the man of fifty, swollen, as it were, by the sense of its own identity, a name formed itself on his lips: Victor Larousselle. . . . With beating heart he resumed his examination of the woman who, quickly realizing that no one else was wearing a hat, had taken off hers, and was shaking out her freshly cropped hair in front of a mirror. He saw, first of all, a pair of eyes that were large and calm: next, a wide forehead, its limits sharply marked by the seven youthful points of her dark hair. All that remained of the legacy of youth seemed concentrated in the upper part of her face. Raymond recognized her in spite of the short hair, the middle-aged "spread", and nature's slow work of destruction, which, beginning at the neck, was busy invading the areas of mouth and cheeks. He recognized her as he would have a road familiar to him in childhood, even though the oaks once shading it had been cut down. He calculated the lapse of time. The sum took him a bare two seconds. She's forty-four, he thought; I was eighteen and she was twenty-seven. Like all those who confound the ideas of happiness and youth, he had a consciousness of the passage of time which was ever active, strive though he might to keep it muffled. His eye was forever measuring the sundering gulf of the dead years. He at once inserted in life's chronology every human being who had played a part in his existence. No sooner did he see a face than he could supply a date.

Will she recognize me? he wondered. But would she have so sharply turned away if she had not already done so? She went up to her companion and seemed to be begging him not to stay, for he replied very loudly, and in the tone of a man who craves an admiring audience, "What nonsense! it's not a bit gloomy. In a quarter of an hour it'll be as tight-packed as an egg with meat!" He pushed out a table not far from the one at which Raymond was leaning on his elbow, and sat down heavily. The blood had rushed to his face, sure sign of hardening arteries. But apart from that its expression was one of unruffled satisfaction. The woman was still standing motionless. "What are you waiting for?" he asked. Gone, suddenly, from the eyes, from the coarse and purplish lips, was all look of pleasure. In what he thought was a low voice, he said: "It's enough for me to like being here for you to start sulking—of course!" She must have told him to be careful, have warned him that he could be overheard, for his next words were almost shouted: "So I don't know how to behave, don't I? What does it matter if they *do* hear?"

Seated not far from Raymond, the woman seemed to have recovered her composure. In order to see her the young man would have had to lean forward. It was for her now to avoid his eyes. He realized her renewed sense of security, and was made suddenly aware, with a quick feeling of terror, that the opportunity which, for the last seventeen years, he had so eagerly desired might slip through his fingers. He thought that he was still, after all that time, determined to humiliate the woman who had so deeply humiliated him, to show her what manner of man he was— the sort that doesn't let a bitch get the better of him without hitting back. For years he had found pleasure in thinking what would happen when fate at last should bring them face to face, how he would skilfully contrive matters so as to ride rough-shod over, and reduce to tears, the woman in whose presence he had once cut so ridiculous a figure. . . . Doubtless, if to-night he had recognized not this woman, but some other trivial familiar of his eighteenth year—the boon companion of that distant time, the miserable usher whom he had loathed—he would, at sight of them, have found in himself no trace either of the affection or of the hatred, now outgrown, which the callow schoolboy had then felt. But, faced by this woman, did he not feel now just as he had felt on that Thursday evening of 19—, when he had walked in the fading light along a dusty suburban road smelling of lilies, and stopped before a gate whose bell would never again ring to the pressure of his finger?

Maria! Maria Cross! Of the shy and grubby youth he had been then she had made a new man, the man he was to be for ever after. How little she had changed! The same questioning eyes, the same radiant forehead. Courrèges reminded himself that his favourite school friend of 19— would, by this time, be heavy, prematurely bald, and bearded. But the faces of a certain type of woman remain steeped in childhood until well on into maturity, and it is that quality of childhood, perhaps, that produces in us a fixation of love kept inviolate from the weapons of time. There she was, as she had always been, after seventeen years of passions about which he knew nothing, like one of those black Virgins whose smile the flaming fanaticisms of Reform and Revolution have been powerless to change. She was still being "kept" by this same man of substance who was noisily venting his ill-humour and impatience because the people for whom he was waiting had not yet turned up.

"I expect it's Gladys as usual who's making them late. . . . I'm always on the dot myself . . . can't stand unpunctuality in others. I suppose I'm odd in that way. I just can't bear the thought of keeping other people waiting—some sort of an instinct, I suppose—no use fighting against it. But good manners are a thing of the past. . . ."

Maria Cross laid a hand on his shoulder, and must have said again: "Everyone can hear what you're saying," because he growled out that he wasn't saying anything he minded people hearing, and that it really was a bit too much *her* teaching *him* how to behave.

Her mere presence had the effect of delivering Courrèges bound hand and foot to the vanished past. Though he had always had a keen sense of days long gone, he had a hatred of reviving the memory of their details, and feared nothing so much as the shuffle of ghosts. But he could do nothing this evening to disperse the crowding procession of faces brought by Maria's presence to the surface of his consciousness. He could hear again, in memory, the clock striking six, and the banging of desk lids in

Upper School. Not enough rain had fallen to lay the dust: the
light in the trolley was too bad for him to finish reading *Aphrodite*—in the trolley filled with work-people to whose faces the
exhaustion of another day had imparted a look of gentleness.

❀ *I I* ❀

HE WAS a grubby brat. Much of his time at school he spent
being turned out of the classroom, wandering about the passages
or leaning against old walls. When he left it in the evening, and
before he got to his suburban home, there was a long interval
of time, spent, most of it, in the trolley, which stood in his mind
for freedom, for deliverance. At last he could feel himself alone,
surrounded by indifferent faces and incurious eyes. This especially
was so in winter, because then the darkness, shredded only at
intervals by scattered street-lamps and the glare of occasional
bars, shut him away from the world, isolated him in a universe
that reeked of damp working-clothes. Dead cigarettes dangled
from sagging lips; faces seamed with coal-dust lay tilted back in
sleep; newspapers slipped from hands gone numb; a hatless
woman held up her novelette to catch the light of the lamps, her
lips moving as though in prayer. But the end of the journey
came at last, and, just after they had passed the church at
Talence, he had to get out.

The trolley—a moving Bengal candle—lit up for a few brief
moments the yews and naked elm-branches of a private park.
Then the boy heard the noise of the trolley-wheels diminish as
he stood in the puddle-pocked road. His nose was filled with
the scent of rotting wood and leaves. He turned up the lane that
ran by the Courrèges garden wall and pushed open the half-
closed gate leading to the back-yard. The light from the dining-
room window lay across a clump of bushes where, in spring, the
fuchsias were planted, because they love the shade. At this point
in the return journey his face took on the sullen look it wore at
school; his eyebrows drew together till they showed as a single
matted line above his eyes, and the right-hand corner of his
mouth began to droop. Entering the drawing-room he threw a
collective "Good evening" to the occupants, who sat grouped

about a single niggardly lamp. His mother asked how often must he be told to wipe his feet on the scraper, and did he mean to sit down to dinner with his hands "like that"? Madame Courrèges, the elder, murmured to her daughter-in-law: "You know what Paul says: don't nag the boy unnecessarily." His very appearance seemed to start an exchange of bitter words.

He sat down where the light could not reach him.

Crouched over her embroidery, Madeleine Basque, his sister, had not so much as raised her head at his entrance. He was of less interest to her, he thought, than the dog. In her opinion, Raymond was the family's "running sore". "I don't like to think what *he'll* grow up into", she was for ever saying, to which her husband, Gaston Basque, would contribute his mite by adding: "It's all because his father's so weak."

She would look up from her work, sit for a moment with her ears pricked, say suddenly, "There's Gaston", and lay aside her task. "I don't hear a thing," Madame Courrèges would remark. But—"Yes, it's him," the young woman would repeat, and then, though no sound had reached any ear but her own, would run out onto the terrace and disappear into the garden, guided by an infallible instinct, as though she belonged to a species of animal different from all others, where it was the male, and not the female, who exhaled the odor that would draw his partner to him through the darkness. In a moment or two the Courrèges would hear a man's voice followed by Madeleine's gratified and submissive laughter. They knew that the couple would not come back through the drawing-room, but would use a side door and go straight upstairs to the bedroom floor, from which they would not descend until the gong had been sounded twice.

The company round the dining-room table, beneath the hanging lamp, consisted of the elder Madame Courrèges, her daughter-in-law, Lucie Courrèges, the young couple, and their four little girls, all with their father's reddish hair, all dressed alike, all with the same complexion and the same patches of freckles. They sat huddled together like tame birds on a perch. "No one's to say a word to them," ordered Lieutenant Basque. "If anyone addresses them, it's they who will be punished. Now don't say I didn't warn you."

The doctor's chair remained empty for some considerable time, even when he happened to be at home. He would come in half-way through the meal, carrying a bundle of learned jour-

nals. His wife said, Hadn't he heard the gong? and complained
that with everything in the house at sixes and sevens, it was
quite impossible to keep any servant for long. Shaking his head,
as though to chase away a fly, he proceeded to bury himself in
one of his journals. This was not affectation on his part, but
merely a way of saving time devised by a man who was in a
constant condition of overwork, never free from worries, and
fully aware that every minute was precious. At the other end of
the table, the Basques sat isolated and aloof, supremely indifferent to everything that did not directly concern either them or
their little ones. Gaston would be explaining how he was pulling
strings to avoid being moved from Bordeaux, how the Colonel
had written to the Ministry . . . his attentive wife all the while
keeping a watchful eye on the children and maintaining an unin-
terrupted flow of educative comment: "Don't you know how to
use a knife?" "Don't sprawl." "Keep your hands on the table—
hands, I said, not elbows." "Now mind what I say, you won't get
any more bread." "You've had quite enough to drink already."

The Basques formed an island of secrecy and suspicion. "They
never tell me anything"—all Madame Courrèges' grievances
against her daughter could be summed up in that phrase—"they
never tell me anything". She suspected that Madeleine was pregnant, kept a careful eye on her figure, and drew her own conclusions when the girl complained of not feeling well. The servants, she maintained, always knew everything before she did.
She believed that Gaston had taken out an insurance policy on
his life, but for how much? She had no idea what money they
had come into on old Basque's death.

In the drawing-room, after dinner, when she grumblingly inquired whether Raymond hadn't any homework to do, any essay
to write, he made no answer. He would take hold of one of the
little girls, look as though he were about to crush her in his great
hands, toss her up over his head so that she could touch the
ceiling, and swing the lithe little body round and round, while
Madeleine Basque, like a ruffled and uneasy hen—though disarmed by the child's excitement, would exclaim: "*Do* be careful;
I'm sure you'll do her some injury"; and then, turning to the company in general, would remark: "He's so *rough*", at which Grandmamma Courrèges, laying down her knitting and pushing up her
spectacles, while her whole face crinkled into a smile, would at
once embark on a brisk defence of Raymond: "Why, he *adores*

children", she would say. "You can't deny that children are all he cares about . . ." for it was one of the old lady's convictions that he wouldn't be so devoted to them if he hadn't a heart of gold. "You've only got to see him with his nieces to realize that there's nothing really to worry about."

But did he really care so very much about children? The truth was he made use of anything that came his way, provided it was warm and living, as a weapon against those whom he called the "corpses". Depositing the young body on the sofa, he would, on these occasions, make for the door, rush from the house, and stride along the leaf-encumbered paths.

Between the branches a lighter patch of sky guided his steps. Doctor Courrèges' lamp glowed from behind a window on the first floor. Should he go to bed without looking in on his father to say good-night? The three-quarters of an hour of hostile silence each morning were all that he could stand. Every day, early, the brougham set out, carrying father and son. Raymond got out at the Barrière de Saint-Genès, from which he walked, by way of the boulevards, to school, while the doctor continued on to the hospital. For three-quarters of an hour they sat side by side in a smell of ancient leather, between streaming windows. The doctor, who a few moments later would be speaking eloquently, authoritatively, to his helpers and his students, had been vainly seeking for months some word that would provoke a response from this being of his own flesh and blood. How was he ever to succeed in blazing a path to this heart which was always bristling with defences? Each time he congratulated himself on finding a joint in the young man's armour, and began speaking to Raymond in phrases planned long in advance, his words seemed suddenly like the words of a stranger: his very voice, dry and mocking, had, he felt, turned traitor—no matter how hard he tried to make it sound natural. This powerlessness to give expression to his feelings was his habitual martyrdom.

It was only through his actions that Dr. Courrèges' kindness of heart was widely recognized, for they alone bore witness to the good that lay so deeply embedded in him that it was like a man entombed. He could never hear a word of gratitude without a growl and a shrug. Bumping along through rainy dawns beside his son, he was for ever addressing silent questions to the withdrawn and sullen face there at his elbow. In spite of himself he could not help interpreting the signs that showed upon that face as those of some dark angel—the deceptive sweetness, for instance, that he caught in eyes that were more deeply shadowed than they should have been. The poor boy regards me as his enemy, thought the father, and the fault is mine, not his. But he was reckoning without the sure instinct for those who love him which is for ever active in the adolescent. Raymond heard the unvoiced appeal, and never confused his father with the others. But he deliberately turned a deaf ear to what never found release in words. Nor could he, on his side, have thought of anything to say to the victim of shyness at his side, for the effect of his presence was to numb the older man with timidity, and so turn him to ice. Nevertheless, the doctor could not refrain, now and again, from remonstrating with him, though he always did so as gently as possible, and in terms of a friendship between equals.

"I've had another letter about you from the headmaster. Poor Abbé Farge, you'll really send him out of his mind! It seems to be proved without a shadow of doubt that it was you who passed round that treatise on obstetrics—I suppose you sneaked it off my shelves. I must confess that his air of outraged virtue seems to me somewhat excessive. After all, you're old enough now to know about the facts of life, and it's a good deal better that you should get them from solid, scientific books. That's the line I took in my reply. . . . But I gather, too, that a number of *La Gaudriole* was found in the newspaper-rack in Upper School, and, very naturally, you are under suspicion. All the sins of Israel are laid to your charge. Better look out, my boy, or you'll find yourself expelled with the final exams still a good six months off."

"No."

"What do you mean—no?"

"Because I'm working extra hard and stand a good chance of not being flunked a second time. I know their sort! They're not going to get rid of the only fellow who's likely to pass. Besides, if they showed me the door, the Jesuits would snap me up in a jiffy! They'd far rather let me go on contaminating the others, as they put it, than run the risk of losing a good item in the school records. Think how triumphant old Farge will look on Speech Day: thirty candidates—twenty-three 'Honors' and two 'Passes.' . . . Thunderous applause. . . . What a lot of swine they are!"

"No, my boy, that's where you're wrong." The doctor stressed those words, "my boy". Now, perhaps, was his oppotunity to pene-

trate the lad's stubborn heart. For a long time his son had obstinately refused to show the slightest sign of weakening. The glow
of a trusting confidence showed through the cynical words. What
should he say that might have the effect, without putting the
boy on the defensive, of proving to him that there *are* men who
don't resort to tricks and calculations, that sometimes the cleverest
are those Machiavellis of high causes who wound us when they
wish us well? . . . He felt about in his mind for the most suitable
formula, and even while he pondered the problem, the suburban
road had turned into a city street filled with the bright and
melancholy radiance of morning and the jostle of milk-carts. A
few moments more and they would reach the city limits, that
Croix de Saint-Genès where once the pilgrims to St. James of
Compostella had knelt in momentary adoration, and where now
only bus inspectors leaned against the walls. Unable to find any
suitable words, he took the other's warm hand in his, said in a
low voice, "My boy" . . . and then noticed that Raymond, his
head pressed to the window, was asleep, or pretending to be
asleep. The young man had closed his eyes, perhaps for fear that
they might, for all his efforts to the contrary, betray a weakening,
a desire to yield. He sat there, his face fast shut to all approaches,
a bony face that looked as though carved in granite, in which
the only sign of sensitiveness was the vulnerable line of the eyelids.

Very gradually the doctor withdrew his hand.

Was it before that scene in the brougham, or later, that the
woman sitting over there on the settee, separated from him by
no more than a single table, so that he could have spoken to her
without raising his voice, had come into his life? She seemed
calmer now, and was sipping her drink with no fear, it seemed,
that Raymond might have recognized her. Every now and again
she looked at him, only to look away almost at once. Suddenly
her voice—and how well he remembered it!—rose above the
babble of noise: "There's Gladys!"

The newly arrived couple came over at once and sat down between her and her companion. They all started talking at once.
"We were waiting for our cloak-room tickets." "We're always
the first to arrive—well, anyhow you've come, that's the main
thing."

No, it must have been more than a year before the scene between father and son in the brougham that one day at dinner (it would have been in the late spring, because the lamp in the dining-room had not been lit) Madame Courrèges the elder had said to her daughter-in-law: "I know whom the white hangings in the church were for, Lucie."

Raymond had thought that one of those endless conversations was about to begin, full of trivial phrases that dropped dead about the doctor's chair. As a rule, they had to do with household matters, each of the women present rushing to do battle for her own particular member of the staff, so that the encounter became a squalid Iliad in which the quarrels of the servants' quarters set the various patron Goddesses at one another's throat in the Olympus of the dining-room. Often the two families would set about disputing the favours of the daily sewing-woman. "I've arranged with Travaillotte to come to me next week", Madame Courrèges would say to Madeleine Basque, and then the younger woman would at once protest that the children's underwear needed mending.

"You always grab Travaillotte."

"Well, then, why don't you get old broken-nose Mary?"

"Broken-nose Mary is a much slower worker. Besides, she always insists on my paying her car-fare."

But on this particular evening, the mention of the white hangings in church had given rise to a more serious discussion. Madame Courrèges the elder had more to say.

"They're for that poor little boy of Maria Cross's, the one who died of meningitis. I gather she ordered an extremely expensive funeral."

"How very tactless!"

At his wife's exclamation, the doctor, who sat reading a journal while he drank his soup, raised his eyes. She, as usual when that happened, lowered hers, angrily remarking that it was a pity, all the same, that the curé hadn't managed to instill some sense of guilt into a woman who, as everyone knew, was a kept creature, who flaunted her shame all over the place, with her horses and carriages and all the rest.

The doctor made a gesture with his hand indicative of protest. "It's not for us to judge: she's done *us* no harm."

"What about the scandal? I suppose that doesn't count?"

From his face she could see that he was saying to himself how vulgar she was. She made an effort to moderate her tone, though a few seconds later she exclaimed as loudly as before that women like that gave her the horrors. . . . The house that for so long had been the home of her old friend, Madame Bouffard, Victor Larouselle's mother-in-law, was now occupied by a slut. . . . Every time she passed the door it cut her to the heart. . . .

The doctor, speaking very calmly, and in an almost hushed voice, interrupted the flow to point out that the only person in that house to-night was a mother sitting by her dead child. At this, Madame Courrèges, with one finger raised, announced solemnly:

"It is God's judgment!"

The children heard the scraping sound made by the doctor's chair as he pushed it sharply back from the table. He thrust his journals into his pocket, and, without another word, walked across to the door. He forced himself to move slowly, but the family, all attention now, could hear him running upstairs four steps at a time.

"Did I say anything so very extraordinary?" Madame Courrèges addressed a questioning look at her mother-in-law, at the young couple, at the children, at the servant. The only sounds in the room were the scraping of knives and forks and Madeleine's voice: "Don't nibble your bread—stop playing with that bone. . ."

Madame Courrèges, her eyes fixed on her mother-in-law, said: "I really think he must be ill."

But the old lady, her nose buried in her plate, seemed not to have heard. It was at this point that Raymond burst out laughing.

"If you must laugh you'd better go outside! And don't come back till you can control yourself!"

Raymond threw his napkin on the floor. How peaceful it was in the garden. Yes, it must have been late spring because he remembered the bumbling noise made by the cockchafers, and that they had had strawberries for dinner. He had sat down in the middle of the paddock on the still warm stone rim of a fountain which no human eye had ever seen spouting water. He noticed his father's shadow passing and re-passing the windows of the first floor. In the twilight that poured dusty and heavy over this stretch of country not far from Bordeaux, a bell was tolling at long intervals because death had come for the child of this same woman who now sat drinking so close to him that he could have stretched out his hand and touched her. Since starting on the champagne, Maria Cross had been gazing more boldly at the

young man, as though she were no longer afraid that she might
be recognized. To say that she had not aged was an understate-
ment. In spite of the fact that she had cut her hair, and that
she was wearing nothing that trespassed beyond the winter's
fashion, her whole body had somehow kept the lines that had
been in vogue about 19—. She looked young, but it was as though
her youth had come to flower fifteen years ago and remained unchanged. She was young in the way that no one is young today.
Her eyelids looked no wearier than they had when she had said
to Raymond: "Our eyes have a fellow feeling."

Raymond remembered how, on the morning following the evening on which his father had suddenly left the table, he had sat
very early in the dining-room drinking his chocolate. The windows
were open on the dawn mist, and he shivered a little. There was
a smell of freshly-ground coffee. The gravel of the drive crackled
under the wheels of the ancient bougham. The doctor was late.
Madame Courrèges, in a purple dressing-gown, her hair plaited
and twisted in the way she always wore it when she went to
bed, kissed him on the forehead. He went on with his breakfast without pausing.
"Isn't your father down yet?
She said that she had some letter to give him to mail. But he
could guess the reason for her early appearance. When the
members of a family live cheek by jowl, they get into the habit
of never giving away their own secrets but of ever being on the
alert to probe the secrets of others. The mother said of her daughter-in-law: "She never tells me anything, but there's little I don't
know about her." Each person in the group claimed to know all
about the others, while remaining inscrutable himself. Raymond
thought he knew why his mother was there: "She wants to make it
up." After a scene like that of the previous evening, she would dog
her husband's footsteps, seeking to be taken back into favour.
The poor woman was always discovering too late that she had
the fatal gift of habitually saying what would most get on the
doctor's nerves. As in certain forms of nightmare, the more she
tried to approach him, the farther away she seemed to get. She
could do nothing, say nothing, that was not hateful to him. Tangled in her clumsy efforts at tenderness, she was, as it were, always groping her way forward with outstretched hands. But
whenever she touched him it was to bruise.

As soon as she heard the sound of his bedroom-door closing, she poured out a cup of steaming coffee. A smile lit up her face, which was marked by the traces of a sleepless night and worn by the slow dripping of laborious and identical days. But the smile vanished as soon as the doctor appeared. She was already on her guard, trying to read the expression in his eyes.

"Why, you've got your top hat and overcoat on!"

"That is quite obvious."

"Are you going to a wedding?" . . . "A funeral, then?"

"Yes."

"Who has died?"

"Someone you don't know, Lucie."

"Tell me who it is."

"The little Cross boy."

"Maria Cross's son? Do you know her? You never told me you did. You never tell me anything. Considering that we were talking at dinner of that hussy . . ."

The doctor was drinking his coffee, standing. He answered in his quietest tones, which was always a sign with him that he was exasperated almost beyond bearing, though well under control.

"Haven't you learned, even after twenty-five years, that I prefer to discuss my patients as little as possible?"

No, she hadn't, and insisted that it always amazed her to find out, quite by chance, in the course of a social call, that this or that friend of hers had been attended by Dr. Courrèges.

"It's so awkward for me when people look surprised. 'What,' they say, 'do you really mean to tell me that you didn't *know*?' and then I have to admit that you don't trust me, that you never tell me anything. Were you treating the child? What did he die of? I can't see why you won't tell me. I never repeat things. Besides, with people like that, what can it matter? . . ."

For any sign the doctor gave, he might not have heard or seen her. He put on his overcoat, calling to Raymond: "Get a move on; seven o'clock struck ages ago."

Madame Courrèges pattered along behind them.

"What have I said now? You suddenly put all your prickles out. . . ."

The door slammed. A clump of shrubs hid the brougham from view. The sun began to shred the mist. Madame Courrèges, talking disjointedly to herself, turned back towards the house.

Seated in the carriage, the schoolboy looked at his father with eager curiosity, anxious for confidences. Now, if ever, father and son might have drawn closer together. But the doctor's thoughts were far from the boy with whom, so often, he had longed to come to grips. Here was the young prey ready to his hand, and he did not realize it. He sat there, muttering into his beard, as though he had been alone: "I ought to have called in a surgeon. One can always try trepanning as a last resort." He pushed back his top hat with its nap all brushed the wrong way, lowered one of the windows, and thrust out his hirsute countenance above the traffic-encumbered road. At the city limits he said absent-mindedly: "See you this evening", but he did not gaze after Raymond's retreating form.

❀ III ❀

IN THE course of the following summer Raymond Courrèges had his seventeenth birthday. He remembered it as a season of torrid heat and shortage of water. Never since then had the city of stone lain prostrate under so intolerable a glare, cluttered though his memory was with many summers spent in Bordeaux, a city protected by hills from the north winds, and close invested by pines and sand which concentrated and accumulated the heat— Bordeaux, so poor in trees, except for its Public Gardens, where, to the eyes of children parched with thirst, it seemed as though the last vestiges of green in all the world were being burned to cinders behind the tall and solemn railings.

But perhaps, in retrospect, he was confusing the sun's heat of that particular summer with the inner flame that was burning him up, him and sixty others of his age, who had their being within the limits of a yard separated from other yards by the back walls of a row of latrines. It needed the constant presence of two monitors to control this herd of boys who were dying into life, of men on the verge of being born. Responsive to the thrust of painful growth, the forest of young lives put forth, in a few short months, spindly and ailing shoots. The world and its ways had the effect of pruning the rank growth of these young scions of good families, but in Raymond Courrèges the action of the rising

sap was fierce and uninhibited. He was an object of fear and
horror to his teachers, who kept him with his scarred face (because his tender skin could not endure the razor) as far as possible
from associating with his fellows. The good boys of the school
looked on him as a "dirty beast" who carried photographs of
women in his note-case and read *Aphrodite* (disguised as a
prayer-book) in chapel. He had "lost his faith". This phrase
caused as much terror in the school as would, in an asylum, the
rumour that one of the most dangerous lunatics had broken out
of his strait-jacket and was wandering stark naked through the
grounds. It was matter of general knowledge that on those rare
Sundays when he was not being "kept in", Raymond Courrèges hid
his school uniform and his cap, with the monogram of the Virgin,
in a bed of nettles, put on an overcoat bought ready-made at
Thierry and Sigrand, clapped on his head an absurd bowler which
made him look like a plain-clothes policeman, and hung about the
more disreputable booths at the fair. He had been seen on the
merry-go-round hugging a slut of indeterminate age.

When, in the pompous setting of Commencement day, an attendant multitude of parents sat stupefied by the heat in the
shade of leaves already shrivelled by the sun, and heard the
headmaster announce that Courrèges had "passed with distinction", he alone knew what an effort he had made, in spite of the
apparent lawlessness of his days, not to be expelled. A single
fixed idea had filled his mind to the exclusion even of the sense
of persecution, so that the hours of detention, spent standing
against the rough-cast walls of the playground, had actually
seemed short—the idea of departure, of flight, in the first glow of
a summer morning, along the highroad to Spain which ran past
the Courrèges' garden, a road that looked as though it were weighed
down by the bulk of its great flagstones, a relic of the Emperor, of
his guns and of his convoys. He savoured in anticipation the heady
delight of every step that should put a little more distance between
him, the school, and his depressing family. It was an understood
thing that on the day he passed his examination his father and his
grandmother would each give him a hundred francs. Since he had
already saved up eight hundred, he would thus be owner of the
thousand which, so he thought, would enable him to travel through
the world, miles and miles from his own "people". That was why he
had spent the hours of detention working, untroubled by the sight
of others at play. Sometimes he would shut his book and chew the

cud of day-dreams. In imagination he could hear the scrape of cicadas in the pine-trees along the roads which soon he would be travelling, could see the cool shade of the inn before which, tired out with travelling, he would sit in some unidentified village. The rising moon would wake the cocks, and off he would start again in the freshness of the dawn, with the taste of bread in his mouth. And sometimes he would sleep beneath a mill, a single corn-stook blotting out the stars: and the damp fingers of the early day would rouse him. . . .

But, though teachers and parents had agreed in thinking him capable of anything, he had not, after all, taken to flight. His enemies, though they did not know it, had been too strong for him. Defeat comes to the young because they let themselves be so easily convinced of their own wretched inadequacy. At seventeen the most undisciplined of boys is only too ready to accept the image of himself imposed by others. Raymond Courrèges was blessed with good looks, but thought himself a monster of ugliness and squalor. He was blind to the fine contours of his face, and convinced that he could rouse in others only feelings of disgust. He was filled with a horror of his own person, and felt assured that he could never pay back in kind the emotion of hostility which he caused in those about him. That was why, stronger even than the longing to escape, he felt the desire to hide, to veil his face, to be compelled no more to wipe away the hatred of future enemies yet unknown. This youthful debauchee, whose hand the pupils of the Church School were afraid to touch, was no less ignorant than they of women, and could not conceive that he might be capable of giving pleasure if only to a slattern in the gutter. He was ashamed of his body. It never occurred either to his parents or to his teachers that all his glorying in wildness and dirt was but the miserable bravado of the young which he assumed because he wanted to make them believe that he revelled in his own uncomeliness. His attitude was no more than the threadbare pride of adolescence, a sort of despairing humility.

The holidays that followed his examination, far from opening a way of escape, were a period of secret cowardice. Paralysed by timidity, he thought he could read contempt in the eyes of the servant-girl who did his room, and quailed before the brooding look which, at times, his father turned on him. Since the Basques were spending August at Arcachon, he had not even the consolation of the children with whose young bodies, supple as growing plants, he loved to play so roughly.

As soon as the young family had gone, Madame Courrèges heaved a sigh of relief.

"It's nice to have the place to ourselves for a bit," she said, in this way taking her revenge on a remark of her daughter's to the effect that "Gaston and I really need a little course of solitude."

Actually, the poor woman lived for nothing but the daily letter, and could not hear the muttering of a storm without seeing in imagination the whole Basque family being dashed to destruction in an open boat. The house was only half full, and the empty rooms weighed heavily on her spirits. Of what comfort to her was a son who spent his time running wild about the roads, and came back sullen-tempered and dripping with sweat, to dash at his food like a ravenous animal?

"People say, 'Well, you've got your husband.' My husband!—I ask you!"

"You forget, darling, how busy Paul is."

"He doesn't have any rounds to make, mother. Most of his patients are on holiday."

"Not his poorer patients. Besides, he's got his laboratory work, the hospital, and all those articles he has to write. . . ."

The embittered wife shook her head. She knew that her husband's active temperament would never lack employment, that never, till the day of his death, would there be a moment's pause in which, for a few brief instants, she might count on his whole and undivided attention. It never occurred to her that such a thing could be possible. She did not know that in even the fullest lives love can hollow out its little nest; that the harassed statesman will stop the wheels of the world when the moment comes for his mistress to pay him a visit. This ignorance spared her much suffering. Though she was only too familiar with the kind of love that dogs the feet of someone beyond the power to touch, someone who will not so much as turn his head to take a moment's notice, the mere fact that she had always been powerless to hold his attention for no matter how brief a while made it impossible for her to imagine that for some other woman the doctor might be a totally different person. She would have hated to think that somewhere a woman might exist who was capable of charming him from that incomprehensible world in which he lived, made up of statistics and observations, of blood and pus imprisoned between glass slides; and it was many years before she discovered that there were evenings when the laboratory remained deserted, when the sick had to wait in vain for the man who, when he might have eased their pain, preferred to stand motionless in a dark and stuffy drawing-room gazing down at a woman stretched upon a sofa.

In order to contrive such secret oases in his days of toil the doctor had to work with twice his normal intensity; had to hack his way through every kind of obstacle that he might win as his reward those few moments filled with concentrated watching and impassioned silence, when to look was all the satisfaction he desired. Sometimes, just when the long-expected hour had almost sounded, a message would reach him from Maria Cross saying that she was no longer free, that the man on whom she was dependent had arranged a party in some restaurant on the outskirts of the city. When that happened he would have found the thought of life intolerable had she not added a postscript to her note suggesting another day. Then, in a flash, the miracle occurred, and at once his whole existence centred about the thought of the new meeting promised by her words. Though every hour of every day was filled with duties, he included in a single sweeping act of vision, like a skilful chess-player, all the possible combinations that might enable him so to arrange matters that, when the time and date arrived, he could be there, motionless and disengaged, in the stuffy and encumbered room, gazing at the figure stretched upon its sofa. And when the moment came and went at which, had she not put him off, he might have been with her, he was filled with happiness, thinking: "It would have been over by now, but, as things are, I still have that happiness in front of me. . . ." There was something then with which he could fill the empty days that lay between. At such times the laboratory in particular took on the quality of a haven. Within its walls he lost all sense of the passing hours, even of love itself. Absorbed in research, he felt freed from time, filling with work the moments that must be lived till, suddenly, the longed-for hour would come when he could push open the gate of that small house where Maria Cross lived behind the church at Talence.

Devoured by his obsession, he gave, that summer, less and less attention to his son. He who had been made party to so many shameful secrets often said to himself: We always think that the

happenings tucked away in newspaper paragraphs don't concern
us, that murders, suicides, and scandals are what come to other
people, while, all the time . . . And yet, all the time, he did not
know that there had been moments in the course of that dev-
astating August when his son had been within an ace of taking
an irreparable step. Raymond longed to run away, but longed,
too, to hide, to become invisible. He could not pluck up courage
to go into a café or a shop. He would walk up and down a dozen
times before a door before he could bring himself to open it.
This mania made all flight impossible, though he felt stifled in his
home. There were many evenings when death seemed to him to
be the simplest of all solutions. He would open the drawer in
which his father kept an old-fashioned revolver, but it was not
God's will that he should find the cartridges. One afternoon he
walked between the drooping vines down to the pond that lay
beyond the sun-baked paddock. He hoped that the weeds, the
growing water-plants, might knot a tangle round his feet, that he
might be unable to extricate himself from the muddy liquid,
that his eyes and mouth might be filled with slime, that no one
might ever see him again, nor he see others watching him. Mosquitoes were skimming the surface, frogs were popping in the
eddying shadows like so many stones. Caught in the weeds a
dead animal showed white. What saved Raymond then was not
fear but disgust.

Fortunately, he was not often alone. The Courrèges' tennis
court was a focus of attraction for all the young people of the
neighbourhood. It was one of Madame Courrèges' grievances that
the Basques should have involved her in the expense of having
it made, and then, when they might have played on it, had
gone away. Only strangers got the benefit of it. Young men in
white, with rackets in their hands, moving inaudibly on san-
dalled feet, appeared in the drawing-room at the hour of siesta,
greeted the ladies, barely bothered to ask after Raymond, and
went out again into the glare which echoed soon to their cries
of "Play" and "Out", to the sound of their laughter. "They don't
even trouble to shut the door", grumbled Grandmother Courrèges,
who thought of nothing but keeping out the heat. Raymond
might have been willing to play, but the presence of the young
women frightened him—especially of the Cosserouge girls, Marie-
Thérèse, Marie-Louise, and Marguerite-Marie, all three fat and
fair and suffering from headache because of the weight of their

hair, for they were condemned to wear upon their heads enormous structures of yellow tresses imperfectly secured with combs
and always on the point of falling down. He hated them. Why
must they always laugh so much? They were in a constant state
of wriggling convulsions, convinced that everybody else was a
"scream". They didn't, as it happened, laugh more at Raymond
than at anybody else, but it was his particular curse to feel himself the centre of a universal derision. But there was one reason,
in particular, why he hated them. The day before the Basques
went away, he had found it impossible any longer to refuse to
keep a promise he had made to his brother-in-law that he would
ride a monstrous great horse that the lieutenant was leaving behind in the stables. He was at the age when no sooner was he in
the saddle than he was seized with giddiness. Consequently, he
cut a poor figure as a horseman. One morning the Cosserouge
girls had come on him suddenly in a forest ride, clinging desperately to the pommel of his saddle. A moment later and he
was sprawling on the sandy ground. He could never see them
after that without hearing again the giggling screams in which,
at that moment, they had indulged. Each time they met him they
took delight in reminding him of every circumstance of that humiliating fall. What storms does teasing, however harmless in intention, raise in a young man's heart in the spring-time of life!
Raymond was incapable of distinguishing one Cosserouge from
another, but lumped them collectively within the orbit of his
hatred, regarding them as a sort of fat, three-headed monster,
always sweating and clucking beneath the motionless trees of
that August afternoon of 19—.

Sometimes he took the trolley, crossed the blazing inferno of
Bordeaux, and reached the docks, where human bodies, devoured by poverty and scrofula, were splashing about in the stag-
nant water with its iridescent scum of oil. Their owners laughed,
chasing one another, and leaving on the flags the faint, damp
outline of their feet.

October returned. The perilous passage had been accomplished.
Raymond had passed the dangerous crisis of his life. It was written that he should be saved, and indeed he was already saved
when, at the beginning of term, the new school-books (he had
always loved the smell of them) brought to him a sort of concentrated vision as he stood upon the threshold of the year which
was to initiate him into the study of philosophy, of all the dreams
and systems that have beguiled the human mind. Yes, he was to

be saved, though not by his own unaided efforts. The time was
near when a woman would come into his life—that same woman
who, this evening, was watching him through the smoky haze
and crowding couples of the tiny bar, whose wide and tranquil
brow no passage of time had had the power to change.

During the winter months through which he had lived before
they met, his spirit had lain in a profound torpor. A sort of dull
passivity had left him weaponless. Stripped of his old aggres-
siveness, he was no longer the eternal whipping-boy of fate.
Once the holidays had passed that had tormented him with the
twin obsession of escape and death, he found himself acquiescing
in the expected conduct of his days. Discipline came to his assistance by making life a good deal easier. But he savoured even
more intensely his daily journey home, the evening passage from
one suburb to another. The College gate once left behind, he
plunged into the secret darkness of the damp little lane which
was sometimes filled with the smell of fog, sometimes with the
hard, dry breath of frost. With the sky, too, in its many aspects,
he became familiar—overcast, swept clear and corroded with
stars, veiled with a covering of cloud that seemed to be lit from
within by a moon he could not see. And then, in a short while,
would come the city limits, with the same crowd of tired, dirty,
submissive men and women waiting to lay siege to the trolley.
The great glowing rectangle plunged ahead into a land, half
town, half country, rumbling on between pathetic little gardens
that lay submerged beneath the fathoms of the winter night.

At home he no longer felt himself to be the object of a never-
ceasing curiosity. General attention was now concentrated upon
the doctor.

"I'm worried about him," said Madame Courrèges to her mother-
in-law. "You're lucky to be able to take things so calmly. I envy
temperaments like yours."

"Paul is rather overworked. He does too much, there's no doubt
about that. But he has a magnificent constitution, so I'm not
really concerned."

The younger woman shrugged her shoulders, making no effort
to hear what the other muttered half to herself: "He's not ill, I'm
sure of that. All the same, he *is* suffering."

Madame Courrèges said, not for the first time, "Trust a doctor
never to take care of himself."

During dinner she kept a watchful eye on him. How emaciated his face looked, she thought, when he raised his eyes from his plate.

"It's Friday, why cutlets?"

"You need a good body-building diet."

"What do you know about it?"

"Why won't you go and see Duluc? No doctor can ever prescribe for himself."

"My poor Lucie, why have you made up your mind that I am ill?"

"You can't see yourself. Why, the mere look of you is enough to frighten one. Everybody says the same thing. Only yesterday, someone—I forget who—said: 'What *is* the matter with your husband?' You ought to take choline. I'm sure it's your liver."

"Why my liver rather than some other organ?"

Her reply was peremptory: "My impression is that it *must be* your liver."

Lucie's impression to that effect was very definite, and nothing would induce her to give it up. Her comments buzzed round the doctor like so many flies, only far more irritating: "You've already had two cups of coffee—I must tell the cook to see that the pot isn't filled. That's your third cigarette since lunch. It's no good your denying it. There are three stubs in the ash-tray."

"What proves that he knows he's ill", she said one day to her mother-in-law, "is that I caught him yesterday looking at himself in the glass. As a rule, he never bothers about his appearance, but there he was, peering at his face and running his fingers over it. It was as though he wanted to smooth out the wrinkles on his forehead and round his eyes. He even opened his mouth and examined his teeth."

Madame Courrèges the elder looked at her daughter-in-law over the top of her spectacles, as though fearful of detecting upon that puzzled countenance something more than mere anxiety, something more in the nature of suspicion. The old lady had a feeling that her son's good-night kiss had recently been less perfunctory than usual. Perhaps she knew what that momentary surrender to emotion meant. Ever since he was a young man she had got into the way of guessing the precise nature of those wounds which one person alone, the owner of the hand that deals them, can cure. But the wife, though for many years frustrated in her instinct of tenderness, had thoughts only for physical ailments. Each time the doctor sat down opposite her and raised

his clasped hands to his face with its look of suffering, she said:
"You really *ought* to see Duluc: we *all* think so."
"Duluc could tell me nothing I don't already know."
"Can you listen to your own heart?"

To this question the doctor made no reply. His whole attention was concentrated upon the pain at his heart. It was as
though a hand were holding and just faintly squeezing it. Ah!
who better than he could count its beats, for were they not the
evidence of what he had just been through with Maria Cross?
How difficult it was to slip a more than usually tender word, a
hinted declaration, into a conversation with a woman who showed
herself always so submissive, who insisted on regarding her doctor as an almost god-like creature, and forced upon him the dignity of a spiritual fatherhood!

He went over in his mind the circumstances of his most recent
visit. He had got out of the carriage on the main road, opposite
the church at Talence, and had walked up the puddled lane. So
swift had been the progress of the dusk that it was almost dark
before he reached the gate. At the far end of an untidy path a
lamp threw a ruddy glow from the ground-floor windows of a low-
built house. He did not ring. No servant preceded him through
the dining-room. He entered the drawing-room without knocking.
Maria Cross was lying on a sofa and did not get up. Indeed, for
a second or two she went on reading. Finally:

"So there you are, doctor; I'm quite ready for you," she said,
holding out both hands, and moving her feet so as to make room
for him on the end of the sofa. "Don't take that chair, it's broken.
I live, you know, in a jumble of luxury and squalor. . . ."

Monsieur Larousselle had set her up in this suburban villa
where the visitor was liable to trip over tears in the carpet, and
only the folds of the curtains concealed the holes in the fabric.
Sometimes when he went to see her she said nothing. He was
prevented from starting a conversation fitted to his role of suppliant lover—a conversation which he had made up his mind *must*
take place—by the presence, over the sofa, of a mirror which reflected the image of a face eaten away by a mass of beard, of two
bloodshot eyes dimmed as the result of constant application to a
microscope, of a forehead from which the hair had already begun
to recede when he was still a house physician. Nevertheless, he
was determined to try his luck. One of her small hands was
trailing over the edge of the sofa, almost touching the floor. He

took it, and said in a low voice: "Maria . . ." Such was her confidence in him that she did not withdraw it. "I'm not feverish,
doctor; really I'm not." As always, she spoke of herself. "Dear
friend," she said: "I've done something of which you'll thoroughly
approve. I've told Monsieur Larousselle that I no longer need
the car, that he'd better sell it and get rid of Firmin. You know
how it is with him, how incapable he is of understanding any
delicacy of feeling. He just laughed, and said what was the point
of upsetting everything merely because of a moment's whim? But
I mean it, and I never use anything but the trolley now, whatever the weather. I came back in it today from the cemetery.
I thought you'd be pleased. I feel less unworthy of our poor dead
darling . . . less . . . less like a kept woman."

The last two words were barely audible. The eyes which she
raised to the doctor's face were brimming with tears, and seemed
humbly to implore his approval. He gave it to her at once, gravely,
coldly. She was forever invoking him. "You're so *big* . . . you're
the noblest human being I have ever known . . . the mere fact
that you exist makes me believe in the reality of goodness." How
he longed to protest, to say: "I'm not the man you think me,
Maria; only a poor, a very poor creature, eaten up by desire
just like other men. . . ."

"You wouldn't be such a saint," she replied, when he tried
to put these thoughts into words, "if you didn't despise yourself."

"No, no, Maria: not a saint at all; you don't, you can't know . . ."

She gazed at him with a fixed stare of admiration, but it never
occurred to her to worry about him, as Lucie worried, to notice
how ill he looked. The concentrated worship which was her tribute to him made of his love a despair. His desire was walled up
within this admiration. He told himself in his misery, when he was
far from her, that his love could surmount all obstacles; but as
soon as she was there before him, deferential, hanging on his
words, he could no longer deny the evidence of a wretchedness
that was beyond all cure. Nothing in the world could change the
nature of their relation. She was not his mistress but his disciple.
He was not her lover but her spiritual director. To have stretched
his arms towards her supine body, to have pressed it to his own,
would have been as mad an act as to break the mirror hanging
above her head. He knew, too, with horrible clarity, that she was
waiting for him to go. The realization that she was an object

of interest to the doctor was, for her, a matter of pride. Surrounded by the wreckage of her life, she prized very highly the intimacy of so eminent a man. But how he bored her! He, without having the slightest idea that his visits were a burden to her, felt increasingly that his secret was becoming more and more obvious, so obvious, indeed, that only her complete indifference could explain her inability to guess it. Had Maria felt even a vestige of affection for him, his love must have stared her in the face. Alas! how utterly insensitive a woman can be when confronted by a man whom, otherwise, she may esteem and even venerate, whose friendship fills her with pride, but who bores her! Of this truth the doctor had some faint realization only, but it was enough to crush him.

He got up, cutting her short in the middle of something she was saying.

"I must say, you *are* a bit abrupt in your manner of taking leave," she remarked; "but there are so many other sufferers waiting for you. . . . I mustn't be selfish and keep you all to myself."

Once again he crossed the empty dining-room and the hall. Once again he breathed in the smell of the frost-bound garden, and in the carriage on his way home, thinking of Lucie's attentive, worried face—no doubt she was already getting anxious, and would be straining her ears for the sound of his return—said to himself: The great thing is not to *cause* suffering. It's quite enough that *I* suffer: I mustn't create suffering in others.

"You're looking much worse this evening. Why *will* you put off seeing Duluc? If you won't do it for your own sake, you might at least do it for ours. You're not the only person concerned. It affects all of us."

Madame Courrèges called the Basques to witness the truth of her pronouncement. They emerged from the low-voiced conversation which they were carrying on, and obediently backed her up.

"It's quite true, Papa, we all want to have you with us as long as possible."

At the mere sound of the hated voice the doctor felt ashamed of the strength of his dislike for his son-in-law. He's really quite a decent fellow . . . it's unforgivable on my part . . . But how was he to forget the reasons he had for hating him? For long years one thing only in his marriage had seemed to be precisely as he

had always dreamed it would be—the narrow cot standing beside
the vast conjugal bed, and he and his wife each evening watching
the slumber of Madeleine, their first-born. Her breathing was
scarcely perceptible. One innocent foot had kicked off the coverlet. A small hand, soft and marvellous, hung down between the
bars. She was such a sweet-natured child that they could afford
to spoil her without fear of consequences, and such advantage
did she take of her father's infatuation that she would play for
hours in his study without making a sound. "You say she's not
very intelligent," he would say; "she's much *more* than intelligent."
Later, though he hated going out with Madame Courrèges, he
loved to be seen in the company of the young girl. "People
think you're my wife!" It was about then that he had made up
his mind that the right man for her would be Fred Robinson,
the only one, he felt, of all his pupils who really understood him.
He already called him "My son", and was just waiting until Madeleine should turn eighteen to conclude the marriage, when, at the
end of the first winter after she had "come out", she told him
she was engaged to Lieutenant Basque. The doctor's furious opposition had lasted for months. No one could see any sense in it,
neither his family nor the world at large. Why should he prefer
a penniless young student, who came from heaven knew where,
to a well-off officer of good ancestry with a brilliant future before
him?

His reasons were too personal to himself to make it possible
for him to discuss them. From the first moment that he had
started to raise objections he felt that in the eyes of this dearly
loved daughter he had become an enemy. He told himself that
his death would have been a matter to her of rejoicing, that she
looked on him now merely as an old wall that must be battered
down so that she could join the male who was calling to her.
Because he wanted to see precisely where he stood, because he
wanted to be sure to what extent this child, on whom he had
lavished all his affection, hated him, he had intensified his stub-
bornness. Even his old mother was against him and joined forces
with the young people. Plots were hatched under his own roof to
enable the lovers to meet without his knowledge. When, finally,
he had given in, his daughter had kissed him on the cheek. He
had pushed away her hair, as he used to do, so as to touch her
forehead with his lips. Everyone said: "Madeleine adores her
father. She has always been his favourite." Until the day of his

death, no doubt, he would hear her calling him "Darling Papa".
Meanwhile he must put up with this Basque fellow. But no matter
how hard he tried, he could not help betraying the fact of his
antipathy. "It really is extraordinary", said Madame Courrèges.
"Here he is with a son-in-law who shares his views about everything, and yet he doesn't like him!" It was just this that the doctor
could not forgive, this seeing all his most cherished ideas turning
to caricature in the distorting mirror of the young man's mind.
The lieutenant was one of those persons whose approval flattens
us out, and makes us doubt the very truths for which, previously,
we would have shed our blood.

"Really, Papa, I mean it. You must take care of yourself for
your children's sake. You must allow them to take sides with
you against yourself."

The doctor left the room without answering. Later, when the
Basques had sought the refuge of their bedroom (so sacred was
it held to be that Madame Courrèges was wont to say, "I never
set foot in it. Madeleine has made it perfectly plain that she
doesn't want me there. There are some things that don't have to
be said twice; I can take a hint"), they undressed in silence. The
lieutenant, on his knees, his head buried in the bed, turned round
suddenly and put a question to his wife:

"Was this house part of your parents' marriage settlement? . . .
What I mean is, did they buy it after they were married?"

Madeleine thought so, but was not certain. "It would be interesting to know, because in that case, should anything happen
to your poor father, we should have a legal right to one-half of
it."

He said no more for a few moments, and then, after a pause,
asked how old Raymond was, and seemed annoyed to learn that
he was only seventeen.

"What difference does that make? Why do you ask?"

"Oh, nothing. . . ."

He may have been thinking that a minor always complicates
an inheritance, because, getting to his feet, he said:

"Naturally, I hope that your poor father will be with us for
a long time yet. . . ."

In the darkness of the room the huge bed yawned to receive
them. They went to it, just as twice a day, at noon and at eight
o'clock, they sat down to table—when they were hungry.

About this same time Raymond woke in the night. Something that had a flat taste was trickling over his face and down his throat. His hand felt for the matches. He lit one, and, by its light, saw that blood was spurting from his left nostril and staining his nightshirt and the sheets. He got up and stood, petrified with fear, in front of the mirror, staring at his long thin body all speckled with scarlet. He wiped his fingers, which were sticky with blood, on his chest, and thought how funny his smeared face looked. He began to play a game in which he was both murderer and murdered.

❖ *IV* ❖

THE EVENING was just like any other evening at the end of January, when, in those latitudes, winter is already on the wane. Raymond, seated in his workmen's trolley, was jarred by the sight of the woman opposite. Far from being distressed at the thought that he formed but one anonymous unit of this human freight, he enjoyed pretending that he was an emigrant in the steerage while the ship drove ahead through the darkness. The trees were coral reefs, the people and the traffic on the road outside, denizens of the vasty deep. The journey, which while it lasted kept from him all sense of humiliation, was all too short. Every one of the bodies round him was as much neglected as his own, as badly dressed. When, as occasionally happened, his eyes met other eyes, he saw in the answering look no hint of mockery. All the same, his linen was cleaner than the unbuttoned shirt, say, of the man with as much hair on his chest as a wild animal. He felt at ease among these people. It never occurred to him that one spoken word would have been enough to conjure up the desert that separates classes as surely from one another as it does individuals. But such communion as might be possible was, no doubt, achieved by this contact, this shared immersion of a trolley-car driving through the suburban night. Rough though he was at school, here he made no effort to shake himself free of the head that was bumping up and down on his shoulder, the head of an exhausted urchin of his own age whose body sagged in sleep, as loosely articulated as a bunch of flowers too lightly bound.

But on this particular evening he noticed, opposite, a woman, a lady. She was dressed in black, and was wedged between two men in greasy overalls. There was no veil over her face. He was to wonder, later, how it was that beneath her gaze he had not, at first, been conscious of that shy awkwardness which the humblest servant-girl could usually produce in him. He was troubled by no feeling of shame, no embarrassment—perhaps because in this trolley-car he felt himself to be without identity, and could imagine no circumstances which might establish a relation between himself and this particular stranger. But the chief reason was that her expression was entirely devoid of anything that might have been taken for curiosity, mockery, or contempt. But, Lord, how she stared! It was as though, absorbed in that concentration, she was saying to herself: The sight of this face brings consolation for all the tedium to which one is exposed in a public vehicle. Confronted by what might well be a sullen angel, I can forget the whole miserable scene. Nothing now has any longer the power to rasp my nerves. Merely to look brings me deliverance. He is like some unknown country. The lids of his eyes are a barren stretch of sea-sand. Two troubled lakes lie drowsing between their bordering lashes. The ink on his fingers, his grimy collar and cuffs, that missing button—all these things are no more than the earth that dirties a ripe fruit ready to fall from the tree, and only waiting the touch of a careful hand to gather it. . . .

He, too, feeling safe because he had nothing to fear from this stranger, not even a word, since nothing had built a bridge between them, stared back with that tranquil intensity with which we gaze upon a distant planet. . . . (What innocence still clung about her brow. Courrèges, this evening, cast a furtive look at it. The radiance which bathed it owed nothing to the glare of the tiny bar, all to that intelligence which is so rarely found in a woman's face, though, when it is, how deeply it moves us, how convincingly persuades us that Thought, Idea, Intelligence are words of the feminine gender!)

In front of the church at Talence the young woman got up, leaving with the men she was deserting only the fragrance of her presence, and even that had vanished by the time Raymond reached the end of his journey. It was scarcely cold at all on this January evening. He was not even tempted to run. Already there was a promise in the foggy air of the secret sweetness of the coming season. The earth was stripped but not asleep.

Raymond, intent on his own thoughts, noticed nothing that evening as he sat at table with his family, though his father had
never looked so ill. Madame Courrèges made no reference to the
fact. He mustn't be "pestered", as she said to the Basques as soon
as he had gone upstairs with his mother. All the same, she had
made up her mind to talk to Duluc without his knowledge. The
room reeked of the lieutenant's cigar. Leaning against the mantelpiece, Gaston said: "There's no doubt about it, mother: something's the matter with him." There was a military quality of
command about the jerky brevity of his speech, and when Madeleine, taking an opposite line to her mother, remarked: "It may
be only some temporary upset . . ." he interrupted her.

"No, Madeleine, it's serious. Your mother is quite right."

The young woman had the temerity to argue. He raised his
voice:

"I say that your mother is right, and that should be enough
for you!"

Up on the first floor Madame Courrèges the elder knocked
gently at her son's door. She found him seated with a number
of books open before him. She asked no questions, but sat knitting, saying nothing. If her silence, her reticence, became more
than he could bear, if he felt the sudden need to speak, she was
ready to listen. But a sure instinct kept her from forcing his
confidence. For a moment he was tempted to choke back no
longer the cry which was stifling him. But to speak now would
mean going so terribly far back in thought, would mean
telling over one by one the beads of his misery up to the moment
of to-night's discomfiture. . . . How could he explain the dispro-
portion between his suffering and its cause? What had happened
would seem so trivial. It was merely that when he had called on
Maria Cross at the time they had arranged, the servant told him
that she had not come in. The news had inflicted the first stab
of pain. He had agreed to wait in the empty drawing-room where
a clock was ticking—though less quickly than his heart. A lamp
shone on the pretentious beams of the ceiling. On a low table
beside the sofa he noticed an ash-tray filled with cigarette ends.
She smokes too much . . . she's poisoning herself, he thought.
What a lot of books there were, but in none were the last pages
cut. His eye took in the torn folds of the great curtains of faded
silk. To himself he repeated: "Luxury and squalor, squalor and

luxury" . . . looked at the clock, then at his watch, and decided
that he would wait only another fifteen minutes. How quickly,
then, did time begin to fly. That it might not seem too short, he
refused to let his thoughts dwell on his laboratory, on his interrupted experiment. He got up, went over to the sofa, knelt
down, and, after first glancing nervously towards the door,
buried his face in the cushions. When he got up his left knee
made its usual cracking sound. He planted himself in front of the
mirror, touched with his finger the swollen artery at his temple,
and thought to himself that if anyone had come in and seen him,
he would have been thought mad. With the characteristic aridity
of the intellectual worker who reduces everything to the terms
of a formula, he said, "All men are mad when they are alone.
Yes, self-control is active only when it is backed by the control
imposed upon us by the presence of others." Alas! that one little
piece of reasoning had sufficed to exhaust the fifteen minutes'
grace he had allowed himself. . . .

How could he explain to his mother sitting there, eager for confidences, the misery of that moment, the degree of renunciation it
had demanded, the fact that it had had the effect of tearing him
up by the roots from the melancholy satisfaction of his daily conversation with Maria Cross? What matters is not the willingness
to confide even when we have a sympathetic listener, even when
that listener is a mother. Which of us is skilled enough to compress a whole inner world into a few words? How is it possible
to detach from the moving flow of consciousness one particular
sensation rather than another? One can tell nothing unless one
tells all. How could he expect this old lady to understand the
music that sounded so deep down in her son's heart, with its
lacerating discords? He was of another race than hers, being of
another sex. They were separated more surely than people living
on two different planets. . . . There, in his mother's presence, the
doctor recalled his misery but did not put it into words. He remembered how, tired of waiting, he had just picked up his hat,
when he heard the sound of steps in the hall. It was as though
his whole life hung suspended. The door opened, but instead of
the woman he expected he saw Victor Larousselle.

"You know, doctor, you're spoiling Maria."

Not a hint of suspicion in the voice. The doctor smiled at the
sight of the impeccable figure with its full-blooded face and light-
coloured suit, bursting with self-satisfaction and contentment.

"What a windfall for you doctors these neurasthenics are, these *malades imaginaires*. No, no, I'm only joking. Everyone knows what a selfless fellow you are. . . . Still, it's a bit of damn good luck for Maria that she should have happened on so rare a bird of the species as you. Do you know why she isn't back? Just because she's given up the car—that's her latest fancy. Between ourselves, I really think she's a bit touched—but that's only an added charm in a pretty woman, eh? What do you think, doctor? I must say I'm very glad to see you. Look here, stay to dinner: Maria will be delighted: she adores you. You won't? Well, at least wait until she gets back. You're the only person I can talk to about her."

"You're the only person I can talk to about her." . . . That sudden outburst of tormented words from this fat, resplendent man! This passion of his, said the doctor to himself, as he drove home, is the scandal of the place. All the same, it is the one noble sentiment of which the fool is capable. At fifty he has suddenly discovered that he is vulnerable; that he can suffer because of a woman whose body he has almost certainly conquered. But that is not enough for him. Somewhere, outside his world of business and horses, there will henceforward be a finer principle of suffering. . . . The romantic conception of passion is not, perhaps, as silly as we think it. Maria Cross! Maria! What misery not to have seen her! But even worse than that is the knowledge that she didn't even think of sending me word. How small a place I must occupy in her life! She can break an appointment without so much as a thought . . . I cram infinity into a few short minutes that for her mean nothing. . . .

The sound of spoken words roused him from his reverie. His mother could bear the silence no longer. She, too, had been following the drift of her secret preoccupations, and was no longer dwelling upon her son's load of mysterious sorrow. She was back once more with what so constantly obsessed her—her relation with her daughter-in-law.

"I let her trample on me; I never say anything but 'Have your own way, my dear, do just as you want.' Nobody could say I provoke her, but she's for ever throwing her money in my teeth. Money! as though you didn't make enough! I know, of course, that when you married you had nothing but your future to offer her, and that she was a Voulassier of Elbeuf—though their mills in those days weren't anything like what they have become since.

All the same, she could have made a better match, I realize that. . . . 'When one's got something, one always wants more'— as she said to me one day about Madeleine. But let's not complain. If it wasn't for the servants, everything would be all right."

"There are few worse things in life, my poor, dear mother, than having servants of different masters all living together in the same kitchen."

He touched her forehead with his lips, left the door ajar so that she could see her way, and repeated mechanically, "There are few worse things in life."

The next day Maria's whim about the car must still have been in the ascendant, because, coming home in the trolley, Raymond saw the unknown woman seated in her usual place. Once more her tranquil gaze took possession of the childish face opposite, making the circuit of the eyelids, tracing the line where the dark hair met the forehead, pausing at the glint of teeth between the lips. He remembered that he had not shaved for two days, touched his skinny jaw, and then, in an access of shyness, hid his hands beneath his cape. She lowered her eyes, and he did not at first notice that, since he wore no garters, one of his socks had slipped down, revealing a patch of bare leg. Too nervous to pull it up, he changed his position. He was not, however, conscious of mental discomfort. What he had always hated in other people was their laughter, their smiles—even when suppressed. He could catch the faintest sign of a trembling at the corners of a mouth, knew only too well what it meant when somebody started to bite his lower lip. But the expression on this woman's face as she looked at him was something he had never met before, something at once intelligent yet animal. Yes, it was the face of some marvellous, impassive *beast*, incapable of laughter. He did not know that his father often teased Maria Cross about the way she had of adjusting laughter to her face like a mask, and then letting it fall again without the slightest hint of alteration in the imperturbable melancholy of her gaze.

When she got out of the trolley by the church at Talence, and there was nothing left for him to see except the faint dent in the leather of the seat which she had occupied, he felt absolutely certain that they would meet again next day. He could give no good reason for his hope, but just had faith in the event. That evening, as soon as dinner was over, he carried two jugs of boiling water to his room, and took down his hip-bath from where it hung on the wall. Next morning he got up a good half-hour earlier than usual, because he had made up his mind that henceforth he would shave every day.

The Courrèges might have spent hours watching the slow unfolding of a chestnut-bud without even beginning to understand the mystery of the rising sap. Similarly, they were blissfully unaware of the miracle that was happening in their midst. As the first strokes of a spade may bring to light the fragments of a perfect statue, so the first glance from Maria Cross had revealed a new being in the grubby schoolboy. Beneath the warmth of her contemplative gaze a body, lovely, though ill cared for, had on a sudden stirred as might, in the rough bark of some forest tree, a spell-bound goddess. The Courrèges had no eyes for the wonder, because the members of a family too closely united lose the power to see one another properly. In the course of a few weeks Raymond had become a young man careful of his appearance, converted to the use of soap and water, secure in the knowledge that he could be pleasing to others, eager to attract. But to his mother he was still an unwashed schoolboy. A woman, without uttering a single word, merely by the intensity of her watching eyes, had transformed their child, moulding him afresh, though they were incapable of detecting so much as a trace of this strange magic.

In the trolley-car, which was no longer lit now that the days were lengthening, Raymond, at each encounter, ventured on some new gesture. He crossed his legs, displayed his clean and uncreased socks, his shoes shining like mirrors (there was a shoe-shine boy at the Croix de Saint-Genès). He had no longer any reason to conceal his cuffs. He wore gloves. There came a day when he took one of them off, and the young woman could not suppress a smile at sight of the overpink nails on which a manicurist had been working hard, though, because for years he had been in the habit of biting them, it would have been better had they not as yet been allowed to draw attention to themselves. All this was but the outward sign of an inner, an invisible, resurrection. The fog that for so long had been collecting in the boy's most secret heart was thinning by degrees under the influence of that serious and still wordless gaze to which custom had already given a certain intimacy. Maybe he wasn't a monster after all; perhaps, like other young men, he could hold the attention of a woman—

and, perhaps, more than her attention! In spite of their silence, the mere passage of time was weaving between them a web of contacts which no word or gesture could have strengthened. They felt that the moment was coming when, for the first time, they would speak, but Raymond did nothing to hasten its approach. Shy galley-slave that he was, he found it enough that he no longer felt his chains. For the moment, all the happiness he needed lay in this feeling of his that he had become someone entirely different. Was it really true that until this unknown woman had begun to look at him he had been nothing but a dirty little brat? We are, all of us, moulded and remoulded by those who have loved us, and though that love may pass, we remain none the less *their* work—a work that very likely they do not recognize, and which is never exactly what they intended. No love, no friendship can ever cross the path of our destiny without leaving some mark upon it for ever. The Raymond Courrèges who sat this evening in a small bar in the rue Duphot, the man of thirty-five, would have been someone quite different if, in 19— when he was just embarking on his philosophy course, he had not seen, sitting opposite him in a trolley on his way home from school, Maria Cross.

⚘ V ⚘

IT WAS his father who first noticed the new man in Raymond. One Sunday, towards the end of that same spring, he was seated at the family table, more deeply buried in his own thoughts even than usual, so far buried, in fact, that he scarcely heard the noise which had started as the result of a dispute between his son and his son-in-law. The subject of the argument was bull-fighting, a sport of which Raymond was a passionate devotee. He had come away that afternoon after seeing four bulls killed, so as not to miss the six-o'clock trolley. But the sacrifice had gone unrewarded, because the unknown woman was not in her seat. He might have guessed as much, it being Sunday. And now she had made him miss two bulls. Thus was he busy with his thoughts while Lieutenant Basque was holding forth.

"I can't understand how your father comes to let you watch such an exhibition of slaughter."

Raymond's reply, "That's a bit comic, I must say: an army officer who can't stand the sight of blood!" started a real row.

The doctor suddenly became aware of what was going on.

"And what, may I ask, do you mean by that?"

"That you're just yellow."

"Yellow?—say that again!"

They were both on their feet. Every member of the family was now taking sides. Madeleine Basque cried to her husband:

"Don't answer him! He's not worth it! What does it matter what *he* says!"

The doctor begged Raymond to sit down.

"Get on with your meal, and let us have no more of this!"

The lieutenant shouted that he had been called a coward. Madame Courrèges maintained that Raymond had meant nothing of the sort. Meanwhile, they had all resumed their seats. As the result of a sort of secret connivance they one and all set about throwing water on the flames. Family feeling made them view with extreme repugnance anything that might upset the smooth running of their little circle. They were a crew embarked for life in the same ship, and an instinct of self-preservation made them careful to see to it that no one should start a fire. That was why silence now descended on the room. A light rain had been falling, but the sound of drops on the steps outside suddenly stopped, and the newly released fragrance of the garden drifted in to where they all sat saying nothing. Someone remarked hastily that it was already cooler, and another voice replied that the rain hadn't amounted to anything, and would barely lay the dust. The doctor, with a feeling of bewilderment, looked at the tall young man who was his son. He had hardly thought of him at all for some time, and now scarcely recognized him. He himself had just emerged from a long nightmare. He had been caught up in it ever since the day, now long past, when Maria Cross had failed to keep her appointment, and had left him closeted with Victor Larousselle. The Sunday now drawing to a close had been one of the most horrible days of his whole life, but at last it had given him back his freedom (or so he thought!). Salvation had come to him as the result of an overwhelming fatigue, an indescribable lassitude. His sufferings had been too much for him. All he wanted now was to turn his back on the battle, to go to ground in old age. Almost two months had elapsed between the ordeal of his profitless vigil in the "luxury and squalor" of Maria Cross's drawing-room and this hideous afternoon which had witnessed his ultimate surrender. Seated at the now silent table, he once again forgot his son, letting his memory recall each separate circumstance of the hard road that he had travelled. In imagination he could see once more its every milestone.

The intolerable agony had started on the very morning after the broken appointment. Her letter of apology had struck the first note.

"It was to some extent *your* fault, my dear, good friend"—Maria had written in the missive which he had read and re-read over and over again, in the course of those two months:

"... because it was the thought of you that gave me the idea of turning my back on a hateful luxury which had begun to make me feel ashamed. Not having the car any longer, I couldn't get back by our usual time. Being without it meant that I reach the cemetery later, and that I stay there longer, because my conscience is clear. You've no idea how quiet it is there at the end of the afternoon, full of birds perched on the gravestones and singing. I felt that my baby-boy approved of what I had done, that he was satisfied with me. I feel already rewarded for my action by having been allowed to sit with all those working people in the trolley. You'll think I'm becoming too romantic, but indeed it is not so. It makes me feel happy to be there with all those poor people of whom I am so little worthy. I can't find words in which to tell you what that coming home in the trolley means to me. 'A certain person' is ready to go down on his bended knees, so anxious is he that I should take back the car which 'a certain person' gave me. But I won't. Dear, dear doctor, what does it really matter if we *don't* see one another? Your example, your teaching, is enough for me. We are so closely united that mere physical presence has no importance. As Maurice Maeterlinck has so wonderfully written—'A time will come, nor is it far off, when human souls will be aware of one another without the intervention of any physical organ.' Write to me. Your letters are all I need, dear spiritual director!

M. C.

"Ought I to go on taking the pills and the injections? I've only got three doses left. Must I buy another box?"

Even had it not so cruelly wounded him, this letter would have aroused the doctor's displeasure, so eloquent was it of self-satis-faction and the pleasure that comes of sham humility. There was no secret of the human heart to which he had not been made privy, and, as a result, his tolerance, where his fellow-men were concerned, was almost unlimited. One vice, and one vice only, irritated him beyond bearing: the effort of the morally depraved to put a mask of beauty on their depravity. For him the last infirmity of the human creature lay in the ability to be dazzled by its own filth as by a diamond. Not that this sort of lie in the soul was habitual with Maria Cross. In fact, what had first charmed the doctor had been a power in her to see herself as she was, a refusal to embellish what was naturally ugly. One of her favourite themes had always been the noble example which her mother, a poor schoolmistress in a small country town, wid-owed while still young, had given her.

"She worked like a slave to pay my school fees, and had quite made up her mind that I should go to a teachers' college. She had the great happiness, before she died, of being present at my marriage, a happiness for which she had never dared to hope. Your son-in-law was well acquainted with my husband, who was a medical officer in his regiment. He adored me, and I was very happy with him. Left, as I was, with a child, I had scarcely enough to live on when he died, but I could have managed some-how. It wasn't sheer necessity that was my undoing, but some-thing that is really much more hateful—the desire to cut a figure, the longing for the security that marriage gives. . . . What, now, keeps me from leaving 'him' is the fact that I am too cowardly to take up the struggle again, to work my fingers to the bone for an inadequate salary."

Often, since the time of those first confidences, the doctor had heard her deprecate herself, mercilessly pass sentence on her weaknesses. Why then had she suddenly fallen a victim to the de-testable vice of self-praise? But what most hurt him in her letter was something quite different. His grievance against her came from the fact that he had lied to himself, that he dared not probe a far deeper wound, the only wound of which he could not en-dure the pain. Maria showed no desire to see him, could quite

gaily envisage the possibility of their separation. Time and time
again, while he was listening to some patient endlessly elaborating
the details of his ailments, or to some floundering candidate hemming and hawing over the definition of hemoptysis, he heard an
inner voice repeating that phrase of Maeterlinck's about human
souls being aware of one another without the intervention of
any physical organ. He must have been mad ever to have believed for a single moment that a young woman could feel the
need for his bodily presence. Mad, quite mad: but then, what resource of reasoning can save us from the unendurable pain of
knowing that the adored creature whose "being there" is a necessary condition of our continued existence, even of our physical existence, can resign herself with complete indifference (perhaps,
actually, with a certain sensation of relief) to the prospect of
never seeing us again? At such times we realize that we mean
nothing to the one person who means everything to us.

During all this period the doctor made an effort to get the
better of himself. "I caught him again the other day looking at
himself in the glass," said Madame Courrèges: "that means he's
beginning to get worried." What sight better calculated to bring
tranquillity and the apathy of complete despair than that of his
own face, with all the telltale marks left upon it by fifty years of
exhausting work? There was only one thing for him to do—to
think of Maria only as he might have thought of someone dead
and buried; to await the coming of death, and hasten it by dou-
bling his daily dose of work—yes, to drive himself without mercy,
to kill himself with work, to achieve deliverance through the
opium of forced labour. But he who showed so little mercy to
those of his fellow-men who lived a lie was still the dupe of his
own thoughts: She needs me: I must give her what I would give
any sick person. He answered her letter with one of his own, in
which he said that he felt it necessary to continue his treatment.
She was perfectly right, he told her, to travel by trolley, but was
it necessary for her to go out every day? He begged her to let
him know when he should find her at home. He would so arrange matters as to be free to come at the usual hour.

A whole week passed without a further word from her. Each
morning he had only to glance at the pile of prospectuses and
newspapers to see that she had not written. He gave himself
up to a calculation of probabilities: I posted my letter on Saturday. There is only one delivery on Sundays. She can't have got it

till Monday. Assuming that she has waited two or three days
before replying, it would be very extraordinary if I heard from her
to-day. If nothing happens to-morrow it will be time enough for
me to start worrying.

And then, one evening, when he came in from a particularly
hard day, he found a letter.

"I regard my daily visit to the cemetery as a sacred duty. I
have quite decided to make my little pilgrimage no matter what
the weather. It is just when evening is falling that I seem closest
to my lost angel. I have a feeling that he knows when I shall
come, that he lies there waiting for me. I know it is ridiculous,
but the heart has its reasons, as Pascal says. I am happy and
at peace when I get into the six-o'clock trolley. Have you any
idea what a workers' trolley is like? But I feel no fear. I am not
so very far removed from 'the people', and though there may
be an apparent gulf between us, am I not linked with them in
another way? I look at all those men, and it seems to me that
they are just as lonely as I am—how shall I put it?—no less
uprooted, no less socially at sea. My house is more luxurious
than their houses; still, it is nothing but a series of ready-
furnished rooms. Nothing in it belongs to me any more than
what is theirs belongs to them. That is true even of our bodies.
Why not call one day, very late, on your way home? I know that
you don't like meeting Monsieur Larousselle. I'll tell him that I
want to see you alone. All you need do when our interview is
over is just exchange a few polite words with him. . . . You
forgot to say anything about the pills and the injections. . . ."

The doctor's first instinct had been to tear the letter up, and
scatter the fragments. Then he went down on his knees, gathered
them all together, and scrambled to his feet again with considerable difficulty. Didn't she realize that he couldn't bear even the
proximity of Larousselle? Everything about the man was hateful
to him. He belonged to just the same general type as Basque.
The lips that showed beneath the dyed moustache, the heavy
dewlaps, the stocky figure, all proclaimed a complacency that
nothing could shake. The fat thighs below the covert coat were
expressive of an infinite self-satisfaction. Because he deceived
Maria Cross with the lowest of the low, it was said in Bordeaux
that he "just kept her for show". Scarcely anybody but the doc-

tor knew that she was still the one great passion of his life, the
secret weakness which drove him almost beside himself. The man
might be a fool, but the fact remained that he had bought her,
that he alone possessed her. Now that he was a widower, he
would probably have married her had it not been for the existence
of his son, the sole heir to the Larousselle fortune, who was being
prepared for his august destiny by an army of nurses, tutors,
and priests. It was unthinkable that the boy should be exposed
to contact with such a woman, unthinkable that he should inherit
a name degraded by a *mésalliance*.

"There's no getting away from it," Basque was fond of saying
—for he was deeply attached to all that made for the greatness
of his native place—"there's no getting away from it, Larousselle's
out of the top drawer all right, he's a gentleman through and
through, and what more can one ask?"

Marie knew that the doctor loathed Larousselle. How, then,
could she dare to make an appointment for the one time of the
day when he would be sure to be brought face to face with the
object of his execration? He went so far as to persuade himself
that she had deliberately planned the meeting so as to get rid of
him. After spending several weeks writing and tearing up a number of mad, furious letters, he finally sent her one that was both
short and dry, in which he said that since she could arrange to
be at home on only one afternoon, it must be because she was
perfectly well and had no need of his ministrations. By return
of post came four pages of excuse and protestation. She would,
she said, be at home to him at whatever hour he might like to
come on the next day but one, which happened to be a Sunday.

"Monsieur Larousselle is going to a bull-fight. He knows that
I don't like that sort of thing. Come for tea. I shall wait for you
until half-past five."

Never had the doctor received from her a letter in which the
sublimities played so small a part, in which matters of health and
treatment were not even mentioned. He re-read it more than
once, and frequently touched it as it lay in his pocket. This meeting, he felt, would be different from all that had preceded it. At
last he would be able to declare his passion. But, man of science
that he was, and taught by repeated experiences that his presenti-
ments had a way of never being realized, he kept on saying to

himself: No, it's *not* a presentiment . . . my attitude of expectancy is wholly logical. I wrote her a churlish letter to which she has sent a friendly answer. Therefore, it is up to me to see to it that our first words shall give to our talk a tone of frankness and intimacy. . . .

As he drove from his laboratory to the hospital, he rehearsed the coming interview; again and again asked *her* questions, again and again framed the replies he would have her make. He was one of those imaginative persons who never read novels because for them no work of fiction can ever be nearly so enthralling as the one they invent for themselves, the one in which they play the leading role. No sooner had he signed a prescription and found himself on the way downstairs from his patient's room, than he was back, once more, like a dog digging up a buried bone, with his fond imagined reveries. Sometimes he felt ashamed of yielding to them, but they served his ordinarily timid nature as a means of bending things and people to the all-powerful will he would have liked to possess. Scrupulous though he was in daily life, he knew no inhibitions of any kind in these adventures of the mind. He would gladly have countenanced the most appalling massacres, would even, in imagination, have blotted out every member of his family, if by so doing he could have created for himself a new and different existence.

During the two days that elapsed before his meeting with Maria Cross he did not, it is true, have to suppress any fancies of this bloodcurdling kind, but that was because in the particular episode which he had invented for his pleasure it was unnecessary to wipe out anybody. All he had to do was to break with his wife, as he had seen many of his colleagues do with theirs, and for no better reason than that he found the thought of living any longer with her unutterably boring. At fifty-two a man may still hope for a few more years of happiness, even though they may be poisoned by feelings of remorse. But why should one who has never known happiness resist a chance of tasting even its make-believe? His continued presence no longer served to bring contentment to an embittered partner, and, as to his son and daughter, well, he had long ago given up all hopes of waking any feelings of affection in *them*. Ever since Madeleine had got herself engaged he had known only too well what the love of his children amounted to. . . . And Raymond? Surely when a person is so inaccessible there is no reason why one should sacrifice oneself in vain efforts to make contact?

He realized well enough that the imagined delights in which he was now indulging were altogether different from his habitual day-dreams. Even when, at a single imagined blow, he blotted out, in fancy, a whole family, he could still feel faintly ashamed, though not at all remorseful. What he was really conscious of on those occasions was a faint sense that he was making himself ridiculous. Such fantasies were purely superficial and did not involve the depths of his being. No, it had never occurred to him that he might be looked upon as a monster, or that he was in any way different from other men who, in his view, were all of them mad as soon as they were alone with their thoughts and freed from the control of others.

But, during the whole of the forty-eight hours which had got to be lived through until the appointed Sunday arrived, he knew he was clinging with all the strength that was in him to a dream that was rapidly becoming a hope. So obsessed was he by the anticipated interview with this woman that he could think of nothing but the words he had decided must pass between them. He occupied himself with putting the finishing touches to a scenario, the central situation of which could be summed up in the following piece of dialogue:

"We are both of us, Maria, at a dead end. There is only one alternative before us. Either we must die with our backs to the wall, or we must retrace our steps and—live. I know you can't love me, because you have never loved anybody. There is nothing for you to do but put yourself wholly into the hands of the one man capable of demanding nothing in exchange for his own devotion."

At this point he could hear in imagination the sort of protest she would make:

"You must be mad! What about your wife, your children?"

"They don't need me. When a man is buried alive he has the right, if he has the strength, to lift the stone that is choking him. You can have no idea of the desert that lies between me and my wife, between me and my son and daughter. The words I speak to them scarcely reach their ears. Animals, when their young have become full-grown, drive them out. More often than not the males do not even recognize them as their own. It is only human

beings who invent sentiments which survive the activities of function. Christ knew this well when He said that those who followed Him must leave father and mother for His sake, who
gloried in the knowledge that He had been sent to separate husband from wife, and children from those who had brought them
into the world."

"You can't compare yourself to God."

"Am I not God's image in your eyes? Is it not to me that you
owe your taste for a certain kind of perfection?" (But here the
doctor would break off: Better keep metaphysics out of it.)

"But what about your position, your patients, the career of
beneficent activity which you have built up? Think of the
scandal. . . ."

"If I were to die they would have to do without me. No one is
indispensable. And when I say die, I mean die, Maria. For I shall
set the equivalent of death between me and the wretched her-
mit existence, so full of grinding labour, which I have been leading. With you I shall be re-born. What money belongs to my wife
she shall keep. I can make enough for our needs. I have been
offered a professorship in Algiers, another in Santiago. . . . I will
hand over to my children what I have managed to save up to
date."

The imagined scene had reached this point when the carriage
stopped at the hospital. With his thoughts still far away, the
doctor passed through the door. His eyes were the eyes of a man
who is just emerging from some mysterious enchantment. As soon
as his rounds were finished he returned to his day-dreaming,
driven on by a secret hunger, saying to himself: I am quite mad
. . . all the same. . . . Among his colleagues there were men, he
realized, who had made dreams like that come true. To be sure,
their undisciplined lives had done something to prepare public
opinion for the scandal of their break with the proprieties, whereas
it was the opinion of the whole town that Doctor Courrèges was a
saint. But what of that? It was just because he had got this reputation without wanting it that it would be such a relief to shed the
tiresome load. Once free of it, he would no longer have to spend
his time urging Maria Cross to act nobly, or in giving her edifying
lectures. He would be a man with a woman to love. He would be
a man strong enough to take by force everything he wanted.

At last Sunday dawned. On that one day of the seven it was
the doctor's custom to attend only his most important cases. He

was careful not to go near the consulting-room which he kept in
town. It was always swarming with patients, but he used it only
three days a week. He hated the ground-floor room in a building
entirely given over to offices. He couldn't, he said, have written
or read a line in it. As, at Lourdes, the most trivial little thank-
offerings find a place, so, between those four walls, he had accumulated the various gifts showered upon him by grateful
"cases". He had begun by hating the "artistic" bronzes, the Austrian terra cottas, the composition cupids, the objects in porcelain,
and the combined barometers and calendars. But gradually he
had developed a kind of taste for the whole horrible museum, so
that he was filled with joy each time that some more than
usually hideous piece of "art" found its way into his hands. "Mind,
nothing *old*," his patients would say to one another when discussing how best they could please Doctor Courrèges.

But on the particular Sunday which was to enshrine his meeting with Maria Cross, the meeting that was to change the whole
course of his life, he had agreed to see, at three o'clock in this
same consulting-room, a business man suffering from neurasthenia
who could not manage to visit the doctor on any other day of the
week. He had resigned himself to the necessity. At least it would
provide him with an excuse for going out immediately after luncheon, and would occupy the few last moments before that fatal
meeting so eagerly awaited, so deeply dreaded. He did not use
the carriage, nor did he attempt to get into any of the over-
crowded trolleys. Groups of human beings were festooned about
their platforms, for there was to be a big football match, and it
was also the day of the first bull-fight of the season. The names of
Albagene and Fuentes stared from great red-and-yellow bills.
Though the spectacle was not due to begin until four o'clock,
the gloomy Sunday streets, with their shuttered shop-fronts, were
already filled with crowds making their way towards the arena.
The young men wore straw hats with coloured bands, or hats of
light gray felt which they fondly imagined had a Spanish look.
They laughed in a thick cloud of cheap tobacco smoke. The
cafés breathed into the street the clean smell of absinthe. He could
not remember how long it was since he had last wandered aimlessly through the hurly-burly of the city with no other preoccupation than to kill time until a certain hour should strike. To be
thus unemployed was a very strange experience for a man who
was usually so overworked. He had lost the secret of doing noth-

ing. He tried to think of the experiment he had recently begun, but could see nothing with his inner eye but Maria Cross lying on a sofa with a book.

Suddenly the sun stopped shining, and the walking folk turned apprehensive eyes to where a heavy cloud was creeping across the sky. Someone said that he had felt a drop of rain, but after a few moments the sun once more came out. No, the storm would not break until the last bull had been put out of its agony.

Perhaps, reflected the doctor, things would not turn out precisely as he had imagined they would. But one thing was certain, mathematically certain: he would not leave Maria Cross without making her privy to his secret. This time he would put his question. . . . Half-past two: another hour to kill before he was due at his consulting-room. At the bottom of his pocket he could feel the key of his laboratory. No, if he went back there it would mean leaving again almost as soon as he had arrived. The crowd swayed as though in the grip of a blustering wind. A voice cried: "There they are!" In a procession of ancient victorias, driven by coach-men who had caught something of reflected glory for all their shabbiness, sat the glittering matadors with their *quadrillas*. It surprised the doctor that he could discern no baseness in the emaciated faces of this strange priesthood clad in red and gold, in violet and silver. Once again a cloud blotted out the sun, and they turned their thin profiles to the tarnished azure of the sky. He thrust a way through the crowd. He was walking now along narrow and deserted thoroughfares. His consulting-room, when he reached it, was as cool as a cellar. Women in terra cotta and alabaster smiled down on him from columns of malachite. The ticking of a sham antique timepiece was slower than that of an imitation Delft clock which stood in the middle of the table, where a "modern-style" female, seated on a block of crystal, did duty as a paperweight. All these various figures seemed to be singing in unison the title of a revue which had stared down on him from every corner of every street—*N'y a que ça de bon!*—including the bull in bogus bronze, his muzzle resting on the back of a companion cow. With a quick glance he took in the whole motley collection. Very quietly he said: "The human race could sink no lower!" He pushed open a shutter and set a dusty sun-beam dancing. Then he began to walk up and down the room, rubbing his hands. There must be no beating about the bush, he assured himself. With my very first words I must make her realize how terribly I suffered when I made up my mind that she no longer wanted to see me. She will express surprise. I shall tell her with all the earnestness I can command that it is impossible for me any longer to live without her . . . and then, perhaps . . . perhaps . . .

He heard the sound of the bell, went to the door, and admitted his visitor. No interruption to this day-dreaming would come from *him*. All *he* asked was to be allowed to talk and talk. Neurasthenics of that sort seem to demand nothing of their doctors beyond a patient hearing. This one must have endowed the members of the profession with a kind of priestly aura, so eloquent was he in pathological confession, so anxious to display the most secret wounds of his soul. The doctor was once more, in imagination, with Maria Cross: I am a man, Maria, a poor creature of flesh and blood like other men. No one can live without happiness. I have discovered that truth rather late in life, but not too late—say it is not too late—for you to throw in your lot with mine. . . . By this time his patient had stopped talking, and the doctor, with that air of noble dignity which had earned him such universal admiration, said:

"The essential thing is that you should believe in the power of your own will. If you refuse to regard yourself as a free agent, I can do nothing for you. Even the art of healing can be wrecked on the reef of a wrong mental attitude. If you persist in thinking of yourself as the helpless victim of heredity, how can you hope that I shall be able to do anything for you? Before going further I demand from you an act of faith. You must believe that it is in your power to control all those wild beasts in yourself that are not the real you at all."

The other kept on eagerly interrupting him, and all the time he was speaking, the doctor, who had risen and gone over to the window, pretended to be looking into the empty street through the half-closed shutters. It was with something amounting to horror that he noted in himself the survival of all these lying phrases which expressed nothing but a faith long dead. Just as we perceive the light given off by a star which has been cold for centuries, so those around him heard the echo of beliefs which he had ceased to hold. He came back to the table, saw that the sham Delft clock marked four o'clock, and hastily got rid of his patient.

I've got plenty of time, he told himself as he all but ran along

the pavement. When he reached the Place de la Comédie he saw
that the trolleys were being besieged by the crowds of people
who were pouring out of the theatres. Not a cab was to be seen.
He had to take his place in a queue, and kept consulting his
watch. Accustomed as he was to driving everywhere, he had
left himself too little time. He tried to calm his nervousness. Even
putting things at their worst he would be no more than half an
hour late—no unusual thing for a doctor. Maria always waited for
him. Yes, but in her letter she had said "until half-past five", and
it was already five! "Just you stop pushing!" exclaimed a fat and
angry woman, the feather of whose hat was tickling his nose.
Inside the trolley, which was packed to suffocation, he regretted
that he was wearing an overcoat. He was sweating, and hated the
thought of arriving with a dirty face and a strong smell.

Six o'clock had not yet struck when he got out in front of the
church at Talence. At first he walked quickly, then, mad with
anxiety, broke into a trot, though his heart was troubling him. A
great storm-cloud had darkened the sky. In this ominous light the
last bull must even now be bleeding. Between the railings of the
little gardens branches of dusty lilac thrust out little begging
hands, craving for rain. Under the warm slow drops he ran towards the woman whom he could see already, in imagination,
stretched on her sofa. She would not immediately, on his entry,
raise her eyes from her open book. . . . And then, just as he
reached her front door, he saw her coming out. They both
stopped. She was out of breath. Like him she had been running.
There was a hint of annoyance in her voice as she said:

"I *did* say half-past five in my letter."

He took in her appearance with an observant eye.

"You're not in mourning."

She glanced down at her summer frock and replied:

"Doesn't mauve count as half-mourning?"

How different, already, everything was from what he had
been imagining! Oppressed by a great weight of cowardice,
he said:

"Since you had given me up, and probably have an appointment somewhere else, we had better put off our meeting to another day."

She spoke eagerly, quickly:

"With whom *should* I have an appointment? What an odd
creature you are, doctor!"

She turned back towards the house, and he followed her. She let her skirt of mauve taffeta drag in the dust. When she bent her head he could see the back of her neck. She was thinking that if she had chosen Sunday for the doctor's call it was because she felt sure that the unknown boy would not be in the six-o'clock trolley. All the same, beside herself with joy and hope when he did not come at the hour named, she had run down the road, just on the off-chance, saying to herself:

There is just one possibility in a thousand that he has taken his usual trolley because of me. Whatever happens, I must not let such a chance of happiness slip.—But, alas! she would never know now whether the stranger had been struck with gloom when he saw that she was not in her usual seat. The heavy rain was splashing on the front steps as she hurried up them, and she could hear behind her the old man's laboured breathing. How importunate are those who do not touch our hearts, those whom we have not chosen! They are wholly external to ourselves. There is nothing about them that we want to know. Should they die, their death would mean no more to us than their lives . . . yet it is they who fill our whole existence.

They went through the dining-room. She opened the drawing-room shutters and took off her hat. Then she lay down and smiled up at the doctor, who was trying desperately to pick some shreds and tatters from the words he had so carefully prepared. She said to him: "You are out of breath. I made you walk too fast."

"I am not as old as all that."

He raised his eyes, as he always did, to the mirror that hung above the sofa. What! was he even now not familiar with his own appearance? Why was it that on each occasion he felt that stab at the heart, that sense of numb misery, as though he had expected to see his own youth smiling back at him? But already he was putting the usual question: "And how are we to-day?" in that tone of paternal concern, with that half-serious inflection, which he always adopted when he spoke to Maria Cross. Never had she felt so well, and in telling the doctor so she felt a pleasure which to some extent compensated her for the earlier disappointment. No, to-day, Sunday, the unknown boy would almost certainly not have been in the trolley. But to-morrow, yes, to-morrow he would be there: of that there could be no doubt, and already her whole being was turned towards the joy to come, the hope that, every day, was doomed to disappointment and rebirth, the hope that something fresh might occur, that the moment would come when he would speak to her.

"I see no reason why you shouldn't leave off the injections." (He saw reflected in the glass his skimpy beard and barren brow, and remembered the burning words he had prepared.)

"I'm sleeping well: I don't feel bored any longer—just think of that, doctor! And yet, somehow, I have no wish to read. I couldn't finish *Voyage de Sparte*; you'd better take it away with you."

"You still see nobody?"

"You don't really think that I should suddenly let myself get mixed up with all these men's mistresses, do you? I, who till now have always avoided them like the plague? In the whole of Bordeaux there is no one of my kind, as you must realize, nobody of whom I could make a friend."

Yes, she had said so often enough, but always, in the past, on a note of self-pity, never, as now, with peace and happiness in her voice. It was borne in on the doctor that her long and tapering flame would no longer point heavenward a flickering tongue, would no longer burn in a void, that somewhere, close to the earth, it had found, unknown to him, fuel on which to feed. He could not keep himself from saying with aggressive emphasis that though it might be true that she did not frequent the women, she nevertheless occasionally saw the men. He felt himself blushing as he realized that the conversation might, even now, take the very tone he had so ardently desired. Indeed, Maria did actually say with a smile:

"Don't tell me you are jealous, doctor! I really do believe you're going to make a scene! No, no, don't be frightened, I was only joking," she added immediately. "I know you too well."

It was obvious that she had been within an ace of laughing outright, that it had never even occurred to her that the doctor might really be capable of such weakness. A worried look came into her eyes.

"I haven't said anything to hurt you, have I?"

"Yes, you have."

But she failed entirely to understand the nature of the hurt he spoke of. She said that her feeling for him was one of veneration and respect. Hadn't he lowered himself to her level? Hadn't he sometimes deigned to raise her to his? With a movement as insincere as her words had been, she seized his hand and drew it to her lips. He snatched it away. Annoyed by the action, she got up, went over to the window, and stared out at the drenched garden. He, too, had risen. Without turning her head, she spoke: "Wait till the shower's over."

He made no move, but stood there in the dark room. In all things a man of method, he employed the agonizing moments in rooting from his heart all desire and all hope. Everything was over, really over. From now on, nothing that had to do with this woman would ever more concern him. He had withdrawn from the battle. With his hand he made in the empty air the gesture of a man sweeping some obstacle aside.

Maria turned her head.

"It has stopped raining," she said.

Seeing that he still did not move, she hastened to add that it wasn't that she wanted to get rid of him, but wouldn't it be as well to take advantage of this momentary break? She offered him an umbrella which at first he accepted, only, a moment later, to refuse, because he had caught himself thinking, I shall have to bring it back: that will give me a chance to see her again.

He felt no pain, but only a sense of enjoyment in the tail-end of the storm. His thoughts ran on about himself, or rather one part of himself. He was like a man who finds consolation for the death of a friend in the certainty that he has ceased to suffer. He had played and lost. No use crying over spilled milk. Henceforward nothing would matter to him but his work. Yesterday they had phoned him from the laboratory to say that the dog had not survived the removal of its pancreas. Would Robinson manage to find another at the Lost Dogs' Home? The trolleys swept by, crammed with an exhausted, singing crowd. But he had no objection to walking along these suburban roads filled with lilac and smelling of the real country because of the rain and the effect of the failing light. He was done with suffering, with beating, like a prisoner, against the walls of his cell. The vital force which had been his since childhood, but which the pressure of so many human creatures had led him to dissipate, he now took back, thrusting it deep, deep into himself. Complete renunciation. In spite of staring posters and gleaming trolley-lines, in spite of cyclists bent double over handlebars adorned with bunches of faded lilac, the suburb merged gradually into open country, the bars gave place to inns full of mule-drivers preparing to set off

by moonlight. Onward through the darkness they would trundle,
like so many corpses stretched out in the bottom of their wagons,
their faces to the stars. On the doorsteps of houses children were
playing with drowsy cockchafers. Never again would he kick
against the pricks. For how long now had he been exhausting
all his energies in this dreary battle? He saw himself by the light
of memory sobbing (it must be almost half a century ago) beside
his mother's bed on the last day of the holidays. "Aren't you
ashamed of crying, you lazy little silly-billy?" she had exclaimed,
not knowing that what had provoked the outburst had simply
been despair at the thought of leaving her: and later . . . once
more he made that sweeping gesture with his hand, as though
he were clearing a space before him. Now, what have I got to
do to-morrow morning? he thought, inoculating himself, as with
an injection of morphine, with the thought of daily duties . . . of
the dead dog, of the need to start the whole business over again
from the beginning. Surely he had tabulated a sufficient number of observations already to enable him to confirm his hypothesis? What a lot of time he had wasted. Through what thickets
of shame he had been wandering! Convinced that the whole
human race must be hanging on his every movement as he worked
away in his laboratory, he had yet been willing to see day after
day go by spoiled and empty. Science must be served with an
undivided passion. It brooks no rival. I shall never be more
than an amateur scientist, he thought. He imagined he saw fire
burning in the branches and realized that it was the rising moon.
He caught sight of the trees that hid from view the house which
harboured that group of beings whom he had the right to call
"my people". So often already he had been false to his vow,
only later to renew it in his heart: From this very evening I will
make Lucie happy. He hastened his pace, impatient to prove
that this time he would not weaken in his resolve. He thought
of their first meeting, twenty-five years before, in a garden at
Arcachon—a meeting engineered by one of his colleagues. But
what he saw with his inward eye was not the betrothed of that
distant time, not a pale and faded photograph, but a young
woman in half-mourning, wild with joy because he was late, and
hurrying to a meeting with someone else . . . but with whom?
He felt a sharp stab of pain, stopped dead for a moment, and
then broke into a run so as to put as great a distance as possible
between himself and the man whom Maria Cross loved. The ac-

tion brought comfort, ignorant though he was that each step he
took was bringing him closer to the unknown rival. . . . And yet
it was on this very evening that, scarcely across the threshold of
the room where Raymond and his brother-in-law stood at odds,
he became conscious of a sudden burgeoning, a sudden rising of
the spring sap, in the stranger whom he had brought into the
world.

Those present had risen from the table, the children offering
their foreheads for their elders absent-mindedly to kiss. This done,
they went off to their rooms under an escort provided by their
mother, their grandmother, and their still more ancient ancestress.
Raymond moved across to the French window. The doctor was
struck by the way in which he took a cigarette from his case,
tapped it, and lighted it. There was a rosebud in his buttonhole,
an orthodox crease in his trousers. The doctor thought: How
extraordinarily like my poor father he is! Indeed, he was the living image of the surgeon who, until he was seventy, had frit-
tered away on women the fortune he had amassed by the practice of his art. He had been the first to introduce into Bordeaux
the blessings of antiseptic treatment. He had never paid the
slightest attention to his son, to whom he habitually referred as
"the young 'un", as though he had forgotten his name. One night
a woman had brought him home. His mouth was twisted and
dribbling. His watch, his note-case, and the diamond ring which
he wore on his little finger were all missing. Paul thought: From
him I have inherited a heart capable of passion, but not his gift of
pleasing—that is a legacy reserved for his grandson.

He looked at Raymond, who was staring into the garden—at
this grown man who was his son. After the day of feverish emotions just past he would have dearly loved to confide his troubles
to a friendly ear, or, rather, to indulge in a burst of maudlin self-
pity, to say to his child: "Why do we never have a good talk? Is it
that you think I would not understand you? Is the gulf that
separates father and son so unbridgeable? I have the same heart
to-day as I had when I was twenty, and you are the flesh of
my flesh. There is at least a good chance that we have in common the same set of tastes, antipathies, and temptations. . . .
Which of us shall be the first to break this silence that divides
us?" A man and a woman, no matter how completely estranged
they may be, can at least come together in the ardour of an em-

brace. Even a mother may take between her hands the head of her grown-up son and kiss his hair. But a father can do no more than the doctor did when he laid his hand on Raymond's shoulder. The boy trembled and turned his head. His father averted his eyes and asked:

"Is it still raining?"

Raymond, upright upon the threshold, stretched his hand into the darkness.

"No, it's left off."

Then, without looking round, he added: "Good-night," and the sound of his footsteps died away.

About the same time, Madame Courrèges was feeling completely "bowled over" because her husband had just suggested that she should take a turn with him in the garden. She said she would go in and fetch a wrap. He heard her go upstairs and then come down again with unwonted speed.

"Take my arm, Lucie: there's a cloud in front of the moon, and it's difficult to see one's way."

"But the path shows white."

She leaned rather heavily on him, and he noticed that her body still smelled the same as it had in the old days of their engagement, when they sat together on a bench in the long June evenings. The mingled scent of human flesh and summer dusk was, as it were, the very essence of their betrothal.

He asked whether she, too, had not noticed the great change that had taken place in their son. No, she said, he was still as surly, as sullen, as pigheaded as he had always been. The doctor pressed his point. Raymond, according to him, was now far less undisciplined. He seemed to have more control over himself. It showed, if in nothing else, at least in the care he was giving to his personal appearance.

"That reminds me. Julie was complaining only yesterday that he wants her to press his trousers twice a week."

"Julie must be made to see reason. Don't forget that she has known him ever since he was a baby."

"Julie is devoted to us, but there are limits even to devotion. It's all very well for Madeleine to talk: *her* maids do nothing at all. I know that Julie is difficult, but I do understand why she should feel annoyed at having to sweep the back stairs as well as the front."

A skinflint nightingale uttered three short notes. Husband and wife caught the hawthorn's scent of bitter almonds as they sauntered on. In a low voice, the doctor continued:

"Our little Raymond . . ."

"We shan't find it easy to replace Julie, and the sooner we realize that, the better. I know you'll say that she drives every cook we have out of the house, but more often than not she is in the right. . . . For instance, Léonie . . ."

With weary resignation he asked:

"Which of them was Léonie?"

"Surely you remember?—the fat one, not the last, but the woman who only stayed with us for three months. She objected to doing the dining-room. But it isn't part of Julie's work."

He said: "Servants to-day are very different from what they used to be."

It was as though some tide in him were suddenly ebbing, and drawing back as it receded all desire in him to confide, to confess, to abandon pretence, to let his tears flow.

"We had better go in."

"Madeleine is for ever saying that the cook is stubborn, but that's not Julie's fault. The woman wants us to raise her wages. They don't make as much out here as they do in town, though things are cheaper. If it wasn't for that they wouldn't stay at all."

"I'm going in."

"Already?"

She had a feeling that she had disappointed him, that she ought to have waited, to have let him do the talking.

"We don't often get a chance to talk," she murmured.

From somewhere beyond the wretched fabric of words that she had built up, from somewhere beyond the wall that her vulgarity had erected, with ant-like patience, day by day, Lucie Courrèges could hear the stifled cry of a man who was buried alive, the shout of an imprisoned miner, and deep within herself, too, another voice replied to his, a sudden tenderness fluttered.

She made as though to lean her head upon her husband's shoulder, but guessed how his body would stiffen, his face take on an expression of hard remoteness. Raising her eyes towards the house, she could not resist saying:

"You've left the light on in your room!"

She regretted the words as soon as she had uttered them. He hurried on so as to be free of her, ran up the steps, and sighed

with relief at finding the drawing-room empty, because it meant
that he could reach his study without meeting anybody. Safe
there at last, he sat down at his table, kneaded his careworn
face with both hands, and once more made that motion of sweeping something aside. . . . The dog's death was a nuisance. It
wasn't easy to find animals for his experiments. With all the
ridiculous nonsense that had been bothering him of late, he had
lost something of his grip on things. I've been relying too much on
Robinson, he thought. . . . He must have miscalculated the time
of that last injection. . . . The only solution would be to begin
again. From now on Robinson must confine his activities to taking the animals' temperature, to collecting and analysing their
urine. . . .

❀ *VI* ❀

A FAILURE of the current had brought the trolleys to a standstill.
They stood all along the boulevards, looking like a procession of
yellow caterpillars. It had needed this incident to establish, at
long last, some sort of direct contact between Raymond Courrèges
and Maria Cross; not but what, on the day following the Sunday
when they had not seen one another, a terrified feeling that they
might never meet again had laid hold on both, with the result
that each had separately decided to take the first step. But to
her he was a shy schoolboy whom the slightest thing might
frighten; and how, he felt, would he ever summon up enough
courage to speak to a woman? Although for the first time she was
wearing a light-coloured dress, he sensed rather than saw her
presence in the crowd, while she, for all her shortsightedness,
recognized him from afar. There had been some sort of ceremony, and he was dressed in his school uniform, with the cape
unfastened and hanging loose about his shoulders (in imitation
of the cadets of the Naval Medical School). A few intending
passengers got into the trolley and settled down to wait until it
started. Others wandered away in groups. Raymond and Maria
found themselves side by side at the far end, close to the platform. Without looking at him, so that he might not think she was
speaking for his benefit, she said in a low voice:

"After all, I haven't very far to go. . . ."

And he, with head averted and cheeks all flame:

"It might be rather nice to walk home for once."

It was then that she brought herself to look him full in the face. Never before had she been so close to him.

"We've been travelling back together for so long that we mustn't lose the habit."

They walked a short distance in silence. Furtively she looked at his hot and scarlet face, at the tender skin of youth scraped and sore from the razor. With a boyish gesture he was hugging to his body with both arms a well-worn portfolio crammed with books, and the idea that he was little more than a child became firmly fixed in her mind. This realization produced in her a sense of uneasy shyness in which scruple, shame, and pure delight played an equal part. He, for his part, felt no less paralysed with nervousness than when, in earlier days, he had decided that only the exercise of superhuman will-power could induce him to enter a shop. Recognition of the fact that he was the taller of the two came as a staggering surprise. The lilac straw hat that she was wearing hid most of her face, but he could see her bare neck and one shoulder which had slipped free of her dress. The thought that he might not be able to find a word with which to break the silence, that he might ruin this precious moment, filled him with panic.

"You don't live very far away: I was forgetting."

"Not very far. The church at Talence is only about ten minutes' ride from the boulevards."

He took from his pocket an ink-stained handkerchief, mopped his forehead, noticed the ink, and put the handkerchief away again.

"But perhaps you've got farther to go?"

"Oh no I haven't: I get out just after passing the church—"

Then, very hurriedly, he added: "I'm young Courrèges."

"The doctor's son?"

There was an eager note in his voice as he asked:

"He's pretty well known, isn't he?"

She had raised her face, the better to see him, and he noticed that the colour had gone from her cheeks. But even as the fact was borne in on him, she said:

"It really is a very small world. But you mustn't talk to him about me."

"I never talk to him about anything. Anyhow, I don't know who you are."

"That's just as well."

Once more she fixed on him a long and brooding look. The doctor's son! In that case, he must surely be just a very innocent and very pious schoolboy who would turn from her in horror as soon as he heard her name. It was impossible that he should not know about her. Young Bertrand Larousselle had been at school with him until last year. The name of Maria Cross must be a by-word among the boys. Less from curiosity than sheer nervousness he pressed her to disclose it.

"You really *must* tell me your name. After all, I've told you mine."

The level light touched to flame a basket of oranges standing in the doorway of a shop. The gardens looked as though they had been daubed all over with dust. At this point a bridge crossed that very same railway line which once had been to Raymond an object of thrilling excitement because trains ran along it to Spain. Maria Cross was thinking: If I tell him who I am, I may lose him. . . . But isn't it my duty to scare him away? This inner debate was rich for her with pain and pleasure. She was quite genuinely suffering, but at the same time felt a vague satisfaction in murmuring to herself: "What a tragedy!"

"When you know who I am . . ." (she could not help thinking of the myth of Psyche, of *Lohengrin*).

His laugh was rather too boisterous. When he spoke, it was without restraint:

"Sooner or later we should have been bound to strike up an acquaintance in the trolley. You must have realized that I made a point of always taking the one that leaves at six. . . . You didn't? Oh, I say, come off it! I often get to the terminus early enough to catch the one before that leaves at a quarter to, but I always give it a miss, just so as to see you. Yesterday I actually came away from the fight after the fourth bull in order not to miss our meeting, and then you weren't there! They tell me that Fuentes was on the top of his form in the last kill. But now we've broken the ice why should I care *what* your name is? There was a time when I didn't care about anything, but from the moment I realized you were trying to catch my eye . . ."

Had anyone else been speaking, Maria would have found such language atrociously vulgar, but in his mouth it had a delicious freshness, so that, later, each time she passed this particular spot

on her journeys to and fro, she was to be reminded vividly of the
sudden access of tenderness and joy that had been released in
her by his schoolboy chatter.

"You can't get out of telling me your name. After all, I've only
got to ask Papa. That'd be easy—the lady who always gets out
of the trolley by the church at Talence."

"I'll tell it to you, but only on condition you swear never to
talk about me to the doctor."

She no longer believed that the mention of her name would
frighten him off, though she pretended to herself that the threat
was real. Fate must decide, she thought—because, deep down,
she was quite certain that she held the winning cards. Just before they reached the church she asked him to continue his journey alone—"because of the neighbours" who would recognize her
and start gossiping.

"All right, but not until I know . . ."

Very hurriedly, and without looking at him, she said:

"Maria Cross."

"Maria Cross?"

She dug the point of her umbrella into the ground and added,
precipitately:

"Wait until you know me . . ."

He was staring, as though dazzled by the sight of her:

"Maria Cross!"

So this was the woman whose name he had heard whispered
one summer's day in the Allées de Tourny, when he and his
companions were going back to school after the break. She had
just passed them in a two-horse brougham. One of the other boys
with whom he was walking had said: "Really, women like
that! . . ." And suddenly another memory came back into his
mind. There had been a time when he was taking a course of
medicated baths, which meant that he had to leave school at four
o'clock. On this particular occasion he had overtaken young Bertrand Larousselle. He was striding alone, his long legs encased in
gaiters of undressed leather. Already, in spite of his tender years,
he was a bullying and overbearing youth. The younger boy was,
as a rule, accompanied by either a servant or a black-gloved priest
with his coat-collar turned up. Among the "juniors" Raymond
enjoyed the worst reputation of all the "uppers", and, whenever
the two of them met, the pure and pious Bertrand would devour
the notorious "dirty beast" with his eyes. It never even occurred
to him that to this same dirty beast he was himself an object

of mystery. At this time Madame Victor Larousselle was still alive, and many ridiculous rumours about her were rife in town and school. Maria Cross, it was said, had set her heart on marriage, and was demanding that her lover should turn his family out of doors. Others announced as a fact that she was waiting until Madame Larousselle should have died of cancer, so that she could then be married in church. More than once Raymond had caught sight of Bertrand behind the closed windows of a car, driving with his corpse-like mother. The women of the Courrèges and Basque families, speaking of her, used to say: "Poor thing! With what dignity she bears her martyrdom! If ever anybody had their purgatory here on earth, it's she! . . . If *my* husband behaved like that, I'd spit in his face and just clear out. *I* wouldn't stand it!"

On the day in question Bertrand Larousselle was quite alone. He heard behind him the whistling of the dirty beast and increased his pace. But Raymond kept on a level with him and never took his eyes off his short covert coat and cap of handsome English tweed. Everything that had to do with the younger boy fascinated him. Suddenly, Bertrand broke into a run, and a notebook slipped from his satchel. By the time he noticed his loss Raymond had already picked it up. Its owner turned back, his face pale with fear and anger. "Give it to me!" he cried: but Raymond read out in a low voice the title on the cover—"My Diary"— and sniggered.

"Young Larousselle's diary—that ought to be pretty juicy!"

"Give it to me!"

Raymond sprinted ahead, turned into the Parc Bordelais, and ran down one of the deserted paths. Behind him he could hear a miserable, breathless voice panting out, over and over again, "Give it to me! I'll tell them you took it!" But the dirty beast, hidden from view by a thick shrubbery, was engaged in mocking young Larousselle, who, by this time at the end of his tether, was lying full length on the grass and sobbing.

"Here's your lousy notebook, your precious diary. Take it, you little idiot!"

He pulled the boy to his feet, wiped his eyes, and brushed down the overcoat of English tweed. Whoever would have thought that the great bully could be so kind! The brat smiled his gratitude at Raymond, who, suddenly, could not resist putting into words a vulgar whim of curiosity:

"I say, have you ever seen her—this Maria Cross woman?"

Bertrand, scarlet to the tips of his ears, picked up his satchel and took to his heels. It never even occurred to Raymond to run after him.

Maria Cross . . . it was she now who was devouring *him* with her eyes. He had expected her to look taller, more mysterious. So this small woman in the lilac dress was actually Maria Cross. Noticing his confusion she mistook the cause.

"Please don't think . . ." she stammered. "You mustn't, really . . ."

She trembled in the presence of this judge whom she had viewed in the light of an angelic messenger. She saw no sign of the grubby thoughts of youth, did not know that spring is often the season of mud, and that this growing lad might be mostly composed of filth. She could not endure the contempt which she imagined him to be feeling, and, with a few hurried murmurs of farewell, was already beating her retreat. But he ran after her.

"To-morrow, same time, same trolley?"

"Are you sure that's what you want?"

She made off then, but twice turned her head. He was standing where she had left him, thinking: Maria Cross's got a crush on me!—As though he could not believe his good luck, he spoke the words aloud: "Maria Cross's got a crush on me!"

He breathed in the dusk as though it contained the very essence of the universe, as though he could savour it in every nerve and fibre of his exultant body. Maria Cross had got a crush on him! Should he tell his pals? Not one of them would believe it. He could already see before him the leafy prison where the members of one single family dwelt side by side, yet no less cut off from one another than the worlds which make up the Milky Way. How inadequate, this evening, was that cage to house the stature of his pride! He skirted it, and plunged into a plantation of pines—the only one that was not fenced in. It was called the Bois de Berge. The earth on which he flung himself was warmer than a human body. The pine-needles left deep imprints on the palms of his hands.

When he entered the dining-room his father was cutting the pages of a journal, and saying something in reply to an observation of his wife's.

"I'm *not* reading—just looking at the titles of the articles."

No one but his grandmother seemed to have heard his "good-evening."

"So it's you, you young rascal!"

As he passed her chair, she put out her hand and drew him to her:

"You smell of resin."

"I've been in the pine-woods."

She looked him up and down with an air of knowing tolerance, murmuring an abusive epithet as though it had been an endearment:

"You little horror!"

He lapped up his soup noisily, like a dog. How insignificant all these people seemed to him! He was way up above them, soaring in the sunlight. Only with his father did he feel that he had some connection, because *he* knew Maria Cross, had been in her house, had attended her professionally, had seen her in bed, had pressed his ear to her chest, her back . . . Maria Cross! . . . Maria Cross! . . . the name choked him like a clot of blood. He could taste its warm saltiness in his mouth. The hot tide of it flooded his cheeks, broke from his control.

"I saw Maria Cross this evening."

The doctor fixed him with a stare.

"How did you recognize her?"

"I was with Papillon—he knows her by sight."

"Hullo!" exclaimed Basque; "Raymond's blushing!"

One of the little girls took up the phrase:

"Oo! Uncle Raymond's blushing!"

He made an ill-tempered movement of the shoulders. His father questioned him again, this time averting his eyes:

"Was she alone?"

At his son's reply—"Quite alone"—he returned to his occupation of cutting pages. Madame Courrèges said:

"It really is extraordinary how much more interested you are in that woman than in any other. What's so very odd, after all, in his having seen that creature in the street? In days gone by, when she was a domestic servant, you wouldn't have paid the slightest attention to her."

There was an interruption from the doctor: "My dear, she never *was* a domestic servant."

"Well, even if she had been," put in Madeleine, and there was a sharp edge to her voice, "that's nothing to be ashamed of— very much to the contrary, I should have thought!"

The maid having left the room with one of the dishes, she turned angrily on her mother:

"It almost looks as though you were deliberately trying to upset the servants and hurt their feelings! Irma has an extremely sensitive nature!"

"So I've got to handle the staff with kid gloves, now, have I? Really, no one would believe the things that go on in this house!"

"You can behave exactly as you like with your own servants: all I ask is that you shouldn't drive other people's away . . . especially when you expect them to wait at table!"

"You're not exactly tactful yourself where Julie is concerned, and you've got the reputation of never being able to keep a maid when you do get one. . . . Everyone knows that the only reason *my* servants ever give notice is because they can't get on with yours!"

At this point the maid came back and the altercation was interrupted. But as soon as she had once again returned to the pantry it was resumed in a series of whispers. Raymond studied his father with amusement. Had Maria Cross been a domestic servant, would *he* have so much as noticed her existence? Suddenly, the doctor raised his head, and, without looking at any of those present, announced:

"Maria Cross is the daughter of the woman who was principal of the St. Clair school when your beloved Monsieur Labrousse was curé there, Lucie."

"What? The harpy who used to plague the life out of him? Who preferred to stay away from Mass unless she and her girls could have the front seats in the nave? Well, I can't say I'm surprised: like mother, like daughter."

"Don't you remember," said Madame Courrèges the elder, "that story of poor Monsieur Labrousse's about how, when the Marquis de Lur-Saluces was beaten in the elections by a wretched little attorney from Bazas, she came round in the evening attended by the whole school, and stood under the presbytery windows jeering at him, and how her hands were quite black with letting off fireworks in honour of the new Deputy? . . ."

"A nice lot they were, I must say."

But the doctor did not wait to hear more. Instead of going upstairs as usual to his study, he followed Raymond into the garden.

Both father and son wanted to talk. Unknown to themselves some strong influence was forming a bond between them. It was as though they were harbouring the same secret. In just such a

way do initiates and conspirators recognize and seek one another. Each found in the other the one being in the world to
whom he could unburden himself of his precious obsession. As
two butterflies, separated by miles and miles, meet at the spot
that houses the odorous female, so had they followed the con-
vergent tracks of their desires, and alighted side by side on the
invisible body of Maria Cross.

"Have you got a cigarette, Raymond? I've forgotten what tobacco tastes like. . . . Thank you. . . . What about taking a turn?"

He heard his own words with amazement. He was like a man
who, having been cured by a miracle, sees the wound that he
had thought healed suddenly open again. No longer ago than
that morning, in his laboratory, he had been conscious of the
lightness of spirit that comes to the devout penitent when he has
received absolution. Seeking in his heart some trace of his recent
passion, he had found none. How solemnly, and rather priggishly, he had lectured Robinson, who, ever since the spring, had
been somewhat neglecting his work for a lady of the chorus.

"My dear chap, the scientist who really loves his work and is
consumed with the desire to make a reputation will always regard
the hours and minutes given over to sexual passion as so much
time wasted."

Robinson had swept back his tousled hair, rubbed his spectacles on his acid-stained overalls, and ventured a protest:

"All the same, sir—love . . ."

"No, my boy, for the real scientist, except in brief moments of
purely temporary surrender, his work must always take prece-
dence of love. He will, if he sacrifices it, always be haunted by
bitter thoughts of the noble satisfaction he might have known if
only he had been faithful to his vocation."

"It certainly is true", Robinson had replied, "that most great
scientists do occasionally indulge their sexual impulses, but I
know scarcely any whom you would call men of really strong
passions."

The doctor understood now why it was that this acquiescent attitude on the part of his disciple had brought the colour to his
cheeks.

Raymond had only to say, "I saw Maria Cross", for the passion
he had thought dead to stir again. Alas! it was merely in a state
of torpor . . . a single word could bring it back to life, provide it
with the food it craved. It was already stretching its limbs,

yawning and getting to its feet. If it couldn't embrace in flesh-
and-blood reality the woman of its choice, it would find relief
in speech. No matter what the cost, he *must* talk about Maria
Cross.

Though they had been drawn together by a mutual desire to
sing Maria Cross's praises, their very first words set father and
son at odds. Raymond maintained that a woman of her emotional
scope could not but outrage the anemic susceptibilities of the
devout. What he admired in her was her boldness, her limitless
ambition, the dissolute life which he imagined her to have led.
The doctor, on the contrary, insisted that there was nothing of
the courtesan about her, that one must not believe what people
said:

"I *know* Maria Cross! I was her best friend during all that time
when her little François was so desperately ill, and I still am. . . .
She unburdened herself to me. . . ."

"My poor dear father, what you mean is that she pulled the
wool over your eyes. . . ."

The doctor controlled himself with an effort. His reply, when
it came, was given with considerable warmth:

"You're quite wrong, my boy. She confided in me with quite
extraordinary humility. If it is true to say of anybody that their
actions bear no resemblance to themselves, it is certainly true to
say it of Maria Cross. Incurable laziness has been her undoing.
Her mother, the St. Clair principal, got her to work for the entrance examination for the Sèvres Training College, but when she
married an army doctor of the 144th regiment all that went by
the board. The three years she spent as his wife were uneventful,
and if he had lived she would have led an ordinary decent and
humdrum existence. The only cause of complaint he had against
her was that temperamental indolence to which I have already
referred, because it meant that she didn't run his house well.
He used to grumble a bit, she told me, when he came home of
an evening, at finding that there was nothing for dinner but a
dish of noodles heated up over a spirit-lamp. Her favourite
occupation was to lie in a torn dressing-gown and slippers, reading all day long. People call her a courtesan, but you'd be surprised
if you knew how little mere luxury means to her. Why, only a
short time ago she decided to give up using the car which was
Larousselle's present to her, and now she travels by trolley like
anybody else. . . . What are you laughing at? I don't see anything

particularly amusing about that. . . . Stop it! it's getting on my
nerves. . . . When she found herself a widow with a child, you
may imagine how ill-equipped for work an intellectual woman
like that would feel. . . . Unfortunately, a friend of her husband's
got her the post of secretary to Larousselle. She was completely
innocent of any sort of scheming, but—well, though Larousselle
had the reputation of being a harsh employer, he never said a
word to her, though she was always late at the office and was
hardly ever up to time with her work. That alone was enough
to compromise her, and by the time she realized the situation it
was too late to do anything about it. The others treated her as
the boss's little bit, and their hostility made her position impossible. She spoke to Larousselle about it, which was just what he
had been waiting for. He had a small property close to Bordeaux
for which, just then, he had failed, or perhaps not wanted, to
find a tenant. He suggested that she should act as caretaker until
she could land another job. . . ."

"And I suppose she found the suggestion all innocent and above
board?"

"Not at all. Obviously, she realized perfectly well what he was
after: but the poor woman was saddled with an establishment
far too expensive for her straitened circumstances, and, to crown
it all, the child was struck down with enteritis, and the doctor
thought it essential that he should have country air. Finally, in
view of the fact that she was already so deeply compromised,
she just hadn't the courage to refuse such a windfall. She let
herself be over-persuaded. . . ."

"You're telling *me!* . . ."

"Don't talk like that! You know nothing whatever about her.
She stood out for a long time. But what was there for her to do?
She couldn't prevent Larousselle from bringing his friends out to
dinner. I realize that she was weak and irresponsible, that she
ought to have refused to act as his hostess; but I can assure you
that those famous Tuesday evenings were very far from being the
hideous orgies of popular imagination. The only thing at all scandalous about them was that they occurred at a time when Madame Larousselle's health had taken a turn for the worse. I can
swear that Maria had no idea that her employer's wife was in
danger. 'My conscience was clear,' she told me. 'At that time I had
not permitted Monsieur Larousselle so much as a kiss. There was
nothing between us, absolutely nothing. What harm was there in
my presiding over a tableful of fools? . . . I admit that the idea

of dazzling them did go to my head. I enjoyed playing the
blue-stocking. I knew that my employer was proud of me. He
had promised to do something for the boy.' "

"And you really swallowed all that? . . ."

What a simpleton his poor father was! But the thing that Raymond really resented was that the doctor should have diminished Maria Cross to the stature of a respectable, weak-willed
little schoolteacher—and thereby reduced his sense of conquest to
nothing.

"She didn't yield to Larousselle's suggestions until after his
wife's death, and then only from lassitude, from a sort of despairing apathy—yes, that exactly describes it. She used the phrase
herself when describing the situation—a *despairing apathy*. She
had no illusions, was perfectly clearheaded. She was not taken
in by his assumption of the role of inconsolable widower any
more than she was by his promise of eventual marriage. She knew
too much about men of his type, she told me, to be deluded. As
his mistress she was a distinct asset, but things would be very
different if she were his wife! I suppose you know that he sent
young Bertrand to the Collège de Normandie so that he wouldn't
be exposed to contact with her? In his heart of hearts he thought
her no different from the common-or-garden drabs with whom he
was for ever deceiving her. Besides, I happen to know that their
physical intimacy doesn't amount to much. I am convinced of
that; you can take my word for it. He, of course, is mad about
her, and he's not the sort of man to be content with having her
just for show purposes, as is generally supposed in Bordeaux: but
she is adamant. . . ."

"You're not going to tell me that Maria Cross is a saint?"

They could not see one another, but each could sense hostility
in the other, though they kept their voices low. They had been
brought together for a moment by the name of Maria Cross,
and it was her name that separated them now. The man walked
with head high: the youth kept his eyes fixed upon the ground
and vented his ill-humour by kicking at a pine-cone.

"You think me a fool, but of us two, it is you who are the innocent. If you think only ill of people, you'll never get to know
them. You have stumbled on precisely the right word. I know
what Maria Cross has been through, and I know that somewhere
in her there are the makings of a saint . . . yes, really, a saint. . . .
But you could never understand that."

"Don't make me laugh!"

"What do you know about her? You've merely been listening to gossip. I *do* know about her."

"I know what I know."

"And how much may that be?"

The doctor stopped dead in the middle of the path where the chestnut-trees threw a deep shade. He gripped Raymond by the arm.

"Oh, let me alone! It's all one to me whether Maria Cross does, or does not, go to bed with Larousselle—but he's not the only pebble on her beach!"

"Liar!"

Raymond was brought up with a shock. "Oh, look here . . ." he muttered. A suspicion had dawned in his mind, only to die out again almost at once, or rather to withdraw from his immediate consciousness. Exasperating his father might be, but he found it no more possible than did Maria to connect the idea of love with the rather neutral image of him which had been his since childhood. He had always seemed to him to be a man without passions and without sin, a man impervious to evil, incorruptible, living in a world far above the rather earthy concerns of other men. He heard the sound of his rather heavy breathing in the darkness.

The doctor made a violent effort to control his feelings. In a tone that was half mocking and almost cheerful, he repeated:

"Yes, liar and humbug. All you want to do is to destroy my illusions. . . ."

And, since Raymond remained obstinately silent, he added: "Go on, out with it. . . ."

"I don't know anything. . . ."

"You said just now—'I know what I know.' "

The boy replied that he had spoken without thinking. His manner was that of someone who has made up his mind to say nothing. The doctor did not press him. This son of his, so close that he could feel the warmth of his body and catch the smell he exuded as of some young and untamed animal, would never understand him.

"I shall stay out here a bit. Won't you sit down a moment, Raymond? There's a breeze getting up at last."

But his son said that he would rather go to bed. For a moment or two longer the doctor heard the sound he made as he kicked at the pine-cones, then he was alone under the dense and drooping

leaves—alive to all the passionate melancholy flung heavenward
by the sleeping fields. With an immense effort he rose from his
seat. The light was burning in his study. . . . I suppose Lucie
thinks I'm still working. What a lot of time I've wasted! I'm fifty—
no, fifty-three. What tittle-tattle has that Papillon boy been repeating? . . . He let his hands wander over the bark of a chest-
nut-tree where he remembered that Madeleine and Raymond
had once carved their initials, and suddenly, flinging his arms
about the trunk, closed his eyes and laid his cheek against the
smooth surface of the wood. Then he stood back, dusted the
sleeves of his jacket, straightened his tie, and walked towards the
house.

Sauntering between the vines, Raymond was still amusing himself by kicking a pine-cone. With his hands stuck deep in his
trouser pockets, he muttered to himself: "What a simple-minded
old fool! there can't be many of his sort left!" Well, he at least
would be equal to his opportunity; no one would lead *him* by the
nose. He had no intention of prolonging his happiness through
the dragging hours of this stifling night. The stars meant nothing
to him, nor the scent of the pale acacia blooms. The assault of the
summer darkness was powerless against this well-armed young
male who was so sure of his strength in the splendid present, so
sure of his young body, so utterly indifferent to all that it could
not subdue and penetrate.

❂ *VII* ❂

WORK, the one and only opium. Each morning the doctor woke,
cured of his obsession, as though what had been gnawing at his
heart had been cut out by the surgeon's knife. He left the house
unaccompanied (in fine weather Raymond did not use the brougham). But his mind raced ahead of him. Already, in imagination,
he was at work on his experiments. His passion diminished to a
dull throb which made itself felt as a threat rather than an actuality. Whether it would become more than that, would wake
again into active life, depended upon him, and upon him alone.
Let him but touch the sore spot, and the sudden pain would make
him cry out. . . . But yesterday his pet hypothesis had been

brought tumbling to the ground by one single fact—or so Robinson assured him. What a triumph for X, who had accused him before the Biological Society of using faulty methods.

One of women's curses is that they can never free themselves of the enemy who preys upon their vitals. And so it happened that while the doctor, intent on his microscope, was blissfully unaware of his own wretchedness and of the world outside the walls of his laboratory, a prisoner pent within the confines of his observations, Maria Cross, lying on a sofa behind closed shutters, could think of nothing but the moment when she would see Raymond again, of that brief flame which alone brought warmth and brightness into the dreary sequence of her days. But how disappointing the moment was when it came! Almost at once they had had to give up their plan of travelling together as far as Talence church. Maria Cross went on ahead and met him in the Park, not far from the school-buildings. He was less forthcoming now than he had been on the occasion of their first exchanges, and his attitude of shy mistrust did much to convince her that he really was only a callow boy, though an occasional snigger, a sudden furtive glance, should have put her on her guard. But she clung to her darling theory of his angelic purity. With infinite precautions, as though she were dealing with an untamed and still unsullied bird, she, as it were, crept closer and closer, walking on tiptoe and holding her breath. Everything about him conspired to strengthen the outlines of that false image of him which she had constructed: the cheeks so prone to blush, the schoolboy slang, the still visible traces of childhood that hung like morning mist about the strong young body. She was terrified by what she thought she had discovered in Raymond, though it had no existence in fact. The candour of his glance set her trembling, and she felt guilty of having brought into that frank gaze a hint of trouble and unease. Nothing occurred to warn her that when they were together he wanted only to run away, the better to gloat on the thought of her and to decide what line he had better take. Should he hire a room? Papillon knew an address, but it was a bit too squalid for a woman of her type. Papillon had told him that one could get rooms by the day at the Terminus. He'd have to find out about that. He had already walked up and down outside the hotel without being able to summon up courage enough to make inquiries at the desk. There might be other difficulties, too, of a physical nature. Over these he brooded until he had made mountains out of molehills.

Maria Cross was playing with the idea of asking him to her house, but of this plan she had, so far, said nothing. She was resolved not to smirch, even in thought, this child of nature, this untamed bird. In the stiffness of her drawing-room, in the drowsy heat of the garden, their love would burgeon into words, and the storm within her breast would find relief in rain. Beyond this point she would not let imagination go. The extreme of her permitted indulgence was to fancy the feel of his head pressed to her body. He would be to her as a fawn domesticated by kindness . . . she would feel the warm, soft muzzle in her hand. . . . She seemed to see before her a long, long vista of caresses. They must be fond yet chaste. She would not let herself, even in imagination, dwell upon a fiercer pilgrimage of love, upon that ultimate bliss of tangled forest undergrowth into which they might plunge and be lost to all the world. . . . No, no—passion must never be allowed to sweep them to such extremes! Not for all the world would she destroy the childish innocence which filled her with such fear, such adoration. How to convey, without startling him into flight, that this very week he might take advantage of Monsieur Larousselle's absence on business in Belgium and venture into the stuffy and encumbered intimacies of her drawing-room? Surely, if she put such a thought into words, he would at once suspect some evil intention? What she did not know was that he took his pleasure of her with far greater satisfaction to himself when they were not together, that she was with him in fancy wherever he went, or that he possessed her, turned from her, and possessed her, again and again, like a famished puppy.

At dinner the doctor kept his eyes upon him. He watched him greedily lapping up his soup, and saw, not his son, but a man who had said, speaking of Maria Cross, "I know what I know. . . ." What could that Papillon possibly have told him? It was no use deceiving himself. Quite obviously, someone of whom he knew nothing was monopolizing Maria's thoughts. I go on expecting her to write, he thought, when it should be perfectly clear that she doesn't want to see me ever again. And if that is true, it means, further, that she has given herself to another . . . but to whom? Impossible to sound the boy any more than I have done. If I insist on his telling me what he knows I shall merely be betraying myself. . . . At that point in his ruminations his son got up and left the room, without deigning to answer his mother, who called after him: "Where are you off to?"

"He goes into Bordeaux almost every evening now," she said. "I know that he gets the key of the gate from the gardener, and comes in at 2 a.m. by the scullery-window. You ought to hear what he says when I question him. It's for *you* to do something about it, but you're so weak!"

The doctor could only stammer: "The wisest thing is to keep our eyes shut."

He heard Basque's voice: "If he was *my* son I'd bring him to heel soon enough. . . ."

The doctor got up from the table in his turn and went into the garden. He would have liked to cry aloud: "My torment is the only thing that has any reality for me!" No one realizes that it is a father's passions, more often than not, that alienate him from his son. He returned to the house, sat down at his worktable, opened a drawer, took out a packet of letters, and settled down to re-read what Maria had written to him six months earlier:

> "Only the desire to become a better woman reconciles me to the necessity of living. . . . I care little what the world should know of my salvation, or that others should continue to point at me the finger of scorn. . . . Humbly I accept their censure."

He no longer remembered that, when he had read those words for the first time, such extravagance of virtue had filled him with despair, that the obligation to walk with her in so rarefied an air had been his martyrdom, that it was maddening to think that he was expected to show the way of salvation to the one woman with whom he would so gladly have gone to perdition. He thought how, reading this letter, Raymond would laugh; grew indignant at the fancy, and voiced a protest in a half whisper as though someone were walking at his side. "Bogus, you say? . . . bogus? . . . The trouble is that whenever she gets a pen in her hand she becomes too 'literary'. . . . But was that humility of tenderness when she sat by her dying child bogus, that acquiescence of hers in suffering, as though the mysterious heritage of faith had come down to her through all her mother's tedious rehash of Kantian principles? In the presence of that small bed beneath its load of lilies" (how isolated and alone the body of the dead child had looked, how silently it had seemed to be accusing her!) "she gave expression to her sense of guilt, beating her breast and groaning aloud that all was for the best, finding consolation in the thought that he had been too young to feel ashamed of her. . . ." But here

the man of science intervened: The truth is rather more compli-
cated. She *was* sincere in her grief, but, all the same, she got a
certain amount of satisfaction out of her heroics—they gave her
the excuse to strike an attitude. . . . Maria Cross had always had
an appetite for situations of high romance. Hadn't she even gone
so far as to play with the idea of having an interview with Madame Larousselle on her death-bed? It was only with the utmost
difficulty that he had made her realize that scenes of that kind
never "come off" except on the stage. She had given up the plan,
but only on condition that he should undertake to plead her cause
with the wife. Luckily, he had been able to assure her that she
had been forgiven.

He went to the window, and, leaning out in the half darkness,
occupied his mind with analysing the various night sounds—a continuous scraping of crickets and grasshoppers, the croaking of two
frogs in a pond, the intermittent notes of a bird that probably
wasn't a nightingale, the clanging of the last trolley. "I know what
I know", Raymond had said. Who could it be that had caught
Maria's fancy? The doctor pronounced one or two names, but at
once rejected them. She had a horror of those particular men.
But of whom *hadn't* she a horror? He thought: Remember what
Larousselle told you in confidence that time he came to have his
blood-pressure tested—"Quite between ourselves, she doesn't
really enjoy—you know what I mean. She puts up with it from
me because, well, with me it's rather different. . . . It really was
screamingly funny the first time I asked all these chaps to the
house. They fluttered round her like moths. When a man introduces one to his mistress, one's first thought, isn't it? is whether
one can cut him out. . . . Go ahead, my fine fellows, said I to
myself . . . and, of course, nothing happened. They were all quite
quietly kept in their place. No one knows less about love than
Maria, and takes so little pleasure in it—and I'm speaking about
what I know. She's as innocent as you make 'em, doctor, a great
deal more innocent than most of the fine respectable ladies who
turn up their noses at her." He had said, too: "It is because Maria
is so completely unlike other women that I'm always terrified
that, some time when I'm not there, she may make some absurd
decision. She spends her whole day in a sort of dream, and only
leaves the house to go to the cemetery. Do you think it's possible
that she has been influenced by something she's read?"
It may be something she's read, thought the doctor: but, no;

if it were I should have heard about it: books are my line of
country. A book sometimes turns a *man's* life upside down, or so
one's told, but does the same hold true of women? It's only life
that really and truly affects them deeply, things of flesh and blood.
A book?—he shook his head. The word book brought "buck" to
his mind, and he had a sudden vision of some wild young animal
rearing at Maria's approach.

Some cats in the grass set up a prolonged miaowing. A footstep
sounded on the gravel: there was the noise as of a window being
opened. It must be Raymond coming back. A moment later the
doctor heard someone in the corridor. There was a knock at his
door. It was Madeleine.

"Not in bed yet, Papa? I'm worried about Catherine. She suddenly started a nasty hacking cough. I was afraid it might be
croup."

"Croup doesn't come on suddenly like that. I'll be along in a
moment."

Some time later, as he was coming out of his daughter's room,
he felt a pain in his left side, and stood leaning against the wall
in the darkness, clutching at his heart. He did not call for help. His
brain was perfectly clear, and he could catch from behind the
door the sounds of a conversation that had just started between
husband and wife.

"I know all about his being a good scientist, but science has
made him skeptical. He no longer believes in medicines. But
how can illness he cured without them?"

"He assured us it was nothing, not even a false croup."

"Don't kid yourself: if it had been one of his own patients
he'd have prescribed something, but because it's one of the family he's not going to spend an unnecessary penny. There are
times when it's an awful nuisance not being able to call in an
outside man."

"But it's very convenient having him always on the spot, especially at night. When the poor old thing's no longer there, I
shall never know what it is to sleep in peace, worrying about the
children."

"You ought to have married a doctor, that's what *you* ought to
have done!"

There was a sound of a laugh being quickly silenced by a kiss.
The doctor felt the hand that was squeezing his heart loosen its

grip. Very quietly he stole away. He turned in, found that he could not lie at full length without pain, and spent the night sitting upright on his bed. The whole world was asleep. The only sound was the fluttering of the leaves. . . . Has Maria ever known what it is to love? I know she's had crazes for people—for instance, there was that little Gaby Dubois girl, she tried to make her break with young Dupont-Gunther, but that was a romantic passion. She must have had some apostolic ancestor from whom she inherits that taste of hers for saving souls. Who was it, by the way, who told me a lot of ugly things about her, in connection with this same Gaby? . . . Can she be "one of them"? I remember other crazes of the same kind. . . . There may be a touch of it in her case. I've always noticed that an excess of romanticism . . . Dawn already!

He lowered his pillow, and with many precautions lay down in such a way that his wretched carcass suffered no hurt. In a few moments he had lost consciousness.

❀ VIII ❀

"BUT WHAT am I going to say to the gardener?"

In one of the deserted paths of the Parc Bordelais Maria Cross was trying to persuade Raymond to pay her a visit at home. In her own house there would be no risk of their meeting people. She urged him to agree, and felt ashamed of doing so, felt that, in spite of herself, she was corrupting him. How was it possible not to see in the unreasoning terror of a boy who had once walked up and down in front of a shop because he didn't dare go in, the indisputable evidence of frightened innocence? With that thought in her mind she hastened to say:

"But, Raymond, you mustn't think I want . . . you mustn't start imagining. . . ."

"It'll be so awkward if I run into the gardener."

"But there *isn't* a gardener: I've told you so already. I'm living in an empty house which Monsieur Larousselle had not succeeded in renting. He has installed me there as caretaker."

Raymond burst into a guffaw of laughter:

"A lady-gardener, eh?

The young woman looked down so that he should not see her face, and stammered out:

"I *know* appearances are against me. After all, people can't be expected to know that I accepted the situation in perfect good faith. . . . François had to have country air. . . ."

Raymond was familiar with this particular refrain. Talk away, he said to himself, and broke in with:

"So I needn't worry about the gardener, but what about the servants?"

She reassured him on that point too. On Sundays she always let Justine, her only maid, go out. She was a married woman whose husband, a chauffeur, slept in the house so as to ensure there being a man about the place, which was none too well protected. The suburban road was not very safe. But on Sunday afternoons Justine and he always went out together. Raymond would merely have to enter by the front door and go through the dining-room on the left. He would find the drawing-room at the far end.

He dug his heel into the gravel with a thoughtful air. The creaking of a swing could be heard coming from behind a privet hedge. An old woman was hawking stale cakes and bars of chocolate done up in yellow paper. Remarking that he had had no lunch, he bought a crescent and a chocolate praline. As she watched him munching his meagre meal, Maria suddenly saw with perfect clarity the inexorable nature of her destiny. The desire that had come to birth in her heart had been pure and limpid, yet her every action had the appearance of a monstrous depravity. When, in the trolley, her eyes had first found rest and refreshment in the young face opposite, there had been no trace of evil intention in her mind. Why should she have fought against a temptation that was so little suspect? A thirsty traveller has no reason to beware of the stream he happens on. I *do* want him to come to my house, she thought, but only because in the streets, on the bench of a public garden, I shall never succeed in probing his secret self. . . . But that doesn't alter the fact that, so far as appearances go, here is a young kept woman of twenty-seven luring a young boy into her web—the son of the only man who has ever believed in me and has never cast a stone. . . . A little later, after they had parted, and just before reaching the Croix de Saint-Genès, her thoughts returned to the subject: I want him to come, but with no evil design, not the least in the world. The very idea of such a thing makes me feel sick. But he doesn't trust me, and why should he? Everything I do is double-faced: to me it looks innocent enough, but to the world, hateful, abominable. Perhaps the world sees more truly than I do. . . . She spoke first one name, then another. If it were true that she was held in contempt for actions in which she had become unintentionally involved, she could remember others that she had done in secret, others of which no one knew but herself.

She pushed open the gate which, next Sunday, Raymond would unlatch for the first time, and walked up the drive which was overgrown with grass (there was no gardener). So heavily did the sky seem to sag that it was hard to believe the over-arching cloud would not burst with its own weight—it was as though the heavens had caught discouragement from a thirsty world. The leaves hung blighted from the trees. The maid had not closed the shutters, and great bluebottles were bumping against the bottom of the window-frames. She had only just energy enough to throw her hat onto the piano. Her shoes left dirty marks on the sofa. There was only one thing possible to do—light a cigarette. But she was aware, too, of something no less habitual, the physical apathy that accompanied the activity of her imagination, no matter how wrought-up that might be. What an endless number of afternoons she had wasted lying just here, feeling slightly sick as the result of over-smoking! How many plans of escape, of self-betterment, she had elaborated, only to see them fall in ruins! To bring them to fruition she would have had, first, to stop lying there supine, to do something positive, to see people. . . . But even if I abandon all attempts to improve the external conditions of my life, I can at least refuse to do anything of which my conscience would disapprove, which might cause it to feel uneasy. Take, for instance, this case of young Courrèges. . . . She had quite decided that if she were about to lure him into her house it was only because she wanted to indulge that sweet and harmless sentiment which had come to her, originally, in the six-o'clock trolley; that sense of comfort in another's presence, that melancholy pleasure of quite quietly letting her eyes take their fill—though here, in this room, she would taste it more intimately than had been possible in the trolley, and at greater leisure. But was that really all? When the presence of another person thrills us emotionally, our imagination leaps ahead, though we may not always realize it, opening up vistas the very vagueness of which has something about it that is not wholly innocent. She thought: Very soon I should have grown tired merely of looking at him had it not been that I felt convinced that he would respond to my handling, that, sooner or later, we should speak to one another. . . . This room, so far as I can foresee, will witness nothing but motherly caresses and unimpassioned kisses, will hear nothing but spoken confidences. . . . Oh, come now, be honest with yourself! Admit that you *are* aware of the existence, beyond such innocuous happiness, of a whole region of the emotions, forbidden, it is true, yet open to exploration. There will be no barrier to break down. The field of action will lie open before you. You have only to work your way cautiously forward, to lose yourself in the misty distance as though by accident. . . . And afterwards? Who is there to forbid you the enjoyment of this delight. . . . Don't you know that you could make the boy happy? . . . Ah, that's where you begin to be the dupe of your own appetites. . . . He is the son of Dr. Courrèges, of the saintly Dr. Courrèges. . . . *He* wouldn't admit that the case was even open to argument. You once told him jokingly that the moral law within him was as bright and shining as the starry sky above his head. . . .

She could hear the raindrops on the leaves, the tentative rumble of the storm. She closed her eyes, tried to fix her thoughts, concentrated her mind on the beloved face of the young boy whose innocence was wholly unsmirched (or that was what she wanted to believe), the boy who, at that very moment, was hurrying along in an attempt to outstrip the coming storm, and thinking: Papillon says it's always best to take the bull by the horns. With women of that kind, he says, brutality's the only thing that counts, the only thing they really like. . . . With his thoughts in turmoil he looked up at the growling heavens. Suddenly he began to run, his cape flung over his head, took a short cut, and jumped over a patch of shrubbery as nimbly as a buck. The storm was moving away, but it was still there. The very silence betrayed its presence. Maria had a sudden inspiration which she felt certain could not be misunderstood. She got up, sat down at her desk, and wrote:

"Don't come Sunday—or any other day. It is for your sake, and for your sake only, that I agree to this sacrifice. . . ."

She should have left it at that, and just signed her name. But some devilish counsellor persuaded her to add a whole page more:

". . . You will have been the one and only happiness of a
tormented and hopeless life. As we travelled home together all
through this last winter, the sight of you brought me peace,
though you did not know it. But the face that was your gift to
me was but the outward and visible sign of a soul which I
longed to possess. I wanted there to be nothing about you that
I did not know. I wanted to provide the answer to your uncer-
tainties, to smooth the path before your feet, to become for you
someone who would be more than a mother, better than a
friend. I live in my dream of that. But it is not in my power to
be other than I am. In spite of yourself, in spite of me, you
would breathe the corruption with which the world has choked
me."

On and on she wrote. The rain had settled in for good, and the
only sound to be heard was that of falling water. The windows
of all the rooms were shut. Hailstones rattled in the hearth. Maria
Cross took up a book, but it was too dark to read, and, because
of the storm, the electricity was not working. She sat down at the
piano, and leaned forward as she played. It was as though her
head were drawn by some attraction to her hands.

The next day, which was Friday, she felt vaguely pleased that
the storm had broken the spell of heat, and spent the whole day
in a dressing-gown, reading, making music, idling. She tried to
recall every word of her letter, to imagine the effect it would have
on young Courrèges. On Saturday, after a close and heavy morning, the rain began again. She realized then the reason for her
pleasure. The bad weather would prevent her from going out on
Sunday, as she had meant to do, so that should the boy after all
keep their appointment in spite of her letter, she would be there
to receive him. Stepping back from the window through which
she had been watching the rain splashing on the garden path,
she said aloud in a firm, strong voice as though she were taking
a solemn oath: "Whatever the weather, I shall go out."
But where would she go? If François were alive she would
take him to the circus. It was her habit, sometimes, to go to a
concert, where she would sit alone in a private box, or—and this
she preferred—would take a seat in a public one. But on these
occasions the audience always quickly recognized her. She could
guess, from the movement of their lips, that people were talking about her. Levelled opera-glasses delivered her up, at close

range and utterly defenceless, to a world of enemies. A voice would say: "When all's said, women like that *do* know how to dress—but then, of course, with all that money it's not difficult; besides, they've nothing to think about *except* their bodies." Occasionally one of Monsieur Larousselle's friends would leave the Club Box and pay her a visit. Half turned towards the audience he would laugh loudly, proud of being seen in conversation with Maria Cross.

Except for the Saint-Cecelia concert she had, even during François' lifetime, given up going anywhere. This change in her habits had occurred after several women had insulted her at a music-hall. The mistresses of all these various men hated her because she had never shown herself willing to be on terms of familiarity with them. The only one of them who, for a short while, had found favour in her eyes was Gaby Dubois. The girl, she had decided on the strength of a brief exchange of talk one evening at the Lion Rouge, where Larousselle had dragged her, was a "sweet creature". The champagne had had a good deal to do with Gaby's spiritual effervescence on that occasion. For a whole fortnight the two had met daily. With dogged determination Maria Cross had vainly tried to break the links that bound her new friend to her various other acquaintances. Then they had begun to see less and less of one another, and a little while later, during a matinée at the Apollo into which Maria had drifted from sheer boredom, alone as usual, and, as usual, drawing all eyes, she had heard, coming from a row of stalls just beneath the box where she was sitting, Gaby's shrill laughter. Other laughs had mingled with it, and odds and ends of insulting comment had reached her ears, though the voices had been kept low. "That tart who gives herself the airs of an Empress . . . who's always putting on a virtue act. . . ." It had seemed to Maria that all the faces in the theatre were turned towards her—and the faces were the faces of wild beasts. Then the lights had gone down, all eyes had been riveted on a naked dancer, and she had slipped away.

After that she would never leave the house without her little boy François. And now, even though a year had passed since he had vanished, it was still he alone who could tempt her out, or rather, that gravestone, no longer than a child's body, though to reach it she had to walk along the special avenue in the cemetery marked "Adults". But Fate had ordained that on the way leading to the dead boy another, living boy should cross her path.

On Sunday morning there was a great wind—not one of those
winds that serves to dandle the piled clouds, but a roarer from the
south with the smell of the sea, and driving before it a sweep of
muffled sky. The note of a solitary tit only emphasized the silence of
a million other birds. There could be no question of going out in
such weather, which was a nuisance: but by this time young
Courrèges would have had her letter. Aware of the extent of his shyness, she felt sure that he would obey her injunction. Even had she
not written he would probably never have dared to cross her threshold. She smiled to herself as she conjured up a vision of him digging
his heel into the gravel of the drive, and saying to himself, with
that mulish expression which she knew so well: "What about the
gardener?" While she ate her solitary luncheon she could hear the
storm raging round the house. The flying horses of the wind gal-
loped madly on, and now, their task accomplished, were whinnying
and snorting among the trees. No doubt from the cloven turmoil of
the deep Atlantic they had brought flights of gulls seeking the sanctuary of the river, and kittiwakes that hold the air and do not settle.
A livid colouring of seaweed seemed to tint the clouds of this
suburban sky, a salty scud to splash the inland foliage. Leaning
from her window that looked on the garden, Maria had the taste
of it upon her lips. No, he would not come: how could he in such
weather, even if she had not sent her letter? Had she not been
sure of that she would have known an agony of apprehension
that he might suddenly appear. Far, far better to feel that she
was safe, to know for certain that he would not come. And yet,
if expectation was wholly absent, why should she open the sideboard cupboard just to make sure that there was some port
left?

At last the rain began to fall in a solid curtain shot with vagrant
sunlight. She opened a book, but her eyes would not take in the
sense of what she read. Patiently she went back to the top of the
page, but in vain. Then, seated at the piano, she began to play,
but not so loudly that she could not hear the sound made by the
opening of the front door. She was overcome by dizziness, and
just had time to say to herself: It's the wind, it must be the wind,
and, a moment later, though the shuffle of hesitating footsteps
reached her from the dining-room—It's just the wind. She had not
strength enough to get up from her chair. He was already in the
room, awkward, embarrassed, not knowing what to do with his
streaming hat. He did not dare to take a step forward, nor did she
call to him, so powerless was she in the tumult of a passion that

had burst its banks and was sweeping all before it, vengeful and
frantic. In a moment it engulfed her, leaving no inch of body or
soul unfilled, topping the peaks, drowning the roots, of her
being. Nevertheless, when she did at last manage to speak, her
expression was stern, her words no more than ordinary.

"Didn't you get my letter?"

He stood there dumbfounded ("She wants to lead you up the
garden," Papillon had said. "Don't let her put you where she
wants you. Just stroll in on her with your hands in your pockets.")
But, faced by what he took to be her anger, he hung his head like
a schoolboy in disgrace. And she, tense and trembling with emotion, as though what she had caught in this stuffy trap of her
over-furnished interior were a frightened fawn, could venture on
no movement. He had come, though she had done everything in
her power to keep him away. Therefore no remorse could poison
this, her happiness. She could surrender to it wholly. To that destiny which had precipitated the boy into this room as food for
her hunger, she swore that she would be worthy of the gift. Of
what had she been afraid? There was nothing in her mind at
this moment but love at its noblest. If that truth needed to be
proved, proof lay in the tears which she checked, thinking of
François. In a very few years he would have grown to be just
such a boy as this. . . . She could not know that Raymond had
interpreted the face she made in her effort not to cry as a sign
of ill-humour, perhaps of anger.

She said: "After all, why not? You did well to come. Put your
hat down on one of the chairs. It doesn't matter if it's damp; it's
not the first wet hat their Genoa velvet has seen. . . . I'm sure
you'd like a glass of port now, wouldn't you? Yes, of course you
would."

While he was drinking she went on:

"Why did I write that letter? Honestly, I don't know. . . .
Women do funny things . . . and then, of course, I knew you'd
come in any case."

Raymond wiped his lips with the back of his hand.

"All the same, I nearly didn't come. I said to myself—she'll
probably be out, and I shall look an awful fool."

"I hardly ever go out—since I've been in mourning. I've never
talked to you about my little François, have I?"

François had come tiptoeing as though he were in very truth
alive. Just so might his mother have kept him by her to break a
dangerous tête-à-tête. But Raymond saw no more in her words

than a trick designed to make him keep his distance, though
Maria's only thought was to put him at his ease. Far from fearing
him, she thought that she was an object of fear. Besides, this
intrusion of the dead child was not of her contriving. The little
boy had forced his presence on them. He had come as children
do, when, hearing their mother's voice in the drawing-room, they
enter without knocking. The mere fact that he is there, she
thought, proves, you poor dear, the purity of your intentions.
What's worrying you? François is standing by your chair, not blushing but smiling.

"It's rather more than a year since he died, isn't it? I very
well remember the day of the funeral. Mother made a
scene . . ."

He broke off. He would have unsaid the words if he could
have done so.

"A scene, why? Ah, yes, I understand. Even on that day there
was no pity in people's hearts."

She rose, fetched an album, and laid it on Raymond's knees.

"I should like to show you his photographs. No one but your
father has seen them. That's him at a month old, in my husband's
arms. When they're as young as that they look like nothing on
earth—except to their mothers. Look at this one, with a ball in
his arms—laughing. That was taken when he was two. *This* was
when we were at Salies. He was already ailing. I had to sell out
some of my tiny capital to pay for our trip. But the doctor there
was kindness and generosity itself. He was called Casamajor . . .
that's him, holding the donkey's bridle. . . ."

As she leaned over Raymond to turn the pages, she was quite
innocently pouring oil on the flames, stoking the blaze. Her
breath fanned the fire within him. She could not see the look of
fury on his face. There he sat, the heavy album weighing down
his knees. He was breathing heavily and trembling with frustrated violence.

"Here he is at six and a half, just two months before he died.
He looks much better, doesn't he? But I can't help wondering
whether I didn't make him work too hard. When he was six he
read everything that came his way, even books he couldn't understand. Living as he did, all the time with grown-ups.

"You see," she said, "he was my companion, my friend"—because, at this moment, she could make no distinction between
what François had been for her in actuality and what she had
hoped he might become.

"Even then he used to ask me questions. What nights of torment I went through thinking that one day I should have to explain. The only thing that consoles me now is the realization that he went without knowing . . . that he never knew . . . that now he never will know. . . ."

She was standing upright, her arms hanging at her sides. Raymond dared not raise his eyes, but he could hear the rustling of her movements. Struck though he was by her words, he had an uneasy suspicion that her grief was not altogether genuine. Later, when he was walking home, he said to himself: She was playing a game, and taking herself in with it. . . . She was running the dead-child business for all it was worth. Still, there's no getting away from it, she *was* crying. . . . He was shaken in the idea he had formed of her. In his youth and inexperience he had painted for himself a picture of "bad women" that was entirely theological in character and modelled on what his masters had told him, convinced though he was that he had successfully resisted their influence. Maria Cross hemmed him in like an army ordered for battle. On her ankles tinkled the bangles of Delilah and of Judith. There was no treachery, no trickery that he would have put beyond one whose glance the saints had dreaded like the glance of death.

Maria Cross said to him: "Come and see me whenever you like: I am always here." With tears in her eyes and peace in her heart, she went with him to the door, without even fixing another day for their next meeting. When he had gone, she sat down by François' bed, carrying her sorrow like a sleeping child in her arms. The tranquillity she felt may have been the result of disappointment. She did not know that she would not always be safe. The dead cannot help the living. In vain do we invoke them from the edge of the abyss. Their silence, their absence, seem to take sides against us.

❀ *I X* ❀

IT WOULD have been far better for Maria Cross if this, Raymond's first visit, had not left her with an impression of security and innocence. She was amazed that everything had gone so smoothly.

I worked myself up unnecessarily, she thought. She believed her predominant feeling to be one of relief, but already she felt unhappy in the knowledge that she had let Raymond go without arranging for another meeting. She was careful now never to go out at the times he might be likely to come. So simple is the squalid game of passion that a youth can master it on his very first adventuring into love. It needed no worldly-wise counsellor to persuade this one to "let her cook in her own juice".

After waiting for four days, she was in a fit state to lay all the blame for his silence on herself, thinking: I talked to him about nothing but my own troubles, and about François. It must have been terribly depressing for him. What possible interest could he take in my album? I ought to have asked him about his life. . . . I ought to have laid myself out to win his confidence. . . . He is bored with me . . . thinks me just a tedious woman. . . . What if he never comes back?

What if he never came back? To such an extent did she worry over the possibility that it was well on the way to becoming a torment: I may wait as long as I like, he won't come. I have lost my hold on him. He's at the age when young men don't suffer bores gladly. Better face it, the whole thing is over and done with. . . . The evidence was too shattering, too terrible. He would never come back. Maria Cross had filled up the last well to be found in her desert. Nothing now but sand. The most dangerous of all things in love is the flight of one of the parties to the plot. The presence of the adored is, more often than not, an obstacle to passion. When she was with Raymond Courrèges she saw, in the first place, a young creature whose innocent heart it would be a crime to disturb. She remembered whose son he was. The last traces of childhood in his face reminded her of her own lost boy. Even in thought she could not draw near that young body save with a sense of ardent modesty. But now that he was no longer there, now that she feared she might never see him again, of what use was it any longer to mistrust the muddied waters of her heart, the dark confusion of her feelings? Now that this fruit was to be dashed from her thirsty lips, why deprive herself of the satisfaction of imagining the flavour she would never know in fact? Whom would she wrong by so doing? What reproach need she fear at sight of the headstone on which the name of François was engraved? Who was there to see her shut away in this house, without a husband, without a child, without servants? Madame Courrèges'

endless lamentations about the quarrels of her domestic staff
might be trivial enough, but how glad would Maria Cross have
been to occupy her mind with such things? Where was there for
her to go? Beyond the drowsing garden stretched the suburban
roads, and further still the stone-built city where, when a storm
bursts, one knows for certain that nine days of stifling heat will follow. A fierce and torpid beast seems to prowl, to growl, to crouch
in a sky drained of all colour. She too, pacing like a beast the garden or the empty rooms, yielded (how else could her misery find
an issue?) little by little to the fascination of a hopeless love, a
love that could offer nothing but the wretched happiness of a self-
consuming anguish. She gave up all attempt to put out the fire—
no longer suffered from aimlessness and lassitude, since she had
no thoughts now for anything but the blaze. A nameless devil
whispered in her ear: "You may be dying, but at least you are
not bored!"

What is strange about a storm is not its tumult but the silence,
the torpor which it imposes upon the world. Maria could see the
leaves lying motionless against the panes of the window, almost
as though painted on them. There was something human about
the drooping melancholy of the trees. It was as though they
were conscious of their lifelessness, their numbed and sleeping
state. Her mood was one in which passion takes on the semblance
of a physical presence. She scratched at the sore place in her
soul: she kept the fire in her heart alive. Her love was becoming
a choking contraction which, had she so wished, she could have
localized in her throat, in her chest. A mere letter from Monsieur
Larousselle had the power to make her shudder with disgust. As
to the idea of his making approaches to her, *that* from now on
would be no longer possible for her to endure. He would not be
back for another fortnight—time enough in which to die. She
gorged her imagination on thoughts of Raymond, on certain memories that formerly would have overwhelmed her with a sense
of shame: I looked at the leather lining of his hat, where it presses
against his forehead . . . seeking in it the very smell of his hair.
. . . She yearned for his face, for his neck, for his hands, for all
and each of them had become the incomparable signs and sym-
bols of a secret reality which was filled to overflowing with delight. . . . How inconceivable was this new tranquillity at the heart
of her despair. Sometimes the thought came to her that so long
as he was alive nothing was lost; that maybe he would return.

But as though there were something terrifying in the hope which such dreaming implied, she hastened to immure herself once more in an absolute renunciation, in the peace of mind that refuses to expect. There was for her a horrible pleasure in digging still deeper the gulf which separated her from the being whom she forced herself to see as pure. The inaccessible youth blazed in her firmament bright as the hunter Orion, and no less remote from her passion. I am already a woman burned up by life, she thought, a woman lost, while he has about him still the magic of childhood. His purity has set great spaces of sky between us, across which my longing refuses even to blaze a trail.

All through these days winds from the west and south drew after them great tumbled ranks of cloud, legions of grumbling vapour which, just as they were about to burst in a torrential downpour, suddenly hesitated, turned round about the charmed and toppling peaks of ether, and disappeared, leaving behind them that sudden sense of freshness which comes when somewhere rain has fallen.

In the night hours between Friday and Saturday the rain at last set in with an unbroken sound of murmuring waters. Thanks to the chloral that she had taken, Maria, at peace with all the world, breathed in the scented air which the garden wafted through the blinds to her tumbled bed. Then she fell into a dreamless sleep.

Lying there relaxed under the early morning sun, she thought with amazement of all the suffering she had been through. She must have been mad. Why had she seen everything in such gloomy colours? The boy was alive: he was merely waiting for a sign from her. The crisis past, she felt once more clearheaded, balanced, perhaps even slightly disappointed. Is that all it was? she thought. He'll come, and just to make doubly sure, I'll write. . . . I'm going to see him again. . . . At all costs she must confront her misery and the youth that caused it. She forced herself to contemplate in memory only a simple, inoffensive child, and was surprised to find that she no longer trembled at the thought of his head upon her knees. She thought: I'll write to the doctor telling him that I have made the acquaintance of his son (but she knew that she would not). Why shouldn't I? What harm are we doing? . . . In the afternoon she went into the garden with its waste of puddles. She felt really at peace, too wholly at peace, so much at peace that she was vaguely frightened. The less she felt her passion, the more she felt the threat of nothingness. Reduced in stature, her love no longer obliterated her inner emptiness. Already she was regretting that her round of the garden had lasted only a bare five minutes, and made the circuit once again, following the same paths. Then she hurried back because the grass had made her feet wet. . . . She would change into slippers, would lie down, smoke, read . . . but what? She had no book on hand that really interested her. As she approached the house she raised her eyes to the windows, and there, behind the drawing-room panes, saw Raymond. He was pressing his face to the glass, amusing himself by squashing his nose flat. Was this rising tide of feeling in her, joy? She walked up the front steps, thinking of the feet that, but a moment before, had pressed them. She pushed open the door, her eyes fixed on the latch because of the hand that had rested on it, crossed the dining-room at a slower pace, composed her features.

It was Raymond's misfortune that he should have come immediately after the long train of days during which she had dreamed so exclusively of him, and suffered so much on his account. Seeing him there in the flesh, she could not fill the void between the endless agitation of her heart and the being who had caused it. She did not know that she was disappointed. That she was, her first remark soon proved:

"Have you just been to the barber?" She had never seen him look like this before, with his hair cut far too short, and shining. She touched the faint scar left above his temple by some blow.

"I got that falling off a swing when I was eight."

She looked at him, trying to bring into focus her desire, her pain, her hunger, her renunciation, and this long, lean youth who looked so like an overgrown puppy. A thousand feelings, all to do with him, surged up within her, and those of them she could retain grouped themselves, for good or ill, about the taut, congested face. But she failed to recognize the peculiar expression in his eyes that betokened the blind fury of the timid man who has decided to try his luck, of the coward who has screwed himself to the sticking point. Never to her had he looked so much like a child, and she said with an air of kindly authority what, so often, in the old days, she had said to François:

"Are you thirsty? I'll give you some red-currant syrup in a moment: but you must cool down first."

She directed him to an armchair, but he chose to sit on the sofa where she had already lain down. He protested that he wasn't a bit thirsty:

". . . and if I were, it wouldn't be for syrup."

Her legs were rather too much exposed, and she pulled down her skirt. The action provoked a compliment:

"What a pity!"

She changed her position and sat down beside him. He asked her why:

"It couldn't be that you're afraid?"

His words made Maria realize that that was precisely what she was. But afraid of what? This was Raymond Courrèges, young Courrèges, the doctor's son.

"How is your dear father?"

He shrugged his shoulders and stuck out his lower lip. She offered him a cigarette which he refused, lit one herself, and leaned forward, her elbows on her knees:

"You told me once before that you aren't on very intimate terms with your father. That's natural enough. . . . Relations between parents and children are never easy. . . . When François used to hide his face against my knees, I always thought to myself—make the most of it, it won't always be like this."

She had misinterpreted the movement of his shoulders, the pouting of his lips. Just now he wanted to push the memory of his father into the background—not from any feeling of indifference, but, on the contrary, because the thought of the elder man had become an obsession with him since something odd that had happened two evenings before. After dinner the doctor had joined him on the path that ran between the vines, where he was smoking a solitary cigarette, and had walked beside him in silence, like a man who has something to say but does not say it. What's he after? Raymond had wondered, indulging to the full the cruel pleasure of silence—that same pleasure which he gave himself on early autumn mornings in the carriage, with the rain streaming down the windows. Mechanically, he had quickened his pace, because he saw that his father had difficulty in keeping up with him, and was lagging a little behind. Realizing suddenly that he could no longer hear the sound of his breathing, he had turned his head. He could see the vague outline of the doctor standing there motionless on the path between the vine-shoots. His two hands were clutching at his chest, and he was swaying on his feet like a drunken man. He took a few paces forward, and then sat down heavily between two of the rows. Raymond dropped to his knees and raised the seemingly dead face to rest on his shoulder. Only a few inches separated them. He had looked at the closed eyes, at the cheeks that had taken on the colour of dough.

"What's the matter, Papa, Papa, *dear?*"

The sound of his voice, at once beseeching and authoritative, roused the sick man as though it possessed some peculiar virtue. He tried to smile, but looked bewildered, and his words, when they came, were breathless.

"It's nothing. . . . I shall be all right. . . ."

He fixed his eyes on his son's worried face, heard in his voice the same note of tenderness that it had had when he was a boy of eight.

"Rest your head against me: haven't you got a clean handkerchief? Mine's dirty."

Very gently Raymond wiped the face in which, now, there were signs of returning life. The eyes were open, gazing at the boy's hair which the wind was lightly fluttering. Behind him was the dense foliage of a vine-plant, and, further still, a yellowish sky full of growls and grumblings. It sounded as though it were emptying cartloads of stones. Leaning on his son's arm, the doctor returned to the house. The warm rain splashed their shoulders and their cheeks, but it was impossible to walk any faster. He had said to Raymond:

"It's this false angina—just as painful as the real thing. I'm suffering from a form of auto-intoxication. . . . I'll stay in bed for forty-eight hours on a diet of water . . . and remember, not a word about this to your granny or your mother."

But Raymond broke in on him with words of his own:

"You're not kidding me? You're *sure* it's nothing? Swear to me that it's nothing."

In a low voice, the doctor said:

"Would you mind so much, then, if I . . ."

But Raymond would not let him finish. He put his arm about the body that was shaking with its gasping efforts to draw breath, and his protest came in a sudden cry:

"What an old *idiot* you are!"

The doctor was to remember later the sweet insolence of the words, to remember it in the bad times when once again his

child had turned into a stranger and an enemy . . . into someone
whose heart was deaf to all appeals, who was incapable of responding. . . .

They went together into the drawing-room, but the father
dared not venture an embrace.

"Let's talk about something else: I didn't come here to chat
about Papa . . . we've got better things to do than that . . .
haven't we?"

He thrust forward a large and awkward paw, but she caught
hold of it before it had attained its goal, restraining it with
gentle insistence.

"No, Raymond, no. You live too close to him really to understand. Those closest to us are always the ones we know least
about. . . . We reach a point at which we can't even see what lies
beneath our eyes. Do you know, my relations always thought of
me as ugly, because when I was a child I had a slight squint. I
was amazed, when I went to school, to find that the other girls regarded me as pretty."

"That's right, tell me nice little stories about when you were
at school!"

His fixed obsession made him look prematurely old. Maria
dared not let go of the great hand. She could feel it growing
damp, and a feeling that was almost disgust took hold of
her. This was the same hand whose touch, ten minutes ago, had
made her turn pale. There had been a time when merely to hold
it in hers had compelled her to shut her eyes and turn away her
head; and now, it was just a flabby, clammy object.

"I want to show you what the doctor's really like, and when
I've made up my mind I can be as obstinate as a mule."

He stopped her by saying that he, too, could be obstinate.

"Look here, I swore that to-day I wouldn't be played with. . . ."

He spoke in a low voice, stumbling over his words; so low,
indeed, that it was not difficult for her to pretend that she had
not heard. But she increased the space between them. Then, after
a moment, she got up and opened one of the windows: "It's
stifling in here—just as though it hadn't rained at all! But I
can still hear the storm, unless it's gunfire from Saint-Médard."

She pointed to where, above the trees, a dense, dark cloud
showed a wind-tossed summit edged with sunlight. But he seized
her forearm in both his hands and pushed her towards the sofa.

She forced a laugh—"Let go!"—and the more she struggled, the more she laughed, to prove that this wrestling match was just a game, and that she regarded it as such. "Let me alone, you nasty little creature! . . ." The lines of laughter about her lips became a grimace. She stumbled against the divan, and saw, only a few inches away, the myriad drops of sweat on his low forehead, the blackheads on his nose. She could smell his sour breath. But the young faun strove to hold both her wrists in one hand so as to have the other free for what he wanted to do, and with one convulsive wriggle she freed herself. There was now between them the sofa, a table, and an armchair. She was rather breathless, but again forced herself to laugh.

"So you really think, my child, that you can take a woman by force?"

He did not laugh, the young male humiliated and infuriated by defeat, touched in the most sensitive part of that pride of body which was already abnormally developed in him, so that it bled. All his life he was to remember this particular moment when a woman had found him not only repellent but grotesque. No matter how often he might be victorious in days to come, no matter how many victims he might subdue and make miserable, nothing could assuage the burning smart of this first humiliation. For many years, remembering this moment, he would bite his lips till the blood came, would tear his pillow with his teeth in the watches of the night. . . .

He fought back the tears which sheer frustrated anger had brought to his eyes—never for an instant imagining that the smile on Maria's face might be no more than a mask, never for an instant understanding that she was seeking, not to hurt an oversensitive boy, but rather to keep herself from betraying by any sign the sense of the disaster and the ruin in which she found herself involved. . . . If only he would go away! If only she could be left alone!

It was only such a short while ago that he had been struck with amazement to feel that the famous Maria Cross was actually within his reach. Again and again he had said to himself, This simple little creature is Maria Cross! He had only to stretch out his hand, and there she would be, inert, submissive to his will. He could take her when and how he chose, let her fall and then pull her to her feet again—and now, the movement of his outspread arms had sufficed to send her dizzily spinning out of reach. She was still there in the flesh, but he knew with a sure knowledge that from now on he could no more touch her than he could have touched a star. It was then that he realized how beautiful she was. Entirely occupied in thinking how to pluck and eat the fruit, without for a moment doubting that it was meant for him, he had never really looked at her. And now, all he could do was to devour her with his eyes.

She said, gently, for fear of irritating him, but with a terrible fixity of purpose: "I want to be alone. . . . Please listen to me, Raymond . . . you *must* leave me to myself. . . ." The doctor had suffered because he felt that Maria did not want to have him with her. Raymond knew an anguish still keener—the certainty which comes to us that the beloved object can no longer pretend, no longer hide the fact that it is the imperative need of her being not to see us any more, that she has rejected us and spewed us up. We realize, then, that our absence is necessary to her life, that she is on fire to forget us. She would hustle us from the room were it not that she is afraid we might resist.

She held out his hat, opened the door, flattened herself against the wall, while he, once more the adolescent youth, filled with horror of himself, wanted only to vanish, babbled idiotic excuses, was paralysed with shame. But no sooner was he out on the road again, no sooner had the door closed behind him, than he found the words he should have thrown in the trollop's teeth. But it was too late! For years to come he was tortured by the thought that he had turned tail without so much as telling her what he thought of her.

While the boy, as he walked home, was voiding his heart of all the abuse with which he had been unable to smother Maria Cross, that young woman, having first closed the door and then the window, lay down. Somewhere beyond the trees a bird was uttering a fragmentary song that sounded like the broken mutterings of a man asleep. The suburban air echoed to the noise of trolleys and factory-whistles. Drunken singing reached her from the Saturday streets. Yet, for all that, Maria Cross lay swaddled and stifled in silence—a silence that came not from without but from within, from the depths of her being, filling the empty room, invading the house, the garden, the city, the whole world. She lived at its airless centre, her eyes fixed on that inner flame which, though suddenly all fuel was lacking, burned inextinguishably. Whence, then, did it derive its sustenance? She was reminded how, sometimes, at the fag-end of her lonely evenings, a last flicker would sometimes start from the blackened ashes in the hearth where she had thought all life was dead. Eagerly she sought the loved face of the boy whom so often she had seen in the six-o'clock trolley, and could not find it. All that had reality for her was a little tousled hooligan, driven beside himself with shyness, forcing himself to overcome his own timidity —a vision as different from the real Raymond Courrèges as had ever been that idealized portrait which had given beauty to her love. Against him on whom she had bestowed the transfigured features of divinity she raged and fumed: Did I suffer the torments of hell and the ecstasies of heaven for a grubby little urchin like that? . . . What she did not know was that it had been sufficient for her glance to fall upon this unformed boy for him to become a man whose dishonesties many women were to know to their cost, submitting to him as lover and as bully. If it were true that she had *created* him by virtue of her love, it was no less true that by scorning him she had added the last finishing touch to her work. She had let loose upon the world a young man whose mania it would be to prove to himself that he was irresistible, even though a Maria Cross had successfully resisted him. From now on, in all the amorous intrigues of his future, there would always be an element of unexpressed antagonism, a longing to wound, to extract a cry of pain from the female lying helpless at his mercy. He was to cause many tears to flow on many nameless faces, and always they would be *her* tears. Doubtless he had been born with the instincts of a beast of prey, but, had it not been for Maria Cross, their violence might have been softened by some touch of weakness.

How fathomless her disgust for this "hooligan"! Yes, the inextinguishable flame burned on within her though there was nothing now for it to feed upon. No human being would ever have the benefit of all this light, all this warmth. Where should she go? To the cemetery where François' body lay? No, no; far better to admit at once that the dead body of her son was nothing now to her but an alibi. She had been content in her visits to the child's grave only for the sake of the sweet homeward way which she had trodden with another, a living, child at her side. Hypocrite! What could she do, what could she say, before that tomb? She could but cast herself upon it as upon some doors she could not open, a woman damned to all eternity. As well might she fall

upon her knees in the dusty street. . . . Little François was no more
than a handful of ashes, he who once had been so full of laughter
and of tears. . . . Whom did she wish to have near her? The
doctor?—*that* bore?—no, not a bore. But what availed all her striving to attain perfection since it was her destiny to set her hand
to nothing that did not turn awry, no matter how excellent her
intentions? Many had been the glorious goals on which she had
set her heart, yet in each of them only the worst part of herself
had found its satisfaction. She wanted no one with her, nor
yearned to find herself elsewhere than in this room with its torn
curtains. Perhaps at St. Clair? St. Clair had seen her childhood.
. . . She remembered the park into which she had crept as soon as
the church-going family, so antagonistic to her mother, had gone
away. Nature, it had seemed, was only waiting for their departure
after the Easter holidays to break the coverings of all its shoots.
The bracken grew high and rank, touching with formless, frothy
green the lowest branches of the oaks. Only the pines swayed, unchanged, the same gray tops that seemed indifferent to the
spring, and even for them a moment came when they, too, saw
torn from their entrails the cloudy plenty of their pollen, the yellow immensity of their passion. At a turn in the path she would
find, in those days, a broken doll, a handkerchief caught on a furze-
bush. But to-day she was a stranger to that world. Nothing would
greet her there but the sand on which so often she had lain face
downward. . . .

When Justine came to tell her that dinner was ready, she tidied her hair and sat down before her steaming plate of soup.
But because nothing must stand in the way of her maid's visit to
the movies with her husband, she was once again, half an hour
later, alone at the drawing-room window. The fragrant lime had
as yet no fragrance. Below her the rhododendrons already
showed dark with coming colour. The fear of nothingness, the
longing for a breathing space, led her to seek some piece of
wreckage to which she might cling. I yielded, she thought, to
that instinct for flight which comes over all of us when confronted by a human face made ugly by exigence and hunger.
I convinced myself that the young brute and the young creature
whom I once adored were different persons—but they were the
same, the same child, only wearing a mask. As pregnant women
wear a mask of fretfulness, so men, obsessed by love, have, too,
close-moulded on their faces that look, so often hideous and al-

ways terrible, of the beast of prey that stirs within them. Galatea
fled from what frightened her, yet lured her on. . . . I had
dreamed of a long pilgrimage of kisses along which, making scarce
noticeable progress, we should have passed from the regions of
temperate warmth to those of enervating heat. But the young
buck was too headstrong. Why did I not surrender to his fumbling urgency! In my raped and ravished body I might have
found peace beyond imagining, something, perhaps, even better
than peace. . . . Maybe, where human beings are concerned,
there is no severing gulf that kisses will not bridge. . . . But
kisses of what sort? Remembering the rictus of his grin, she gave
vent to an "Ugh!" of disgust. A whole gallery of pictures forced
themselves into her mind. She saw Larousselle turning from her
with a muttered growl, his face suffused: "What *is* it you
want? . . . You're just a lump of wood, not flesh and blood at all!"

What, if it came to that, did she want? She wandered about
the deserted room, sat for a while by the window, looking out,
elbow on sill and head on hand, dreamed of some mysterious, un-
visited land of silence where she might have felt her love, yet
not demand of it speech or sound, though the beloved would
have heard it, would have understood the nature of her desire
even before desire was born. The touch of hands and lips implies
between two persons a physical separation. But so deeply inter-
fused would they have been one with the other, that no grip
and clasp of limbs would have been necessary, that brief encounter so quickly loosed again by shame. Shame? She seemed to
hear the laugh of Gaby Dubois, the light o' love, the words that
once she had spoken: "Speak for yourself, my dear . . . *that's* the
only consolation I've got in the bloody awful life I lead. . . ."
Whence came this feeling of disgust? Did it really mean anything
at all? Was it something positive and personal? A thousand formless thoughts woke in her mind and disappeared again, like, in
the empty sky above her head, the shooting stars and falling,
burned-out meteors.

Is not my lot, thought Maria, the common lot of all woman-
kind? Without husband, without children, no one, indeed, could
be more lonely than herself. But was this solitude more actual
or more intense than the sense of isolation from which no family
life, however happy, could have saved her—the sense of being
alone which comes to all of us as soon as we learn to recognize

in ourselves the distinguishing marks of that accursed species, the race of lost souls whose instincts, needs, and mysterious ends we alone can interpret? A truce to such exhausting analysis! Pale though the sky might be with traces of the lingering day, with the promise of a rising moon, beneath the still leaves darkness was massing. Leaning out into the night air, drawn, almost physically absorbed, by the quietness of the vegetable world, Maria Cross yielded not so much to a desire to drink deep of the branch-encumbered air as to a temptation to lose herself in it, to feel herself dissolved and atomised, till the inner desert of her heart should become one with the emptiness of space, till the silence within her should in no way differ from the silence of the spheres.

❖ X ❖

MEANWHILE, Raymond Courrèges, having, as he walked the road, emptied his mind of all its foul abuse, and inwardly raging that he had not turned the flood on Maria Cross, felt an urgent need to spatter her with still more mud. Obsessed by that craving, he longed, as soon as he got home, to see his father. The doctor, true to his expressed intention, had decided to spend the next forty-eight hours in bed, eating nothing and drinking only water—to the great satisfaction of his wife and mother. The onset of his false angina was not alone in determining him to act in this manner. He was curious to observe the effect upon his own constitution of such a regimen. Robinson had already looked in to see him on the previous evening.

"I'd rather it had been Duluc," said Madame Courrèges, "but Robinson's better than nothing: after all he *is* a doctor, and knows all about testing the heart."

Robinson crept cautiously through the house, keeping close to the wall, and furtively climbed the stairs, dreading lest he find himself suddenly face to face with Madeleine, though they had never been actually engaged. The doctor, his eyes closed, his head feeling empty but his mind curiously lucid, his body free from pain beneath the light encumbrance of the sheets, and screened from the blaze of the sun, found no difficulty in following the tracks made by his thoughts. Here for a moment lost, there recovered, tangled and confused, they stretched before him, and his mind nosed its way along them as a dog might beat the bushes while his master walked, but did not shoot, amid the undergrowth. Without the slightest sense of fatigue he composed whole articles, to the last word, so that all that was left for him to do was to set them down on paper. Point by point he answered all the criticisms that had been provoked by the paper he had recently read to the Biological Society. His mother's presence was sweet to him—but so, also, was his wife's, and that was a matter to give him pause. Brought to a standstill at last, after an exhausting chase, he was ready to acquiesce now in Lucie's company. He noticed with appreciative wonder how careful his mother was to efface herself, and so avoid all risk of conflict. Without a shadow of mutual recrimination, the two women seemed content to share the prey, now that he had been torn for a few brief moments from his professional duties, from his private research, and from a passion which, for them, remained anonymous. He did not put up a struggle, but appeared to take an interest in all that they said, however trivial. His world had suddenly contracted to the dimensions of their own. He actually wanted to know whether Julie was really leaving, or whether there was a chance that she might come to terms with Madeleine's maid. The feel of a woman's hand upon his forehead, his mother's or his wife's, gave him back the sense of security which he had known in the days of his childhood ailments. It rejoiced him to know that if he was to die, he would not die in solitude. It seemed to him that death in that room, with its familiar mahogany furniture, with his wife and his mother forcing themselves to smile, would be the most normal, the simplest, occurrence in all the world; for would not the bitter taste of his last moments be disguised by them as always, in the past, had been the nasty taste of medicine? . . . Just to slip away, wrapped in the warm folds of a lie, knowing himself a dupe. . . .

A flood of light invaded the room. Raymond came in, grumbling that he couldn't see a thing. He approached the man lying in the bed. In his presence alone he could relieve himself of all the vicious hatred that he felt for Maria Cross. Already he could taste in his mouth the sour flavour of what he was about to vomit forth. The sick man said: "Give me a kiss." A great warmth of feeling was in the eyes which he turned upon his son who, two evenings ago, among the vines, had wiped his face. But the young man, coming straight from the daylight into the darkened room, could not make out his father's features very distinctly. There was a harsh note in his voice as he put a question:

"Do you remember our talk about Maria Cross?"

"Yes, what of it?"

Raymond, leaning above the supine body, as though for an embrace or a murderous blow, saw beneath him two tormented eyes fixed upon his lips. He realized that someone else, besides himself, was suffering. I have known it, he thought, ever since that evening when he called me a liar. . . . But he felt no jealousy. He was incapable of imagining his father in the role of lover: no, not jealousy, but a strange desire to cry, with which was mingled a sense of irritation and of mockery. The poor cheeks looked gray under the thinning beard, and there was a tightness in the voice that begged him to go on:

"Well, what is it you know? Don't keep me on tenterhooks: tell me!"

"I was misled, Papa; you are the only person who really knows Maria Cross. I just wanted to tell you that. Now try and get some sleep. How pale you look. Are you sure this diet is agreeing with you?"

It was with amazement that he heard his own voice saying the very reverse of what he had meant to say. He laid a hand upon the sad and arid brow—the same hand which Maria Cross had held such a short while before. The doctor found it cool, was afraid that it might be taken away.

"My opinion of Maria dates from far back. . . ."

At that moment, Madame Courrèges came back into the room. He put his finger to his lips, and Raymond noiselessly withdrew.

His mother was carrying a paraffin-lamp (because in the doctor's weak state the electric light would have hurt his eyes). She put it on the table and lowered the shade. The restricted circle of illumination, the old-fashioned nature of its source, brought suddenly to light the mysterious world of rooms now vanished for ever, where a night light had been wont to struggle with a thick darkness full of furniture half drowned in obscurity. The doctor loved Maria, but he could see her with detachment. He loved her as the dead must love the living. She made one with all the other loves of his life, from boyhood on. . . . Feeling his way along the pathway of this thought, he now saw that one and the same sentiment had always held him in thrall down the years.

It had always been like the one that had caused him the torment
from which he had only just been released. He could feel his way
back along the dreary sameness of that eternal pilgrimage, could
have put a name to each one of all the passionate adventures,
most of which, like this one, had ended only in frustration. Yet,
in those days he had been young. It wasn't, then, age alone that
stood between him and Maria Cross. No more successfully at
twenty-five than now could he have crossed the desert separating
this woman and himself. He remembered how, just after he had
left college, when he was the same age as Raymond, he had
loved, yet never known a moment's hope. . . . It was the law of
his nature that he could never make contact with those he loved.
He had never been more conscious of that truth than in those moments of partial success when he had held in his arms the object
so long desired, and found it suddenly poor and dwarfed and
utterly different from what it had been in the agonies of his desire. No reason to seek in the mirror the reasons for that solitude
in which he was fated to remain until his death. Other men—his
father had been one such, Raymond would be another—can follow the law of their being into old age, obedient to the demands
of their vocation of love. But he, even in his youth, had been obedient only to the call of his predestined solitude.

The ladies having gone downstairs to dinner, he heard a sound
that came straight out of his childhood, the tinkle of spoons on
china. But closer to his ears and to his heart were the noises made
by rustling leaves, by the crickets, by a frog pleased at the coming of the rain. Then the ladies returned. They said:
"You must be feeling very weak."
"I certainly couldn't stand upright."
But because this diet of his was a form of "treatment" they
were pleased that he felt weak.
"Wouldn't you like a little . . .?"
The sense of weakness helped him on his way of exploration
into the distant past. The two ladies were carrying on a conver-
sation in undertones. The doctor heard a name mentioned, and
questioned them:
"Wasn't that a certain Mademoiselle Malichecq?"
"So you heard what we were saying? I thought you were
asleep. No, it's her sister-in-law who's a Malichecq. . . . She's a
Martin."

The doctor had gone to sleep by the time the Basques put in an appearance, and did not open his eyes until he heard the doors of their rooms shut. Then his mother rolled up her knitting, rose heavily from her chair, and kissed him on the forehead, the eyes, and the neck.

"Your skin's quite cool," she said.

He was alone with Madame Courrèges, who at once embarked upon a grievance:

"Raymond took the last trolley into Bordeaux again. God knows what time he'll come in. He looked terrible this evening; I felt quite frightened. When he's spent the money you gave him, he'll run into debt, if he hasn't started already!"

In a low voice the doctor said: "Our little Raymond . . . nineteen already," and shuddered, thinking of certain streets in Bordeaux that were always deserted after dark. He remembered the sailor over whose body he had tripped one evening. The man's face and chest had been blotched with stains of wine and blood. . . . Somebody was still moving about upstairs. A dog in the stable-yard started to bark furiously. Madame Courrèges listened intently:

"I can hear somebody moving about. It can't be Raymond as early as this. Besides, if it were, the dog wouldn't be making all that noise."

Somebody was coming towards the house. There was nothing furtive about his movements, indeed, he seemed to be going out of his way to avoid concealment. The shutters of the French window were shaken. Madame Courrèges leaned forward.

"Who's there?"

"An urgent message for the doctor."

"The doctor doesn't go out at night: you ought to know that by this time. Try Doctor Larue in the village."

The man, who was holding a lantern in his hand, was insistent. The doctor, who was still half asleep, cried out to his wife:

"Tell him it's useless. I didn't come to live in the country just in order to be pulled out of bed by night-calls."

"It's out of the question. My husband only sees patients by appointment. He has an arrangement with Doctor Larue . . ."

"But, Madame, it's about one of his patients that I've come, a neighbour of his. . . . He'll come soon enough when he hears the name. It's Madame Cross, Madame Maria Cross. She's had a fall—on her head."

"Maria Cross? Why should you think he'd put himself out for her more than for anybody else?"

But at the sound of the name the doctor had got out of bed. He elbowed his wife aside and leaned out of the window.

"Is that you, Maraud? I didn't recognize your voice. What has happened to your mistress?"

"She's had a fall, sir, on her head. She's delirious and asking for the doctor."

"I'll be with you in five minutes; just give me time to get something on."

He shut the window and started looking for his clothes.

"You're not really going?"

He made no reply but muttered to himself: "Where are my socks?" His wife protested. Hadn't he just said he wouldn't be disturbed at night for anybody? Why this sudden change of mind? He could scarcely stand up: he would faint from sheer weakness.

"It's one of my patients. Surely you see that I can't *not* go?"

There was sarcasm in her voice as she answered:

"Oh yes, I see right enough. . . . It has taken me some time, but I see now."

She did not yet actually suspect her husband. For the moment she was intent only on wounding him. He, confident in his detachment, in the fact of his renunciation, had no qualms on her account. After the long torment of his passion, nothing, he felt, could be less blameworthy, less guilty than his feeling now of friendly alarm. It never occurred to him that though he might, his wife could not draw a comparison between the past and present states of his love for Maria Cross. Two months earlier he would not have dared to show his anxiety so openly. When passion is a flaming fire we instinctively dissimulate. But once we have given up all hope of happiness, once we have accepted an eternal hunger, an eternal thirst, the least we can do—or so we think—is not to wear ourselves out with pretending.

"My poor Lucie, you're quite wrong. All that is very far away now . . . quite, quite finished. Yes, I *am* deeply attached to the poor creature . . . but that has nothing to do . . ."

He leaned against the bed, murmuring: "She's right; I've eaten nothing," and proceeded to ask his wife to make him some chocolate on the spirit-lamp.

"Where do you think I'm going to find milk at this time of night? I don't suppose there's a scrap of bread in the kitchen, either. But no doubt, when you've seen to this—this woman, she'll make you a nice little supper. It will be well worth while having been disturbed for that!"

"What a fool you are, my dear. If only you knew . . ."

She took his hand and came close:

"You said—all that's quite finished . . . all that's very far away— then there *was* something between you? What was it? I have a right to know. I won't reproach you, but I want to know."

The doctor felt so breathless that he had to make two attempts before he could get his boots on. He muttered:

"I was speaking generally: what I said had nothing to do with Maria Cross. Look at me, Lucie . . ."

But she was busy going over in her mind the events of the past months. She had the key to it all now! Everything hung together: everything was as clear as clear. . . .

"Paul, don't go to that woman. I've never bothered you with questions . . . you must do me the justice to admit that."

He answered gently that it was not in his power to do what she asked. His duty was to his patient—she might be dying: a fall on the head might well prove fatal.

"If you keep me from going out, you will be responsible for her death!"

She loosed him, finding no more to say. As he moved away from her she began speaking to herself, stumbling over her words: "It may be all a trick . . . they may have fixed it up between them." Then she remembered that the doctor had had nothing to eat since the previous evening. Seated on a chair, she listened to the murmur of voices in the garden.

"Yes, she fell out of the window . . . it must have been an accident. She wouldn't have chosen the drawing-room one, which is on the ground floor, if she had meant to throw herself out. Quite delirious . . . complaining about her head . . . doesn't remember a thing."

Madame Courrèges heard her husband tell the man to get some ice in the village: he would find some at the inn or at the butcher's. He must get some bromide, too, at the chemist's.

"I'll go by the Bois de Berge: it'll be quicker that way than if I had the horse put in."

"You won't want the lantern, sir: it's as bright as day with this moon."

The doctor had only just passed through the small gate leading

to the stable-yard when he heard someone running after him.
A voice panted out his Christian name. He saw that it was his
wife, in her dressing-gown, with her hair in plaits, ready for bed.
She was too breathless to say more, but held out to him a piece
of stale bread and a large bar of chocolate.

He went through the Bois de Berge. The clearings were stained
with moonlight, though the full strength of the white radiance
could not penetrate the leaves. But the great planet sat in throned
majesty above the road, shining as though in a river-bed cut for
its brightness. The bread and chocolate recalled the taste of
all his schoolboy snacks—the taste of happiness—at dawn, when
he used to go out shooting, in the days when his feet were soaked
with dew and he was seventeen. Numbed by the shock of the
news, he only now began to feel the pain. Suppose Maria Cross
was going to die? Who was it that had made her want to die? But
had she wanted it? She could remember nothing. How completely
knocked out are those victims of shock who never remember anything, who smother up in darkness the essential moment of their
destiny! But he mustn't question her. The important thing for the
time being was that she should work her brain as little as possible.
Remember, he thought, you are only a doctor attending his patient. There can be no question of suicide. When people have
made up their minds to die, they don't choose a ground-floor window. She doesn't take drugs, or not as far as I know, though it's
true that there was a smell of ether in her room one evening when
I was there; but she'd been suffering from headache. . . .
Beyond the area of his stifling torment, on the very edge of his
consciousness, another storm was growling. When the appointed
moment came, it would burst: Poor Lucie—jealous! what a
wretched business . . . but time enough to think about that
later. . . . Here I am. The moon makes the garden look like a
stage scene. It's as puerile as a setting for *Werther*. . . . No sound
of raised voices. . . . The main door was ajar. From sheer habit he
went straight to the empty drawing-room, then turned and
climbed the stairs. Justine opened the door of the bedroom. He
went across to the bed, on which Maria was lying, moaning to
herself, and trying to push away the compress from her forehead. He had no eyes for her body beneath the close-clinging
sheet, the body which so often he had undressed in imagination.
He had no eyes for her disordered hair, nor for her arm, naked to

the armpit. All that mattered was that she recognized him, that her delirium was only intermittent. She kept on saying: "What happened, doctor?—what was it?" He made a mental note: amnesia. Leaning over the naked breast whose veiled loveliness had once made him tremble, he listened to her heart, then, very gently touching her injured forehead with his finger, he traced the extent of the wound. "Does it hurt you here . . . or here . . . or here?" She complained, too, of pain in her hip. Very carefully he drew down the sheet so as to expose no more than the small bruised surface; then covered it up again. With his eyes on his watch, he felt her pulse. This body had been delivered to him for cure, not for possession. His eyes knew that they were there to observe, not to be enchanted. He gazed intently at her flesh, bringing all his intelligence to bear. The clearness of his mind barred all roads of approach to his melancholy passion.

"I'm in pain," she moaned; "I'm in such dreadful pain."

She pushed away the compress, then asked for a fresh one, which the maid proceeded to soak in the kettle. The chauffeur came in with a bucket of ice, but when the doctor tried to apply it to her head, she pushed away the rubber skull-cap and, in commanding tones, insisted on a *hot* compress. To the doctor she exclaimed: "Don't be so slow: it takes you an hour to carry out my orders!"

He was extremely interested in these symptoms, which were similar to others he had noticed in cases of shock. The body lying there before him, which once had been the carnal source of all his dreams and reveries and delight, roused in him nothing but an intense curiosity, a concentrated and enhanced attention. The patient's mind was no longer wandering, but she poured forth a spate of words. He noticed with surprise that she, whose powers of speech were normally so defective that she had to make an effort, and not always a successful effort, to find the right words for what she wanted to express, had suddenly become almost eloquent. She had complete command of her vocabulary, and seemed capable of calling on technical terms at will. What a mysterious organ, he reflected, is the human brain. How extraordinary it is that it can develop its scope in this amazing way merely as the result of shock.

"I never meant to kill myself—you must believe that, doctor. I absolutely forbid you to think that such an idea ever came into my mind. I can remember nothing. The only certain thing is that what I wanted was not to die but to sleep. I've never truly longed for anything in my life but peace and quiet. If ever you hear anybody boasting that he dragged me down to the point of making me want to kill myself, I tell you you mustn't believe it. Do you understand me? I prohib-it anything of the sort."

"Yes, dear lady. I swear to you that nobody has ever uttered such a boast in my hearing. . . . Now, just sit up and drink this. It's only bromide: it will soothe your nerves."

"I don't need soothing. I am in a good deal of pain, but I am perfectly calm. Move the lamp farther away. There now, I've messed the sheets. But I don't care—I'll empty the drug all over the bed if I want to. . . ."

When he asked whether the pain was less acute, she replied that it was excruciating, but that it didn't come only from her injury. In an access of talkativeness she once more raised her voice and spoke in such an unbroken flow that Justine observed that Madame was talking like a book. The doctor told the woman to go and get some sleep. He would sit up with the patient, he said, until daybreak.

"What other way out is there, doctor, except sleep? I see everything so clearly now. I understand what I never understood before . . . the people we think we love . . . the passions that end so miserably . . . now, at last, I know the truth. . . ." (The compress had grown cold and she pushed it away with her hand. The damp hair clung to her forehead as though she were sweating.) "No, not passions, but one single passion. It goes on inside us, and from a casual meeting, from the eyes and lips of some perfect stranger, we build up something that we think corresponds with it. . . . Only by physical contact, by the embraces of the flesh, by, in short, the sexual act, can two persons ever really communicate. . . . But we know only too well where that road leads, and why it was traced—for the sole purpose of continuing the species, as you would put it, doctor. We choose the one path open to us, but it was never designed to lead us to our hearts' desire."

At first he had lent but half an ear to this outburst. He made no attempt to understand what she was saying. What interested him was her irrelevant talkativeness. It was, he noticed, as though the physical disturbance she had suffered had sufficed partially to bring into the open ideas that had been lying repressed in her mind.

"One's got to love the pleasure of the body, doctor. Gaby used to say—it's the only thing in the world, darling, that has never disappointed me—but, unfortunately we can't, all of us, do that. And yet it *is* the only thing that makes us forget the object of our search, forget so far that it actually becomes that object. Stupefy yourself . . . that's easier said than done."

How curious it was, thought the doctor, that she should speak of sexual pleasure precisely as Pascal had spoken of faith. In order to quiet her at all costs so that she might get some sleep, he held out some syrup in a spoon. But she pushed it away, and once again made a stain upon the sheets.

"No, I don't *want* any bromide. I shall empty it all over the bed if I like: *you* can't prevent me!"

Without the slightest subtlety of transition she went on: "Always between me and those I have longed to possess there has stretched this fetid region of swamp and mud. But they didn't understand. . . . They always thought I was calling to them because I wanted to wallow in the dirt."

Her lips moved, and the doctor thought that she was muttering names, Christian names. He leaned over her eagerly, but did not hear the one name which would have utterly destroyed his peace of mind. For a few moments he forgot that she was his patient and saw only a woman who was lying to him. In an agony of misery he murmured:

"You're just like all the others. You want one thing, and one thing only, pleasure. . . . It's the same with all of us. It's the only thing we want."

She raised her lovely arms, hid her face, uttered a long-drawn moan. In a low voice he said: "What's the matter with me? I must be mad!" He renewed the compress, poured some more syrup into a spoon, and supported the sufferer's head. Maria at last consented to drink: then, after a moment's silence:

"Yes, I too, I too. You know, doctor, how sometimes one sees the lightning and hears the thunder simultaneously—well, with me pleasure and disgust are all confused, just like the lightning and the thunder: they strike me at the same moment. There is no interval between the pleasure and the disgust."

She grew calmer and stopped speaking. The doctor sat down in an armchair and watched beside her, his mind a confusion of thoughts. He believed that she was asleep, but suddenly her voice, dreamy now and at peace, rose again:

"Someone with whom we might make contact, someone we might possess—but not in the flesh—by whom we might be possessed. . . ."

Fumblingly she pushed the damp cloth from her brow. The room was filled with the silence of the dying night. It was the hour of the deepest sleep, the hour at which the constellations change their pattern in the sky so that we no longer recognize them.

Her pulse was calm. She was sleeping like a child whose breathing is so light that one gets up to make sure that it is still alive. The blood had once more mounted to her cheeks and gave them colour. Her body was no longer that of a sufferer: not now did pain divorce her from desire. How long must his poor tormented flesh keep watch beside this other flesh deadened at last to suffering? The body has its agony, thought the doctor: To the simple, Paradise lies wide open. . . . Who was it said that love was the pleasure of the poor? I might have been the man who, his day's work ended, lay down each night beside this woman. But then, she would not have been *this* woman. . . . She would have been a mother more than once. All her body would bear signs of the purpose it had served, the traces of a life spent in degrading tasks. . . . Desire would be dead: nothing would remain but a few grubby habits. . . . Dawn already! How long the servant is in coming!

He was afraid that he would never be able to walk as far as his house. He told himself it was hunger that made him weak, but he dreaded the treachery of his heart whose beats he could so clearly hear. Physical anguish had freed him from love's sickness. But already, though no sign came to warn him, the destiny of Maria Cross was imperceptibly drifting away from his own. . . . The mooring-ropes are loosed, the anchor raised: the vessel moves, but as yet one does not realize that it is moving, though in another hour it will be no more than a dark stain upon the sea. He had often observed that life takes no heed of preparations. Ever since the days of his youth, the objects of his affection had, almost all of them, disappeared with dramatic suddenness, carried away by some other passion, or, with less fuss and bother, had just packed up and left town. Nothing more was ever heard of them. It is not death that tears from us those we love; rather, it keeps them safe, preserving them in all the adorable *ambiance* of youth. Death is the salt of love: it is life that brings corruption. To-morrow the doctor would be stretched upon a sick-bed, with

his wife sitting beside him. Robinson would be keeping a watchful
eye on Maria Cross's convalescence, and would send her to
Luchon to take the waters, because his best friend had set up in
practice there, and he wanted to help him with a few patients.
In the autumn, Monsieur Larousselle, whose business often took
him to Paris, would decide to rent a flat close to the Bois, and
would suggest to Maria that she move there, because, by that
time, she would have said that she would rather die than go back
to the house at Talence, with its worn carpets and torn curtains,
or put up any longer with the insults of the Bordeaux folk.

When the maid came into the room, even had the doctor not
felt so weak that he seemed to be conscious of nothing but his
weakness—even had he been full of life and vigour, no inner
voice would have warned him to take his last long look at the
sleeping Maria Cross. He was fated never to enter this house
again, yet all he said to the maid was: "I'll look in again this
evening. . . . Give her another spoonful of bromide if she seems
restless." He stumbled from the room, holding to the furniture to
keep himself from falling. It was the only time in his life that he
had left Maria Cross without turning his head.

He hoped that the early morning air would sting his blood to
activity, but he had to stop at the bottom of the steps. His teeth
were chattering. So often in the past, when hastening to his love,
he had crossed the garden in a few seconds, but now, as he looked
at the distant gate, he wondered whether he would have strength
enough to reach it. He dragged himself through the mist and was
tempted to turn back. He would never be able to walk as far as
the church, where, perhaps, he might find somebody to help him.
Here was the gate at last, and, beyond the railings, a carriage—
his carriage. Through the window he could see the face of Lucie
Courrèges. She was sitting there quite motionless and as though
dead. He opened the door, collapsed against his wife, leaned his
head on her shoulder, and lost consciousness.

"Don't agitate yourself. Robinson has everything under control
in the laboratory, and is looking after your patients. At this very
moment he is at Talence, you know where. . . . Now don't talk."
From the depths of his lassitude he noticed the ladies' anxiety,
heard their whispering outside his door. He believed that he was
seriously ill, and attached no importance to what they said: "Just
a touch of influenza, but in your anemic state that's quite bad

enough." He asked to see Raymond, but Raymond was always out. "He came in while you were asleep, but didn't want to wake you." As a matter of fact, for the last three days Lieutenant Basque had been in Bordeaux hunting everywhere for the boy. They had taken no one into their confidence but a private investigator. "Whatever happens, he must never know. . . ."

At the end of six days Raymond suddenly appeared in the dining-room while they were at dinner. His face looked thin and tanned by exposure. There was a bruise under his right eye where somebody had hit him. He ate as though he were famished, and even the little girls did not dare to question him. He asked his grandmother where his father was.

"He's got a touch of influenza . . . it's nothing, but we were rather worried because of the state of his heart. Robinson says that he mustn't be left alone. Your mother and I take turns at sitting with him."

Raymond said that to-night he would relieve them, and when Basque ventured to remark, "You'd much better go to bed: if you could only see what you look like! . . ." he declared that he wasn't the slightest bit tired, and that he had been sleeping very well all the time he was away:

"There's no shortage of beds in Bordeaux."

The tone in which he made the remark made Basque lower his eyes. Later, when the doctor opened his, he saw Raymond standing beside him. He made a sign for him to come closer, and, when he did so, murmured: "You reek of cheap scent . . . I don't need anything: go to bed." But towards midnight he was roused by the sound of Raymond walking up and down. The boy had opened the window and was leaning out into the darkness. "It's stifling to-night," he grumbled. Some moths flew in. Raymond took off his jacket, waistcoat, and collar. Then he sat down in an armchair. A few seconds later the doctor heard his regular breathing. When day came, the sick man woke before his watcher and gazed in amazement at the child sitting there, his head drooping, seemingly without life, as though sleep had killed him. The sleeve of his shirt was torn, and revealed a muscular arm that was the colour of a cigar. It was tattooed with the sort of obscene design favoured by sailors. The congested patch beneath his eye had obviously been caused by a fist. But there were other scars on his neck, on his shoulder, and on his chest, scars that had the form of a human mouth.

※ *XI* ※

THE REVOLVING door of the little bar never remained still for a moment. The circle of tables pressed closer and closer on the dancing couples, beneath whose feet the leather floor covering, like the wild ass's skin, continually shrank. In the contracted space the dances were no more than vertical jerkings. The women sat jammed together on the settees and laughed when they noticed on bare arms the mark of an involuntary caress. The one called Gladys and her companion put on their fur-coats.

"You staying?"

Larousselle protested that they were leaving just as things might get amusing. With his hands thrust into his pockets, unsteady on his feet, and his paunch sticking out provocatively, he went across and perched himself on a high stool. The barman burst out laughing, as did the young men to whom he was explaining with considerable pride the ingredients of a special aphrodisiac cocktail of his own invention. Maria, alone at her table, took another sip of champagne and put down her glass. She smiled vaguely, utterly indifferent to Raymond's proximity. What passion might occupy her mind he could not know. She was armed against him, separated from him, by the accumulated experiences of seventeen years. Like a dazed and blinded diver he fought his way to the surface, up from the dead past. But the only thing in the unclear backwash of time that really belonged wholly to him was a narrow path, quickly traversed, between walls of clotted darkness. With his nose to the ground he had followed the scent, oblivious to all others that might cross it. But this was no place for dreaming. Across the smoky room and the crowd of dancing couples Maria gave him a hasty glance, then turned away. Why had he not even smiled at her? He dreaded to think that after all these years the youth that once he had been might again take visionary form in this woman's eyes, that image of the shy young boy in the grip of an impotent and furtive desire. Courrèges, notorious for his audacities, trembled with anxiety this evening lest, at any moment now, Maria might get up and disappear. Wasn't there anything he could try? He was the victim of that fatality which condemns us to play the role of a man in whom a woman makes exclusive, unalterable choice of certain elements, for ever ignoring those others that may, too, be part of him. There is nothing to be done against this particular chemical law. Every human being with whom we come in contact isolates in us a single property, always the same, which as a rule we should prefer to keep concealed. Our misery, on these occasions, consists in our seeing the loved one build up, beneath our very eyes, the portrait of us that she has made, reduce to nothing our most precious virtues, and turn the light full on our one weakness, absurdity, or vice. And not only that. We are forced to share in the vision, to conform to it, for just so long as those appraising eyes, with their single, fixed idea, are bent on us. Only to others, whose affection is of no value to us, will our virtues glow, our talents shine, our strength seem superhuman, our face become as the face of a god.

Now that he had become, under Maria Cross's gaze, once more an abashed and foolish youth, Courrèges no longer wanted to revenge himself. His humble desire went no further than that this woman might learn the details of his amorous career, of all the victories he had won from that moment when, shortly after he had been thrown out of the house at Talence, he had been taken up, almost kidnapped, by an American woman who had kept him for six months at the Ritz (his family believed that he was in Paris working for his exam). But it was just that, he told himself, that was so impossible—to show himself as someone totally different from what he had been in that over-furnished drawing-room, all "luxury and squalor," when she had said, averting her face, "I want to be alone, Raymond—listen to me—you *must* leave me to myself."

It was the hour at which the tide begins to ebb. But those regular patrons of the little bar who left their troubles with their coats in the cloak-room stayed on. A young woman in red was whirling round ecstatically, her arms extended like wings, while her partner held her by the waist—two happy May flies united in full flight. An American showed the smooth face of a schoolboy above a pair of enormous shoulders. With ears only for the voice of some god within him, he danced alone, improvising steps which were probably obscene. To the applause which greeted his efforts he responded awkwardly with the grin of a happy child.

Victor Larousselle had resumed his seat opposite Maria. Now and again he turned his head and stared at Raymond. His large face, of a uniform alcoholic red (except under the eyes, where there were livid pouches), had the look of a man eager for a sign of recognition. In vain did Maria beg him to turn his attention elsewhere. If there was one thing above all others about Paris that Larousselle could not bear, it was seeing so many strange faces. At home there was scarcely one that did not immediately bring to mind some name, some married relationship, someone whom he could immediately "place"—whether publicly, as a person demanding social acknowledgment, or surreptitiously, as a member of the half-world whom he might know but could not openly greet. Nothing is commoner than that memory for faces which historians attribute only to the great. Larousselle remembered Raymond perfectly well from having seen him driving with his father in the old days, and from having occasionally patted his head. At Bordeaux, in the Cours de l'Intendance, he would have made no sign of recognition, but here, apart from the fact that he could never get used to the humiliation of passing for ever unnoticed, he was secretly anxious that Maria should not be left alone while he played the fool with the two Russian girls who were so obviously wearing nothing under their frocks. Raymond, acutely conscious of Maria's every gesture, concluded that she was doing her best to prevent Larousselle from speaking to him. He was convinced that, even after the lapse of seventeen years, she still saw him as an uncouth and furtive oaf. He heard the man from Bordeaux snarl: "Well, I *want* to, and that ought to be enough for you!" A smile lay like a mask on his unpleasant countenance as he picked his way towards Raymond with all the self-confidence of a man who believes his handshake to be a privilege. Surely, he *couldn't* be mistaken? he said. It was, wasn't it, the son of that excellent doctor Courrèges? His wife remembered quite clearly that she had known him at the time when the doctor was attending her. . . . He was completely master of the situation, took the young man's glass, and made him sit down beside Maria, who held out her hand, and then, almost immediately, withdrew it. Larousselle, after sitting down for a few moments, jumped up again and said without the slightest show of embarrassment:

"Forgive me, will you?—back in a minute."

He joined the two young Russian women at the bar. Though it might be only a matter of moments before he would be back again, and though nothing seemed to Raymond more important

than to turn this short respite to the best advantage, he remained
silent. Maria turned away her head. He could smell the fragrance
of her short hair, and noticed with deep emotion that a few of
the strands were white. A few?—thousands perhaps! The strongly
marked, rather thick lips seemed miraculously untouched by age,
and still gave him the impression of fruit ripe for the picking.
In them was concentrated all the sensuality of her body. The
light in her eyes, under the wide, exposed brow, was astonish-
ingly pure. What did it matter if the storms of time had beaten
against, had slowly eaten away and relaxed, the lines of neck and
throat?

Without looking at him, she said:

"My husband is really very indiscreet. . . ."

Raymond, as sheepish now as he could ever have been at eighteen, betrayed his amazement at the news that she was married.

"Do you mean to say you didn't know? It's common knowledge
in Bordeaux."

She had made up her mind to maintain an icy silence, but
seemed astounded to find that there was anybody in the world—
least of all a man from Bordeaux—who was ignorant of the fact
that she was now Madame Victor Larousselle. He explained that
it had been many years since he'd lived in that city. At that she
could no longer keep from breaking her vow of silence. Monsieur Larousselle, she said, had made up his mind the year after
the war . . . he had waited until then because of his son.

"Actually, it was Bertrand who begged us, almost before he
was out of the army, to get the whole thing settled. It didn't matter to me one way or the other. . . . I agreed from the highest
motives only."

She added that she would have preferred to go on living in
Bordeaux:

"But Bertrand is at the Polytechnic. Besides, Monsieur Larousselle has to be in Paris for a fortnight every month, so we thought
it better to make a home there for the boy."

She seemed suddenly overcome by shyness at having spoken
like this, at having confided in him. Once again remote, she said:

"And the dear doctor? Life has a way of separating us from our
best friends. . . ."

How delightful it would be to see him again! But when Raymond, taking her at her word, replied: "As a matter of fact,
my father is in Paris at this very moment, at the Grand Hotel.

He would be more than pleased . . ." she stopped short, and appeared not to have heard him.

Eager to touch her on the raw, to rouse her to a show of anger, he took his courage in both hands and proceeded to voice his one burning preoccupation:

"You don't still hold my boorishness against me? I was only a clumsy child in those days, and really very innocent. Tell me you don't bear me a grudge . . ."

"Bear a grudge?"

She pretended not to understand. Then:

"Oh, you're referring to that ridiculous scene . . . really, there's nothing to forgive. I think I must have been slightly mad myself. Fancy taking a little boy like you seriously! It all seems to me so entirely unimportant now . . . so very, very far away."

He certainly had touched her on the raw, though not in the way he had expected. She had a horror of all that reminded her of the old Maria Cross, but the adventure in which Raymond had played a part she looked on as merely ridiculous. Suddenly grown cautious, he found himself wondering whether he had ever known that she had tried to kill herself. No, for if he had he would have been prouder, would have seemed less humble.

As for Raymond, he had discounted everything in advance— everything except this worst of all foreseeable possibilities, her complete indifference.

"In those days I lived in a world of my own, and read the infinite into all sorts of nonsensical trifles. It is as though you were talking to me of some perfectly strange woman."

He knew that anger and hatred are but extensions of love, that if he could have roused them in Maria Cross his cause would not have been entirely hopeless. But the only effect his words had had upon this woman was to irritate her, to make her feel ashamed at the thought that once she had been caught out with such a wretched trick and in such paltry company.

"So you actually thought", she went on, "that a piece of silliness like that could mean something to me?"

He muttered that it had certainly meant something to him—an admission that he had never before made to himself, but now, at last, scarcely knowing what he said, put into words. He had no idea that the whole pattern of his life had been changed by that one squalid incident of his youth. He was caught in an uprush of suffering. He heard Maria's calm, detached voice:

"How right Bertrand is to say that we don't really begin to live until we've reached twenty-five or thirty."

He had a confused feeling that the remark was not true; that by the time we are beginning to grow up the future is wholly formed in us. On the threshold of manhood the bets have already been placed; nothing more can be staked. Inclinations planted in our flesh even before birth are inextricably confused with the innocence of our early years, but only when we have reached man's estate do they suddenly put forth their monstrous flowers.

Completely at sea, fighting his losing battle against this inaccessible woman, he remembered now what it was that he had so longed to tell Maria, and even though he realized increasingly as he spoke that his words were about as ill-timed as they possibly could be, declared that "our little adventure certainly hasn't stood in the way of my learning about love". Oh, very far from it! He was quite sure that he had had more women than any young man of his age—and women who had something to them, not just your common-or-garden tarts. . . . In that respect she had brought him luck.

She leaned back and, through half-closed eyes, looked at him with an expression of disgust. What, then, she asked, was he complaining of?

"Since, I presume, that sort of filth is the only thing you care about."

She lit a cigarette, leaned her cropped neck against the wall, and watched, through the smoke, the gyrations of three couples. When the jazz-players paused for breath the men detached themselves from their partners, clapped their hands, and then stretched them towards the Negro instrumentalists in a gesture of supplication—as though their very lives depended upon a renewal of the din. The Negroes, moved by compassion, resumed their playing, and the May flies, borne aloft on the rhythm, clasped one another in a fresh embrace and once again took wing. But Raymond, with hatred in his heart, looked at this woman with the short hair and the cigarette, who was none other than Maria Cross. He searched for the one word that would shake her self-control, and at last he found it.

"Well, anyhow, you're—here."

She realized that what he meant was—we always return to our first loves. He had the satisfaction of seeing her cheeks flush to a deep red, her brows draw together in a harsh frown.

"I have always loathed places like this. To say that sort of thing shows how little you know me! Your father, I am sure, remembers the agonies I went through when Monsieur Larousselle used to drag me off to the Lion Rouge. It wouldn't be of the slightest use my telling you that the only thing that brings me here is a sense of duty—yes, of duty. . . . But what can a man like you know of my scruples? It was Bertrand himself who advised me to yield—within reason—to my husband's tastes. If I am to retain any influence, I mustn't ride him on too tight a rein. Bertrand is very broad-minded. He begged me not to resist his father's wish that I should cut my hair. . . ."

She had mentioned Bertrand's name merely in order to lessen her nervous tension, to feel at peace and mollified. By the light of memory, Raymond saw once again a deserted path in the Public Park in Bordeaux. The time was four o'clock. He could hear the panting of a small boy running after him, the sound of a tear-thickened voice: "Give me back my notebook." What sort of a man had that delicate youth become? Intent on wounding, he said:

"So you've got a grown-up son now?"

But she wasn't wounded at all; she smiled happily:

"Of course, you knew him at school. . . ."

Raymond suddenly took on for her a real existence. He had been one of Bertrand's schoolfellows.

"Yes, a grown-up son, but a son who can be at once a friend and a master. You cannot imagine how much I owe to him. . . ."

"You told me—your marriage."

"Oh *that!* . . . my marriage is the least of my debts. You see, he has revealed—but it's no good, you wouldn't understand. It was only that I was thinking how you'd known him at school. I'd so much like to have some idea of what he was like as a little boy. I've often asked my husband about him, but it's extraordinary how little a man can tell one about his son's childhood: 'A nice little chap, just like all the others'—that's as much as he can say. I've no reason to believe that you were any more observant. In the first place, you were much older than he was."

"Four years—that's nothing," Raymond muttered, and added: "I remember that he had a face like a girl."

She showed no sign of anger, but answered with quiet contempt that of course they could not have had much in common. Raymond realized that in the eyes of Maria Cross her stepson floated in an airy world far above his head. She was thinking of Bertrand: she had been drinking champagne; there was a rapturous smile upon her lips. Like the disunited May flies, she, too, clapped her hands, eager for the music to renew its spell about her. What remained in Raymond's memory of the women he had possessed? Some of them he would scarcely have recognized. But hardly a day had passed during the last seventeen years that he had not conjured up in his mind, had not insulted and caressed, the face which to-night he could see in profile close beside him. He could not endure that she should be so far from him in spirit. At all costs he must bridge the gap, and to that end he took the conversation back to Bertrand.

"I suppose he'll be leaving college very soon now?"

She replied with a show of polite interest that he was in his last year. He had lost four years because of the war. She hoped that he would graduate very high, and when Raymond remarked that no doubt Bertrand would follow in his father's footsteps, said, with some animation, that he must be given time in which to make up his mind. She was quite sure, she added, that he would make his influence felt no matter what profession he adopted. Raymond could not make out in what way he was so remarkable.

"The effect he has on his fellow-students is quite extraordinary. . . . But I don't know why I am telling you all this. . . ."

She gave the impression that she was coming down to earth, coming down a long way, when she asked:

"And what about you. What do *you* do?"

"Oh, I just potter about, in the business world, you know."

It was suddenly borne in on him what a wretched mess he had made of his life. But she was barely listening. It wasn't that she despised him—that, in its way, would have been something definite, but that for her he simply did not exist. She half rose from her chair and made signs to Larousselle who was still holding forth from his stool. "Just a few more minutes!" he called back. In a low voice she said, "How red he looks—he's drinking too much."

The musicians were packing up their instruments with as much care as though they had been sleeping children. Only the piano seemed incapable of stopping. A single couple was revolving on the floor. The other dancers, their arms still intertwined, had collapsed onto seats. This was the moment of the evening which Raymond Courrèges had so often sipped and savoured, the moment when claws are retracted, when eyes become veiled by a sudden softness, when voices sink to a whisper and hands become insidiously inviting. . . . There had been a time when, at such moments, he had smiled to himself, thinking of what was to come later, of men walking homeward in the early dawn, whistling to themselves and leaving behind, in the secrecy of some anonymous bedroom, a jaded body sprawled across a bed, so still, so spent, that it might have been that of a murdered woman. . . . Not thus would he have left the body of Maria Cross! A whole lifetime would have been all too short to satisfy his ravenous hunger.

So completely indifferent was she to his presence that she did not even notice how he had moved his leg closer to her own, did not even feel the contact. He had no power whatever over her. And yet in those distant years he had been hers for the taking. She had thought she loved him—and he had never known. He had been an inexperienced boy. She should have explained what it was she wanted of him. No whim, however extravagant, would have rebuffed him. He would have proceeded as slowly as she wished. He could, at need, make smooth and easy the voyage of pleasure . . . it would have brought her joy. But now it was too late. Centuries might pass before their ways should cross again in the six-o'clock trolley. . . . He looked up and saw in a mirror the wreckage of his youth, the first sure signs of creeping age. Gone were the days when women might have loved him. Now it was for him to take the initiative, if, indeed, he were still worthy of love.

He laid his hand on hers:

"Do you remember the trolley?"

She shrugged her shoulders, and, without so much as turning her head, had the effrontery to ask:

"What trolley?"

Then, before he could reply, she hurried on:

"I wonder whether you would be so very kind as to bring Monsieur Larousselle over here and get his coat for him from the cloak-room . . . otherwise we shall never make a move."

He seemed not to have heard her. She had asked that question, "What trolley?" quite deliberately. He would have liked to protest that nothing in his whole life had ever meant so much to him as those moments when they had sat facing one another in a crowd of poor work-people with coal-blackened faces and heads drooping with sleep. He could see the scene in imagination—a newspaper slipping to the floor from a hand gone numb; a bare-

headed woman holding up her novelette to catch the light of
the lamps, her lips moving as though in prayer. He could hear
again the great raindrops splashing in the dust of the lane behind
the church at Talence, could watch the passing figure of a workman crouched over the handlebar of his bicycle, a canvas-sack,
with a bottle protruding from it, slung over his shoulder. The
trees behind the railings were stretching out their dusty leaves
like hands begging for water.

"Do, please, go and fetch my husband. He's not used to drinking so much. I ought to have stopped him. Liquor is so bad for
him."

Raymond, who had resumed his seat, got up again and, for the
second time, shuddered at what he saw reflected in the mirror.
He was still young, but what good would that do him? True, he
might still awaken love, but no longer could he choose in whom.
To a man who can still flaunt the passing glories of the body's
spring-time, everything is possible. Had his age been five years
less than it was, he might, he thought, have had a chance. Better
than most he knew what mere youthfulness can achieve with a
woman who has been drained dry, how magically it can overcome
antipathies and preferences, shame and remorse, what pricking
curiosity, what appetites it can wake. But now he was without a
weapon. Looking at himself he felt as a man might who goes into
battle with a broken sword.

"If you won't do what I ask, I suppose I must go myself. They're
making him drink. . . . I don't know how I can manage to get
him away. How disgusting it all is!"

"What would your Bertrand say if he could see you now, sitting
here with me . . . and his father in that state?"

"He would understand everything: he *does* understand everything."

It was at that moment that the noise of a heavy body crashing
to the ground came from the bar. Raymond rushed across the
room and, with the help of the barman, tried to lift Victor Larousselle, whose feet were caught in the overturned stool. His hand,
streaming with blood, still convulsively clutched a broken bottle.
Maria tremblingly threw a coat round the shoulders of Bertrand's
father, and turned up the collar so as to hide his now purple
face. The barman said to Raymond, who was settling the bill,
that one could never be sure it wasn't a heart-attack, and half
carried the great hulking body to a taxi, so terrified was he of
seeing a customer die before he had got clear of the premises.

Maria and Raymond, perched on the bracket-seats, held the drunken creature in a sitting position. A bloodstain was slowly spreading over the handkerchief which they had wrapped round the injured hand. "This has never happened to him before," Maria moaned. "I ought to have remembered that he can't touch anything but wine. Swear you won't breathe a word of this to anyone." Raymond's mood was exultant. In an access of joy he greeted this unexpected turn in his affairs. No, nothing could have parted him from Maria Cross this evening. What a fool he had been to doubt his lucky star!

Although winter was on the wane, the night was cold. A powdering of sleet showed white on the Place de la Concorde under the moon. He continued to hold up on the back seat the vast mass of flesh from which came the sound of hiccups and a confused burble of speech. Maria had opened a bottle of smelling-salts. The young man adored their faint scent of vinegar. He warmed himself at the flame of the beloved body at his side, and took advantage of the brief flicker of each passing street-lamp to take his fill of the face that looked so lovely in its humiliation. At one moment, when she took the old man's heavy and revolting head between her hands, she looked like Judith.

More than anything she dreaded that the porter might be a witness of the scene, and was only too glad of Raymond's offer to help her drag the sick man to the elevator. Scarcely had they got him on to his bed than they saw that his hand was bleeding freely, and that only the whites of his eyes were visible. Maria was worse than useless. She seemed quite incapable of doing the simplest things that would have come naturally to other women. . . . Must she wake the servants, who slept on the seventh floor? . . . What a scandal there would be! She decided to ring up her doctor. But he must have taken off the receiver, for she could get no answer. She burst into sobs. It was then that Raymond, remembering his father's presence in Paris, had the happy idea of ringing him, and suggested to Maria that he should do so. Without so much as a "Thank you", she started to hunt through the directory for the number of the Grand Hotel.

"He'll come as soon as he gets dressed and finds a taxi."

This time Maria did take his hand. She opened a door and switched on the light.

"Would you mind waiting in here: it's Bertrand's room." She

said that the patient had been sick and felt better. But his hand was still giving him a good deal of pain.

As soon as she had left the room Raymond sat down and buttoned his overcoat. The radiator was not giving much heat. His father's sleepy voice was still in his ears. How far away it had sounded. They had not seen one another since old Grandmamma Courrèges had died three years before. At that time Raymond had been in pressing need of money. Perhaps there had been something rude and aggressive in the way he had demanded his share of the inheritance, but what had really got under his skin and precipitated a rupture had been the way in which his father lectured him on the subject of his choice of a profession. The mixture of cadging and pimping by which he had elected to earn a living had horrified the elder man, who regarded such an occupation as being unworthy of a Courrèges. He had gone so far as to try to extract a promise from Raymond that he would find some regular occupation. And now, in a few moments, he would be here, in this apartment. What ought his son to do—kiss him, or merely offer him his hand?

He tried to find an answer to the question, but all the time his attention was being drawn to, was being held by, one particular object in the room—Bertrand Larousselle's bed, a narrow iron bed, so unaccommodating, so demure beneath its flowered cotton coverlet that Raymond could not keep himself from bursting out laughing. It was the bed of an elderly spinster or a seminarist. Three of the walls were quite bare, the fourth was lined with books. The work-table was as neat as a good conscience. If Maria came to my place, she'd get a bit of a shock, he thought. She would see a divan so low that it seemed part of the floor. Every woman who ventured into that discreetly dimmed interior was at once conscious of a dangerous sense of being in some strange new world, of a temptation to indulge in activities which would no more commit her than if they had taken place in a different planet—or in the innocent privacy of sleep. . . . But in the room where Raymond was now waiting, no curtains hid the windows frosted by the winter night. Its owner wished, no doubt, that the light of dawn should wake him before the sounding of the earliest bell. Raymond was entirely insensitive to all the evidences of a life of purity. In this room designed for prayer he could see merely a cunning piece of trickery, a deliberate exploitation of refusal, of denial, designed to increase the de-

lights of love by suppressing all obvious allurements. He looked
at the titles of some of the books. "What an ass!" he murmured.
These volumes that spoke of another world were quite outside his
experience and gave him a feeling of disgust. . . . What a time
his father was taking! He did not want to be alone much longer.
The room seemed to mock at him. He opened the windows and
looked out at the roofs beneath a late moon.

"Here's your father."

He closed the window, followed Maria into Victor Larousselle's
room, saw a figure bending over the bed, and recognized his
father's huge bowler-hat lying on a chair, and the ivory-knobbed
stick (which had been his horse in the days when he had played
at horses). When the doctor raised his head he hardly knew him.
Yet he realized that this old man who smiled and put his arm
about his shoulder was his father.

"No tobacco, no spirits, no coffee. Poultry at lunch and no
butcher's meat at night. Do as I say, and you'll live to be a
hundred. . . . That's all."

The doctor repeated the words "That's all", in the drawling voice
of a man whose thoughts are elsewhere. His eyes never left
Maria's face. She, seeing him standing there motionless, took the
initiative, opened the door, and said:

"I think what we all need is a good night's sleep."

The doctor followed her into the hall. Very shyly he said: "It
was a bit of luck, our meeting like this." All the time he had been
hurriedly dressing, and later, in the taxi, he had been quite convinced that as soon as he had said that Maria would break in
with—"Now I've found you again, doctor, I'm not going to let
you get away so easily." But that wasn't at all the answer she
had made when, from the open door, he had eagerly remarked,
"It was a bit of luck. . . ." Four times he repeated the phrase he
had so carefully prepared, as though by stressing it he could force
from her the hoped-for answer. But no; she just held up his overcoat and did not even show signs of impatience when he failed
to find the sleeve. Quite unemotionally she said:

"It really is a very small world. This evening has brought us
together after many years. It is more than likely that we shall
meet again."

She pretended not to hear him when he said: "But don't you
think it is up to us to put a spoke in fortune's wheel?"

He repeated the same remark more loudly: "Don't you think
we might manage to put a spoke in fortune's wheel?"

If the dead could come back how embarrassing they would be!
They do come back sometimes, treasuring an image of us which
we long to destroy, their minds full of memories which we passionately desire to forget. These drowned bodies that are swept
in by the flooding tide are a constant source of awkwardness to
the living.

"I am very different from the lazy creature whom you once
knew, doctor. I want to get to bed, because I've got to be up by
seven."

She felt irritated by him for saying nothing. She had a sense of
discomfort beneath the brooding stare of this old man who merely
went on repeating: "Don't you think we might put a spoke in
fortune's wheel?"

She replied with a good grace, though rather brusquely, that
he had her address.

"I scarcely ever go to Bordeaux these days; but perhaps you . . ."

It had been so kind of him to take all this trouble.

"If the staircase light goes out, you'll find the switch *there*."

He made no movement, but stayed obstinately where he was.
Did she never, he asked, feel any ill effects from her fall?

Raymond emerged from the shadows: "What fall was that?"

She made a gesture with her head expressive of utter exhaustion.

"What would really give me pleasure, doctor, would be to think
that we could write to one another. I'm not the letter-writer I used
to be . . . but for you . . ."

He replied: "Letters are worse than useless. What's the point of
writing if we are never to see one another?"

"But that's precisely the reason."

"No, no. Do you think that if people knew they were never
going to see one another again they would want to prolong their
friendship artificially by corresponding, especially if one of the
two realized that letter-writing imposed a dreary duty on the
other? . . . One becomes a coward, Maria, as one grows older.
One has had one's life and one dreads fresh disappointments."

He had never put his feelings so clearly into words. Surely she
would understand now!

Her attention had strayed because Larousselle was calling for her,
because it was five o'clock, because she wanted to get rid of the
Courrèges.

"Well, I shall write to you, doctor, and you shall have the dreary duty of replying."

But a little later, when she had locked and bolted the door and gone back to the bedroom, her husband heard her laugh and asked what she was laughing at.

"The most extraordinary thing's just occurred to me . . . promise you won't mock. I really believe that the doctor was a bit in love with me in the old Bordeaux days . . . it wouldn't surprise me."

Victor Larousselle replied thickly through clammy lips that he wasn't jealous if that was what she meant, and followed up the remark with one of his hoariest jokes: "He's just ripe for the cold stone." He added that the poor fellow had obviously had a slight stroke. Many of his old patients, who didn't like to abandon him, secretly consulted other doctors.

"Not feeling sick any longer? Sure your hand doesn't hurt?"

No, he was quite comfortable.

"I only hope that the story of what happened to-night doesn't make the rounds in Bordeaux. . . . Young Courrèges is quite capable . . ."

"He never goes there nowadays. Try to get some sleep. I'm going to put out the light."

She sat in the darkness, motionless, until a sound of quiet snoring rose from the bed. Then she went to her room, passing, on the way, Bertrand's half-open door. She could not resist the temptation to push it wide. Standing on the threshold she sniffed. The mingled smell of tobacco and the human body filled her with a cold fury: I must have been mad to let him come in here! . . . She opened the windows to let in the cold air of dawn, and knelt down for a moment at the head of the bed. Her lips moved. She buried her face in the pillow.

❈ *XII* ❈

THE DOCTOR and Raymond drove away in a taxi. It was like the old days when they had sat together in the carriage with its streaming windows on a suburban road. At first they said no more to one another than they had used to do in that forgotten time. But there was a difference in the quality of their silence. The old man was sagging with weariness and leaned against his son. Raymond held his hand.

"I had no idea that she was married."

"They didn't tell anybody: at least, I believe and hope that they didn't. They certainly didn't tell me."

It was said that young Bertrand had insisted on the situation being regularised. The doctor quoted a remark made by Victor Larousselle: "I am making a morganatic marriage." Raymond muttered: "What dam' cheek!" He stole a glance in the half-light at the tormented face beside him, and saw that the bloodless lips were moving. The frozen expression, the features looking as though they were carved in stone, frightened him. He said the first thing that came into his head.

"How's everybody?"

Flourishing. Madeleine, in particular, said the doctor, was being splendid. She lived for nothing but her two girls, took them out to parties, and hid her sorrow from the world, showing herself worthy of the hero she had lost. (The doctor never neglected an opportunity of praising the son-in-law who had been killed at Guise, striving, in this way, to make honourable amends for the past. He blamed himself for having been wrong about him. So many men in the war had been surprisingly unlike themselves in death.) Catherine, Madeleine's eldest daughter, was engaged to the Michon boy, the youngest of three brothers, but there was to be no public announcement until she was twenty-two:

"You mustn't breathe a word about it."

The voice in which he uttered this injunction was his wife's, and Raymond caught back the words he had been about to say: "Why should anyone in Paris be interested?" The doctor broke off as though suddenly silenced by a stab of pain. The young man began silently to calculate: He must be sixty-nine or seventy. Is it possible to go on suffering at that age, and after all these years? . . . He became suddenly aware of his own hurt, and the consciousness of it frightened him. It wouldn't last . . . very soon it would pass into forgetfulness. He remembered something that one of his mistresses had said: "When I'm in love and going through hell, I just curl up and wait. I know that in a very short while the particular man in question will mean absolutely nothing to me, though at the moment I may be ready to die for him, that I shan't so much as spare a passing glance for the cause of so much suffering. It's terrible to love, and humiliating to stop loving. . . ." All the same, this old man had been bleeding from a mortal wound for seventeen long years. In lives like his, hedged about with routine, dominated by a sense of duty, passion becomes concentrated, is put away, as it were, in cold storage. There is no way of using it up, no breath of warm air can reach it and start the process of evaporation. It grows and grows, stagnates, corrupts, poisons, and corrodes the living flesh that holds it prisoner.

They swung round the Arc de Triomphe. Between the puny trees of the Champs Élysées the black road flowed on like Erebus.

"I think I've done with pottering around. I've been offered a job in a factory. They make chicory. At the end of a year I shall be managing director."

The doctor's reply was perfunctory: "I'm so glad, my boy." Suddenly he shot a question: "How did you first meet?"

"Meet whom?"

"You know perfectly well what I mean."

"The friend who offered me this job?"

"Of course not—Maria."

"It goes back a long way. When I was in my last term at school, we got to exchanging a few words in the trolley. I think that's how it all began."

"You never told me, though once, if I remember correctly, you did mention that some friend had pointed her out to you in the street."

"Perhaps I did . . . one's memory gets a bit hazy after seventeen years. Yes, it all comes back now: it was the day after that meeting that she first spoke to me—actually, it was to ask after you. She knew me by sight. I think that if her husband hadn't come over to me this evening she'd have cut me."

This brief interchange seemed to have set the doctor's mind at rest. He leaned back in his corner. He muttered: "Anyhow, what does it matter to me? What does it matter?" He made the old familiar gesture of sweeping away some obstacle, rubbed his cheeks, sat up and half turned towards Raymond in an effort to escape from his thoughts, to occupy his mind only with his son's concerns.

"As soon as you've got an assured position, my boy, hurry up and get married."

Raymond laughed, protested, and the old man was once more driven in upon himself:

"You can have no idea what a comfort it is to live in the middle of a large family. Yes, I mean it. One's all the time got to think about other people's troubles, and those thousands of little hypodermic pricks keep the blood flowing. Do you see what I mean? One has no time to think of one's own secret miseries, of the wounds that strike deep into the very roots of one's being. One gets to rely on all these family concerns. . . . For instance, I meant to stay in Paris until the end of the Conference, but I've suddenly decided to catch the eight-o'clock train this morning. I just can't help myself. The great thing in life is to make some sort of refuge for oneself. At the end of one's existence, as at the beginning, one's got to be borne by a woman."

Raymond mumbled something about rather seeing himself dead first. He looked at the shrunken, moth-eaten old figure at his side.

"You can have no idea how safe I've always felt with all of you round me. To have a wife, children, about one, pressing in on one, is a sort of protection against all the undesirable distractions of outside life. You never used to say much to me—I don't mean that as a reproach, dear boy—but I don't think you'll ever realize how often, just as I was on the point of yielding to some delicious, maybe criminal, temptation, I would feel your hand on my shoulder gently guiding me back into the right path."

"How ridiculous to think that there are such things as forbidden pleasures," Raymond muttered. "We're completely different, you and I; I'd have overturned the whole apple-cart in next to no time."

"You're not the only one who made your mother suffer. We're not really so different. Scores of times I've sent the apple-cart spinning—in imagination. You don't know. . . . No, you *don't*. A few casual infidelities would have brought me far less sorrow than the long-drawn-out disloyalty of desire of which I have been guilty for the last thirty years. It is essential that you should know all this, Raymond. You'd find it pretty difficult to be a worse husband than I have been. Oh, I know my orgies never went beyond day-dreaming, but does that make it any better? The way your mother takes her revenge now is by being over-attentive. Her fussing has become a necessity of my existence. The endless trouble to which she goes. She never lets me out of her sight day or night. I shall die in the lap of comfort, never fear. We're not looked after now as we used to be. Servants, as she says,

are no longer what they were. We've never replaced Julie—do you
remember Julie? She's gone back to her native village. Your
mother does everything. I have to scold her, often. There's nothing she won't turn her hand to—sweeping out the rooms, polishing the floors."
He stopped, then, with a note of supplication in his voice:
"Don't live alone," he said.
Raymond had no time to reply. The taxi stopped in front of
the Grand Hotel. He had to get out, feel for his money. The
doctor had only just enough time to do his packing.

These early hours of the morning, all given over to street-
sweepers and market-gardeners, were familiar to Raymond Courrèges. He breathed in the dawn air, rejoicing in the well-known
sights, remembering how he always felt as he walked home in
the small hours, physically exhausted, his senses gorged and satisfied, happy as a young animal wanting nothing but to find its
burrow, to curl up and sleep. What a blessing that his father
had decided to say good-bye at the door of the Grand Hotel. How
he had aged! How he had shrunk! There can never be too many
miles for my liking, between me and the family, he thought: The
farther away one's relations, the better. . . . It came over him
that he was no longer thinking about Maria. He remembered that
he had a whole lot of things to do to-day. He took out his engagement book, turned the pages, and was amazed to discover
how vast the day had become—or was it that the things with
which he had proposed to fill it had diminished in number?
The morning?—an empty waste: the afternoon?—two appoint-
ments which he had no intention of keeping. He leaned over
his day like a child over the rim of a well. Only a few pebbles
to drop into it, and they wouldn't fill the yawning void. Only one
thing could do that—going to see Maria, being announced, being
welcomed, sitting in the same room with her, talking to her—it
wouldn't matter about what. Even less than that would have
sufficed to fill these empty hours and many, many more—even
just to have known that he had arranged a meeting with her, no
matter how far ahead it might be. With the patience of a marks-
man, he would have shot down the days separating him from that
longed-for moment. Even if she had put him off, he would have
found comfort somehow—provided she had suggested an alternative date, and the new hope thus started on its way would have

been enough to fill the infinite emptiness of his life. For life now
had become for him nothing but a feeling of absence which he
had got to balance by a feeling of anticipation. "I must think the
whole business out seriously," he told himself, "and begin only
with what is possible. Why shouldn't I get in touch with Bertrand again and worm my way into his life?" But they had no
single taste in common, did not even know the same people.
Anyhow, where was he to find him?—in what sacristy run this
sacristan to earth? In imagination he obliterated all the interven-
ing stages which separated him from Maria, jumped the gap,
and reached the point at which he was holding that mysterious
head in the crook of his right arm. He could feel on his biceps
the touch of her shaven neck, like the cheek of a young boy. Her
face swam towards him, closer, closer, enormously enlarged as
on a movie-screen, and no less intangible. . . . It struck him
with amazement that the early wayfarers he met did not turn to
look at him, did not notice his mania. How well our clothes conceal our real selves! He dropped on to a seat opposite the Madeleine. This seeing her again . . . that was the trouble. He ought
never to have seen her again. All the passions in which he had
indulged for seventeen years had, unknown to him, been lit to protect himself from her—as the peasants of the Landes start small
fires to keep the greater fire from spreading. . . . But he *had*
seen her, and the fire had got the better of him, had been increased by the flames with which he had thought to combat it.
His sensual aberrations, his secret vices, the cold technique of self-
indulgence, so patiently learned, so carefully cultivated, all had
added fuel to the conflagration, so that it roared upward now,
sweeping towards him on a vast front with a sound of crackling
undergrowth.

"Lie low, curl yourself up into a ball," he kept on saying to himself. "It won't last, and until it's over, find some drug with which
to stupefy yourself—float with the current." Yes, but—his father
would know no lessening of *his* pain until the day of his death.
What a dreary life he'd led! But would a course of debauchery
have freed him from his passion?—that was the question. Everything serves as fuel for passion: abstinence sharpens it; repletion
strengthens it; virtue keeps it awake and irritates it. It terrifies and it fascinates. But if we yield, our cowardice is never ab-
ject enough to satisfy its exigence. It is a frantic and a horrible
obsession. He should have asked his father how on earth he had

managed to live with that cancer gnawing at his vitals. . . . Of what use is a virtuous existence? What way of escape can it provide? What power has God over passion?

He concentrated his attention on the minute-hand of the great clock away to his left, trying to catch it in the act of moving. By this time, he thought, his father must already have left the hotel. He suddenly felt that he would like to give the old man one last kiss. There was more than paternity between them, there was another tie of blood. They were related in their common feeling for Maria Cross. . . .

Raymond hastened towards the river, though there was plenty of time before the train was due to leave. Perhaps he was yielding to that species of madness which compels those whose clothes have caught fire to run. He was oppressed by the intolerable conviction that he would never possess Maria Cross, that he would die without ever having her. Though he had had his will of many women, taken them, held them for a while, abandoned them, he felt himself to be in the grip of the same sort of wild despair which sometimes overwhelms men who have never known physical love, men condemned to a life of virginity, when they face the horror of dying without ever having known the delights of the flesh. What he had had in the past no longer counted. Nothing seemed worth the having save what he would never have.

Maria! He was appalled to think how heavily one human being may, without wishing it, weigh in the scales of another's destiny. He had never given a thought to those virtues which, radiating from ourselves, operate, often without our knowing it and often over great distances, on the hearts of others. All the way along the pavement that stretches between the Tuileries and the Seine he found himself, for the first time in his life, compelled to think about things to which, up till then, he had never given a moment's consideration. Probably because on the threshold of this new day he felt emptied of all ambitions, of all plans, of all possible amusements, he found that there was nothing now to keep his mind from the life that lay behind him. Because there was no longer any future to which he might look forward, the past swarmed into his mind. For how many living creatures had not his mere proximity meant death and destruction? Even now he did not know to what lives he had given purpose and direction, what lives he had cut adrift from their moorings; did not know that because of him some woman had killed the young life just

stirring in her womb; that because of him a young girl had died,
a friend had gone into a seminary; and that each of these single
dramas had given birth to others in an endless succession. On the
brink of this appalling emptiness, of this day without Maria,
which was to be but the first of many other days without her, he
was made aware, at one and the same moment, of his dependence
and his solitude. He felt himself forced into the closest possible
communion with a woman with whom he would never make contact. It was enough that her eyes should see the light for Raymond
to live for ever in the darkness. For how long? If he decided that,
at no matter what cost, he must fight his way out of the dense
blackness, must escape from this murderous law of gravity, what
choices were there open to him but the alternatives of stupor
or of sleep?—unless this star in the firmament of his heart should
go suddenly dead, as all love goes dead. He carried within him
a tearing, frantic capability of passion, inherited from his father
—of a passion that was all-powerful, that would breed, until he
died, still other planetary worlds, other Maria Crosses, of which,
in succession, he would become the miserable satellite. . . . There
could be no hope for either of them, for father or for son, unless,
before they died, He should reveal Himself who, unknown to
them, had drawn and summoned from the depths of their beings
this burning, bitter tide.

He crossed the deserted Seine and looked at the station clock.
By this time his father must be in the train. He went down on to
the departure platform and walked along the row of waiting
coaches. He did not have to search for long. Through the glass
of one of the windows he saw the corpse-like face etched on the
darkness of the interor. The eyes were closed, the clasped hands
lay on a spread of newspaper, the head leaned slightly backward,
the mouth was half open. Raymond tapped with his finger. The
corpse opened its eyes, recognized the source of the sound,
smiled, and, with uncertain steps, came out into the corridor. But
all the doctor's happiness was ruined by his childish fear that the
train might start before Raymond had had time to get out.

"Now that I've seen you, now that I know you wanted to see
me again, my mind is at rest. Better go now, dear boy. They're
closing the doors."

It was in vain that the young man assured him that they had
a good five minutes before the train would start, and that, in any
case, it stopped at the Austerlitz station. The other continued to

show signs of nervousness until his son was once more safely on
the platform. Then, lowering the window, he gazed long and lov-
ingly at him.

Raymond asked him whether he had got everything he wanted.
Would he like another paper or a book? Had he reserved a seat
in the restaurant-car? To all these questions the doctor replied,
"Yes, yes." Hungrily he fixed his eyes on the young man who
had asked them; the man who was so different from himself,
and yet so like him—the part of his own flesh and blood that
would survive him for a few more years, but that he was fated
never to see again.

The Knot of Vipers

PART ONE

". . . CONSIDER, O GOD, THAT WE ARE WITHOUT
UNDERSTANDING OF OURSELVES; THAT WE DO NOT
KNOW WHAT WE WOULD HAVE, AND SET OURSELVES
AT AN INFINITE DISTANCE FROM OUR DESIRES. . ."
Saint Theresa of Avila

THE man here depicted was the enemy of his own flesh and blood. His heart was eaten up by hatred and by avarice. Yet, I would have you, in spite of his baseness, feel pity, and be moved by his predicament. All through his dreary life squalid passions stood between him and that radiance which was so close that an occasional ray could still break through to touch and burn him: not only his own passions, but, primarily, those of the lukewarm Christians who spied upon his actions, and whom he himself tormented. Too many of us are similarly at fault, driving the sinner to despair and blinding his eyes to the light of truth.

It was not money that this miser really treasured, nor, in his blind fury, was it vengeance that he sought. What it was that he truly loved you may discover who have the strength of mind, and the courage, to follow his story to the end, to that ultimate moment of confession which death cut short.

❖ I ❖

W HEN YOU FIND this letter lying on top of a bundle of securities in my safe you will be surprised. I might have been better advised to entrust it to my solicitor, with instructions to hand it to you after my death, or to leave it in that locked drawer of my desk which my children will almost certainly force before my body has grown cold. But for years I have written and rewritten it in imagination, and always, in my bouts of sleeplessness, have seen it staring at me from the shelf of a safe empty of everything except this single act of vengeance upon which I have been brooding for almost half a century.

You need not be afraid. As a matter of fact, any cause for fear that you might have had will have been dissipated before you read these lines. "The securities are there all right!" I can hear your raised voice in the hall as you announce the good news on your return from the Bank. "The securities are there all right!" you'll say to the children through the folds of your mourning-veil.

But you've had a very narrow escape! I had taken all the necessary steps. Had I so willed it, you would stand to-day stripped of everything but the house and lands. You can thank your lucky stars that I have outlived my hatred. For years I believed that it was the most vital part of me. But now, quite suddenly, and for the time being, at least, it has ceased to mean anything to me. I find it difficult in my old age to recapture the vindictive mood of earlier years when I would lie in my sick-bed, night after night, not so much planning the method of revenge (the delay-action bomb had already been "set" with an attention to detail which was a matter of considerable pride to me) as wondering how I might derive the maximum of satisfaction from its detonation. I wanted to live just long enough to see your faces when you got back from the Bank. It was merely a matter of not giving you authority to open the safe too soon, of waiting just long enough to enjoy the sound of your despairing question—"but where *are* the securities?" I felt that no death-pangs, however frightful, could spoil that pleasure for me. Of such calculating malice was I capable! And yet, by nature I am not a monster. How came it, then, that I was brought to such a pass?

It is four o'clock, and my luncheon tray is still standing on the table, with flies buzzing round the dirty plates. I have rung, but with no result. Bells never work in the country. I am lying quite patiently in this room where I slept as a child, and where, no doubt, I shall die. When that moment comes, the first thought of our dear daughter Geneviève will be to claim it for her children. It is the largest in the house, and has the best outlook. It has been earmarked entirely for my own use. You will, I hope, do me the justice to admit that I did offer to move out in Geneviève's favour, and would have done so had not Dr Lacaze expressed the opinion that the dampness of the ground-floor might be bad for my bronchitis. I have no doubt that I should have been as good as my word: but I should have harboured such a sense of grievance that the doctor's refusal to countenance the change was, perhaps, fortunate. All through my life I have made sacrifices, and the memory of them has poisoned my mind, nourishing and fattening the kind of rancorous resentment which grows worse with the passage of the years.

The love of quarrelling is, with us, a family trait. I have often heard my mother say that my father quarrelled with his parents, and that they themselves died without ever again setting eyes on the daughter whom they had driven from home thirty years earlier (she married and produced that brood of Marseilles cousins with whom we have never had anything to do). None of us ever knew the rights and wrongs of the squabble, but we took the hatreds of our forebears so wholeheartedly on trust that, if I ran across one of those Marseilles cousins in the street to-day, I should turn my back on him. But, after all, one needn't have anything to do with one's distant relations. It is a very different matter with wives and children. No doubt united families *do* exist: but when I think of the number of households in which two individuals live a life of constant exasperation and mutual loathing, for ever sitting at the same table, using the same washbasin, lying between the same sheets, it is really remarkable how few

divorces there are! They live in a constant state of mutual detesta-
tion, yet can never escape an enforced proximity!

Why should I have felt the itch to scribble on my birthday? I am
entering on my sixty-eighth year, but no one else knows it. There
are always cakes and flowers and little candles for Geneviève
and Hubert and their children when birthdays come round. . . .
If I have never, for years past, given you anything on yours,
that is not because I have overlooked it. No, it is my form of
revenge, and I get a certain satisfaction from it. . . . The last
bunch of birthday flowers that ever came my way was picked by
the crippled fingers of my poor mother. In order to get them, she
had, in spite of her weak heart, paid one last, painful visit to the
rose-garden.
    Where was I? Oh yes, you will doubtless be wondering why
I have been suddenly seized by this mania for writing. "Mania"
is the right word. You can judge of its strength from the way all
the letters lean the same way, like pine-trees under the impact of
a westerly wind. Listen: I began this letter by referring to a
vengeance on which I had long brooded but now renounce. There
is, however, something in you, some part of you, that I long to
overcome—your silence. Don't mistake my meaning. You have a
ready enough tongue, and can talk about poultry and vegetables
for hours on end with Cazau. With the children, even with the
youngest of them, you can jabber, day after day, until I can
scarcely hear myself think. Many's the time I have got up from
the table with my head feeling as empty as a rotten nut, obsessed
by business cares and worries of every kind, which I could not
share with a soul . . . especially after the Villenave case, which
led to my being recognized (to quote the newspapers) as a
"great Criminal Pleader". The more tempted I was to believe in
my own importance, the more determined did you seem to make
me feel my insignificance. . . . But it's not that I am referring to
now. The silence I want to get my own back on is of quite a different kind. It comes of your determined refusal ever to discuss
our own affairs, our own utter failure to understand one another.
Many and many a time, watching a play or reading a novel, I
find myself wondering whether, in actual fact, there ever are
lovers or married couples who have "scenes", who lay all their
cards on the table and find relief in unburdening their hearts.
    For forty years we have suffered side by side. In the whole of

that time you have always managed to avoid saying anything
that went below the surface, have always avoided committing
yourself.

I believed at one time that this attitude of yours was deliberate,
the expression of some fixed determination the reason for which
escaped me. And then, quite suddenly, I realized the truth—
which was that discussions of the kind I longed for just didn't
interest you. So utterly alien was I from all your concerns, that
you shied away, not because you were frightened but because
you were bored. You became an expert at scenting danger, and
could see me coming a mile off. If, sometimes, I managed to
take you by surprise, either you succeeded, without difficulty, in
avoiding the issue, or you patted my cheek, gave me a kiss, and
made for the door.

I might have some reason to fear that, having read thus far,
you will tear this letter up and read no farther. But somehow, I
don't think that is likely to happen. For some time now I have
caught you looking at me with a certain amount of surprise and
curiosity. You may not be very observant where I am concerned,
but even you can hardly fail to have noticed a change in my
mood. I feel pretty well assured that, this time, you will not avoid
the issue. I want you to know, you, and the rest of your brood,
your son, your daughter, your son-in-law and your grandchildren,
what manner of man it is who has lived out his solitary existence
in your midst, and against whom you have closed your ranks; the
overworked lawyer who has had to be handled with tact because
he held the purse-strings, but whose sufferings might have been
those of somebody living on a different planet. What planet? It
has never occurred to you to try to find out. Don't be alarmed. I
am no more concerned here to compose an advance Obituary of
myself than to draw up a Brief for the Prosecution in the case
of Me versus You. The one outstanding quality of my mind—
which would have impressed itself on any other woman—is a
terrifying lucidity.

I have never possessed the power of self-deception which is
most men's stand-by in the struggle for existence. When I have
acted basely, I have always known precisely what I was doing. . . .

At this point I had to break off . . . no one brought me a lamp,
or came to close the shutters. . . . I sat here looking out at the

roof of the bottling-shed, the tiles of which are as vivid in colour as flowers or the breasts of birds. I could hear the thrushes in the ivy on the Carolina poplar, and the noise made by somebody rolling a cask. I am fortunate in being able to wait for death in the one spot of all the world where everything is as I remember it, the sole difference being that the stutter of a motor-engine has replaced the creaking of the old bucket-and-chain well worked by a donkey. (And of course, there's the loathsome mail-plane which announces tea-time, and leaves its horrible smear across the sky.)

Few men are lucky enough to be able to find again in their actual physical surroundings, and within their range of vision, the world which most discover only if they have the courage and the patience to search their memories. . . . I lay my hand on my chest and feel the beating of my heart. I look at the glass-fronted medicine-cupboard containing the hypodermic syringe, the little bottle of nitrite of amyl, and such other odds and ends as might be needed should I have one of my attacks. Would anybody hear me if I called? You're all so insistent that it's only a *false angina*, not so much because you want to convince *me*, but because you'd like to believe it yourselves, and so feel justified in sleeping soundly at night. I am breathing more easily now. It is exactly as though a hand were gripping my left shoulder and keeping it rigid in a strained position, so that I may never be allowed to forget, for a moment, what's lying in wait for me. In my case, death certainly won't come by stealth. It has been snuffing round me for years. I can hear it and feel its breath. It treats me with patience because I make no effort to resist, because I submit to the discipline which its approach imposes. I am ending my life in a dressing-gown, surrounded by all the paraphernalia of incurable disease, sunk in the great winged chair where my mother sat waiting for her end. There is a table beside me, as there was beside her, laden with medicine-bottles. I am ill-shaven and evil-smelling, a slave to all sorts of disgusting little habits. But don't be too sure. In the intervals between attacks I am my old self. Bourru, the solicitor, who thought me as good as gone, has got used to seeing me turn up as hale and hearty as ever, and I can still spend hours in the safe-deposit vault, snipping off dividend coupons unaided.

I must manage to live long enough to complete this confession, to *make* you listen. During all the years in which I shared your

bed, you never failed, each time I got in beside you, to say—
"I'm simply *dropping*, I'm half-asleep already. . . ."

It was less my endearments than my words that you were
trying to avoid.

True, our unhappiness began with the sort of interminable
discussions which are the delight of young married couples. We
were little more than children. I was twenty-three, you eighteen,
and perhaps love was less of a pleasure to us than the confidences, the talks, in which we gave free play to all our thoughts.
Like young children in their earliest friendships, we had sworn to
tell one another everything. So little had I to confess, that I was
driven to elaborate and embellish such squalid little adventures
as had come my way, nor did it ever occur to me that your
experience had been any fuller than my own. I never dreamed
that, before I came into your life, you might have murmured
another man's name to yourself, and in this belief I continued,
until . . .

It was in this very room where I sit writing now. The wallpaper has been changed, but the mahogany furniture still stands
precisely where it did then. There was then, as now, a tumbler
of iridescent glass upon the table, along with a tea-set which had
been won in a raffle. Moonlight flooded the matting, and the south
wind, blowing across the Landes, brought the smell of heath-fires
to our very bedside.

That night you spoke once more of Rodolphe—the old friend
whom you had often mentioned, and always in the dusk of our
room, as though you wanted to make sure that his ghost should
be between us in the moments of our closest union. Have you
forgotten? It was not enough for you now merely to mention his
name.

"There are things, darling, I ought to have told you before we
got engaged. I feel rather guilty about having kept them back—not
that there was ever anything the least bit serious—so please don't
start worrying. . . ."

I was quite easy in my mind, and did nothing to provoke a
confession. But you forced it on me. So eager were you to tell me
the whole story that, at first, I felt rather embarrassed. It wasn't
that you wanted to ease your conscience: it wasn't that you felt
you owed it me to make a clean breast of this particular chapter
in your past—though that was the reason you gave, and that was
what I think you really believed.

No, the truth of the matter was that you were revelling in a delicious memory. You could no longer resist the sweet temptation. Perhaps you suspected that the incident might constitute a possible threat to our happiness. However that may be, the whole thing was, as they say, beyond your power to control. The shadow of this Rodolphe hung over our marriage bed, and there was nothing you could do about it.

But I don't want you to run away with the idea that our unhappiness started in jealousy. Later, it is true, I was to become furiously jealous, but I certainly felt nothing remotely resembling that passion on the summer night of '85 which I am now recalling, the night on which you confessed that, while on holiday at Aix, you had become engaged to this unknown young man.

How odd to think that I should have had to wait forty-five years before explaining what I felt about it all! I am not even sure that you will read this letter. The whole thing is of so little interest to you. *My* concerns are, to you, sheer boredom. Very early on, the children began to come between us, so that you neither saw nor heard me, and now there are the grandchildren. . . . Well, it can't be helped. I am going to make this one last effort. It may be that I shall exert greater power over you when I am dead than I ever did while living . . . anyhow, at first. For a few weeks I shall once again occupy a place in your life. If only as a matter of duty you will read these pages to the end. That I *must* believe. I do.

❀ *II* ❀

As I have said, at the time of your confession I felt no jealousy. How am I to make you understand what it was that it destroyed in me?

I was the only child of the woman whom you knew as a widow, or, rather, in whose society you lived for many long years without ever really knowing her at all. But even if you had been sufficiently interested to try to discover the precise nature of the bond uniting that particular mother and that particular son, I doubt whether you would have succeeded in doing so. *You* were one of the many component cells of a powerful and numerous middle-class family, one element in a hierarchy, one cog in a highly organized machine. You could not begin to grasp the extent to which the widow of a minor official at the Prefecture could be wrapped up in a son when he was all that she had left to her. She took pride in my school successes, and in them I, too, found all my happiness. At that time I was fully convinced that we were very poor. The evidence was all around me, in the narrow pattern of our lives, in the strict economy which my mother made the law of our being. Not that I was allowed to want for anything. I realize to-day how spoiled I was as a child. My mother's farms, at Hosteins, furnished us with a quantity of inexpensive food, and I should have been much surprised had I been told that it was of exceptional quality. Corn-fed chickens, hares, goose-paté, were not my idea of luxury. I had always heard it said that our land was of no great value, and, indeed, when my mother came into her inheritance it had consisted only of stretches of grassland on which my grandfather, as a child, had herded cattle. What I did not know was that my parents' first care had been to make it productive, and that at twenty-one I should find myself the owner of two thousand hectares of mature timber already yielding a great number of pit-props. My mother managed, also, to save some part of her modest income. Even during my father's lifetime, the two of them had "bled themselves white" so as to be able to buy Calèse (forty thousand francs they paid for those vineyards which now I wouldn't part with for a million!). We lived in the Rue Sainte-Catherine, on the third floor of a house belonging to us (it had, together with a number of vacant lots, formed my father's inheritance). Twice each week we received a hamper from the country. My mother went as seldom as possible to the butcher. The only ambition I had at that time was to enter the École Normale. There was a battle royal on Thursdays and Sundays before I could be induced to take a little exercise in the fresh air. I was not in the least like those boys who are always head of the class without any apparent effort. I was a "swot", and proud of it: just a common or garden plodder. I cannot remember ever having taken the least pleasure, while at school, in studying Virgil or Racine. They were "set books" for me, and nothing more. I segregated from among the achievements of the human spirit such subjects as formed part of the curriculum—no others seemed to me to have the slightest importance—and wrote just the sort of essays that one had to write in order to satisfy the examiners: in other words, precisely what had already been written by generations of candidates. That was the kind of little idiot I was, and probably would have continued to be, but for an attack of blood-spitting which terrified my mother and, two months before the École Normale entrance examination, compelled me to abandon all hope of my chosen career.

That was the price I had to pay for an overworked childhood and an unhealthy adolescence. A growing youth cannot, with impunity, sit crouched over a table far into the night, and despise all forms of physical exercise. Am I boring you? I am terrified of boring you. You mustn't skip a line. You must take my word for it that I am confining myself strictly to the essentials of my story. The drama of our two lives, yours and mine, was conditioned by things which happened to me as a young man, things you never knew or, having known, promptly forgot.

At any rate, these first few pages will have shown you that I have no intention of letting myself off easily—and that must be not a little satisfying to your hatred. . . . Please don't protest. . . . If you have begun to think about me now, it is solely in the hope of finding nourishment for your hostility.

I don't want to be unjust in my attitude to the undersized and sickly creature whom I left, just now, poring over his lexicons. When I read other men's recollections of childhood, and take notice of the paradise which seems to fascinate their backward gaze, I cannot help feeling a sharp spasm of pain. "How about myself?" I ask; "why this sense of a waste-land ever since my earliest years? Maybe I have forgotten what these others remember: maybe I, too, trailed clouds of glory. . . ." But, alas, I can recall nothing but desperate struggles, nothing but the embittered rivalry in which I was involved with one chap called Hennoch and another called Rodrigue. I instinctively repulsed all friendly advances. There were some, I remember, on whom the prestige of my successes exerted a species of attraction, so that they were fascinated by my very churlishness. I did not suffer affection gladly: I had a horror of "sentiment".

Were I a professional writer, I could not compose a single "touching" passage from the record of my school years. . . . But wait, I *do* recollect one incident, trivial though it may appear. I recalled very little about my father, but there were moments at which I felt convinced that he was not really dead at all, but only that, as the result of a combination of circumstances, he had

somehow vanished. On such occasions I would run all the way
along the Rue Sainte-Catherine on my way home from school,
keeping to the middle of the road, and dodging the traffic, because I was afraid that the crowded pavement would slow me
down. I would take the stairs four at a time—only to find my
mother darning by the window, and the photograph of my father
hanging in its usual place to the right of my bed. Then, scarcely
responding to my mother's kiss, I would settle down to my books.

After the blood-spitting incident which changed the whole pattern of my future, I spent several melancholy months in a cottage
at Arcachon. The ruin of my health had put a full-stop to any hope
of a university career. My poor mother got on my nerves. She
seemed to take no account of my changed circumstances, and to
be wholly unconcerned about what was to happen to me. Each
day, she lived for "thermometer-time". All her sorrow, all her joy,
seemed to hang upon the record of my weekly weighings. When,
later, it was my fate to lead the life of an invalid, without anybody
showing the least interest in the state of my health, I realized
that I was suffering the just punishment for my hardness of
heart, for the unyielding resentment of the spoiled child which I
had shown in those earlier years.

With the first of the fine weather I began, as my mother put it,
to "look up". Indeed, I was like somebody reborn. I broadened
out and grew stronger. My body had suffered cruelly from the
discipline I had imposed upon it, but now, in the dry air of the
forest, with its furze and arbutus, which surrounded Arcachon
in the days when it was no more than a village, it began to put
forth new blossoms of health.

About this time I learned from my mother that there was no
need for me to worry about the future; that we were the possessors of a handsome fortune which was increasing year by year.
I could well afford to wait, since, almost certainly, I should be
released from military service. All my masters had been struck
by my unusual fluency in speaking. My mother was anxious for
me to read law, and seemed convinced that, without fatiguing
myself unduly, I could easily become a success at the bar, unless,
of course, I felt attracted to politics. . . . On and on she talked,
pouring out all her plans for me, and I sat there listening, in a
mood of sulky hostility, staring out of the window.

I began to run after women. Noticing this new development,
my mother adopted an attitude of frightened tolerance. In later

years, as a result of living in close contact with your relations, I have learned how seriously sexual irregularities are regarded in religious families. The only thing that worried my mother was the possible ill effect of such indulgences on my health. Once she was assured that I was being reasonably careful she shut her eyes to my nocturnal outings, though always stipulating that I should be home by midnight. Don't be afraid that I am going into the details of my amorous adventures. I know how all that side of life disgusts you, and, anyhow, they were too trivial and too squalid to deserve recording.

But this I will say, that even in those early days I paid a high price for them. I suffered from the fact that I was deficient in charm, that my youthfulness paid such poor dividends. It was not, I think, that I was ill-looking. My features were "regular", and Geneviève, who is the living image of me, was very pretty as a girl. No, my trouble was that I am one of those who, in popular parlance, have never known what it is to be young. There had been an over-plus of gloom, a lack of freshness, about my early years. The very look of me was enough to produce in others a sense of chill, and the more I realized this, the less accommodating did I become. I have never learned how to wear my clothes, how to choose a tie, or tie it when chosen. I have never in all my life known what it is to be unself-conscious, or to laugh or play the fool. I cannot imagine myself forming one of a party on the "spree". I am by nature one of Nature's wet blankets. At the same time, I am cursed with an excess of sensitiveness, and I was never able to stand being laughed at, no matter how good-humoured the laughter might be. On the other hand, whenever I made a joke at other people's expense, I always, without meaning to, struck so savagely that my victims never forgave me. I invariably chose to make fun of the one thing, some physical infirmity, for instance, about which I ought to have kept silent. Because of my shyness, and because of my pride, I adopted to women that superior attitude of the hectoring schoolmaster which, of all things, they most resent. I never noticed what they were wearing. The more conscious I was of their dislike, the more intolerable did I become. My youth was a prolonged condition of suicide. I was deliberately uncouth simply because I was afraid of being unconsciously so.

Rightly or wrongly I blamed my mother for this temperament of mine. I had got the idea that I was paying for the fact that,

ever since my childhood, I had been cosseted, supervised and
looked after far too much. I was abominably brutal to her at this
time. She doted on me, as I have said, to a ridiculous extent. I
could not forgive her for lavishing on me the affection which I
was fated to have from nobody else. You must forgive me for
harping on this subject. Only the thought of what she gave makes
it possible for me to endure that failure to give which has always
marked your attitude to me. It is right and proper that I should
pay the price of my misdeeds. She has been dead now, poor
woman, for many years, and the memory of her lives only in
the heart of an old and worn-out man. How terribly she would
have suffered could she have foreseen how the future was to
avenge her!

Yes, I was a brute. In the little dining-room at the cottage,
under the hanging lamp at meal-times, I would answer her timid
questions with the barest monosyllables, or would fly into sullen
rages on the slightest excuse, and often on no excuse at all.

She made no attempt to understand, never tried to discover
the reasons for my outbursts of temper, but submitted to them as
to the whim of some angry God. It was because I had been ill, she
said: I must learn to relax. And then she would go on to explain
that she was too ignorant ever to hope to be able to understand
me. "I realize that an old woman is no fit companion for a boy of
your age. . . ." In the past she had been careful, not to say
miserly, about money, but now she gave me far more than I
asked for, encouraged me to spend lavishly, and used to bring me
back from Bordeaux the most ridiculous ties which I obstinately
refused to wear.

We made friends with some neighbours, to whose daughter I
proceeded to lay siege—though I did not care two pins about
her. She had been ill, and was spending a winter of convalescence
at Arcachon. My mother was terribly worried. She was afraid I
might catch something from her, or compromise her by my attentions and be jockeyed into an engagement. I realize now that I
went on with my courtship (which, as it happened, was entirely
without effect) simply and solely with the intention of hurting
her.

We returned to Bordeaux after a year's absence. We had
moved. My mother had bought a house on one of the boulevards,
but had said nothing to me about it, because she wanted to

spring it upon me as a surprise. I was staggered when the front-door was opened by a man-servant. The whole of the first floor was reserved for my especial use. Everything looked brand new. I was secretly dazzled by a luxury which, looking back, I now see must have been pretty awful. But I kept my pleasure to myself, and, such was my cruelty, spoke to her only in disparagement of her efforts, and nagged at her about the expense.

It was then that she gave me a triumphant account of her stewardship—though there was absolutely no need for her to do so, since most of the money came from her side of the family. An income of fifty thousand francs, to say nothing of what the timber brought in, constituted at that time, and especially in the provinces, a very "tidy" fortune. Any other young man would have used it to make a career for himself, and to buy his right of entry into the highest ranks of local society. In my case, it was not ambition that was lacking, but the dislike which I felt for my companions in Law School and concealed with difficulty.

Most of them were the sons of leading families in the city, and had been educated by the Jesuits. As a mere Secondary-School product, and the grandson of a shepherd, I could not forgive them for the hateful sense of envy which their manners roused in me, though I regarded them as my intellectual inferiors. Envy of those whom one despises is a degrading passion and may well poison a whole life.

But I did envy them, and I did despise them, while their contempt of me (probably the product of my imagination) served to exacerbate my resentment. To a youth of my temperament it never even occurred to try to win their friendship. In fact, I did all I could to make common cause with their adversaries. That hatred of religion which, for so long, has been my dominant passion, which has caused you so much suffering and has set a wall of enmity between us, started in Law School, in 1879 and 1880, when Article 7 was voted by the Chamber. It was the year which saw the famous Decrees and the expulsion of the Jesuits.

Until that time I had been indifferent to such matters. My mother never talked to me about religion, except to say—"I am quite easy in my mind: if people like ourselves are not saved, then nobody will be." She had me baptized. My first Communion, which I took while at school, left on me the impression merely of a boring formality, and my memory of it is extremely vague. In any case it was unique. I never took Communion again. My ignorance in all matters touching religion was profound. When, as a child, I used to pass priests in the street, I always thought of them as of people wearing a disguise, as a species of maskers. I never grappled with problems of faith, and when, later, I came up against them, I approached them only from the political angle.

I founded a study-circle which used to meet at the Café Voltaire. Its value to me was that of a training-ground in public speaking. The boy who was so shy in his personal dealings with others became a totally different person in open debate. I had a number of followers, and thoroughly enjoyed the feeling that I was their leader, but this did not prevent me from despising them, just as I despised the middle-class youths among my fellow students. I resented the simple-minded way in which they exhibited their petty motives, because it forced me to realize that my own motives were precisely similar. They were the sons of minor Civil Servants, former scholarship boys, intelligent, ambitious, but embittered. There was no affection in the flattery they offered me. I asked them to dinner once or twice, and those evenings were for them red-letter occasions, much talked about. But their manners disgusted me, and a time came when I could no longer resist the temptation to make fun of them. They were mortally offended, and never forgot.

Nevertheless, my hatred of religion, and of all that had to do with it, was perfectly sincere. My social conscience was beginning to give me trouble. I made my mother pull down the wattle-and-daub cottages in which our farm-hands lived on an insufficient diet of thin wine and black bread. For the first time in her life she tried to stand up to me: "You'll get no thanks for it. . . ."

I did not press the point. I knew only too well that my adversaries and I had the same ruling passion—land and money—and I hated having to admit it. There are, in all societies, the "haves" and the "have-nots", and I realized that I should always belong to the "haves". My fortune was as large as, if not larger than, that of the solemn asses who, I thought, averted their eyes when they saw me, but would be only too glad to take my hand if I should offer it. There was no lack of those, both of the Right and of the Left, who were delighted at a chance of throwing my two thousand hectares of timber and vineyard in my teeth on the public platform.

You must forgive me for dwelling on this subject. It is essential that you should have a thorough grasp of these details if you are to understand what our meeting meant to the sort of disgruntled creature I had become, and what wonderful hopes I built on our mutual love. That I, the son of peasants, whose mother had gone about with her head tied up in a handkerchief, should actually marry into the Fondaudège family, was something at which the imagination boggled. It was beyond my power to conceive.

✿ *III* ✿

I BROKE off in my writing because the light was getting bad, and because I could hear voices below. Not that any of you were making much noise. Far from it, you were being particularly careful to keep your voices down, and that was what worried me. Formerly, I could always overhear your conversations from this room, but now you have grown suspicious, and have taken to whispering. You told me the other day that I was getting "hard of hearing", but that is not true. I can catch the sound of trains rumbling over the viaduct perfectly well. No, I certainly am not deaf. The truth of the matter is that you are all of you talking in low voices. You want to make quite certain that I shall not know what you are talking about. What is it that you want to keep from me? Business worries? There they all are, hanging round you, on the look-out for what they can pick up—our son-in-law in the rum trade, and our grandson-in-law who does nothing, and our son, Hubert, the stockbroker . . . the chap who pays 20 per cent and has everybody's money to play with!

Don't rely on me: I'm not shelling out! "It would be so easy" —you'll murmur to me to-night—"to fell some of the pines." You will remind me that Hubert's two girls have been living with their parents-in-law since their marriage, because they can't afford to furnish homes of their own. "We've got masses of stuff just rotting away in the loft: it wouldn't cost us anything to lend them some of it. . . ." That's the suggestion you'll be making to me in an hour or so. "They resent our attitude. They never come to see us. I'm being cheated out of my own grandchildren. . . ." That's what you've all been whispering about so busily.

I've been reading over the stuff I wrote yesterday evening. I must have been suffering from a sort of delirium. How could I so let my feelings get the better of me? I started this as a letter, but it's a letter no longer. It has become a diary, now and then broken off, now and then resumed. . . . Shall I tear it up and begin all over again? No, I can't do that: time is pressing. What I have written I have written. After all, didn't I want to make a clean breast to you of everything?—didn't I want to force you to look into the bottom of my mind? For thirty years I have been nothing to you but a machine for dealing out thousand-franc notes, a machine that has been running badly, a machine that you've got to patch up until the happy day when you'll be able to break it open, empty it, and plunge your hands into the treasure it contains.

There, I'm letting my temper run away with me again. I'm back at the point where I left off. I must trace this evil mood of mine to its source, must recall that fatal night. . . . But first of all, I would have you cast your mind back to the occasion of our first meeting.

In August, 1883, I was staying with my mother at Luchon. At that time the Hotel Sacarron was crammed with heavily uphol-stered furniture, cushions, and stuffed chamoix. After all these years it is the limes of the Allées d'Ettigny that I smell when the season comes round for the limes to flower. The patter of mules, the tinkling of bells, the crack of whips, used to wake me in the mornings. The water of the mountain torrents gurgled in the streets. The air was full of voices calling *croissants* and milk loaves. Guides rode by on horseback. I used to watch the parties of climbers setting out.

The whole of the first floor was occupied by the Fondaudège family. They had King Leopold's suite. "They must be making the money fly!" said my mother. But that didn't prevent them from being always in arrears when it came to settling their busi-ness debts (they had taken a lease of a big plot of land which we owned in the docks, for purposes connected with their shipping interests).

My mother and I always dined at the *table d'hôte*, but you and your family had meals served to you separately. I can still remember that round table in the window, and your fat grand-mother who concealed her baldness under an arrangement of black lace with quivering jet ornaments. I felt convinced that she was smiling at me, but it was the way her tiny eyes were set in her face, and her great slit of a mouth, which produced that impression. A nun waited on her, a woman with a puffy, bilious face swathed in starched linen. How beautiful your mother was! She wore nothing but black, being in perpetual mourning for the two children she had lost. It was she, not you, who was the first object of my furtive admiration. The nakedness of her throat, her arms and her hands, set my heart beating. She wore no jewellery. I played with the idea of stalking her à la Stendhal, and gave myself until the evening to murmur a word to her, or to slip a note into her hand. You I scarcely noticed. I had an idea that young girls did not interest me. Besides, you had that particular arrogance which takes the form of never looking at other people, and is tantamount to denying their existence.

One day, on my way back from the Casino, I came on my mother in conversation with Madame Fondaudège. The latter's manner was obsequious, and just a little too friendly. She gave me the impression of somebody who knows that it is useless to try to lower herself to the level of her companion. Mother, on the other hand, was speaking in a loud voice. She was dealing with a tenant, and, in her eyes, a Fondaudège was no more than a debtor in arrears. A countrywoman by nature, and an owner of land, she had a profound distrust of big business and of the kind of fortunes it produced, none of them built on a foundation of solid property. I broke in on the discussion just as she was saying: "Of course I have complete confidence in Monsieur Fondaudège's signature: all the same——"

For the first time in my life I intervened in a business argument. Madame Fondaudège got the extension she wanted. I have often thought, since then, that my mother's peasant shrewdness did not mislead her. Your family has cost me a pretty penny, and if I had just sat back and let myself be sucked dry, your son, your daughter and your grandson-in-law would very soon have made ducks and drakes of my fortune and swallowed it up in their business speculations. Business indeed!—what has it ever amounted to?—a ground-floor office, a telephone and a typist! . . . Behind that setting the money has been drained away by the bucketful. . . . But I anticipate: we are still in 1883 at Bagnères-de-Luchon.

That powerful family of yours was now all smiles. Your grandmother went on talking the whole time because she was deaf. No sooner did I have an opportunity of chatting with your mother after dinner than I found that she bored me and completely upset all my preconceived romantic ideas. You will, I am sure, forgive me if I point out that her conversation was tedious in the extreme. So limited was the world in which she lived, and so jejune was her vocabulary that, after the first few minutes, I had had enough and was at my wits' end to keep the talk going at all. My attention, thus diverted from the mother, became fixed upon the daughter. I failed, at first, to notice the suspicious absence of all obstacles to our intimacy. But then, why should it have occurred to me that your family might be congratulating themselves on having made a good "catch"? I remember one drive, in particular, up the Valley of the Lys. Your grandmother and her nun were in the back of the victoria: you and I occupied the little let-down seats facing them. God knows there were carriages and to spare in Luchon! Only the Fondaudèges would have dreamed of bringing their own!

The horses proceeded at a walking pace, moving in a cloud of flies. The good sister's face was shiny, and her eyes half shut. Your grandmother sat flapping a fan which she had bought in the Allées d'Ettigny. It was decorated with a picture of a matador giving the *coup de grâce* to a black bull. You had long gloves, in spite of the heat. Everything you wore was white, down to your high-laced boots. Ever since the death of your two brothers, you said, you had had "a devotion to white". I did not know what "having a devotion to white" meant. I have learned since what a point your family made of these rather exotic "devotions". In my then state of mind I thought it all rather poetical. How can I possibly make you understand the emotion that you roused in me? I had become suddenly aware that I was no longer unpleasing, had ceased to repel, was not odious any more. One of the most important moments of my life was when you said: "How extraordinary that a man should have such long lashes!"

I was careful to keep my advanced ideas dark. I remember how, in the course of that drive, we got out in order to lighten the carriage on a hill, how your grandmother and her nun told their beads, and how the old coachman, long trained in the way he should go, made his responses to their *Ave Marias*. You looked at me with a smile, but I remained solemn. It cost me nothing to accompany you to eleven o'clock Mass on Sundays. There was, for me, no metaphysical idea attached to the ceremony. It was merely the religious exercise of a class in which I was proud to find myself numbered, a species of ancestor-worship adapted to the use of the bourgeoisie, a hotch-potch of rites with nothing but a social significance. Occasionally you would give me a sidelong glance, and the memory of those Masses remains associated in my mind with the staggering discovery which I made at that time, that I was capable of arousing interest, pleasure, and emotion in another. The love which I felt was all mixed up with the love which I inspired—or thought I inspired. There was nothing real about my own feelings. What counted for me was my belief in the love which *you* felt. I caught my reflexion in the mirror of somebody else's personality, and in the image thus presented there was nothing repulsive. In that blissful state of relaxation I blossomed and flowered. I remember how I thawed in the warmth of your gaze, how emotion gushed from the opened freshets of my being. The most ordinary expressions of affection —the pressure of a hand, a flower laid between the pages of a book—were wholly new to me, and I succumbed to their enchantment.

The only person who did not benefit from this change in me was my mother. I felt that she was hostile to the dream (the lunatic dream, I thought) which was forming in my mind. I resented the fact that she was not dazzled. "Can't you see," she kept on saying, "that these people are trying to land you?" It never occurred to her that by talking like that she might well destroy the immense happiness I was feeling just because, for the first time, I believed that I had found favour in a young woman's eyes. There was at least one woman in the world, I told myself, who found me attractive, who might actually entertain the idea of marrying me. For that was what I believed, in spite of my mother's scepticism. You were too great and powerful as a family (so ran my silent argument) to find any advantage in a marriage with such as me. Nevertheless, I regarded my mother almost with hatred for throwing even a shadow of doubt on the reality of my bliss.

She went her own way, and set about finding out what she could. The sources of her intelligence were the leading Banks. It was a great day for me when she had to admit that the House of Fondaudège, in spite of occasional difficulties, still enjoyed a high reputation. "Their profits are fantastic, but they are living at too high a rate," she said. "Everything goes on horses and liveried servants. They are more intent on cutting a dash than on putting money by."

This verdict of the Banks set the seal upon my happiness. The disinterestedness of your family was proved. Your people were smiling on my suit because they liked me. It seemed to me, suddenly, the most natural thing in the world that I should be generally liked. I was allowed to walk alone with you, of an evening, in the Casino gardens. How strange it is that when life is just beginning for us, and when a little happiness comes our way, no warning voice is heard. "However long your life, you will never know any bliss comparable to these few hours. Drink them to the dregs, because Fate holds nothing more in store for you. This first gushing of cool water is also the last. Quench your thirst once and for all, for you will never again have an opportunity to drink." If only someone had said that!

For I was convinced, on the contrary, that a long life of passionate happiness was opening out before me. I set too little store on the evenings which we spent together, motionless, under the sleeping trees.

Signs there were, however, though I failed to interpret them aright. Do you remember one night in particular, when we were sitting on a bench by the winding path that climbs the hill behind the Hot Baths? All of a sudden you started to sob. The fragrance of your wet cheeks comes back to me still, as of an unknown sorrow. I thought your tears were those of happy love. I was too young to know the meaning of that choking misery. True, you hid it from me. "It's nothing," you said: "it's just being here with you."

You were not lying to me, liar though you are. It was, indeed, because I was with you that you cried, with me; and not with someone else, with that other whose name, at long last, you told me in this very room where I sit writing now, an old man near his death, surrounded by a battery of eager eyes strained for the coming kill.

There, on that bench by the winding path at Superbagnères, we sat. My face was pressed against your neck, your shoulder, and in my nostrils was the scent of a very young girl in tears. It was mingled with the scent of wet leaves and of mint in the warm, moist Pyrenean night. The branches of the lime-trees round the bandstand on the Place des Thermes below us caught the glint of lamps. An old Englishman from the hotel was catching the moths that fluttered round them in a long-handled net. "Lend me your handkerchief," you said. I wiped away your tears, and treasured the handkerchief against my heart.

I need say no more than that I had become a different person.
There was a radiance in my face—I knew it from the way the
women looked at me. Those evening tears brought no suspicion
in their train.

Besides, for one night such as that there were many when you
were all happiness, when you leaned on me and clung to my arm.
I walked too quickly for you, and your efforts to keep up with me
made you out of breath.

I was, as a lover, very self-controlled. You appealed to some
part of me that was untouched, unspoiled. Never once was I
tempted to abuse the confidence which your parents placed in me.
I did not so much as dream that their attitude might be the
result of cold calculation.

I was a changed being, so completely changed that one day—
it's only now, after forty years, that I can pluck up sufficient
courage to make this confession. It won't, I think, when you read
this letter, give you much cause to feel triumphant. Here it is.
One day, when we were driving through the Lys Valley, we got
out of the victoria. The streams were gurgling. I was rubbing a
leaf of fennel between my fingers. The lower slopes of the mountains were growing dark, but the light was still secure upon their
peaks. . . . An intense feeling suddenly came over me, an almost
physical certainty that another world *did* exist, a reality of which
we know only the shadow.

That feeling lasted for a moment only. In the course of a long
and miserable life I have had comparable experiences, but only
at wide intervals. The very strangeness of what happened to me
then gave it an enhanced value in my eyes. That is why, in our
terrible religious squabbles of a later date, I had to keep the
memory of it from my mind. I owe it to you to make this admission. But the time has not yet come for me to embark upon that
subject.

There is no point in my recalling our engagement. The whole
thing was settled one evening. It happened without my meaning
it to. I rather think that you interpreted something I said in a
sense different from the one I intended. I found myself bound to
you, and was too staggered to protest. What is the use of going
over all that old ground again? There was, however, one horrible
incident which I still cannot get out of my mind.

There and then, on the spot, you made a condition. In what
you called the "interests of harmony" you flatly refused to con-

sider the idea of my mother living with us, or even of having her
under the same roof. You and your parents had quite made up
your minds. You wouldn't even discuss the matter.

How vividly, after all these years, I remember that stifling
hotel room with its open window giving on to the Allées d'Ettigny!
Through the lowered venetian blind a golden powdering of dust
drifted in on us. In our ears was the cracking of whips, the sound
of a Tyrolean tune. My mother had a headache and was lying on
the sofa, dressed in a skirt and a petticoat-bodice (she had never
in her life possessed a dressing-gown, a peignoir or a wrap). She
would, she said, give up the ground-floor suite to us and make do
with one room on the third floor. I snatched at this opportunity,
and took the plunge.

"Isa thinks that it would be very much better . . ."—and all
the time I was talking I kept glancing furtively at her old face,
and looking away again. She was crumpling the trimming of her
bodice between her gnarled fingers. If only she had put up a
fight I could have dealt with the situation, but her silence made
anger impossible.

She pretended not to be hurt, or even surprised. When at last
she did speak she chose her words carefully, so as to lead me to
suppose that she had always known our separation to be inevitable.

"I shall spend most of the year at Aurigne," she said: "it's in
better condition than the other farms, and you can have Calèse.
I'll have a little garden-room run up at Aurigne. Three rooms
will be quite enough for me. It won't cost much, but it's a nuisance, all the same, to incur even a small expense when I may
be dead by next year. But you'll find it will come in useful, later,
for the duck-shooting. It'll be pleasant living there in October. I
know you don't care much about shooting, but you may have
children who will."

No ingratitude of mine could ever exhaust the treasures of
her love. Driven from one position, it re-formed its ranks elsewhere. It took what I left, and made do. But that same evening
you said:

"Is there anything wrong with your mother?"

Next day she looked just as usual. Your father arrived from
Bordeaux with his eldest daughter and his son-in-law. Somebody
must have told them what was going on. They looked me up
and down. I could almost hear them comparing notes: "D'you

think he'll do? That old mother of his is really the last straw. . . ."
I shall never forget my surprise when I saw your sister, Marie-
Thérèse—the one you called Marinette. She was older than you
by a year, but looked younger, with her slim body, her long
neck, the great coil of hair that looked too heavy for her, and
those childlike eyes. The old man to whom your father had sold
her, Baron Philipot, gave me the horrors. But since his death I
have often thought that that sexagenarian was one of the un-
happiest men I have ever come across. What tortures the poor
fool must have suffered in his efforts to make his young wife
forget that he was old! He was so tightly buckled into his stays
that he could scarcely breathe. His high, wide, starched collar
scarified his jowl and his dewlaps. The refulgence of his dyed
moustache and whiskers merely accentuated the purple ruin of
his face. He scarcely listened when anyone spoke to him, was
always looking round for a mirror, and, when he found one,
how we laughed (do you remember?) at the way the old idiot
mopped and mowed at his reflexion, and could never keep his
eyes off himself! He was incapable of smiling, because of his
false teeth. By an exercise of will-power—which never failed—
he kept his mouth perpetually shut. We used to notice, too, the
peculiar way in which he put on his hat so as not to disarrange
the extraordinary lock of hair which started from the nape of his
neck and spread out over his skull like the delta of a half-dried-
up river.

Your father, who was his contemporary, was still attractive to
women, in spite of his white beard, his baldness and his paunch.
Even in business matters he laid himself out to exert his charm.
My mother was the only person who stood out against him.
Maybe the blow I had just dealt her had had a hardening effect.
She argued every clause of the marriage contract as though it
had been a deed of sale or a lease. I pretended to be indignant at
her demands—though I was secretly overjoyed to think that my
interests were in such good hands. If, to-day, my fortune is entirely separate from yours, if you have so little hold on me, I owe
it all to my mother who insisted on the most rigorous form of
settlement, and behaved as though I were a daughter who had
made up her mind to marry a debauchee.

As soon as it became clear that the Fondaudège family was
not going to use these demands as an excuse for breaking off the
engagement, I was able to sleep calmly in my bed. They put up

with me—or so I thought—because you had set your heart on
having me as a husband.

Mamma would not hear of an "allowance", but insisted that
your dowry should be paid down in cash. "They keep on quoting
Baron Philipot as a precedent," she said: "apparently, he took
the eldest without a sou . . . and so I should think! They must
have got a pretty return from handing over the poor child to
that nasty old man! But with us, the shoe's on the other foot.
They thought I should be dazzled at the prospect of marrying
my son into their precious family. That shows how little they
know me!"

We two, the "turtle-doves", made a great show of not being
interested in the discussion. I imagine that you felt no less confidence in the genius of your father than I did in that of my
mother. As a matter of fact, I suspect that neither of us quite
realized what a store we both of us set by money.

No, that's unfair. You've never been fond of money except for
the children's sake. No doubt you'd gladly have murdered me if,
by doing so, you could have made them richer. But, then, you'd
have gladly given them the bread out of your own mouth.

I, on the other hand, adore money, and I don't mind admitting
it. It gives me a sense of security. So long as I remain in control
of my fortune, you have no weapon against me. "At our age one
needs so little"—that is your constant refrain; but how wrong
you are! An old man lives only by virtue of what he possesses.
As soon as he's got nothing, out he goes on the scrapheap. For us
the only choice is between the alms-house, the workhouse and a
private fortune. One is always hearing of peasants who let their
old parents starve to death after they have stripped them of
everything. The same holds good, as I know from experience,
though with rather more form and ceremony, of the middle-
classes. Yes, I *am* afraid of being poor. I have the feeling that I
can never pile up enough gold. You want it because it attracts
you. I want it because it is my only protection.

The hour of the Angelus has gone by, and I did not hear the
bell. . . . But, of course, it wouldn't have been rung to-day, because it's Good Friday. The men of the family are arriving to-
night by car. I shall come down to dinner. I want to see the
whole gang. I feel much stronger when they're all ranged against
me than I do when they tackle me separately. And there's

another reason. I like making a point of eating my cutlet on this day of penitence—not out of bravado, but just to show you that I have kept my will-power intact, that I am not prepared to yield on a single point.

All the positions which I have occupied for the last forty-five years, and from which you have failed to dislodge me, would fall one by one if I made the least concession. With the rest of the family fasting on beans and salt fish, my Good Friday cutlet will serve as a sign that you don't stand a chance of skinning me so long as there is breath in my body.

❦ IV ❦

You see, I wasn't wrong. My presence among you yesterday evening completely upset your plans. Only the children, sitting apart at their own table, were happy, because on Good Friday they have chocolate and bread-and-butter for supper. I must say I find it difficult to tell who's who among them. Janine, who's my granddaughter, has a child of her own old enough to walk. . . . I let everyone see that there was nothing wrong with my appetite. So that the children shouldn't get any false ideas about my cutlet, you had told them that the state of my health and my great age made it necessary. . . . What really did terrify me was Hubert's optimism. He said he felt confident that the market would show an upward trend soon—but with the air of a man for whom that hypothetical trend was a matter of life and death. I can never get over the fact that he's my son—but he is. Yes, this man of forty's my son. My reason admits it, but not my imagination. For some curious reason I can't face it. And suppose things do go wrong for him? After all, a stockbroker who offers such high dividends plays high and takes big risks. . . . One of these days I shall be told that the family honour is in jeopardy. . . . The family honour, indeed! That's an idol before which I will *not* sacrifice. The sooner I make up my mind on the point, the better. I've got to stand my ground and not allow myself to get sentimental—more especially as there is always that old Fondaudège uncle in the background who'll play up even if I don't. . . . But I'm digressing, going off on a false scent, or, rather, I'm shirking

the recollection of that night when, though you did not realize it
at the time, you destroyed all our hopes of happiness.

It's odd to think that you've probably forgotten all about it.
A few hours in the warm dusk of this room decided our destinies.
Every word you spoke increased the distance between us, and
yet, you noticed nothing. Your memory, which is a junk-shop of a
thousand trivialities, has retained not one single iota of that disaster. You make a great to-do about believing in the life everlasting, but you didn't seem to realize that what you were gambling
with at that moment, what you were endangering, was my immortal soul. The birth of love in my heart had made me sensitive
to the climate of faith and adoration which was the ambiance in
which you lived. I loved you, and I loved the spiritual elements
in your being. When you knelt down in your long, schoolgirl's
night-gown, I felt deeply moved.

We occupied this room where I now sit writing. Why did we
come to Calèse, to my mother's, when we got back from the
honeymoon? (I had refused her offer of the place. It was her
creation, and she loved it.) When, later, I sought out food for
my rancour, I remembered a number of circumstances which
had, at first, escaped me, or from which I had deliberately averted
my gaze. In the first place, on the ground that an uncle once
removed had just died, your family had insisted on keeping the
wedding ceremony as quiet as possible. It was as plain as houses
that they felt thoroughly ashamed of the connexion. Baron
Philipot had put it about that his young sister-in-law had fallen
madly in love with a young man at Bagnères-de-Luchon, a
charming enough fellow, with a future before him and plenty of
money, but of doubtful birth. "Fact is," he said, "he doesn't belong." To hear him speak you'd have thought I was somebody's
bastard. On the whole, however, he thought my lack of family a
good thing. At least there was no need to blush for my relations.
All things considered, my old mother was quite presentable, and
seemed to know her place. According to him you were a spoiled
child who could twist her parents round her little finger, and my
fortune had seemed big enough to persuade the Fondaudège clan
to consent to the marriage while shutting their eyes to its many
disadvantages.

When this tittle-tattle reached my ears it told me nothing,
really, that I did not know already. I was so happy that I refused
to attach any importance to it. Truth to tell, the almost secret

way in which the wedding was carried through suited me very well—for how could I have possibly found groomsmen in the down-at-heels circle of which I was the centre? Pride kept me from making advances to those who had so recently been my enemies, though my brilliant marriage would have made reconciliation easy. I have already, in the course of this confession, shown myself in such ugly colours, that I may as well go further and make no effort to conceal this trait in me which may be described as independence of mind or inflexibility. I refuse to bow the knee to anybody, and I remain true to my ideas. In connexion with this latter point, I may as well say that my marriage had given me a few twinges of conscience. I had promised your parents that I would do nothing which might alienate you from the practice of your religion, but I had in no way compromised my own freedom of action, except in so far as I had undertaken not to become a Freemason. As a matter of fact, you none of you thought of making any further demand on me. In those days the general view was that religion was the wife's affair. In your world, the husband—to use the accepted formula, "accompanied his wife to Mass". I had already, at Luchon, given you ample proof that I wasn't likely to kick at that.

When we returned from Venice in September '85, your parents made excuses for not receiving us in their château of Cenon, where, owing to the presence of their friends, and Philipot's, there was no room available. We found it convenient, therefore, to stay for a while with my mother. The memory of the brutal way in which we had treated her did not embarrass us in the least. We were perfectly prepared to live with her for as long as it suited us.

She was careful to give no outward sign of triumph. The house was ours, she said, and we were free to invite whom we liked: she would make herself scarce, and nobody need see her. "I know how to disappear," she added: "I spend almost all my time out of doors." This was true, for she gave much of her attention to the vines, the cellar, the chickens, and the laundry. After meals she went for a while to her own room, and always apologized when she found us in the drawing-room when she came down. She regularly knocked before coming in. I had to explain to her that she mustn't do that, that it wasn't "the thing". She even suggested that you should take over the housekeeping, but you

did, at least, spare her that mortification. But that was only because you had no wish to saddle yourself with her duties. How
terribly condescending you were to her, and what a humble gratitude she showed!

You did not come between her and me as much as she had
feared you would. Actually, I was a great deal nicer to her than
I had been before our marriage. Our mad fits of laughter were a
never-ending cause of surprise to her. She could scarcely believe
that the happy young husband whom she saw before her was the
same person as the repressed, unyielding son she had formerly
known. She explained the change by the fact that she hadn't
known how to handle me. I had always been too far "above"
her. You were repairing the damage that she had done.

I remember her admiration when she saw you daubing away
at screens and tambourines, and when you sang or played—
always breaking down in the same places—one of Mendelssohn's
"Songs Without Words" on the piano.

Young women friends sometimes came to see you. "You're
going to meet my mother-in-law," you would tell them: "one of
the genuine old ladies from the country. You don't come across
many of them nowadays." You decided that she had what you
called a "style of her own". She had got into the habit of speaking
patois to the servants, and that, you thought, was very "smart".
You even went so far as to show your visitors a daguerreotype
of her at the age of fifteen, in which she appeared with her head
tied up in a handkerchief. You were fond of quoting a saying
about old peasant families having "more true distinction than
many of noble rank. . . ." How very conventional you were in
those days! It was motherhood that restored you to your natural
self.

I keep shying away from the story of what happened that
night. It was so hot that we had left the blinds up, in spite of
your terror of bats. When the branches of a lime tree brushed
against the house we knew precisely what it was, though the
sound was exactly like that of someone breathing at the far end of
the room. Sometimes the wind in the leaves was like the noise
of rain. The waning moon lit up the floor and the pale phantoms
of your scattered clothes. We no longer heard the murmurs of
the meadow grass, so much had they become part of the general
silence.

"We really must go to sleep," you said . . . but all the time a
shadow roamed about our inert and weary bodies. Not alone did
we struggle up from the depths: the unknown Rodolphe came
with us. Each time I took you in my arms I woke the memory
of him in your heart.

When I loosed you from my embrace, we felt his presence. I
did not want to suffer: I was afraid of suffering. The instinct of
self-preservation applies to happiness as to other forms of life. I
knew I must not ask you any questions. I let his name burst like a
bubble on the surface of our life. Beneath the waters there slept
a principle of corruption, a putrid secret, and I did nothing to
stir it from the mud. But you, wretched woman, felt the need to
liberate in words the cheated passion that still hungered for satisfaction. One question of mine sufficed to bring it into the open.
"Who, precisely, was this fellow Rodolphe?" "I'm afraid there's
a lot I ought to have told you—oh, nothing really serious, don't
worry."

You spoke hurriedly, and in a low voice. Your head no longer
lay against my shoulder. Already the tiny space that separated
our stretched bodies had become unbridgeable.

He was the son of some Austrian woman and of a big indus-
trialist from the north. . . . You had met him at Aix when you
had been there with your grandmother the year before we had
got to know one another at Luchon. He had just left Cambridge.
You made no attempt to describe him, but I knew that he possessed all the graces which I felt myself to lack. The moonlight
on the sheet illuminated my coarse peasant hands with their
spatulate fingers. You had done nothing "wrong", though he was,
you said, less respectful than I had been. My recollection of what
you confessed is vague: not that it mattered. *That* wasn't what
worried me. If you had been genuinely in love with him I could
have forgiven one of those short, sharp surrenders in which the
innocence of childhood melts into nothingness. But my mind was
already full of questions. "How could she have fallen in love with
me scarcely twelve months after so great a passion?" I felt frozen
by terror. "It was all a sham," I told myself: "she lied to me.
That liberating influence was all a make-believe. How could I
have been such a fool as to fancy that a young girl could love
me—me whom nobody could love?"

The stars of the night's end were twinkling. A blackbird woke.
The breeze which we could hear among the leaves, even before

we felt it on our bodies, filled the curtains and brought refreshment to my eyes as in the days when I was happy. Only ten
minutes before, that happiness had been real to me, and now I
was thinking about the "time when I was happy". I asked another question:

"Was it that he didn't want you?" You felt the sting of that. I
can still hear the special voice you put on when your vanity was
touched. On the contrary, you said, he had been madly in love,
and very proud at the thought of marrying a Fondaudège. The
trouble was that it had come to the ears of his parents that you
had lost two brothers from consumption before they were grown
up. In view of the fact that he, too, suffered from delicate health,
they wouldn't hear of the match.

I asked my questions very calmly. No words of mine could
possibly have given you any idea of what it was you were so
busily pulling to bits.

"Actually, darling," you said, "it was quite providential for us,
the way things turned out. You know how proud my parents are
—rather absurdly so, I must admit. It was their obsession about
this marriage which never came off that made our happiness—
mine and yours—possible. You must have noticed the importance
that people in my little world attach to health where marriage is
concerned. Mamma got it firmly fixed in her head that the whole
town knew what had happened, and that no one would ever want
to marry me. She was quite convinced that I should die an old
maid. I can't tell you the life she led me—oh, for months and
months—as though I hadn't enough troubles of my own! . . . In
the end she persuaded us, both Papa and me, that I was out of
the marriage market for good!"

I carefully refrained from saying anything that might have
made you suspicious. You repeated what you had said before,
that the whole thing had been providential.

"I fell in love with you from the moment we met. We had
said many, many prayers at Lourdes before going to Luchon, and
as soon as I set eyes on you I knew that they had been answered."

You were far from guessing how those words grated on my
nerves. Those who oppose you in religion have, really, a very
much nobler idea of it than you realize, or than they realize
themselves. Why, otherwise, should they be so affronted at the
way in which you debase it? Can you honestly think it right and
proper to ask for tangible rewards from the God whom you call

your Father? . . . But that's beside the point, which was, quite simply, that you'd all pounced hungrily on the first snail that popped its head out of its shell. After hearing what you had said I could have no doubt of that.

How monstrous a thing our marriage was I realized only at that moment. Before it could take place at all your mother had had to have a brain-storm and infect both you and your father with her own temporary lunacy. . . . You told me that the Phili-pots had gone so far as to threaten to disown you should you marry me. Actually, at Luchon, while we were all laughing at the old fool, he was doing all he could to persuade your family to break it all off.

"But I stuck to you, darling, and he got nothing for his pains."

Again and again you told me that you had no regrets. I let you talk, and saved my breath. You could never, you assured me, have been happy with the precious Rodolphe. He was too good-looking. Love, for him, meant not giving but taking. The first woman who tried could have got him away from you.

You were blissfully unaware that your voice changed when-ever you mentioned him—lost some of its sharpness and became tremulous, with a sort of a cooing sound in it, as though old sighs, treasured within your breast, found freedom when his name was spoken.

He could never have made you happy because he was hand-some, charming and beloved! The logical deduction from that was that I could be the joy of your life because I was nothing much to look at and put people off with my surly manners! I gathered from your description that he had the intolerable arro-gance of all young Frenchmen who have been to Cambridge and learned to ape the English. . . . Would you really rather have had a husband who couldn't choose a suit or tie a tie, who hated games and was incapable of the sophisticated frivolity which consists in avoiding all serious subjects, in shying away from emotional entanglements or any show of feeling, and living with care-free elegance? You had accepted the inferior me (so I was to believe) merely because I happened to have swum into your ken just when your mother, afflicted by her change of life, had convinced herself that you would never find a husband, because you would not, or could not, remain unmarried a moment longer, and because I happened to have enough money to provide an excuse in the eyes of the world. . . .

I did my best to control my breathing. I clenched my fists, I
bit my lips. Many times since then I have felt such a loathing of
myself that I have turned with revulsion from the very thought
of my body and of my feelings, and always, in such moments, my
thoughts have gone back to the young man of 1885, the husband
of twenty-three, sitting with his arms tightly crossed in a frenzied
attempt to stifle his young love.

I shivered. You noticed it and broke off in the middle of what
you were saying:

"Are you cold, Louis?"

"It was nothing," I said: "just a touch of goose-flesh."

"You're not going to tell me you're jealous?—that would
really be too ridiculous!"

I swore to you that I did not feel the least twinge of jealousy—
and it was true. How could I possibly have made you understand
that my personal drama was something far beyond mere jealousy?

You were worried by my silence, but you had not the least
idea how deeply I had been wounded. Your hand felt for mine
in the darkness; you stroked my face. Your fingers felt no trace
of tears, but perhaps the rigidity of my clenched jaws struck you
as strange. You took fright. In your effort to light a candle you
were lying half across me. The match wouldn't strike. I lay there
half stifled under the weight of your hateful body.

"What's the matter with you? Don't lie there saying nothing!
You're frightening me!"

I pretended to be surprised. I assured you that there was nothing to be frightened about.

"How silly of you, darling, to give me such a shock! . . . I'm
going to put out the light and try to get some sleep."

You said no more. I watched the new day come, the day
which would mark the beginning of a new life for me. The swallows were twittering under the eaves. A man crossed the yard,
dragging his clogs. All I heard then I can hear still, after forty-
five years—cocks crowing, bells ringing, a goods-train on the viaduct. All I smelled then I can smell still—the scent that I love
above all scents, of ashes carried by the wind from heath-fires by
the sea.

Suddenly I started up:

"Isa, that night you cried when we were sitting on a bench by
the winding path at Superbagnères—was it because of him?"

You didn't say anything. I gripped your arm, but you shook

yourself free with a sort of animal snarl, and rolled over on your side. Your long hair was all about you as you slept. You lay curled up like some wild young creature of the woods, the blankets piled higgledy-piggledy on your body because of the dawn chill. What should I have gained by rousing you from your child-like slumbers? I knew already what I needed to know without hearing it from your lips.

I got up quietly and padded across on bare feet to the wardrobe mirror. I stared at myself as though I had been a stranger, or, rather, as though I had suddenly become myself again—the man whom nobody loved, on whose account no one in the world had ever had a moment's suffering. I was filled with self-pity, thinking of my youth. I passed a great peasant hand across my unshaven cheeks which were already showing dark beneath a harsh growth of beard with red lights in it.

I dressed in silence and went down to the garden. Mamma was in the rose-walk. She always got up before the servants so as to air the house.

She spoke to me:

"Enjoying the cool of the day?"

Then, pointing to the mists on the low land:

"It's going to be a scorcher. I must have every shutter closed by eight."

I kissed her with more show of affection than usual. She murmured, very low . . . "Dear boy. . . ." My heart (do you find it odd that I should speak of my heart?) felt ready to burst. A few hesitating words came to my lips . . . but how should I begin what I had to say? . . . would she understand? . . . Invariably I yield to the temptation of silence.

I walked down to the terrace. The young fruit-trees were showing shadowy above the vines. The shoulder of the hill was thrusting the mist aside, breaking it into wisps and shreds. A belfry emerged from the thin fog, then the church to which it belonged, like a living body. It has always been your fixed opinion that churches, and all they stand for, leave me cold . . . let me tell you, then, what I felt at that moment. I felt that a man whose heart is broken as mine had been broken may be impelled to seek the reason for, the meaning of, his undoing: that, possibly, what has happened to him may conceal some significant secret, that what happens—especially in the world of the feelings— may, perhaps, carry a message the meaning of which he must interpret. . . . So, you see, there have been moments in my life when I have been capable of glimpsing things which might, perhaps, have drawn us together. . . .

But on that particular morning my emotion lasted for only a few moments. I still have a picture of myself going back towards the house. It was not yet eight o'clock, and already the sun was hot. You were leaning from your window, holding your hair in one hand, while, with the other, you brushed it. You did not see me. I stood still for a few seconds, looking up at you. I had been caught by a sudden spasm of hatred. After all these years, I can still taste its bitterness.

I ran to my desk and opened the drawer which I kept always locked. From it I took a little crumpled handkerchief, the same that you had used to wipe away your tears one evening at Super-bagnères. I, poor fool, had pressed it to my heart. I took it now; I tied a stone to it as I might have done to a puppy I meant to drown, and threw it into the pond, which local country-people call the "gutter".

❈ *V* ❈

THEN began that era of the Great Silence which has scarcely been broken for forty years. There was no outward sign of collapse. All went on as in the days of my happiness. We remained united in the flesh, but no ghost of Rodolphe was now born of our embrace, nor did you ever mention the dreadful name. At your bidding he had come, had prowled about our bed, had accomplished his work of destruction. All he could do now was to remain silent and await the long sequence of events, the delayed working of cause and effect.

You may, perhaps, have felt that you had done wrong to speak at all. It was not that you expected anything very serious to occur as a result of your admission. Still, it might have been wiser to keep his name out of our talk. I don't know whether you noticed that we no longer indulged in nightly chats. Those interminable discussions of ours were now a thing of the past. Whatever we said to one another we said only after due and careful thought. We were, each of us, on the defensive.

I used to start awake in the middle of the night. It was pain

that woke me. I was fastened to you like a fox to the trap. Sometimes I tried to imagine what might have been said between us
had I shaken you roughly, had I thrown you out of bed. "You're
wrong"—you might have cried: "I didn't lie, and for the very
good reason that I was in love with you."—"Yes, at second best,
because it's always easy to consent to the physical act—which
means nothing—in order to make your partner believe that you
love him. I was no monster: any young girl who had truly loved
me could have done with me what she would. . . ." Sometimes I
groaned in the darkness, but you never woke.

Your first pregnancy made all attempts at explanation useless.
Little by little it changed the nature of our relationship. It began
before the time of the grape-harvest. We went back to town. You
had a miscarriage, as a result of which you were in bed for
several weeks. By the following spring you were again with child.
I had to take great care of you. Then began that long series of
pregnancies, mishaps, and childbed, which gave me more pre-
texts than I needed for keeping away from you. I plunged into a
secret life of debauchery—very secret, for I was beginning to appear more and more frequently in Court—was "feeling my feet",
as Mamma said—and had to be careful about my reputation. I
had my special times, my regular habits. The man who would
live an irregular life in the country has to develop the cunning of
the hunted hare. Don't be afraid, Isa, I shall spare you all details
of what, I know, fills you with horror. You may rest assured that I
shall paint no picture here of the Hell into which I descended almost every day. It was you, once, who had fished me out: it was
you, now, who threw me back again.

Even had I been less prudent, you wouldn't have twigged a
thing. After the birth of Hubert, you came out in your true
colours. You were a mother, and nothing but a mother. You no
longer paid the slightest attention to me. You didn't even notice
my existence. It is quite literally true that you had eyes only for
your young. In sowing the necessary seed, I had done all you
wanted of me.

So long as the children were in the grub stage, and did not
interest me, there was no cause for quarrel between us. We never
met except to perform those ritual acts which the body carries
through as a matter of habit, and in which the man and the
woman are, each, a thousand miles removed from their own
flesh.

You began to take notice of me only when I, in my turn,

started to prowl around our young family. You began to hate me
only when I claimed my rights in them. It was not paternal instinct
that dictated my attitude. I can bring myself now to make
that admission, and you ought to be very grateful to me for doing
so. I very soon became jealous of the passion that had waked
in you. I tried to entice the children away for the sole purpose
of punishing you. I deceived myself with any number of high-
sounding reasons—duty, for instance, and my refusal to let a
bigoted woman stunt young minds. But those were just excuses!

Shall I ever come to the end of my story? I began it for you,
and already I feel it to be in the highest degree unlikely that you
will be able to bear with it much longer. It is, fundamentally,
for myself that I am writing. True to my character of an old
barrister, I want to get my brief sorted out, to docket and arrange
the various exhibits in that lost cause—my life. . . . Oh, those
bells!—of course, to-morrow's Easter. I shall join you all downstairs in honour of the sacred feast—as I promised I would. "The
children are always complaining that they never see you"—that's
what you said to me this morning. Geneviève was standing beside
you, close to my bed. She had something she wanted to ask me. I
had heard you whispering together in the passage: "It'll be much
better if you speak first . . ."—you said to her . . . I suppose it's
something to do with her son-in-law, that blackguard, Phili. How
cleverly I kept her from bringing him into the conversation, or
mentioning what it was that she was after! She left the room without having managed even to broach the subject. I know perfectly
well what it's all about. I overheard your conversation the other
evening. The drawing-room window is just below mine, and,
when it's open, I only have to lean forward a little. She wants me
to advance Phili the capital he needs to buy a quarter share in a
Broker's firm. . . . It'd be as good an investment as any other. . . .
Oh yes, I know all about that. . . . As though I hadn't seen the
storm blowing up, as though I didn't know it was time now to
tuck one's money away in a safe place! . . . If only they knew how
much I made last month by anticipating the slump!

They've all gone to Vespers. Easter has emptied the house and
the fields. I sit here alone, an old Faust separated from the world's
joy by the wall of my abominable old age. They've no idea what
old age means. During luncheon, they were all ears for what I
was saying about business and the Stock Market. I was talking

deliberately at Hubert, so that he might get out while there is
still time. How worried he looked. . . . Not a born bluffer, our
Hubert! He polished off his food. You had piled his plate with
the obstinacy of an unhappy mother who sees that her son is
devoured by anxiety, and forces him to eat, as though that were
so much to the good, were something gained. And his only thanks
was to snap your head off. It was me and Mamma over again.

How careful young Phili was to keep my glass filled! What
a show of interest his wife, Janine, exhibited in my well-being!
"Grandpapa, you *oughtn't* to smoke, really you oughtn't: even
one cigarette's too much. Are you *sure* they haven't made a mistake? Is this coffee really free of caffeine?" She's a poor hand at
deception, poor dear: her voice gives her away. She's just like you
in the early days of our marriage, when you used to put on an
act. But that all went by the board when your first child was
born, and you became yourself again. Until the day of her
death, Janine will be a woman "in the know", repeating everything she hears, provided she thinks it gives her an air of distinction, trotting out second-hand views about this, that and the
other, and not understanding a word. How Phili, who's nothing
if not natural, an unashamed scavenger, can bear to live with
such a little half-wit, beats me. But, no, I'm wrong: one thing
about her is perfectly genuine, and that's her passion for him.
The reason she's so transparent is that nothing matters for her,
nothing really exists for her, but her love.

After luncheon we all sat out on the steps. Janine and Phili
kept their eyes fixed on Geneviève, like a couple of dogs begging
for crumbs, while she looked at no one but you. You said "no"
with an almost imperceptible shake of the head, at which Geneviève got up and turned to me:

"How about taking a turn with me, Papa?" You're all so
frightened of me! I took pity on her. I had made up my mind not
to budge, but, all the same, I got up and took her arm. We walked
round the meadow. The family watched us from the steps.

She lost no time in coming to the point. "I wanted to have a
word with you about Phili."

She was trembling. It's horrible to know that one's children
are frightened of one. But at sixty-eight a man's not free to decide
whether he shall seem unapproachable or not. By that age the general cast of our features is set, and the heart, when it finds that
it can no longer give expression to its feelings, grows discour-

aged. . . . Geneviève had decided what she wanted to say, and out it all came in a rush. . . . It had to do, as I had expected, with Phili's buying a share in a Broker's firm. She stressed the one point of all others best calculated to antagonize me—the fact that Phili's having nothing to do was a constant threat to Janine's married happiness. He was beginning to stray from the domestic hearth. I told her that a share in a Broker's firm would merely serve to supply a man like her son-in-law with convenient alibis. She stood up for him. Phili was universally popular. Why should I be harder on him than Janine was? . . . I protested that I neither judged nor condemned him, that I took not the slightest interest in his love-life.

"Why should I bother about him? He certainly doesn't bother about me."

"He admires you enormously."

This impudent lie gave me the chance to trot out what I was keeping up my sleeve.

"That's as may be, my dear, but it doesn't prevent your precious Phili from referring to me as the 'old crocodile'. It's no good denying it. Many's the time I've heard him say it behind my back . . . and I've no wish to deny the imputation: crocodile I am, and crocodile I shall remain. There's nothing to hope for from an old crocodile—except his death. And even when he's dead"—I was foolish enough to add—"even when he's dead, he can still be up to his old tricks." (I'm sorry I said that: it only roused her suspicions.)

She was knocked of a heap. She tried to explain it all away (as though I care two hoots what Phili calls me!). What I detest about him is his youth. How can she have the faintest idea what a hated and despised old man feels at the sight of a young creature in the pride of life, who has had showered upon him, from youth up, those very things which I have tasted only once in half a century? I loathe and detest all young men, and Phili more than most. Like a cat slipping silently through the window, he has padded into my house, attracted by the smell of what was inside. My granddaughter may not have had much in the way of a dowry—but, oh! her "expectations"—only over our dead bodies do young gentlemen get within touching distance of our children's "expectations"!

Then as Geneviève started snuffling and dabbing at her eyes, I adopted a tone of sweet reasonableness.

"After all, my dear, you've got a perfectly good husband in
the rum trade. Surely dear Alfred can find some sort of a job for
his son-in-law? Why should I be more generous than you are
yourselves?"

Then she started to talk about poor Alfred. What a change!
What contempt! what disgust! According to her he's a mean-
spirited coward who is drawing in his horns more every day.
Once upon a time his business was a large and prosperous affair,
but now there isn't a living in it for more than one person.

I congratulated her on having such a husband. When a storm's
brewing one's got to shorten sail. The future, I said, belongs to
men like Alfred who can take a limited view. In these days, the
only hope of making a success of business is to keep going in a
small way. She thought I was laughing at her. But I was voicing
my profound belief—as is shown by the fact that I keep my own
money under lock and key and won't even take chances with
the Savings-Bank.

We walked back to the house. Geneviève didn't dare to say
another word. I was no longer leaning on her arm. The members
of the family, seated in a circle, watched us coming, and, no
doubt, were already busy interpreting the unfavourable omens.
It was obvious that our return had interrupted an argument between Hubert's little lot and Geneviève's. What an unholy squabble there would be over my pile if ever I agreed to relax my
grip! Phili was the only one on his feet. The wind was blowing
in his rebellious hair. He was wearing an open-necked shirt with
short sleeves. I have a horror of these modern young men who
look like athletic girls! His baby cheeks flushed scarlet when, in
reply to Janine's stupid question—"Well, have you had a nice
chat?"—I replied, very quietly, "We have been talking about an
old crocodile. . . ."

Let me repeat, it's not because of that piece of ill-conditioned
rudeness that I hate him. They've no idea what old age means.
You can't imagine the torment of having had nothing out of life,
of having nothing to look forward to but death, of feeling that
there is no other world beyond this one, that the puzzle will
never be explained, the key never given to us. . . . You haven't
suffered what I have suffered. You never will suffer what I am
suffering now. It is not for your death that the children are
impatient. They are fond of you in their own way, they love
you. . . . From the very first they took sides with you against me.

I had a very warm feeling for them. I can remember Geneviève —this fat, forty-year-old woman who, a moment or two back, was trying to wheedle four hundred thousand-franc notes out of me for her scamp of a son-in-law, as a little girl perched on my knee. As soon as you saw me paying any attention to her, you called her away. . . . But if I go on mixing present and past like this, I shall never get to the end of my confession. I really must try to put a little order into my thoughts. . . .

❀ *VI* ❀

I DON'T think that I began to hate you from the first year after that disastrous night. My hatred grew, by slow degrees, as I came to realize how completely indifferent you were to me, how nothing really existed for you outside the circle of your pulling, screaming, greedy little scraps of humanity. You did not even notice how, though I was not yet thirty, I had become an over-worked Chancery barrister with a big reputation at the most important Bar in all France after that of Paris. It was the Vill-enave case (1893) which gave me the chance to prove myself a great Criminal lawyer as well (it is exceedingly rare to excel in both branches). You were the only person who remained deaf to the universal applause of my gifts as a pleader. That was the year, too, in which our misunderstandings turned to open warfare.

The notorious Villenave case set the seal on my reputation. It also gave a further twist to the vice which was crushing out my life. Perhaps up till then I had still retained a tiny shred of hope, but I saw now, beyond all power to doubt, that, so far as you were concerned, I had ceased to exist.

I wonder whether you remember the story of that Villenave couple? They had been married for twenty years, and were still so devoted to one another that they had become almost a legend. People talked of being as "loving as the Villenaves". They lived with an only son of fifteen in their château at Ornon, just out-side the city, seeing very few people, and utterly self-sufficient. "It's the sort of thing one reads about in books," said your mother, using one of those ready-made phrases the secret of which her granddaughter Geneviève has inherited. I don't mind betting that you have forgotten everything to do with their story. If I tell it over again now, you'll just laugh at me as you always did when I described my triumphs of cross-examination at the dinner table. . . . Well, that can't be helped.

One morning, their servant, who was doing the downstairs rooms, heard a pistol-shot on the first floor, followed by a cry of pain. He rushed upstairs. The door of his master's bedroom was locked. He could hear low voices, the sound of things being moved about, and agitated steps in the bathroom. He kept on rattling the handle, and, in a moment or two, the door was opened. Villenave was lying on the bed in his night-shirt, covered in blood. Madame de Villenave, her hair disordered, and wearing a dressing-gown, was standing at the foot of the bed with a revolver in her hand. She said: "I have wounded Monsieur de Villenave. Get a doctor, a surgeon and the Police Inspector— hurry! I will stay here." They could get nothing more out of her than that single statement—"I have wounded my husband" —and this was confirmed by Monsieur de Villenave as soon as he was able to speak. He refused to give any further information.

The accused would do nothing about appointing Counsel to represent her at the trial. I was entrusted—as the son-in-law of a friend of theirs—with her defence. She maintained an attitude of unshakable obstinacy. Though I went every day to see her in prison, I could get nothing out of her. The city was filled with the most ridiculous rumours. Personally, I was convinced of her innocence from the very first. She was accusing herself, and the husband who loved her remained completely acquiescent. What an unerring nose do the unloved have for the scent of passion in others! This woman was entirely possessed by conjugal love. She had not fired at her husband. Might it be that she had tried to fling herself between him and a rejected lover? There had been no visitor to the house since the previous evening . . . there was no intimate friend who came regularly to see them . . . well, it's all ancient history now, and I won't go into details.

Up to the morning of the day of the trial I had decided to adopt a purely negative attitude, and merely to argue that Madame de Villenave could not have committed the crime which she was as good as confessing. But, at the very last moment, the evidence of her son Yves, or, rather (for in itself that evidence was quite unimportant and shed no light on the mystery), the beseeching and commanding look which his mother kept steadily fixed on him all the time he was in the witness box, as well as the obvious relief which she showed when he left it, told me the truth. I denounced the son. I described him as a morbid adolescent who had been driven to a jealous frenzy by the love lavished upon his father. I flung myself with a sort of passionate logic into a spur-of-the-moment argument which has since become famous, and in which Professor F——, on his own admission, found the essential germ of his theory. It has shed new light not only on the psychology of adolescence, but on the treatment of its neuroses.

If I stir these old memories, it is not, my dear Isa, because I have the slightest hope of rousing in you, after forty years, the admiration which you did not feel at the moment of my triumph when my picture was appearing in the newspapers of two hemispheres. Your complete indifference in this supremely important moment of my career revealed to me the extent of my solitude and abandonment. But there was more to it than that. For weeks on end I had had before my eyes, between the four walls of a cell, a woman who was sacrificing herself with the sole purpose of saving, not so much *her* child, as her husband's, the heir to his name. It was he, the victim, who had implored her to take the blame. So great was her love that she had been willing to let the world believe that she was a criminal, that she had tried to murder the man whom she adored to the exclusion of everybody and everything in the world. Conjugal, not maternal, love had been the mainspring of her action (as was proved by the sequel, for she separated from her son, and has always found some excuse or other for living away from him ever since). I, too, might have been loved as Villenave was loved. Of him, too, I saw a good deal at the time of the trial. What had he got that I hadn't? True, he was well-born and averagely good-looking, but I don't think he was very intelligent. His hostile attitude to me after the trial proved that. I, on the other hand, was in my own way something of a genius. If, at that moment, I had been blessed with a wife who loved me, to what heights might I not have risen? Nobody can go on indefinitely believing in himself unless he gets some help from outside. There must be some other person to give him assurance of his abilities, someone to crown him when the day of recognition comes. When, as a schoolboy, I used to walk back from the dais on Prize Day, with my arms full of books, it was always my mother's eyes that I tried to catch in the crowd, and it was she who, to the sound of a military band, really placed the laurel-wreath upon my freshly cropped head. At the time of the Villenave case she was beginning to fail, though I realized it only by degrees. The extent to which she was entirely wrapped up in a little black dog, which barked furiously every time I approached her, gave me my first inkling of her declining powers. Whenever I went to see her she would talk about nothing else. She no longer listened to anything I said.

In any case, her feeling for me could never have been a substitute for the love which might have saved me at this turning-point of my life. Her ruling vice was the love of money, and this I have inherited. The passion is in my blood. She would have done everything she could to keep me in a profession which, to use her own words, brought in "big money". At that time, the idea of writing attracted me. Many newspapers, and all the important Reviews, approached me with offers. In addition, the Left-wing parties wanted me to stand at the next election for the constituency of La Bastide (the man who finally accepted, in my place, got in without the slightest difficulty), but I refused to listen to the call of my ambitions because I didn't want to give up the chance of earning "big money".

In that, I was falling in with your wishes, too. You had made it quite clear to me that you would never leave the provinces. A genuinely loving wife would have taken pleasure in my fame, would have taught me that the art of living consists in abandoning a base passion for one more noble. Those idiot journalists who make a great show of indignation when some man of law takes advantage of his position as a Deputy or a Minister to enjoy a few trivial pickings would be better employed in expressing admiration of those who have succeeded in establishing an intelligent hierarchy among their passions, and have preferred glory in the field of politics to big profits in business. If you had had any real love for me you could have saved me from my ingrained habit of never setting anything above immediate gain, of being incapable of giving up the mediocre and squalid temptation of big fees for the shadow of power. After all, there is no shadow without a reality that projects it. The very shadow itself is a reality. As things turned out, there was nothing for me to do but go on making "big money", just like the grocer at the corner.

That's all I have left—the money I earned in the course of those terrible years, the money you're mad enough to want me to give away. The very idea that you might enjoy it after my death is intolerable to me. I told you, at the beginning of this screed, that I had, at one time, taken steps to see that you should be left with nothing, at the same time giving you reason to believe that I had now abandoned this particular plan of revenge. But I had not then taken into account the tidal movement of my hatred. Sometimes it ebbs, and I grow soft . . . sometimes it flows, and then the muddy waters engulf me.

After what happened to-day, after this Easter incident, this concerted attack undertaken with the object of stripping me bare in the interests of dear Phili, I feel differently. I have had a view of the family pack sitting back on its hunkers round the door, and spying on my movements. I am obsessed by the idea of so dividing up my property that you'll all be at one another's throat. Oh yes, you'll fight like dogs over the land and over the securities. Don't bother—you're going to get the land all right, but the securities no longer exist. The ones I mentioned on the first page of this letter I sold last week at the top of the market. Since then, they've been falling every day. Ships have a way of foundering as soon as I abandon them. I'm never wrong. My millions of liquid capital you shall have—but only if I decide in your favour. There are days when I make up my mind not to leave you a penny of it.

I can hear the whole lot of you whispering your way upstairs. You stop: you talk freely without fear of waking me (the accepted view is that I am deaf). I can see the light of your candles underneath the door. I recognize Phili's falsetto (anybody would think his voice is still breaking), and catch a sudden burst of stifled laughter, the sound of young women clucking. You're calling them to order: you're just going to say—"He isn't asleep, I know he isn't." . . . You creep up to my door; you listen; you look through the key-hole. The lamp gives me away. You've returned to the pack. I think you must be whispering—"He's still awake; he's listening to you. . . ."

They tip-toe away: the stairs creak: door after door closes. On this Easter night the house is full of couples. I might be the living trunk from which these young shoots have sprung. Most fathers are beloved: but you were my enemy, and my children have gone over to the enemy.

It is to this war between us that I must turn now. I feel too weak to go on writing, yet hate the thought of going to bed, even of lying down in the rare moments when the state of my heart permits it. At my age, sleep attracts the attention to death. One mustn't look as though one were dead. I have a feeling that so long as I am on my feet death can't come near me. What is it that I dread about death?—physical pain? the awful struggle at the end?—no, not that, but the feeling that to die is to become nothing, that our state in the grave can be expressed only by the symbol ——

❊ *VII* ❊

So long as our three little ones remained in the limbo of infancy, the enmity between us was still disguised. But there was a heavy atmosphere about our home. Your indifference to me, your complete detachment from everything that had to do with me, kept you from feeling any discomfort on that account, or even from noticing it. Besides, I was never there. I lunched alone at eleven, so as to get to the Courts by midday. Work took up most of my time and—well, you can guess what I did with such brief snatches of leisure as I might have been able to give my family. Why did I turn to this hideous, bare skeleton of debauchery? It was stripped of everything that usually provides some excuse even for animal passion. It had been reduced to pure horror, without a hint of feeling to justify it, without the least pretence of sentiment. I might so easily have had the kind of adventures that the world approves. A lawyer of my age could scarcely avoid certain temptations. There were many young women ready and eager to get under the skin of the public figure, and rouse the man. . . . But I had lost faith in the creatures, or rather, in my power to attract any of them. I at once detected the self-interest which animated those who were "ready and willing", those of whose charms I was conscious. The fixed idea that what they were looking for was a certain security of tenure chilled my ardour. Why should I mind admitting that, in addition to the tragic certainty of feeling myself to be somebody whom no one would ever love, I was a victim to the suspicion which afflicts most rich men, and makes them feel that they are being deceived and exploited? I had put

you on a fixed allowance, and you knew me too well to expect
a penny more than the agreed sum. It was calculated on a generous basis, and you never exceeded it. I felt no threat of danger
from that quarter. But with other women it was quite a different
kettle of fish! I was one of those fools who believe that there are
only two classes of women—those who indulge in love for its own
sake, and those debased creatures who are out only for what they
can get. In fact, most women oscillate between the two. They want
to give free rein to their amorous tendencies, and they want to be
"kept", protected and spoiled. At sixty-eight I look back with a
lucidity which, at times, makes me want to howl, at all that I
rejected in those days, not from any sense of virtue, but because
I was mistrustful and cowardly. The few "affairs" which I did
begin soon ended, either because my naturally suspicious nature
misinterpreted even the most innocent of requests, or because I
made myself odious by reason of those manias of mine which you
know only too well—endless quarrels with waiters or cab-drivers
on the subject of tips. I like to know in advance precisely what
I've got to pay. I like to work to a tariff. It's not easy to confess
this. What I found attractive in mercenary love was, probably,
that it had a fixed price. But in a man of my sort what possible
connexion could there be between mere self-indulgence and the
cravings of the heart? I had ceased to believe that the cravings
of the heart could ever be satisfied, and I took good care to stifle
them as soon as they showed their heads. I was a past master in
the art of destroying all sentiment at the precise moment when
the will begins to play a decisive part in matters of love, when a
man can still stand on the sidelines of passion and is free to
surrender or to hold back while there is still time. I chose the
simplest satisfactions—those that may be had for an agreed out-
lay. I hate being "done", but what I owe I pay. You're always
girding at me for being "close", but that doesn't prevent me from
having a horror of debts. I pay cash for everything. My trades-
men know this and bless me. I can't bear the thought that I owe
any man a penny. Love, I thought, was something in which one
was perpetually giving . . . and I found it disgusting.

Perhaps I'm making too much of all this, and fouling my own
nest. I have loved, and even perhaps been loved. It was in 1909,
when my youth was already on the wane. Why should I pass over
that particular adventure in silence? You knew all about it. You
made no bones about recalling it when you wanted to drive me
into a corner.

She was a young schoolteacher, who had been charged with
infanticide, and I saved her. She gave herself to me at first out of
sheer gratitude, but later . . . yes, for one year I knew what real
love was. What ruined everything was my inability to keep my
demands in check. Not content with letting her live in mean
circumstances which were only just one degree above actual poverty, I had to have her constantly at my beck and call. I never
let her see anybody. She always had to be there when I wanted
her during my brief periods of leisure, and not there when I
didn't. She was my property. My passion for possession, and for
using and abusing what I possess, extends to human beings. I
ought to have been a slave-owner. For this one and only time I
thought I had found a victim really made to the measure of my
demands. I kept a close watch even on the expression of her
face. . . . But I'm forgetting my promise not to tell you about this
side of my life. The long and the short of it is that she ran away to
Paris. She couldn't stand it any longer.

"It's not only us you can't get on with. Everyone's afraid of
you, and keeps out of your way. You must know that, Louis!"
If you've said that once, you've said it a hundred times, and it's
perfectly true. At the Law Courts I was always a lone wolf. I
was elected to the Bar Council—but only at the last possible moment. They'd chosen too many fools in my stead for me ever to
be ambitious of the Presidency. I'm not sure, as a matter of fact,
that I ever really wanted it. It would have meant being a representative, entertaining. Honours like that cost a deal of money,
and the game's not worth the candle. You wanted it for the sake
of the children. You've never wanted anything for me. "Do it for
the sake of the children."

During the year immediately following our marriage, your
father had his first stroke, and the château of Cenon was closed
to us. You very quickly adopted Calèse. The only thing of mine
you've ever really made your own is my land. You took root in
my soil, but our roots never met. Your children spent all their
holidays in this house and garden. Our little Marie died here.
But, so far from her death giving you a horror of the place, you
have invested the room in which she lived her last days with a
sort of sacred character. . . . It was here that you hatched your
brood, that you tended the sick, watched by the cradles, and sent
an endless succession of nurses and governesses packing. It was
on lines strung to the apple trees that Marie's tiny dresses were

hung out to dry, and a long sequence of innocent garments. It was in this drawing-room that the Abbé Ardouin used to group the children round the piano and make them sing choruses which, so as to avoid my anger, were not always sacred in character.

Smoking in front of the house on summer evenings, I used to hear their pure young voices. I can still recollect that air of Lulli's, "*Ah! que ces bois, ces rochers, ces fontaines. . . .*" There was about it all a sense of quiet happiness from which I felt myself excluded. It was a zone of dreamlike innocence which I was forbidden to enter. It was a quiet sea of love which died into nothingness a few feet from the rock of my presence.

When I entered the drawing-room, the voices fell silent. Geneviève took herself off with a book. Marie was the only one who wasn't frightened of me. I called to her and she came. I snatched her up in my arms, and she nestled there happily enough. I could feel her little bird's heart beating. I let her go, and at once she fluttered away into the garden. . . . Marie!

Very early on the children began to show surprise at my absence from Mass, and at my Friday cutlet. But the struggle that you and I were waging very rarely flared up when they were present, and if it did, I was usually beaten. After each one of my defeats, the war went underground again. Calèse was the battlefield, for when we were in Bordeaux, I was scarcely ever at home. But the legal vacation coincided with the school holidays, and August and September found us all together here.

I remember one occasion when we had a head-on clash (it had to do with some joke I had made in Geneviève's hearing, when she was reciting her Scripture lesson). I asserted my right to defend my children's minds, you, yours to protect their souls. I had been routed once already when I agreed that Hubert should be entrusted to the Jesuit Fathers, and the younger children to the Ladies of the Sacred Heart. I had yielded to the prestige which the traditions of the Fondaudège family always enjoyed in my eyes. But I was hungry for revenge, and, on that particular occasion, what mattered to me was that I had hit on the one subject capable of making you really wild. When *that* was under discussion you had to abandon your attitude of indifference and listen to what I was saying, no matter how much you might hate it. At last I had found a way of bringing you to battle. Formerly my irreligion had been no more than a mould into which I ran the various humiliations which, as the son of a peasant father who had made money, I had had to endure from my superior middle-class companions. But now I filled it with all the frustrations I had met with in love, and an almost limitless extent of rancorous resentment.

The dispute started again during luncheon (I had asked what possible satisfaction it could give the Eternal Being to see you eating salmon-trout instead of boiled beef). You left the table. I remember the expression on the children's faces. I followed you to your room. Your eyes were dry: you spoke quite calmly. I realized then that you hadn't been so wholly unaware of the life I had been leading as I had supposed. You had come across certain letters which contained quite enough evidence to get you a separation. "I have stayed with you for the sake of the children," you said. "But if your presence here is going to endanger their spiritual well-being, I shall not hesitate for a moment."

No, you certainly would not have hesitated to leave both me and my money. Ruled though you might be by self-interest, you would have consented to any sacrifice that might have been necessary to keep the teachings of the Church—that agglomeration of habits, formulae and general nonsense—unsullied in those little brains.

I did not keep the letter of abuse you sent me after Marie's death. You were too strong for me. Any legal proceedings between us would seriously have imperilled my own position. In those days, and in provincial circles, such things were not taken lightly. There was already a rumour going about to the effect that I was a Freemason. My opinions had made me more or less of an outcast from local society. But for the prestige enjoyed by your family, they might have done me a lot of harm. Worst of all, had there been a legal separation, I should have had to surrender the Suez Canal shares which formed part of your dowry. I had come to regard them as my own property. I couldn't face the thought of having to give them up—(to say nothing of the allowance your father made us).

I ate humble pie and agreed to all the conditions you laid down. But I made up my mind to devote my leisure to the task of winning over the children. I came to that decision at the beginning of August, 1896. Those sad and blazing summers of long ago have become confused in my mind, and my memories of that time cover a period of, roughly, five years (1895–1900).

I thought it would not be difficult to renew my hold over the children. I reckoned on my authority as their father, and on my intelligence. It would be a mere nothing, I thought, to work on a boy of ten and two little girls. I remember the surprise and uneasiness which they showed when I suggested one day that they should go for a long walk with Papa. You were sitting in the courtyard, under the silver lime. They looked at you enquiringly. "There's no need for you to ask my permission, my pets!"

We started off. How does one talk to children? Accustomed though I am to standing up to the Public Prosecutor, to Defending Counsel when I'm appearing for the defendant in a Civil suit, to a whole courtful of hostile lawyers, and though Assize Judges go in fear of me, I confess that children get me down—children, and members of the lower orders, even peasants, though I am a peasant's son myself. In their presence I become unsure of myself and tongue-tied.

They were very nice to me, but obviously on their guard. You had long ago thrown a holding-force into those three hearts! You controlled all the approaches. Not one step could I take without your permission. You had made no attempt to undermine my authority—oh, you were far too scrupulous for that! but you had let them see pretty clearly that a lot of praying would have to be done for poor Papa. No matter how erring I might be, I occupied a perfectly definite place in their scheme of things—I was the "poor Papa", the object of their prayers, the misguided pagan ripe for conversion—and anything I might say or hint on the subject of religion merely confirmed the rather crude idea they had of me.

They lived in a world of marvels. Its landmarks were the feast-days of the year, each of them celebrated with solemn piety. *You* could get them to do anything you wanted just by talking about the First Communion which they had either made recently or were about to make. When, in the evening, they sang on the front steps at Calèse, it was not always the airs of Lulli—which were included for my especial delectation: there were psalms, too. From far away I could see the vague blur made by your little group, and, when there was a moon, could make out the three little lifted faces. The sound of my footsteps on the gravel interrupted their singing.

On Sundays I was awakened by the bustle you all made in getting off to Mass. You were always afraid of being late. The horses pawed the ground: the cook hadn't turned up and had to be called. One of the children had forgotten a prayer-book. A shrill voice cried: "Which Sunday after Pentecost is it?"

When they got back and came in to give me a kiss they always found me still in bed. Little Marie, who must have recited all the prayers she knew with a special "Intention" for me, stared solemnly into my face, doubtless hoping to discover some slight improvement in my spiritual state.

She was the only one of them who did not irritate me. The two elder were already smugly ensconced in the beliefs to which you clung with so sure a feeling for that middle-class comfort which, at a later date, was to make them turn their backs on all the heroic virtues and sublime lunacies of the Christian faith. In her, on the contrary, there was a touching ardour, a genuine feeling of compassion for the farm labourers and the poor. People said of her: "She'd give everything she has: money just trickles through her fingers. It's all very charming, of course, but that sort of generosity needs careful watching. . . ." They said, too: "No one can resist her, not even her father." She used to climb on my knee of an evening of her own accord. Once she fell asleep with her head on my shoulder. Her curls tickled my cheek. I was suffering agonies, because I had to keep so still, and I wanted to smoke. But I sat there like a graven image, and, when the nurse came to fetch her at nine o'clock, I carried her all the way up to her room. You all stared at me in amazement, as though I had been the wild beast in the legend who licked the feet of the child martyrs. Shortly after that—it was on the morning of the 14th of August, she said to me—you know how children do:

"Promise—there's something I want to ask you, but you must promise first to do what I say. . . ."

She reminded me that you were going to sing at the eleven o'clock Mass next day, and that it would be nice of me to go and listen.

"You've promised! you've promised!" she kept on saying as she kissed me: "you've given your word!"

She took my kiss for a promise. The whole house was told about it. I felt that I was under observation. The "master" was going to Mass next day—fancy that! he who never, as a rule, put his foot inside a church! It was an event of immense significance.

I sat down to dinner that evening in a mood of irritability which I could not long conceal. Hubert asked you something— I forget what—about Dreyfus. I remember protesting furiously against your reply, and leaving the room. I did not come back, but packed my bag, took the 6 A.M. train on the 15th, and spent a hideous day in Bordeaux where the heat was stifling and everybody seemed to have gone away.

It seems odd to me now that you should ever have seen me again at Calèse after that. How came it that I always spent the school holidays with the family instead of in travelling? No doubt I could concoct all sorts of admirable explanations, but the real truth was my dislike of incurring a double expense. The idea that anyone could set off on a trip and spend a lot of money without first emptying the larder and locking up the house, never occurred to me. All the pleasure of going away would have been ruined for me by the knowledge that the household expenses were piling up all the time. So, I just crawled back to the family swill-pail. There was food waiting for me at Calèse, so why should I feed elsewhere? My mother had bequeathed to me her mania for "economy", and I had made a virtue of it.

Back I came, then, but with such resentment in my heart that not even Marie could soften me. I began to use tactics of a different kind against you. Instead of delivering a frontal attack on your beliefs, I did all I could, no matter how trivial the circumstances, to show how ill your practice squared with your faith. You must admit, my poor Isa, that, good Christian though you were, I had an easy enough task! You had forgotten, if, indeed, you had ever known, that charity is synonymous with love. You gave its name to what you regarded as your duties to the poor. These you scrupulously observed, always with a weather eye open on your eternal salvation! I realize that a profound change has come over you in recent years. To-day you visit cancer cases in hospital—I know all about that: but, at the time I am speaking of, once you had helped the poor—*your* poor—you felt all the freer to demand from those who were dependent on you what you regarded as your due. You made no compromise with the duty of the housewife, which is to get the largest possible amount of work in return for the lowest possible wages. The wretched old crone who came every morning to our front door with her cart could never sell you so much as a lettuce without your whittling down her meagre profit to the last farthing. If she had been a beggar, you would have given freely of your "charity".

When your frightened servants ventured to ask you for a "rise", you were at first amazed, and then so furiously indignant that you always ended by getting your way. You had a sort of genius for being able to demonstrate that they really had all they could reasonably want. You managed to pile up the total of their advantages: "You have a roof over your heads, a cask of wine, and half of a pig which you fatten on my potatoes, to say nothing of a garden in which you can grow vegetables." The poor devils never realized, till you told them, how well off they were! Your maid, you said, could save every penny of the forty francs you paid her every month! "She gets all my old clothes and underlinen and shoes. What can she find to spend her money *on*? If I gave her more, she'd only hand it over to her family!"

I admit, of course, that you looked after them devotedly when they were ill. You never left them to their own resources. I am well aware that you were, for the most part, always respected, and sometimes loved, by your staff. It is the foible of domestics to despise weak mistresses. In all such matters you were a true representative of the ideas of your class and period. But you could never bring yourself to admit that the Gospel condemned them. "*I* always thought"—I would say—"that Christ laid it down . . ." Remarks of that kind invariably brought you up short. You didn't know what to answer, and you were furious because of the children. You unfailingly finished up by falling into the trap. "We're not meant to take those things literally . . . ," you would stammer, and that gave me just the chance I needed to triumph over you. I would floor you with examples, all going to show that sanctity consists, precisely, in taking the Gospels literally. If you were foolish enough to reply that you were not a saint, I would quote the precept: "Be ye perfect, even as your Father in heaven is perfect."

You must admit, my poor Isa, that I did what I could in my own way, and that if, now, you visit cancer cases, it is to me in part that they owe your devotion! In the old days, your love of your children obsessed you to the exclusion of every other consideration. All your reserves of kindness and self-sacrifice were used up on them. They filled your vision: you couldn't *see* anybody else. It wasn't only from me that they had alienated you, but from the whole of the rest of the world. The only thing you could speak about to God was their health and their future. That's where I got my chance. I would ask whether, as a Christian, you ought not rather to demand for them every kind of cross—poverty, sickness. You would cut me short: "I'm not going to an-

swer you: you're talking about what you don't understand. . . ."
Unfortunately for you, we had as a tutor a young seminarist
of twenty-three, the Abbé Ardouin. I was merciless in my appeals
to him for support, and caused him much embarrassment, since
I never asked his opinion except when I knew that I was in the
right. He was incapable of saying anything but what he really
thought. As the Dreyfus case developed, I found innumerable
opportunites for setting him at odds with you. "So you're in favour"—you would say—"of undermining our whole military system for a . . ." The mere word "Jew" released the full spate of
my pretended indignation, and I would keep on until I had
forced the Abbé to admit that no true Christian ought to connive
at the condemnation of an innocent man, even though the safety
of the country might be at stake.

But I made no attempt to convince you and the children,
whose whole knowledge of the "affair" was derived from cari-
catures which appeared in the "right-thinking" newspapers. You
closed your ranks against me, and presented an impenetrable
front. Even when I seemed to be in the right, you suspected me
of trickery. Things got to such a pitch that you deliberately said
nothing when I was within earshot. I had only to come near—
and it's just the same now—for all discussion to stop. But there
were times when I hid in the shrubbery without your knowing I
was there, and then I would put in my oar before you had time
to retreat. You couldn't avoid the issue then.

Talking of the Abbé Ardouin to your friends, you would say:
"The man's a perfect saint. He's no more capable of thinking evil
than a child. My husband plays with him like a cat with a mouse.
That's the only reason he puts up with him. As a rule, he hates
the very sight of a cassock. . . ."

The only reason I'd agreed to having a priest for tutor was, as
a matter of fact, that no layman would have agreed to work all
through the holidays for a hundred and fifty francs. At first I
treated the tall, black-haired, shy young man with the weak eyes
as completely insignificant. I took no more notice of him than I
did of the furniture. He saw to it that the children did their work,
took them out for walks, ate very little, and never uttered a word.
As soon as dinner was finished, he went up to his room. Sometimes, when there was nobody about, he played the piano. I
know nothing of music, but he was, as you said, "a nice person
to have about the place".

One incident there was which I am sure you have not forgotten. What you have never known is that it established between the Abbé Ardouin and me a secret current of sympathy. One day the children told me that the Curé had called. I at once took refuge in the vineyard, as I always did on such occasions. But you sent Hubert to fetch me back. The Curé had something urgent to say to me. With much grumbling I returned to the house, because I was really rather frightened of the little old man. He had come, he said, to unburden his conscience. It was he who had recommended the Abbé Ardouin as a thoroughly reliable young seminarist who had been prevented, by ill health, from taking Orders at the normal time. He had just learned, in the course of a retreat, that this postponement had actually been a disciplinary measure. The Abbé was, to be sure, very pious, but he was mad about music, and had been tempted by one of his co-seminarists to slip out one night and go to a charity concert at the Grand Theatre. They were in lay dress, but were recognized and denounced. What made matters worse was that one of the performers was Madame Georgette Lebrun, and she had sung excerpts from *Thaïs*. At sight of her bare feet and Greek tunic, held up under the arms by a silver girdle ("and that was all: not so much as a hint of a shoulder-strap"), there had been an "Oh!" of indignation. In the Union Club Box an old gentleman had exclaimed: "This is really going a bit *too* far . . . where does she think she is?" Such was the spectacle to which the Abbé Ardouin had been exposed. One of the delinquents had suffered immediate expulsion: the other—the Abbé—had been pardoned. He was a prize student. But his Superiors had postponed his ordination for two years.

We were all of us unanimous in declaring that he enjoyed our full confidence. From then on, however, the Curé showed the greatest coldness to the young man who, he said, had deceived him. No doubt you remember the incident. What you have never known is that, on the same evening, while I was smoking on the terrace, I saw coming towards me in the moonlight the emaciated figure of the guilty man. He addressed me with considerable embarrassment, and asked to be forgiven for having introduced himself into my family without first explaining that there was a slur upon his character. When I told him that the escapade which had caused all the trouble made me like him the more, he suddenly adopted an intransigent attitude, and proceeded to argue against himself. I couldn't, he said, realize the heinousness of his offence. It was not merely that he had broken his vow of obedience: he had sinned against his vocation and against the moral code. He had been a cause of scandal. The whole of the rest of his life would not be long enough to enable him to make proper reparation for his misdeed. . . . . I can still see that tall, bowed back, and his shadow in the moonlight, cut in two by the parapet of the terrace.

Prejudiced though I might be against men of his cloth, I could not, witnessing his shame and sorrow, suspect him of the faintest tinge of hypocrisy. He excused his silence to us on the ground of his need. But for the job we had offered him, he would have had to live for two months at the cost of his mother, a poor widow of Libourne, who went out charring. When I replied that, so far as I could see, there had been no obligation upon him to mention something that had to do merely with seminary discipline, he took my hand and uttered the following extraordinary words. It was the first time that anything of the sort had been said to me, and I don't mind confessing that I felt knocked sideways.

"You are," he said, "a very good man." You know that laugh of mine which, even in our first years together, got on your nerves, that sort of private chortle which has the effect of killing any gaiety within the radius of my presence?—well, it racked me that evening as I looked at the shocked and gawky seminarist in front of me. After a while I was able to get out:

"You can't know, Monsieur l'Abbé, how comic that sounds. Ask those who know me whether I am good! Question my family, my professional colleagues! Why, malevolence is my leading characteristic!"

He replied, rather shyly, that those who are truly malevolent don't talk about it.

"I defy you," said I, "to find what you would call a single good action in the whole course of my life."

Then, intending a reference to my calling, he quoted the words of Christ: "I was in prison, and ye visited Me. . . ."

"That's how I make my living, Monsieur l'Abbé. I act from purely self-interested motives. There was a time when I even bribed the gaolers to mention my name, at suitable moments, to those awaiting trial . . . not much goodness there, eh?"

I have forgotten what he said to that. We strolled together under the lime-trees. How surprised you'd have been if I had told you that the presence of that frocked priest somehow brought me peace of mind. But it did.

It was my habit to get up before sunrise and go down into the garden to breathe the morning coolness. On those occasions I used to watch the Abbé setting off for Mass. He walked quickly, and was so much absorbed in his own thoughts that he sometimes passed quite close to me without so much as being aware of my presence. Those were the days when I was lashing you with my mockeries, and doing everything I could to prove that your actions were at odds with your principles. . . . Nevertheless, my conscience was not altogether comfortable. Each time I caught you out in some meanness, some lack of charity, I pretended that there was not a trace of Christ's spirit among the lot of you. But I knew perfectly well, all the time, that beneath my roof, and unsuspected by the other inmates, there dwelt a man who lived in strict obedience to its promptings.

❀ VIII ❀

THERE was one occasion, however, when you really did fill me with genuine and unfeigned horror. At some time in '96 or '97— you will remember the exact date—our brother-in-law the Baron Philipot died. Your sister, Marinette, woke one morning and said something to him. He did not answer. She opened the shutters and saw the old man's upturned eyes and sagging jaw. It took her quite a little while to realize that she had been sleeping for a considerable time beside a corpse.

I don't think any of you fully realized the beastliness of that old wretch's will. He left his wife an enormous fortune, on one condition—that she should never marry again. If she did so, the bulk of the money was to go to his nephews.

"We shall have to take great care of her," your mother kept on saying. "Fortunately, we are a very united family. The poor darling mustn't be left alone for a moment."

At that time Marinette was about thirty, though she looked, as you will remember, little more than a girl. She had let herself be married off to an old man without a word of protest, and had put up with him very patiently. It never occurred to you that she might find some difficulty in shouldering the responsibilities of perpetual widowhood. You entirely discounted the shock of her release, the effect upon her of emerging suddenly from a dark tunnel into the full light of day.

Don't be afraid, Isa, that I am going to abuse the advantage which that situation offered me. It was only natural that you should want all those millions to stay in the family, that you should hope our children would ultimately enjoy them. It was wrong, you thought, that Marinette should get no reward for ten years of slavery to an old man's whim. You behaved as all good parents would have behaved in the circumstances. Celibacy seemed to you to be a perfectly natural condition. I don't suppose you remembered the time when you have been a young wife. That chapter had been long since closed. You were a mother. The other implications of marriage had ceased to exist for you and for your parents. Imagination has never been an outstanding characteristic of your family. In this matter of sexual relationships, your attitude was neither that of brute beasts nor of ordinary human beings.

It was agreed that Marinette should spend the first summer of her widowhood at Calèse. She accepted the suggestion gladly, not that there was much intimacy between you, but she was fond of our children and especially of Marie. I scarcely knew her. What at first struck me about her was her gracefulness. She was a year older than you, but seemed very much your junior.

Recurrent pregnancies had given you a heavy look, whereas she, apparently, had emerged intact from the old man's bed. Her face was the face of a child. She wore her hair high, in the fashion of the day, with a fluff of darkish fair strands in the nape of the neck (people to-day have forgotten that outmoded marvel—a tousled nape!). Her eyes were rather too round, and gave her the appearance of perpetual surprise. I used to encircle her "wasp-waist", jokingly, with my two hands. But the prominence of her breast and hips would, to-day, have seemed almost monstrous. Women at that time looked like hot-house flowers. Her gaiety surprised me. The children thought her great fun, for she organized games of hide-and-seek in the loft, and played with them at Tableaux Vivants in the evenings. "She's a little too feather-headed," you used to say, "and doesn't seem to realize her position."

You found it already a strain on your patience to see her going about all week in white dresses; and when she attended Mass without a veil, and refused to wear so much as a border of crape, you considered her behaviour definitely shocking. The heat, according to you, was not an adequate excuse.

She had shared only one amusement with her husband—riding. Baron Philipot had been a champion horseman, and until the last day of his life had rarely missed his morning canter. She had had her mare sent to Calèse, and, since there was nobody to accompany her, had taken to going out alone. This you thought doubly scandalous. It was unseemly for a three-months-old widow to take any kind of exercise, but that she should go riding without somebody in attendance passed all bounds.

"I shall let her know what the family thinks of such behaviour," you said more than once. And so you did, but she continued to have her own way. At last, tired of squabbling, she asked me to act as her escort, and promised to find me a very quiet mount (she, of course, paying for everything).

We used to start off at dawn, because of the flies, and because we had to walk the horses for two kilometres before reaching the nearest stretch of pine-wood. We used to mount at the front steps. Marinette would stick her tongue out at the closed shutters of your room, pin a dew-drenched rose to her habit, and say, as she did so, "*Quite* unsuitable for a widow!" The church bell would be ringing with short sharp strokes for early Mass, and the Abbé Ardouin would give us a shy greeting before vanishing into the mist which hung above the vines.

We spent the time until we reached the woods in chatting. I realized that I enjoyed a certain degree of prestige in my sister-in-law's eyes, not so much because of my position at the Bar, but because of the subversive ideas which I preached in the bosom of the family. Your principles were too much like those of her late husband. A woman always thinks of ideas, whether about religion or anything else, in terms of a *person*. For her they take tangible form, and the form may be either hated or adored. It would not have been difficult for me to take advantage of rebellious youth; but though I found it easy enough to act as her echo so long as it was all of *you* she inveighed against, I found it impossible to approve the contemptuous way in which she spoke of the millions she would lose in the event of her marrying again. I had every reason in the world to agree with her, and to take a high line of romantic nobility, but I could not pretend, even half-heartedly, to agree with her when she spoke of the loss of such a fortune as something not worth worrying about. If I am to be perfectly frank, I think I ought to admit that the idea of her

dying, and of the money coming to us, was not wholly absent
from my mind (and when I say "us", I don't mean the children
—to whom I scarcely gave a thought—but, primarily, to myself).

Try as I might to school myself to use the words she would
have liked to hear, it was no good. What I actually said was:
"My dear Marinette, you can't be serious! Think of it, seven
million! It is impossible to be indifferent to seven million! No man
in the world is worth the sacrifice of even a fraction of such a
sum!"—and, when she maintained that happiness was more important than money, I told her that nobody could give up such a
fortune and be happy.

"It's all very well for you to say you hate them!" she exclaimed:
"You're really one of them, you know!"

Then she set off at a gallop, with me following. Her verdict
had been passed on me: all hope was lost. What a price I was
paying for my lunatic love of money! I might have found in
Marinette a younger sister, a mistress. . . . You'd like me,
wouldn't you, to sacrifice to you that to which I've sacrificed
everything else? Oh no, my money's cost me far too dear for
me to give up a single penny of it until I've breathed my last!

But you never give up, do you? I can't help wondering whether
Hubert's wife, who forced her presence on me last Sunday, was
really acting as your delegate, or whether she came of her own
accord. Poor Olympe! (why on earth did Phili nickname her
Olympe?—we've all forgotten what her real name is) . . . on the
whole, I'm inclined to believe that she said nothing to you about
her coming to see me. You've never made her one of yourselves,
you don't regard her as belonging to the family. She is completely
indifferent to everything outside the boundaries of her narrow
world. She knows nothing of the laws of the "tribe", and has no
idea that I am "the enemy". That's not because she is either
benevolent or sympathetic, but simply because she never thinks
about other people, and doesn't even bother to hate them.

"He's always very nice to me," she says, whenever my name
is mentioned in her hearing. She is entirely unaware of my bitterness, and because, simply from a spirit of contradiction, I
take up the cudgels in her favour against the lot of you, is convinced that I find her attractive.

Reading between the lines of her confused outpourings, I
gather that Hubert has "got out" in time, but that he has had to
call on the whole of his private fortune, as well as on his wife's

dowry, to save the business. "He says he's bound to get his money back, but that he must have an advance . . . he calls it a mortgage on his expectations. . . ."

When she said that, I nodded my head. I agreed with everything, and pretended not to have the remotest idea what it was she wanted. I can play the innocent very successfully at such times!

If only poor Olympe knew what I sacrificed to money in the days when I was still relatively young!

On those mornings of my thirty-fifth year, we used to jog back, your sister and I, letting the horses take their own pace, along the road which was already feeling the heat of the sun, between the sprayed vines. She sat there in the saddle mocking at me while I talked about the millions that she mustn't, on any account, lose. Each time that I managed to free myself from the obsession of that menaced fortune, she would laugh at me with a sort of contemptuous kindness. I tried to defend myself, but only succeeded in getting into deeper water.

"It's in your own interest, Marinette, that I'm talking like this. You don't really think, do you, that I'm the sort of man to let himself be hag-ridden by the problem of his children's future? I know that Isa doesn't want the money to slip between their fingers, but I . . ."

Then she would laugh, and say between partly clenched teeth: "You're quite horrid enough as it is. . . ."

I protested that I was thinking only of her happiness. She shook her head with an air of disgust. What really made her envious, though she never admitted it, was not so much marriage as motherhood.

Oh, she despised me all right! But when, after luncheon, in spite of the heat, I left the dark, cool house where the members of the family were dozing, sprawled on the leather sofas and in the wicker chairs, when I threw back the shutters of the French windows, and slipped out into the blazing blue, I didn't have to look back. I knew perfectly well that she would follow. I could hear her footsteps on the gravel. She walked with difficulty, catching her high heels in the baked earth. We stood together with our elbows on the parapet of the terrace. She played a sort of game with herself, which consisted in seeing how long she could keep her bare arm on the hot stone.

The plain beneath gave itself to the sun in a silence as deep as when it sleeps under the moon. The Landes ringed the horizon in an immense black semicircle on which the metallic sky pressed like a weight. Not a man, not an animal, would stir out of doors till four o'clock. The flies buzzed, but made no effort to move away. They were no less motionless than the pillar of smoke rising from the plain straight and still in the airless heat.

I knew that the woman at my side could never love me, that everything about me was odious to her. But we were the only two living things in that lost land, imprisoned in its summer torpor. She was young and tormented, spied upon by her family, and she turned to me as unconsciously as the heliotrope turns to the sun. And yet, had I betrayed by a single word the emotions of my heart, she would have given me only mockery in return. I was perfectly well aware that she would have repulsed with disgust any advances on my part, however timid. There we stood together, on the edge of that immense vat in which the future harvest of the grapes was fermenting under the blue-tinted leaves, drowsing in the sun.

And what did you think, Isa, about those morning rides and close confabulations while the rest of the world was sunk in siesta? I know what you thought, because on one occasion I overheard you. Through the closed shutters of the drawing-room I heard you say to your mother, who was staying with us at Calèse (no doubt she had come to reinforce the watch that was being kept on Marinette):

"He's a bad influence on her, but only because of his ideas. Apart from them he serves as a distraction. I can see no harm in their going about together."

"Yes, he *is* a distraction for her, and that's all that really matters," your mother replied.

You were delighted to think that I was a distraction for Marinette. "But after the holidays," you said more than once, "we shall have to find some other way of keeping her amused." You may have despised me, Isa, but your contempt was nothing to mine when I heard you talk like that. I suppose it never occurred to you that there might be any danger. Women have a way of not remembering what they have ceased to feel.

Nothing, to be sure, could possibly happen during those after-luncheon intimacies poised above the plain. Empty though the world was, we were standing, as it were, bang in the middle of a stage. Had there been but one peasant who had not surrendered to siesta, he would have been bound to see us there, a man and a woman motionless as two trees, gazing down at the incandescent earth, and so close together that neither could have made the slightest movement without touching the other.

But our nightly strolls were no less innocent. I remember one August evening in particular. Dinner had been made stormy by a discussion of the Dreyfus case. Marinette, who, with me, represented the party for revision, had by now surpassed me in the art of bringing the Abbé Ardouin into the open and forcing him into taking sides. You had mentioned with enthusiasm some article of Drumont's, and Marinette, as though butter wouldn't melt in her mouth, had said:

"Do tell me, Monsieur l'Abbé, is it permissible for us to hate the Jews?"

That evening, much to our delight, he did not take refuge in easy evasions. He spoke of the greatness of the Chosen People, of the part they had played as witnesses to the truth, of their conversion, which had been foretold and would herald the end of the world. And when Hubert protested that we needs must hate our Lord's butchers, the Abbé replied that each of us had the right to hate one of Christ's butchers, and one only—himself, but no one else.

Thoroughly put out, you retorted that the only result of such highfalutin theories would be the surrender of France into the hands of her enemies. Fortunately for the Abbé, you then turned the conversation on to Jeanne d'Arc—and she made all well again. One of the children, out on the steps, exclaimed:

"How lovely the moon is to-night!" I went out. I knew that Marinette would come too. I heard her say in a low voice, "Wait for me." . . . She was wearing a "boa" round her neck.

The moon was rising full in the east. She expressed admiration of the long shadows cast by the elms on the grass. The farmworkers' cottages stood blind-eyed in the white radiance. A few dogs were barking. She asked me whether it was the moon that made the trees so motionless. She said that on such a night the whole of creation was but a torment to the lonely. "An empty stage!" she said. Everywhere, at this very moment, lips were pressed to lips, shoulders touched, heart responded to heart. I could distinctly see a tear quivering on her lashes. In the world's stillness her breathing was the only sign of life. . . . It was

eager, it was hesitant. . . . You died in 1900, Marinette. What remains of you now? What remains of the body that was buried
thirty years ago? I can remember the smell of it in the darkness.
Perhaps, only if we have conquered the body can we believe in
the body's resurrection. The punishment of those who have
abused it is that they cannot even imagine that it will rise again.

I took her hand, as I might have taken the hand of an unhappy
child, and, like a child, she leaned her head upon my shoulder.
I received the gift of it merely because I happened to be there.
The earth receives the fallen peach. Most human beings come
together not as the result of any deliberate choice, but like trees
which have grown side by side, their branches interlacing in the
simple process of their growth.

But what made me infamous at that moment was that I
thought of *you*: thought how I might be revenged on you, how I
might make use of Marinette to cause you suffering. It may have
been for a fleeting second only, but it is true, nevertheless, that
the idea of such a crime did enter my head. We took a few uncertain steps outside the zone of moonlight towards a clump of
syringas and pomegranate trees. But Fate intervened. At that
precise moment I heard steps in the lime walk—the walk which
the Abbé Ardouin used every morning on his way to Mass. It
was almost certainly he. . . . I thought of what he had said to me
one evening—"You are a very good man." If only he could have
read my heart at that moment! Perhaps the shame that overcame
me at the thought was my salvation.

I led Marinette back into the light, and made her sit down. I
dried her eyes with my handkerchief, and spoke to her as I
might have spoken to Marie if she had fallen and I had picked
her up under the limes. I pretended that I had not noticed the
hint of an emotional disturbance in her tears, and in the soft
yielding of her body.

❈ *IX* ❈

NEXT morning she did not ride. I went into Bordeaux (I spent
two days of each week there, even in vacation time, so as not to
interrupt my consultations).

The Southern Express was standing in the station just as I was getting into the train to go back to Calèse, and great was my astonishment to see, through the window of a coach labelled *Biarritz*, Marinette in a grey tailor-made suit and without a veil. I remembered that a friend of hers had been pressing her for some time to join her at Saint-Jean-de-Luz. She was reading an illustrated paper and did not see the signs I made. That evening, when I mentioned the incident to you, you paid little attention to what you thought was a brief indulgence in liberty. You told me that, shortly after I had left, Marinette had received a telegram from her friend. You seemed surprised that I did not know this. Perhaps you had suspected us of having arranged to meet secretly in Bordeaux.

Besides, you had other things to think of. Little Marie had been sent to bed with a temperature. She had been suffering for some days from diarrhoea, and you were uneasy. I will do you the justice to say that whenever any of the children were ill, nothing else mattered to you.

I want to pass quickly over what followed. After more than thirty years it is only with an immense effort that I can bring my mind to dwell on it.

I know the substance of your charge against me. You had the effrontery to tell me to my face that I was against having a second opinion. I have no doubt that if we had called in Professor Arnozan he would have diagnosed what we took to be influenza as typhus. But cast your mind back. Once, but only once, you did say, "Mightn't it be as well to have Arnozan?" My reply to that was: "Dr. Aubrou tells me that he's been attending more than twenty cases of this type of influenza in the village. . . ." You didn't insist. You pretend now that you raised the point again next day, that you begged me to send a telegram to Arnozan. Had you done so I should have remembered it. That fact is, I've chewed old memories over and over through so many days and nights, that I'm no longer sure what actually did happen. I know I've always been a miser about money, but not to the extent of trying to save expense where Marie's health was concerned. So it can't have been that, apart from the fact that Arnozan worked for the love of God and humanity. If I didn't call him in, the reason is that we were still convinced that it was simply a case of influenza which had "gone to the bowels". That ass Aubrou

made Marie eat so as to keep up her strength. It was he who
killed her, not I. You were entirely of my opinion, and if you
say now that you urged me to call in Arnozan, you are lying. I
was not responsible for Marie's death. That you should ever have
accused me of such a thing is horrible. All the same, you *believe*
I was: you've always believed it.

Oh, that relentless summer! the frenzy of the heat, the fero-
cious scraping of the grasshoppers. It was impossible to get any
ice. All through those endless afternoons I sat wiping the sweat
from her tiny face, which seemed to be a target for every fly
within reach. Arnozan came at last, but too late. He changed the
treatment, but by that time all hope of saving her was gone. It
was probably only because of her delirium that she kept on
saying—"for Papa!—for Papa!" . . . Do you remember the sound
of her voice when she suddenly cried out, "Please, God, I am
only a child . . . " and how she stopped, and went on, "No, I can
stand it, I can . . ."? The Abbé gave her some water from Lourdes
to drink. Our heads, yours and mine, came together above her
exhausted body: our hands touched. When it was all over, you
thought me callous.

Do you really want to know what was going on in my mind?
I was thinking how strange it seemed that you, a Christian, should
set such store by the *corpse*. You wouldn't leave it. We tried to
get you to eat: we kept on telling you that you would need all
your strength. But only by using force could we make you leave
the room. You sat beside the bed, touching her cold forehead
and her cheeks in a sort of fumbling way. Her hair, which still
had life in it, you kissed, and now and again you slipped to your
knees, not to pray, but so that you could press your face against
the cold and rigid hands.

The Abbé Ardouin raised you up, and spoke of how we must
make ourselves like little children if we are to enter the Kingdom
of the Father. "She lives, she sees you, she is waiting for you."
But you shook your head. The words did not even penetrate to
your brain. Your faith was useless to you. You had thoughts for
nothing but that flesh of your flesh, which was going to be laid
in the earth and would soon know corruption. It was I, the un-
believer, who realized, as I looked at what was left of Marie,
the full meaning of the word "remains". I was overwhelmed by a
sense of departure, of absence. She was no longer there. *That*

was not her: "Is it Marie that ye seek . . .?—she is no longer here. . . ."

Later, you accused me of being quick to forget. Only I know what broke in me when I kissed her for the last time as she lay in her coffin. But what lay there was not really her. You held it against me that I did not accompany you to the cemetery, when you visited it almost every other day. "He never sets foot inside the place"—that was your constant complaint. "And yet," you would say, "she was the only person he seemed to have any feeling for. . . . The truth of the matter is—he's quite heartless. . . ."

Marinette came back for the funeral, but left again three days later. You were blinded by your grief and never saw the threat that was gathering in that direction. You even seemed relieved when your sister went away. Two months afterwards, we heard of her engagement to a literary gent, a journalist whom she had met in Biarritz. It was too late, then, to put a spoke in her wheel. You showed yourself to be utterly unforgiving. It was as though some long-repressed hatred of Marinette had suddenly burst free. You didn't, you said, want to know the "creature"—who, as a matter of fact, was quite an ordinary sort of chap, pretty much like any other. His only crime was that he had deprived our children of a fortune. Not that he derived any benefit from it himself, since most of it went to Philipot's nephews.

But reason was never your strong suit. You were quite unscrupulous. I have never known anybody who could be so serenely unjust. God knows what peccadilloes you may have confessed in the secrecy of your heart—but there was certainly not one of the Beatitudes which you did not deny by the actions of your life. You thought nothing of accumulating false reasons against those you hated. You had never seen your sister's husband, and knew nothing whatever about him, but that did not prevent you from saying: "She fell a victim to some sort of adventurer she met at Biarritz, a regular lounge-lizard type. . . ."

When the poor girl died in child-bed (I don't want to judge you as harshly as you judged me in the matter of Marie), it wasn't only that you showed next to no regret. Events had proved you right. It had been bound to end like that. She had dug her own grave, and you had nothing with which to reproach yourself. You had done your duty. The wretched woman had known perfectly well that her family would always take her back if she

made the slightest sign. You, at least, had had nothing to do with
the business—that must have been a comforting thought! You
had been firm—but at what a cost! "There are times when one
has got to learn to trample on one's feelings!"
I don't want to be too hard on you. I realize that you behaved
well to little Luc, Marinette's son, when there was no one to
bother about him after your mother's death. You made yourself
responsible for him during the holidays, and went to see him
once each winter in the school just outside Bayonne where he
had been placed. "You did your duty"—such were your words
—"even if his father didn't do *his*."
I have never told you how I came to meet Luc's father. It was
in Bordeaux, in the September of 1914. I was trying to find a
safe-deposit at a Bank. The fugitives from Paris had taken them
all. At long last, the manager of the Crédit Lyonnais notified me
that one of his clients was returning to the capital and might,
perhaps, consent to let me have his. When he told me his name I
realized that it was Luc's father. He was very far from being the
monster you thought him. I tried in vain to recognize, in this man
of thirty-eight, lean, hollow-cheeked and worried to death by the
constant threat of medical boards, the being whom, fourteen
years earlier, I had seen at Marinette's funeral. I had a business
talk with him. He expressed himself with the utmost frankness.
He was living with a woman, but didn't want Luc to have anything to do with her. It was out of consideration for the boy that
he had handed him over to the tender mercies of his grandmother. My poor Isa, if only you and the children had known
what I offered him at that meeting! I can tell you now. My suggestion was that he should keep the safe-deposit in his own name,
giving me power of attorney. I, for my part, was to leave all my
liquid assets there, with a document stating that they were Luc's
property. So long as I lived he would have been powerless to
touch them, but, after my death, could have taken possession
without your knowing a thing. . . .
Obviously, I should have been putting myself and my fortune
into his hands. How I must have hated you at that moment!
But the man wouldn't play. He was too frightened. He spoke of
his "honour".
How came it that I could have entertained such a mad idea?
At the time I am speaking of our children must have been within
measurable distance of their thirties. They were married, were

definitely on your side, were opposed to me on every conceivable issue. You were working in secret. I was the enemy. God knows you were not on particularly good terms with any of them, and especially not with Geneviève. Your grievance against her was that she left you out of everything, that she never asked your advice. But against me you maintained a common front. Nevertheless, everything between us was conducted in a muted key, except on solemn occasions. For instance, there were terrible battles over the children's marriages. I set my face against giving anything in the nature of a dowry, and insisted on an allowance in each case. I refused to render an account of my financial position to either of the families concerned, and stuck to my point. I had all the cards in my hand. Hatred was my strong suit, hatred and love—the love that I felt for young Luc. And the families put up with me, because they felt so sure that my fortune was immense.

My silence worried you. You wanted to know. Sometimes, Geneviève tried to get on the soft side of me. I could hear the poor ungainly creature clumping along in her clogs a mile off! I often said to her, "You'll bless me when I'm dead," just for the pleasure of seeing the greedy glint in her eyes. She passed on those wonderful words of mine to you. The whole family was in a state of trance. And all the time I was trying to find some way of leaving you nothing beyond what could not be concealed. I thought only of young Luc. I even played with the idea of mortgaging the land. . . .

But on one occasion I did let myself be taken in by your play-acting. It was the year after Marie's death. I was ill. Some of my symptoms were not unlike those of the disease which had carried off our little daughter. I hate being fussed over. I have a horror of doctors and drugs. You nagged me until I agreed to stay in bed and see Arnozan.

You nursed me devotedly—that goes without saying—but also with a certain uneasiness. Sometimes, when you asked me how I was feeling, I thought I heard a note of anxiety in your voice. When you felt my forehead, you did it much in the same way as you would have done if I had been your child. You wanted to sleep in my room. If I was restless in the night you got up and fetched me a drink. "She is really fond of me," I used to say to myself: "who *would* have thought it!—I suppose it's because of

what I make!" But there I was wrong. You don't love money for
its own sake. It's more likely that what was worrying you was the
thought that my death would leave the children poorer. But it
wasn't that either.

When Arnozan had finished examining me, you had a conversation with him out on the steps, and you raised your voice
once or twice as you so often do. It's a habit that's always giving
you away. "I want you to let it be known, doctor, that Marie died
of typhoid. People are saying it was consumption because of
what happened to my poor brothers. There's so much ill-nature
in the world. Once an idea gets about, it has a way of persisting.
I'm so terribly afraid of the harm that sort of talk might do to
Hubert and Geneviève. If my husband had been seriously ill it
might have given substance to that sort of gossip. For some days
I felt very anxious about him—thinking of the children. One of
his lungs, you know, was affected before his marriage. That's a
matter of general knowledge. People do so love that sort of thing.
Even if he had died of some infectious disease, they wouldn't
have believed it any more than they did in the case of Marie.
And my poor darlings would have been the ones to suffer. It used
to make me wild to see how little care he took of himself! He
wouldn't even stay in bed—as though he had only himself to
think of! But he never worries about anybody else, not even the
children! . . . Men like you, doctor, find it difficult to believe that
people like him exist. You're just like the Abbé Ardouin—who
never thinks evil of anybody. . . ."

I lay there in bed, laughing to myself, and when you came
back you asked me what I was laughing at. "Oh, nothing," I
said. It was a kind of private language of our own. "What are
you laughing at?" one of us would say.—"Oh, nothing." "What
are you thinking about?"—"Oh, nothing."

❦ X ❦

I TAKE up this narrative again after an attack which has kept me
in your power for close on a month. When illness weakens me, the
family circle closes about my bed. The whole lot of you are there,
watching me.

On Sunday Phili came to keep me company. It was hot: I
answered him in monosyllables. I lost the thread of my ideas . . .
for how long I can't say. The sound of his voice woke me. I saw
him there in the half-light with his ears pricked. His eyes were
glittering like a wolf-cub's. He was wearing a gold chain just
above his wrist-watch. His shirt was open, and his chest looked
like a child's. I dozed off again. The creaking of his shoes roused
me, and I lay watching him through half-closed eyes. He was
feeling my jacket, just were the inside pocket is in which I keep
my note-case. My heart was thumping, but I forced myself to lie
still. Perhaps his suspicions were aroused: anyhow, he went back
to his chair.

I pretended that I had just woken up, and asked him whether
I had been asleep for long.

"Only a few minutes, Grandpapa." I felt that terror which
visits old men when they know that young eyes are watching
them. Am I going mad? I got the idea that he was quite capable
of killing me. Hubert once said that Phili would stick at nothing.

I want you to know, Isa, how wretched I have been. By the
time you read these pages it will be too late for you to show me
pity, but I like to think that you may feel a little. I do not believe
in the everlasting hell-fire of your creed, but I do know what it
is to be damned in this life, and outcast. I realize only too clearly
that whatever road I choose I am bound to lose my way. All
through my life I have chosen wrongly. I have never learned
how to live—not in the sense that those of this world understand
living. Of the art of life I have, quite literally, known nothing. I
am in torment, Isa. The south wind is burning up the air. I am
thirsty, and have nothing with which to assuage my thirst but a
luke-warm tap. I am the owner of millions, but am without so
much as a glass of cold water to my name.

Phili's presence terrifies me. I think I put up with it only because he reminds me of somebody else, of that young Luc, our
nephew, who would now be a man of over thirty. I have never
denied your virtues, but he gave you no opportunity to show
them. You never liked him. There was nothing "Fondaudège"
about Marinette's boy. He had jet-black eyes. His hair grew low
over his forehead and swept back from his temples in what
Hubert used to call a couple of "love locks". In that school at
Bayonne where he was a boarder his reputation for work was

bad. But that, you said, was no concern of yours. You had quite enough to do looking after him in the holidays. He took no interest in books. Though this countryside is poor in game, he managed to find something to kill every day, contriving to "get" the one and only hare that lurked, each year, in the trenched earth of the vineyard. I can see him still, holding the dead beast by the ears, its muzzle smeared with blood, and waving triumphantly to us as he tramped back between the growing grape-shoots. I used to hear him starting out at dawn. I would open my window, and his clear young voice would call up to me through the mist: "Just off to take a look at my night-lines."

He invariably looked me straight in the face. There was nothing shifty about his eyes. He wasn't frightened of me: the idea of being frightened of me never entered his head. If I happened to come home unexpectedly after a few days' absence, and caught the smell of cigar smoke in the house, or found the carpet up in the drawing-room with all the signs of a hastily interrupted party (I had only to turn my back for Geneviève and Hubert to provoke an "invasion"—in spite of my strict injunctions to the contrary—and you always aided and abetted their disobedience, because, you said, "one must return hospitality"), it was invariably Luc they sent to make their peace with me. The terror I inspired just made him laugh. "I went into the drawing-room while they were dancing, and called out, 'Here's Uncle, he's come by the short cut!'—and, by Jove, you should have seen them hop it! Aunt Isa and Geneviève spirited the sandwiches away into the pantry! What a hullabaloo!"

That boy was the only person in the world I couldn't scare. Sometimes, when he set off on a day's fishing, I used to go down to the river with him. Usually, he could never keep still, was for ever dashing about here, there and everywhere, but on those occasions he was capable of standing perfectly motionless for hours on end, all eyes. It was exactly as though he had been turned into a tree: the slow, noiseless movements of his arm were like that of a swaying branch. Geneviève was perfectly right when she said that he would never be "literary". He couldn't be bothered to go out on the terrace at night to look at the moon. He was entirely without a feeling for nature, because he *was* nature, was wholly absorbed into it, was one of its forces, a living spring among its many springs.

I used to think of all the drama his young life had known—a

THE KNOT OF VIPERS

dead mother, a father who was never mentioned in our presence, a lonely life in a remote school. Much less than all that would have sufficed to fill *me* with bitterness and hate. Everybody loved him, and that seemed strange to me, whom everybody loathed. Yes, everybody loved him—even I. He had a smile for all, including me—but not more for me than for the others.

His nature was purely instinctive, and what struck me more and more, as he grew older, was his purity, his unawareness of evil, his utter disregard of it. I don't mean to imply that our children weren't "good". Hubert, as you always said, was a model youth. In that respect, I must admit, your early training had borne fruit. I wonder whether, if Luc had lived into manhood, he would have remained so utterly untroubled. I never got the impression that, with him, purity was something he had been taught, something of which he was conscious. It had the limpid quality of water running over a stony bed. It glittered on him like the dew on grass. I dwell on this because it had a profound effect on me. Your parade of high principles, your hints, your expression of distaste, your pursed lips—these things never made me so truly aware of evil as did that boy, though I was not conscious of it at the time, nor for many years afterwards. If, as you hold, humanity carries in its flesh the stigma of original sin, then, all I can say is that no living eye can ever have seen the mark in Luc. He had come from the hand of the potter uncracked and lovely. I felt myself, in comparison with him, deformed.

Is it accurate to say that I loved him like my own son? No, because what I loved in him was that complete absence of all trace of myself. I know only too well what of myself I have bequeathed to Hubert and Geneviève—sharpness of temper, the exorbitant value which they attach to material things, and a certain violence of contempt (in Geneviève's treatment of her husband, Alfred, there is a relentless quality which I recognize only too well). I could always feel quite sure that I should never bump up against myself in Luc.

During the rest of the year I scarcely thought of him. He spent Christmas and Easter with his father, and returned to us only with the coming of the summer holidays. In October he migrated with the other birds.

Was he religious minded? You used to say: "Even in a young animal like Luc one can see the influence of the good Fathers. He never misses taking Communion on Sundays. . . . I know, of course, that he hurries through his act of contrition, but, after all, no more is asked of any of us than we can give."

He never spoke to me about religion, even indirectly. His talk was always of the concrete. Sometimes when he pulled from his pocket a knife, a float, or a whistle for luring larks, his little rosary of black beads would fall to the ground. When that happened, he would hurriedly pick it up. But perhaps on Sunday mornings he did seem a little less scatter-brained than on other days, less evanescent, less imponderable, and as though charged with some unfamiliar current.

The links that bound me to Luc were many, but one of them may cause you some surprise. At times, on those Sunday mornings, I thought I could detect in the young fawn whose leapings were, for the moment, stilled, the brother of the little girl who had fallen asleep twelve years earlier—of our Marie. And yet, how different they were! She, you will remember, could never bear to see an insect crushed, and loved to line a hollow tree with moss, and set in it a statue to the Virgin. All the same, in Marinette's son, in the boy whom you used to call "a little animal", I seemed to see Marie again: or, rather, what I felt was that the same fresh spring, which had bubbled up in her and then gone underground again, was once more gushing at my feet.

When the war broke out Luc was not quite fifteen. Hubert was mobilized into the auxiliary forces. The medical boards to which he submitted with philosophic resignation, filled you with anxiety. For years his narrow chest had been a nightmare to you, but now your hopes were centred on it. When the deadliness of office work, and occasional jeers, made him eager to volunteer for active service (he really did try), you began to speak openly of what, for so long, you had been careful never to mention. "With your heredity . . ."—that was how you put it.

My poor Isa, don't be afraid. I'm not going to throw stones at you. You have never taken the slightest interest in me, have never really noticed me at all, and in those days you did so less even than usual. You had no idea of the mounting terror in me as winter followed winter. Luc's father was called up in one of the Ministries, and we had the boy with us, not only in the summer holidays, but at Christmas and Easter as well. The war filled him with enthusiasm. The only thing he was afraid of was that it might be over before he was eighteen. Formerly, he had never opened a book, but now he took to poring over maps and military manuals. He embarked methodically on a course of physical exercises. At sixteen he was already a full-grown man—and a tough one at that. He had no feelings to spare for the wounded and the dead. I gave him to read the grimmest accounts I could find of life in the trenches, but the picture he derived from them was of some terrible and magnificent form of sport in which all were not privileged to take a part. He would have to hurry up! How fearful he was of being too late! His idiot of a father had already given him written permission to offer himself as a volunteer, and this he carried in his pocket always. As the fatal day in January '18 approached, I followed with frightened concentration old Clemenceau's career, always on the watch for something to happen. I felt as must have felt those parents of men held prisoner, who used to watch for Robespierre's fall, hoping against hope that the tyrant would be laid low before their loved ones came to trial.

When Luc was under instruction in the training-camp at Souges, you used to send him knitted mufflers and all sorts of little comforts, but you used to say things, my poor Isa, which made me feel like murder—for instance: "Of course it would be terrible if anything happened to the poor boy—but, at least, he wouldn't leave anyone behind him." . . . I know you didn't mean any harm. . . .

A day came when I realized that it was no longer any good hoping that the war might be over before Luc was called up. When the front was broken on the Chemin des Dames, he came to say good-bye, a full fortnight earlier than he had expected. Well, it couldn't be helped. . . . And now I must pluck up courage to tell you of an incident so horrible that it still wakes me at night and makes me cry aloud. On the day to which I have referred, I went into the study to fetch a leather belt which I had got the local saddler to make to my own specification. Then, I climbed on a stool and tried to pull towards me a plaster cast of the head of Demosthenes which stood on top of the book-shelves. But I could not move it. It was full of gold coins which I had hidden there since the war began. I plunged my hand into all that gold which represented for me what I most valued in the world, and began to stuff the leather belt with money. When I got down from the stool, the swollen snake, gorged with metal, was hanging round my neck and weighing me down.

Shyly I held it out to Luc. At first he did not grasp what it was
that I was offering him.

"What on earth do you expect me to do with that, Uncle?"

"It may come in useful in billets, or if you're taken prisoner . . . or in other ways. With money you can do anything."

"Oh!" said he, with a laugh. "I've got quite enough to carry
as it is. . . . You didn't really think, did you, that I'd load myself
up with all that money? The first time I went into the line, I'd
have had to bury it in the woods!"

"But, my dear boy, at the beginning of the war, everyone who
had any gold took it with him."

"That's because they didn't know what they were in for,
Uncle."

He was standing in the middle of the room. He had thrown
the money-belt on the sofa. Strong though he was, he looked
terribly frail in his ill-fitting uniform. The collar was far too big
for him, and his neck looked like a drummer-boy's. His cropped
hair had taken all character from his face. He had been made
ready for death, decked for the sacrifice. He was just another
item in the mass, without identity, anonymous, as good as vanished. For a moment he stared at the belt, then he raised his
eyes to mine with an expression of mockery and contempt. All
the same, he gave me a hug. We went down with him to the
front-door. He turned his head and shouted back: "Much better
take all that to the Banque de France." By that time I could no
longer see anything, but I heard you say, with a laugh:

"Don't be too sure of that! it's asking a lot of him!"

Somebody shut the door. I stood in the hall quite motionless.
You said:

"You knew perfectly well, didn't you, that he wouldn't accept
the money? It was a perfectly safe gesture on your part."

I remembered that the belt was still on the sofa. One of the
servants might quite easily have found it there: one could never
be sure. I hurried upstairs, looped it round my neck again, and
emptied the contents back into the head of Demosthenes.

I scarcely noticed my mother's death, which took place a few
days later. Her mind had been wandering for years, and she no
longer lived with us. It is only now that I think of her every day,
remember her as the mother of my childhood and young manhood. The picture of her in those last years has faded from my

mind. Though I hate cemeteries, I still go, at times, to visit her
grave. I used to take flowers, but I have given up doing that,
because I noticed that they were always stolen. The poor sneak
the roses of the rich for the benefit of their own dead. I ought to
have a railing put up, but everything's so expensive nowadays.

Luc has no grave. He just disappeared, was one of the "missing". I keep in my note-case the only card he had time to send
me. It was one of the printed Field-Service affairs: "All well:
have received your parcel. Love." The word love was in his own
handwriting. That message at least I did get from my poor child.

❀ X I ❀

TONIGHT I woke, fighting for breath. I felt a compulsion to get
up. I dragged myself to my chair, and sat, reading over, to the
accompaniment of a howling wind, the last few pages I had
written. I was appalled by the light they shed on my deepest self.
Before settling down to go on with them, I leaned for a while at
the window. The gale had dropped. Calèse was wrapped in sleep.
There was not so much as a breeze, and the sky was full of stars.
Suddenly, about three o'clock, there was another squall. The
sky rumbled, and heavy, icy drops began to fall. They rattled on
the tiles so loudly that I feared they might be hail. I thought that
my heart had stopped beating.

The grapes have barely "set". Next year's harvest covers all
the slopes. But it seems that it may be with it as it is with those
young animals which the hunter tethers and then leaves in darkness to attract the prowling beasts of prey. Clouds, heavy with
thunder, are snuffling round the proffered vines.

But what do I care now about the grape-harvest? I have nothing left to harvest in this world. The only thing left for me to do
is to get to know myself a little better. Pay attention, Isa. After
my death, among my papers, you will find a statement of my
last wishes. They date from the months immediately following
Marie's death, those months during which I was ill, and you were
worried on account of the children. You will find, too, my profession of faith. It runs something like this: "Should I agree, at the
moment of my death, to accept the ministrations of a priest, I

herewith, while my mind remains clear, protest against the advantage that will have been taken of my weakening powers—physical as well as mental—to extort from me what my reason rejects." I owe you that confession. It is, on the contrary, when I study myself, as I have been doing for the past two months, with a closeness of attention which is stronger than my feeling of disgust, and when I feel my mind to be at its clearest, that the temptations of Christianity most torment me. It is then that I feel it impossible to deny that a way does exist in me which might lead me to your God. If I could reach the point of feeling satisfied with myself, I could fight this sense of pressure with more hope of success. If I could despise myself unreservedly, then the issue would be settled once and for all. But when a man is as hard as I am, when his heart, as in my case, has become dead wood, when he can inspire only hatred, and create about himself nothing but a waste land, then he has no defence against the onrush of hope. . . . I wonder if you really understand what I am getting at, Isa? Perhaps it is not for you, not for the army of the just, that your God came into the world, if come He did, but for us. You have never known me, have never realized the kind of man I am. Do I seem less horrible to you, now that you have read these pages? You must surely see by this time that there does exist in me a secret string which Marie could touch merely by snuggling into my arms, or little Luc, when, returning from Mass on Sundays, he would sit down on the bench in front of the house and stare at the distant plain.

Don't please think that I am painting too pretty a picture of myself. I know my heart—it is a knot of vipers. They have almost squeezed the life out of it. They have beslavered it with their poison, but, underneath their squirming, it still beats. Impossible now to loosen the knot. I can fight free only by cutting it with a knife, by slashing it with a sword: *I am come to bring not peace but a sword.*

It may well be that to-morrow I shall deny what I here confess, just as, to-night, I have denied those final wishes which I confided to paper thirty years ago. I have seemed to hate, with a hatred for which I may yet make atonement, all that you profess: and I shall still go on hating those who call themselves Christians. But is it not because so many of them degrade hope and distort a Countenance, *that* Countenance, *that* Face? You will say that a

man, heavy as I am with abominations, has no right to sit on them
in judgment. But isn't there, Isa, in my very vileness something
(I don't know what) which, more than all their virtues, resem-
bles the Sign of your adoration? What I am writing here must
seem to you nothing but an absurd blasphemy. But you must
prove it to me. Why do you not speak to me? Why have you
never spoken to me? Perhaps, who knows? some word of yours
might rend my heart. I feel to-night that even now it is not too
late for us to start again. Suppose I don't wait until I am dead to
let you see these pages? Suppose I beg you, in the name of your
God, to persevere with them to the end? Suppose I wait until you
have reached the last word? Suppose I saw you come into my
room with tear-stained face and open arms? Suppose I asked
your pardon? Suppose we knelt down, side by side, and prayed?

It seems as though the storm is over. The dawn stars are
twinkling in the sky. I thought the rain had started again, but it
was only the dripping of the trees. If I lie down again I shall
have to fight for breath. I can't write any more. Now and again
I drop my pen, and let my head fall against the hard back of the
chair.

A hiss like that of a wild beast, then a deafening din and a
great glare filling all the sky. In the panic silence that followed,
I heard the sound of fireworks on the hills, set off by the vinegrowers to scatter the clouds or resolve the hail to water. Rockets
were leaping into the air from the darkness where shrouded Barsac
and Sauterne were waiting in terror for the coming of the scourge.
The bell of St. Vincent's, which keeps the hail away, has been
ringing with might and main. The sound of it is like that of
someone singing in the night because he is afraid. Suddenly, from
the roof there came that noise as of a handful of flung pebbles . . .
hailstones! Time was when I should have rushed to the window. I
could hear the sound of shutters flung back, and your voice crying down to a man who was hurrying across the yard: "Is it
serious?" . . . " 'Tis all mixed with rain," he replied; "and that be
lucky: but 'tis coming down proper hard." A frightened child has
just run barefoot down the passage. I find myself, from force
of habit, reckoning: "A hundred thousand francs gone west . . ."
—but I have not stirred. Nothing, in the old days, could have
kept me from rushing downstairs—one night they found me out
among the vines, wearing my slippers, holding a candle, and

bare-headed under the hail. Some profound peasant instinct had driven me out as though to fling myself upon the ground and cover the beaten vines with my body. But to-night I have become a stranger to all that was once best in me. Those restricting bonds have, at last, been loosened, by what or by whom I do not know. The cables have been cut, Isa, and I am adrift. What power is leading me on? Is it blind—or is it love? Perhaps it may be love. . . .

PART TWO

❈ *XII* ❈

WHAT induced me to pack this note-book? What has this long-drawn-out confession to do with me now? I have broken with my family for ever. She for whom I laid myself bare in these pages can exist for me no longer. Why, then, resume the task? The answer to that question is, I suppose, that, though I did not know it at the time, the setting down of all my thoughts on paper brought me comfort and release. What a revelation of my state of mind those last lines contain, written on the night of the hailstorm! I must have been within measurable distance of madness. . . . No, no, I won't even mention that word: I mustn't, because they are quite capable of quoting any mention of it against me, should these pages ever fall into their hands. They are no longer addressed to anybody in particular, and, when I feel myself getting worse, I shall have to destroy them, unless, of course, I decide to leave them to the unknown son in search of whom I have come here to Paris. I longed to reveal the fact of his existence to Isa in that passage which deals with my love affair of 1909. I was actually on the point of confessing that when my mistress ran away it was because she was with child and had made up her mind to find a hiding-place in Paris.

I thought I was being very generous because I allowed mother and child six thousand francs a year before the war. It never occurred to me to increase the sum. If the two people I have found here are ground down and enslaved by sordid toil, the fault is mine. On the pretext that they live in this district, I am staying at a *pension* in the Rue Bréa. There is scarcely room, between the wardrobe and the bed, for me to write: and, oh! the din! In my days Montparnasse was quiet. Now it appears to be inhabited exclusively by lunatics who never go to bed! The family made considerably less noise on the front steps at Calèse that night when I saw with my own eyes and heard with my own ears . . . but

359

what's the point of reviving that memory? . . . I suppose that by
giving it shape and form I shall free my mind of an obsession, at
least for a while. . . . After all, why should I destroy these pages?
My son and heir is entitled to all the information about myself
that I can give him, and this confession will, to some extent, fill
out the gap which I have set between us ever since he was born.
We have had two meetings, and I can now, alas, make up my
mind about him. He is not the kind of man to take the slightest
interest in what I have written. How can a miserable junior clerk,
a numskull who spends all his spare time betting on horses, hope
to understand?

All that night in the train, between Bordeaux and Paris, I spent
the time imagining his reproaches and formulating my defence.
What a hold the tawdry conventions of novelists and play-
wrights have over one! I felt so sure of finding myself confronted
by the bastard of fiction, all bitterness and noble sentiments! I
endowed him, turn and turn about, with Luc's nobility and Phili's
looks. I was ready for anything—except only that he would turn
out to be the living image of myself! Are any fathers really pleased
to be told that their sons are "just like" them?

I realized the full extent of my self-loathing when I was brought
face to face with this pale image of myself. In Luc I had loved a
son who was utterly unlike me. In Robert's case, there is only one
difference between us—he has shown himself to be quite incapable of passing even the simplest examination. He has tried
again and again, but always with the same result, failure. His
mother, who has worked herself to the bone, despises him for
this lack of success. She can't help constantly referring to it. He
hangs his head. He hates the idea of so much money being thrown
down the drain. In that respect he is indeed my son! But the
fortune I am bringing him is beyond the power of his miserable
comprehension to grasp. It means nothing to him: he doesn't
really believe in it. The truth of the matter is, both he and his
mother are thoroughly frightened—"It's not legal . . . we might
be caught."

This pale, flabby woman with the faded hair, this caricature of
the girl I loved, just sat and stared at me when I went to see her
(she still has beautiful eyes). "If I'd passed you in the street,"
she said, "I'd never have recognized you!" Should I have recognized her? I had steeled myself against possible reproaches,
against her wish to be revenged for what had happened, against

everything, in fact, except this dreary indifference. Embittered, worn down by eight hours a day at the typewriter, she lives in a constant dread of scandal. Years ago she ran foul of the Law, and since then has had a morbid terror of it. I explained my whole scheme to them. The idea is that Robert should rent a safe-deposit in his own name, and that I should at once transfer to it such of my fortune as can be moved. He would give me power of attorney to have access to it, and take a solemn oath not to touch a penny of it till I am dead. Naturally, I should insist on his giving me a signed statement to the effect that everything in the safe-deposit belongs to me. I am not going to put myself in the hands of a complete stranger. But both mother and son have raised an objection. At my death, they say, the paper will be found. The fools don't trust me!

I have tried to make them realize that we should be perfectly safe in the hands of a country lawyer, some fellow like Bourru, who owes everything to me, and with whom I have done business for forty years. He is keeping, locked away, an envelope on which I have written: "Please burn on the day of my death," and I am quite sure he will burn it, with all its contents. Into that envelope I should put Robert's signed statement. I am the more certain that Bourru will burn the packet because there are in it certain documents which it is very much to his interest to see out of the way. But Robert and his mother are afraid that, once I am dead, Bourru won't burn anything, and will start blackmailing them. The same idea, I confess, had occurred to me, and, to guard against it, I am prepared to put evidence into their hands which would be sufficient to send him to penal servitude. I should make it a condition that the paper must be burned in their presence, and that then, and then only, they give back to him the weapon with which I shall have provided them. What more can they want?

But they can't grasp it. They're too pigheaded. One is a fool, the other an imbecile. I am offering them millions, and instead of going down on their knees in gratitude—as I fully expected they would—they go on arguing and splitting hairs! . . . Even supposing the thing is a bit risky, surely the game is worth the candle? But no, they won't sign. "In the first place, the Income Tax authorities might make difficulties."

The fact that I didn't slam the door in their faces proves how bitterly I hate the rest of my family. Incidentally, they're fright-

ened of the family, too. "They'd smell a rat, they'd bring an action
against us. . . ." They've already got it firmly fixed in their heads
that my relations have warned the police, and that I'm being
watched. They won't see me except after dark, and in odd, out-
of-the-way places. Do they expect a man in my state of health to
sit up half the night and spend my life in taxis? I've no reason to
suppose that anybody at home is suspicious. This isn't the first
time I've taken a trip alone. They can't know that I was present,
though invisible, at the council of war they held the other night
at Calèse. In any case, they won't have got on my trail yet. This
time, nothing's going to keep me from reaching my goal. The day
Robert consents to play ball I can sleep in peace. He's too great
a coward to be careless.

It's the thirteenth of July to-night, and there's a band playing
in the open air. Couples are dancing at the end of the Rue Bréa.
Oh, for the peace and quiet of Calèse! I remember my last night
there. In spite of doctor's orders I had taken a tablet of veronal,
and had fallen into a deep sleep. I awoke with a start and looked
at my watch. It was one o'clock in the morning. I could hear
several voices, and that frightened me. I had left the window
open. There was no one in the courtyard nor in the drawing-
room. I went into my dressing-room which looks north and is on
the same side of the house as the steps. It was there that the
family, contrary to habit, was making a night of it. At that late
hour they had no reason to believe they would be overheard. The
only windows on that side of the house are those of the various
dressing-rooms and of the corridor.

The night was still and warm. Every now and then there was
a pause in the conversation, and I could hear Isa's rather wheezy
breathing, and the sound of a match being struck. There was not
enough breeze to rustle the leaves on the dark elms. I didn't dare
lean out, but I could recognize my enemies by their voices and
their laughter. They were not arguing. Isa or Geneviève would
say something, and then there would be a prolonged silence. But
all of a sudden, Hubert spoke. At once Phili flared up, and then
they all started talking at once.

"Are you quite sure, Mamma, that the papers in his study safe
are really of no value? Misers are always careless. Don't you remember all the money he wanted to give young Luc . . . where's
he hidden that?"

"He realizes that I know the combination: it's 'Marie'. He never

THE KNOT OF VIPERS

opens the safe except when he wants to look at an Insurance
Policy or a Tax Return."

"But, Mamma, there might be some record of how much this
money amounts to. . . ."

"There's nothing in the safe but papers relating to his house
property; I'm sure of that."

"Don't you think all that's terribly significant?—I mean, doesn't
it show that he's taken every possible precaution?"

There was a yawn from Phili: "What an old crocodile!" he muttered; "just my luck to hit on a crocodile like that!"

"If you want my opinion," said Geneviève, "you won't find anything in his safe-deposit at the Crédit Lyonnais either. What do
you think, Janine?"

"But there are times, Mamma, when it really does look as
though he's got a sort of feeling for you. Wasn't he ever nice to
you when you were children? If not, that must have been because
you didn't know how to get round him, because you weren't
clever. You ought to have tried to appeal to his better nature
and win him over. I'm sure I could have succeeded if he hadn't
had such a horror of Phili."

Hubert broke in with a bitter comment: "There's no doubt your
husband's insolence has cost us pretty dear."

I caught the sound of Phili's laugh, and leaned forward a little.
The flame of a cigarette lighter lit up for a moment his cupped
hands, his flabby chin and thick lips.

"It didn't need me to set him against you!"

"That's not true: he hated us much less in the old days."

"Don't forget what Grandmamma told us, about how he behaved
when the little girl died," went on Phili: "how he didn't seem to
care, and never set foot in the cemetery."

"That's going a bit too far, Phili: if ever he cared for anyone in
the world it was for Marie."

But for this protest of Isa's, made in a faint and trembling voice,
I could not have controlled myself. I sat down on a low chair
and leaned forward, resting my head against the windowsill.
Geneviève was speaking:

"If Marie had lived, nothing of all this would have happened.
He would have been bound to watch over her interests."

"Oh, come! he'd have got his knife into her, as he has into
everybody else! He's a monster, and doesn't know what human
feelings mean!"

Once again Isa protested:

"You mustn't talk about my husband like that, Phili, in front of me and his children! You do owe him *some* respect."

"Respect?"

I thought I heard him mutter something like—"If you think it's fun for me to have got mixed up with a family like this! . . ."

His mother-in-law broke in dryly:

"Nobody forced you!"

"Every kind of glittering expectation was dangled before my eyes. . . . Oh, now Janine's blubbering . . . what have I said that's so extraordinary?"

The sound of his voice faded away in a sort of exasperated grumble. I could hear nothing but the noise Janine made in blowing her nose. A voice which I could not identify murmured: "How bright the stars are!" St. Vincent's clock struck two.

"Time for bed, children."

Hubert protested that they couldn't separate before something had been decided. It was high time to act. Phili agreed. He didn't think I could last much longer, and once I was dead it would be too late. It was a pretty sure thing that I had taken steps.

"Children, children, what do you expect me to do? I've tried my best, and there's nothing more to be done."

"Oh yes there is," said Hubert; "you could . . ." What was he whispering? Just what I most wanted to know I couldn't hear. I gathered from the tone of Isa's voice that she was shocked, scandalized.

"No, I couldn't possibly agree to that. . . ."

"It's not a question of personal feelings, Mamma, but of saving our inheritance."

There were more vague murmurings, cut short by Isa:

"But that would be a terrible thing to do!"

"But, don't you see, you're playing his game, Grandmamma? He can't disinherit us unless you agree, and this is a case of silence giving consent. . . ."

"Janine, my dear, how can you!"

Poor Isa! She had spent endless nights sitting up with this squalling little brat, and had even taken her into her own room because her parents wanted to sleep, and no nurse would put up with her. . . . There was an edge to Janine's voice which I wouldn't have let pass for a moment. She went on:

"I don't like saying things like this to you, Grand'ma, but it's my duty. . . ."

Her duty! that was the name she gave to the urgencies of her body, to the terror she felt at the idea of being abandoned by the scoundrel whose idiotic laugh now floated up to me.

Geneviève backed up her daughter. It was quite true, she said: weakness might so easily turn to complicity.

Isa sighed:

"Perhaps the best thing would be to write him a letter . . ."

"Oh, for Heaven's sake, no letters!" Hubert protested. "Letters are always our undoing! I do hope, Mamma, that you haven't already written to him?"

She admitted that she had, just once or twice—"but nothing threatening or abusive." She was obviously embarrassed. I laughed to myself. Oh yes, there had been letters all right, and I was taking good care of them. Two contained passages of pretty serious abuse, but the third was couched in almost affectionate terms, quite affectionate enough, anyhow, to make it certain that she would lose any suit for separation which those idiotic children might persuade her to bring.

The feeling of uneasiness was now general. It was just as when a dog starts growling, and the rest of the pack follow suit.

"Oh, don't say that you've written him any letters that might be dangerous to us, Grand'ma."

"I don't *think* I have, though I'm afraid there was one . . . I know that Bourru, the lawyer over at St. Vincent . . . I think my husband's got some hold over him (anyhow, he's a nasty creature, a hypocrite to boot) . . . did say that it was most unwise of me to have written. . . ."

"What was it you wrote? Nothing abusive, I do hope?"

"There was one in which I reproached him a little too violently after Marie's death, and another in 1909 referring to a liaison of his which was rather more than usually persistent. . . ."

Hubert groaned out something about it's being "very serious, extremely serious," but she tried to reassure him by adding that she had made everything all right since by expressing her regrets and admitting that she had been wrong. . . .

"That just about puts the lid on it! . . . so he knows he can't be dragged into court now! . . ."

"But, after all, why should you think he means to treat you all so badly?"

"You'd realize soon enough if you weren't completely blind. The dark mystery of his financial operations: the hints he drops: that remark he made to Bourru, in front of witnesses, when he said: 'They'll look pretty silly when the old man dies. . . .' "

They went on talking as though Isa had not been present. She struggled out of her armchair with a groan. She oughtn't, she said, to stay out after dark, with her rheumatism. The children did not so much as answer her. I heard the inattentive "good-nights" they gave her without bothering to interrupt what they were saying. It was she who had to move round the circle distributing good-night kisses. They none of them budged. I thought it safer to lie down again in bed. I heard the sound of her heavy steps on the staircase. She came right up to my door. I could clearly catch the noise of her uneasy breathing. She put her candle down and opened the door. She came across and stood close to my bed, leaning over me, with the object, no doubt, of making quite sure that I was asleep. What a long time it seemed! I was afraid of giving myself away. Her breath was coming in little gasps. At last she went out and closed the door. As soon as I heard her bolt her own, I went back to my listening-post in the dressing-room.

The children were still there, but now they were talking in whispers. Much of what they said escaped me.

"Don't forget," observed Janine, "that he came of a different social class. . . . Phili, darling, you're coughing, *do* put on your overcoat."

"Actually, it's not his wife he most hates" (Geneviève now), "but us. What a fantastic situation—if you read of it in a novel you wouldn't believe it! It's not for us to judge our mother," she wound up, "but I do think she's been a bit too forgiving. . . ."

"Damn it all!" (Phili). "She can always get her marriage settlement back. Old man Fondaudège's Canal shares must have gone up a good deal since '84!"

"B-but they've been . . . sold."

I recognized the hesitant tones, the hemming and the hawing, as coming from Geneviève's husband. Until that moment the wretched Alfred had not opened his lips. His wife cut him short. She spoke in the sharp, shrill voice which she keeps for him:

"You must be mad! The Suez Canal shares sold?"

Alfred explained how, in the May of that year, he had gone into his mother-in-law's room and found her signing some documents. She had said: "I'm told that now's the moment to sell. They're standing very high, and will almost certainly drop."

"And you mean to say you never told us?" exclaimed Geneviève. "Really, I believe you must be half-witted! He actually made her sell the Suez?—is *that* what you're trying to explain? You just casually mention it as though it were the most natural thing in the world!"

"But, Geneviève, I thought your mother would tell you what she'd done. In any case, by the terms of her settlement, she remains mistress of her own property."

"That's all very well, but it's more than likely that he pocketed the profits of the sale! What's your opinion, Hubert? To think he never breathed a word—and that's the man I'm tied to for the rest of my life!"

At this point Janine told them to speak lower, so as not to wake her little girl. For the next few moments I heard scarcely a word. Then, once again, Hubert's voice rose above the general buzz.

"I've been thinking about what you were saying just now. . . . But, you know, we should never get her to agree, and even if we did manage to convince her, it would be a long, slow business. . . ."

"She might prefer it to a separation. Separation, you see, is bound to lead, sooner or later, to divorce, and that would involve a case of conscience. . . . Of course, what Phili proposes does sound a bit shocking at first, but after all, *we're* not going to have to say the word: it won't be for *us* to make the final decision. All we've got to do is to get the thing started. Nothing will happen unless the competent authorities think it necessary. . . ."

"Well, as I said before," remarked Olympe, "you'll all of you be going to a lot of trouble for nothing. . . ."

Hubert's wife must have been thoroughly outraged to raise her voice as she did. She maintained that I was a perfectly sensible man, a man of sound judgment. "I don't mind admitting," she said, "that we quite often agree about things, and that if you weren't for ever butting in, I could do anything I liked with him. . . ."

Phili must have made some pretty insolent reply, though I couldn't hear what it was. They all laughed, as they always do when Olympe joins in. I caught a few disjointed phrases.

"He hasn't conducted a case for five years . . . hasn't been up to it."

"Wasn't that because of his heart?"

"His heart's bad *now*, but when he gave up practising there was nothing particularly wrong with him. The real trouble was he was always getting at odds with his colleagues. There were quite often scenes when he was conducting a conference—I've got first-hand evidence of that. . . ."

I strained my ears, but it was no good. Phili and Hubert had drawn their chairs together. All that reached me was an indistinct murmur. Then, suddenly, there was another outburst from Olympe:

"He's the only one of the whole lot of you I can talk to about books, or discuss general ideas with, and you want . . ."

Phili said something in reply. I caught the word "looney." One of Hubert's sons-in-law, who scarcely ever says anything at all, gave a sort of a splutter:

"You might be at least decently polite to my mother-in-law. . . ."

Phili protested that he was only joking. Weren't they both of them playing the part of victims in this business? Hubert's son-in-law asserted, in a trembling voice, that he didn't look on himself as a victim, and that he'd married his wife for love, at which there was a chorus of "Same here!—Same here!—Same here!" Geneviève mockingly remarked to her husband:

"You'll be saying next, I suppose, that *you* married me without knowing how much my father was worth?—But *I* happen to remember that on the night we became engaged you whispered: 'What's the odds? It doesn't matter if he won't talk about it, we *know* it's enormous. . . .' "

There was a general burst of laughter, followed by a babble of voices. Once again it was Hubert who dominated the meeting. For a moment or two nobody interrupted him. It was only his final remark that I heard:

"The one thing that really matters in all this affair is justice and morality. We are defending our inheritance, the sacred rights of the family. . . ."

In the deep hush that comes before the dawn, I could hear more clearly:

"Have him watched? he's too well in with the police! I've proof of that—they'd put him wise . . ." (then, a few moments later) ". . . everyone knows he's as hard as nails and as greedy as you make 'em. I've even heard it whispered that he hasn't been all he should be in business . . . though, of course, no one's ever doubted his good sense and his judgment. . . ."

"Well, there's no denying that his feelings for us are inhuman, monstrous and unnatural. . . ."

"But do you really think, Janine, my dear," said Alfred to his daughter, "that *that* would be sufficient to get him certified? . . ."

It had been beginning to dawn on me, and now I knew! I felt perfectly calm: certainty had brought a sense of peace. It was they who were the monsters, I who was the victim. The fact that Isa had been absent gave me pleasure. So long as she had been with them, she had, to some extent, protested. In her presence they had not dared to mention the plan which I had just overheard. Not that it terrified me. Poor fools!—as though I were the kind of man to let himself be put under restraint or shut away! Long before they so much as raised a finger, I could put Hubert in a hopeless position. He had no idea what a hold I had over him. As to Phili—there was a whole dossier about *him*. . . . I have never really seriously intended to make use of it . . . and I shan't have to. It'll be quite enough if I show my teeth.

For the first time in my life I felt the satisfaction of being outdone in malevolence. I did not in the least want to be revenged on them, or, rather, the only vengeance I envisaged was to snatch from their grasp the inheritance over which they were hanging in a fever of impatience, and sweating with anxiety.

"A shooting star!" cried Phili: "I had no time to make a wish."

"One never does have time," said Janine. Her husband, with that childish gaiety which he has never lost, said:

"Whenever you see one you should cry 'millions'!"

"What an ass you are, Phili!"

They all got up. The garden chairs scraped on the gravel. I heard them shoot the bolts of the front door, and the smothered laughter of Janine in the passage. One after the other the bedroom doors were shut. I had decided what to do. I had had no attack now for two months. There was nothing to keep me from going to Paris. As a rule, when I started on a trip I said nothing about it. But I did not want them to think I was running away. I spent the time until morning in going over the plans I had already made, dotting the i's and crossing the t's.

❧ *XIII* ❧

WHEN I got up at midday, I had no feeling of fatigue. I put a
call through to Bourru and he arrived after luncheon. For nearly
three quarters of an hour we walked up and down under the
limes. Isa, Geneviève and Janine were watching us from a distance, and I thoroughly enjoyed the thought of how anxious they
must be. What a pity that the men were all in Bordeaux!
"Bourru," they were fond of saying, "is his evil influence"—that
wretched, petty attorney who was more wholly in my power
than any slave could have been! It was a sight for sore eyes to see
the poor devil twisting and turning in his terror lest I might leave
my heir some weapon which could be turned against him. "But,"
I told him, "don't you see, once you've burned the signed receipt,
we'll hand everything over. . . ."

When he left, he made a profound bow to the ladies, who
scarcely acknowledged it, and rode off on his squalid bicycle. I
joined the three females and explained that I was leaving that
evening for Paris. When Isa protested that I was much too ill to
travel alone, I said:

"I've got to see about my investments. You may not believe it,
but it's of you I'm thinking."

They looked at me uneasily. The note of irony in my voice gave
me away. Janine, with a glance at her mother, plucked up courage to say:

"Grand'ma or Uncle Hubert could easily go instead. . . ."

"There's something in that, my dear . . . but, you see, I've always been in the habit of seeing to these things myself. I know
it's very wrong of me, but I don't trust anybody."

"Not even your own children? Oh, Grand'pa!"

She stressed the word "Grand'pa" in a rather priggish way.
Her coaxing manner was hard to resist. How exasperating that
voice of hers could be—the same voice that I had heard the
night before mingled with the others.

I gave vent to a laugh, that dangerous laugh of mine which
makes me cough. It plainly terrified them. I shall never forget
the look of exhaustion on poor Isa's face. They must have been at

her already. Janine would probably return to the charge as soon as
I had left them: "Don't let him go, Grand'ma! ..."

But my wife was in no mood to attack. She was at the end of
her tether, completely done up. I had heard her, a few days back,
say to Geneviève: "I'd like to go to sleep and never wake up. ..."
She produced a softening effect on me, just as my poor mother
used to do. Worn out though she was, a broken-down old machine, good for nothing, the children were still trying to set her
against me. Of course they were fond of her in their own way.
They made her see the doctor and keep to a diet. ...

As soon as her daughter and granddaughter moved away, she
came up to me.

"I need some money ..." she began hurriedly.

"To-day's the tenth: I gave you your month's allowance on the
first. ..."

"I know, but I had to lend some of it to Janine. They're terribly
hard up. I can save while we're at Calèse. I'll pay you back out of
my August allowance."

I said it was no business of mine, but that I was certainly not
going to keep that fellow Phili.

"I've got several bills outstanding, too, with the butcher and
baker, for instance, look. ..."

She took them out of her bag. I felt sorry for her, and offered to
write out cheques for them. "In that way I shall know that the
money won't go into anyone else's pocket." She agreed. I took out
my cheque-book, and noticed that Janine and her mother in the
rose-garden were looking at us.

"I don't mind betting," I said, "that they think you're talking to
me about something quite different."

Isa trembled. In a low voice she said: "About what?" At that
moment I felt a tightening in my chest. I clutched at it with my
two hands in a way that she knew only too well. She came close
to me:

"Are you in pain?"

I clung to her arm for a moment. There, under the limes, we
must have looked like an old married couple ending their lives
after long years of happy union. "It's better now," I brought out.
She must have thought that this was the moment to speak, a
unique opportunity: but she had no strength left. I noticed
that she, too, was struggling for breath. Ill though I was, I had

put up a fight. She had surrendered, given in. She had nothing with which to fight.

She seemed to be looking for the right words, glancing furtively the while at her daughter and granddaughter, as though to draw courage from their proximity. In the face she turned to me I saw an indescribable weariness. There may have been something of pity in it, there certainly was something of shame. The children must have wounded her to the heart on that memorable night.

"I'm worried at the thought of you going off alone."

I said that should anything happen to me while I was away, it wouldn't be worth having me brought back here.

She begged me not to talk like that. I said: "It would be just a waste of money, Isa. Cemeteries are much of a muchness everywhere."

"I feel the same," she said. "They can bury me anywhere they like, for all I care. There was a time when I wanted to lie near Marie . . . but what is there left of her?"

Once again I realized that, for her, Marie was no more than dust and ashes. I dared not tell her that, for years past, I had felt my child to be alive, that I had, as it were, breathed her in, had been conscious of her as of a fresh breeze blowing through the darkness of my days.

Geneviève and Janine did not get much satisfaction from their spying. Isa seemed to be utterly exhausted. Was it that she realized at last the nothingness of what she had been fighting for all these years? Geneviève and Hubert, goaded by their own children, had set this old woman on to me, Isa Fondaudège, the young, sweet-scented girl of those nights at Bagnères.

For close on half a century we two had been enemies, and now, on this heavy afternoon, the enemies had suddenly become aware of the bond created, in spite of the long-drawn-out struggle, by a shared old age. We might seem to hate one another, but, for all that, we had reached the same point in the road. There was nothing now beyond that promontory on which we stood awaiting death. Nothing, at least, for me. She had her God, or should have had. All the things to which she had clung with such bitter determination (and I, too, had clung with desperation) were fallen away; all the greedy desires which had stood between her and the Eternal Being. Could she see Him now that there was nothing to impede her sight? No, there were still the demands and ambitions of her children. It was *their* greediness that now hung about her neck like a burden. She must begin all over again, and be hard

on their account. Worries about money, worries about health,
schemes of ambition and of jealousy. There they all were in wait
for her, like a schoolboy's exercise on which the master has written—"To be done again."

She turned her head and looked again towards the walk where
Geneviève and Janine, armed with pruning clippers, were making
a pretence of trimming the roses. From the bench on which I had
sat down to recover my breath, I watched my wife move away.
She was hanging her head like a child in fear of a scolding. The
excessive heat of the sun was sure portent of a storm. She was
walking with the gait of those to whom walking is painful. I could
almost hear her groaning, "Oh, my poor legs!" Husbands and
wives of long standing never hate one another as much as they
think they do.

By this time she had reached the children. Obviously they were
blaming her for something. All of a sudden, I saw her coming
back towards me red in the face, and out of breath. She sat down
beside me with a groan.

"This stormy weather tires me so! My blood-pressure's very
high these days. . . . Listen, Louis, there's something I'm worried
about. . . . How have you reinvested the money from those Suez
Canal shares which were part of my settlement? I know there
were some other documents you got me to sign. . . ."

I gave her the figure of the enormous profit I had realized for
her by selling just before the market broke, and explained that
I had put the proceeds into debentures.

"Your settlement has been breeding, Isa. Even allowing for
the depreciation of the franc, you'll be amazed. Everything's in
your name at the Westminster Bank, your original settlement, and
the profits. . . . It's nothing to do with the children . . . you can
be quite easy in your mind. My money is my own, and what
that money has produced, but what was yours is yours still. You
can reassure those angels of unselfishness over there."

Suddenly she gripped my arm:

"Why do you hate them so, Louis? Why do you hate your own
flesh and blood?"

"It's you who hate me, or rather, it's my children. *You* merely
ignore me, except when I get on your nerves or frighten you. . . ."

"You might add 'or when I torture you'. Don't you know that
I have suffered abominably at times?"

"Oh come! you had eyes for nobody but the children. . . ."

"I had to cling to them. What had I got but them?"—and, in a

374   *François Mauriac*

lower voice, she added: "You know perfectly well that you neglected me, that you were unfaithful to me from the very first year of our marriage."

"My poor Isa, you can't make me believe that my occasional wild oats really meant anything to you . . . as a young wife you may, perhaps, have been a bit hurt in your pride, but . . ."

"You really sound as though you mean what you say. . . . Why, you never even noticed whether I was there or not! . . ."

A feeling of hope set me trembling—which was strange, when you come to think that we were talking of emotions long since dead—of the hope I had entertained, unknown to myself, forty years before, that perhaps I was loved. . . . But no, it was asking too much that I should believe that now. . . .

"You never spoke a word, you never uttered a sound. All you needed was the children."

She hid her face in her two hands. I was more conscious than I had ever been before of their prominent veins and discoloured patches.

"My children! Do you realize that when we took to having separate rooms, I never, for years and years, had one of them to sleep with me, even when they were ill, because I was always half expecting, half hoping, that you would come!"

Her old woman's hands were wet with tears. This was Isa. I alone could see, in that thickened, almost crippled body, the young girl "with a devotion to white" whom I had known on a road in the Valley of the Lys.

"It's disgraceful, it's ridiculous, at my age, to recall such memories . . . ridiculous, especially . . . Please forgive me, Louis."

I stared at the vines and said nothing. I was a prey to sudden doubt. Is it possible that a man can live for nearly half a century noticing one side only of the person who shares his life? Can it be that, from long habit, he picks and chooses from among her gestures and her words, keeping for use only those that feed his grievances and perpetuate his resentments? There is a fatal tendency in all of us to simplify others, to eliminate in them everything that might soften the indictment, give some human lineaments to the caricature which our hatred craves in order to justify itself. . . . Perhaps Isa noticed my uneasiness; I wonder. At any rate, she was a shade too quick about scoring her next point.

"Say you won't go to-night!"

I fancied that I caught the familiar glint in her eye which always tells me when she thinks she's "got" me. I pretended to be surprised, and answered that I saw no reason for putting off my journey. We went back to the house together. Because of my heart we did not climb the slope by the elms, but took the lime walk which leads round to the far side. In spite of everything, I still felt doubtful and uneasy. What if I didn't go? What if I gave Isa what I have written? . . . What . . .

She laid her hand on my shoulder. How many years was it since she had last done that?

The lime walk ends in front of the house, on the north side.

"Cazau never tidies up the garden chairs. . . ."

I gave them an absent-minded glance. The empty chairs were still set in a close circle. Those who had occupied them had felt it necessary to draw them together so that they could keep their voices low. I could see heel-marks on the ground. The butts of Phili's special brand of cigarette were lying all over the place. Only a night or two ago the enemy had camped there, taking council under the stars, discussing in my own home, in front of the trees which my father had planted, the advisability of putting me under restraint, of having me shut away. Once, in the dark hours, in a moment of self-deprecation, I had compared my heart to a knot of vipers. How wrong I had been! The knot of vipers was outside myself! On that night of plotting they had wriggled free of me and twined themselves into a tangle, into a hideous circle at the foot of these steps. Their slime was still visible on the ground.

You shall have that money back, Isa, I thought: the money of yours which I have set to breed, but nothing more, nothing else. I would even find some way of keeping the estate out of their hands. I would sell Calèse and the stretch of heath. Everything that had come to me from my family should go to that unknown son of mine, to the boy whom I was to see in two days' time. Whatever he might turn out to be, at least he had one great advantage —he didn't know you. He had taken no part in your plotting. He had been brought up far from my sight, and could not hate me, or, if he did, the object of his hatred was an abstract being having no connexion with myself.

Angrily I broke free and hurried up the steps, forgetful of my old man's heart. Isa called after me: "Louis!" But I did not even turn my head.

❀ *X I V* ❀

I COULD not sleep, so I dressed and went out into the street. In order to reach the Boulevard Montparnasse I had to force my way through the dancing couples. In the old days, even a dyed-in-the-wool Republican such as I was avoided the 14th July merry-making. No respectable citizen would have dreamed of taking part in the festivities of the street. But this evening, in the Rue Bréa, and in front of the Rotonde, the men who were dancing were far from being rowdies. There was nothing vicious about them. For the most part they were well-set-up, bare-headed young fellows. Some of them wore short-sleeved, open-necked shirts. Very few of the girls were tarts. They clung to the wheels of such taxis as broke up the dancing, but gaily and without hostility. A young man who had jostled me by accident cried: "Way for the noble ancient!" I moved between a double row of radiant faces. "Not sleepy, Grand'pa?" a chap with a dark complexion and hair growing low over his forehead flung at me. Luc would have learned to laugh just like that, to dance in the streets, and I, who had never known what it meant to relax and enjoy myself, would have caught the secret from my poor boy. He would have revelled in the scene, would have taken his fill of it, and he wouldn't have wanted for money. . . . Fill? . . . it was with earth his mouth was filled now. . . . So ran my thoughts, while, conscious of the old familiar tightness in my chest, I sat in front of a café with the fun going on all round me.

And then, quite suddenly, in the crowd that swarmed along the pavement, I saw myself. It was Robert in the company of a rather seedy individual. How I hate Robert's long legs, his stocky body, so like my own, and his absence of neck! In him my defects are exaggerated. *My* face is long, but his is like a horse's—the face of a hunchback; and his voice is a hunchback's too.

I called to him. He broke away from his companion and looked about him uneasily.

"Not here," he said; "meet me on the right-hand pavement of the Rue Campagne-Première."

I pointed out that we could not be more effectively concealed than at the heart of this hubbub. He let himself be persuaded, took leave of his friend, and sat down at my table.

He had a sporting paper in his hand. To break the silence I tried to talk about horses. I'd got into the way of it with old Fondaudège, years ago. I told Robert how, when my father-in-law betted, he always took all sorts of considerations into account— not only the animal's pedigree to the third and fourth genera- tion, but the ground-conditions that suited it best and . . . He interrupted me:

"I get my tips at Dermas's" (Dermas is the name of the draper's shop in the Rue des Petits-Champs, where he's fetched up high and dry in a job).

The only thing he cared about was winning. Horses as horses bored him.

"Give me bicycles every time!" he said, and his eyes sparkled.

"Soon it'll be motors," I said.

"That's what you think!"

He moistened his thumb, took out a slip of cigarette-paper and rolled himself a cigarette. Silence once more descended between us. I asked whether the slump had made itself felt in his business. He replied that some of the staff had got the sack, but that he was safe enough. Not once did his talk stray outside the narrow circle of his personal concerns. It was into the lap of this nit-wit that millions were to fall! Suppose I give it all to charity, I thought; or distribute it piecemeal? . . . No, for in either case *they* would have me put away. By Will, then?—impossible to ex- ceed the legally stipulated proportion. Oh, Luc, if only you were alive! . . . True, he wouldn't have accepted it, but I could have found some way of enriching him without his knowledge . . . by settling money, for instance, on the woman he might have loved. . . .

"Look here, sir. . . ."

Robert stroked his chin. His hand was red, the fingers spatulate.

". . . I've been thinking things over. What if that lawyer fellow, Bourru, should happen to die before we had burned the paper? . . ."

"Well, his son would succeed him, and the weapon I've given you against the father could, should the occasion arise, be used against the son."

Robert went on stroking his chin. I made no attempt to say more, so fully occupied was I with the feeling of tightness, with the agonizing constriction, in my chest.

"And again, what if Bourru burns the paper and I hand over what you'd given me to make him act proper? What's to stop him from going to your family and saying, 'I know where the dough

is, and I'm ready to sell the secret—so much for giving you the
low-down, and a bit extra if you get your hands on it'—making
it a condition that his name shan't be mentioned? . . . *He'd* be
in the clear. There'd be an enquiry, and it'd come out as I really
was your son, and that since your death Mother and I had been
blowing it. . . . And we should either have to make a correct tax
return or keep the whole thing dark."

He was expressing himself with precision. His mind was no
longer sluggish. It had been slow in getting started, but now there
was no holding it. The dominating instinct in this wretched coun-
ter-jumper was peasant caution, peasant mistrust and a horror of
taking risks. He wasn't going to leave anything to chance. No
doubt he would have preferred a hundred thousand francs in
cash to the danger involved in having to conceal so vast a fortune.

I waited until my heart felt easier and the tightness had loosened.
Then:

"There's something in what you say," I replied, "and I'll do what
you want. You needn't sign anything. I'll trust you. As a matter of
fact it would be perfectly easy for me to prove that the money
is mine. Not that it really matters, because in six months, or a
year at most, I shall be dead."

He made no gesture of protest. The commonplace that anyone
else might have uttered was quite beyond him; not that he was
more callous than other young men of his age, but simply that
he had been badly brought up.

"That might work," he said.

He chewed my suggestion for a few moments, and then continued:

"I'd have to look in now and again at the safe-deposit, even
with you alive, just so's the Bank people'd get to know my face.
I might go and get some of the money for you when you wanted
it."

"If it comes to that, I've got several safe-deposits abroad. If
you'd rather, if you believe it would be less risky . . ."

"What, leave Paris! . . . what do *you* think!"

I pointed out that he could go on living in Paris and take an
occasional trip when necessary. He asked whether my fortune
was in securities or cash.

"I'd rather you gave me some sort of paper, something like you
being of sound mind had left everything to me . . . just in case
anything leaked out and I was accused of theft—one never knows.
Besides, my conscience would be easier. . . ."

He stopped speaking, bought some peanuts and started to eat them voraciously, as though he were hungry. Suddenly:

"What's your family done to you?" he asked.

"Take what I offer," I said dryly, "and don't be inquisitive."

A little colour showed in his flabby cheeks. His smile was of the uncomfortable, self-conscious kind which he probably assumed when he was being hauled over the coals by his employer. It revealed the strong, pointed teeth which were the only good feature in his otherwise unpleasing face.

He went on shelling peanuts without saying anything more. There was nothing in his expression to show that he was in the least dazzled. Obviously his imagination was getting to work. I had stumbled on the one person incapable of seeing anything in this marvellous windfall but the very small risks involved. But dazzled was just what I wanted him to be. . . .

"Haven't you got a girl?" I asked him point-blank. "You could marry her and live in solid, respectable comfort."

He made a vague gesture and shook his head with a hang-dog expression. I pressed my point.

"You could marry anybody you like. If there's any girl who seems out of your reach . . ."

He pricked up his ears at that, and, for the first time, I saw a glimmer of excitement in his eyes.

"I could marry Mademoiselle Brugère!"

"And who is Mademoiselle Brugère?"

"I was only joking. She's one of the heads at Dermas's. Proper stuck up—won't so much as look at me; doesn't even know I exist. I say, that's an idea!"

I assured him that with a twentieth part of my fortune he could marry any "head" in Paris.

"Mademoiselle Brugère!" he said again. Then, with a shrug, "No, that's too much to expect!"

My chest was hurting. I signed to the waiter. It was then that Robert did a most surprising thing.

"No, look here, it's the least I can do. . . ."

I put my money back in my pocket with a feeling of satisfaction. We got up. The musicians were packing their instruments. The festoons of electric lights had been extinguished. There was no longer any reason why Robert should be afraid of being seen with me.

"I'll walk back with you," he said. I asked him to go slowly because of my heart. I was surprised that he did nothing to hasten the execution of our plans. I told him that if I died in the night he would lose a fortune. He showed complete indifference. All I had done was to throw him out of his stride. He was about my own height. Would he ever manage to look like a gentleman? This son and heir of mine was a poor creature! I tried to give an intimate turn to the conversation. I told him that I was filled with remorse to think that I had left him and his mother to their own resources. This seemed to surprise him. He thought it "very handsome" of me to have made them an allowance. "There's lots as wouldn't have done that." Then he said something quite horrible: "After all, you weren't the first. . . ." Obviously, he had no illusions about his mother!

When we reached my door he said:

"I've got an idea . . . what about my taking a job which would keep me hanging round the Stock Exchange? That'd explain my good luck, wouldn't it?"

"You watch your step," I said; "you'd very soon lose everything."

He stared at the pavement in a preoccupied manner. "I was thinking about the Income Tax people. . . . What if the collector started making enquiries?"

"But this is a cash transaction, an anonymous fortune tucked away in a safe-deposit which no one but you in all the world would have the right to open. . . ."

"Oh, I know all about that, still . . ."

I was out of all patience, and slammed the door in his face.

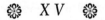

❀ *X V* ❀

CALÈSE.

A FLY is buzzing against the window. I can see the slope of the hill. It looks numbed and lifeless. The wind is moaning and driving a mass of sagging cloud before it. Its shadow lies across the plain. This deathlike stillness means that everything is waiting for the first rumble of the thunder. On just such a day of summer, thirty years ago, Marie said: "The vines are frightened. . . ." I have reopened this note-book. Yes, no doubt of it, the handwriting is mine. I examine the letters closely. I can see under each line the

mark made by the nail of my little finger. I will tell the story
to the end. I know now for whom it is intended. This confession
had to be set down in black and white, but many pages of it I
shall have to suppress, because the reading of them would be
more than they could bear. Even I can't look through them without a pause. Every now and again I break off and hide my face
in my hands. Here is the portrait of a man, of a man among other
men. This is I. You may spew me forth, but that doesn't alter
the fact that I exist.

On that night of the 13th/14th July, after leaving Robert, I
was barely strong enough to undress myself and lie down on my
bed. It was as though a huge weight were crushing the life out of
my body. All the same, I did not die. The window was open . . .
had my room been on the fifth floor . . . but it was on the first,
and if I had jumped I should probably not have been killed.
It was that probability alone which kept me from trying. . . . I
could scarcely stretch out my hand for the pills which usually
bring me relief.

At dawn someone did at last answer my bell. A local doctor
came along and gave me an injection, as a result of which I was
able to breathe normally again. He told me that I was to make no
movement of any kind. As the result of extreme pain one becomes
as submissive as a young child. There was not the slightest danger
of my budging. I was no longer distressed by the ugliness, by
the disgusting smell, of the room and the furniture, or by the noise
of that stormy 14th July. Nothing distressed me now because I
was no longer in pain. To be free from pain was all I asked.
Robert came to see me in the evening, but did not repeat the
visit. His mother sat with me for two hours on her way home from
the office, did me a few small services, and brought me my mail
from the *poste restante* (no letter from the family).

I made no complaint, and was very docile. I drank everything
the doctor had prescribed. When I spoke of my plan, she changed
the subject. "There's no hurry," she kept on saying. I sighed. "But
there is," I said; "and the proof of that is here"—pointing to my
chest.

"My mother's attacks were worse than yours, and she lived
to be almost eighty. . . ."

One morning I felt better than I had done for a long while. I
was very hungry. The food in my *pension* was uneatable. I was
seized by a sudden desire to lunch at a little restaurant on the

Boulevard Saint-Germain where I knew the cooking was good.
The size of the bill there caused me less astonishment and anger
than in most of the squalid eating places I usually frequented in
my terror of spending too much money.

The taxi put me down at the corner of the Rue de Rennes. I
took a few steps to test my strength. All was well. It was barely
noon. I decided to have a bottle of Vichy at the *Deux Magots*.
I found a seat inside, on the settee that runs along the wall, and
gazed absent-mindedly out of the window at the Boulevard.

My heart gave a little jump. Just outside, separated from me by
no more than the thickness of the glass, I saw a familiar vision
of narrow shoulders, bald patch, grizzled nape and undistin-
guished, projecting ears. . . . It was Hubert, peering so near-
sightedly at a paper that it was almost touching his nose. Obviously, he had not seen me come in. The beating of my sick heart
quietened down. A horrible joy possessed me. I was spying on
him, and he did not know that I was there!

It was difficult to imagine Hubert anywhere but in one of the
fashionable cafés of the Grands Boulevards. What was he doing
in this part of the town? His presence there was certainly not ac-
cidental. I had only to wait, having paid for my Vichy, so as to be
free to get up and go out should it be necessary.

It was clear that he was waiting for somebody. He looked at
his watch. I thought I knew who it was who would worm his
way to him between the tables, and was almost disappointed
when I saw Geneviève's husband get out of a taxi. Alfred was
wearing a straw hat cocked over one ear. When he was away
from his wife, this fat little man in his forties reverted to type.
His provincial dandyism was in striking contrast to Hubert's dark
clothes. Hubert, said Isa, always dressed "like a Fondaudège".

Alfred took off his hat and mopped his shining forehead. He
ordered an aperitif and swallowed it at a gulp. His brother-in-
law was already on his feet, consulting his watch. I made ready
to follow them. No doubt they would take a taxi. I would do the
same and try to follow them, by no means an easy thing to do.
But even to have got wind of their presence was something
gained. I waited until they were on the kerb before leaving my
retreat. They did not, however, hail a cab, but crossed the Square,
and made towards Saint-Germain-des-Prés, talking all the while. I
was surprised and gratified to see them enter the church. A de-
tective who watches a thief walking straight into a trap could not

have had a more delicious emotion than the one that made me catch my breath. I took my time. They might have looked behind them, and, though my son is near-sighted, my son-in-law has extremely good eyes. In spite of my impatience, I waited for two good minutes on the pavement. Only then did I enter the porch in their wake.

It was a little after noon. I moved carefully up the almost empty nave, but soon realized that the objects of my search were not there. It occurred to me for a moment that they might have seen me, that they had come into the church in order to throw me off the scent, and had left it again by one of the doors in the side-aisles. I retraced my steps and went into one of the transepts —the one on the right, being careful to conceal myself behind the enormous pillars. Suddenly, in the darkest part of the apse, I saw them against the light. They were sitting on two chairs, and between them was a third person, a person with humble, drooping shoulders, whose presence there in no way surprised me. It was the same individual whom, a while back, I had expected to see gliding towards my legitimate son between the tables. It was my other son, that miserable worm, Robert.

I had foreseen this treachery, but from weariness or laziness had not given it much thought. From the moment of our first meeting I had realized that this lily-livered creature had no stomach for the fight, and that his mother, haunted by memories of the Law, would advise him to come to terms with the family and sell his secret for what he could get. I looked at the back of his idiotic head. He was firmly wedged between the two solid citizens, one of whom, Alfred, was what is commonly called a "good sort" (though with a keen eye to his own interests, even if he was inclined to take the short view—and, as a matter of fact, he found the short view pretty remunerative), while the other, my charming Hubert, was as sharp as you make 'em, and had just that air of arrogant authority (his legacy from me) against which Robert would be powerless. I looked at them from my pillar, much as one might look at a spider busy with a fly, when one has made up one's mind to kill both fly and spider. Robert's head drooped more and more. He had probably begun by saying "Fifty-fifty", secure in the belief that he held all the cards. But merely by making himself known to them, the poor fool had put himself in their hands, and couldn't do anything but throw up the sponge. Watching the unequal battle, which I alone knew to be vain and

futile, I felt like a god preparing to crush these miserable insects
with my powerful hand, to stamp these twined snakes into the
ground. I laughed.

Only ten minutes were necessary to reduce Robert to silence.
Hubert was displaying a fine eloquence, and was, no doubt, issuing his orders. The victim was expressing his agreement with brief
movements of the head, while his servile back grew rounder and
rounder. Alfred, lolling as though in an armchair, with his right
foot resting on his left knee, had tilted his seat and thrown his
head backwards, so that I got an upside-down view of his flabby,
bilious, black-bearded face.

At last they got up. I followed them, still taking great care not
to be seen. They were walking slowly. Robert was between them
with hanging head, and I half expected to see handcuffs on his
wrists. His great red hands were kneading a soft felt hat of dirty
grey. I had thought that nothing in the world would ever surprise
me again, but I was wrong. Alfred and Robert made straight for
the door, but Hubert dipped his fingers in the Holy Water stoup,
turned towards the High Altar, and made a flamboyant sign of
the cross.

I was in no hurry now. I could afford to be calm. There was no
point in following them. I knew that that evening, or the next day,
Robert would at last urge me to carry out my plans. What should
be my attitude? I had plenty of time in which to think about that.
I was beginning to feel tired, and sat down. What was uppermost
in my mind at the moment, dominating everything else, was a
feeling of irritation at Hubert's pious gesture. A young girl in the
row in front of me, decently dressed and with no particular claim
to looks, put a cardboard hat-box on the ground beside her, and
knelt. I had a side-view of her. Her head was slightly bent, and
her eyes were fixed on the same distant little door which Hubert,
his family duty done, had just so gravely saluted. She was smiling
faintly, and was quite motionless. Two seminarists came in next.
One of them, tall and very thin, reminded me of the Abbé Ardouin; the other was short, and had a chubby face. They made
their genuflexion side by side, and, like the girl, seemed stricken
into immobility. I looked at what they were looking at, and tried
to see what they were seeing. But there's nothing here, I said to
myself, but silence, coolness and the smell of old, sunless stones.
Once again the face of the little work-girl held my attention. Her
eyes were shut now. Their lids, with their long lashes, reminded

me of Marie's as I had seen them on her death-bed. I could feel, almost within reach of my hand, and at the same time infinitely distant, the presence of an unknown world of goodness. Isa had often said to me: "You never see anything but evil—you find it everywhere. . . ." That was true . . . and yet, it was not true at all.

❀ XVI ❀

I HAD my luncheon. My mind felt relaxed and almost gay. I had not felt so well for a long time. It was as though Robert's treachery, far from upsetting my plans, had given them a helping hand. A man of my age, I thought, who has been living under sentence of death for years, does not seek elaborate reasons for his changes of mood. They are organic. The myth of Prometheus means that all the sorrows of the world have their seat in the liver. But it needs a brave man to face so humble a truth. I was conscious of no physical discomfort. I digested my underdone steak without the slightest difficulty. I was glad it was so large because that meant I shouldn't have to spend money on another course. I would just have some cheese, which is both nourishing and cheap.

How should I behave to Robert? I must train my guns now on a new target. But I could not concentrate my mind. Besides, why burden myself with a plan? I should be better advised to trust to the inspiration of the moment. I dared not admit to myself that I was thoroughly looking forward to the fun of playing, like a cat, with this dim little field-mouse. Robert wasn't within miles of suspecting that I had smelt a rat. . . . Am I cruel? Yes, I suppose I am, but no more so than anybody else, than all the other men in the world, than women, than children, than all except those (I thought of the little work-girl whom I had seen in Saint-Germain-des-Prés) who are in the service of the Lamb.

I took a taxi back to the Rue Bréa, and lay down on my bed. The students who formed the main clientele of the house were away on holiday. I rested in peace and quiet. The fact that the top half of the door was glazed, though a grubby half-curtain concealed the panes, removed all sense of privacy. Several small pieces of wooden moulding belonging to the "Renaissance" style bedstead had come unstuck, and lay, carefully gathered together, in a gilded bronze "tidy" which stood on the mantelpiece. The wall-paper, designed to imitate watered silk, was disfigured by a number of spreading damp-stains. Even with the windows open, the room was filled with a smell from the pretentious, red-marble-topped commode. A cloth, with a mustard-coloured ground, covered the table. I found the general effect pleasing. It seemed to sum up the whole of human ugliness and ostentation.

I was awakened by the rustling of a skirt. Robert's mother was sitting by my bed. The first thing I noticed about her was her smile. Her obsequious attitude would have sufficed to put me on my guard, even if I had known nothing, and to warn me that I had been betrayed. There is a particular species of kindliness which always goes with treachery. I returned the smile, and told her that I was feeling better. Twenty years before her nose had not been so big, In those days, too, her large mouth had been adorned by a handsome set of teeth which Robert had inherited. But to-day her smile revealed a "plate". She must have been walking fast, and the sour smell of her body battled successfully with the emanations from the marble-topped commode. I begged her to open the window wider. She did so, and then came back, still smiling. Now that I was feeling well, she said, Robert was entirely at my disposal for the "business in hand". To-morrow, Saturday, he would be free from midday on. I reminded her that the Banks are closed on Saturday afternoons. In that case, she decided, he had better ask for some time off on Monday morning. There wouldn't be any difficulty about his getting it. Besides, there was no longer any need for him to keep on the right side of his employers. She seemed surprised when I insisted that Robert should stick to his present job for a few weeks longer. When she took leave of me, she said that she would come again with her son next day to see me. I begged her to let him pay his visit unaccompanied. I wanted, I said, to have a little talk with him, so that I might get to know him better. . . . The poor fool made no attempt to disguise her anxiety. She was pretty obviously afraid that her son would give himself away. But when I adopt a certain tone of voice, no one thinks of questioning my decision. I had no doubt that it was she who had urged Robert to come to terms with my family. I knew that frightened, uncomfortable young man too well by this time not to realize that he must be feeling very uneasy in the part he had agreed to play.

When the poor fool entered the room next morning, I saw at
once that I had underrated the effect of the situation on him. It
was obvious, from the appearance of his eyes, that he had not
slept, and he seemed quite unable to look me in the face. I made
him sit down and told him that I thought him looking far from
well. I was affectionate, almost tender, in my manner. I described,
with the eloquence of a practised lawyer, the perspectives of happiness now opening before him. I drew a picture of the house and
park I was going to buy, in his name, at Saint-Germain. It was
to be furnished throughout in "period" style. There would be a
pond well stocked with fish, a garage for four cars, as well as
many other "features" which I improvised as I went along. When
I spoke about a car, and suggested one of the biggest American
makes, he was like a man in mortal agony. Obviously, he had
promised not to accept a penny of my money during my lifetime.

"All your troubles are over," I said. "There is nothing for you
to do now but to sign the deed of purchase. I have already arranged to hand over to you on Monday a sufficient number of
securities to bring you in an income of a hundred thousand
francs a year. That will keep you going. But the bulk of my
liquid capital is in Amsterdam. We must go there together the
week after next so as to get everything straightened out. . . . Is
there anything wrong, Robert?"

"I . . . I . . . won't touch a penny during your lifetime," he
stammered. ". . . I shouldn't like to . . . I don't want to deprive
you of anything. Please don't insist. . . . It'd only make me feel
awful!"

He was leaning against the wardrobe, his left elbow supported
in his right hand, and biting his nails. I gave him the look that
opposing counsel have learned to dread. In just such a way had
I been used to fix my victim in the box, keeping my eyes riveted
on him until he collapsed into the arms of the attendant police
officer.

Actually, I forgave him. I felt that a burden had been lifted
from my shoulders. How frightful to have had to end my days
in the company of such a worm! I didn't hate him—merely, as it
were, dropped him in the ash-can. All the same, I could not resist
the temptation to have a little more fun with him.

"I must say, Robert, your feelings do you credit. How charming of you to want to wait until I am dead! But I am not going
to accept such a sacrifice. Everything shall be yours on Monday.
By the end of next week a large part of my fortune will be in

your name. No," I went on dryly (he had begun to protest),
"not another word. I have made my offer and it's up to you to
take it or leave it."

He still refused to meet my eyes. He needed, he said, a few
days in which to think things over—by which, of course, the poor
idiot meant to write to Bordeaux for orders.

"Your attitude surprises me, Robert. It really is very odd."

I thought I was looking at him more kindly, but my expression
is apt to be a good deal fiercer than the feelings which inspire it.
In a perfectly expressionless voice, Robert muttered:

"Why are you staring at me like that?"

I could not help imitating him. "Why am I staring at you like
this? I might equally well ask why you can't look me in the face."

Those who are accustomed to being loved instinctively make
all the gestures, and say all the things, most likely to win over
their interlocutors. I, on the other hand, have grown so used to
being hated and to frightening people, that my eyes, my brows,
my voice and my laugh automatically become the servants of
this detestable gift of mine, so that they deliver their message
even before I mean them to. The poor lad was twisting and
turning under a gaze which I had thought to make sympathetic:
but the more I laughed, the more ominous did my gaiety seem
to him.

Much in the manner of a slaughterman giving the *coup de
grâce* to an animal, I fired a point-blank question at him:

"How much did they offer you?"

I had used the second person singular, and the effect of this,
whether I liked it or not, was to give to my words a tone not
so much of friendliness as of contempt.

"Who d'you mean?" he stammered.

He was clearly prey to an almost superstitious terror.

"The two gentlemen," I said; "the fat one and the thin one . . .
yes, the thin one and the fat one."

I wanted to get the whole thing over and done with. The idea
of prolonging the scene gave me the horrors (as when one can't
bring oneself to crush a centipede under one's boot). "Come, don't
take it so hard," I said; "I've forgiven you."

"*I* didn't want to do it . . . it was . . ." I put my hand over
his mouth. I couldn't have borne to hear him accuse his mother.

"Ssh! no names! . . . how much *did* they offer you?—a million?—
five hundred thousand?—less than that? Oh, surely not!—three
hundred?—two hundred?"

"Not any sum down at all, but a regular allowance. That was what tempted us: it gives us a greater feeling of security. Twelve thousand francs a year."

"Starting from to-day?"

"No, from when they come into their inheritance. . . . They hadn't foreseen that you'd want to put everything in my name now, at once. . . . But is it too late? . . . Of course, they might sue us . . . unless we could keep the whole thing on the q.t. . . . Oh, what a fool I've been! I deserve everything that's coming to me!"

He sat on the bed, shedding squalid tears. One of his hands hung down, red and enormous.

"After all, I *am* your son," he whined; "don't let me down."

With a clumsy movement he tried to put his arm round my neck. I freed myself—but not roughly. I went over to the window, and, without turning round, said:

"From the first of August you will receive a monthly sum of fifteen hundred francs. I shall take immediate steps to see that this amount is paid to you for life. Should you predecease your mother, it will revert to her. My family must never know that I got wind of the little plot hatched in Saint-Germain-des-Prés" (the name of the church made him jump), "and I need scarcely point out that the least indiscretion on your part will mean that you lose everything. All I ask in return is that you shall keep me informed of anything they may be planning against me."

He knew now that nothing escaped me, and realized precisely what any future treachery would cost him. I made it quite plain that I wished never to see him or his mother again. They must write to me, *poste restante*, at the usual office.

"When are your accomplices of Saint-Germain-des-Prés leaving Paris?"

He assured me that they had taken the late train on the previous night. He made a great show of gratitude and of promises for the future, but I cut him short. He was, no doubt, flabbergasted by what had happened. A fantastic God, moving in a mysterious way, whom he had betrayed, had seized him, let him go, and picked him out of the abyss into which he had fallen. . . . He shut his eyes and went limp. Squirming like a mongrel cur, his ears flattened to his head, he cringingly took the bone I had flung to him, and made off.

Just as he was going out of the door, a thought occurred to

him. How, he asked, would he receive this allowance? Through what channel?

"You will receive it," I said dryly. "I always keep my promises. The rest does not concern you."

With his hand on the latch, he still hesitated.

"I'd rather have it in the form of a Life Insurance Policy, or something like that, taken out with a good, reliable firm. . . . I should feel easier in my mind . . . I wouldn't have to worry . . ."

With sudden violence I wrenched open the door which he was holding ajar and pushed him into the passage.

❀ *X V I I* ❀

I LEANED against the mantelpiece and mechanically counted the scraps of varnished wood in the "tidy".

For years I had dreamed of this unknown son of mine. Never, in the whole course of my wretched existence, had I lost the feeling that he was there. In some sport of the earth there lived a child born of my body whom I might one day find again, who might, perhaps, at some distant date, bring me comfort. That he was of humble condition served to tighten the bonds between us. I had liked to think that he resembled my legitimate son in nothing. I had endowed him in my mind with simplicity and strength of affection, two qualities which are by no means rare among the common people. And now, after all these years, I had played my last card. There was nothing to be hoped from him, nor from any living person. There was nothing left for me to do but curl up and turn my face to the wall. For forty years I had cheated myself into believing that I could accept the fact of hatred—both of the hatred I inspired and the hatred that I felt. But, like other human beings, I had cherished a hope and assuaged my hunger as best I could, waiting until I should be driven back on my last reserves. That moment had come, and it was all over.

I could not even look forward to the horrible pleasure of scheming how best to disinherit those who had wished me ill. Robert had put them on the scent, and, sooner or later, they would discover my hoards, even the ones that did not stand in my own name. Think of some other way? . . . Oh, if only I could go on living, could have time enough in which to spend everything and *then* die . . . leaving behind me not even enough to pay for a pauper's funeral! But all my life long I had saved. For years I had satisfied my lust for "putting by". How, at my age, could I learn to be a spendthrift? Besides, thought I, the children have got their eyes on me. Anything of that sort I might do would merely put a dangerous weapon into their hands. . . . I should have to ruin myself secretly, by driblets. . . .

But alas! I shouldn't know how! I was quite incapable of losing my money. If only it were possible to stuff my grave with it, to return, earth to earth and dust to dust, clasping in my arms my gold, my notes, my shares! If only I could give the lie to those who preach that, when we die, we must leave the goods of this world behind us!

There was, of course, "Charity". Good works are trap-doors opening into depths which can swallow everything. Why not send anonymous gifts to the Relief Committee, to the Little Sisters of the Poor? Why not, at this fag-end of my life, begin to think of others, of those who were not my enemies? But the horror of growing old consists in this, that one's age is the sum total of one's life, and not one figure of it can we change. It has taken me sixty years—I thought—to "create" this old man now dying of hatred. I am what I am. I should have to become somebody else. . . . Oh God! . . . Oh God . . . if only You existed! . . .

It grew dark, and a maid came in to turn down my bed. But she did not close the shutters. I lay down in the half-light. I dozed, in spite of the noise in the street and the glare of the lamps. Every now and again I returned to full consciousness for a brief moment, as one does on a journey when the train comes to a stop. Then, once more, I dropped off. Though I did not feel any worse, I got the idea that I had only to stay as I was and wait patiently until my sleep should become eternal. I still had to make arrangements for the promised allowance to be paid regularly to Robert. I wanted, too, to look in at the *poste restante*, since there was nobody now to do that for me. For the last three days I had not read my mail. One of the most ineradicable of human beliefs is that *some* day a mysterious letter will turn up. What better proof could there be that hope springs eternal in the human breast? We are none of us without it.

It was this preoccupation with the idea of letters that got me

out of bed next day, about noon, and sent me off to the post
office. It was raining. I was without an umbrella, and kept close to
the walls. My appearance aroused curiosity. People began to look
round at me. What's so odd about me?—d'you take me for a lunatic? . . . If you do, you mustn't let on—my children might take
advantage of a thing like that! Don't stare at me so! I'm just like
everybody else—except that my children hate me and that I
ought to take steps to protect myself from them. But that doesn't
mean I'm mad. There are times when I am under the influence
of all the drugs that an angina patient has to take. Yes, I *do* talk to
myself, but that's because I am always *by* myself. Conversation
is a necessity of all human creatures. What is there so extraordinary in the words and gestures of a lonely old man?

The packet I was given contained some printed matter, some
letters from the Bank, and three telegrams. They probably had
to do with Stock Exchange transactions which it had been impossible to put through. I delayed opening them until I should
be seated in a cheap eating-house. . . . Several builder's labourers,
looking like pierrots of varying ages, were seated at a long table
eating their not very generous portions, drinking their litres, and
scarcely speaking a word. They had been working in the rain all
morning. At half-past one they would start again. It was the end
of July. The stations were full of holiday-makers. . . . Would they
have understood anything of the torment seething in my mind?—
Of course they would: how could an old lawyer doubt it? My first
case had had to do with children who had gone to law in some
quarrel about looking after their father. The wretched man went
to one or other of them every three months, only to be received
with curses. The one point on which he had found himself in
agreement with his sons was in calling loudly on death to bring
them all release. Many was the form in which I had witnessed
this drama of the old father obstinately refusing, year after year,
to hand over the money-bags, and then, finally, letting himself
be wheedled out of his rights, only to die of overwork and hunger
at the hands of his children. Oh yes, the emaciated labourer with
the gnarled hands, seated only a few feet from me, and slowly
mumbling his bread between toothless gums, would surely know
all about that.

No one, in these days, shows any surprise at the sight of a
well-dressed old man in a cheap eating-house. I cut up a piece

of pallid rabbit and amused myself by watching the raindrops
running together on the window-pane. I spelled out the name of
the proprietor upside down. In feeling for my handkerchief, I
came on the packet of letters. I put on my spectacles and opened
one of the telegrams at random. "Mother's funeral to-morrow 23
July nine St. Louis church." It was dated that morning. The other
two, sent off the evening before, must have followed one another
at a few hours' interval. One of them said: "Mother desperately ill
return." The other: "Mother dead. . . ." All three were signed
"Hubert".

I crumpled up the telegrams and went on eating, my mind
preoccupied with the thought that, somehow, I should have to
muster up sufficient strength to take the night train. For several
minutes I was concerned with nothing else. Then another feeling
began to emerge—a feeling of amazement that I should have survived Isa. It had long been an understood thing that I was under
sentence of death. Neither I, nor anybody else, had doubted for
a moment that I should be the first to go. Plans, intrigues, plots—
all had been centred on the days immediately following my death,
which could not now be long delayed. I had been as certain of
that as any member of my family, had always seen my wife in
the character of a widow, encumbered by crape when she went
to open my safe. No astronomical disaster could have caused me
more surprise—or uneasiness—than this death. Automatically, the
business-man side of me began to take stock of the situation,
began to wonder how it could be used to advantage against my
enemies. Such were my feelings until the train actually started.

It was only then that my imagination began to take a hand. For
the first time I conjured up a vision of Isa as she must have looked
in her bed on the previous day, and on the day before that. I saw
the whole scene—her room at Calèse (I did not know then that
she had died in Bordeaux). "Putting her into her coffin," I murmured to myself, and yielded to a cowardly feeling of relief. What
would have been my attitude had I been there? How should I
have behaved under the watchful and hostile eyes of my children? That problem no longer arose. Furthermore, the fact that I
should have to go straight to bed as soon as I arrived would settle
every difficulty of that kind. There could be no question of my
being at the funeral. Only a moment ago I had made an effort
to go to the lavatory, and had had to give it up. This evidence
of my weakness did not frighten me. Now that Isa was gone, I

no longer lived in hourly expectation of my end. My turn had
gone by. But I *was* afraid of having an attack, the more so since
I was alone in the carriage. I should be met at the station (I
had sent a telegram) no doubt by Hubert.

But it was not Hubert who was waiting for me. What a relief
it was to see Alfred standing there with his fat face showing all
the marks of a sleepless night! The sight of me seemed to frighten
him. I could not manage to get into the car unaided, and had to
take his arm. We drove in the gloom of a rainy Bordeaux morning through a district given over to slaughter-houses and schools.
There was no need for me to talk. Alfred went into the smallest
details. He described the exact spot in the Public Gardens where
Isa had collapsed (in front of a clump of palms just before one
gets to the green-houses), the chemist's shop into which she had
been taken, the difficulty they had had in getting her heavy body
upstairs to her room on the first floor, the blood-letting, the tap-
ping. . . . She had been fully conscious all night, though she was
suffering from cerebral hæmorrhage. She had kept on asking for
me by means of signs, and had fallen asleep just as the priest arrived with the consecrated oils. . . . "But she had taken Communion the day before. . . ."

Alfred wanted to drop me at the front door (which was already
draped in black) and hurry home, explaining that he had barely
time in which to get dressed for the ceremony. But he had to resign himself to the necessity of helping me out of the car. He
gave me his arm up the first few steps. I did not recognize the
hall. In the dim interior great stands of candles were burning
round a massed bank of flowers. I blinked my eyes. I felt lost, as
one sometimes does in dreams. There were two motionless nuns.
They must have been provided by the undertaker along with
the other fittings. Behind this hotch-potch of fabrics, flowers and
lights, the familiar staircase, with its shabby carpet, climbed
into the region of everyday life.

Hubert came down. He was in evening dress, and looked very
correct. He held out his hand to me and said something, but
his voice seemed to come from very far away. I tried to answer,
but failed to make a sound. His face drew closer and became
enormous. Then I lost consciousness. I learned later that my faint-
ing fit lasted for a bare three minutes. I came to myself in what
had once been my waiting-room in the days when I was still

practising at the Bar. There was the sharp prick of smelling-salts
in my nose. I recognized Geneviève's voice: "He's coming round."
I opened my eyes. They were all there, bending over me. Their
faces seemed different—red, puffy, and some of them with a
greenish tinge. Janine, more robust than her mother, had the
appearance of being her contemporary rather than her child.
Hubert's face, in particular, showed the effects of tears. He had
the same ugly, pitiful look as when, a child, he had been taken
by Isa on her lap, and she had said, "The poor little mite's really
unhappy. . . ." Only Phili appeared to be completely unchanged.
Wearing the dress-suit which he had dragged through all the
night-haunts of Paris and Berlin, he looked at me with the customary expression of bored indifference on his handsome face. He
might have been just off to a party, or, rather, just back from one,
drunk and slovenly, for he had not yet tied his tie. Behind him
I could make out a number of anonymous veiled women, who
must have been Olympe and her daughters. Other shirt-fronts
gleamed in the half-light.

Geneviève held a glass to my lips, and I gulped down some of
its contents. I told her that I was feeling better. In a gentle,
kindly voice she asked whether I would like to go to bed at once.
I said the first thing that came into my mind:

"I should so much have liked to go with her to the end, not
having been here to say good-bye."

I repeated the phrase, like an actor seeking the correct in-
flexion—"not having been here to say good-bye . . ."—and the flat
words, serving no purpose beyond that of saving appearances.
They had come to me only because they belonged to the part
I was playing in the funeral ceremony, and suddenly awoke in
me, with a sudden jerk, the very feeling of which they were the
expression. It was as though I had told myself something which,
till then, I had not realized. I should never again see my wife.
There could never, now, be an explanation between us. She
would never read these pages. Things would remain for all eternity in exactly the same state in which they had been when I
left Calèse. We could not start afresh, wipe the slate clean, and try
again. She had died without knowing me, without understanding
that there was more in me than the monster, the tormentor, she
thought me to be, that behind the mask there did exist a totally
different man. Even if I had arrived at the last moment, even
though no word had passed between us, she would have seen the

tears which were now running down my face, and would have
died in the knowledge of my despair.

Only my children, speechless with astonishment, were witnesses of the scene. Probably, in the whole course of their lives,
they had never seen me cry. The old surly, terrifying face, the
Medusa's head at which they had none of them been able to
look, had undergone a metamorphosis, had become simply that of
a human being.

I heard a voice (it was probably Janine's):

"If only you hadn't gone away! Why did you?" Yes, why, indeed, had I gone? But I *could* have got back in time had the telegrams not been addressed to the *poste restante*, but delivered to
me at the Rue Bréa. Hubert was foolish enough to add:

"Going away like that, without leaving an address . . . how
could we possibly guess?"

A thought, till then vague in my mind, became, on a sudden,
crystal-clear. Pressing with my two hands on the arms of the chair,
I struggled to my feet, trembling with anger, and shouted in his
face the one word—"Liar!"

He was taken aback. "Papa!" he stammered, "you must be
mad!"

But I went on: "Yes, you're liars, the whole lot of you. You
knew my address perfectly well. I dare you to tell me to my face
that you didn't!"

He protested feebly: "But how could we have known it?"

"You were in touch with somebody very close to me . . . you
can't deny that, you know you can't!"

The whole family stared at me in a sort of petrified silence.
Hubert shook his head like a child caught out in an untruth.

"You didn't give him much for his treachery: you weren't exactly generous. Twelve thousand francs a year in return for a
fortune isn't much!"

I laughed and laughed until I was caught in a fit of coughing.
They could none of them find anything to say. Phili muttered in a
low voice: "Dirty trick. . . ."

I went on with what I had been saying, though I lowered my
voice in deference to a gesture of appeal from Hubert, who was
striving in vain to get a word in:

"You were the cause of my not coming back. You were being
kept informed of my every movement; but I mustn't be allowed
to know that. If you had sent me a telegram addressed to the

Rue Bréa, I should realize at once that I had been betrayed.
Nothing in the world would have induced you to take such a
step, not even the prayers of your dying mother. No doubt you
felt sorry, but you were cold and calculating. . . ."

All this I said to them, and other things still more horrible.
Hubert begged his sister to intervene. "Make him stop! Make him
stop! Somebody will hear him!" he said in a choking voice.
Geneviève put her arm round my shoulders and made me sit down
again.

"Not now, Father; not now. We'll talk about all that later when
we're not so upset. I beg you, in the name of her who is still
with us . . ."

Hubert's face was livid. He put a finger to his lips. The chief
undertaker's man came in with a list of the pall-bearers. I took
a few steps. I did not want any of their supporting arms. I
stumbled, and they drew aside to let me pass. I was able to
cross the threshold of the mortuary chapel, and squat down on
a *prie-Dieu*.

Hubert and Geneviève followed me. Each taking an arm, they
led me away, and I made no effort to resist. They got me upstairs
with considerable difficulty. One of the nuns agreed to keep an
eye on me during the ceremony. Hubert, before leaving, with a
great show of ignoring what had just passed between us, asked
me whether he had done right in arranging for the President of
the Bar Council to be one of the pall-bearers. I turned away to the
streaming window and said nothing.

Already there was a sound of many feet. The whole town would
come to sign the visitors' book. On the Fondaudège side there
were innumerable connexions, and on mine, the Bar, the Bank,
and the world of business. . . . I was conscious of a lightness of
heart. I felt like a man who has just been acquitted of a crime,
whose innocence has been declared to the world. I had convicted
my children of lying, and they had made no attempt to deny
their responsibility. While the whole house was echoing to the
sound of feet—as though some strange ball without music was in
progress—I forced myself to concentrate my thoughts upon their
guilt. It was they alone who had prevented me from hearing Isa's
last farewell. I stuck spurs deep into my ancient hatred, but,
like a foundered horse, it would not respond. Perhaps the reason lay in my physical prostration, or in my satisfaction at the
knowledge that I had had the last word. I cannot be sure.

I could no longer hear the sing-song of the priest's voice. The sounds of the funeral died away, and a silence as deep as that of Calèse filled the huge house. Isa had emptied it of its inhabitants. Behind her corpse she trailed the paraphernalia of her home. No one was left within its walls but I and the nun, who was finishing, at my bedside, the telling of her beads which she had begun beside the bier.

The silence made me sensitive once more to the fact of eternal separation, to that departure from which there is no return. Again I felt a tightness round my heart because now it was too late, and all was over between us. Propped up against the pillows of my bed, that I might breathe the more easily, I looked round at the Louis XIII furniture which we had chosen in Bardie's shop at the time of our engagement. It had been hers until she inherited her mother's. This bed it was, this melancholy bed, which had been the silent witness of our bitter wordlessness.

Hubert and Geneviève came in alone. The others had stayed outside in the passage. I realized that they could not get used to the sight of my tears. They stood beside my pillow, the brother, a bizarre figure dressed for the evening at midday, the sister, a mound of black picked out by a white handkerchief, and her veil thrown back to reveal a round and puffy face. Grief had unmasked us all, and we did not recognize one another.

They were worried about my health. Geneviève said:

"Almost everybody was at the cemetery: she was much beloved."

I asked them about the day before her stroke.

"She wasn't feeling well. She may, I think, have had a presentiment, because the day before she was due to go to Bordeaux, she spent hours in her bedroom, burning piles of letters. We thought the chimney must be on fire."

I broke in. A sudden idea had occurred to me. . . . Why hadn't I thought of it before?

"Geneviève, do you think my going away had anything to do with it?"

She answered with a satisfied air that, no doubt, "it had been a blow".

"But you didn't tell her, didn't keep her informed of what you had discovered?"

She shot a questioning glance at her brother: ought she to seem to understand? I must have presented an odd appearance at that moment, for, certainly, they seemed very much afraid. While Geneviève helped to prop me up in bed, Hubert hurriedly replied that his mother had been taken ill more than ten days after my departure, and that they had decided, throughout that period, not to include her in their melancholy discussions. Was he speaking the truth? In tremulous tones, he added:

"If we had yielded to the temptation of mentioning to her the uneasiness we were feeling, then, indeed, the prime responsibility would be ours."

He half-turned away, and I could see his shoulders moving convulsively. Somebody pushed the door open, and asked whether they were *ever* going to have something to eat. I heard Phili's voice: "Well, I can't help it, can I, if I'm starving?". . . Geneviève asked me through her tears what I would like for luncheon. Hubert said that he would come back after the meal, and that we must have everything out, once and for all, if I felt strong enough to listen. I nodded my agreement.

When they had left the room, the good sister helped me to get up. I was able to take a bath, dress myself, and drink a cup of beef-tea. If there was to be a discussion I did not want to play the part of a sick man to be dealt with gently and protected.

On their return I was a very different person from the old gentleman who had aroused their compassion. I had taken the necessary drugs, and was sitting upright. I felt less congested, as I always do when I leave my bed.

Hubert had changed into a day suit, but Geneviève was swathed in an old dressing-gown belonging to her mother. "I've nothing black to wear," she said. They sat down facing me. After a few conversational phrases:

"I've thought a good deal about this," Hubert began.

He had carefully prepared his speech, and addressed me as though I had been a meeting of shareholders. He weighed each word, and seemed anxious to avoid any show of anger.

"While I was sitting by Mamma, I scrupulously examined my conscience. I made a great effort to alter my point of view and to put myself in your place. We had regarded you as a father whose fixed idea was to disinherit his children, and that, to my mind, makes our behaviour legitimate, or, at least, excusable. But we have given you a certain advantage over us by the violence with which we fought our cause, and by . . ."

He seemed to be looking for the right word. I murmured, very quietly, "and by your cowardly plots".

His cheeks showed a patch of colour. Geneviève at once reacted:

"Why 'cowardly'? You're in a much stronger position than we are. . . ."

"Oh, come! . . . a very sick old man against a pack of healthy young animals!"

"In a family like ours," said Hubert, "a very sick old man is distinctly privileged. He never leaves his room: he can be constantly on the watch: he has nothing to do but observe the habits of his children and take advantage of them. He can make his plans undisturbed, and arrange his moves at leisure. He knows all there is to be known about those round him, while they know nothing whatever about him. He has reconnoitred the best vantage-points for listening . . ." (here I could not help smiling, and they smiled too). "Yes," Hubert went on, "the members of a family are always lacking in prudence. They argue, they raise their voices. In a very short while everyone is shouting without realizing it. They rely too much on the thickness of the walls in an old house, oblivious of the fact that the floors are flimsy, and that there are always open windows to be reckoned with. . . ."

These allusions had the effect of, to some extent, diminishing the tension between us. It was Hubert who first brought the conversation back to its serious level.

"I see now that we must have seemed blameworthy. It would be easy enough for me to plead legitimate self-defence, but I want to avoid anything that might embitter this discussion. It is no part of my intention to name the aggressor in this wretched quarrel. I am even prepared to plead guilty. But you must realize . . ."

He had got up, and was wiping the lenses of his spectacles. The eyes blinked in his worn and harassed face.

". . . You must realize that I was fighting for the honour, for the very existence, of my children. It is impossible for you to imagine the situation in which we find ourselves. You belong to a different century. You have lived your life in a fabulous period when a careful man could plan his future on a basis of safe investments. Oh, I know that you are fully aware of what is happening in the world, that you saw the storm coming before anybody else did, that you realized in time . . . but that was because you had

retired from active business, because you were, if I may say so, an
onlooker. You could judge the situation quite coolly; you dominated it, you were not, as I am, up to the ears in it. . . . The
awakening has been too sudden. . . . It's been impossible, as yet,
to look round. . . . This is the first moment that all the branches of
the tree have given way at the same moment. There is nothing
left to cling to, nothing on which one can get a hold. . . ."

There was something of desperation in the way he repeated
those words—"nothing, nothing at all. . . ." How deeply *was* he
committed?—on the edge of what abyss was he struggling? Afraid
that he might have given himself away, he checked his flow of
eloquence, fell back on the usual commonplaces—the drive for
industrial re-equipment in the post-war period, over-production,
the fall in purchasing power. What he said did not matter: it
was this desperation of his that held my attention. It was borne
in on me at that moment that my hatred was dead, and dead, too,
my desire for reprisals. Perhaps they had been dead for a long
time. I had been piling coals on my anger, had been tearing myself to pieces. But what was the use of refusing to look facts in
the face? My feelings, as I sat there in my son's presence, were
confused, but my dominant emotion was one of curiosity. How
strange it all seemed—the wretched man's obvious agitation and
terror, the horrors which it needed only a word from me to dissipate! I thought of the fortune which, so it seemed, had been
my life's obsession. I had tried so hard to give it away or lose it.
I had not been free even to dispose of it as I had wished, and
now I felt, suddenly, wholly detached. It no longer interested me,
was no longer any concern of mine. Hubert had left off speaking,
and was watching me from behind his spectacles. What was I
scheming?—what new blow preparing? There was already a sort
of fixed grin on his face. He drew himself up and raised his arm
like a child preparing to ward off attack. He began again to
speak, and now his voice was timid:

"All I ask is that you should set me on my feet. Taking into consideration what will be coming to me from Mamma, I shan't now
need more than . . ." (he hesitated a moment before naming the
figure) . . . "more than a million. Once I've wiped the slate
clean, I shall be able to manage. Do what you like with the
rest. . . . I undertake to bow to your wishes. . . ."

He swallowed, and continued to observe me furtively. I was
careful to keep my face a blank.

"And what about you, my dear?" I asked, turning to Gene-

viève. "You're right as rain, aren't you?—married to a clever husband. . . ."

It always irritated her to hear her husband praised. She protested that the business was on its last legs. Alfred had bought
no rum, now, for two years. At least that meant that he had made
no bad deals, which was a comfort. They'd got enough to live on,
certainly, but Phili was threatening to desert his wife and child,
and was waiting only until he knew for certain that all hope of
getting some of the family fortune was gone. "Good riddance!"
I muttered, but she took me up sharply.

"Oh, we all know he's a rotter—Janine no less than the rest of
us—but if he leaves her she'll die. I mean it—she'll die. That's
something you can't understand, Father: you're not made that
way. Janine knows a great deal more about Phili than all the
rest of us put together. She has often told me that he is far worse
than we could possibly imagine. But that doesn't alter the fact
that she would die if he left her. I know it must sound nonsense
to you. Things like that are beyond your comprehension. But
surely a man as intelligent as you can understand a thing even
if you don't feel it?"

"You're tiring Papa, Geneviève. . . ." It had occurred to Hubert
that his clumsy sister might have "put her foot in it", that I might
be hurt in my pride by what she had said. He could see from my
face that I was suffering, but he could not know why, could not
know that Geneviève had opened an old wound and was jabbing
at it.

"Lucky Phili!" I sighed.

I could read amazement in the glance that passed between my
two children. They had always, quite honestly, believed me to be
half-mad. Perhaps if they had had me locked up, they would
have done so with an easy conscience.

"A blackguard!" muttered Hubert; "and he's got a hold over us!"

"His father-in-law looks on him with a rather kindlier eye," I
said. "Alfred is always saying that he's a queer fish, but not really
bad at heart."

Geneviève flared up:

"That's because he's got a hold over Alfred, too! The son-in-
law has corrupted the father-in-law—everyone knows that!
They're constantly being seen together consorting with women. . . .
The shame of that was one of the things that made Mother's life
a misery. . . ."

She dabbed at her eyes. It was clear that Hubert thought I was trying to distract their attention from what really mattered. "That's not the point, Geneviève," he said with a show of irritation. "To hear you talk one would imagine that you and your children are the only people in the world."

She turned on him in a fury. Of the two of them, which was the most selfish?—that's what *she* would like to know!

"It's only natural," she went on, "to put one's own children first. I have always done everything for Janine, and I'm proud to admit it, just as Mamma did everything for us. I'd go through fire . . ."

Her brother broke in on her. I recognized myself in the sharpness of his tone. "And see that others went through it, too!" he said.

What fun I should once have got from their quarrel! I should have hailed with delight these preliminary signs of a battle to the death over the few leavings of my fortune which I could not keep from them. But the only feeling of which I was conscious now was one of faint disgust and boredom. . . . If only the whole wretched business could be settled once and for all! If only they would leave me to die in peace!

"It's odd, my children," I said to them, "that I should end by doing what I've always considered as the height of folly. . . ."

Their snarlings were all forgotten in an instant! They turned on me a hard, suspicious look. They were waiting, their guard was up.

"I've always thought of myself in terms of the old farmer robbed of his livelihood, and left by his children to die of hunger. If he took too long over his dying, well then, a few eiderdowns piled conveniently on his face would hasten the processes of nature. . . ."

"Father, *please* . . ."

The look of horror with which they protested was not assumed. Hastily I changed my tone.

"You're going to be busy, Hubert. Sharing out the pickings won't be easy. I've got my money stowed away in a great number of places—here, in Paris, abroad. Then there's the real estate, my various houses. . . ."

At each word their eyes grew rounder. They couldn't believe their ears. I saw Hubert's thin hands open and shut.

"I want everything to be settled before my death, at the same time as you wind up your mother's estate. I shall retain Calèse

for my own use, both the house and the park (the cost of upkeep
and repairs to fall on you). I don't want to hear another word
about the vines. A monthly income—the amount of which remains
to be settled—will be paid me by my lawyer. . . . Just hand me
my wallet . . . yes, it's in the left-hand pocket of my coat."

Hubert gave it to me with a trembling hand. I took out an envelope.

"This will give you some idea of the total amount of my fortune . . . you had better take it to Arcam, the barrister. . . . No, on
second thoughts, it would be better to ring him up and ask him to
come round. I'll give it him myself, and confirm my dispositions
in your presence."

Hubert took the envelope, and said with an air of acute anxiety:
"You're not laughing at us, are you?"

"Ring up the lawyer: you'll soon see whether I'm laughing. . . ."

"No," he said; "not to-day, it would be scarcely decent. . . . We
ought to wait a week."

He passed one hand over his eyes. Clearly, he was feeling
ashamed, was forcing himself to think of his mother. He turned
the envelope over and over in his fingers.

"All right then, open it," I said; "open it and read what's inside.
You have my authority to do so."

He went quickly across to the window and broke the seal. He
fell on the letter like a starving man on food. Geneviève could restrain herself no longer, but got up, joined him, and peered
greedily over his shoulder.

I looked at the brother and sister. There was nothing in the
sight to cause me horror. A man of business threatened with ruin:
a father and a mother who had suddenly come into the millions
which they had thought lost to them for ever. No, they caused
me no sense of horror. But my own indifference astonished me.
I was like a patient who comes round from an operation and says
that he has felt nothing. I had torn out of myself something which
I had always thought was deeply rooted in my being—and I felt
nothing but relief, nothing but a sort of physical lightness! I was
breathing more easily. What, after all, had I been doing for years
but trying to get rid of this fortune, trying to load it on to somebody who was not a member of my family? But always I had
been deceived in the object of my wishes. We do not know what
we desire: we do not love those whom we think we love.

I heard Hubert say to his sister: "It's enormous, simply enormous—a vast fortune!" They exchanged a few words in low
voices. Geneviève declared that they could not accept such a sacrifice, that they had no wish to strip me naked.

The words "sacrifice" and "strip" sounded strange in my ears.
Hubert was insistent.

"You have been influenced by the emotion of the moment. You
think you are more ill than you are. You're not seventy. People
with your ailment live to a great old age. After a while you will
regret what you have done. I will relieve you of all business
worries, if you like, but you must enjoy in peace what belongs to
you. We want only what is just. We have never asked for anything but justice. . . ."

I was overcome by a sense of weariness. They saw my eyes
close. I told them that my mind was made up, that I would say
no more on the subject except in the presence of a lawyer. They
were already at the door. Without turning my head, I called
them back.

"I forgot to tell you that a monthly allowance of fifteen hundred francs is to be paid to my son Robert. I have promised him
that. Remind me of it when we draw up the agreement."

Hubert blushed. This particular arrow had taken him by surprise. But Geneviève read no malice into what I had said. Round-
eyed, she made a rapid calculation:

"Eighteen thousand francs a year," she said. "Don't you think
that's rather a lot?"

🏵 XVIII 🏵

THE grass looks lighter than the sky. A thin vapour is rising from
the soaked earth. The ruts, brimming with rain, reflect a muddy
blue. I feel as interested in everything as I used to do when
Calèse still belonged to me. Now, I am possessed of nothing, yet
do not feel my poverty. The sound, at night, of rain upon the
rotting vines makes me no less sad than when I was the owner
of the threatened crop. What I thought of as love of my land was
no more than the physical instinct of the peasant; for I come of a
long peasant line and was born of those who, through the cen-

turies, had scanned the sky with anxious looks. The money to be
paid to me each month will accumulate at the lawyer's. I have
never wanted for anything. All my life long I have been the
prisoner of a passion which never really possessed me. Like a
dog barking at the moon, I was held in thrall by a reflection.
Fancy waking up at sixty-eight! Fancy being reborn at the very
moment of my death! If only I may be granted just a few more
years, a few months, a few weeks. . . .

The nurse has gone. I am feeling much better. Amélie and
Ernest, who served Isa, are to stay on with me. They know how
to give injections. Everything lies ready to my hand, the little
bottles of morphine and of nitrite. The children are so busy that
they scarcely ever leave town. They turn up here only when
they want to know something about a valuation. . . . They get
along without too much quarrelling. They are so terrified of being
"done down" that they have agreed, rather foolishly, to divide up
all the complete sets of damask linen and glassware. They would
cut a piece of tapestry in two rather than let any one of them
have the benefit of it. They would prefer to see everything spoiled
than get unequal shares. It is what they call having a "passion
for justice". They have spent their lives giving high-sounding
names to sordid instincts. . . . No, I ought to scratch that sentence
out. For all I know, they may be prisoners, as I was, of a passion
that does not really go deep.

What do they think of me? That I have been beaten, pre-
sumably, that I have been forced to surrender. They've "got me".
All the same, each time they visit me they show respect and
gratitude. But that doesn't prevent them from being in a constant state of amazement at my attitude. Hubert, in particular,
keeps a watchful eye on me. He is suspicious. He is not quite
sure that I have been disarmed. You can be quite easy in your
mind, my poor boy. I was never really an object of terror even
when I returned as a convalescent to Calèse, and now . . .

The elms along the roads and the poplars in the meadows
stand massed together. Between their dark-hued trunks the mist
accumulates, and the smoke of bonfires, and the breath of the
huge earth when it has drunk deep. For we have waked to find
the autumn all about us. The grapes still glittering from the recent
storm will never recover what this rainy August stole. But for us,
perhaps, it is never too late. I must never stop telling myself
that it is never too late.

It was from no feeling of devotion that I went into Isa's room the day after I got back. What led me there was idleness, that complete lack of occupation which seizes me in the country. I never know whether I most enjoy or dislike it. I was tempted to push the half-open door, the first door on the left at the top of the stairs. The window was flung back; the wardrobe and the chest of drawers were empty. The servants had swept the place clean, and the sun, even in the farthest corners, had eaten up the last impalpable remains of a completed destiny. The September afternoon was buzzing with sleepy flies. The thick round tops of the lime trees looked like bruised fruit. The blue, deep at the zenith, showed pale behind the dozing hills. A burst of laughter came up to me from some girl I could not see. Sun-bonnets were moving among the vines. The grape-harvest had begun.

But the wonder of life had withdrawn from Isa's room. A pair of gloves and an umbrella lying on the floor of the wardrobe looked dead. I gazed at the old stone mantelpiece on the spandrel of which were carved a spade, a sickle and a blade of corn. These old-fashioned hearths, in which whole trunks can burn, are masked in summer by large screens of painted canvas. This particular one had a picture of two oxen ploughing. One day, when I was very young, I had slashed it with a pen-knife in a fit of temper. It was only leaning against the fireplace. I tried to adjust it properly, but it fell, revealing the black square of the grate, filled with ashes. Then I remembered what the children had told me about Isa's last day at Calèse: "She was burning papers: we thought there was a fire." . . . I realized how strongly she must have felt the approach of death. It is impossible, at one and the same time, to think of one's own death and that of another person. Obsessed by the certainty of my approaching end, I had, quite naturally, not felt worried by Isa's blood-pressure. "It's nothing—just old age," our idiotic children had gone on saying. But she, when she had kindled this great fire, had known that her hour was at hand. She had wanted to disappear utterly, and so had set about effacing every tiny trace of herself. I stared into the hearth, at the scraps of grey fluff which the wind was gently fluttering. The tongs she had used were still in their place, between the chimney and the wall. I took them, and started to rummage in the heap of dust, that last remains of an utter nothingness.

I searched as though the secret of my life lay hidden there, the secret of our two lives. The farther I probed with the poker, the thicker lay the ashes. I brought out a few scraps of paper which the thickness of the bundles must have saved from the flame. But all I could recover were a few words, a few broken phrases, which conveyed no meaning. All were in the same handwriting. I could not recognize it. My hands were trembling: I worked feverishly. On one tiny fragment, smeared with soot, I could make out the word PAX. Beneath it was a small cross, a date, 23 February, 1913, and the words *"my dear daughter. . . ."* I set myself to assemble the letters written on the margin of some other pieces of charred paper, but all I could get was this: *"You are not responsible for the hatred which this rouses in you. Only if you yielded to it would you be to blame. Far from that being so, you try . . ."* As the result of much effort, I succeeded in reading a little more: *". . . judge the dead rashly . . . the affection which he feels for Luc does not prove"* . . . Soot hid all of the rest, except one single phrase: *"Forgive, not knowing what it is that you have to forgive. . . . Offer for him your . . ."*

There would be time enough later for me to think of what I had read. My only concern at the moment was to find more. I searched every nook and cranny of the hearth, crouching so awkwardly, that I found it difficult to breathe. The discovery of a note-book bound in American cloth set my heart beating. It looked intact, but, on examining it, I found that none of the pages had escaped the fire. The only words I could decipher were on the inside of the cover, in Isa's hand: FLOWERS OF THE SPIRIT, and, underneath, *"My name is not the name of Him who damns: I am called Jesus"* (Christ to Saint François de Sales).

There were several more quotations, but all of them illegible. I spent some time longer bending over the burned-out ashes, but in vain. I could find nothing more. I scrambled to my feet and looked at my black hands. In the mirror I could see my smeared forehead. Suddenly, as in the days of my youth, I was seized with a longing to go for a walk. Forgetful of my heart, I hurried downstairs, far too fast.

For the first time for weeks I made my way to the vines. Half stripped of their fruit, they were slipping back into their winter sleep. The landscape was light and limpid. It seemed to have become distended, like those blue-tinted bubbles which Marie used to blow from the end of a hollow straw. Already the ruts

and the deep hoof-marks of oxen were hardening under the influence of sun and wind. I walked on, carrying within me the picture of an unknown Isa, of a woman racked by powerful passions which only God could master. The busy housewife had,
all the while, been a wildly jealous sister. Luc had been to her
an object of loathing. . . . How could a grown woman have
brought herself to hate a little boy? . . . Was it the thought of her
own children that had been at the bottom of that bitter resentment, the knowledge that I loved Luc so much more deeply
than I ever loved them? But Marinette, too, she had detested.
. . . It was *I* who had caused her all that suffering. Yes, it was
true, I had had it in my power to torture her! What a mad
dance it had been! Marinette was dead, Luc, too, and now Isa:
and here I was, an old man, still on his feet, it was true, but
standing at the very edge of that same grave which had swallowed the rest of them, and filled with a wild delight because
at last I knew that I had not been an object of indifference to
her, but had raised a storm to beat about her heart.

It was laughable. I actually laughed aloud, panting a little,
leaning against one of the vine-stakes, and looking at the pale
sea of mist in which villages and village churches and poplar-
lined roads lay drowned. The setting sun pierced through with
difficulty to light that buried world. I could feel, I could see,
I could touch my guilt. It was not only that my heart had become a nest of vipers, that it had been filled with hatred for
my children, with a lust for vengeance and a grasping love of
money. What was worse than that was that I had refused to look
beyond the tangle of vile snakes. I had treasured their knotted
hideousness as though it had been the central reality of my
being—as though the beating of the life-blood in my veins had
been the pulse of all those swarming reptiles. Not content with
knowing, through half a century, only of myself what was not
truly me at all, I had carried the same ignorance into my
dealing with others. The expression of squalid greed on the
faces of my children had held me fascinated. Confronted by
Robert, I had been able to see only his stupidity, because it was
all I had wanted to see. I had never once realized that the superficial appearance of others was something I must break through,
a barrier that I must cross, if I was ever to make contact with
the real man, the real woman beyond and behind it. That was
the discovery I ought to have made when I was thirty or forty. . . .

But now I am an old man. The movement of my heart is too sluggish. I am watching the last autumn of my life as it puts the vines to sleep and stupefies them with its fumes and sunlight. Those whom I *should* have loved are dead, and dead, too, those whom I *could* have loved. I have neither the time now, nor the strength, to embark upon a voyage of exploration with the object of finding the reality of others. Everything in me, even my voice, even my gestures, belongs to the monster whom I reared against the world, the monster to whom I gave my name.

Were those, in strict accuracy, the thoughts on which I brooded as I stood leaning against a vine-stake at the far end of one of the planted rows, with my face turned towards the gleaming hill-slopes of Yquem under the setting sun? One incident there was—and I must mention it here—which doubtless made them clearer in my mind. But it did not create them. They were there already on that evening, as I walked back to the house, my heart filled with the peace that lay upon the earth. The shadows were lengthening. The whole earth was wide open, awaiting the bounty of nature. In the distance the half-glimpsed hills were like bowed shoulders patiently hoping for the darkness and the mist to cover them so that they might stretch themselves, perhaps, lie down and fall into a human sleep.

I had expected to find Geneviève and Hubert at the house. They had promised to dine with me. For the first time in my life I was looking forward to their company, was thinking of it in a mood of pleasurable anticipation. I was impatient to show them my change of heart. Not one minute must I lose in getting to know them, in getting them to know me. Would there be time, before I died, to put my new discovery to the test? I longed to drive post-haste to the goal of my children's affection, to break through every obstacle that stood between them and me. At last I had cut through the knot of vipers. So quickly would I win their love that when the moment came for them to close my eyes, they would do so with tears.

They had not yet arrived. I sat on the bench close to the road, listening to the passing cars. The more they delayed, the more did I long for them to come. Several times I had a return of my old anger. What did they care about keeping me waiting! It didn't matter to them if I suffered on their account! They were doing it on purpose! . . . But I took a hold on myself. There might be reasons for their lateness of which I knew nothing, and it was unlikely that they would be those on which I habitually fed my resentment. The gong sounded for dinner. I went to the kitchen to tell Amélie that we must wait a little longer. Only on very rare occasions did I venture into her world of black rafters and pendent hams. I sat down in a wicker chair close to the fire. Amélie, her husband, and Cazau, the bailiff, were there. I had heard their loud laughter while I was still some way off. As I entered the room they all fell silent. An atmosphere of respect and terror enveloped me. I never talk to servants. It is not that I am a difficult or unreasonable master, but simply that, for me, they don't exist. I don't see them. But this evening I found their presence comforting. Because my children had not turned up, I should have liked to eat my dinner on the corner of the table which the cook used for chopping up the joints.

Cazau had made his escape. Ernest was putting on a white jacket, preparatory to serving at table. I tried to find something to say, but all in vain. I knew absolutely nothing about these two human beings who had been our devoted attendants for the past twenty years. At last, I remembered that, in the old days, their married daughter from Sauveterre de Guyenne had been in the habit of coming to see them, and that Isa had always refused to pay her for the rabbit she brought, on the ground that she had so many meals in our house. Without turning my head, I rather hurriedly asked:

"And how is your daughter, Amélie? Still living at Sauveterre?"

She bent her sun-tanned face to mine and stared.

"Surely, sir, you know that she is dead? . . . It'll be ten years on the twenty-ninth, Michaelmas Day . . . have you forgotten, sir?"

Her husband said nothing, but his eyes looked hard. He thought I had been only pretending to forget. I stammered out: "Oh, I'm so sorry! . . . this old head of mine . . ."—but, as always when I am embarrassed or nervous, I giggled. I just could not help it. Then the man announced in his usual voice that dinner was ready.

I got up at once, went into the ill-lit dining-room, and sat down opposite the ghost of Isa. There, next to her, was where Geneviève has always sat, and then, in order, the Abbé Ardouin, Hubert. . . . My eyes wandered to Marie's high-chair, standing between the sideboard and the window. It had descended, first to Janine,

then to Janine's daughter. I went through the pretence of swal-
lowing a few mouthfuls. . . . The expression on the face of the
man who was serving me was horrible.

A fire of vine-shoots had been lit in the drawing-room. Here,
each generation as it ebbed had left its shells—its albums, caskets,
daguerreotypes and patent lamps. The small tables were covered
with knick-knacks from which all life had drained away. The
heavy tread of a horse in the night, the sound of the wine-press
which is built on to the house, tore at my heart-strings. "Oh,
my children, why didn't you come?" The words were the formula-
tion of my wretchedness. Had the servants been listening outside
the door, they would have thought there was a stranger in the
room with me, for neither voice nor words would they have connected with the miserable old man, who, as they believed, had
deliberately pretended not to know that their daughter was dead.
   All of them, wife, children, masters and servants, were in
league against my soul. I must play my hateful part at their dic-
tation. I was painfully caught in the rigidity of the expected attitude. I had modelled myself on the image projected by their
hatred. What madness, at sixty-eight, to hope to swim against
the stream, to impose on them a new vision of the person I
really am and have always been! We see only what we are
accustomed to see. You, too, my poor children, I do not truly see.
Were I younger, the lines would be less deeply graven, the habits
less unalterably rooted. But I doubt whether, even in my youth,
I could have broken the spell. Some especial strength was needed,
I said to myself. Yes, but what strength? The aid of some *person*,
of someone in whom we might all have been reunited, of someone who would, in the eyes of my family, have guaranteed the
victory which I had won over myself, of someone who would
stand my witness, who might relieve me of my hideous burden,
and bear it on his own shoulders. . . .
   Even the genuinely good cannot, unaided, learn to love. To
penetrate beyond the absurdities, the vices, and, above all, the
stupidities of human creatures, one must possess the secret of
a love which the world has now forgotten. Until that secret shall
have been rediscovered, all betterment in conditions of life will
be in vain. I used to think that it was selfishness which kept me
uninterested in questions of sociology and economics, and to

some extent that was true, for I have been a monster of solitude and indifference. Still, I had a feeling, an obscure certainty, that it was no use merely to revolutionize the face of the world, that what was needed was the power to reach the world through the medium of the heart. Him whom I seek can alone achieve that victory, and he must needs be the heart of all hearts, the burning centre of all love. The desire I felt may well have been a prayer. On that night I was within an ace of falling on my knees with my arms on the back of a chair, as Isa used to do, long summers ago, with the three children pressing round her. In those days I would come back from the terrace towards the lighted window. I would muffle my footsteps and, invisible in the darkness of the garden, look on the group at prayer within. *"Prostrate at Thy feet, O God"*—Isa would say—*"I thank Thee that Thou hast given me a heart to know and love Thee. . . ."*

I remained standing in the middle of the room, swaying on my feet as though I had received a blow. I thought of my life and saw what it had been. No one could swim against such a current of mud. I had been a man so horrible that he could have no friend. But wasn't that, I asked myself, because I had always been incapable of wearing a disguise? If all men went through life with unmasked faces, as I had done for half a century, one might be surprised to find how little difference there was between them. But, in fact, no one lives with his face uncovered, no one. Most men ape greatness or nobility. Though they do not know it, they conform to certain fixed types, literary or other. This the saints know, and they hate and despise themselves because they see themselves with unclouded eyes. I should not have been so universally condemned had I not been so defenceless, so open and so naked.

Such were the thoughts which haunted me that evening, as I wandered about the darkened room, stumbling against those heavy pieces of furniture in mahogany and rosewood, poor wrecks buried in the sands of a family's past, on which so many bodies, now turned to dust, had at one time leaned and lain. Children's boots had soiled the sofa where they had snuggled with a volume of *Le Monde Illustré* of 1870. The dark stains on its covering were as they had always been. The wind was moaning round the house, stirring the dead leaves of the limes. In one of the rooms the shutters had been forgotten and left open.

❀ *X I X* ❀

NEXT day I waited impatiently for the coming of the postman. I
paced up and down the garden as Isa used to do when the children were late and she felt anxious. Had they quarrelled? Was
one of them ill? I fretted myself "into a fever", and became as
clever as Isa had ever been in the art of formulating and encouraging fixed ideas. I walked among the vines with the absent-
minded and remote look of those who brood upon a trouble. But
I remember, too, that I noticed this change in myself and derived
no little pleasure from the realization that I was ill at ease. The
mist was a sounding-board. I could hear the plain, though I
could not see it. Wagtails and thrushes were making merry in the
furrows where the grapes were not yet rotting. Luc, as a child,
when the holidays were ending, had loved these sober-footed
mornings. . . .

A line from Hubert, dated Paris, did little to reassure me. He
had been obliged, he said, to leave in a hurry. Something serious
had happened. He would tell me about it on his return, which
would be, he hoped, in two days' time. My mind immediately
went to difficulties of a financial nature. Had he, perhaps, been
doing something illegal?

By the afternoon I could stand the suspense no longer. I had
myself driven to the station, where I took a ticket to Bordeaux,
though I had promised not to do any more travelling alone. Geneviève was now living in our old house. I ran into her in the hall,
just as she was saying good-bye to someone I did not know, but
who looked like a doctor.

"Hasn't Hubert told you?"

She took me into the waiting-room where I had fainted on the
day of the funeral. I breathed more freely when I knew what
the trouble was. Phili had run away. I had feared something
much worse. But he had gone in company with a woman who
had "a hold on him", and after a terrible scene which had left
Janine without a vestige of hope. The poor child was in a state
of complete prostration from which it seemed impossible to rouse
her, and the doctor was worried. Alfred and Hubert had pursued
the fugitive to Paris. Judging from a telegram which had just
arrived, their efforts had been fruitless.

"When I think of the allowance we made them . . . Of course
we were wise to possible risks and had not given them control of
any capital. Still, the income was by no means inconsiderable.
Janine was always terribly weak with him. He could get anything
he wanted out of her, and was constantly threatening to abandon
her, because he felt convinced that you were not going to
leave us anything. It's so extraordinary to me that he should
have chosen just the very moment when you'd handed over the
whole of your fortune to run away—how do you explain it?"

She came to a dead stop, her eyebrows raised, her eyes dilated.
Then she leaned against the radiator, rubbing her hands together.

"This woman," I said, "is, I suppose, rich?"

"Far from it—she's a teacher of singing. You know her quite
well: it's Madame Vélard. She's by no means young, and she's
knocked about a bit. It's all she can do to make a living. How
do you explain it?" she said again.

She did not wait for my answer, but went on talking. At that
moment Janine came into the room. She was wearing a dressing-
gown, and put up her face for me to kiss. She was no thinner,
but despair had wiped the heavy, unattractive face clean of all
that, at one time, I had hated in it. The poor creature, formerly
so daubed and mannered, had become frighteningly simple and
bare. The crude light of a hanging lamp beat down on her, but
she stood there unblinking. All she said was, "I suppose you
know", and collapsed on to the sofa.

I don't think she even heard what her mother was saying, the
interminable catalogue of grievances which Geneviève must have
been pouring out over and over again since Phili left.

"When I think . . ."

Every sentence began with that "When I think . . ."—a surprising statement from one who thought so little. They had, she
said, consented to the marriage, although, at twenty-two, Phili
had already run through a considerable fortune which had come
to him while he was still very young (in view of the fact that
he was an orphan and had no near relations, it had seemed
best to give him full control of his money). The family had shut
their eyes to the very unsavoury life he had been leading . . . and
this was all the thanks they got! . . .

I tried in vain to control my mounting irritation. My old perversity stirred in its sleep. As though Geneviève herself, Alfred,
Isa, and all their friends, had not been continually at Phili,
holding out a thousand dazzling prospects!

"What I find quite extraordinary," I said, "is that you seem really to believe what you're saying. And yet, you must know that you were all of you running after him. . . ."

"I won't have you stick up for him, Father! . . ."

I protested that it was not a question of sticking up for him. But we had been wrong to paint Phili blacker than he was. No doubt he had been made to see too clearly that, once the fortune was assured, he would have to swallow every kind of insult, that they were banking on his becoming resigned to having his wings clipped. The trouble was that human beings are never so base as we believe them to be.

"When I think that you can stand there and defend a wretched creature who has abandoned his young wife and his little girl . . ."

"Geneviève!" I cried in exasperation. "You don't begin to understand what I am saying. Do at least make an effort. I quite agree that it is a shocking thing for a man to abandon his wife and child, but the culprit might have yielded to ignoble motives instead of to higher ones. . . ."

"So you think it noble," said Geneviève, with mulish obstinacy, "to abandon a wife of twenty-two and a young child. . . ."

That was the limit of her vision. She simply had no idea of what I was talking about.

"Oh, don't be such a fool . . . unless it is that you are deliberately pretending not to understand. My point is that I find Phili a good deal less despicable now that . . ."

Geneviève cut me short, saying that I might at least wait until Janine had left the room before insulting her with this defence of her husband. But the girl who, until now, had not opened her lips, suddenly said, in a voice which I had difficulty in recognizing:

"What's the use of denying it, Mamma? We treated Phili like mud. Don't pretend you've forgotten. When all this business of sharing out Grand'pa's money began, we thought we'd got him where we wanted him. He was just like a dog I was dragging about on a lead. I had resigned myself to the fact that he didn't love me. That didn't hurt any more. I had got him: he was mine: he belonged to me. I held the purse-strings and I could make him pay through the nose. That was your expression, Mamma. Don't you remember how you said to me: 'Now you can make him pay through the nose . . .'? We thought that money was the only thing he cared about. He may have thought so, too, but his anger and his sense of humiliation were too much for him.

Because, you see, he doesn't love this woman who's stolen him away. He told me so himself, before he left, and he flung so many horrible things in my face that I am sure he was speaking the truth. The point is that she doesn't despise him, and doesn't make him feel like a worm. She gave herself to him: she didn't snatch him. I was just handed to him on a plate!"

She repeated the last words as though she were flagellating herself. Her mother shrugged, but was pleased to see her tears. . . . "She'll feel better after this." Then she went on: "Don't worry, darling, he'll come back. Hunger drives the wolf out of the woods. . . . When he's been roughing it for a bit . . ."

I felt sure that talk like that would only disgust Janine. I got up and took my hat. The idea of spending the rest of the evening with my daughter was more than I could stand. I told her that I had hired a car and was going back to Calèse. Suddenly Janine said:

"Take me with you, Grand'pa. . . ."

Her mother asked her whether she had gone mad. She must stay where she was. The lawyers needed her presence. Besides, she would be "miserable" at Calèse.

She followed me out on to the landing, and attacked me violently for having humoured Janine.

"You must admit that if she gets rid of that creature it'll be a case of good riddance. One can always get an annulment, and with all that money Janine might make a splendid marriage. But she's got to be quit of him first. . . . You always detested Phili, and now you must needs go singing his praises to her. . . . Whatever happens, she mustn't go to Calèse . . . a nice state she'd come back in! Sooner or later, if she stays here, we shall manage to take her mind off her troubles . . . she'll forget. . . ."

Unless she dies, I thought, or drags on a miserable existence with a pain that never lessens, that no lapse of time will ever change. It may be that Janine belongs to that peculiar race of human beings which an old lawyer is best fitted to understand. She may well be one of those women in whom hope is a disease, who can never be cured of hoping, and, at the end of twenty years, still watches the door with the eyes of a faithful dog. I went back into the room where Janine was still seated, and said to her:

"When you're ready, my child. . . . You are always a welcome visitor."

She gave no sign that she had taken my meaning. Geneviève

had followed me in, and now said, suspiciously: "What was that you were saying to her?" I learned later that she had accused me of having "changed Janine's mind" during the few seconds I was alone with her, of having "filled her head with all sorts of ideas". I went down the stairs, remembering only that the girl had said "take me with you. . . ." She had asked me to take her. Instinctively, I had, when talking of Phili, said just what she needed to hear. Maybe I was the first person who had not wounded her susceptibilities.

I walked through Bordeaux. It was the first day of the new term, and the streets were all a-glitter. The mist had left a dampness on the pavements of the Cours de l'Intendance, and they shone. The voices of the noonday crowd drowned the rattle of the trams. I was no longer aware of the smells of my childhood. I might have found them again in the melancholy surroundings of the Rue Dufour-Dubergier, of the Rue de la Grosse Cloche. There, perhaps, I might have come, at some dark street corner, on an old woman hugging a steaming pot of those boiled chestnuts which smell of aniseed. I did not feel sad. Someone had listened to me and had understood. The two of us had come together, and that, in itself, spelled victory. But with Geneviève I had failed. When I am faced by a certain type of idiocy I can do nothing. One can touch a living soul through a curtain of vice and crime no matter how dense and dark: but vulgarity is an insurmountable barrier. Well, it couldn't be helped. I would follow my own line. Impossible to shatter the stones of all these graves. It would mean happiness for me if I could reach to the heart of one single being before I died.

I slept at an hotel and did not return to Calèse until the following morning. A few days later Alfred came to see me, and from him I learned that my visit had had disastrous results. Janine had written Phili a crazy letter in which she said that she had been to blame for everything, and had asked him to forgive her. "Women are all the same. . . ." I knew what the fat idiot was thinking, though he did not dare to put it into words: "She's her grandmother all over again."

He made it quite clear that a suit for separation would now stand no chance of success, and that Geneviève held me responsible. I had worked on Janine. I asked my son-in-law with a smile what possible motives I could have had for doing a thing like that. He didn't, he said, share his wife's point of view, but explained that, according to her, I had acted from malice, from a desire to revenge myself, perhaps even from a sheer love of mischief.

The children did not come to see me again. Two weeks later, Geneviève wrote me a letter in which she explained that they had had to send Janine to a nursing-home. There was no question, of course, of insanity. They had great hopes that, if she were left to herself, she would get better.

I, too, was left to myself. I felt perfectly well. Never had I had so long a respite from my heart. For the whole of that fortnight, and well beyond it, the autumn sunshine lay upon the earth, as though reluctant to depart. Not a leaf had fallen yet, and the roses bloomed again. This new estrangement from my children should have made me suffer. Hubert put in an appearance only when there was business to discuss. He was dry and formal, perfectly polite, but on his guard. The influence which, my children insisted, I had brought to bear on Janine had lost me all the ground that I had gained. In their eyes I was once more the enemy, a treacherous old man, capable of anything. The only one of them all who might have understood me was shut away, and cut off from all communication with the living. But I was conscious only of a deep sense of peace. Stripped of everything, isolated, and with a terrible death hanging over my head, I remained calm, watchful, and mentally alert. The thought of my melancholy existence did not depress me, nor did I feel the burden of my empty years. . . . It was as though I were not a sick old man, as though I still had a lifetime before me, as though the peace of which I was possessed was Somebody.

❦ X X ❦

IT IS a month now since Janine ran away from the nursing-home and came here. She is not yet cured. She believes that she has been the victim of a plot, and says that she was shut away because she refused to attack Phili and ask him for a separation and an annulment. The others imagine that it is I alone who have put these ideas into her head, and have set her against them, whereas, if the truth be told, I have been fighting tooth

and nail, all through the interminable days at Calèse, against her
illusions and her fancies.

Outside, the rain has been rotting the leaves and making them
indistinguishable from the mud. Heavy clogs crunch the gravel
of the courtyard. A man passes, his head enveloped in a sack. So
stripped has the garden become, that there is nothing left to disguise the few poor concessions made to pleasure—mere skeletons
of hedgerows, sparse shrubberies shivering under the eternal rain.
So penetrating is the dampness of the rooms that, when night
comes, we lack the courage to move far from the drawing-room
fire. Midnight sounds, but we cannot bring ourselves to go to bed.
The embers, patiently piled, collapse in ashes, and I have to
renew the old wearisome effort to convince the poor girl that her
parents, her brother and her uncle have no malevolent designs
on her. I do my best to keep her mind from dwelling on the
nursing-home. The conversation always, in the end, comes back
to Phili: "You've no idea what he was really like, the kind of man
he was at bottom. . . ." I can never feel sure whether these
phrases are a prelude to a list of grievances, or to a lyrical outburst. Only the tone in which they are spoken gives me a clue,
makes it possible for me to know whether she is about to sing
his praises or bespatter him with mud. In either case, the facts
which she produces seem to me to be equally insignificant. The
poor creature is entirely without imagination, but love has given
her an extraordinary power of distortion and amplification. I know
her Phili only too well. He is one of those completely negative
human beings whom youth, for one fleeting moment, manages to
invest with glamour. To this spoiled child, born with a silver spoon
in his mouth, she attributes subtleties of feeling, capabilities of
villainy and premeditated treacheries—though, as a matter of fact,
he is nothing but a mass of automatic reflexes.

What she won't understand is that what he really needs is to
feel that he is strong. It was no use trying to bully him. Dogs of
his type don't respond to that kind of treatment. They merely
slink away and pick up what they can find lying to hand.

She hasn't got the remotest idea of what he is really like. All
she knows is that she longs to have him with her. All she feels is
a hunger for the endearments which he withholds, and bitter
jealousy and horror at the thought that she has lost him. Without
eyes to see, a nose to smell, nerves to feel, she runs after him in
a demented way, without having the faintest idea of what it is

she is pursuing. . . . Are fathers ever really blind? Janine is my granddaughter, but were she my daughter I should still see her for what she is—one of those women who are incapable of receiving anything from another person. With her regular features, her thick, heavy body, and her foolish voice, she is marked with the sign of those who never catch the eye or fill the mind. Nevertheless, when I sit talking to her at night, I find a sort of beauty in her, a beauty not her own but borrowed from despair. Surely there must be a man somewhere whom this display of heat and flame might attract? At present she is burning away unhappily in a waste land beneath a darkened sky, with nobody to see her but an old crock.

Though I have come to pity her in the course of our long vigils, I never tire of making comparison between Phili, who is as like a million others as one white butterfly is like all other white butterflies, and this frenzy of passion which he alone can rouse in his wife, so that nothing else in the whole world, visible or invisible, exists for her. Janine can, quite literally, see nothing but this slightly shop-soiled male who prefers drink to most other forms of self-indulgence, and looks on love as a labour, a duty and a bore. . . . What a tragedy it is!

Sometimes her daughter slips into the room, but she scarcely looks at her, just kisses her curly head in a mechanical sort of way. Not that the child is wholly without influence on her. It was because of her that Janine screwed herself to the point of abandoning her pursuit of Phili (she is quite capable of hounding him, goading him, and making scenes in public). I couldn't have stopped her. It is for the child's sake that she has stayed on here. But motherhood has brought her no consolation. It was in my arms, on my knees, that the little girl sought refuge one night as we sat waiting for dinner to be announced. There was a bird-like, nest-like fragrance in her hair which brought back memories of Marie. I closed my eyes and pressed my lips to her head. I restrained myself from hugging her too tightly, while, in my heart, I called upon my long-dead child. It was Luc, too, whom I felt I was embracing. When she was hot from play she had the same salty taste that I used to find in his cheeks when, tired out from running, he fell asleep at table. On those occasions he could not even wait for the dessert, but would go round the company holding up his drowsy face for good-night kisses. . . .

So it was that I dreamed, while Janine moved about the room, pacing, pacing, within the prison of her love.

I remember another evening when she asked: "What can I do to get rid of this pain? . . . do you think it will ever go away?" There was a frost. I watched her open the window and push back the shutters. She bathed her face, her breast, in the frozen radiance of the moon. I led her back to the fire, and, though I am inexpert in the gestures of love, sat awkwardly beside her with my arm about her shoulders. Was there nothing, I asked, that could bring her comfort? "You have your faith." "Faith?" she said vaguely, as though she had not understood. "Yes," I went on, "God. . . ." She raised her ravaged face, and her eyes were full of suspicion. At last she said that she "couldn't see the connexion", but I was insistent, and she continued:

"I'm religious, if that is what you mean. I go to church. Why do you ask me a question like that? Are you laughing at me?"

"Are you quite certain," I went on, "that Phili is really worth all this pain and torment?"

She looked at me with the same morose, irritated expression that I am used to seeing on Geneviève's face when she doesn't understand what has been said to her, doesn't know what answer to make, and fears a trap. Finally, she plucked up courage to say that the two things "had nothing to do with one another" . . . that she didn't like mixing up religion with matters of this kind, that she was a practising Christian and regularly performed her religious duties, but that she had a horror of morbidity. She might have been saying that she always paid her taxes. It is precisely the attitude that, all my life, I have loathed and detested, the caricature and mean interpretation of the Christian life which I had deliberately chosen to regard as the essence of the religious mind, in order that I might feel free to hate it. One must have the courage to look what one hates full in the face. . . . But had I not already been guilty of self-deception, I asked myself, when, on the terrace at Calèse, the Abbé Ardouin had said: "You are a very good man"? Later, I had shut my ears so as not to hear Marie's words as she lay dying. Nevertheless, at her bedside the secret of death and of life had been revealed to me. . . . A little girl had been dying for me . . . that was something that I had tried to forget. With untiring assiduity I have always tried to find some way of losing the key which a mysterious hand has invariably given to me at

the great turning-points of my life (the expression of Luc's face
after Mass on Sunday mornings when the grasshoppers were beginning to scrape, and again this spring, on the night of the hailstorm . . .).

So ran my thoughts that evening. I remember getting up and
pushing back my chair so violently that Janine gave a start.
The silence of Calèse at that late hour, a thick, an almost solid
silence, numbed and muted her grief. She let the fire die down,
and, as the room grew colder, moved her chair closer to the
hearth until her feet were almost touching the embers. The
dying flames seemed to exert a kind of attraction on her hands
and face. The lamp on the chimney-piece shone down on her
heavy, crouching figure, while I wandered about among the mahogany and rosewood in the encumbered dark. Impotently I
prowled around that lump of humanity, that bruised and beaten
body. "My child . . . ," I began, but could find no words for
what I wanted to say. . . . Something, as I sit to-night writing
these lines, is stifling me, something is making my heart feel as
though it would burst—it is the Love whose name at last I know,
whose ador . . .

                    *   *   *   *   *

                                Calèse, 10th December, 193. . .
My dear Geneviève:
    The drawers here are positively bursting with papers, but I
hope, by the end of this week, to have got them into some sort
of order. My immediate duty, however, is to send on to you at
once the strangest of strange documents. You know that our
father died at his desk, and that Amélie found him on the morning of the 24th November with his face fallen forward on an
open note-book. It is this book which is now on its way to you by
registered post.
    I am afraid that you will be as pained as I was when you read
it. . . . Fortunately, the writing is so bad that the servants will
make nothing of it. At first, from motives of delicacy, I decided to
keep it from you, thereby saving you a good deal of distress, for
it contains passages in which father speaks of you in a way that
cannot but wound your susceptibilities. But then I wondered
whether I had any right to keep to myself something which is
yours as much as mine. You know how scrupulous I am in all
that pertains to our parents, and I feel sure that you will understand what prompted me to change my mind. None of us, if it

comes to that, shows up very well in these embittered pages. They tell us, alas! nothing that we have not long known. The contempt with which father treated me poisoned my early years. For a considerable period of my life I had no confidence in myself. I quailed beneath that pitiless eye, and it was a long time before I even began to realize my true worth.

I have forgiven him, however, and perhaps I ought to add that what now urges me to bring this document to your notice is, for the most part, a sense of filial duty. Judge him how we may, there can be no doubt that our father emerges from these pages—in spite of the horrible things he says—I won't say as more noble, but certainly as more human (I am thinking, in particular, of his love for our sister Marie, and for young Luc— of which there is much moving evidence). I am in a far better position now to understand the grief which he displayed when our mother died, grief which, at the time, came to us as a staggering surprise. You thought it, I remember, to some extent put on. Should what is there written do no more than throw a light on the feelings which lay so deeply buried beneath the surface of his relentless pride, your reading of his confession will amply compensate for the pain it must otherwise, my dear Geneviève, cause you.

I am grateful for it—as I think you too will be—if only because it serves to ease our conscience. I am by nature a worrier. No matter how many reasons I may have for feeling that I am in the right, a very little will start me on a long process of self-examination. For one who has developed moral sensibility, as I have done, to a high degree, life can never be easy. Pursued by a father's hatred, I have never had recourse to even the most legitimate methods of defence, without being oppressed by feelings of anxiety—I would even say, of remorse. Had it not been that I was the head of the family, and, as such, responsible for the honour of our name and the well-being of our children, I should often have been tempted to give up the struggle rather than suffer those torments and strugglings of the spirit of which you have, more than once, been a witness.

I thank God who, in His mercy, has seen fit to justify me through these, our father's, written words. In the first place they provide confirmation of what we had long suspected about his various schemes for depriving us of our birthright. It is not without a sense of shame that I read about the ways in which he hoped to establish a hold over both Bourru the lawyer and that young chap Robert. Over these disgraceful incidents it is well that we should cast the mantle of Noah. Still, the fact remains that it was my bounden duty to frustrate, at any cost, his many abominable machinations. This I did, and with a success of which I see no reason to be ashamed. Of one thing, my dear sister, you may rest assured, that you owe your fortune to *me*. In what he has written, the wretched man tried hard to convince himself that the hatred which he felt for us died a sudden death. He takes pride in announcing that all concern for worldly goods left him in a flash. I must confess that when I read that I found it very difficult not to laugh! But it is worth noticing the precise moment of this unexpected change of front. It occurred just when his schemes had gone awry, when his natural son had agreed, for a price, to tell us what he knew of them. It was not easy for him to get rid of so huge a fortune. Plans which it had taken him years to perfect could not be rearranged in a few days. The truth of the matter is that the poor man felt his end to be near, and had neither the time nor the means to disinherit us except in the manner which he had decided to adopt, and which we providentially discovered.

As a lawyer he was unwilling to lose his case in the court either of his own or of our judgment. Consequently, he was cunning enough—though half-unconsciously, I admit—to transform actual defeat into moral victory. He persuaded himself that he was no longer interested, that he had become detached from the things of this world. . . . What else could he have done? I, certainly, am not prepared to have dust thrown in my eyes, and I feel pretty sure that you have enough good sense to agree. We need not, I think, go out of our way to admire or to be grateful.

There is another point of which this narrative lifts a weight from my conscience. It is something about which I have long indulged in heart-searchings, though I have never succeeded, I must admit, in altogether ridding myself of a pricking sense of guilt. I refer to the efforts we made—though they came to nothing—to get the view of a specialist on the subject of father's mental condition. I ought, I think, to make it clear that much of my uneasiness on this score sprang from the attitude taken by my wife. I never, as you know, attach very much importance to her opinion. No one could well be less capable than she of holding balanced views on any subject. But in this matter of the specialist she gave me no rest, night or day, and was for ever dinning into my ears arguments, some of which, I now admit, did go home and did make me feel uncomfortable. She succeeded at last in convincing me that father, who had been a great Chancery barrister, a shrewd man of business, and a profound student of psychology, must be good-sense incarnate. . . . Nothing is easier than to paint an ugly picture of children who try to get their old father certified so as not to lose their inheritance . . . you see, I am not mincing words . . . and I have, God knows, spent many a sleepless night brooding on the problem.

Well, my dear Geneviève, this note-book, especially in its final pages, provides ample evidence that the poor man was suffering from intermittent delirium. I am prepared to go further, and to say that we should have been fully justified in submitting the case to a psychiatrist. But what is now far more important is that pages containing so much that might prove dangerous to our children must on no account be divulged to any living soul. I may as well say, at once, that I consider it to be your duty to burn what I have sent as soon as you have read it to the end. We *must not* run the risk of it falling under the eyes of a stranger. You cannot but realize, my dear Geneviève, that though *we* have always maintained the strictest secrecy about our family affairs, that though *I* have always taken steps to see that nothing should leak out concerning the uneasiness we have all felt about the mental state of him who, when all's said and done, was the head of the clan, others, not strictly members of it, have been far from showing the same discretion, or even common prudence. Your wretched son-in-law, especially, has been guilty of spreading the most dangerous stories. We are paying a high price for them now, and I am sure that I am not telling you anything that you don't know already when I say it is common talk in Bordeaux that there is a close connexion between Janine's neurasthenia and the eccentricities popularly attributed to your father as a result of Phili's gossiping.

Tear the thing up, then, and don't talk of it to a soul. I would go further, and say—let there be no mention of it even among ourselves. I don't mind admitting that this extreme caution may, in some ways, be a matter for regret. There are in our father's narrative certain psychological observations, certain impressions of nature, which show that his oratorical training had left him with a real gift for writing. That is but one reason the more for destroying it. A nice thing it would be, wouldn't it, if, at some later date, one of the children should think of publishing it?

But there can be no reason why you and I should not call things by their proper names. Now that we have read this record through, we can have few illusions about father's semi-insanity. I can see now what your daughter meant (at the time I took it for a sick woman's whim) when she said: "Grand'pa is the only truly religious person I have ever met." The poor child had let herself be taken in by his vague aspirations and hypochondriacal fancies. All through his life he had been the enemy of his family, hated by everybody, and without a single friend. He had been unfortunate in love, as you will see (there are some very comic details in this connexion!), and so jealous of his wife that he could never forgive her for having indulged in a harmless flirtation when she was a girl. Is it conceivable that, towards the end of his life, he should have felt a desire for the consolations of prayer? I don't think so. What emerges from these pages with dazzling clarity is a state of well-defined mental instability, taking the form of persecution mania and religious hallucination. Is there no trace, you will ask, of genuine Christianity? None at all. Anyone as deeply informed as I am about such matters knows only too well the real value of such outbursts. Not to put too fine a point on it, bogus mysticism of this kind makes me feel physically sick.

But you, being a woman, may feel differently. Should you be inclined, then, to take his religiosity at its face value, all I can say is this: remember that father, with his extraordinary gift for hatred, never loved anything unless it provided him with a *weapon against somebody*. This religious exhibitionism of his amounts only to a criticism, direct or oblique, of the principles in which our mother brought us up from childhood. If he indulged in a murky mysticism, it was only that he might use it as a stick to beat that rational and moderate faith which has always held a place of honour in our family. Truth is poise . . . but I will not plunge deeper into those regions of abstract thought where you would have difficulty in following me. I have said enough. Read the document for yourself. I am impatient to know what you make of it.

I have little space left in which to reply to the important matters on which you have asked my opinion. My dear Geneviève, we are living in days of crisis, and the problems with which we are faced are agonizing. If we keep these piles of bank-notes tucked away in a safe, we shall have to live on capital—and that is always a misfortune. If, on the contrary, we instruct our broker to buy shares, the dividends we may get will be small consolation for the continual fall in the capital value of our investments. Since whatever we do we are bound to lose, the wiser course will be to keep our Bank of France notes. The franc is worth only four sous, but it is backed by an immense gold reserve. On this point father was clear-sighted, and we ought to follow his example. There is one temptation, my dear Geneviève, against which you must fight tooth and nail—the temptation to invest at any price. It is deeply rooted in the French temperament. We shall, of course, have to watch every penny we spend. Should you ever want any advice, you know that I am only too ready to give it. Times are bad, but profitable opportunities may occasionally present themselves. I am, at the moment, keeping a very close eye on a Cinema concern and a new liqueur. Those are the type of investment which the crisis will not touch. In my opinion, it is things of that kind that we ought to watch. We must be bold, but, at the same time, prudent.

I am delighted to know that you have better news of Janine. I don't think that her excessive religious devotion which makes you uneasy need be considered as a serious danger. The important thing is that she should stop thinking about Phili. Her natural sense of proportion will reassert itself. She belongs to a race which has always known how not to misuse the *really good things*.

Until Tuesday, my dear Geneviève,   HUBERT.

Janine to Hubert

My dear Uncle:

I am writing to ask whether you will act as judge between Mamma and me. She won't let me read Grand'pa's Journal, because she says it would damage the devotion I have to his memory. But if she's so keen that it shouldn't be damaged, why does she keep on saying: "You've no idea what awful things he says about you. He doesn't even spare your looks . . ."? I am even more surprised that she should be so eager for me to see the very harsh letter in which you expressed your views about the Journal. . . .

Now, for the sake of peace and quiet, she says she'll let me have it if you think I may, and that she leaves the decision entirely to you. I am making this appeal, therefore, to your sense of justice.

Let me dispose at once of the first objection. It concerns me, and me alone. No matter how hard Grand'pa may be on me, he can't be harder than I am on myself, and I am quite sure that the sharp edge of his criticism spares the unhappy girl who spent one whole autumn with him in the house at Calèse, up to the time of his death.

Forgive me, Uncle, if I contradict you on one essential point. I am the only witness in a position to pronounce on the state of Grand'pa's feelings during those last weeks of his life. You denounce what you call his vague and morbid religiosity. But let me tell you this: he had three interviews (one at the end of October and two in November) with the Curé of Calèse, whose evidence, for some reason that I can't fathom, you refuse to accept. According to Mother, the Journal, in which he set down the most trivial incidents of his life, says nothing about those interviews, which wouldn't be the case if they had really been the occasion of a change in himself. . . . But she says, too, that it breaks off in the middle of a word. I have no doubt at all that death surprised your father at the very moment when he was about to make his declaration of faith. It's no use your saying that if he had received absolution he would have taken Communion. I can only repeat what he told me the day before he died, that he was weighed down by a sense of unworthiness. The poor man had made up his mind to wait until Christmas. What reason have you for not believing me? Why treat me as though I were the victim of an hallucination? His voice is fresh in my memory. I can hear it now as it was when he spoke to me on the Wednesday, which was the day before his death, in the drawing-room at Calèse. He said how eagerly he was looking forward to Christmas. It sounded as though he was in a condition of great mental suffering. Maybe the shadow of death was already upon him.

Don't be afraid, Uncle. I am not trying to make him out a saint. I agree with you that he was a terrible, even at times a dreadful, man. That doesn't alter the fact that a great light shone upon him during those last days of his life, and that it was he, and he alone, who, at that moment, took my face between his hands, and entirely changed my way of looking at things. . . .

Doesn't it occur to you that your father might have been quite a different man if only *we* had been different? Don't accuse me of throwing stones at you. I know your good qualities, and I know that Grand'pa was cruelly unjust both to you and to Mother. The real misfortune for all of us was that he took us for exemplary Christians. . . . Don't protest. Since he died I have seen much of people who, in spite of all their faults and weaknesses, live according to their faith and move about their daily tasks in the fullness of Grace. If Grand'pa had lived among them, mightn't he have discovered years ago the harbour which he reached at last only on the very threshold of death?

Let me say again that it is not my intention to abuse my family in the interest of its implacable head. I don't forget (far from it) that poor Grand'ma's example might, in itself, have been enough to open his eyes, had he not preferred to glut his feelings of resentment. But I do want you to know why, in the last resort, I feel that he was right in his attitude towards us. Where our treasure was, there were our hearts also. We thought of nothing but the threat to our inheritance. No doubt there was ample excuse for us. You were a business-man, I was a poor weak woman. But that doesn't alter the fact that, with the single exception of Grand'ma, we never let our principles interfere with our lives. Our thoughts, our desires, our actions, struck no root in the faith to which we paid lip-service. All our strength was employed in keeping our eyes fixed on material things, while Grand'pa . . . I wonder whether you will understand what I mean when I say that where his treasure was, there his heart was *not*? I am quite sure that on this point the document which you won't let me read contains conclusive evidence.

I do hope, Uncle, that you will see what I mean, and I await your reply with confidence.

JANINE.

Woman of the Pharisees

❧ I ❧

COME HERE, BOY!"
I turned round, thinking that the words were addressed to one of my companions. But no, it was to me that the one-time Papal Zouave had spoken. He was smiling, and the scar on his upper lip made the smile hideous.

Colonel the Comte de Mirbel was in the habit of coming once every week into Intermediate School yard. On these occasions his ward, Jean de Mirbel, who was almost always in a state of being "kept in", would move away from the wall against which he had been made to stand, while we, from a distance, watched the arraignment to which his terrifying uncle subjected him. Our master, Monsieur Rausch, called upon to act as witness for the prosecution, replied obsequiously to the Colonel's questions. The old man was tall and vigorous. On his head he wore one of those caps known as a "cronstadt", and his coat, buttoned up to the neck, gave him a military air. He was never to be seen without a riding-switch, probably of raw-hide, tucked under his arm. When our friend's conduct had been particularly bad, he would be marched away across the yard between Monsieur Rausch and his guardian, and the three of them would disappear into a staircase in the left wing of the building, which led to the dormitories. We would stop whatever game we were playing and wait until a long-drawn wail struck sharply on our ears. It sounded like the yelp of a beaten dog (though that may have been due to our imaginations). A moment later, Monsieur Rausch would reappear, accompanied by the Colonel, the scar showing livid in his purple face. His blue eyes would look faintly bloodshot. Monsieur Rausch was all attention. He kept his head turned towards his companion and his lips were stretched in a servile grin. That was

433

the only occasion on which we ever saw that pale, terrifying face, topped by its red, crimped hair, distorted into a grimace of laughter. Monsieur Rausch, the terror of our lives! Whenever we went into class and found his seat still empty, I used to pray: "O God, please let Monsieur Rausch be dead! Blessed Virgin, please let him have broken his leg, or make it so that he's ill— not seriously, but just a little!" . . . But he had an iron constitution, and his hard, dry hand at the end of its skinny arm was more to be feared than a slab of wood. Jean de Mirbel, fresh from the mysterious punishments inflicted upon him by his two executioners (vastly exaggerated, no doubt, in our boyish fancies), would come back into the form-room with his eyes red and his grubby face streaked with tears, and make his way to his desk. The rest of us kept our eyes fixed firmly on our notebooks.

"Do as you're told, Louis!" barked Monsieur Rausch. It was the first time he had ever called me by my Christian name. I stayed hesitating on the threshold of the parlour door. Jean de Mirbel was standing inside the room, his back towards me. On a small table there lay an open parcel containing two chocolate éclairs and a bun. The Colonel asked me whether I liked cakes. I nodded my head.

"Well, those are for you, then . . . Go on; what are you waiting for? It's young Pian, isn't it?—know his family well—doesn't look as though he had any more spunk than his poor father. . . . Brigitte Pian, his stepmother, now there's a woman for you—reg'lar Mother of the Church. . . . You, there! stop where you are!"—this he shouted at Jean, who was trying to slink away. "You're not going to get off as lightly as that! You've got to watch your young friend having a good time. . . . Come on, make up your mind, you little fool!" he added, his two eyes fixing me, from either side of the short, firm nose, with a stare in which a glint of anger already showed.

"He's shy," said Monsieur Rausch; "don't wait to be asked twice, Pian."

My friend was looking out of the window. His turn-down collar had come unfastened, and I could see his dirty neck above it. No one in the world had such power to frighten me as the two men now bending down and smiling into my face. I knew from of old the harsh, animal-like smell that hung about Monsieur Rausch. I stammered out that I wasn't hungry, but the Colonel retorted that a boy didn't have to be hungry to eat cakes. Seeing

that I was persisting in my obstinacy, Monsieur Rausch told me
to go to the Devil, adding that there were plenty of others who
wouldn't be so stupid. As I was making my escape into the yard,
I heard him call to Mouleyre, an unnaturally fat boy who always
ate anything on which he could lay his hands in the dining-hall.
He ran up at the summons, sweating. Monsieur Rausch shut the
parlour door, from which Mouleyre emerged later, his mouth
smeared with cream.

It was a June evening, and still swelteringly hot. When the
day-boys had gone home we were allowed to remain outside for
a bit because of the heat. Mirbel came up to me. We could hardly
be described as friends, and I am pretty sure that he despised
me because, in those days, I was a rather spiritless and well-be-
haved boy. He took from his pocket a pill-box and half raised the
lid.

"Look!"

It contained two stag-beetles. He had given them a cherry for
food.

"They don't like cherries," said I. "They live on the rotten bark
of old oaks."

We used to catch them on Thursdays, near the School Lodge,
on our way out. These particular insects always start flying at
sunset.

"You can have one of them. Take the bigger, but be careful—they're not tame yet!"

I couldn't tell him that I didn't know where to put the beetle.
But I was pleased that he should speak so kindly to me. We sat
down on the steps that led to the main block of the school-buildings. Two hundred boys and about twenty masters were crowded
into what had once been a beautifully proportioned town house.

"I'm going to train them to pull a cart," said Jean.

He took from his pocket a small box which he fastened with
thread to the beetle's claws. We played with it for a while. During these special recreation periods on summer evenings no boy
was ever kept in, and there was no insistence on community
games. Elsewhere on the steps other boys were busy spitting on
apricot-stones and polishing them. This done, they made a hole
in each and took out the kernel, using the empty shell as a
whistle. The heat of the day was still intense within the space
surrounded on four sides by buildings. Not a breath of air stirred
the leaves on the sickly plane-trees. Monsieur Rausch, his legs

apart, was in his usual place over by the outdoor toilets, to see
that we didn't stay too long in them. They gave off a powerful
stench which fought a losing battle with the smell of chlorine
and disinfectant. From the other side of the wall came the sound
of a cab bumping over the rough cobbles of the rue Leyteire. I
was filled with envy of the unknown passenger, of the coachman, and even of the horse, because they were not shut away in
school, and didn't have to go in fear of Monsieur Rausch.

"I'm jolly well going to thrash Mouleyre", said Jean suddenly.

"I say, Mirbel, what's a Papal Zouave?" I asked him.

He shrugged his shoulders. "I'm not quite sure, but I think
he was one of the chaps who fought for the Pope before 1870,
and got beaten." He was silent for a few moments, and then
added: "I don't want him and Rausch to die before I'm grown
up."

Hatred made him look ugly. I asked him why he was the only
one of us who was treated as he was.

"My uncle says it's for my good. He says that when his brother
was dying, he swore by God that he'd make a man of me. . . ."

"And your mother? . . ."

"Oh, she believes everything he says . . . or maybe she doesn't
dare contradict him. She didn't really want me to be a boarder
here. She would have liked me to stay at home at La Devize
with a tutor. But he wouldn't allow that. He said my character
was too bad."

"*My* mother", said I proudly, "has come to live in Bordeaux for
my education."

"But you're a boarder just the same."

"Only for these two weeks, because Vignotte—he's the agent
over at Larjuzon—is sick, and my father's got to do his work. But
she writes to me every day."

"Madame Brigitte Pian isn't your real mother, is she?"

"It's the same thing, though . . . it's just as if she were."

I stopped at that and felt my cheeks burning. Had my real
mother heard? Are the dead always listening to find out what
the living are saying about them? But if Mamma knew everything, she would realize that no one had ever taken her place in
my heart. It didn't matter how kind my stepmother was to me.
It was quite true that she wrote to me every day, but I hadn't
even opened the letter that had come from her that morning. And

when I cried that night, in the stifling dormitory, before going
to sleep, it would be because I was thinking of my father, of my
sister Michèle, or of Larjuzon, and not of Brigitte Pian. Still, my
father would have liked me to be a boarder all the year round,
so that he could have gone on living in the country. It was my
stepmother who had insisted. They had taken a little flat in Bordeaux, to make it possible for me to go home every evening. My
sister Michèle, who hated our father's wife, always maintained
that she had used me as an excuse for breaking the promise she
had made when she married, that she would live at Larjuzon.
No doubt Michèle was right. If my stepmother never tired of
saying that I was "too nervous and too sensitive to be sent to
boarding-school", it was because this was the only argument that
could persuade my father to stay on in Bordeaux. I knew that
well enough, but it didn't make any difference. The grown-ups
could settle their own affairs. It was enough for me that my stepmother had had the last word. But I knew that Papa was unhappy
when separated from his woods, his horses, and his guns. He
must be enjoying himself now. . . . That thought was a great
comfort to me during this fortnight of trial. Besides, it would
soon be Prize Day, and then Brigitte Pian would have to resign
herself to going back to Larjuzon.

"Prize Day soon!" I exclaimed.

Mirbel had a beetle in each hand and was pressing them together.

"They're kissing!" he said, and added without looking at me:
"You don't know what a rotten trick my uncle's thought up if I
don't get a good report: I'm not going to be allowed to spend vacation with my mother. I'm not to go to La Devize at all. I'm
to be sent to board with a priest, the Curé of Baluzac. It's actually only a few miles from where you live. He's been told to
make me work six hours a day and to break me in. . . . I gather
that's his line."

"Then why not try to get a good report?"

He shook his head. It couldn't be done; not with Rausch. He'd
often tried.

"He never takes his eyes off me. You know my desk's just under
his nose. You'd almost think he had nothing to do but watch me.
All I have to do is glance out of the window . . ."

It was true enough, and nothing could be done to help Mirbel.
I promised that if he spent his holidays at Baluzac I'd see a lot

of him. I knew Monsieur Calou, the Curé, very well. There was
nothing especially terrible about him. As a matter of fact, he was
very decent.

"No, he's horrible. My uncle says that bad boys are sent to him
to be broken in. I've heard that he drove the two Baillaud boys
nearly crazy. But I won't let him lay a finger on me."

Perhaps the Curé of Baluzac was kind only to me? I didn't
know what to say to Mirbel. I suggested that perhaps his mother,
who never saw him, wouldn't give up the chance of having him
home for the holidays.

"She will, if he says so. She does everything he wants!" replied
Mirbel in a fury. I realized that he was very close to tears.

"How about letting me help you with your lessons?"

He shook his head. He had too much back work to make up.
Besides, Rausch would spot it. "Whenever I hand in a decent
exercise he always accuses me of cribbing."

At that moment Rausch put a whistle to his lips. He wore a
long frock-coat with stains down the front. In spite of its being
summer, he still had his feet stuffed into padded felt slippers. His
crinkled, carroty hair grew well back from a bony forehead covered with pimples. His eyes were of different colours and blinked
from beneath reddened lids. We marched off in a long line towards the dining-hall. I hated the smell of greasy soup that came
from it. It was still broad daylight but no sky was visible through
the dirty windows. I noticed that Mirbel was the only boy at our
table who did not eat ravenously. The Papal Zouave had hit on
the one punishment that could get under his ward's skin—spending the holidays with the Curé of Baluzac, away from his mother.
I should be able, with my bicycle, to see him every day. I felt
a little stab of happiness. I would speak about Jean to the Curé
who was so kind to me and let me gather nuts in his garden.
True, I was "young Pian", the stepson of Madame Brigitte, his
"benefactress". But that made it all the better. I would ask my
stepmother to intercede on Jean's behalf. I told him as much
on our way upstairs to the dormitory. Twenty of us slept in a
room that was ventilated by one window only, which gave on to
the rue Leyteire. At the foot of each bed stood a washstand
with a basin. In this we put our tooth-glasses in such a way that
the man who came round with a jug could fill both glasses and
basins at the same time. In five minutes we were all undressed
and in bed. The assistant master, Monsieur Puybaraud, lowered

the gas, and in a trembling voice recited three prayers which brought the tears to my eyes. I cried because I was lonely, because some day I should have to die, because I was thinking of my mother. I was thirteen. She had been dead for six years. She had vanished so quickly! One evening she had kissed me, so full of life and sweetness, and the next day . . . the horse had bolted and brought home the trap empty. I never knew how the accident had happened. No one had told me much about it, and my father, now that he had married again, never mentioned his first wife's name. As though to make up for that, my stepmother often exhorted me to pray for the dead woman. She used to ask me each evening whether I had a thought for her. She seemed to believe that Mamma had more need of prayers than other dead people. She had always known my mother, who had been her cousin, and had sometimes invited her to the house during the holidays. "You ought to ask your cousin Brigitte to come to Larjuzon," said my father. "She can't afford a holiday: she gives away all she has. . . ." My mother would do her best to stand out against this appeal, although she professed to admire Brigitte. Perhaps she was afraid of her. That, at any rate, was what my sister Michèle thought. "Mamma saw through her: she knew only too well what an influence her cousin had over Papa."

I attached little importance to such statements. But my stepmother's exhortations made an impression on me. It was only too true that Mamma had had no time in which to prepare herself for death. The sort of education I had had helped me to understand Brigitte's insistence. It was indeed necessary that I should intercede for that poor departed spirit.

That evening, snuffling beneath the sheets, I had begun to tell my beads for Mamma while Monsieur Puybaraud lowered the gas until he had reduced the butterfly of flame to no more than a bluish flicker. He took off his frock-coat and started on a last round of the beds. The rhythmic breathing of the sleepers was already audible. As he passed close by me he must have heard the sob that I was doing my best to smother, for he came close and laid his hand on my tear-stained cheek. With a sigh he tucked me in as Mamma used to do, and then, bending down suddenly, kissed me on the forehead. I flung my arms around his neck and kissed his bristly cheek. He crept away very quietly to his cubicle. I could see his shadow moving behind the thin curtain.

Almost every evening Monsieur Puybaraud consoled me in the same way. "Much too soft-hearted, and dangerously over-sensitive", said my stepmother, who had a good deal to do with him, since he acted as general secretary to the Charity Organization.

A few days later when my parents returned to Bordeaux and the butler came at about six to take me home, I ran into Monsieur Puybaraud, who seemed to have been on the lookout for me, in the yard. After smoothing back my hair from my forehead with his rather damp hand, he gave me a sealed letter which he begged me to post. This I promised to do, astonished that he had not given the letter to the censor, whose business it was to take charge of the school correspondence.

I waited until I was in the street before reading the address. The envelope bore the name of Mademoiselle Octavia Tronche, teacher at the Free School, rue Parmentade, Bordeaux. I knew her well. She used to come to the house between her classes, and my stepmother employed her on various tasks. On the reverse side of the envelope, in a fair round hand, Monsieur Puybaraud had written: *Go, little letter, and bring to my heart a gleam of hope.* . . . Walking a few paces behind the butler, who had put my satchel under his arm, I read and re-read this strange invocation. I pondered over it there on the pavement of the Cours Victor-Hugo, just where it joins the rue Sainte-Cathérine, in the dusk of the evening before Prize Day. And in my nostrils was the faint smell of absinthe.

❧ *II* ❧

IT WAS then that I was guilty of the first bad action of my life— of an action, I mean, the thought of which even now fills me with a sense of remorse. Monsieur Puybaraud had made no attempt to extract from me any promise about the letter, but I knew, nevertheless, that he regarded me as more deserving of his trust than any of my comrades. I tried later to persuade myself that I had not realized what was at stake for the assistant master. That is not true. I understood perfectly well what was involved, and had a pretty shrewd idea of the dramatic touch that his semi-religious cast of mind gave to the incident. It was a matter of common knowledge that he belonged to a lay society (now long since dispersed), a sort of Third Order, the members of which were bound by no vows. Sometimes, indeed, quite frequently, one or other of the so-called "Brethren" would, with the consent of his superiors, leave the Community in order to marry. But Monsieur Puybaraud's position was rather peculiar. His work kept him in close contact with the diocesan officials of the Charity Organization Society, and with several of the boys' parents. Everyone in the town knew him, and not only the higher clergy and the rich middle-class families. He was a familiar figure in the poorest slums, where the children flocked round him as soon as he appeared at the corner of a street: for he always brought them sweets. His frock-coat and the curious high beaver hat that he affected drew no surprised glances. His kindly face looked longer than it was by reason of the short whiskers that stopped at the level of his cheekbones. In summer he held his hat in his hand, and continually mopped his bald forehead and the sparse, silky hair which he wore long behind. His small features were almost too "pretty" for a man. There was about his eyes something of the look of a wounded animal, and his hands were always damp. My stepmother was loud in praise of his virtues, though she held strong views on the subject of his "excessive and morbid sensibility". I, of all people, should have kept myself from mentioning to her the secret of his letter, but it was precisely to her that I burned to impart my knowledge. The possession of it filled me with a sense of self-importance. Young as I was, I wanted to shock, to scandalize. Nevertheless, I was too frightened to say anything so long as other members of the family were present.

I have a vivid recollection of that evening. The flat that my father had consented to lease was on the second floor of a house in the Cours de l'Intendance. On summer evenings the noise of traffic on the cobblestones and the clang of the electric cars—which had only recently begun to operate in the city—made conversation difficult. A fortnight spent in the country had brought the colour back to my father's cheeks, and the prospect of the approaching holidays had put him in a good humour. At a word from his wife, however, he left the table to put on a bow tie and a black coat. She could not bear the untidy clothes that he always wore at Larjuzon.

In spite of the heat she had on a high-necked dress with a lace collar that swathed her to the ears. Her large face, with its heavy, lustreless cheeks, was surmounted by a mass of hair puffed out with curls, and kept in place by an almost invisible net. Her black, staring eyes had a hard look, but her mouth was always smiling, though she scarcely ever opened it wide enough to show her long yellow teeth, which were generously filled with gold and stood out firmly from the gums. A double chin gave her an air of dignity which was accentuated by the way she carried her head, by the way she walked, and by her deep voice which was never heard to better advantage than when she was engaged in issuing orders. The right place for her would have been at the head of some Community. After the death of her father, Baron Maillard, who had been Prefect of the Gironde at the time of the Empire, Brigitte had devoted the bulk of her fortune to the purchase and reconditioning of a small convent in the outskirts of Lourdes, where it was her intention to house young women of fashion under a new Rule inspired in part by her Director, the abbé Margis. The material part of the work was completed, but nothing more was ever heard of the scheme.

Brigitte Maillard had more than once, in connection with this undertaking, consulted my father, who in his youth had worked as an unpaid clerk in the office of a Bordeaux solicitor and knew a good deal about the ins and outs of legal business. He dissuaded her from bringing a suit which would have caused considerable scandal and could not possibly have succeeded. He, on his side, valued the advice that she gave him about the domestic difficulties in which he was at that time involved, though they were later to be solved so tragically by the death of my mother.

Those who knew nothing of the events which, at a certain period of my father's life, had led to the forming of a deep intimacy between him and Brigitte Maillard found it hard to imagine how two such dissimilar characters had come to link their destinies. Seen in company with this tall, bilious-looking Madame de Maintenon, my poor father aroused feelings of pity. His appearance was eloquent of weak good-nature. He spoke hesitatingly, there was a greedy look about his mouth, and his drooping moustache seemed as though it should be forever trailing in little "nips" and rich gravies. Overfeeding had given him a red face, and his eyes were prominent.

I can see my sister now as she sat that evening between husband and wife when the Puybaraud affair came to a head. Michèle was at that time fourteen. The general opinion was that her skin was too swarthy. The lower part of her face was abnormally heavy, and her hair grew too low on her forehead. But her really beautiful eyes softened all hearts, and she had very fine teeth which she showed whenever her wide mouth parted in a smile. Some might think that her arms were rather too muscular, but the same could not be said of her legs. They were a matter of great pride to her, and she did her best to show them in spite of the rather long skirts which our stepmother insisted on her wearing even then.

As a matter of fact Brigitte was always extremely patient with her, and as a rule was careful not to get herself involved in arguments with the headstrong little girl. She was always saying: "Since I can exercise no sort of influence over the child, it is my duty to keep peace in the home at all costs." She derived a feeling of triumph from the fact that the Ladies of the Sacred Heart failed equally to elicit any sort of response from Michèle. "The girl is filled with a spirit of contradiction and bad temper," she would remark to our father. But against this sentence he protested. "You are quite wrong, my dear. You do so love to dramatize things! She is wilful, that's all, and flares up quickly like my poor mother. . . . But a good husband will settle all that."

Brigitte shook her head with a sigh. She looked on life from a higher standpoint. It was her mission, her glory, to view it from that higher standpoint.

The evening on which the Puybaraud complication burst into flame was a Saturday. We were listening to the sound of the crowds on the pavements of the Cours de l'Intendance where the garrison tattoo was in progress. Michèle and my father were leaning on their elbows at one end of the balcony. I was some little distance off with my stepmother. The sharp-winged swifts were skimming the roof-tops. The flow of traffic was continuous. The walls still held the heat of the day. An occasional gust brought the sweet scent of limes and, with it, that smell to be found only in big cities before the days of motor-cars—a rich mixture of horse-droppings, wet roadways, and circus tanbark. I was still wrestling with the temptation to reveal Monsieur Puybaraud's secret. But I knew that I should succumb. My stepmother was questioning me methodically about the end-of-term examinations. She wanted to know all about the examination in each subject, and how I had answered. I knew that this interest came only from a sense of duty, and that her thoughts were elsewhere. But she said what she had to say. Always, in every circumstance of life and in all her relations with other people, she knew precisely what her words, what her attitude, ought to be.

I made up my mind.

"Mother," I said, "there's something I want to tell you. But"— I added with a touch of hypocrisy—"I'm not sure whether I ought."

A spark of attention began to glow in the black eyes which, till then, had shown no interest in me.

"My dear child, I have no idea what you have to say. But there is one rule which you would do well to follow blindly, and that is, never to keep anything from your second mother. For on her has devolved the duty of bringing you up."

"Even when it is a secret involving others?"

"If it involves others that is all the more reason why you should tell me," she replied sharply. Hungry for my revelations, she asked: "Whom does it concern?—your sister?"

She already suspected the worst of Michèle, although the girl was only fourteen years old. I shook my head. No, it wasn't about Michèle: it was about Monsieur Puybaraud and Octavia Tronche.

She choked back an exclamation. "What's that?" She grabbed my arm. "Monsieur Puybaraud? Octavia?"

I was too ignorant as yet about love to have noticed that my stepmother could never approach the subject calmly, but that as soon as it was mentioned she became, as it were, all worked up. No sooner had I mentioned the letter and the sentence written on its flap than she interrupted me.

"Give it to me, now, at once."

"The letter?—but I posted it."

She seemed to be disappointed. "That was very wrong of you. You should have given it to me. I am responsible for Octavia's moral well-being. She holds an important position at the Free School, and hopes one day to be headmistress. It is not only my right, but my duty, to know everything about her. . . . Never mind, I shall manage to have a look at the letter, somehow or other", she added more calmly.

She saw that I was worried. Monsieur Puybaraud was so fond of me. What on earth would he think? She made it clear to me

that I need take no action in the matter. She felt sure that she
could persuade Octavia to tell her what it was all about.

"It is not, my dear child, that I suspect anything *wrong*. So
estimable a person as Monsieur Puybaraud deserves my complete
confidence. After all, if he wishes to leave his Order and go back
into the world, he has a perfect right to do so. We must not hold
him guilty of anything worse than imprudence. Not, that is, unless
we have proof to the contrary. I have always thought that his
rather over-emotional form of piety might lead him to act rashly.
Thanks to you, I can now intervene while there is still time."

In a low voice, from behind clenched teeth, she added, with
sudden violence: "Octavia, of all people! But they're all the
same—all bitches, every one of them!"

The sound of the brass-band playing the tattoo came from the
direction of the rue Vital-Carle. The people of Bordeaux were
delighted with a recent innovation in the ceremony. The bands-
men had electric bulbs in their caps instead of pompons. My stepmother went back into the drawing-room, while I remained, leaning on my elbows above the heads of the crowd. Boys and girls
were marching in step with the soldiers. They walked arm in
arm and made a living chain across the pavement. They were
shouting and laughing. I struggled no longer with my sense of
shame and with the agony of spirit which oppressed me. What
was going to happen to poor Monsieur Puybaraud? I was too
young fully to understand the paternal instinct that had made
him lean over my bed, tuck me in, and kiss me on the forehead.
But I did feel that I had betrayed a man whose loneliness was
such that he had turned to a boy of thirteen for comfort. I remembered Alphonse Daudet's *Enfant Espion,* and what the Ger-
man soldiers had said to young Sten: "Not nice, that, not nice."
Had I done wrong? My stepmother said that I had done my
duty . . . why, then, should I feel so remorseful?

I joined her in the room. She was seated close to the window,
trying to read. We could not have any light because of the mosquitoes, and it was too hot to close the windows. A vague
longing to "make up" for what I had done made me feel that I
wanted to perform some kind action. So I mentioned Mirbel, begging her to speak to the Curé of Baluzac on his behalf. I watched
her large pale face in the dusk. It was much too dark to read.
She was sitting there quite motionless and very upright. Her
early convent training had taught her never to lean back in a

chair, nor do I remember ever seeing her cross her legs. I knew
that she was only half paying attention, and that her thoughts
were busy with the Puybaraud-Tronche affair.

"The Curé of Baluzac?" she said at last. "Poor abbé Calou!—
it can't be very easy for him to pose as an ogre! . . . Well, I suppose the extra money helps him to buy a few books. I wonder
whether I ought to tell the Colonel how misinformed he has
been?"

I begged her to do nothing of the sort. Her words confirmed
me in my feeling that the abbé Calou would not be a very terrifying gaoler, and I was particularly anxious not to be deprived
of the pleasure of having Jean de Mirbel as a companion during
the holidays. But she added that, on second thought, she felt
sure that the young good-for-nothing could get only what was
good from living in the company of Monsieur Calou, and that
God's will must be done.

All the next week I watched Monsieur Puybaraud with considerable apprehension. But I was still his "pet" (as the other boys
called me), and up to the end of term he was as kind to me as
ever. The examinations were almost over, and the heat became
too oppressive to make much work possible. Even Monsieur
Rausch relaxed and read *Le Soldat Chapuzot* to us in form. In
Senior Yard the carpenters were busy putting up stands for the
Prize-giving. Every day we rehearsed Mendelssohn's choruses
from *Athalie:*

> All the world is filled with His glory:
> Oh, come, let us adore Him!

But for Michèle I should probably have known nothing of the
opening rounds of the Puybaraud-Tronche scandal. Though her
nature was of the frankest, and she, of all people, would be the
last to dream of listening at keyholes, her attitude towards our
stepmother was defensive. She watched Brigitte Pian with a clear-
sighted mistrust which she never for one moment relaxed. Besides, Octavia Tronche was devoted to her, and could not for
long hold out against her questions. Consequently, I was kept informed about the deplorable results of my indiscretion.

Octavia Tronche worked at my stepmother's on Thursdays and
Saturdays—the only times at which she was free from school

classes—from eight to eleven in the mornings. She had thin, lifeless hair, but, though without any freshness of youth, was not
wholly devoid of charm. This she owed to her eyes, though they
were small and of an indeterminate colour, and to the very sweet
smile that hung about her rather bloodless lips. The children
adored her, and, because of this, she was constantly exposed to
the malicious pin-pricks of her jealous colleagues. Her clothes
drooped from thin shoulders, and no one could well have had less
indication of a bosom. Below the waist, however, she was more
markedly feminine, and even her nun-like skirt could not altogether conceal the fullness of her hips.

When, on that particular morning, she entered the small
drawing-room where Madame Pian—"Madame Brigitte"—was sitting, Octavia was greeted with an unaccustomed smile.

"I am afraid you are feeling the heat, my dear: I can see it in
your face."

Octavia assured her patroness that she was not at all tired.

"And in your work even more than in your face." Brigitte Pian's
voice had taken on a sudden note of sternness. "You made several mistakes in addressing when you sent out the last number
of the *Bulletin*. I have had complaints from a good many ladies
that it arrived late."

Octavia, in some confusion, began to make excuses.

"That, in itself, would not be very serious," went on my stepmother; "but the circular I dictated to you, and neglected to read
over (yes, *neglected:* please observe that I do not spare myself
when I have been worthy of blame), was full of errors and omis-
sions. Some of the sentences did not even make sense. . . ."

"I am afraid that my head has not been very clear these last
few days," Octavia stammered.

"Your head or your heart?" asked Brigitte in a voice whose
sweetness was belied by her severe and haughty expression.

"Oh, Madame Brigitte, what *can* you mean?"

"I am not asking you to tell me your secrets, my dear: confidences cannot be forced." And then, as Octavia began to protest that she had no secrets from Madame Brigitte: "You know
how scrupulous I am in respecting the consciences of others. You
are one of our old girls. I trust you—not blindly, but with my
eyes open, and with a sense of almost maternal responsibility. We
all have difficult times to go through, my dear."

This was more than Octavia could stand. Falling on her
knees, she hid her face in Madame Brigitte's lap. The latter

looked at the thin neck beneath the tight little bun into which
the girl's hair was drawn, at the pale skin, and at the topmost
vertebra which the twisted collar of her dress left exposed. It
was as well that the poor creature could not see the expression of
disgust that came over the older woman's face. *Even she is no exception, ill-favoured though she is,* it seemed to say. Aloud, but
quite gently, Madame Brigitte said:

"And so, my poor Octavia, you too think that you have a
lover?"

Octavia Tronche looked up, protesting: "That I have a lover?
Oh, no, Madame: I am not quite such a fool. It is not that!"

In those few seconds her face had become transfigured. Shyness had given to it a delicate loveliness, something of the adorable charm that comes from utter humility.

"All I ask is that *he* should let me live for him alone and for
the children which God in His mercy may see fit to give us."

"Naturally, my dear Octavia, naturally", said my stepmother,
helping her to her feet. "Come and sit down beside me and control yourself. That I once looked on you as one called to a higher
vocation is no matter. It will make me very happy to think of
you with a home and a Christian family of your own. What could
be more natural, more simple? The excess of your emotion surprises me."

"But it is not simple at all, Madame—far from it. If you only
knew . . ."

I imagine that my stepmother realized, at that moment, what
it was to be completely happy. She was tasting the pleasure that
belongs, of right, to God alone: the pleasure of knowing to the
full the destiny of someone who thought that she was imparting
a piece of unsuspected news; of feeling that it was in her power
to mould that destiny as she willed. For she did not doubt her
hold over the scrupulous conscience of Monsieur Puybaraud. Had
she been tempted to do so, Octavia's attitude would have restored
her confidence. With masterly skill she let her tone range through
every shade of expression from that of confidential friendship to
suspicion. At last she said: "I feel your trouble as keenly as you
do yourself", and then went on to ask the poor girl, with every
mark of anxiety, whether the man in question was married or
divorced. At that, her victim hid her face and struggled to conceal her tears. When next Madame Brigitte spoke there was a
note almost of horror in her voice.

"Wretched girl! Am I to understand that this man is already
bound to somebody whose claims are absolute? Are you setting
yourself against the ordinances of God?"

"No, Madame, no! He is free: his superiors have raised no
difficulty. Monsieur Puybaraud (you must have guessed already
that it is he) has arranged to leave the college at the end of
this week. As soon as he has done so, we have permission to
consider ourselves engaged."

My stepmother rose, cutting her visitor's protestations short.
"You need say no more! I do not wish to *hear* more. The responsibility lies with your respective spiritual directors. It may be
that I should not see eye to eye with them in this matter . . ."

"But that is why I am so upset, Madame Brigitte!" cried Octavia between her sobs. "You see, Monsieur Puybaraud will not
let himself be convinced that he has the right to act as he wishes.
He keeps on saying that you alone can clarify his mind, that you
alone are sufficiently instructed to give him peace of mind. But
please, please, Madame, understand that the situation is not as
you think it. . . . You have only got to look at me to see that.
Monsieur Puybaraud is not the slave of mere physical desire. He
says the thought that he may one day have a son like your
Louis makes him almost sob with joy."

"That I can quite realize," responded my stepmother in gloomy
tones. "The Evil One always employs tricks and subterfuges when
he sets out to attack men of a frank and upright nature."

"Oh, Madame, surely you are not going to persuade him that
this is a trap set by the Evil One?"

Impulsively she seized the hand of my stepmother, who was
seated in her usual chair in front of a desk littered with circulars
and files.

"Unless he asks me, I shall say nothing at all to him, my child.
If he does ask, I shall say only what I feel moved by the Holy
Spirit to say. But whatever that may be, I shall speak out fear-
lessly and directly, as it has always been my rule to do."

Octavia clasped her hands and gazed at the expressionless face
with eyes that resembled those of a defenceless lamb.

"But surely there is nothing wrong in his wish to be a father?
His director doesn't think so. For years Monsieur Puybaraud has
fought against his feelings. May it not be that his failure to overcome them is in itself a sign that he is called upon to follow this
particular vocation?"

My stepmother nodded her head. "We should do wrong altogether to dismiss such an hypothesis," she remarked; "though
it is not God's way to set the feet of His servants on the heights
only to cast them down into the valleys. I shall need more definite
evidence before I can bring myself to believe that Heaven has
asked of Monsieur Puybaraud such an abandonment of his post,
so dire a retreat, so sad a return to a less austere way of life.
Nothing should be allowed to shake our faith."

"He says that he has been guilty of the sin of pride, that he has
over-estimated his strength. It is a blessing vouchsafed him by
Heaven, he thinks, that he should have been permitted to see
his way clearly before it was too late", urged Octavia in a voice
of supplication.

"If he is so certain"—my stepmother interrupted her dryly—
"what need is there for him to seek further? Why should I be
brought into the matter at all?"

Octavia realized that this was precisely where the trouble lay.
He was *not* certain: his mind changed from day to day. Bursting
into tears she declared that she could see how it was: Madame
Brigitte's mind was made up, she would be inexorable.

At this my stepmother became more human. "You are wrong,
Octavia. You must not think that I am hostile *in principle* to these
promptings of nature. There are others concerned, besides Monsieur Puybaraud. It would, indeed, make me very happy to know
that you, at least, had been called upon to fulfill the duties of a
wife and mother. Yes"—she went on, her gaze fixed upon her humble suppliant (and perhaps seeing already in anticipation the
swollen figure beneath its smock, the plain face made plainer
still by pregnancy)—"it may be that the intentions of the Almighty on your behalf have made necessary this deviation of Monsieur Puybaraud from a higher vocation. I realize that he may
have to be humbled if you are to be saved."

Thus it was that Brigitte Pian attributed to our Father in
Heaven the complexities and perversities of her own nature. But
Octavia Tronche, snatching at this straw of hope, was already
recovering like a flower in water. She raised her gentle, suffering
face.

"Oh, Madame Brigitte!" she exclaimed in tones of exaltation.
"Now indeed you are speaking with God's voice. You know everything, I admit everything. Unworthy though I am, it is for me
that Monsieur Puybaraud is willing to renounce the joys of a

higher vocation, to turn his back on the peace which might await him within the walls of an institution on which he has already brought so much credit."

"And you would quite calmly accept such a sacrifice, my child?" asked Brigitte Pian sharply.

Octavia was nonplussed.

"I am not saying that you ought to refuse it. All I wish to point out is that, all other considerations apart, you have to ask yourself this question: Have you, or have you not, the right to accept such a sacrifice? Are you willing that a man like Monsieur Puybaraud, who is infinitely superior to you in spiritual gifts and in the degree to which Grace has been accorded him, should, for your sake, abandon the fruits of his apostolic mission, and lose the glory he enjoys in the sight of God as well as the honour he has won in the eyes of men? For it is no good disguising the fact that if he deserts his present post he *will* suffer a loss of credit, even (and especially) in the opinion of his neighbours. You must face the facts. Every door will be closed to him. No one could well be more helpless than he in all that pertains to the day-to-day struggle for existence, and you must realize that, owing entirely to you, he may find himself condemned to a life of care and even of poverty. . . ."

Octavia Tronche's face was irradiated, not for the first time, by a smile of pure humility.

"*That* does not trouble me, Madame Brigitte, I am strong and healthy. So long as there is breath in my body he shall lack for nothing, no, not even if it means that I have to work by the day. He shall want neither for the necessities nor yet for the luxuries. . . ."

"You know perfectly well that you are *not* strong. Why, even your secretarial work here (which amounts to practically nothing) is almost too much for you when added to your duties at school: though I don't want you to think that I am complaining."

It was true enough that Octavia Tronche could not stand up to long hours, and that the work of organizing charity sales, coming on top of her teaching, very soon exhausted her. My stepmother repeated that it was her duty to face that aspect of the problem, however painful she might find it to do so. When Octavia shyly suggested that they had hoped he might get some appointment on the staff of the Charity Organization, in which for years he had been doing unpaid work, Brigitte expressed surprise that

she should have been guilty of such an offence against all tact
and propriety. How could she dream that any such thing was possible? There are certain facts, surely, that need no explanation.

"You must be out of your senses, my poor child. Quite apart
from anything else, it is not customary to use money that belongs to the poor to pay for work which can be performed by almost any priest, to say nothing of pious laymen. No, the most
we shall be able to do will be to recommend Monsieur Puybaraud
—so far, that is, as we can recommend *honestly* any man who
has sunk so low through no fault but his own, and who, so far as I
know, has no particular qualification and holds no diploma."

Whenever my stepmother had cast a fellow human creature
into the depths of affliction, it then gave her pleasure to raise
the victim by a spontaneous act of mercy. Since, in her view, Octavia had been driven to the lowest level of despair, she was now
at pains to bring her slowly back again and to give her grounds
for hope. It was only later, on the evening before Prize Day, and
from the lips of Monsieur Puybaraud himself, that I learned what
had been decided between them.

We had been working hard all day, hanging banners and grouping the Papal and Republican flags. Monsieur Puybaraud appeared, walking across the yard, and I hastened to join him. This
I always did. It was a special privilege that none of the other
boys ever thought of disputing. He made me sit down on the
steps of the platform, and told me that he was on the point of
making a very grave decision. Madame Brigitte, "who, like all
real saints, conceals much true goodness of heart beneath a forbidding exterior", realized that he needed a period of calm and
solitude in which to collect his thoughts and decide what it would
be best for him to do. She had had the great kindness to suggest
that he should spend the vacation at Larjuzon.

"At Larjuzon!" I exclaimed in amazement. There are places
into which certain persons do not fit. I found it impossible to think
of one of my schoolmasters in the country surroundings which
were the background of my summer holidays.

The official explanation of his presence at Larjuzon would be
that he was there to coach me in Latin.

I tried to imagine what Monsieur Puybaraud would look like
in his frock-coat and high-hat on a blazing summer's day walking
the garden paths at Larjuzon. I asked him whether he would
wear the same clothes that he always did. He told me that he

would have to invest in a country outfit, and that he might therefore not arrive for a few days.

Monsieur Rausch had moved from his usual position and now,
in his shirt-sleeves, perched on a ladder and armed with a ham-
mer, he was expending his natural ferocity on a nail. The boys
were exchanging addresses. The school orchestra was busy in the
Hall rehearsing the opening bars of *Travels in China.* Jean de
Mirbel, leaning as usual against the wall, though punishments
were over for the term, even for him, had his eyes fixed on the
ground. His hands were in his trousers pockets, and he wore his
cap untidily (his appearance did no credit to the school) on the
side of his head. The slight down on his cheeks made him look
much older than the rest of us (he was two years behind in his
school work). It was probably his age even more than his bad behaviour that cut him off from his companions. He lived alone in
a stormy world, with no one to give him a helping hand, the victim of some mysterious fate which seemed to hang over his future.
What it might be he did not know, and there was no one whom
he could take into his confidence.

❧ *III* ❧

THE HIRED victoria from Langon stopped in front of the presbytery garden. The Colonel was the first to get out. The luncheon
which he had just devoured had had the effect of heightening
to an unusual degree the mottled purple of his face, so that the
scar looked white by comparison. His cap was tilted slightly over
his left ear. The short fawn top-coat, reaching only to his thighs,
had a faded red rosette on its lapel. His skinny legs, clad in very
tight trousers, were like those of a cock. He wore white spats.

Jean, encumbered with a suitcase and a haversack, followed
him into the garden, where it was almost impossible to tread
without stepping on serried rows of vegetables. The presbytery
was surrounded—jostled is the better word—on all sides by potatoes, beans, tomatoes, and green-stuff of every description. Currant-bushes and peach-trees lined the narrow path that led to a
low doorway surmounted by a St. John's cross made from the
pith of an elder-tree.

Neither the nephew nor the uncle had the slightest idea that from behind a dusty window on the ground floor somebody was watching them. As soon as the abbé Calou heard the sound of the knocker he opened the front door. He was a head taller than the Colonel. He wore over his soutane a blue gardening-smock. He had not shaved for several days and the stubble on his face reached as high as his cheekbones. His forehead was low, and his wide blue eyes gave him the look of a child. He had a cleft tip to his nose and strong, healthy teeth. But the only thing that Jean de Mirbel noticed on the occasion of this first meeting was that the priest's huge hands, with their square-tipped fingers, were covered with hair.

"I've brought you your young boarder. Can't say he's a present most people would like to have. . . . Take your hat off to the Curé! . . . Come on, quicker than that! I don't want to have to tell you twice. . . . True to type, you see, from the word go!"

Jean, his beret in his hand, bowed his head without so much as uttering a word.

"A reg'lar young hooligan! I'm not sorry to have you see him in his true colours—gives you an idea of the sort of ill-conditioned cub you've got on your hands. . . . Won't get a how-d'ye-do out of him without a flogging!"

"We've plenty of time to get to know one another," replied the Curé.

There was something cold and impersonal about his tone. Without another word he led them upstairs to the boy's room on the second floor. It was a whitewashed attic, with the bare minimum of furniture, but very clean. The window looked on to the church and the graveyard, with, beyond it, a valley through which, behind a screen of pine-trees, ran the Ciron, a minor tributary of the Garonne. The fresh green of willows marked its course.

"I sleep and work just below. There is nothing but these floorboards between us. I shall almost be able to hear him breathing."

The Papal Zouave expressed his complete approval of the arrangements. The boy, he said, was up to all sorts of tricks. "Doesn't do to let him out of your sight for a single moment, day or night."

They went downstairs again to the large apartment on the ground floor which the Curé dignified with the name of drawing-room. It was furnished with a small table and four armchairs.

The lime, working out of the walls, had eaten away most of the paper. The Colonel whispered to their host:

"I'd like a word with you in private. Run along, you, and stay in the garden till I tell you to come back—now, then, quick march!"

At this point the Curé interrupted quietly: "If you don't mind, Colonel, I would rather he remained here and heard our conversation. It is part of my system that he should do so. You must have complete confidence in me. I consider it important that the young man should know precisely what it is that you complain of in his behaviour, and what it is that we have to correct."

"I warn you that such a step may have serious consequences. You don't know him. I should feel freer. . . ."

The Colonel was displeased, but the Curé would listen to no objection. Jean, therefore, remained standing in the middle of the drawing-room floor, his eyes fixed upon his uncle.

"Don't quite know how to tell you what I want to say. Young hooligan's about the length and breadth of it. Incorrigible, no other word for him—in-cor-ri-gi-ble," he repeated in an acid tone.

It was perfectly true that he could find no other word. Like many people who regard themselves as being above the common herd, he had a very limited vocabulary which he enriched with pantomime, cliché, intonation, and gesture.

"Rather be killed than do what he's told. Usually gives in in the long run, however . . . gets sick of being flogged. . . . No fool, though . . . got abilities. . . . Trouble is, won't do as he's told . . . won't learn his lessons."

"What does he like doing? I mean, what are his special tastes?"

"Like doing?" The Colonel seemed to be taken aback. "Well, what *do* you like doing? Nothing, eh? I know all about that. But what else?—come on, answer, now. . . . You see, not a word—just like him. Answer me, boy, or I'll box your ears!"

The Curé laid his hand on the arm raised to strike. "Let him be: I'll find out soon enough what his tastes are."

"And he'll find out soon enough what your system is . . . nothing very mysterious about it, I don't mind betting"—and he gave the Curé a wink. "Only two ways of getting the better of a vicious horse—spur and whip. At least, *I* don't know any others. . . . And when I say vicious, I know what I'm talking about. . . . There are one or two things I'd have liked to tell you in private. . . ."

Jean de Mirbel's face had become scarlet. So low did he hang his head that the Curé could see nothing but his hair.

"Need I add that I speak as his guardian and in the name of the Comtesse de Mirbel, the young scoundrel's mother? You are at liberty to use any means you may think proper, provided you break him in, *any*—you understand me—short of injuring his health."

"I quite understand", replied the Curé, his eyes still fixed upon the shamefaced object before him.

"To go back to what you were saying about his tastes. He likes reading—and not unnaturally his choice in books is pretty low. Young though he is, he knows a thing or two. Don't think I need say more about that. . . . And he's not always as dumb as he is now—can argue the hind legs off a donkey when he likes. D'you know what he was brazen enough to maintain last Easter to Monsieur Talazac, our Curé at home?—that not only oughtn't Combes to be blamed if he acted sincerely in kicking the Religious Orders out of France, but that he had acquired merit in the eyes of God by doing so!"

"Did he really argue that?" asked the Curé with a show of interest.

"Should damn well think he did. . . . Fine state of affairs, eh? And nothing would budge him—not Monsieur Talazac's reasoning, not the shocked looks of the ladies, nor yet the thrashing I gave him!"

"So you actually argued like that?" repeated the Curé. And he fixed a thoughtful gaze upon the little fox trapped there in his drawing-room, who, with his hair bristling, seemed to be hunting for a way of escape.

"If you have some private recipe for getting brains to work as they should, the family will be eternally grateful. You see, our name, our fortune, and the future of our line are all dependent on this young devil. He says he'd rather be seen dead than take the St. Cyr entrance examination, or volunteer for service with the colours, as the Mirbels have always done. Anyhow, he's so behind in his work that it's too late now for him to start thinking about the professional Army. He has the cynical effrontery to say that he'll do nothing, that he doesn't want to do anything, not even to look after his estates. You see, not a word of denial from him!—just a grin. You, there, stop grinning, or I'll let you feel the weight of my hand!"

Jean had retreated towards the wall. His lips were parted in a smile that showed his side-teeth which, though white and pointed, were irregular. He put up his arm to protect himself—the familiar gesture of a boy who knows what it is to be frequently beaten. "Please don't get worked up, Colonel. From now on this lad is my concern. You can leave him here with an easy conscience. I will send regular reports on his progress to you and the Countess, and he shall write home himself."

"Not if I know it!" exclaimed Jean. They were the first words that he had uttered.

"Till our next meeting, then, young feller-me-lad. I am leaving you in good hands"—he shook the Curé's enormous fist—"in good, strong hands. I am told that they have done wonders in other cases."

He burst into one of his surprisingly shrill guffaws of laughter.

The Curé went with him as far as the carriage. "And no coddling, mind", was the Colonel's final injunction. He handed the priest an envelope containing the first installment of fees. "You're not dealing with a young girl. He's got a hide like a rhinoceros. You needn't be afraid of treating him rough. I'll back you up. Whatever happens, just ignore anything that my sister-in-law may write. I'm captain of this ship, and it's for me to decide what's to be done."

The Curé went back into the drawing-room. Jean had not moved from where he had been standing. He started back as the priest approached, and once again his arm went up as though to ward off an expected blow.

"Come and help me lay the table," said the Curé.

"I'm not your servant!"

"In this house everyone is his own servant . . . except in the matter of cooking. Maria looks after that, but she is seventy-one and suffers from rheumatism. When I said lay the table, I meant for your tea. I never take it myself. Your friend Louis Pian and his sister are bicycling over to see you. They'll be here any moment now."

He opened the dining-room door.

"There's a fruit tart and some plums in the sideboard, and an opened bottle of orange syrup. If you want some water, you'll find a jug in the scullery. See you again this evening, my boy. . . . One thing more. My study, as you know, is just under your room. There are plenty of books, though probably not the kind you like. Still, if you look carefully, you may come on something. . . . You can root about there to your heart's content. You won't disturb me."

Jean listened to the Curé's heavy footsteps on the wooden stairs. Then he heard the sound of a chair scraping on the floor above his head. There followed an interval of complete silence broken only by the noise of grasshoppers, the cluck of fowls, and the buzzing of flies.

"If he thinks he's going to get round me like that! . . ."

Nevertheless, he pushed open the dining-room door and sniffed the odour of fruit tart. The room was better furnished than the rest of the house. It contained an old-fashioned clock, a long Louis-Philippe sideboard, a table of waxed cherry-wood, and several wicker chairs. It felt cool and the air was filled with the faint scent of fruit. Beyond the French windows there was a view on to the low roofs of outhouses and, beyond them, to a sloping field in which the hay stood ready stacked.

Someone may ask: "But how do you know so much about events of which you were not a witness? What right have you to reproduce conversations which you cannot have heard?" Well, if the truth must be told, I have outlived most of my characters, several of whom played an important part in my life. Besides, I am the sort of man who keeps old papers, and I have at my disposition not only a private diary (Monsieur Puybaraud's), but various notes made by Monsieur Calou which Mirbel found after the priest's death. At this very moment, for instance, I have before me the very letter which the abbé was reading—not for the first time—while Jean, alone in the dining-room, was wandering round the table and yielding to the temptation to take an occasional bite at a plum . . . and while I and my sister Michèle were bicycling to see him along the white and dusty roads which, in those days, were still innocent of tar. (At Vallandraut we had seen the Comte de Mirbel driving home in the victoria, his cap perched over one ear, his thin legs crossed. Michèle had drawn my attention to his scar, and to the faded red rosette on the lapel of his fawn top-coat.)

I don't deny that I have exercised my right to arrange my material, to orchestrate the reality which it records—that cross-section of existence which will live for as long as I live, with memory unimpaired, and upon which the passing years have had no effect. I may have given literary form to the talk that went on, but at least I am guiltless of changing so much as a syllable of that letter from the Comtesse de Mirbel which the abbé Calou had received the day before Jean's arrival. It was signed, in a spidery hand, "La Mirandieuze-Mirbel", and was written in blue ink. It ran as follows:

I am venturing to write to you direct because I understand from Madame Baillaud that your methods of educating the young are very different from those attributed to you by my brother-in-law, the Comte Adhémar de Mirbel. I thank God that it did not occur to him to pay the Baillauds a visit, and that he still believes in the reputation you have gained for taming difficult boys and, as he puts it, of using an iron hand with them. Unlike him, I did not stand upon ceremony. It is not easy for me to be on calling terms with the family of a retired chemist whose forebears were my forebears' servants. Nevertheless, I did not hesitate to get into touch with them, and any effort it may have cost me has been amply rewarded by the knowledge I have gained of the kind of man I am dealing with, and by the certainty I now possess that I can have complete confidence in you.

It is essential that I should tell you certain things which will help you to get a clear picture of my unfortunate son. In the first place, you should know that his love for me is very much more violent than that which a boy of his age usually feels for his mother. Jean is convinced that I do not return his affection. He believes that I judge him in the light of his uncle's attitude. To be perfectly frank, he has some reason for so thinking, since it must look as though I were abandoning him without a struggle and handing him over to the tender mercies of a butcher! I trust that you will forgive my choice of phrase. When you have seen the Count you will understand what I mean.

And at this point, I think, I must make a rather painful confession. I do so with the greater readiness because I realize that I am addressing a priest—a man trained in the duty of forgiveness. I am powerless where my brother-in-law is concerned, partly because by my husband's will he was given complete charge of my son, but chiefly because he has a hold over me. My husband, during his last illness, put into Adhémar's hands certain documents which are terribly damaging to me in more ways than one. I will not go so far as to say that I was ever a "guilty" wife. In whatever

I have done my conscience has been clear. I have but exercised my rights as a woman. Imprudent, incapable of deceit or calculation, I may have been. It would have been easy for me to deceive my husband, and it is only fair to myself to say that I should have had every excuse for doing so. What I suffered as a young woman—the bullying and incarceration to which I was subjected as a result of my husband's jealousy, the secret punishments and acts of vengeance that were wreaked upon me with impunity in the solitude of our Armagnac château—would make a novel in themselves. Some day I may write it. For I can write. In a sense writing has been my undoing. Adhémar has in his possession a number of unfortunate letters sent to me by a certain person, together with my replies. I was a fool not to have destroyed them, for, urged on by the demon of literary composition, I expressed on paper, and in extremely passionate terms, sentiments which, in the eyes of the world, a woman may be forgiven for yielding to, though never for putting into words.

That is my secret. Though I no longer believe in the mysteries of religion, I still trust in the virtue and discretion of its ministers. It is necessary that you should know all this. Adhémar has complete power over Jean only because my honour has been betrayed into his hands. If I so much as stumble on the road in which he has set my feet, I am lost. My saying this will show you what manner of man he is. But he fears that his hold over me is insufficient. He would like me to be his wife. My very considerable fortune is an added temptation, but it is only fair to say that it was my husband's dying wish that he should marry me. It was one of his favourite maxims that a woman can be tamed only in marriage. It never occurred to either of them that a Mirbel who was also, on her mother's side, a La Mirandieuze could ever so much as dream of divorce. Adhémar exercises over me a sort of indirect blackmail. He hints that in the event of my consenting to become his wife, he would give his permission for Jean to be brought up at home, here, at La Devize. I gather that if such a course were taken, I should have the deciding vote in all matters affecting his education, and be free to spend part of each year with my parents. Madame de La Mirandieuze, as you probably know, has influential connections, nor have I abandoned the idea that I might even now be able to take a staggering revenge for everything I have suffered through the medium of a literary success.

What am I to do? I have not given my brother-in-law a definite "no": I am playing for time. Adhémar is well over sixty

*and gets very red after meals. The irregularities of his present
way of life—over which I am generous enough to draw a veil—
would be sufficient to encourage in me certain definite anticipa-
tions, were it not for the fact that I am not that sort of woman.
I may have been foolish, but I am incapable of baseness. I have
told you all this because I thought it necessary to do so. I venture
to hope that you will judge me, not by those narrow standards
which I know are abhorrent to you, but by the touchstone of an
enlightened and humane religion, and that you will not withhold
from me the forgiveness which you alone can confer. It is my dear
wish that you should prevail upon Adhémar to allow me to pay
a visit to Jean while he is at Baluzac. If you write to him that in
your opinion it would be good for the boy, he will not refuse. Tell
him that you can let me have a room in your house. Not that I
intend to impose myself upon you. Rather than cause you any
inconvenience, I will sleep at the inn at Vallandraut. I have a
mother's heart, and it waits impatiently for your reply. I beg you
to believe that I am already deeply grateful to the benefactor of
an only and much-loved child.*

The Curé took a red pencil and underlined the words—*I will
sleep at the inn at Vallandraut.* Those marks of red crayon, scarcely
faded by time, lie before me as I write. . . . Did the Curé, even
then, realize that those words formed the very heart and kernel
of the letter?—that all the rest of it was merely an elaborate preliminary? I thought so once, but, truth to tell, I very much doubt
whether he could have had so prophetic an insight. I am inclined
to believe that the words were underlined later, after the events
had occurred which gave them such significance. But he must have
realized at once that nothing would ever have induced Adhémar
de Mirbel to use against his sister-in-law a document which
would inevitably have brought disgrace upon his family. Nor was
it very probable that the Colonel, nearly seventy, and the possessor of a handsome fortune of his own, should be playing with
the idea of marrying the Countess.

Monsieur Calou took from a drawer a folder on which were written the two words—"False Women". In this he placed the letter,
put it back, and closed the drawer. He listened for a while to
our voices in the room below, to our laughter, to the clink of
plates. He stood there motionless, his elbows resting on the top of
the desk, his face hidden in his enormous hands.

❦ *IV* ❦

"KIDS' stuff", said Jean, emptying his glass of orange syrup. "I want something stronger than that."

He started rummaging in the sideboard. I felt pretty sure that it was just swagger meant to impress us, but I was shocked for all that. Might it be true, after all, that Mirbel really was the kind of boy with whom nothing could be done? He brought out several half-empty bottles, uncorked them, and sniffed their contents.

"Probably black-currant or angelica cordial or nut wine—old maid's tipple. . . . But the Curé's not the man to drink that sort of muck. . . . Ah, this is more like it! Here's what he fills himself up on!" he exclaimed suddenly, brandishing an already opened bottle of Armagnac—"1860, too" (he made a clucking noise with his tongue), "the year Uncle Adhémar got his wound at Castelfidardo."

Michèle protested. . . . Surely he wasn't going to drink Armagnac in the afternoon?—you drink it with dessert.

"But when the dessert comes in the Curé will be here."

"Jean, you *can't* do that!"

"Can't I!—and no liqueur glass for me, either!"

I found it difficult to decide just how much was mere playacting. This noisy boaster was so different from the sullen schoolboy who was always in trouble with the authorities. I did not realize at once that his foolhardy mood was the result of having Michèle as an audience, for he hardly addressed a word directly to her, and answered her when she spoke in monosyllables only. He scarcely seemed to be aware of her presence.

"It's too much, Jean: you'll make yourself ill!"

"And at one gulp, too: just you watch!"

He tilted back his head, but choked and started to cough. Michèle slapped his back. The room was filled with the smell of spirits.

"Monsieur Calou will notice," said I.

"We'll fill up the bottle with water: he'll just think the stuff has gone flat."

"But the smell, Jean. You stink of it, and so does the whole house."

We heard the scraping sound of a chair being pushed back, and then the abbé Calou's heavy tread upon the stairs. As soon as he entered the room he sniffed and looked sharply at us.

"So the young rascals have discovered my Armagnac, have they?" he said in high good humour. Then, turning to Jean— "You must admit it's not bad, eh?—and you ought to know. I don't mind betting there's good brandy at La Devize—the best of it comes from round there. . . . Louis, you ought to take your young friend down to the Ciron. Does he like fishing?—He does?— Well then, show him the good pools. The pike are doing a lot of damage, but I expect you'll find something."

He opened the French window which led straight out to the back of the house. We stood for a moment looking out, then started across the half-mown meadow. The storms of this wet summer had interfered with the hay harvest. We walked towards the line of willows. Darting blue dragon-flies announced the proximity of the stream even before we could see it. We trudged on across the marshy ground. It was an afternoon of moist, stifling heat. The brandy must have made Jean bold, for he walked beside Michèle, and far enough behind me to be out of earshot. I led the way. I was conscious of a vague uneasiness. It was the first symptom of that mental and emotional pain which was to infect my whole existence. But I am not telling the story of my own life, and I have no intention of isolating its single thread from the woof of the various destinies with which I am concerned. Still, I can scarcely pass over in silence that consciousness of being hurt of which, as a child, I then became aware. Nothing is so common as ordinary jealousy. But the jealousy which swept over me that day as, a boy of thirteen, I walked through the sodden fields, straining my ears to catch what my friend and my sister were saying, was not of the common kind—at least, I hope not, if only for the sake of humanity in general, whose shoulders already have to bear more than enough of the curses to which flesh is heir.

I did not know then which of my emotions was mainly concerned—my love for my sister or my friendship for Jean. It was hateful to realize that she was talking to him in the low, intimate voice which, till then, she had kept for me alone. Michèle belonged to me. So far I had never shared her with anyone, and now here was Jean taking her away from me, making her laugh; Jean whom, for the last fortnight, I had loved to picture in imagination on the roads about Larjuzon; Jean, who had played

a part in all my holiday plans, whom I had dreamed of having
to myself. He, no less than my sister, had suddenly broken away
from me. Why hadn't I realized that things would turn out like
this?

They're treating me like a kid: they're hiding from me, I told
myself. Sometimes I had to stop to let them catch up. Now and
again, at a twist in the path, I lost sight of them altogether and
had to turn back.

"What are you two talking about?"

They looked at one another, laughing but saying nothing. Jean
was chewing a piece of grass. Michèle was rather red in the face.
The brim of her straw hat was so broad that she had to tilt her
head back in order to see me. I pressed my question: what were
they talking about? Things that couldn't possibly interest a little
boy, Michèle said. Jean's lips approached her ear. This time I
caught what he said. "D'you think he *knows*?" he asked.

Now, to "*know*" meant, in our language, to be informed about
the facts of life, the mysteries of generation. My face flushed
scarlet, and I stalked on ahead, turning over this further grievance
in my mind. They were hiding from me in order to discuss forbidden things. Their guilty secret was another barrier between
us.

My stepmother had given me permission to ask Jean to lunch
with us next day at Larjuzon. I had looked forward to this, but
now decided suddenly not to pass on the invitation. I was terrified at the thought that the day was approaching when either
Michèle would take Jean from me, or Jean would take Michèle.
Rather than have this happen, I would deprive myself of Jean's
company. Let him stay alone at the presbytery and be bored
stiff! After all, his uncle probably knew what he was doing when
he put the screw on. The general view at school was that Mirbel
was a dirty beast. He was allowed to stay on only because his
guardian had been one of the heroes of Castelfidardo. Probably
at this moment he was telling Michèle what I called "one of his
dirty stories". Michèle mustn't be allowed to see him. I would warn
my stepmother. It would be far better for me to give him up,
never to see him again, than to experience this tightness in the
throat, this feeling in the pit of the stomach, this pain, this misery for which there was no cure, since any possible cure was beyond my power to control, and lay within the will, the heart, the
hidden thoughts of my friend and my sister who were now in

league against me! The torments I was suffering were more acute than any words of mine could express. To be sure, here beside the Ciron, looking down on the swirling stream, leaning against the trunk of a pine-tree which had grown to a great height by reason of the water that fed its roots, I did not fully realize that I could find no words for all that I was feeling. It was pride alone, I thought, that compelled me to hide my vexation. Without waiting for them to come up with me, and in the hope of putting them off my trail, I had walked quickly. I dried my tears, got back my breath, and composed my features. They were laughing, and I could hear their laughter long before they came in sight. I caught a glimpse of Michèle's straw hat above the bracken which their movement had set waving. At last I saw them. My sister asked me how Jean de Mirbel was going to get to Larjuzon next day, seeing that he had no bicycle.

"That old beast has confiscated it!" he said.

The old beast was his uncle. I answered coldly that there was nothing I could do about it.

"I was thinking of lending him mine," said Michèle. "I could ride yours this evening and take you back on the frame."

"Five miles on the frame? No, thank you. I have no intention of getting my bike smashed up. Mirbel will just have to walk from Larjuzon. If he's so keen on coming, five miles will be nothing."

"I knew he'd say that!" cried Michèle in a sudden fury. "His wretched old bike's sacred. I knew he would raise a row!"

"Oh, no, he won't," said Jean, taking my arm, half coaxing, half bullying. "You'll let me do it, won't you, Louis?"

I shook myself free and sat down on a root. "He's sulking", said Michèle; "it'll be ages before we can get him to say yes."

But I wasn't sulking, I was suffering. I watched the water-spiders struggling against the current. Long weeds were swaying in the clear stream. Minnows were darting about near the banks. I could see their shadows on the sandy bottom. Till my dying day I shall have in my nostrils the smell of trodden mint and river-plants. They symbolize for me the memory of that moment in which I said good-bye to the happy summers of my childhood, when I made acquaintance with sorrow and the torment of a boy's love. No, I was not sulking, I was wrestling with the miseries of a grown man. The others must have sat down too, some way off, for I could still hear them whispering though the bracken hid them. Suddenly I heard Jean's voice raised. I realized that he was talking loud on purpose.

"Don't worry: he'll come round all right. If he doesn't we'll take matters into our own hands. . . ."

I got up and ran over to them. "How are you going to do that, you great brute? Just you try!"

He seized my wrists. He was hurting me, but I clenched my teeth so as not to cry out.

"Are you going to lend your sister your bike, or aren't you?"

"Let me go, you're twisting my wrists!"

"Don't want to ride home on the frame, eh?"

Suddenly I was free, Michèle had attacked my tormentor. In a furious voice she shouted: "Leave my brother alone!"

"All right, all right, I wasn't going to hurt him!"

They glared at each other. I was conscious of a sudden sense of calm. They were quarrelling, they were going to be enemies. Michèle liked me better than him, and he wasn't in love with her after all. It was because of me that they were fighting. It was lovely to feel the tightness in my chest loosen. As always happens with me, as soon as the trouble grew remote, I thought that it had vanished for good. I no longer hated them. My old affection for them both returned. Of course Michèle and I would go back on my bike. But I wasn't going to give in at once, wasn't going to deprive myself of the pleasure of seeing them walk with a space of enmity between them. Now it was Mirbel's turn to go ahead, chewing his piece of grass, while I followed some distance behind, holding my sister by the hand. So on we went, I clutching Michèle's hand and looking at Jean as he marched ahead. It was pure happiness. The grass was wet. A great storm-cloud darkened the sky above the trees, but there was no thunder. Several men and women were busy round a wagon half piled with hay.

"Really, you know, Mirbel *is* just a great brute," I said.

"Still, he's rather nice. . . ."

"Doesn't alter the fact that he's a brute. . . ."

"But we'll fix it up, won't we, so he can come over to lunch to-morrow?"

Again I felt that tightness in my throat. I asked Michèle whether she was terribly keen on having him come.

"Larjuzon's a bit queer this vacation, don't you think, with that Puybaraud of yours looking like a great white worm, and Brigitte always fussing round him?"

"Oh, Michèle!"

"If she's not careful, she will make life at Larjuzon impossible, even for Papa. Of course I'm going to lend my bicycle to Mirbel."

"Then you'll jolly well walk back!" I said with a flare of temper. Jean had turned. This sudden storm of words between Michèle and me gave him a sense of triumph. That was what came of not letting him show me who was who. *He* knew how to treat kids. . . .

We walked round the presbytery, all shouting at the same time.

"Well, it's my bike, isn't it?" I protested.

"I call it frightfully nice of you to have asked his permission at all," said Jean to Michèle. "Just you jump on it before he can do anything. If he doesn't want to ride on the frame, well, he can do the five miles on foot, that's all!"

I got in before them and seized my bicycle. But Jean did not let me get far. He hung on to the handle-bar and stuck his foot in the wheel, so that I fell off. Monsieur Calou, who must have seen us, came hurriedly out of the house, ran towards us and picked me up. I had merely grazed my arm. He turned to Mirbel.

"Go up to my room and bring down the iodine and the package of cotton that you'll find on the washstand."

He issued this order in his usual quiet way, but his voice held a threat of thunder, and he kept his eyes fixed on Mirbel, who stood there with his great fists half clenched. Still, he obeyed at once. When he came back again the abbé proceeded to bathe my injury at the pump. Without turning to Jean he said:

"Dab it with cotton. . . . Now, put on some iodine—not too much. Stings a bit, doesn't it? What's been happening, Michèle?— tell me."

She embarked on a confused story. She said we were both to blame. Mirbel had been rough, but I had gone out of my way to irritate him.

"Shake hands," said the abbé.

I took Jean's hand and he made no effort to withdraw it. Monsieur Calou then said that he would settle the matter. He wouldn't hear of letting two of us go back on the one bicycle. He said that he'd lend Jean his next day so that he could get over to Larjuzon. It could be spared for a few hours, for there was no one seriously ill among his flock. But something unexpected might turn up, so he asked Jean to be sure to be back before four. "And you two can come with him. In that way you'll be able to spend the rest of the afternoon together."

The threat of thunder had gone from his voice; there would be no storm. The wind had swept the sky clean. He asked us to water his vegetables for him, and advised us to do it barefoot so as not to get our shoes wet. As a reward, he said, we could take as many currants as we liked. Maria had finished her jam-making.

As soon as the abbé had gone back into the house, Jean said that he hadn't come there to do manual work, and wouldn't be treated like a servant. But no sooner had Michèle and I taken off our shoes and stockings than the temptation was too much for him. He got out of his sandals and took one of the watering cans that my sister was carrying. Such is the power of happiness that I remember as a time of calm, unclouded happiness that summer's day when we ran barefoot over the gravel which hurt our feet, and did all we could to splash one another as much as possible. But all the same, my pleasure was streaked with pain because it was Michèle whom Jean splashed. She had tucked her skirt up to her knees and, though pretending to be angry, gave vent to little shrill gusts of laughter which were quite unlike any sound I had heard her make before. But I refused to let myself suffer. Deep within me I carried a load of dumb agony which a trifle would have served to waken, and I shouted louder than either of them to keep it from my mind. When the sun disappeared behind the pines it was time for us to think of going. Jean asked at what hour lunch would be at Larjuzon.

"Twelve, but come early," said Michèle; "we get up at eight. Come as soon as you can get the abbé's bicycle."

I protested that he mustn't be deprived of it for too long. He might be called to some sick-bed. Jean replied in his "nasty" voice that "people could die without the help of a curé". Michèle seemed shocked at this, and I noticed that there was a certain coldness in her tone when she said good-bye. But she turned round twice to give an answering signal to his waving beret. He was wearing a sailor's pea-jacket over a striped red-and-white jersey. His feet were bare, his trousers rolled above his knees and kept in position by an elastic.

Later, he told me about his first evening at the presbytery. For a while he had wandered round the house, not knowing what to do with himself. Baluzac could hardly be called a village. It consisted of a single inn and a store kept by a man called Voyod, with whom the Curé did not wish his charge to have anything to do. In fact, the only order he had issued was that he should keep clear of the place. The abbé Calou had also spoken about the books in his study. In Jean's life books occupied a place which no one who had had to do with him suspected. On his father's side he belonged to a family which would have viewed a taste for reading in a young boy as a disquieting symptom. His guardian and his mother were convinced that he was interested only in scabrous and obscene publications, and, to tell the truth, their suspicions were not wholly without foundation.

Jean could not resist his desires. The knowledge that the house was full of books, even if they were only books for a priest's reading, that there was a library of which he had been given the free run, exercised over his mind a power no less than many worse temptations. But he stood out against it. He did not want Monsieur Calou to think that he could be won over so easily. He was cautious about putting his head into so obvious a trap. Nevertheless, he went upstairs to the first floor, taking care not to make the stairs creak.

There was a strong smell of pipe tobacco. Jean hesitated to approach the door. His pride held him back. He felt quite sure that the Curé had been listening, had caught the sound of his padding footsteps, and was waiting with as keen a sense of expectation as any fisherman watching the trout circling a waiting snare.

Monsieur Calou could contain himself no longer, but opened the door. "Anything you want, you young scamp?"

Jean shook his head.

"A book, perhaps?"

The boy entered the thick haze of smoke. He had never seen so many books. They were ranged in rows from floor to ceiling: they lay scattered over chairs and on the mantelpiece. There were books everywhere, bound in paper covers. There was a set of steps mounted on wheels for reaching the upper shelves, and a desk at which a man could read and write standing. Never had he seen so many marvels! The books must be pretty boring, of course; still, one never knew, and no book, thought Jean, could be wholly boring.

The Curé went back to his table without taking any further notice of him. Jean climbed on to the steps. How tiresome it was that he felt so sick, and had such a pain at the back of his neck. . . .

The Armagnac that he had drunk out of bravado was giving him a lot of trouble, and the smell of the Curé's pipe was the last straw. Hurriedly, he returned to the floor, picked up a volume at random and read the title: *A Treatise on Concupiscence—A Letter and Some Maxims on the Theatre—Logic—A Treatise on Free Will*, by Bossuet. Was he going to be sick? Was he going to faint, here in the Curé's study? On no account must he do that! In an effort to forget his qualms, he opened the book and forced himself to read.

The woman in Proverbs who boasted of the perfumes scattered about her bed, and of the sweet odours that regaled the visitor to her chamber; who said, "Let us take our fill of love, let us solace ourselves with love", showed by her words whither may lead those cunning scents which are prepared with an intent to ensnare the Will, and draw it to an indulgence of the senses through an employment of that which seems not directly to attack the stronghold of our modesty. . . .

"You're very pale, my boy: almost green. Don't you feel well?"
Jean protested that it was nothing, just a little attack of sickness.
"Lie down."
The boy refused. It would pass off of itself. He felt better already. He made another effort to concentrate his thoughts on the page. . . . The abbé heard the sound of Jean's body striking the floor, though not violently, for the sufferer had kept hold of the steps. The boy felt himself lifted by two strong arms, and retched uncontrollably. The Curé, without showing the slightest sign of disgust, handed him a basin and supported his head with his great hand. Jean opened his eyes and asked to be allowed to go down to the garden. He was in despair at the thought that he had been betrayed, unexpectedly like this, into the hands of the enemy.
"I'm coming down too," said the abbé. "I want to finish reading my breviary in the church. You can join me there. It's a lovely little church, built by Bertrand de Gouth, who afterwards became Clement V. I don't suppose you know that he was a fellow-countryman of ours—born at Vallandraut, though there are some who say it was at Uzeste, where he is buried. . . . It wouldn't do to have many Popes like him."

Jean replied that he was not interested in old stones.

"Never mind, come along anyhow, and pay our Lord a little visit."

Aha!—that was the priest for you! Jean muttered that he didn't believe in all those old wives' tales.

"Really?—that's interesting." There was no hint of outrage in Monsieur Calou's tone.

"Does it surprise you?" Jean's tone was smug.

"Why should it?" said the Curé. "The really surprising thing is that a man *should* believe. . . . The really surprising thing is that what we believe should be true. The really surprising thing is that the truth should really exist, that it should have taken on flesh, that I can keep it a prisoner here beneath these old vaults that don't interest you, thanks to the strength in these great hands of mine which your uncle Adhémar admires so much. Yes, you little oddity, I can never get over feeling how absurd, how utterly mad, it is that what we believe should be precisely and literally true!"

Was the Curé laughing at him? Jean tried another fling: "Oh, well, anyhow it doesn't mean a thing to me!"

He tried to carry off his attitude with a swagger, staring his adversary straight in the face. But, in spite of himself, he had to lower his eyes.

"That may be so now, my queer little scrap of humanity, but you may feel different later."

"You shan't get me!" cried the boy defiantly.

"It's not a question of my getting you. How could it be?"

"Well, who else could? There's no one else here, is there, except you and Maria?"

The Curé said nothing. He seemed to be thinking. "How do you manage at school? I don't suppose you're allowed to trifle with Confession or Communion there?"

Jean replied complacently that he had never let that bother him. They had Confession every Saturday. He just said anything that came into his head. And every Sunday they had to go to Communion. But what did it matter whether one believed or not? It didn't make the slightest difference.

He had expected an outburst, but it did not come.

"You really think so?" asked Monsieur Calou.

Jean presented an insolent face to his gaze. But he felt shamed by its gentle sadness.

"Every Saturday and every Sunday, for Heaven knows how long . . . two years at least, O Lord!"

Monsieur Calou looked at the handsome face, at the unsullied brow beneath the mop of dark hair in which one lighter lock shone like a flame. He could say no more than: "Lie down a little before dinner, my boy." Then he hurried off towards the church without looking back. His bent shoulders made him seem less than his real height.

❦ *V* ❦

I FIND it difficult, looking back, to distinguish the first occasion on which Mirbel lunched at Larjuzon from those that came later. All through August we were constantly together. When he didn't come to us, Michèle was for ever hanging about him at Baluzac, and nothing would have induced me not to go with her, since my peace of mind would have been utterly destroyed had I known that they were together away from me. My whole life centred around the need I felt to be always the third party in their meetings.

Nor, at first, was it very difficult for me to be with them. The bad days, when they managed to give me the slip, were far fewer than those on which Michèle railed against us two boys and had to protect herself against the tricks which we invented at the expense of my "kid sister". There was never entire harmony among us. Either she or I had to be the victim. I was never happy unless I was defending Michèle against Jean and his often ill-natured teasing. But almost always, just when I thought that they had quarrelled for good and all, they would quite suddenly make it up. It was precisely when I felt myself most safe from any possible hostile coalition of my sister and my friend that inexplicable scenes would occur which had the effect of putting me to the torture—such as the occasion on which we sent her off into a temper by alluding to "the story of the cakes" which, as Mirbel said, had united him and me till "death should us part".

"What story of what cakes?" asked my sister.

We winked at one another, put our fingers to our lips, and swore our most solemn oath that never, no, never, would we let her into the secret. We began to run round her in circles, pulling her hair, snapping our fingers, and chanting: "Cowardy, Cowardy Custard! . . ." I was careful to keep my distance, but Jean jumped about like a dancing dervish, touching her and then springing back out of reach. . . . Suddenly Michèle leaped at him, her fingers clawed, and made a dash at his face. He did not attempt to defend himself, but stumbled and measured his length on the grass. When he got up we saw that his cheek was bleeding from a scratch. We stood there appalled. Michèle looked quite pale.

"Oh, Jean, wipe your face! I haven't got a hanky."

But he did nothing to staunch the blood. I thought he was going to rush at her, but instead, he stood there grinning. It was so unlike him to act that way that it seemed almost as though he had some hold over her, and she over him, as though he didn't mind her hurting him. Children though they were, they had become, unconsciously, free of that world in which blows mean the same thing as kisses, and insults may express more of love than the tenderest endearments. A sort of curtain seemed to drop between us. They passed from my vision, leaving me, an outsider, on the wrong side of the curtain—a small boy lost in a universe peopled by that inconsequent race of monsters whom we knew as "the grown-ups".

If Mirbel showed signs of becoming less wild, the credit was due entirely to my sister and not to Monsieur Calou (at any rate, until the end of August, when an event occurred which I shall describe in due course). True, the Curé had won a signal victory over his charge on the very day of his arrival, but, during the weeks that followed, he made no noticeable progress in his campaign.

I have a cat here with me in the house [noted Monsieur Calou in his diary that summer]: *a cat that slinks in and out of the library without so much as moving a chair, sniffs round the books, pads into the dining-room, settles itself at the table, and gobbles its soup. It never shows fight, works an hour each day without complaining, and, on Sunday, goes to Mass. I showed my hand too soon. The boy hates my gentleness . . . that "professional gentleness of yours"—as the young spark from Bordeaux put it one day in accents of repulsion. I don't want there to be anything in*

*my looks or speech to put him off. The great thing is not to sicken
him by the slightest hint of unctuousness. How harsh the unction
of Christ is! To cleave their hearts, one must be as hard as a
diamond! Jean would have felt far less dislike for me if I had
been rough and stern. He expected that, and was ready armed
against it.*

It may be that the abbé Calou had stumbled on Jean's secret,
but of mine he had no suspicion. Could anyone really have understood it and explained me to myself? No man can bear a
child's cross. It is something beyond the comprehension of the
fully grown.

Monsieur Puybaraud watched over my studies and the good
of my soul with an ardent singleness of mind for which I was
not at all grateful. That he loved me there could be no doubt,
and the accepted view at home was that I adored him. To this
game of make-believe I willingly lent myself. "Louis swears by
Monsieur Puybaraud: he takes no notice of anyone else. . . ." As
a matter of fact, I shouldn't have cared greatly if I had been told
that I was never going to see him again. The degree of indifference shown by children to grown-ups, even to those to whom
they seem to be most attached, is seldom realized. Except for
Jean and Michèle and, in quite a different way, for my father
and my dead mother, no living creature was altogether real to me.
Those who could be collectively described as "the others" were,
for me, a mere anonymous crowd. They served to fill the stage.
They stood about the centre of my heart when it leaped with
happiness or wallowed in despair according to my relations of the
moment with Jean and Mirbel, but its condition meant nothing
to them.

When I walked in the park with Monsieur Puybaraud, and he
talked to me in a moral or a learned strain, I answered him in
proper wise, responding to his advances with that rather knowing
gentleness which served so well to win me the affection of others
whenever I took the trouble to employ it. The poor man had no
idea that my heart was suffering a thousand miles away, that the
words I uttered had no connection with my thoughts or real feelings, that effortlessly and without the faintest sense of shame I hid
my true self from him, substituting for it the mere image of the
solemn and attentive child on whom he lavished the treasures of
his kindly spirit.

I was in the advantageous position of knowing all about his private life. Not that it really interested me. That summer was Monsieur Puybaraud's moulting season. He was half-way back to the world. He wore a panama instead of his top-hat, a short jacket in place of his frock-coat. But he was loyal to his black trousers and his starched shirts, no matter how stiflingly hot the day might be. His attitude to me was that of a Christian school-master, though he was led to confess more intimate matters than are usually thought fitting for young ears. To-day, after such a long interval of time, when Monsieur Puybaraud has long been dust, I can read his diary and find excitement in the struggle he was waging, in the drama of which I was then the disinterested spectator, because it touches on problems with which I become the more obsessed the older I grow.

During the first week of Monsieur Puybaraud's stay, Brigitte Pian had plenty to occupy her. The days were too short for her happy task of helping a man to straighten the tangled skein of his private problems. She felt that she was not wasting her life, that she was not running counter to her true vocation, which was to make clear to others what God had planned for them from the beginning of time. Here, at her very door, was an unrivalled opportunity for her to show her mettle, though she fully realized the dangers involved. She was, perhaps, too satisfied in the part she felt called upon to play. Not that she was guilty, even in the smallest degree, of self-indulgence: still, at first she did seem to be deriving too much satisfaction from Monsieur Puybaraud's way of listening to her as to an oracle. But, alas, his meekness was superficial only. Very soon it was borne in on Brigitte Pian that she was dealing with a less submissive sheep than she had at first supposed. "He is a wandering soul", she told herself in the course of the second week. She even went so far as to accuse him of deliberately setting his face against the operations of Grace—by which she meant her own advice.

It was Brigitte Pian's way to drive reluctant souls on to the mountain-tops (that was how she phrased it), and she made it her duty to open Monsieur Puybaraud's eyes to that especial trick of the Devil which takes the form of enlisting against a Christian sinner the very sense he has of his own humility. My master was convinced that previously he had had too high an idea of his own strength when he had felt himself called upon to eschew the normal destiny of mankind. He felt that it was his duty, while there might yet be time, to find his way back to the beaten track marked out by those who had gone before him and, like them, to take to himself a wife, have children, and watch over them as a bird watches over its brood. But Brigitte Pian knew well that it is sometimes necessary to tear from human souls that mask of spurious humility behind which they take refuge. She declared, as though she had been the very mouthpiece of God, that Monsieur Puybaraud had been taken from his school work only because, from all eternity, he had been destined for the life of the cloister. She assured him that he had to face one problem and one alone— at what door should he knock? to what Order should he make his submission?

Not only, however, did Madame Brigitte fail to make progress in her struggle with Monsieur Puybaraud, although she was fight-ing him on ground of her own choosing; she was forced to admit that she was at grips with an influence considerably stronger than any that she could bring to bear—and what an influence! for what was defeating her was the persuasive power exercised by Octavia Tronche, who inspired in my stepmother a feeling which the world would have described as contempt. But she knew that we should feel contempt for no human creature, and that even the soul of Octavia Tronche had value in the sight of God.

It was a matter for astonishment to my stepmother that Oc-tavia at a distance had a greater hold over Monsieur Puybaraud than when, back in the city, she had been seeing him every day. The reason for this was that though separated from my master she wrote to him daily. Madame Brigitte devoured the outside of these letters with her eyes. Monsieur Puybaraud read them in her presence at breakfast-time, bringing to the task a degree of con-centration that had to be seen to be believed. The truth was that his former occasional dissatisfaction with Octavia's rather homely appearance (responsive though he always was to the spiritual charm that shone out from her) yielded wholly a feeling of ad-miration and tender respect during this time of her absence, when her contact with him was confined to the pages that she wrote each night before going to bed.

Their correspondence—which I found among Monsieur Puy-baraud's effects—could not possibly be published here, not be-cause it does not deserve publication, but because I doubt whether there are many readers capable of appreciating the charm of true humility, which takes no heed of itself and seems completely ignorant of its effect on others. I cannot, however, pass it by in silence, seeing that Octavia's victory over my stepmother had tragic repercussions on more than one person.

Although Octavia thought highly of Madame Brigitte, she was encouraged by distance to resist her influence, and to warn her lover against indulging in an excessive distrust of the dictates of his own conscience. "No matter how superior in virtue another person may be," she wrote, "her views cannot supersede your own vision of the Divine Will, since that is the fruit of complete surrender to God. . . . My own opinion is that we should most certainly pay attention to the advice of others, but that we should never let it divert our attention from the ever watchful respect which we owe to our own inner voice. Don't you agree, my dear, that it is in the secrecy of our own hearts that we most truly hear the bidding of God? I find it impossible to believe that what I feel for you so strongly can be contrary to His will. Light, for me, is where you are. If I struggle against the instinct which leads me to you, I see nothing but darkness. I am the more convinced that what I say is true, because I know that if your temporal or spiritual welfare depended upon my giving you up, I *could* give you up, not, indeed, without pain and suffering, but certainly without a struggle. Selfish though I am (and God alone knows how selfish that is!), I love you too much to consider my own feelings. So wholly do I love you, that I would not, no, not for a single moment, fight against the influences to which you are exposed at Larjuzon, if I were sure that they are making for your happiness, if I did not feel that too much subtle reasoning may be brought to bear upon what is really a perfectly simple and very ordinary situation. Perhaps a poor creature like me has no right to judge, but I *do* think that there is one point in particular about which Madame Brigitte is wrong. She does not realize, as you and I do, that all flesh, imperfect and corrupt though it may be, is holy; that, in spite of original sin, the birth of a child is still God's loveliest mystery. I have heard her say things on this subject which I may perhaps have misunderstood. What I love most in you, my darling, is that fondness for children which God has implanted in your heart, for those little children like whom we must become if we are to gain the Kingdom of Heaven. We cannot become like them, but at least we can bring them into the world, and that is no small thing. No doubt there are higher vocations . . . still, I do not believe that in becoming

your wife I shall be resisting Christ's summons to His flock, His
insistence that we should leave all and follow Him. For in you,
and through you, beloved, in and through the children who may
be born to us, I submit to that Will which it is our chief delight
to honour. . . . The mere thought that this is so sets me trembling
with happiness. . . ."

Monsieur Puybaraud did not show these letters to me, and I
could judge of my stepmother's defeat only by the increasing
gloom of her demeanour, especially at mealtimes, the atmosphere
of which soon became almost intolerable.

I had a feeling that his affairs were going badly, that his relations with Madame Brigitte were becoming embittered, but I
was far too unhappy myself to pay much attention to what was
going on. Ever since Michèle had scratched Jean's cheek, the
friendship between them had grown closer and closer. Gone were
the happy times when my friend, a child once more, had plotted
with me to tease my "kid sister". Whenever Jean came to the
house they thought of one thing only—how to be alone together.
They were as clever in their efforts to avoid me as I was in trying not to let them out of my sight. I was ashamed of my per-
sistence: it became hateful to me. Yet I dogged their footsteps,
pretending not to notice the glances of irritated impatience that
passed between them.

If my stepmother called me, if Monsieur Puybaraud had a cor-
rected exercise to give back, if I had to be absent for no matter
how short a time, I knew that when I got back Michèle and Jean
would have vanished. In the garden path where but a moment
earlier Michèle's laughter had echoed, or my friend's loud and
breaking voice as he called to the dog, I now heard nothing but
the sighing of wind in the branches left dripping by the recent
storm. I cried their names, "Michèle! Jean!—where are you?" and
then fell silent, knowing full well that even if they had heard,
the only effect of my appeal would be to make them lower their
voices still further, walk on tiptoe, and hide their tracks.

I had no clear idea of the nature of the attraction that held
them in thrall. My senses were not yet awakened: I had felt
nothing of the kind myself. What causes jealousy is a vision of
the delight that a beloved person gives to, and receives from,
another. I do not think that I was capable then of any such
emotion. But their happiness, conditioned as it was in part by
my absence, hurt me to such an extent that I could have cried
aloud.

. I remember the day when Monsieur Puybaraud suddenly decided to leave us. At luncheon scarcely anybody said a word except Monsieur Calou, who had come over to Larjuzon with Jean.
Monsieur Puybaraud answered his questions, but Madame Brigitte
never opened her lips. Her great face was gloomy enough to have
frightened me. Opposite her, my father sat huddled over his
plate, chewing his food and paying not the slightest attention
to anybody. Jean and Michèle, with the whole length of the table
between them, exchanged wordless speeches with their eyes. I,
sitting next to Monsieur Puybaraud, pretended to be absorbed in
his remarks. But I was aware of nothing but that silent interchange between my sister and my friend, was conscious of
nothing but the happy peace of mind that I knew Michèle was
feeling just because Jean was there. For her, I was merely part
of the rest of the world, which meant that I didn't really exist
at all. I was a part of nothingness.

Because of the storm we could not drink our coffee under the
trees. My stepmother apologized for her silence. She had a headache, she said, and asked me to fetch an anti-pyrine tablet from
her room. The two minutes during which I was away sufficed for
Jean and Michèle to make their escape in spite of the bad weather.
I wanted to follow them, but the rain had grown heavier, and my
stepmother forbade me. "If Michèle wants to get wet, that is her
affair. You will stay indoors."

Could it be that she had noticed nothing? Michèle's behaviour
ought to have filled her with horror. But she had eyes for no one
but Monsieur Puybaraud. Her headache, which was genuine
enough, forced her to go to her room. No matter what the company, my father would never give up his siesta. So I was left
alone in the billiard-room, watching the drenched countryside
through the French windows. In the drawing-room Monsieur Puybaraud and the abbé Calou were talking. At first they kept their
voices low, but after a while I could hear every word of their
conversation. Monsieur Puybaraud was complaining of the tactless tyranny to which he was being exposed. Monsieur Calou,
I gathered, was laughing at him for being so timid, and was ad-
vising him to slip his moorings without any further delay.

"They must be hiding", I told myself, "in the abandoned farm."
I conjured up a picture of Michèle and Jean in the kitchen where
only an occasional shepherd ever lit a fire, and where the walls
were scribbled over with pictures and words that made Jean
laugh, but which I did not understand. They were kissing. They

were delighting in one another. Michèle was never gentle with
me. Even when she was kind there was a rough quality in her
kindness. Jean, even when he was in a good mood, always spoke
to me as though he were my master. A hulking great brute, but
not to Michèle. He would say to her, "Your hands are cold", and
hold them in his for a long while. He was never kind to me. I
have always wanted people to be kind. . . .

Looking out on to the rainy fields, I suffered.

Monsieur Calou wanted to take advantage of a break in the
clouds to go back to Baluzac. He asked me to call Jean. I rang the
great bell, but in vain. There was no sign of Jean. The abbé Calou
decided at last that his charge was old enough to get home alone.
He rode off on his bicycle after saying good-bye to Madame
Brigitte. Her headache had gone, and she took a stroll in the
avenue with Monsieur Puybaraud. Standing on the steps, I could
see them pacing up and down. My master was doing all the talking. There were only the briefest of interchanges between them,
and, although I could hear no high words, something told me that
all was not well. Monsieur Puybaraud, on his way back into the
house, stroked my hair. He was very pale.

"I am going away to-morrow morning, Louis. I must see to my
packing."

I scarcely heard him. Where were Michèle and Jean? They
had not come back to tea. I could remember no previous occasion on which they had been alone together for so long. It was
not annoyance that I most felt now, but anger, a desire to hurt
them. I became a prey to all the nastiest instincts that flourish in
us at that period of life when the man we are to be is already
fully formed and fully dowered with his individual portion of inclinations and passions.

The rain had left off. I walked quickly beneath the dripping
trees. Now and again a raindrop splashed on my cheek or ran
down my neck. It was a sunless summer and the grasshoppers
were silent. If only there had been some other boy or girl at
Larjuzon with whom I could have played on my own . . . But
no face, no name came to my mind. At a turn in the path I saw
my stepmother walking towards me. She saw me standing there,
my hand pressed to my forehead. I could not restrain my tears,
and for a while could make no answer to her questions.

"They're running away from me," I managed at last to stammer.

She thought that I was referring to some childish game. "Pretend not to notice. Then they'll have to be 'out'. . . ."

"No, no—that's what they want."

"What *are* you talking about?"

"Yes," I insisted, almost whispering, "to be alone."

She frowned. "What do you mean?" she asked. Her suspicions had been awakened, but as yet they had no definite object. She was too much preoccupied, too wholly confined within her own circle of pain. Still, the seed I dropped had fallen on good soil. Sooner or later it would put forth shoots.

"One is always punished when one attaches too much importance to other people," murmured Brigitte Pian on a note of bitterness. "I sometimes wonder, dear child, whether I don't give too much of myself when I work for the salvation of my neighbours. Oh, I know that the least among them is of infinite worth. I would give my life that one might be saved. But there are moments when I am frightened to think how much time I have wasted (at least, it *seems* wasted, but of that God alone is judge) over insignificant, nay, evil persons. It is the cross laid upon the great-hearted that they shall exhaust themselves in darkness and uncertainty on behalf of the spiritually mean and inferior. . . ."

She uttered the last word from between tightened lips. I realized that when she spoke of the spiritually inferior she meant Monsieur Puybaraud. Why was she so interested in him? Was she in love with him? If she wasn't in love with him, thought I, why did she get in such a state at the mere mention of his name? How can those we do not love affect us for either good or ill?

I caught sight of Michèle in the distance seated on one of the stone steps. Without waiting for me to ask her what she had been doing, she said that she had been for a ride on her bicycle, and that Jean had gone back to Baluzac without returning to Larjuzon. She must have come straight from her room. She had tidied her hair and washed her face and hands. She looked at me, trying to guess what I was thinking. But I pretended not to be interested. I found pleasure in feeling at the same time acutely miserable and completely master of myself.

I went upstairs early, meaning to read in bed, but this I could not do. Through the floor I could hear the rumblings of a violent dispute. Michèle told me next day that my stepmother had lost control of herself and had been very harsh to Monsieur Puybaraud.

He too, finally, had lost his temper, exasperated by the fact that when he tried to explain to my stepmother why it was that he had decided to marry Octavia, she had replied, raising her eyes to Heaven, that this was the cross she had always known was reserved for her, and that she willingly accepted the sacrifice.

"But, Madame Brigitte, there is no question of your being sacrificed. This is my affair, and mine only. . . ."

But Madame Brigitte would not listen. She had been wounded, but forgave the hand that held the weapon. She always behaved like this when people told her that she had been wrong or had committed some injustice. Instead of frankly admitting her fault and sitting in sack-cloth and ashes, she turned the other cheek, protesting that it was well she should be thus misunderstood and vilified. In this way she added another link of mail to the armour of perfection and merit in which she went clad from head to foot. On such occasions her interlocutor was driven to speak angry words, and this gave her a feeling of still greater excellence at the bar of her own conscience and in the sight of God.

On this particular evening, however, she had given full rein to her fury. She must have exceeded all decent limits, for next day at breakfast (which was earlier than usual, because my master was taking the eight-o'clock train), she humbled herself to the extent of apologizing to him in my presence.

"Such behaviour was unworthy of me", she said, not once, but many times, in an access of humility, "and I want Louis to hear me acknowledge my fault. When I have reason to believe that a fellow human soul is straying and in danger of damnation, I can contain myself no longer. . . . But excess of zeal is no excuse for the violence of my words. He who would tame the old Adam must never sleep. I realize, in all humility, that I have a fiery nature." This she said with every sign of satisfaction. "My friend, you must forgive me."

"No, Madame Brigitte," Monsieur Puybaraud protested, "I cannot bear to see you abasing yourself in this way. I am not worthy."

But she would not listen. She wanted to revel in the grandeur of her attitude. She had paid the price asked of her, and it cost her nothing now to tread the path of humiliation to the end, since, by so doing, she forced her adversary to lay down his arms, and increased her own sense of personal merit (one link the more added to the armour of perfection).

"My conduct to you and to Octavia shall prove that I bear you no grudge. What I have said, I felt in conscience bound to

say. But that is all over now, and I confide you both to God.
You will have no trustier friend than me in the new life, so be-
set by snares, so full, I fear, of ordeals, which is opening before
you."

Monsieur Puybaraud seized her hand and kissed it fervently.
What would they do without Madame Brigitte? Octavia's position at the Free School, and his own in the Charity Organization, depended upon her. One word from her . . . He raised
his eyes to the face of his benefactress, which suddenly emptied
itself of all expression. Brigitte Pian's words became vague. She
spoke of the necessity of trusting in Providence, that ever-sure
protector that wrapped us in its loving care when we suffered
most and felt ourselves abandoned by the world. And then, since
Monsieur Puybaraud insisted on mentioning the subject again,
she said that she could decide nothing as yet. She had, she remarked, only one vote in the Organization, like every other member of the Committee.

"Oh, but, Madame Brigitte," he urgently replied, "no one knows
better than you that if only you would take our side . . ."

But my stepmother this morning was in humble mood, and the
more Monsieur Puybaraud assured her that she was all-powerful
in the matter of assuring continued employment for Octavia and
himself, the more she retreated, taking a delight in minimizing
her influence and stressing her utter unimportance.

❦ *VI* ❦

AFTER Monsieur Puybaraud had gone, Larjuzon knew peace for
several days. My stepmother scarcely ever left her bedroom. She
both wrote and received a great many letters. It had now turned
hot and fine, but though the thunder had ceased to crack and
crash behind the trees, it still rumbled deep down in more than
one heart. That week Jean bicycled over only once. He spent the
whole afternoon with me, but I got no pleasure from his companionship. That sixth sense of suffering which I have never yet
found misleading warned me that he was not following his own
inclinations, but was acting in conformity with some plan of action
drawn up in advance by him and Michèle.

She made no effort to come with us when we set off intending to idle our time away on the bank of the stream. Jean was kind to me that afternoon, just as kind as I had long wanted him to be. But in spite of this I had never felt so sad, the reason being that his kindness derived from the same source as my own sense of irritation—from the influence that Michèle had acquired over him. That he who but yesterday had been a misunderstood and tormented child should now be basking in happiness was for me a cause of suffering.

We talked very little. He was deep in a daydream and I was brooding over my suspicion that he had arranged to meet Michèle somewhere else. Almost every day now Michèle went off alone on her bicycle while I was working. There must be some place on the road between Baluzac and Larjuzon where they met. . . . He had come with me today merely in order to put me off the scent. I watched him whittling away at a willow-branch. He said he was making a whistle. His swarthy face was radiant with good humour.

"Monsieur Calou is really pretty decent, you know. He's actually written to my uncle suggesting that Mamma should pay me a visit, and Uncle has given his consent. She's coming next week. She's going to stay at Vallandraut."

"Oh, I *am* pleased!"

And I was. It was the thought of his mother's visit, then, that had caused his happiness. Michèle had something to do with it, of course, but it wasn't only because of her.

"You've never met Mamma, have you? She's lovely"—he made an appreciative noise with his tongue. "Lots of well-known artists have wanted to paint her portrait. But you'll see for yourself. She's planning to call on your stepmother to thank her. She'll enjoy it here, though she doesn't ordinarily go in for paying visits. I've told her a lot about you and Michèle. I'm sure she'll like Michèle. Mamma loves natural people. There's only one thing I'm afraid of, and that is that Michèle will be too careful. You know what she's like when she wants to be thought a perfect young lady—the way she minces when she speaks—and it's not her style, really. I don't think her hair ought to be too neat, do you?"

I said nothing. Actually, he was talking to himself. I didn't really mean a thing to him. He looked at his watch, yawned, suddenly grasped my arm, and gave me a hug. He was overflowing with tenderness, and I had come in for a drop of it because I happened to be available. But I knew that the hug had been meant for Michèle.

That day they said good-bye to one another with a decidedly frosty handshake. But when he had mounted his bicycle they exchanged a few words in a low tone. At dinner my stepmother talked of the Comtesse de Mirbel and her coming visit. To hear her speak one would have thought that Jean's mother represented in beauty of soul and loveliness of body all that was fairest in contemporary society. Of course, she *had* given occasion for a good deal of gossip, but charity should forbid us to believe everything we hear, and certainly she, Brigitte Pian, gave no credence to the abominable stories that were going round. No one should say things like that except on the evidence of his own eyes. Besides, however great the scandal may have been, it could not be denied that, ever since her husband's death, Julia de Mirbel had lived a very retired existence at La Devize. Except for the few months that she spent in Paris with her Mirandieuze relations, she had never left it. Her general conduct had been a perfect example of quiet dignity.

From what was said it became perfectly clear that the daughter of the former Imperial Prefect attached considerable importance to the behaviour of a lady whose parents would not have condescended to recognize the existence of her own. The coming visit stood, on the worldly plane, for the only piece of snobbish gratification which, in those days, was available to my stepmother. For no one could deny that she belonged to the highest circle of local society, less by reason of her family background and considerable wealth than because of the mysterious power she wielded among church-going folk, and her reputation for shining virtue. There could be no doubt that it was the name of Mirbel that had opened the doors of Larjuzon to Jean. Normally, my stepmother would have been loud in her disapproval of him, and certainly the boy had always been spoken of in our family as both headstrong and undesirable.

After dinner the moon rose, and Michèle wanted to go for a walk in the park. My father woke from his doze just long enough to repeat, word for word, the phrase that our mother had always been in the habit of using on such occasions: "Cover up well: there's a damp chill from the river."

I noticed in Michèle the same sort of happiness as that with
which Jean had been overflowing that afternoon, the same excitement, the same appearance of intoxication. The moon lit up her
face with its slightly underhung jaw. The full, projecting lower
lip gave her a hungry, almost animal, expression which to some
extent was an index to her character. Nowhere have I ever met
with anybody who had such an appetite for happiness. It had
always been marked in her and showed itself by the greedy
way in which she bit into fruit or buried her face in a rose, and
by a complete surrender to sleep, which was like an enchanter's
spell, and came upon her at times as she sat beside me on the
grass. But she never waited passively for happiness to come. She
was constantly tormented by the urge to fight, to conquer, and
of this she gave me proof that evening when she spoke of Jean.
For it was in order to talk about Jean that she had suggested
taking this walk in the park. Just before we began to skirt the
mist-drenched meadows, she decided to broach the subject. She
put her bare arm round my neck, and I could feel her breath on
my ear. What she had to tell me was quite mad, so amazing indeed that I could scarcely believe her.

"We're engaged, you know. . . . I mean it. It's terribly serious,
though he's not yet seventeen and I'm going on fifteen. . . . I
know everyone'll just laugh and not believe it . . . so we're not
telling anyone except you—only you, dear, darling Louis. . . .
Why are you crying? Don't you think it's marvellous?"

Marvellous!—it was her favourite word. I hid my face against
her shoulder, and she let me cry, not asking me anything. For
she was accustomed to my tears, which were apt to come on the
slightest pretext. I was conscious of a feeling of peace. No need
to ask more questions: everything was settled now; there was
nothing left for me to hope for, nothing for me to look forward to
except playing the role of confidant for which they had cast
me. Never again should I be the only, the prime, concern of
Michèle's heart. From the meadows came the quiet, cold gurgle
of water. Michèle smelled of warm carnations. She wiped my eyes
with her handkerchief, talking all the while in her low voice.

I had guessed right. They were in the habit of meeting several
times a week behind Monsieur Du Buch's mill. They were terrified lest my stepmother should discover them. Michèle made me
swear to say nothing that might put her on their track. When she
said that, I remembered what I had told Brigitte Pian about their
hiding from me. I had spoken with no thought of making mischief.

(Though was that really true?) Perhaps her suspicions had already been aroused.

"I'm frightened of her, Louis. She hates people to be happy. I have a feeling she's always got it in for me because I don't look miserable. We must be very careful. But Jean is so reckless!"

She spoke to me of him with a freedom of which I should never have been capable. She knew perfectly well the risk she ran. He was much, much worse even than his uncle imagined. I ask myself to-day why she thought that, because he has told me himself that he would have regarded as sacrilege any attempt on his part to give her more than the most chaste of kisses. Perhaps it was that she knew he would not always be so lamb-like. . . . Whatever the reason, she was not frightened of him. She would marry him and nobody else. She had chosen him, and he her, children though they were. If she lived to be a hundred no other man would ever mean anything in her life. That was a truth on which there could be no going back. He was so intelligent, so strong.

"And so handsome, too—don't you think?"

No, I did not think that he was handsome. What meaning can a child attach to the word? He knows strength, of course, when he meets it—physical power. But the question must have made an impression on me, because now, at the end of a long life, I can still remember that spot in the path where Michèle asked me about Jean. Am I in any better position to-day to say precisely what I mean by the word handsome, beautiful? Can I say by what signs I recognize it in a human face, in a landscape, in a stretch of sky, a colour, a word, a tune? All I know is that beauty troubles the senses, for all that it concerns the spirit, that it breeds in one a sort of despairing happiness, leads to a contemplation that never wholly finds its object but is worth a world of kisses. . . .

"Look here, Michèle," I said. "I suppose you know that the boys at school say that Jean is a dirty beast?"

"Yes, I think I do. . . . But Monsieur Calou doesn't think he is. What I am going to say may startle you, but I think it's better to be a dirty beast than to have Brigitte Pian's brand of virtue!"

"Oh, Michèle!"

"I mean it. I'd rather be in Hell without her than in Heaven with her!"

"But, darling Michèle, it's blasphemous to say things like that,"

I protested. "It'll bring you bad luck. Ask to be forgiven, now, at once; make an act of contrition."

Obediently she made a quick sign of the cross, and murmured a few words: *I repent with all my heart the sin which I have committed against Thy adorable Majesty*—then she burst out laughing.

"D'you know what Monsieur Calou said to Jean about Brigitte Pian? He said that there are some people who choose God, but that perhaps God doesn't choose them. . . ."

"Monsieur Puybaraud", said I in shocked tones, "thinks that Monsieur Calou has too much intelligence for a priest: that he is too acute, and that his ideas smell of the stake."

Michèle did not know what the expression "to smell of the stake" meant. She asked me, but I did not answer, for my whole attention was fixed on an idea that had just occurred to me.

"Listen," I said sharply, "there's something I want you to tell me. Don't be angry. . . . Does he kiss you?"

"Of course he does . . . passionately", she said. "You wouldn't understand, but it's marvellous. He doesn't do anything else, though, Louis . . . not anything. . . . You mustn't imagine . . ."

Gracious Heaven! what worse could they do than kiss? My cheeks were on fire. I looked at Michèle, who was my senior by just a year (but she was already a woman, I, still a child), and thought how old she was, how heavily burdened with experience and sin!

"You *are* a silly, Louis: haven't I just told you we're engaged?"

She, too, was trying to reassure herself. Her conscience was far from easy. But a fresh wave of happiness swept suddenly over her and she started humming in that voice of hers which was as yet "unplaced", was still capable of astonishing breaks. The tune was an air of Gounod's which our mother used to sing on just such summer nights as this:

"The darkness brings the silence back. . . ."

It was a long while before I could get to sleep: not that I was more unhappy than usual, but that I was tormented by a sense of remorse. I tried to remember the expression on Brigitte Pian's face when I had complained that Jean and Michèle were hiding from me. I knew her too well to feel comforted because she had shown no overt sign. I was not without experience of her self-control, and was aware that she never yielded to sudden impulses.

She buried her grievances and dug them up weeks later when no one remembered what had caused them. I was often scolded for something I had done in such and such circumstances a year earlier, and about which she had never spoken until then.

Certain slight changes in my stepmother increased my anxiety, and I warned my sister. I pointed out to her that Madame Brigitte kept less often to her room than was usual, despite the heat; that one was likely to come across her at all hours of the day on the stairs or even in the park. She would enter the drawing-room unheralded by any creak of footsteps. Michèle did her best to reassure me by pointing out that our stepmother no longer had Monsieur Puybaraud to get her teeth into. But the very first day that Jean came over to Larjuzon again, I knew from certain signs that he had entered the world of Brigitte's preoccupations. One morning she expressed surprise that Michèle should walk about on the roads during the hours of siesta, when even the farm animals stayed in the barn.

Such remarks were the sharp flashes of lightning that announced the coming storm. But I, at least, had the consolation of being able to tell myself that my fears had been groundless, that, so far as the present unease was concerned, I was without guilt.

I have already mentioned Vignotte. He was the estate agent at Larjuzon, where he had been installed with his wife for only a short while. They had been imported by my stepmother, and it was about them, I feel pretty sure, that my father and she had had their first serious disagreement. Very shortly after her marriage Brigitte had fallen foul of old Saintis, who had been born on the place, and with whose rudeness, drunkenness, and dishonesty my father put up uncomplainingly. People who settle in the country after having spent all their lives in cities soon find themselves at odds with the local folk and make enemies of them. The theme is as old as the hills. Balzac made use of it. But in this case the story had not followed the usual course of fiction, for the country dwellers of Larjuzon had been worsted by the lady from the city. One day, when Saintis had been drinking heavily, he was so rude to my stepmother that my father was compelled to get rid of him. But he never forgave his second wife for having driven him to take this step.

The Vignottes, who regarded Brigitte as their benefactress, were very grudgingly accepted by my father. He could not abide his new agent and regretted old Saintis for all his drunkenness and his thieving propensities.

Ours was a district in which any wagging tongues were feared, but those of the Vignottes most of all. Madame Vignotte, with her lips and cheeks sucked inwards over her toothless gums, looked like nothing so much as a walking proboscis straddled by a pair of spectacles and surmounted by shiny strands of false black hair. She never returned from her shopping expeditions without having some morsel of gossip for Madame Brigitte. She rarely made direct assaults upon the reputations of our neighbours, but delighted in hints and sly jokes at their expense. The odd thing was that nothing ever seemed to shock the pious old dame, who had never in her life been a step from the village. Adultery, needless to say, she took in her stride. But she knew all about, and was quite willing to discuss, incest and every kind of sexual aberration, not excluding the crime of sodomy, chuckling and winking the while.

The market was her happy hunting-ground, and she left the woods and fields to the tender mercies of her husband who, from his pony-trap perched high on its big wheels, dominated the countryside as he drove from farm to farm. Many were the couples philandering in fancied security during the heat of the day or when darkness fell who were marked by his hawk-like eye. Sometimes the actual prey was hidden from view, but the sight of two bicycles, symbolically entwined beneath a bush, would fill him with a wicked joy.

Now it so happened that one day, not far from a hut used for pigeon-shooting, he noticed a tall, dusty bicycle, and, close beside it, looking tiny by comparison, the very machine which Mademoiselle Michèle had asked him, the day before, to oil (as though it was his business to oil bicycles!). True to her usual methods, Brigitte Pian at first made no use of what Vignotte told her. She pretended not to believe him and, by so doing, put him on his mettle. The more she refused to be convinced, the coarser became his charges. He went so far as to say that Mademoiselle Michèle and the young fellow over at Monsieur Calou's . . . All this he asserted to an accompaniment of resounding oaths. He had seen them with his own eyes, or as good as. Nothing was going to persuade him that a young scamp like that would stay for over an hour with a girl in a shooting-hut without . . . Still, one mustn't be too hard. After all, one had been young oneself, and these things happened . . . even to young ladies . . . why, one

had only got to look at her to see . . . Abeline Vignotte had got
wise to it all right, not that it much surprised her. "But I said,
'No, Abeline, fun and games, perhaps, but . . .' 'Get away with
you,' she replied; 'just you look and see how her figure's developing! . . . It's sad, all the same, a girl like that, with the example
of Madame Brigitte always before her eyes. . . .' "

Brigitte had decided to do nothing until Madame de Mirbel
should have paid her expected visit. But the situation was serious
from more than one point of view, and extremely delicate. Monsieur Pian adored Michèle, and it was difficult to foresee the nature of his reactions. I gather from a notebook kept by Monsieur
Calou, which is relevant to this incident, that my stepmother had
certain scruples (for at this time she searched her conscience
with avidity, though never to the point of fanaticism). What
troubled her was that she could not disguise from herself the fact
that she found considerable pleasure in the thought of a disaster
that ought to have brought her nothing but shame and consterna-
tion. For was she not like a second mother to Michèle? But faced
by a difficulty of this complexion, Brigitte Pian set herself to
apply the only solution to which she attached any value. She
must conquer her scruples by force of logic, must find some reason that would make her pleasure seem legitimate and fit it
into the pattern of her moral perfection.

She was helped, on this occasion, by letting her mind dwell,
for the space of a few seconds, upon the alluring prospect of a
marriage into the Mirbel family—though such a prospect, it is
true, was distant and by no means certain, considering the boy's
age. Madame Brigitte rejected the temptation without much difficulty, but she gloried, all the same, in her renunciation, and
wove it diligently into the mail-corselet of her merits. Had she
been a worldly woman, she told herself, she would have taken
full advantage of a scandal of this kind. But no, she would turn
it into a weapon with which to achieve the wretched girl's salvation. That the child should have come as close as she had done
to the edge of the abyss was disaster enough, even if she had not
actually taken the final plunge into the depths, but a rescue
was still possible. The situation should be painted in its true
colours. The scales would fall from Monsieur Pian's eyes, and
the whole spiritual atmosphere of the house would be transformed. There would be nothing but profit for Michèle in being
made to drink this cup of humiliation to the dregs.

Where Michèle was concerned, Madame Brigitte did her utmost

to encourage thoughts of mercy in herself, for mercy is a virtue that must not be neglected. How could she help feeling indulgent when she remembered whose daughter the poor child was? The first Madame Pian had been precipitated into outer darkness through a sudden and terrible death over which had hung the well-founded suspicion of suicide. Brigitte had in her possession a file of documents which only charity had prevented her from opening in the presence of her husband, who insisted on remaining so wilfully blind to the truth. So far she had not done so, in spite of the odious, the actually insulting, comparisons that he allowed himself at times to draw between her and her predecessor. Only the highest kind of virtue—heroic virtue, as God well knew—had kept Brigitte silent. But perhaps the time was coming, was even now at hand, when, for the sake of the girl, she would have to display to the eyes of the outraged father and husband written proofs that the wife he mourned had been far from deserving of his tears. But if the papers proved that, they would prove, too, that the foolish rather than blameworthy daughter should be pardoned because of the heavy legacy that lay so crushingly upon her.

In this way did Brigitte Pian colour the pleasure she savoured in anticipation. She was a logical-minded woman who kept to a straight road marked out by clearly labelled principles. She never took a step that she could not immediately justify. Later she would yield to the onset of those obscure anxieties that she now put from her without excessive difficulty, would leave the highroad to beat the undergrowth of guilty motive.

A day was to come when the memory of deeds that could never be undone would prove her torment, showing her their true face—till then undreamed of and horrible beyond words. But that time was far off. Many were to be her victims before the true vision dawned on her of that love in whose service she thought herself enrolled, but of which she was in fact wholly ignorant.

❧ *VII* ❧

THE only thing that I remember at all vividly about the Comtesse de Mirbel's day at Larjuzon is that Jean appeared to my eyes in an entirely new light. Up till then I had always seen him as the bad boy of the school who knew rather too much about "life" for his age; as the dunce on whom Uncle Adhémar and Monsieur Rausch had to use physical force; as a dangerous sort of chap, though he could be kind enough when he liked—almost gentle, indeed, in his dealings with me. That was the trouble. I was fond of him but could not respect him. As the result of a logical contradiction which I can't say worried me a great deal, I thought less highly of my sister when I knew she was in love with him.

But when his mother was there, Jean seemed a different person. His eyes never left her face except when he glanced round at us to see whether we were sufficiently admiring. Every time the Countess produced a verbal sally, he looked at me with a laugh, as though fearful that I might have missed the point, or might not show myself responsive to such wit. From the very moment of their arrival he showed how pleased he was at our surprise on finding that the mother of this great lout of seventeen was both elegant and young. To-day there is nothing particularly miraculous about the preservation of a youthful figure. It is a thing that can be had by all who are willing to pay for it. But at the time of which I am speaking, it was a matter for astonishment to find a mother who still retained the figure of a young girl. At first, therefore, we were more struck by the apparent youth of the Countess than by her beauty, which, though almost perfect so far as features went, was lacking in brilliance. She was afraid of the sun, and went to as much trouble to avoid it as she would to-day to expose every inch of her body to its rays. The veil in which her face and straw hat were swathed did not, in her opinion, afford sufficient protection, and whenever she had to cross the tiniest patch of sunlight she was most careful to open her elegant parasol. She never so much as half removed her gloves, except at luncheon. In her anxiety to produce a good impression on us she achieved an effect of rather affected simplicity.

When coffee had been served under the oaks, Jean took her off for a stroll along the path which made the circuit of the park, that she might have an opportunity of talking to Michèle. During their brief absence, the abbé Calou and my parents exchanged a number of acid remarks.

"In her own way she's a very superior sort of person, of course," said my stepmother; "but I need hardly add that it's not a way I particularly like, even judging by worldly standards. Don't you think there's something almost idolatrous about the cult of the body when it's carried to quite such extremes?"

Although at that time she still regarded Monsieur Calou as a good and learned priest, though rather on the simple side and quite without ambition, she held that his judgment was both childish and eccentric. She kept, as she said, "a careful eye" on him, for she regarded it as her privilege to watch over every soutane that came within her orbit.

"The Comtesse de Mirbel", said the priest, "is a lady of letters" —and his sudden laugh was out of all proportion to the very mild humour of his remark. "Did you know that she has written novels?"

"Has she ever had any of them published?" I asked.

"No," snapped my stepmother in her most sarcastic tone; "she finds it sufficient to live them."

Heavens!—backbiting, and in front of a child too, who might well be scandalized by such a remark. One link—two—sprang loose from the carefully wrought armour of her perfection. But almost immediately she set herself to repair the damage. She spoke, she said, without any real knowledge, and regretted that she had not resisted the temptation.

"I give you absolution, Madame," said the abbé Calou.

"There are some things about which a priest ought not to joke," replied Brigitte, frowning portentously.

We could see the Countess in the distance, coming towards us flanked by Michèle and her son. Jean had his face turned towards her as he walked. He was laughing and leaning forward in his anxiety to hear what my sister was saying. He did not see us: the two adored creatures at his side completely blotted us out from his consciousness. I suffered, but there was no jealousy in my suffering. I felt I wanted to cry. Jean was not what we had thought him. He was good, though at times he might give the impression of naughtiness. Brigitte gazed at the group as it moved towards us. The corners of her mouth were drawn slightly downward; her large face was like a mask, and I could learn nothing from its carefully assumed expression of composure. The abbé Calou, like her, never took his eyes from them. He seemed preoccupied and sad. By the time they had come within hearing, an argument had broken out between mother and son.

Jean was begging to be allowed to go back with her to Vallandraut. She shook her head. They must be careful to observe every detail of the arrangements made by Uncle Adhémar. It had been agreed that she should have an early dinner with Jean at the presbytery, and then go back in the carriage to Vallandraut in time to get to bed early. The train left at six, which meant that she would have to be ready at dawn. They must say good-bye at the abbé Calou's.

But Jean would never give up anything on which he had set his heart. His mother's arguments went in one ear and out the other. They made no impression on him. Nothing mattered to him except his longing to spend part of the night with her He had secretly planned to sit up in her room and watch the day break.

"But we're *always* apart: I never see you: and now, when I've *got* a chance, you grudge me an evening—a night."

He was speaking in the obstinate tone I knew so well, and his face had assumed the mulish look that Monsieur Rausch found so exasperating. But his mother was as determined in her refusal as he was in his request. Michèle tactfully left them to themselves. The argument grew noisier. We could hear Madame de Mirbel's last words, uttered with a dry finality.

"I said no, and I mean no. You always ask for more than you are given. You're spoiling the whole day for yourself. No . . . I'll not listen."

She came towards us with a smile. Though it seemed to light up her whole face there was something about it that was strained and tremulous. Jean watched her surreptitiously, a look of defiance in his eye. The Countess, after my stepmother had served her with currant syrup and barley water, went back to the carriage, telling her hostess once more how *very* kind she had been, though we got the impression that she was more distant and more preoccupied than she had been when she first arrived. I watched the victoria out of sight. Jean occupied a little let-down seat, and had his back to the horses. He looked obstinate and far from happy, but his face was soon hidden from us by the parasol that the Countess suddenly opened.

What I am now going to relate owes nothing to my imagination, though Jean rarely spoke of it to me. But one whole volume of the abbé Calou's diary is taken up with the details of what happened.

Scarcely had the victoria reached the main road when Jean re-

turned to the attack. At such times he was like a hound on the
scent. But it was no good. His mother maintained her refusal
with an air of irritated firmness. When she had exhausted all her
arguments, she half turned to the abbé Calou, who was looking
on in silence.

"You're in charge of Jean: please make him be sensible."

He answered her dryly that to-day he had "transferred his responsibility". To this she replied, with a touch of insolence in her
tone, that now if ever was the time to show that strong hand
about which she had heard so much. At this Jean, white with
anger, sprang up and, taking advantage of the fact that the
horses had slowed down for a hill, jumped from the carriage and
narrowly escaped falling under the wheels.

The driver tugged at his reins, the horses reared. By the time
the Countess and the priest reached Jean, he had got up. He
was unhurt. For a few moments mother and son glared at each
other in silence, standing there on the deserted highway. It was
an overcast day with occasional bursts of sunlight. The grasshoppers were scraping away at a sort of intermittent prelude. The
coachman had the greatest difficulty in holding in his team, and
kept slashing with his whip at the horseflies which were proving
troublesome.

"I am forced to agree with your uncle. There's no doing anything with you."

But Jean started to argue again. He hadn't seen her for three
months: she had made this trip for his sake, and now she wanted
to spoil the one evening that they might have spent together.

"My dear boy," she said, "I promised your uncle, I gave him
my word. . . . Next time I will keep a whole night for you . . .
and I won't wait until the end of the holidays, either. But we
mustn't set your uncle against us. Now, get back into the carriage
and sit between us. If that won't be too uncomfortable for *you*",
she added, turning to the priest. Then she put her arm round her
son. "Snuggle up to me . . . like a baby," she said.

He stopped fighting, gave up the battle. He had surrendered
at last! The shadows of the pines grew longer, spanning the road
from one side to the other. The abbé Calou turned away his head.

"This is the best time for catching grasshoppers," said Jean;
"they come down the trunks when the sun sinks, and start making their noise when they're about a man's height from the
ground."

The Countess heaved a sigh of relief. He was talking of other things. He had loosened his grip. When they reached the presbytery, she told the coachman that it was not worth while taking the horses out, because she was going to start for Vallandraut before eight. But the man would not listen to her. He meant to feed and water his animals. In hot weather like this they needed a rub-down, too. All the Countess could get from him was a promise that he would leave their harness on.

When they sat down to dinner she complained that Madame Pian's too lavish luncheon had made it impossible for her to do honour to Maria's chicken. It was only seven o'clock, and the horizontal light was flooding the small presbytery dining-room although the blinds were drawn.

"How pleasant it is here!" she said. "Jocelyn's dining-room must have been just like this." *

She took scarcely a thing on her plate, and kept glancing towards the kitchen. The service was slow because Maria had no one to help her. More than once the Curé had to get up and go into the kitchen for a dish, but this he did gloomily and with a grudging air. Perhaps he was still upset by what had happened in the carriage. Jean was not surprised that the priest should remain proof against his mother's charms. It was only to be expected. "They could never get on together", he thought. And then, she made no effort to conceal her anxiety to be gone. She was aware of this herself, and tried to find some excuse. The coachman, she said, had made her feel nervous: he had the look of a gaolbird.

"I don't want to be out late on the roads with a man like that."

Jean interrupted her: "I'll ride back with you, Mamma, on my bicycle."

She bit her lip. "You're *not* going to begin that all over again! You promised me . . ."

He hung his head. Maria brought in the "pastry", which was her masterpiece.

"You won't taste many better," said the Curé.

The Countess did her best to swallow a few mouthfuls. That was the best she could manage. But she liked making herself popular, and did not want to leave with a feeling that she had disappointed her host. She tried, therefore, to be friendly with

* The reference here is to Lamartine's novel in verse, *Jocelyn*—
TRANSLATOR.

him, and gentle to the boy. But the gloom on the Curé's face remained unlightened. As soon as dessert had been served, he left the room in order to read for a short while in his breviary. The Countess realized that he had done this in order to give her an opportunity to be alone with her son before she took her departure. Jean realized it too, and came closer. He could have given a very accurate account of her thoughts at that moment. He knew that she was in a hurry to be off, yet was ashamed to let her anxiety be seen. She forced herself to stroke his hair, but kept on glancing surreptitiously at the clock that hung over the mantelpiece. Jean caught her doing this, and reassured her. "It's fast", he said. She replied eagerly that she could spare him a few more moments. She embarked on some advice, speaking in a rather preoccupied tone of voice. The abbé Calou was quite nice, really. . . . Jean wasn't unhappy, was he?

"No, Mamma, no . . . I'm happy . . . honestly I am—very happy," he added with shy warmth.

She did not see the blush that came to his cheeks, nor feel him tremble. The day before, he had made up his mind to confide in his mother, hoping she would not laugh, would not mock him, would treat the matter seriously. . . . But he had let the right moment slip, and it was too late now to pour out his feelings. . . . Much better to keep Michèle's name from this last-minute conversation. Thus he argued to himself. But there was another reason which he dared not admit: that it was no use giving himself away to someone whose mind was elsewhere. Many years later, when we were seated by my fire in the rue Vaneau in Paris, and Jean was telling me about the saddest moments of his life, he could still remember those few minutes of twilight after the stifling day, with himself sitting in the presbytery dining-room at the side of his adored mother, their knees almost touching, and watching her as she kept on glancing at the clock. Through the glass door he could see the Curé moving up and down in the kitchen-garden, intent upon his breviary.

"I'll come back before the end of the holidays, darling: that's a promise. And next time you shall have a whole evening."

He made no reply. She told the coachman to close the hood of the victoria. Jean jumped on the step and touched her neck with his lips.

"Get down! Don't you see he can't hold the horses in? . . ."

A cloud of dust rose and then subsided. Jean waited until the
carriage had disappeared round the last bend, and then went
back into the garden. He took off his shoes and stockings, got a
watering can, and began to water the chicory that he had trans-
planted the day before. Monsieur Calou said not a word, but went
off to the church to make his devotions. When he returned, Jean
had gone to bed, and called out "good-night" sleepily through the
door. The Curé, before himself retiring, went down again to make
sure that he had bolted the front entrance. Contrary to his usual
custom, he did not leave the key hanging on its nail in the passage, but put it under his pillow. Then, kneeling down beside the
bed, he prayed at greater length than on other nights.

Monsieur Calou thought at first that it was the wind that had
waked him. It was blowing hard, though the night was fine and
moonlight lay along the floor. Somewhere a shutter was banging.
Leaning out of the window he saw that it belonged to the room
above his own, where Jean slept. The fastening must be broken.
He slipped on his soutane, reached the attic landing, and opened
Jean's door as quietly as possible, meaning to shut the window. A
violent gust overturned a vase filled with heather picked by
Michèle, standing on the table. The abbé saw at once that the bed
was empty. He waited a few moments to get his breath, then
went downstairs and tried the front door. The bolt had not been
drawn, nor the lock forced. The young lunatic must have got out
through the window by hanging on to the gutter. The Curé took
the key from under his pillow and went out.

The night was given over to wind and moonlight. All about the
house was a great murmuring of pines. It was not like the intermittent moaning of the sea. No wave, no crash of foam broke
the green swell and surge of the trees. He went first to the shed
where the two bicycles were kept (he had hired one for his
pupil at Vallandraut), and found that only his own was there. At
the corner of the house, where the gutter ended, he could see in
the sandy soil the marks of a fall. Jean must have jumped from
a fair height because the indentations of his two heels were
clearly defined.

The abbé went back to the shed, took out his bicycle, and then
hesitated.

It was almost midnight—too late now to do anything. The harm
was done! What harm? . . . No use letting himself get into a state.

Why make a tragedy of the furious midnight scene that was probably taking place in the inn at Vallandraut? What, in any case, had it to do with the Curé of Baluzac? True, he was in charge of the boy, had made himself responsible for him: but the truant would return before morning, and the simplest thing would be to notice nothing. There were some things that were better ignored. The really wise man never let himself be forced into the position of having to take disciplinary action that might destroy at a blow all the advantages he had previously gained. . . . But that was precisely the problem! The Curé paced for a while among the currant-bushes, pushed open the gate, and gazed down the road which lay empty beneath the moon.

There was no way he could be of help to the boy whom he loved so dearly, who, perhaps at that very moment, was receiving a mortal blow. His mother had had good reason for wishing to be left alone at night. Her opposition to Jean had been obstinate, fierce—almost, it had seemed, inspired by hate. The abbé Calou tried to make himself believe that his thoughts were nonsense. But he knew the type too well! The exigence (which Jean had inherited), the frenzy which would not stop, if need be, at trampling a son into the mud. . . . Perhaps, though, he was exaggerating the danger just because he loved Jean so dearly.

It was the first time he had ever become attached to one of his pupils. Since he had begun to specialize in "difficult cases" no such opportunity for affection had come his way. He had not taken on the work because he had to. His brother, a landed proprietor in the Sauterne country, to whom he had surrendered his share of the family estate, sent him each year a sum of money, the amount of which varied according to the harvest, though it was never more than six thousand francs. This, with his stipend and the small sums that came to him from parishioners, was a great deal more than he needed, for he lived off his own poultry and vegetables and occasional gifts from the neighbours.

If, then, he had decided to undertake the training of boys whom their parents could not manage, it had not been from any desire to make money. No, he just spread his nets and patiently waited, never abandoning hope that some day the one wild bird who might really prove worthy of his care would drop plumb into his house. If that should happen, he would make a man of him. He thought he ran a better chance of finding the right one if he confined himself to the unruly. This predilection for "bad

lots" was doubtless due to the strain of romanticism that still remained in him, to the heritage he had brought with him from the
seminary. But it responded, too, to some deeper and more secret
yearning, to a desire to help young creatures who might be threatened, who might already have been hurt, by life, who did not
care whether they were saved or not, who needed a sponsor at
the Father's throne. It was not a matter of virtue so much as of
preference and inclination.

Until now he had put up with his charges because he was in
love with young life and adolescence. But in every case so far,
the ephemeral charm of youth had overlaid a solid bottom of vulgarity, stupidity, and boorishness. A superficial grace often lent a
glow to the most ordinary and insensitive little middle-class oaf.
In Jean de Mirbel the abbé Calou had found for the first time
what he had always hoped that God might some day send him.
At last a child had come his way who had a soul.

But that soul was hard to reach. Not that it mattered. The
abbé Calou was one of those people who, from their earliest days,
are vowed to a life of disinterested labour, whose affections ask
nothing in return for what they give. The trouble was that Jean
would not let himself be loved or protected. Though he had
had the boy there under his hand, and just a little watchfulness
would have served to make all well, the abbé had not been able
to avert the danger of this nocturnal meeting between mother
and son. What would happen to Jean when he had left the
presbytery and was at large upon the highways of the world? (For
the abbé could not imagine that he would ever be content to vege-
tate in a country château.) Even when he had left his roof, the
abbé would feel himself still bound by the responsibility he had
undertaken. . . . Where was he now? How follow him? How reach
him? Doubtless he would be home before morning. If he were
not, the abbé would simply go out and look for him. Meanwhile,
there was nothing to be done but to make some hot coffee. He
went back to the kitchen, and, after opening the shutters to let the
moonlight in, lit a few twigs. This done, he sat down in Maria's
low chair, took from his pocket a rosary made of olive-stones, and
stayed there motionless. The moonlight touched the back of his
head and shone upon his rough, untended hair. He sat there
with his arms resting upon his thighs. The enormous hands,
hanging down between his legs, took on a strange, exaggerated
significance.

❧ *VIII* ❧

JEAN had waited to put his plan of escape into action until he heard the sound of the Curé's regular breathing through the floor. The clock had not yet struck eleven when he started off down the moonlit road. The wind was at his back, and he rode without effort in a state of tranquil intoxication, certain now that nothing in the world could keep him from accomplishing what he had set his mind upon. He would see his mother this very night, would watch by her pillow until break of day. He was as sure that this would be so as that one day he would hold Michèle in his arms. Never before had he ridden at dead of night by the light of a moon spun by the wind above an empty world. He felt no nervousness about the coming interview with his mother. In the presence of a third person she had seemed to be the stronger: alone with him she would be at his mercy.

He travelled swiftly and was soon enveloped by the river mist where the road dropped into a hollow just before it reached the first houses of Vallandraut. At once he lost his self-assurance. He conjured up a picture of the locked and bolted inn. How could he explain his presence there? How manage to have his mother wakened? What excuse could he contrive? Not that it much mattered. He would say that the thought of not seeing her again had made him ill, and that Monsieur Calou had advised him to take a chance. At dead of night, and in a public inn, his mother could scarcely scold him overmuch, for fear of scandal. He would attack her hard hostility; yes, in the long run, he would soften it. He would not fly into a rage, whatever happened. He would hide his face in her skirt and cry; he would kiss her hands.

He reached the market-square where a few carts with uptilted shafts cast on the ground a shadow as of horned animals. The waning moon shone straight on to the flaking plaster of the Hotel Larrue, picking out the black lettering of a sign that said: "Lodging for Man and Beast." There was still a light in the bar, and he could hear the click of billiard-balls. He leaned his bicycle against the wall, and asked the plump young woman who was dozing in a chair by the deserted counter for a glass of lemonade. She answered him with an ill grace that it was too late, that the hotel ought by rights to be shut, and that no drinks were served after eleven. Then he put to her the question he had long prepared: was the Comtesse de Mirbel staying there? He was the bearer of an urgent message.

"Countess?—what Countess?"

The girl was suspicious and obviously thought that her leg was being pulled. She said that she had other things to do than listen to tall stories, and added that at his age he'd be better off at home than wandering the roads.

"But I know there is a lady staying here" (perhaps, he thought, she had not given her name). "A fair lady, wearing a straw hat and a gray tailor-made suit. . . ."

"A fair lady?—wait a moment. . . ." A flicker of intelligence showed in her stupid eyes.

"In a tailor-made costume", she went on, "and a spotted veil, and carrying a handsome dressing-case which she left here to be taken care of?"

Jean interrupted her with some impatience: where was her room?

"Her room? But she's not sleeping here. She only came in to leave her luggage. She's staying at Balauze"—the girl was insistent —"she gave me a telegram this morning addressed to the Hotel Garbet, reserving a room."

Jean reflected that Balauze was the county town, and that probably his mother had thought she would be more comfortable at the Garbet than here. But, then, why had she told him that she would be sleeping at Vallandraut? He asked how far it was to Balauze. Seven miles? . . . less than an hour's run on his bicycle.

"She meant to sleep at the Garbet", went on the girl, who had suddenly become talkative (and was probably moved by an instinct of hostility towards a lady who had scorned the Hotel Larrue). "But I shouldn't be surprised to hear that she'd spent the night in a ditch. . . ."

Jean became anxious.

"Why? Did she have bad horses?"

"Horses!—I like that! She came in a motor-car. The whole town turned out to see the sight. You've no idea the row it made, and what a stink of gasoline and oil and dust there was. . . . And it ran over Madame Caffin's chicken, though it's only fair to say that they paid her much more than it was worth. . . . You ought

to have seen the gentleman in a pair of goggles that almost covered his face—a regular mask it was, enough to frighten one to
death—and a gray duster down to his heels. . . . The things they
wear nowadays!"

"Then she's at the Hotel Garbet at Balauze, close to the church?
You're quite sure?"

He thanked her, jumped on his bicycle, and turned right from
the Baluzac road. Now the wind was in his face, and he struggled
against its unseen strength, against the hostile power (or was it
pity, perhaps, and not hostility that inspired it?) that was doing
its best to slow down his approach to Balauze. Had he been with
the young Pians he would never have dared confess his weakness,
but since he was alone, he dismounted as soon as the road began
to rise. In spite of the cool night wind, his face was running with
sweat, and his backside was sore. He could think of nothing but
how tired he was. For all his boast of manhood, he was still a
child about anything that concerned his mother. It would never
have occurred to him that she could have any connection with
what he vaguely thought of as human crimes and passions. Both
his father and his uncle figured in his imagination as brutes. From
his earliest years at La Devize he remembered his father's shrill
voice, could see him now, looking like an angry little turkey-cock
strutting round his mother where she sat, an image of silent martyrdom. Uncle Adhémar, who had the same kind of voice, had always shown a certain amount of courtesy in his dealings with his
sister-in-law. Never for a moment had Jean entertained the idea
that she might have deserved their hatred. But, for all that, he
had scarcely ever spent a whole day with his mother without
being made aware that she was not in the least like his private
idea of her. He was constantly noticing her lack of warmth, her
insincerity. The way she had deceived them all about spending
the night at Balauze ought not to have surprised him. At La Devize, as in Paris, where she always stayed with her grandparents,
the Mirandieuzes, from January to June, Jean, home for the Easter
holidays, had more than once caught her in an inconsistency, for
the Countess never bothered to give plausibility to her various lies.
She would say, for instance, that she was simply *longing* to go to
some play of which everyone was talking, quite forgetful of the
fact that she had ostensibly been to see it one evening the week
before, and the next day had given them an enthusiastic, if rather
vague, account of its plot. Often and often had Jean, with the

terrible logic of childhood, disconcerted her by his never-varying comment—"But, Mamma, you *said*"—never dreaming of taking her words at other than their face value. What she had said did not always—did not, indeed, very often—agree with the story she was telling then. But she never troubled to think up an explanation. "Did I *really* say that? You must have dreamed it, darling. . . ." But if ever Jean had been visited by the hint of a suspicion, it did not survive their separation. How should he have dreamed that her soul was less lovely than her face? In his memory of her the idea of sin must ever be a stranger to that serene brow, to the set of her rather too short nose, to those heavy lids veiling eyes that held the colour of the sea (*glaukopis:* he had underlined the Greek word in his lexicon), above all, to the thrilling contralto voice, with its occasional hoarseness: that unforgettable voice that casts its spell over me even to-day whenever I go to see the old lady whose hand alone seems to show the ravages of time, for the structure of her face has remained unaltered beneath the flaccid skin, like some marvel of Greek statuary that has survived the centuries, and her eyelids are like the trampled edges of those same green pools with their reflections of sea anemone and weed.

Jean pushed his bicycle up the last hill on the road to Balauze, not at all worried by what he had heard, but nervous at the thought that the interview between him and his mother would have a witness at the Hotel Garbet. Which of his mother's friends had a motor-car? It must be Raoul . . . for that was how the famous dramatist was known to the Mirandieuzes, who, like all people of fashion, enjoyed being on familiar terms with so well-known a man. He was not in fact called Raoul, but I am not going to set down the real name of a man who was once as celebrated as Donnay, Bernstein, or Porto-Riche, though to-day he is entirely forgotten. If nothing now remains of a body of work which was once highly considered, if the very titles of his most famous plays have passed from human memory, it remains true that he once exercised a profound influence on many who are still alive and who, like the Comtesse de Mirbel, are dragging out the fag-end of their existence before taking the final plunge into nothingness.

It would never have occurred to Jean that there could be any bond between his mother and this fat gentleman in his forties. "She probably thought it would be amusing as well as convenient to do the journey by motor-car," he reflected. "But it was not nice of her to deprive me of a treat that I should have enjoyed so enormously."

He rode down a dark, narrow street that debouched onto the Cathedral square with its arcaded pavements. It was empty. He went round it and had some difficulty in making out the hotel which stood in the shadow of the church. It had been contrived from the outbuildings of the former bishop's palace, and only a narrow alley separated it from the Cathedral. The front door and the entrance to the stable-yard were both closed, and all the shutters were fastened except on the first floor, where two windows seemed to be half open. Should he ring, knock at the door, wake the household in the middle of the night? What excuse could he give? He might ask them to take him in, but he had scarcely any money. Would his mother pay for him? He stood hesitating. Though his mind was innocent of all suspicion, something told him that he had better do nothing of the sort, that it would be wiser to advance no farther along the path on which he had so foolishly set his feet. But he couldn't go back to Baluzac: that would be tantamount to admitting that he was beaten, and for nothing in the world would he have done that. He decided to lie down on a sort of low ledge that he could see between two of the buttresses of the Cathedral, and to wait for morning. The alley was so narrow that this meant he would be as good as directly under the windows of the hotel. When his mother came out, he would give her a hug and say nothing at all. She would be so surprised that it would not occur to her to question him. The fact that he had ridden all that distance through the darkness, that, worn out and hungry though he was, he had kept his vigil there just in order to be able to give her one more kiss, would prove how much he loved her. Within these walls she was sleeping now, doubtless on the first floor, behind those unfastened shutters— she always kept her bedroom windows open.

By this time the moon had disappeared behind the apse of the Cathedral, but its diffused light still cast a pallor on the sky, so that only an occasional twinkling star was visible. Jean was cold, and the stones hurt him. He lay down on the grass, but some nettles that he had not noticed stung him, and he got up again with an exclamation of pain. A dog that had been keeping late hours was wakened by the sound and barked, but soon left off again. The hour of cockcrow was still far off. Jean began to think of Michèle, and his thoughts were chaste, no matter what his life

may have been. In imagination he held her in his arms, though
seeking no other pleasure in the contact than that of finding peace
in the nearness of a faithful heart. And all the time, close to him,
on the other side of the road, behind the half-closed shutters . . .

Later, he was to know everything about his mother. All this
man's affairs were public property, all were marked by the same
horrible character. There are many novels that bear, or might
bear, the title: *A Woman's Heart;* more than one professional psychologist has plumbed the secrets of the feminine mind. . . . The
man who was sharing to-night the Comtesse de Mirbel's bed at
the Hotel Garbet lived for no other object than to reduce this
mystery to its true and rather squalid proportions. His victims
knew precisely what they might expect of him. Those whom he
had possessed all bore about with them the same indelible sign—
the sign of a lust that could know no satisfaction. They became
moral wanderers on the face of the earth, creatures wholly detached from all human responsibility, obsessed by the experiences
they had shared with him. "You don't know yourself", he would
whisper to each in turn; "you are ignorant of your potentialities
and limitations: you have no idea what perspectives lie before
you. . . ." Though he might leave them later, they still retained
from their contact with him the rudiments of that dangerous science of bodily pleasure which is more difficult to learn than the
virtuous think, since beings who are genuinely perverse are almost
as rare in this world as saints. One does not often meet a saint
by the roadside, but neither does one often come across anyone
capable of dragging from one's vitals that particular kind of groan,
that cry expressing horror no less than delight, which becomes
sharper as time lays its hand upon a body already threatened by
decay, already undermined as much by desire as by age, by the
passage of the years, and by passions that can no longer be assuaged. No one has ever written of the torment that old age
brings to women of a certain type. In it they taste of Hell before
death touches them.

Jean slept for a considerable while, his head resting against the
corner made by the wall and the buttress. The discomfort of his
cramped position woke him, or maybe it was the cold, or perhaps
the sound of a man's voice speaking at the window above.

"Come and look. I don't know whether it's the moon or the
dawn that makes the sky so pale."

He was speaking to someone in the room behind him, whom

Jean could not see. He was standing a little back from the window, with his face turned sideways to it. He wore a dressing-gown of dark-coloured silk.

"Put something on," he added; "the night is chilly."

He leaned his elbows on the bar of the window, and made room beside him for the woman. But he occupied most of the opening, and the white, light figure could barely squeeze between the wall and his powerful torso.

"What a wonderful effect of loneliness!—and how still it is! . . . No, darling, I'm not cold."

"But you must be:throw my overcoat round your shoulders."

She disappeared and came back wearing a man's ulster. It made her body look larger and her head very small. The two of them remained there for a long time without speaking.

"How unimportant it makes one feel," said the man. "Do you think that the people now asleep in all these houses have ever seen one of my plays?—that they so much as know my name?"

"They've probably read them in *l'Illustration*."

"That's true," he said more cheerfully; "the Supplement to *l'Illustration* goes everywhere. They must have seen it, if only at the hairdresser's. . . . What a stage-set this square would make, eh? But the open air's not really my line. The stuff I write needs four walls."

She made her answer in a low voice, choking back a little laugh. He, too, laughed, and added:

"With one of the four walls cut away. That's what a play ought to be, the masterpiece of which I dream. . . ."

"And with no dialogue: isn't that what you're thinking?"

They whispered. Jean could hear nothing but the throbbing of the blood in his own ears.

One o'clock sounded.

"No, no . . . really, we must get some sleep."

Once again there was the sound of a choked-back laugh. The woman leaned her head against the shoulder at her side. Jean looked at the gable that crowned the front of the building. The door of the stable-yard must be very old. A horse-shoe was nailed to one of its sides. He read: Hotel Garbet. Weddings and Banquets Catered For. He compared in his imagination the man standing at the window, every note of whose voice he recognized, with the middle-aged person with the dyed hair combed across a bald, white pate, whom the Mirandieuzes knew as Raoul.

The comfort that a child seeks instinctively deep down within
itself when threatened by some terrible pain, he now expressed
out loud. "It's comic!" he said in mocking tones; "it really is . . .
just too comic!" And then: "All right, my fine lady!" He heard the
faint sound made by the window being closed. "Oh, well, I suppose it amuses you, and it doesn't do anyone any harm. . . ." And
suddenly he was seized with panic at the idea that he might be
discovered, might have to listen to her explanations. How awful!
He had a sudden vision of his mother's face, could see her look
of shame, could hear her stammered words. . . . He jumped on
to his bicycle, crossed the square, unconscious at first of his fatigue,
so happy was he at the idea of increasing the distance between
himself and that room at Balauze. But at the first hill his legs felt
weak. He dismounted, dragged his bicycle to a near-by mill,
dropped into some hay, and lost consciousness.

How hot it was in the hay! He felt as though he were on fire in
spite of the cold dawn wind. His head ached. That must be a lark
singing there above him in the mist. Close by his ear a hen and
her brood were scratching the earth and clucking. He tried to get
up. He was shivering. "I'm feverish", he told himself. He took his
bicycle and tried to resume his journey. About a hundred yards
farther on, at the crossing where a road led off to Uzeste, a pine-
branch over a door announced an ale-house. With great difficulty
he reached it and ordered some hot coffee. An old woman looked
at him curiously, muttering something in the local dialect. The sun
was hot upon the seat beside the door onto which he dropped.
What if the motor-car suddenly appeared? But no, they would get
up late. They had the whole day before them, the dirty beasts! . . .
Because they *were* dirty beasts . . . not because they were lovers,
but because they were so horribly mincing and affected. . . . Well,
that was the last time he'd make a fool of himself . . . for anyone.
Everyone slept with everyone else: that was what life was. With
whom did Uncle sleep? and Monsieur Rausch? and Monsieur
Calou? . . . It'd be fun to see the old Curé on the job. He'd ask
them, all of them . . . that is, if he didn't die before he got the
chance.

He moistened his lips with the coffee, swallowed a few mouthfuls, and then turned round and was sick. He leaned his head
against the wall and closed his eyes. He no longer had sufficient
energy even to brush the flies away from his burning face. A

bicycle passed and slowed down. He heard an exclamation, and
then the sound of his own name repeated several times. The huge,
anxious face of Monsieur Calou was close to his own. If he made
an effort perhaps he would be able to understand and answer. But
the Curé was there, so why struggle any more? why not just let
himself go? He felt himself lifted like a little child, put into a bed
in a dark room that smelled of manure. Monsieur Calou wrapped
him in his old black cloak, after which he had a long argument
with the landlord, who didn't want to rent him his cart because it
was market-day at Balauze. "I don't care how much you charge",
said Monsieur Calou in an impatient voice. At last came the clip-
clop of a horse on the cobbles of the yard. Some straw had been
laid in the cart. Jean was asleep when the Curé lifted him, and his
head bumped against the old man's shoulder. The priest laid him
in the straw and covered him with his cloak. He took off the
knitted jersey that he had put on under his soutane in the chill
of the dawn, and rolled it up under the boy's head.

The attack of pleurisy was serious. For a fortnight Jean was in
danger. The Papal Zouave spent forty-eight hours at the presbytery and agreed with Monsieur Calou that it would be better not
to upset the Countess; she was merely told that the boy had a bad
attack of bronchitis, and she didn't worry. Mountain treatment
was not then in vogue, and was only very rarely prescribed. The
doctor summoned from Bordeaux said that the smell of pines was
the best possible thing in such cases, and advised the Colonel to
accept Monsieur Calou's offer. The Curé had undertaken to coach
the boy for his examination, and to get him through in two years
without any danger of overworking him. But what ultimately
decided the Papal Zouave was his dislike of the idea of sending
his nephew back to a school that had recently been dishonoured
by "the scandal of Monsieur Puybaraud's marriage".

The evening on which it was decided to leave Jean at Baluzac,
the Curé wished ardently that God was still incarnate, so that he
might have kissed His hands and embraced His feet in token of
gratitude. Jean maintained a hostile silence, and never opened
his mouth except to ask imperiously for what he wanted. Monsieur
Calou knew nothing about what had happened at Balauze, but he
could see that the boy had suffered a terrible shock. How the
wound had been inflicted and with what weapon he would learn
later. Or perhaps he wouldn't. It did not matter. What mattered
was to prevent the infection from spreading. At dusk he sat by the

dozing boy and asked him whether he didn't dread a winter at Baluzac. Jean replied that anything was better than Monsieur Rausch, but that he was sorry he couldn't "bash his face in", as he had meant to do.

The Curé pretended to think he was joking. "Just you wait till you see what a lovely blaze I get going when we're working and reading in the evenings. We'll take notes and drink walnut juice, while the west wind roars in the pines and flings rain against the shutters. . . ."

In a voice quite unlike his own, Jean said that "there wouldn't be much love knocking around".

Monsieur Calou replied very gently that what was important was to love in one's heart.

"You don't say so!" (The voice was still the voice of another, of a stranger.)

Without any sign of dismay, the Curé returned the rosary to the pocket of his soutane, took out his pipe, and set to sniffing it (he wouldn't let himself smoke in Jean's room).

"I'm an old man", he said, "and I've found my way into port."

"Oh, of course: God and all that. You needn't tell me."

The priest got up and laid his hand on Jean's forehead. "Yes, God first, last, and all the time, naturally."

It was as though he had a son of his own, a naughty son, or rather, a son who would have liked to be naughty, but *his* for all that.

Jean threw himself back on his pillow and exclaimed: "Don't go getting ideas. If you want to know, I loathe and detest everything you stand for!"

"You'll make your fever worse", said the Curé.

How terribly the poor boy was suffering! "He takes it out on me because I happen to be at hand and there's no one else he can snap at." The abbé sat plunged in thought—his elbows on his knees, deliberately keeping his face in shadow because Jean, from the depths of his pillows, was trying to see the effect of his outburst. But even if the lamp had been shining full on it, the sick boy would have seen nothing, so empty of expression was it. Suddenly he felt ashamed of what he had said.

"I wasn't talking against *you*", he muttered.

Monsieur Calou shrugged his shoulders. "Much better to get it off your chest. . . . Very soon, you know, you'll be able to have visitors."

"I don't know anyone."

"What about the Pians?"

"They haven't come near me: they haven't even written."

"They've sent over every day for news."

"But they haven't come," Jean said again, and turned his face to
the wall.

One of our farmers who lived at Baluzac and brought us milk
every morning did, in fact, bring us news of Jean. But the Curé
was surprised that we hadn't given any more definite sign of interest. He was pretty sure that Mirbel felt hurt by this neglect,
though he could not know how deeply wounded he had been by
our seeming indifference. The Curé of Baluzac, however, firmly
convinced that "that Brigitte woman" was behind it all, made up
his mind to go over to Larjuzon as soon as his patient was a little
better, and have it out with her.

❦ *IX* ❦

At Larjuzon the postman always arrived while the family was
gathered round the breakfast-table. My stepmother, whether she
had come back from Mass or had only just emerged from her
room, was, even at this early hour, invariably dressed and buttoned up to the neck with formal precision. On the morning when
I read out the letter from Monsieur Calou announcing Mirbel's
illness she was in one of her bad moods. Her face was set and
hard, and she was frowning. At eleven o'clock she was due to take
a confirmation class in its catechism, and, to judge by the way she
spoke of the children, they were without exception stupid, incapable of learning anything, and interested only in pinching one
another's behinds. In addition to which they were dirty, given to
leaving tracks on the floor, and they smelled. As for the least sign
of gratitude—well, one might wear oneself to the bone for them
and not get so much as a word of thanks. If their parents only got
the chance, they would think nothing of looting the house and
murdering everyone in it.

We knew that on these catechism days the least shock was
enough to set a spark to that inflammable temperament with
which Heaven had seen fit to endow Madame Brigitte.

"We must go over to Baluzac at once!" cried Michèle, as soon as I had come to the end of the letter; "and I'm not dressed yet."

My stepmother's voice broke in on a high note: "Am I to understand that you are proposing to go over to Baluzac this morning?"

"Of course I am!"

"I forbid it!"

"Why shouldn't I go this morning?"

"You'll go neither this morning nor this afternoon!" snapped Madame Brigitte, white with anger.

We looked at one another dumbfounded. Strained though her relations with my sister were, she had always, till now, avoided an open breach.

"What's the matter with you?" replied Michèle, stung to insolence. "There's no reason why I should wait until to-morrow."

"Nor to-morrow either. You're never going to Baluzac again!" said my stepmother. "And don't look as though you'd no idea what I mean, you little hypocrite!"

My father glanced up nervously from his newspaper. "Brigitte, dear, what are you in such a state about?"

"I ought to have asserted myself sooner." Her voice had become solemn.

Michèle asked what it was she was being accused of.

"I am accusing you of nothing. I never believe evil of anyone until I see it with my own eyes."

My father got up. He was wearing an old brown dressing-gown. A few tufts of gray hair showed through the unbuttoned collar of his shirt. "All the same, you seem . . ." he began.

She fixed upon her husband a look of angelic patience. "It hurts me to hurt you: but it is necessary that you should know the truth. I am told that she is in the habit of meeting young Mirbel behind Du Buch's mill."

Michèle replied in a firm voice that it was perfectly true that she did sometimes meet Jean. What harm was there in that?

"Don't look so innocent: it ill becomes you. You have been seen."

"*What* has been seen? There was nothing *to* see."

My father drew her tenderly to him. "Of course there is no harm in your meeting young Mirbel at Monsieur Du Buch's mill. But though you are still only a child, you look older, and

the people of this town, especially the women, are a lot of poisonous snakes."

Brigitte cut him short. "Poisonous snakes, indeed! Don't you
go taking Michèle's part against me! I am interfering now, before
it is too late, simply and solely in order to protect her from idle
gossip—though I am prepared to admit that it may have no
foundation. Young Mirbel is a bad lot. May God forgive me for
ever having had him in the house!" In a lower voice she added:
"The important question is, how far has it gone?"

She had become very gentle all of a sudden. My father took
hold of her by the wrist. "Come on now, out with it! What *is* all
this nonsense?"

"It's . . . let me go!" she exclaimed. "You seem to forget who
I am! . . . If you want the truth you shall have it."

She was furious, and moved back to the other side of the table
where, entrenched behind the china and the silver, she stood
with her hands on the back of a chair. Her eyes were closed,
and, under cover of their veined lids, she seemed to be concentrat-
ing her thoughts.

"Michèle is a young girl who is in love with a young man.
There you have it in a nutshell."

In the silence which followed these words we none of us dared
to exchange a glance. Madame Brigitte, suddenly sobered, fixed
her eyes with a look of pain on father and daughter.

Octave Pian had risen. He looked very tall, and more as I remembered him before Mamma's death. He had been wounded
in his tenderest feelings—the affection of a father for his daughter,
in which respect plays a large part, as well as a modesty so sensitive that the least affront to it is unforgivable. He had been
jerked out of his normal mood of black gloom, and the memory
of his dead wife had for the moment been driven from his
mind by the presence of that other woman who was so terribly
real, so horribly alive.

"A child who is not yet fifteen? How ridiculous to talk like
that! You ought to be ashamed of yourself!"

"Ashamed of what? I am not accusing her of anything", replied
my stepmother, with an obvious effort at self-control. "I want to
believe that she is innocent—or comparatively so: I said it before,
and I say it again." But girl-mothers of fourteen and fifteen *had*
been known. It was only necessary to visit the poor to realize
that! . . .

I can still hear the sound of her voice as she pronounced the words "girl-mothers". Never had two words contained such a concentrated accent of disgust. In a low voice I asked Michèle what girl-mothers were. She said nothing; perhaps she did not know. With her eyes fixed on her father she said: "You don't believe her, do you?"

"Of course I don't, my dear, dear child!" and he drew her to him again.

"Do you wish me to produce her accusers?" asked my stepmother; "the people who say that they saw her with their own eyes?"

"Yes, produce them!" cried the girl.

"I can make a pretty shrewd guess: it's the Vignottes," said my father, suddenly quite calm. "We all know what the Vignottes are like! . . . So you're ready to swallow the tittle-tattle of a pair like that, are you?"

"Who says that I'm *ready* to do anything of the sort? I repeat that I am accusing no one. I am performing a painful duty. I am reporting something that was told me—no more. It is your duty to satisfy yourself whether it is true. *My* task finishes where yours begins."

Brigitte Pian folded her arms. She stood there, impartial, invulnerable, justified in the sight of God and all His angels.

"And what, may I ask, do the Vignottes say that Michèle was doing?"

"You must ask them that yourself. You can hardly expect me to soil my lips. . . . It is bad enough to have to listen to such things. But if it is absolutely necessary, if you insist on my being present, I will find the needful courage in that love which I have vowed to all of you, and especially to *you*, Michèle. . . . Oh, you can laugh if you like! But I have never loved you so fondly as at this moment."

A few tears started to her eyes. She was careful to wipe them away only when she was sure that we were looking.

My father, without the slightest show of heat, told me to go and fetch the Vignottes.

Vignotte came in holding his beret in his hand. His right eye, which had received a charge of slugs out shooting, was closed. The other had a sort of look of concentrated stupidity. Round his mouth with its few stumps of decayed teeth was a growth of

untrimmed beard. He was bandy-legged. He had left his wooden
clogs in the hall, and padded through the half-open door, his
feet encased in list slippers that flapped as he walked. No one had
heard him enter. We turned our heads, and there he was, obsequious, grinning, stinking of sweat and garlic.

He realized what was in the wind as soon as he had crossed
the threshold. My father ordered me out of the room, and told
Michèle, very gently, to go upstairs and wait until she was summoned. I went to the drawing-room, but stayed near the door
in a state of considerable excitement. My chief sensation, I remember, was one of rather shamefaced hope. Michèle and Jean
were going to be separated. My function would be to act as the
link between them. They would be able to communicate only
when I was willing, and under *my* supervision. I had no very
clear idea of all this: I just felt it, sensed it with extreme vivid-
ness. I had run like a mad creature to find Vignotte, and had
hurried back with him. Though haste was no part of that prudent man's make-up, I had made him follow me at once without
giving him time even to put on his "overcoat", as he called his
jacket. Now I could hear him through the door.

"I never said no such thing. . . . I sees what I sees. . . . Not but
what I was in that there hut all right. . . . I can't tell how long
they'd been there not saying a thing . . . and what was they
doin', all silent-like? That's what I asks meself. . . . Didn't
have to use my eyes to know as they was there. . . . S'pose they
was just *lookin'*. . . . Well, I only hopes they was. . . . Though
it don't matter to me."

My father asked some questions which I could not properly
hear. He did not raise his voice, but spoke in his normal slow
drawl. Every now and then he used some word of local dialect,
stressing it in an odd sort of way. Those parts of his talk I understood better than the rest. He had become once more the master
who has no need to shout, who can make himself feared by the
turn of an inflection. He interrupted my stepmother, cutting her
short in the middle of a sentence.

"Let me finish what I have to say to Vignotte."

It was not an argument, not even a discussion, but a sum-
ming-up. When my father had finished speaking, I heard no
more save the trumpeting sound made by Vignotte when he blew
his nose. Then my stepmother opened the door, and I had
barely time to get out of the way. She never so much as glanced

at me. With her garden hat stuck well at the back of her head, her hands concealed in white mittens, she reached the hall, took a parasol and went down the front steps, looking not so much angry as plunged in thought. I learned shortly afterwards from my sister that our father had just shown some of the firmness which had marked him in the old days, but which we children had quite forgotten.

He had apparently given in to his wife to the extent of forbidding Michèle, not only to go to Baluzac, but even to exchange letters with Jean. I was staggered to learn that this ruling was to apply to me as well. As a safeguard against its possible violation, our father confiscated our bicycles for the time being. Sister Scholastique, the Superior of the Free School, who was under considerable obligation to my parents, was to be asked to superintend Michèle's studies during the holidays, when she would have a certain amount of time at her disposal. Actually, my father did not suspect his young daughter, and told her as much, kissing her tenderly. But he knew how merciless the people round Larjuzon could be, and wished to protect her against possible gossip. The whole affair, therefore, would have represented a victory for Madame Brigitte, had it not been for the fact that my father had told the Vignottes that they had better look out for another place. This decision struck directly at their patroness. She argued, but in vain, that her husband was running considerable risk by making enemies of such people, armed as they were. But my father assured her that he had a hold over the Vignottes and could find ways of stopping their mouths.

This scandal, then, which was destined to have serious consequences for so many of us, did produce one happy result at least, though it was unfortunately of short duration. It roused our father from the state of apathy in which he had been living for the past ten years. Brigitte suddenly saw herself opposed by an adversary with whom she had long ceased to reckon. Her husband's love for Michèle derived from the passion he had felt for the first Madame Pian. The real struggle was being fought over a dead woman's body. This, no doubt, my stepmother knew perfectly well—which explains her behaviour during the days that followed.

In every circumstance of her life Brigitte Pian was sincerely anxious to do good. Or this, at least, was what she believed. That fact must never for a moment be forgotten by readers of this

chronicle. I could have painted quite a different portrait of her
from the one on which so pitiless a light is shed in these pages.
I was made too clearly aware of her victims' sufferings to be altogether fair to her. But I feel that even when recounting what
may seem to be some of her blackest acts, I ought not to yield
to the too easy temptation of showing only one side of her forbidding character.

It is important to remember that when, before her marriage,
Brigitte Pian used to spend the summer months at Larjuzon, she
found herself involved in one of those marital dramas which may
well go on, quite silently, for years without any violent arguments
or outbursts of nagging, until one or other of the actors is safely
dead. My father had always before his eyes the vision of his
dearly loved wife Marthe. He had known that she was suffering
because of someone else, had realized that he could do nothing
to help, and had seen that the spectacle of his own pain merely
had the effect of making her own sense of remorse the more acute.
He was a simple man, not much given to introspection, and he
had found comfort in Brigitte's clear-sighted analysis of the situation. A close tie had grown up between them. But when the
circumstances in which it had had its origins no longer existed,
it inevitably grew slack. Brigitte always claimed that she had
saved him from suicide. However that may be, it cannot be denied that when things were at their worst he did relieve his feelings by confiding in an affectionate companion who had never
been far from him, had even guided his footsteps during the most
terrible moments of his ordeal. In her, too, he had found the
only means he had of keeping in touch with his wife, whose
cousin and childhood friend she was.

But when Brigitte Pian became the second Madame Pian, she
quite honestly felt it to be her duty to finish the good work she
had begun by delivering her husband from the obsessive influence
of the dead—all the more so, since he had consented to this second
marriage only in the hope that some such cure might result from
it. Possibly, at some later date, her actions were dictated by a
sense of personal grievance, by feelings of jealousy which she
would not admit even to herself. But at first she had a perfect
right to believe in a mission to which no less a person than her
husband had called her. When, after a few months, she realized
that the influence of Marthe was still in the ascendant, that my
father still believed that her virtue, in spite of all temptations

forced upon her by an overwhelming passion, had never, never
yielded, that the dead woman was still in his eyes a heroine
who might have died for love but would never have been false
to her plighted word, Brigitte thought it incumbent on her to
make sure that this halo of sanctity had been truly merited. If
only she could confront her husband with definite proof that the
first Madame Pian had been guilty of adultery, that she had assumed the appearance of virtue only after her lover had abandoned her, and had finally taken her own life in an access
of despair, then, and then only, she thought, would he be freed
from the shameful spell. For a long while before any real evidence came her way, she had felt quite sure, as a result of
what she had heard, that Marthe had in fact been guilty. Maybe
her ardent desire to step into her shoes was in some sort influenced by her wish to discover this evidence. She knew that it
would be easier to find, once she was free to come and go as she
chose through all the rooms of the house, and to rummage in desks
and drawers unseen by others.

This she did with a pleasure that one finds it difficult to credit.
A very few weeks after her marriage she laid hands on a document that so far exceeded her wildest hopes that she thought it
better, for the time being, to say nothing about it. This reluctance
to make use of so tremendous a weapon shows that Brigitte was
capable of pity. So long as any hope remained of effecting her
husband's cure without opening his eyes, she resisted the temptation of telling what she knew.

Once the Vignottes had gone, it did seem as though he might
perhaps be cured. Defeated on that issue, Brigitte got full satisfaction on every other. She could not but applaud a decision
that my father made a few days later. From the beginning of
the following term, Michèle was to go as a boarder to the Ladies
of the Sacred Heart, whose school she had hitherto been attending as a day-student. Octave Pian did not look on this as a punishment, but only as the best way of insuring that his young
daughter would be removed from the influence of her formidable
stepmother.

Madame Brigitte ought now to have declared herself satisfied.
But she was far from feeling so. In defending his daughter, the
father had, in reality, been defending his dead wife. His sudden return to the world of action had put the coping-stone, not
on Brigitte's victory, but on Marthe's: had proved that he was still

possessed, mind and soul, by the image of the dead woman. This, I have very little doubt, was the truth which my stepmother glimpsed in the dark recesses of her conscience, and it urged her to spring the mine that had been lying so long concealed, which, for so many months, she had refrained from detonating.

My sister and I were still, however, very closely watched. Unfortunately for us, the local postmistress was completely under Madame Brigitte's thumb, and must have received very precise instructions on the subject of our letters. Everything at Larjuzon intended for the post had to be put in the study each evening, to be collected next morning by the postman. Not an envelope could leave the house without our stepmother's knowing all about it.

Michèle, therefore, had to rely on me for getting messages to Jean. She had no wish to break the promise made to our father that she would not write to him, but she badly wanted to send him a little gold locket made in the shape of a heart, which she wore on her breast. It contained a piece of our mother's hair. I was shocked that she should give away such a relic to Mirbel, and showed no very great enthusiasm about making on foot a journey that would be all the longer and more tiring since I should have to go a roundabout way if I was to avoid being seen in the town and promptly denounced. Besides, so prolonged an absence would have aroused the suspicions of Madame Brigitte, who was keeping a more than usually watchful eye on me, though without any appearance of ill-will. At times she would give me a hug, would stroke the hair back from my forehead, murmur, "My poor child!" and heave a deep sigh.

The more insistent Michèle became, the more clearly did I show my dislike of undertaking such an adventure. And so it came about that the last weeks of vacation were spoiled by a series of fruitless arguments. I was deprived of the fun of long days spent with my sister, free of any third person to spoil our intimacy. I had so looked forward to them. As for Mirbel, I should see him again, I thought, when term began, for I did not then know that he was to spend the rest of the year at Baluzac. The fate awaiting me—the worst I could possibly have imagined—remained hidden. At school it was my pleasure to feel that I had to share Mirbel with nobody else. To be sure, it was as Michèle's brother that I should find favour in his eyes. But at least they would not be seeing each other, and would have no means of communicating, while I should always be at hand, the only one among all that tribe of boys whom he would deign to recognize.

One September day at about four o'clock, a priest riding a bicycle turned into the Avenue. Michèle cried: "The abbé Calou!" Brigitte Pian told us to go to our room, and, when Michèle began to protest, she was backed up firmly by our father. On this occasion, too, he stayed where he was, though as a rule, whenever a visitor was announced, he hid himself in the study. I am pretty sure that he wanted to make certain that his wife would say nothing about Michèle beyond what it had been agreed between them should be said. Since I was not present at the interview, I will here reproduce the notes that Monsieur Calou jotted down the same evening in his diary. I give them, succinct and dry, precisely as I found them.

An extraordinary woman—quite a miracle of perversity. In her eyes the appearance of evil is as important as evil itself—when it suits her purpose. A deep nature, but she reminds me of those aquariums in which the spectator can see the fish from every side. Each one of Madame Brigitte's most secret motives, the intention behind her every act, is plainly visible. If ever that gift of judgment and condemnation which she now exercises at the expense of others is turned against herself, she's in for a bad time!

Much shocked that I should plead the case of these young people, and should anticipate nothing but good for Jean from this first love affair. She pursed her lips at me. Obviously thinks me a second "Savoyard Vicar". I ventured to warn her against being overzealous in her desire to act as the mouthpiece of the Divine Will. It is a fault to which pious persons are only too prone. But how unwise of me to include the clergy in my criticism! It was simply asking her to hit back at me with a remark about my denying the rights of the Church to instruct its children! She's quite capable of denouncing me to the Archbishop—I can see her doing it! She's not so much concerned to find out what I think as to remember enough of what I say to incriminate me with the authorities. She would have no hesitation about ruining me if she thought it necessary to do so. I said as much, and though my attitude when I took my leave was respectful enough, hers was decidedly dry—not to say rude.

Just as I reached the door on the way out, Michèle emerged

*from behind the bushes. She was very flushed and wouldn't look
me in the face. When I got to the bottom of the steps, she said:
"Do you believe what they told you?"*

"No, Michèle, I don't."

*"I should like you to know that . . . if I were making my con-
fession to you . . . I should have nothing to say about Jean."*

She was crying. I stammered out—"God bless the two of you!"

*"Tell him that I can't see him or write to him, that I'm going to
be a boarder from the beginning of next term. I shall be closely
watched. Can't you imagine the instructions that will be given
about me? . . . But please tell Jean that I'll wait just as long as
is necessary. . . . You will, won't you?"*

*I tried to turn the whole thing into a joke. "That's an odd sort
of mission to give to an old priest, Michèle," I said.*

*"I don't care whether you're an old priest or not. Except for
me, you're the only person in the whole world who loves him."
She said this as though it were the most natural, the simplest,
the most obvious thing that could be imagined. There was nothing
I could say in reply. I had to turn my head away. Then she held
out a little parcel addressed to him.*

*"I swore not to write to him, but I didn't say anything about
not giving him a little remembrance. Tell him it's the most precious thing I have. I want him to keep it until we meet again.
Tell him . . ."*

*She made a sign to me to go, and jumped back into the bushes.
Sister Scholastique's coif appeared between the trees. . . .*

The abbé Calou found Jean just where he had left him, lying on
a chaise-longue under the west wall of the house. A book was
open on his knees, but he was not reading.

"Well, *you've* started a hornets' next at Larjuzon, my poor boy."

"Have you just come from Larjuzon?" Mirbel tried, though in
vain, to assume a detached and indifferent expression.

"Yes. That Brigitte woman is up to her old tricks again. Just
imagine, Michèle . . ."

At the Curé's first words Jean could contain himself no longer.

"She ought to have sent me an answer," he burst out. "When
one's in love, walls don't mean a thing. One takes any risk. . . ."

"She's only a little girl, Jean . . . though I've never met a
braver one."

Without looking at Monsieur Calou, the boy asked whether he had spoken to her.

"Yes, for a few minutes. I've remembered everything she asked me to tell you. She can't see you or write to you: from the beginning of next term she's going as a boarder to the school of the Sacred Heart. But she will wait—for years, if necessary."

He spoke like someone repeating a lesson learned by heart. In this way he gave the maximum weight to each word.

"Is that all?"

"No, she asked me to give you this . . . it is her most sacred possession, and she wants you to keep it until you see her again."

"What is it?"

The Curé did not know. He laid the little object on Jean's knees and went into the house. Through the half-open shutters he could see the boy holding the little golden heart at the end of its chain in the hollow of his hand. He raised it to his lips as though he would drink it down like a draught of water.

Monsieur Calou sat down at his desk, opened the manuscript of *Descartes and the Theory of Faith,* and read over the last paragraph he had written. But he could not concentrate, and went back to the window. Mirbel's face was hidden in his two hands. No doubt the locket lay there, imprisoned between them and his lips.

For the past two days Jean had been taking his midday and evening meal in the dining-room. About seven o'clock, once more shut away in his old black mood of silence, he sat down at table opposite the Curé. Monsieur Calou had taken to keeping a magazine or a newspaper beside him while he ate. It was obvious from the moment the soup was brought in that the boy was shooting covert glances at his host. If he still maintained silence, that was because he was shy and embarrassed and did not know how to start on what he wanted to say. Nor was the Curé wholly at ease. He was afraid that a clumsy word might ruin all. He therefore confined himself, as always, to keeping a watchful eye on Jean's rather capricious appetite. When, after the meal, they went out into the garden, he asked him what he would like to eat next day. Jean replied that there was nothing he had particularly set his heart on, but he spoke with rather less ill grace than usual. Suddenly he asked:

"Are you really bothered about my health?"

"My dear boy, what a question!"

Murmuring, "No, honestly, I mean it", in a child-like tone, Jean sat down in his chaise-longue and took the abbé's hand. The latter was still standing. Without looking at him, Jean said: "I've been pretty beastly to you . . . and then . . . you went and did a thing like that for me."

He started to cry, as a child cries, making no attempt to hide his tears.

The abbé Calou sat down beside him. He had not withdrawn his hand.

"You can't know what it means. . . . If Michèle had given me up, I should have killed myself. I suppose you don't believe that?"

"Yes, my boy, I do."

"You really believe me?"

How he longed to be reassured, to have his word believed!

"I knew from the very first that this was serious."

But when Jean murmured in a low voice—"Was I dreaming? Did I really see what I thought I saw at Balauze?"—the abbé interrupted him: "Don't tell me anything if it's going to hurt you too much."

"She lied to us. Do you realize that? It was all bunk about her sleeping at Vallandraut. . . . They had booked a room at Balauze, at the Garbet. . . ."

"It is the way of women to say one thing and do another . . . it's a well-known fact. . . ."

"She wasn't alone . . . there was a fellow with her. I saw them at the window of their room, in the middle of the night."

He had seen them, and his staring eyes could see them still.

Monsieur Calou took his head between his hands and shook it gently, as though to wake him.

"It's no use trying to force one's way into other people's lives, if they don't want one there: remember that, my boy. Never push open the door of another person's life, for it can be known only to God. Never turn your eyes upon that secret city, that place of damnation, which is the soul of another, unless you wish to be turned into a pillar of salt. . . ."

But Jean still went on, his gaze fixed on some invisible picture. He described what he could still see by the light of memory, what he would go on seeing until his dying day.

"He was almost an old man. . . . I recognized him—a fellow

from Paris who writes plays. . . . Dyed hair, a paunch . . . and
. . . and . . . that mouth. . . . Oh, it was horrible!"
"You must tell yourself that in her eyes he represents wit, genius, elegance. To love another person means to see a miracle of
beauty which is invisible to the rest of the world." A moment
later he added: "We must go in. It soon gets dark at this time
of year, and you haven't got enough on."
Mirbel followed him without protesting. The abbé held him by
the arm until they reached the library, where the boy was now
sleeping. Jean lay down on the bed. Monsieur Calou lit the lamp
and went over to his armchair.
"And did they", he asked, "see you?"
"No, I was standing against the wall of the church, hidden in
the shadow. I had gone before it was light. Then I slept in a
mill. If you hadn't searched for me I believe I should have died
like a sick dog. When I think of all you have done for me . . ."
"You could hardly expect me to sit here with my slippers on
waiting for you to come back, could you? You are in my charge,
and I am responsible for your welfare. Think of the trouble I
should have got into. . . ."
"That wasn't the reason, was it? Not the only reason?"
"Little idiot!"
"Because you do like me, don't you—just a bit?"
"As if there were no one else but an old curé to care for Jean
de Mirbel!"
"I don't believe it's possible: it can't be!"
"But look at that gold heart . . . where have you put it? Ah,
hung it round your neck, as Michèle used to hang it round hers.
Against your heart—that's the right place for it: like that, you can
always feel it. When things get bad you've only got to touch it."
"But she's such a little girl. She doesn't know me, anything
about me. She's so pure that she wouldn't understand me, no
matter how hard I tried to explain. Even you don't know some
of the things I've done . . ."
Monsieur Calou laid his hand on the boy's head. "You're not
one of the virtuous, I know. You're not that kind. You are one of
those whom Christ came into the world to save. Michèle loves
you for what you are, just as God loves you because you are as
He made you."
"Mamma doesn't love me."

"Passion blinds her to the love she has for you in her heart . . .
but it exists all the same."

"I hate her!" This he said in the rather forced and artificial voice
that he sometimes affected. "You think I don't mean it? But it's
true: I hate her!"

"Of course you do, as we all of us *can* hate those we love. Our
Lord told us to love our enemies. It is often easier to do that
than not to hate those we love."

"Yes," said Jean, "because they can hurt us so frightfully."

He leaned his head against the Curé's shoulder, and went on in
a low voice: "If only you knew how terribly it hurt, and still
does! It's as though I were touching an open sore. It hurts so
much that I want to shriek—to die!"

"My poor child—we must forgive women a great deal. I can't
yet explain to you why. Perhaps you will understand later: I think
you will, because you have it in you to hurt them too. Even those
among them who seem to have everything they want deserve
our pity . . . not a corrupt and furtive pity, but the pity of Christ,
the pity of a man and of a God who knows well from what imperfect clay He has made His creatures. But this is not the time
to speak of such things."

"I'm no longer a child. You must realize that."

"I do realize it: you are a man. You have reached the age at
which suffering begins."

"Ah, *you* can understand!"

They went on talking for a long time, the priest and the boy,
even after Jean had gone to bed. And when weariness lay
heavy on his eyes, he asked Monsieur Calou to say his prayers
beside him there, and not to leave the room until he was asleep.

❦ X ❦

THE crowing of a cock woke me. Was it dawn already? I struck
a match: it was not yet five. I decided to wait a bit. Though
Michèle had never succeeded in making me promise to take that
journey to Baluzac, I had made up my mind to go this morning
on my own account. The evening before, after Monsieur Calou
had gone, I had been told by my stepmother that Mirbel would

not be going back to school for the rest of that year. Had she
seen me tremble? Had she realized what a mortal blow she was
striking at the pale little boy who pretended so hard not to mind?
She added that it would make a great difference to her own plans,
that she and my father had agreed to look for another school,
so that I might be removed from the influence of so black a
sheep. Now, however, that would not be necessary. I should
find Monsieur Puybaraud gone, but about that, too, she was glad.
I was quite sensitive enough as it was, and Monsieur Puybaraud
had been altogether the wrong sort of master for me—a dangerous man.

Jean at Baluzac, Michèle at boarding-school . . . what on earth
would become of me? On that day I looked for the first time
straight in the face of loneliness. He is an old enemy now. We
have learned to rub along together, to know each other. Loneliness has struck me every imaginable blow. There is no spot in me
left to strike. It has set me many traps, and I have fallen into
every one. But it torments me no longer. We sit now, one on
either side of the fire on winter evenings, when the fall of a
fir-cone and the sobbing of the night wind mean as much to me
as the sound of a human voice.

Whatever happened I must see Jean again for the last time. . . .
We must arrange to write. . . . It would be easy for me, but
how should I address my letters? How does one have letters delivered *post restante*? I must see him once more, must be convinced that I still existed for him, that Michèle had not entirely
taken my place.

The roses on my curtains grew faintly pink: the day was breaking. I dressed, holding my breath. Not a creak did I make on
the floor. A single wall stood between me and the huge room
in which the two mahogany beds of Monsieur and Madame Pian
stood as far as possible from each other.

I opened my door without a sound. The stairs, it is true,
creaked a little, but Brigitte was no light sleeper. I would go out
by the kitchen door so as to make sure of not being heard. The
key was hanging in the scullery.

"Where are you off to so early?"

I choked back a cry. There she stood, at the turn of the stairs,
erect in the dawn light. She was wearing an amethyst-colored
dressing-gown. A great coil of hair, like a fat snake with a red
ribbon round its snout, fell to her waist.

"Where are you off to? Tell me now!"

It did not occur to me to lie. She knew everything before I so much as opened my mouth. Besides, despair had sapped my courage. In a panic of escape I flung myself into its waiting arms. I sought safety in that very over-sensitiveness which had only to show its face to terrify any aggressor, however formidable, and compel him to help rather than to punish me. I screamed, I choked: I went further than I intended, and could not stop. Brigitte lifted me in her strong arms and took me to her room, where my father, suddenly wakened, sat up in bed thinking that he was in the throes of a nightmare.

"Quiet, quiet . . . I'm not going to eat you. Drink a little water. It's flavoured with orange."

She had laid me on her own bed.

"It was because I was never going to see him again," I stammered. "I wanted to say good-bye to him."

"It's that Mirbel boy all the trouble's about," said Brigitte to Octave. "See what a state he's in. I sometimes wonder whether it is not too late to do anything about these fits of his. He's so morbidly sensitive." And then, in a lower voice: "Poor child!— what an inheritance!"

"What do you mean, talking about 'inheritance' with him here?" asked my father in the same low tone. "What are you hinting at?"

"Hinting is not one of my failings."

"Oh, isn't it?" He chuckled, shook his head, and said: "Oh, that's rich!"

I had never seen him looking so pale. He was sitting on the edge of his bed. His legs, all covered with black hair, did not reach the floor. Large swollen blue veins showed in his feet with their malformed toes. A mat of gray hair sprouted from his open nightshirt. His thighs were terribly thin, almost emaciated. Brigitte, standing there in her ecclesiastical-looking robe, her hair drawn forward on her prominent forehead, with the long, fat, shining tress hanging down, brooded over him with an eye that was at once hostile and watchful.

My father got up, took me in his arms and carried me back to my own bed. I sobbed into his nightshirt. He tucked me in. A misty sunlight entered through the fleur-de-lis openings cut in the shutters. I can still hear the tone of his voice as he said: "Wipe your eyes, you little fool; blow your nose and go to sleep."

While he was saying this he brushed the hair away from my eyes with his hand, and stared—stared as though he had never seen me before.

I ought never to have known what I am now going to relate—with overwhelming shame and embarrassment, but it must be done. Indeed, I did not learn it until immediately after the First World War, when I became reconciled with my uncle Moulis, one of my mother's brothers from whom I had been separated all my life as the result of a family quarrel into which I need not enter here. He had been devoted to his sister Marthe, and wanted to get to know me before he died. He was an architect, like my grandfather, practising in the city, a Bohemian, artistic sort of man, of the kind that Brigitte Pian loathed. She always maintained that he was responsible for the influences that had surrounded my mother's early life and had led to her undoing. This cynical old bachelor, speaking more than twenty years after the events he was describing, told me about the circumstances that had attended my birth. He could not actually prove that I was not Octave Pian's son, but he thought it more likely that I owed my existence to a first cousin of my mother's, Alfred Moulis—"a regular Adonis", said my uncle. I could see no trace of charm in the photograph he showed me, and the idea that I may be the son of that curly-headed and rather sheepish-looking person gives me no sort of pleasure. From childhood he had adored his cousin, and she responded without reserve. I will not expatiate on this odious subject. I intend to say only what is absolutely necessary to an understanding of the document that my stepmother discovered very soon after her marriage.

According to my uncle Moulis, it was a sort of memorandum written in my mother's hand: a series of calculations and comparisons of dates, from which it seemed clear that, if Octave was really my father, I must have been born two months prematurely. It is true that at the time of my birth I was considerably under normal weight, that I had to be wrapped in cotton-wool, and that I was reared only with the greatest difficulty. But what had been the purpose of this paper? There seems little doubt that it formed part of a letter. That, at least, was what my uncle thought, though he could not be sure.

But Octave Pian had a reason, which he thought was known only to himself, for doubting whether I could really be his son, and to this the document in question lent strong support. Uncle Moulis had had the facts from his sister. . . . It is an extremely delicate subject, and I can broach it only in the most roundabout manner. What I gathered was that Octave belonged to that by no means rare species of men who, when desperately in love, are afflicted with impotence. Such a state of affairs must lead to atrocious suffering, especially when the love is not mutual, and the ridiculous despair of one partner is observed by the other with a cold and mocking eye.

I hope that the reader will realize how very repugnant it is to me to put all this down in words. But it does, at least, prove that what I am relating is true and in no wise invented. Subjects of this kind are as a rule instinctively avoided by the professional novelist, because he knows that most people find them repellent. But those who turn their backs on fiction, and set out to follow up the destinies of persons with whom they have actually been connected, are for ever coming on the traces of these miseries and aberrations of the flesh. And even worse than the aberrations are the inadequacies. For those are just the things that we do not wish to hear about, because so many of us may have been to some extent their victims. Renan once said that the truth may well be depressing. He was thinking in terms of metaphysics. On the level of human affairs it may be not only depressing but ridiculous and embarrassing—so much so that decency forbids us to put it into words. Hence the silence in which such things are usually shrouded. Only when they result in a divorce or a suit for annulment at Rome does the glaring light of publicity beat upon them.

When, in October, I went back to the city with my stepmother, Octave Pian stayed on at Larjuzon. The separation of husband and wife had now become an accomplished fact, even though they had never discussed it in so many words. Everything happened quite naturally. My father had not yet seen the revealing document (though it had been left behind, as by accident, in a drawer of his room where he must sooner or later come upon it), but he had been sufficiently prepared and worked upon by Brigitte to see me go without any real feelings of regret. He preferred winter solitude in the depths of the country to life with a woman whom he hated and a son the very sight of whom opened old wounds. My last memory of him is of a man who had sunk back into the apathetic stupor from which he had roused himself for a brief spell in order to take up the cudgels on Michèle's behalf. It must have been about this time that he started drinking again, but it was only after our departure that the habit grew upon him.

Michèle was now a boarder at the Sacred Heart, and I was left alone with my stepmother. The two years that elapsed before I took my final examination were bleak and dreary, but I suffered a good deal less than I thought I should. Work came easily to me, and Brigitte had little cause to anticipate trouble from the silent schoolboy who spent his evenings studying his lessons and doing his themes without any need of supervision. During the first year my father came into town once every month on Michèle's free day, and took both of us to lunch at a restaurant. I can still remember vividly the peculiar pleasure it gave me to choose my favourite dish from the menu—oysters, jugged hare, or duck hash. The certain knowledge that Michèle and Jean were separated, probably for ever, had the effect of diminishing not only my jealousy, but also my affection, though spasms of both would occasionally recur for a few brief moments. I have never been able fully to realize that I love anybody unless the emotion is accompanied by some degree of suffering.

Here, I think, I ought to recall two incidents which proved to me, once and for all, that my friendship for Mirbel was a thing of the past. One evening during that first winter, when I got back from school, my stepmother said, without raising her eyes from her book: "There's a letter for you." I was not taken in by her assumed indifference. "It's from Mirbel", I remarked, after one glance at the envelope, and immediately, with that instinctive cunning that the young sometimes show when they have to deal with difficult relatives, added with seeming frankness, "Do you think I ought to read it?" At first Brigitte Pian appeared to hesitate, but almost at once decided to leave it to me whether I ought to show it to her. She never so much as glanced at me as I opened it. Jean de Mirbel, after describing the "deadly existence" he was leading at the Baluzac presbytery ("and it's enough to make a fellow want to blow the lid off", he wrote), begged me to send him news of my sister. "Perhaps you could persuade her to scribble a few words at the end of your reply. It would make me awfully happy, and it wouldn't really be breaking her promise. Tell her that no one can imagine what it's like to live in a scrubby little country town tucked away in a pine-forest, cheek by jowl with an old priest—though I don't deny he's a decent enough fellow and does what he can for me. The trouble is that *I'm* not decent. Tell her that three lines would make all the difference to me. She can have no idea how it would help. . . ."

I can remember my feeling of anger when I read on and found that the letter contained nothing whatever about my own affairs. I was more irritated than hurt. If that was how things were, I felt I'd much better think no more about him, but wipe the slate clean. How often in the course of my life have I felt a similar need to terminate some relationship, to throw some person or persons overboard!

I held the letter out to Brigitte, who read it at once, but without any display of haste. When she had finished, she folded it up, baring her large, horse-like teeth in a smile. "The Reverend Mother", she said, "has forwarded me a whole packet in this young man's handwriting. He had the impudence actually to send a number of letters to your sister at the convent. Each one began, though you'd hardly believe it, with an appeal to Reverend Mother—or to whoever might first open the envelope—to deliver it to Michèle! Which goes to prove", she added sententiously, "that corruption of mind may walk hand in hand with stupidity, and that the two things are by no means incompatible." Saying which, she threw the pages into the grate, where they fell a prey to the flickering flames.

I am not sure that the second incident belongs to the same period. I have an idea that my meeting with the abbé Calou took place during the winter of the following year. One Thursday, just as I left the house, someone called my name. I at once recognized the abbé, though he had grown much thinner. His old soutane flapped round his bony shoulders. He must have been watching for me to come out. I told him that I was on my way to Féret's bookshop, and he fell into step beside me.

"How pleased Jean will be when I tell him this evening that I have seen you!"

"Is he all right?" I asked with an air of indifference.

"No," he said; "no, the poor fellow is very far from being all right."

He waited for me to question him, but in vain, for I had stopped at the door of Féret's shop and was turning over the pages of several second-hand books on display there in the open. Was I really so hard? I don't think I can have been, for I was vividly aware of the poor old priest's distress as he leaned over my shoulder, and am even now conscious of the remorse that assailed me at that moment.

"Actually, I'm very worried about Jean. Do you know, he hasn't been home to La Devize once this year? His mother is spending the winter in Egypt. Of course, he's working very hard, and he gets a certain amount of shooting. I took him out after pigeon last October. He bagged a hundred and forty-seven. I've found a horse for him, too, at Du Buch's mill, a sorry old nag, but ridable. It's the lack of companionship that's so bad for him."

"But what about you?" I asked with the ingenuousness of youth.

"Oh, me . . ."

He made a vague movement with his hands, and said no more. He must have realized for a long time how helpless he was. He had none of the qualities that a boy of Jean's age needs for happy companionship. His pupil had no more use for his erudition than for his gentleness. What else could he be but a gaoler in the eyes of a young man whom he would find, of an evening, curled up in a wicker chair by the kitchen fire, in precisely the same position as when he had left him after luncheon, with his book open at the same page. On these occasions Jean never so much as raised his eyes to the abbé's face. Nor did he find much amusement in going out alone on his old nag. When he was not in the house the abbé knew only too well where he had sought refuge. I was not at that time aware of this latest cause for anxiety. The truth was that Jean frequently stayed late in the enemy's camp—at the store kept by that very Voyod who was the abbé Calou's declared foe. The master and mistress of the local school would join the party after school hours. There would be much drinking of coffee in the back shop, and discussion of an article by Jaurès or by Hervé.

Although I knew perfectly well what the abbé was after, I gave him no assistance. He had to launch into his subject without preliminaries.

"I must regret that I have had words with Madame Pian," he said. "I believe her to be quite incapable of yielding to bitterness, and I am sure that only the highest motives led her to act as she has towards Michèle and Jean. I have no wish to discuss her decision, and am perfectly willing to yield to her superior wisdom. But don't you think, my dear boy, that Michèle might occasionally write a few lines to the Curé of Baluzac? What harm could there be in that? I am not suggesting that she should send Jean any direct message, but she could tell me something about her life. That would be an enormous source of comfort to your young friend. I am prepared to go even further, Louis, and to say"—he almost whispered the words into my ear—"to say that it might prove his salvation. For things have got to that pitch now—he has got to be saved. Do you understand what I am talking about?"

I could see his child-like eyes close to mine, could smell his sour breath. But I did not really understand what he was talking about. Still, this time I was touched, and it was for his sake rather than for Jean's that I agreed to do what he asked. I gave him a promise that I would pass on his suggestion to Michèle, and I spared him the embarrassment of having to beg me to say nothing to my stepmother. I gave him that assurance unasked. He enveloped the back of my head in his great hand, and pressed my face to his stained soutane. I went with him as far as the street-car. The men standing round him on the rear platform looked like a lot of midgets.

The correspondence between the abbé Calou and Michèle, which might perhaps have prevented or, at any rate, retarded much unhappiness, was interrupted after the third letter. Michèle had been foolish enough to give it to one of the weekly boarders, because she had not been able to resist the temptation to address it directly to Jean, though the name on the envelope was that of the abbé Calou. The letter was impounded by one of the nuns, who sent it to Brigitte Pian. She related the whole incident to me, though without attaching any blame to Michèle. "It was the priest who led her into temptation," she said; "there can be no doubt of that. Your sister has been guilty of a grave fault, but I thought it my duty to ask Reverend Mother to overlook it, and I must say that she has behaved in the whole affair with exemplary charity. But the account against the Curé of Baluzac grows daily"—she spoke with involuntary satisfaction—"and this letter is the last straw."

In some such words she spoke out her thoughts in my presence. Did she love me? For a long time I was quite convinced that her show of affection was due to the fact that I was the living proof of the first Madame Pian's sin. But I have since changed

my mind. I am inclined to believe now that she lavished on me
all the love of which she was capable, and that I had, in some
way, managed to touch that maternal instinct which is to be
found in even the most insensitive of women.

❦ XI ❦

FROM then on my existence was closely bound to that of Brigitte
Pian. The small drawing-room where she worked and in which
she received visitors separated my bedroom from hers. The door
was always left half open until someone was announced; then
she would close it. But no matter how low she kept her naturally vibrant tones, I could follow all conversations easily
enough, especially in winter, when the windows were kept shut
and only a dull rumble reached the flat from the Cours de
l'Intendance.

Occasionally, when I recognized Monsieur Puybaraud's voice,
I would go and say how-do-you-do to him, though not always.
It was usually he who made the move. He would come into my
room and give me a hug just before taking his leave. My behaviour to him had changed in proportion as his position in the
world had deteriorated. The poor, frail creature whose shoddy
ready-made overcoat offered little protection against the wind,
whose shoes were never shined, could not inspire in me the same
deference as the frock-coated schoolmaster whose favourite pupil
I had been.

In justice to myself I must add that his appearance moved me
to a sense of pity, or at any rate produced in me the sort of
moral discomfort which is always excited by the sight of another's
poverty, and which we are tempted to call by the nobler name.
But when I thought about Monsieur Puybaraud's misfortunes I
could not but feel myself in agreement with Madame Brigitte. I
found it difficult not to despise him for having yielded to an attraction which, though I had never yet felt its power myself, I
was already inclined to view with suspicion and disgust. I should
not have felt quite so keenly repelled by the outward signs of
his deterioration if they had not stood in my eyes for a spiritual
equivalent; if he had not, by marrying, made himself delib-

erately guilty, in my opinion, of disloyalty to a higher vocation.
My views on this matter have not greatly changed. I believe that
all the miseries of our human state come from our inability to
remain chaste, and that men vowed to chastity would be spared
most of the evils that weigh them down—even those that seem to
have no direct connection with the passions of the flesh. From the
lives of a very small number of human beings I have derived an
idea of what happiness might be in this world if it were based on
generosity and love. Wherever I have found it, the movements of
the heart and the promptings of the flesh have been kept under
a strict discipline.

Monsieur Puybaraud came once every fortnight to receive from
the hands of my stepmother the small allowance on which his
household depended. The rest of the time he spent in running
all over the city in search of employment that he never found. Octavia, now pregnant, but threatened with a miscarriage, had to
stay on her back until the child should be born, and could be of
no help to him. I heard it said that a Little Sister of the Assumption went in every morning to do their housework. That was all
I knew about the domestic arrangements of the wretched couple,
and I was too incurious to ask many questions.

I did notice, however, that if the semi-monthly interviews between Monsieur Puybaraud and my stepmother always ended
with the passing of an envelope from one hand to another, they
usually involved a long, low argument diversified by occasional
muted outbursts. On his side the tone was that of an eager beggar, while my stepmother's replies were given in a voice I knew
only too well. She was obstinate in her denials, undeviating in
her refusals. And suddenly she would be left speaking alone,
in the manner of one expounding the law to an inferior who
had been talked down and reduced to silence.

"You know perfectly well that things will happen like that because I mean them to, and the sooner you reconcile yourself
to the fact, the better." This she said one day loudly enough for
me to hear every word. "When I say 'I mean', I express myself
badly, because we should do not what *we* will but what God
wills. It is no use your hoping that I shall back you up in this
matter any longer."

Whereupon, my former master, in spite of all that he owed to
my stepmother and his utter dependence on her good-will, accused her of abiding by the letter of the law rather than the

spirit, and so far forgot himself as to say that her neighbours always had to pay for her scruples, that it was always at somebody else's expense that she displayed her spiritual delicacy and the rigours of her conscience. He added that he would not go away until he had got what he was asking for. (I had not been able to make out through the door what all this was about.) My stepmother, by this time quite beside herself, exclaimed that if such were the case she had better leave him, and I heard her go out of the drawing-room, not without considerable commotion. A few seconds later Monsieur Puybaraud came into my room. His face was dead white. He held in his hand the envelope that she must almost have flung at him. His trousers were mud-spattered to the knees. He was wearing no cuffs. His black tie and starched shirt-front were the left-overs of his old school outfit.

"You heard?" he asked. "Louis, dear boy, you shall judge between us. . . ."

I don't think that many youngsters can have been asked to referee between older persons quite so often as I was. The trust that I had inspired in my master on that evening, now long past, when he gave me a letter to post to Octavia Tronche, urged him once again to have recourse to my good offices. It was a rational trust deriving from that cult of the young which he had always professed. According to him (and he had been foolish enough to develop his views in my hearing), boys between the ages of seven and twelve are the privileged possessors of a remarkable clarity of mind, of something that at times amounts to the inspiration of genius, though older persons find it hard to believe this. It vanishes, however, with the approach of puberty. In spite of the fact that I was now fifteen, I had retained, in his eyes, all the glamour of childhood. Poor Puybaraud! Marriage had not improved him physically. He was now almost bald. A few sparse strands of fair hair waged a hopeless struggle against the encroaching nakedness of his skull. His flushed cheekbones alone gave colour to his bloodless face, and he was continually coughing.

He drew a chair up to mine as he used to do when he explained some Latin text to me in the old Larjuzon days.

"*You* will understand. . . ."

He used the second person singular. This he did only in moments of emotional outpouring, and when he was speaking to one of those young persons whom he regarded as the possessor of an infallible genius. He told me the doctor believed that Octavia could have a child in the normal way only if she were assured of complete rest, both mental and physical. He had thought it best, therefore, to calm her most harrowing anxieties by keeping from her the origin of the small sum of money he brought back to her each fortnight. She did not know that it came from my stepmother, but believed that her husband was earning his living and had succeeded at last in getting some post in the diocesan organization.

"Yes, I lied to her, and I do still, every day, though at the cost of how much shame and moral agony God alone knows! But surely fibs we are obliged to tell a sick woman can hardly rank as lies? I refuse to admit that they *are* lies, in spite of anything that Madame Brigitte may say!"

He gazed fixedly at me, as though expecting some oracular pronouncement.

I shrugged my shoulders. "Surely it doesn't matter what she says, Monsieur Puybaraud, so long as you are easy in your own conscience? . . ."

"It's not so simple as all that, Louis, my boy. You see, Octavia is surprised and worried that Madame Brigitte has never been to see her since she has been confined to bed. Up to now, your step-mother has always refused to come. She won't come—so she had the effrontery to write—until I have repudiated what she calls my 'offence against the truth'. Consequently, I have been led into a series of explanations to Octavia of which I will spare you the details. Lies beget lies. I know that I ought to give way. I am in a maze from which I can find no way out. But so far I have managed, more or less, to save my face. Now, however, Ma-dame Brigitte is beginning to use threats. She says that her con-science forbids her to remain my accomplice any longer in this deception. She insists that I tell Octavia where the money comes from. . . . Can you imagine such a thing?"

I could, very easily, and I told Monsieur Puybaraud that what really astonished me was that my stepmother should have con-sented to keep Octavia in the dark for so long. I made it pretty clear that I admired this scrupulous honesty on the part of my stepmother, though I did not say so in words. I was just then beginning to make the acquaintance of Pascal in the little Brunschwieg edition. The Brigitte Pian type appealed to me. I found it beautiful. It reminded me of Mother Agnès, of Mother Angélique, and of those other proud ladies of Port-Royal. I can see myself now, implacable in my youthful fervour, seated beside the

log-fire in front of a little table loaded with dictionaries and notebooks with, opposite me, that poor, worn-out figure stretching two
small, grubby white hands to the blaze, his uncobbled shoes
smoking in the heat. There, in the flames, his gentle and defeated
eyes could see the image of a woman lying in bed with her
precious, menaced burden. That was a reality that Brigitte Pian
refused to recognize, a reality that he could not make me see.
My stepmother had said to him more than once: "I warned
you before it all happened: you have no cause of grievance
against me." It was true that everything was turning out precisely as she had foreseen, that in the light of events she could
feel no doubt of the illumination which had descended from
God upon her spirit.

"She left me with a threat. She warned me that she would
call on Octavia late tomorrow afternoon," said Monsieur Puybaraud in a gloomy voice. "She is going to bring her some broth,
but she insists that between now and then I shall prepare Octavia for the news of my real situation. What am I to do? I want
to spare my poor wife the spectacle of my shame. As you very
well know, I am incapable of self-control. I shall not be able to
keep myself from crying. . . ."

I asked him why he didn't get some pupils. Couldn't he do
some tutoring? He shook his head. He had no degree, and his
marriage had closed against him most of the houses in which
he might have found some chance of employment.

"What a pity that I don't need a tutor," I said in a self-satisfied
voice; "but you see, I am always top of the class."

"Oh, you!" he answered on a note of tender admiration. "You
already know as much as I do. Pass your examination: get as
many diplomas as you can, my boy. You don't need them now,
but one never knows. . . . If only I had a degree!"

Child of a poor family, and educated out of charity by his future
colleagues because they saw great possibilities in him, Léonce
Puybaraud had found no difficulty in learning, and might have
gone far, had he not been asked, when he reached the age of eighteen, to deputize for some of the teachers when the school happened to be short of staff. He had to continue his own education
while acting as a teacher, and knew no more of literature than
what he had managed to pick up from anthologies and school
textbooks. On the other hand, he had read more deeply than most
university students in the great classic writers of Greece and
Rome. But today all his erudition could not help him to earn

the three hundred francs a month which was the minimum on which his family could live.

I longed for him to go, and began turning over the pages of my dictionary in an effort to make it clear that I had no time to waste. But he allowed himself to relax in the warm, cosy atmosphere of the room, in the presence of the youth to whom he was devoted. He sat there, wondering and wondering what he could do to disillusion Octavia without causing her too great an emotional disturbance.

"Why tell her yourself?" I suggested. "Couldn't you get somebody else to do it for you?—the Little Sister of the Assumption, for instance, who comes every day?"

"What a good idea, Louis!" he cried, slapping his skinny thighs. "No one but you would have thought of such a solution! She's a little saint, that girl. Octavia is devoted to her, and she to Octavia. It is quite curious to see two human beings each so convinced that she is inferior to the other. I only wish that Madame Brigitte could share the spectacle with me. It would teach her the nature of true humility. . . ."

He stopped because I pursed my lips. He felt that I was more completely under the influence of Madame Brigitte than he had ever been.

Next day, about the middle of the afternoon, Brigitte Pian descended from a landau in front of the house in the rue du Mirail where the Puybarauds lived in furnished rooms which she had chosen for them and whose rent she paid. Her arms were so loaded with a variety of parcels that she could not lift the hem of her skirt as she climbed the appallingly squalid staircase. The water from the household sinks ran in an open gutter. The smell was not unfamiliar to her: she met it constantly in the course of her charitable visits. The prevailing stench of urban poverty is always the same: a mixture of stews and privies. But it is not my intention to underrate what was best in Brigitte Pian's life, tempting though it is to do so. Whatever her true motives may have been, she was always a great giver of alms, and at times, when visiting the genuinely sick, showed herself capable of real personal devotion. She worked on the principle that it was better to provide solid help for a few than to spread inadequate relief over a wide field. I remember that when I accompanied her on her shopping rounds, she would buy cotton or groceries at out-of-the-way shops kept by protégés whom she had helped out of their diffi-

culties, and would send her friends on similar errands. She spared
these petty trades-people neither advice nor criticism, and was
for ever complaining of the ingratitude of those who resolutely refused to make a success of their lives, no matter how much pecu-
niary aid she might bring them.

She had been less generous than usual with the Puybarauds
and, though she kept them alive, left them to struggle along as
best they could. I find it hard to say whether this was deliberate
policy on her part. It is conceivable that she did not know the full
facts of the case. I am inclined to think she considered it a good
thing that they should remain in the state of penury which she
had always predicted for them; should so obviously suffer the
punishment that had come upon them as a result of their refusal
to follow her advice. She never ceased to find a source of triumphant satisfaction in her knowledge that they were entirely dependent on her. Had she recognized the true nature of her feelings
for Octavia, they might have caused her a passing tremor.

The first object that caught her eye as she entered the sick-room
was an upright piano standing at right angles to the bed, close to
the pillow. It took up so much space that it was difficult to move
freely between the wardrobe, the table, and the dresser, on top
of which lay a litter of bottles, cups, and dirty plates. (Each morning Monsieur Puybaraud in his haste would destroy the order that
the little Sister of Mercy left behind her.)

While the first courtesies were being exchanged and their visitor
was inquiring about the patient's health, the Puybarauds noticed—
with what anxiety may be imagined—that the piano had already
"caught Madame Brigitte's eye". They realized that at any moment she might begin to ask them about it. The shop from which
they hired it had promised to take it away, but had not done so.
That very morning Monsieur Puybaraud had started another
hopeless discussion on the subject. How were they ever going to
explain to Brigitte Pian that they had been guilty of so absurd an
act of self-indulgence?—absurd, because neither of them could
play a note, although they both loved picking out hymn tunes
with one finger on the keys. Even had they not been in the last extremes of poverty, their hiring of the instrument would have been
difficult to excuse: but dependent as they were for the very means
of life on another's charity . . .

Octavia hurriedly embarked on a subject designed to divert
Madame Brigitte's attention. She thanked that lady from the bot-

tom of her heart for not having allowed Léonce to deceive her any longer about the source of the money that he brought home every other week. He had acted as he had with the best possible intentions and out of consideration for her. But for some time now she had suspected a trick, and had thought at first that it was of Madame Brigitte's own devising, since, as all the world knew, she would do good by stealth as others did evil. (Octavia was not wholly innocent of a fault, so widespread in the circles in which she had been brought up, where flattery causes few pangs when it is addressed to rich and influential patrons with the power of life and death over those around them.) She added that she understood and shared Madame Brigitte's scruples of conscience. That lady listened with but half her mind. Her eyes kept constantly returning to the piano. She interrupted the invalid to say how sorry she was that she had caused Monsieur Puybaraud any distress of mind. She might, she said, have been weak enough to yield to him had she been dealing with one of those many worldly persons who know nothing of the ways of God. But she had decided that a Christian like Octavia ought not to remain ignorant of the consequences of her acts, that she ought to face the trials that Providence had seen fit to lay upon her. "Since it was clearly part of the Divine plan that you should live on the charity of a devoted friend and that Monsieur Puybaraud should be unable to find suitable employment, I felt that I had no right to spare you the effects of so salutary a lesson."

Monsieur Puybaraud, having noted these words in his diary, and stigmatized them as "damnable", adds: "I won't swear that she spoke them with conscious irony, but I am pretty sure that she felt considerable satisfaction at being able to find a watertight excuse (from the religious point of view, I mean) for the pleasure it gave her to know that she had such a hold over us: that nothing stood between us and starvation but the little envelope that I had to accept from her twice a month."

"It is odd," she said, "but somehow I don't remember that piano in the inventory sent me when I took these rooms for you."

"No," replied Octavia in a voice that trembled; "it is a piece of silliness for which I alone am responsible."

She looked at the elder woman with that sweet, disarming smile which few could resist. But the expression of hauteur on the face of her patroness showed no sign of softening.

"Forgive me, darling," broke in Monsieur Puybaraud; "it was I who suggested it, and I was thinking more about my own pleasure than yours."

It was foolish of him to call his wife "darling" in front of Brigitte Pian. She had always hated the lack of reserve in married couples who, presuming on the legitimacy of such endearments, stressed by word and gesture the fact of their squalid intimacy. In the case of this particular pair it was quite intolerable.

"Am I to understand", she inquired in tones that were suspiciously gentle, "that you have hired this piano?"

The accused nodded.

"One of you, then, must be capable of giving music lessons. I had an idea that you were both so ignorant of the art as not even to know your notes."

Octavia explained that they had agreed to give themselves this small indulgence.

"What indulgence? Picking out tunes with one finger as I often used to see you doing at school, though it made you ridiculous in the eyes of the girls?" Madame Brigitte, who scarcely ever laughed, emitted a sort of sharp bark.

Octavia hung her head. Her faded yellow hair was parted in the middle and drooped low on either side of her face. Her breast rose and fell rapidly beneath her coarse cotton slip.

"I know that it was wrong of us, Madame Brigitte," said Monsieur Puybaraud; "but please do not distress Octavia"—he dropped his voice to a whisper—"we will discuss the matter, if you don't mind, on the occasion of your next visit. I will explain it all. . . ."

"Yes"—she had adopted the same low tone—"we will go into it another time. You can tell me then where the money came from. . . ."

"It is yours: I am not denying that. . . . I realize that for people who are living on charity it is unpardonable to spend twenty francs a month on a piano that neither of them knows how to play. But I'd rather not discuss it now. . . ."

"What is there to discuss? You have already made the whole matter abundantly clear." Brigitte was still speaking in the same low voice (but Octavia had not lost a single word). "There is nothing you can add. You neither of you seem to realize that you have done anything at all out of the ordinary. It is not the money I am worrying about. . . . It is not a question of money. . . ."

Monsieur Puybaraud broke in by reminding her that she her-

self had remarked that there was no more to be said. He put his
arms round Octavia, who was choking back her sobs. But Brigitte
Pian, alarmed by the woman's tears, was in the grip of one of
those fits of temper which she found it extremely hard to control,
and regarded, in all humility, as a sign of that volcanic temperament with which it had pleased Heaven to endow her. Though
she tried hard not to raise her voice, the fury of her mood came
from behind clenched teeth in a spate of words.

"Well, I suppose I've got to make the best of it, but there is a
limit, even to virtue! It is my duty not to be weak: however charitable I may have been towards you, I am not going to push
kindness to the point of idiocy!"

"I beg of you either to stop talking or to go! Can't you see that
you are distressing Octavia?" Monsieur Puybaraud so far forgot
himself as to seize her by the arm and push her towards the door.

"How dare you lay a finger on me!" This attempt at physical
interference with her movements had had the immediate effect
of once more seating Brigitte Pian on the familiar throne of her
perfection.

"No, Léonce!" groaned Octavia. "She is our benefactress. It is I
whom you hurt when you fall short of the behaviour she has a
right to expect from us."

At this, Monsieur Puybaraud allowed himself to be carried
away by one of those sudden outbursts of temper to which weak
natures are prone. Seeing that Brigitte was already on the landing,
he exclaimed rather too loudly: "After all, darling, this is our
house, isn't it?"

My stepmother, framed in the doorway, drew herself to her
full height. "*Your* house, indeed!"

Such an easy triumph enabled her to recover an almost divine
complacency. The statement with which she had just silenced
her wretched adversary stood in no need of being elaborated.
But she could not resist the temptation of levelling a parting shot.

"Would you like me to send you the lease? You will find, I think,
that the name in which it is drawn up is not yours!"

Monsieur Puybaraud slammed the door and went across to the
bed where Octavia lay with her face in her hands, sobbing.

"It was wrong of you to act so, Léonce. We owe everything to
her . . . and, really, you know, that piano . . ."

"Calm yourself, beloved: you'll do some injury to our child."

They always spoke of "our child" when referring to the still unborn life, the adored baby which might never come into the world.
Holding his wife's head pressed close to him, he said, more than
once: "Horrible creature!"

But Octavia protested. "No, Léonce, no; it is wrong to speak
like that. Temperament is a stumbling-block to us all. It is easy
enough not to commit crimes for which God has seen fit to spare
us the opportunity. But only a special gift of Grace can enable
us to overcome in our daily lives the real weaknesses of character with which we are burdened. It would have been better,
perhaps, if Madame Brigitte had lived under convent discipline."

"If she ever had, she would soon have bossed the whole community. She'd have made them all tremble, and she'd have had
plenty of time to pick out her particular victims. We ought to re-
joice, rather, that she is not in a convent where she would have
had complete authority over the lives and thoughts of the sister-
hood. A woman like Brigitte Pian would be in her element there.
We, at least, are free to starve, free never to set eyes on her
again! . . ."

"I agree with you that she would have made it her business to
insure the sanctity of the Sisters," said Octavia, still tearful, but
with the faint glimmer of a smile. "You must have noticed that
the history of the great Orders is full of instances of Superiors
like Brigitte Pian. They have always helped the Community to
take the stoniest way to Heaven—and the shortest, for people
subjected to that sort of discipline do not live long. . . . But I
oughtn't to talk like this", she added; "after all she *is* our benefactress. . . . Oh, it's wicked of me!"

For a while they said no more. Monsieur Puybaraud, seated on
the bed, began to nibble one of the biscuits that Brigitte had
brought with her. At last: "What's going to become of us?" he
asked.

"You must go and see her to-morrow morning," replied Octavia.
"I know her. She will spend to-night wrestling with her scruples,
and will be the first to ask forgiveness. In any case, things will be
different when little Louis arrives."

He could not share her conviction. Never, no, never, would he
expose himself to such treatment again!

"It is hard to have to humble oneself, darling; for a man, and a
really good man like you, it's the hardest thing in the world.
But it is what God asks of us."

"What I find hardest to bear is her assumption that God has

justified her belief that things would turn out exactly as they have. Do *you* think we are being punished for what we have done?"

"No", she exclaimed with eager passion. "Not punished but tested. We were right in what we did. Our lives belong together. Madame Brigitte does not understand that we were meant to suffer together."

"You're right. From our suffering has come all our happiness." She flung her thin arms round his neck. "You regret nothing?"

"I suffer because I cannot support us . . . but once the child is born, nothing else will matter. Our happiness will be complete."

She whispered in his ear: "Don't set too much store on it, don't be too hopeful."

"What makes you think . . . Has the doctor said anything you haven't told me?"

He pressed her with questions, but she shook her head. No, the doctor had said nothing; it was only that she had an idea that the ultimate sacrifice might be asked of them. "No", said Monsieur Puybaraud again, as she went on to say that he must be ready to accept whatever God might think best for them, must acquiesce wholeheartedly in the possible ordeal, as Abraham had acquiesced, and that then, and then only, their Isaac might be given back to them. Monsieur Puybaraud continued to say "No", but more gently now, until at last he slid to his knees, pressed his forehead against the bed, and in a strangled voice made the responses to the evening prayer which Octavia had begun to recite.

When it was over she relapsed into silence and closed her eyes. Then her husband lit a candle, went over to the piano, the keys of which reflected the light, and, with one hesitating finger, tried to pick out her favourite hymn, the hymn sung by little children at their first Communion. As he did so he whispered the words: "Heaven has come down to earth, my beloved rests in me."

❦ *XII* ❦

BRIGITTE PIAN was no sooner in the street than she turned what remained of her anger against herself. How could she so utterly have lost control of her temper? What would the Puybarauds think? They did not, as she did, see her perfections from within, nor could they measure the height, breadth, and depth of her virtue. They would judge her in the light of an outburst which, if the truth were told, had made her feel thoroughly ashamed. How could human nature be relied upon, she thought as she walked up the rue du Mirail towards the Cours Victor-Hugo, if, after a whole lifetime spent in the conquest of herself, at an age when she might reasonably expect to be exempt from the weaknesses that disgusted her in others, the mere sight of a piano was enough to break down all her self-control?

Though the maintenance of her armour of perfection was one of her most constant preoccupations, there was nothing so very extraordinary in a link's occasionally working loose. She could always console herself for such an occurrence—provided there had been no witness. But the Puybarauds, and especially Octavia, were the last people in the world before whom she would willingly have shown signs of weakness. "They'll take me for a beginner", said Brigitte to herself, and the idea was painful, because she measured her progress in the spiritual life very much as she would have done in the study of a foreign language. She was made furious by the thought that the Puybarauds should have no idea how she had "moved up" in class during the last few months; should, on the evidence of a moment's ill-humour, rank her with ordinary church-going females. Just how far Brigitte Pian had been "promoted" it was not for her, conscious of the need for humility, to say, but she would gladly have climbed all the way upstairs again to the Puybarauds' rooms just to remind them that even great saints have sometimes been the victims of bad temper. Was she a saint? She was making great efforts to be one, and, at each step forward, fought hard to hold the ground she had gained. No one had ever told her that the closer a man gets to sanctity the more conscious does he become of his own worthlessness, his own nothingness, and that he gives to God, not from a sense of duty but because the evidence is overwhelming, all credit for the few good activities with which Grace has endowed him. Brigitte Pian pursued an opposite course, finding each day ever stronger reasons for thanking her Creator that He had made her so admirable a person. There had been a time when she was worried by the spiritual aridity that marked her relations with her God; but since then she had read somewhere that it is as a rule the beginners on whom the tangible marks of Grace are showered, since it is only in that way that they can be extricated from the slough of this world and set upon the right path. The kind of insensitiveness that afflicted her was, she gathered, a sign that she had long ago emerged from those lower regions of the spiritual life where fervour is usually suspect. In this way her frigid soul was led on to glory in its own lack of warmth. It did not occur to her that never for a single moment, even in the earliest stages of her search for perfection, had she felt any emotion which could be said to have borne the faintest resemblance to love: that she had never approached her Master save with the object of calling His attention to her own remarkably rapid progress along the Way, and suggesting that He give special heed to her singular merits.

Nevertheless, here, on the pavement between the rue du Mirail and the Cours de l'Intendance, as she made her way up the rue Duffour-Dubergier and the rue Vital-Carle, all blanketed in their customary fog, Brigitte Pian found herself yielding to a mood of spiritual discomfort which was far more profound than could be accounted for merely by the fact that she had cheapened herself in the Puybarauds' eyes. A sense of suppressed anxiety (which, though it was sometimes in abeyance, never wholly vanished from her consciousness) made her aware that the balance-sheet of her soul had not been truly audited, and that she too might one day be weighed in those unchanging standards of the Infinite by which, so she had always understood, the Uncreated Being was in the habit of judging the world of men. There were days—more particularly those on which she had been to see Octavia Tronche—when a flash of lightning would tear holes in the mists that shrouded her soul, and show her to herself as she really was. When that happened, she realized beyond all possibility of denial (the mood never lasted for more than a moment) that her way of life was not the only way of life, nor her God the only God. The sense of satisfaction in being Brigitte Pian, which as a rule was so overpowering, fell away from her suddenly, and she shivered, feeling herself naked and miserable, cast upon an arid waste of sand beneath a copper sky. Far away she could hear angelic choirs, and, mingled with them, the hateful voices of the Puybarauds. The feeling soon passed, and she always managed, by dint of certain impromptu prayers of proved efficacy, to recover her spiritual equilibrium. When the need for such rehabilitation came on her, she would pause before an altar somewhere (as now in the Cathedral) until silence once more filled her heart. She not only felt the silence, but adored it as a sign sent to her from her hidden Master that she had again found grace in His eyes. But to-day, first before the Holy Sacrament and, later, before the statue of the Virgin which stands behind the choir (looking for all the world like the Empress Eugénie), she was conscious of a voice within her that spoke in tones of disapproval. "It has been sent to try me", she thought; "I must submit in all humility"— which was her way of saying: "Notice, I beg, O Lord, that I do not kick against the pricks, and enter my acquiescence, please, on the credit side of the account." But since peace of mind still would not come to her, she went into a confessional and accused herself of violence of thought, though not of injustice (for her anger had been fully justified), of having failed to keep her legitimate indignation within the bounds of a duly disciplined charity.

If, after luncheon next day, Monsieur Puybaraud had seen Brigitte in her own home, he would have found himself in the presence of a woman now utterly defenceless and only too willing to exhibit herself as an object-lesson in humility. In the matter of humility she feared competition with none. But when, pale with emotion, he asked the servant whether her mistress was at home, he was told that she had been summoned back to Larjuzon by telegram, and that the young people had gone with her. Monsieur Pian had been taken suddenly ill, and the wording of the telegram had been sufficiently alarming to make Madame pack at once; she had taken "the nearest thing to mourning that she happened to have".

There was nothing suspicious about my father's death. Saintis (who had been re-established in the vacancy left by the dismissal of Vignotte) had found him early in the morning, lying on his face by the side of his bed and already cold. Like many of his comfortable country neighbours, Octave Pian had always eaten and drunk too much; but after he had been left alone in the house, his drinking had taken on frightening proportions. The evening before his death he must have surpassed himself, for the bottle of Armagnac which he had opened that day was found empty in the study, where it was his custom to sit smoking by the fire until the stroke of midnight.

I know today that Brigitte Pian's scruples had crystallized around the paper to which I have already referred. Rightly or wrongly, she held that it must strike a final blow at my mother's memory. I long believed that when she went from Larjuzon she had deliberately left that document in a drawer where she was certain that sooner or later my father must find it. That was, doubtless, to let my imagination outstrip events. Knowing what I do to-day, I can read their true meaning into the phrases my stepmother endlessly repeated as she lay in her bedroom through the long nights that preceded and followed my father's funeral. Lying wide-eyed in the dark, I listened in a state of terror, firmly convinced that Brigitte Pian had gone mad. Beneath the door, whose woodwork had been gnawed by rats, the light showed, obscured at regular intervals by the passage of her body as she paced up and down. Though she was wearing bedroom slippers, the floor creaked beneath her tread. "I must think, I must think," she kept on saying in a loud voice. I can hear the words still, words spoken by someone intent on getting order into the confusion of her mind at any price. She could have shown him the paper, but she had not done so. She had always hesitated to cause him anxiety, although it would have been a simple matter for her to destroy the kind of worship with which he surrounded the memory of Marthe. But she had never allowed herself to do so. It was far from certain that he would open that drawer. The only thing for which she can be truly blamed is that she did not burn the paper. . . . She never did, but it was not because she still had a lingering hope that one day he would discover it. "Into Thy hands, O Lord, I commit myself." God must be the judge. Whether or no Octave opened the drawer must depend on God, and even if he did, it must still depend on God whether the poor man would understand the meaning of what he read, would attach any significance to it. There is nothing to prove that he *would* have caught its drift. "I know, of course, that the document is no longer in the drawer, and that the stove in the hall is full of the fragments of papers that he burned. But he got rid of everything that had belonged to his first wife, and of that paper along with the rest. . . . He didn't know what he was doing. He was drinking hard at the time, had made up his mind to get as drunk as possible. . . ."

These are not, I need hardly say, her actual words. I have reconstructed them from memory, giving full weight to what I have learned since, but did not know at the time. I have set myself the task of getting at the heart of her scruples. The only ones

to which I can bear witness are "I must think," which expressed
the eager necessity to which her wandering mind still clung during the long night.

Michèle pretended not to see Brigitte—poor Michèle, who had
to face the torment of her own remorse, a remorse which I shared
with her, which for some time had been a part of both our lives,
but of which now in the evening of my days I can recapture no
trace. However genuine Michèle's sorrow may have been—and she
had loved her father dearly—her chief preoccupation just before
the funeral, when she was at Larjuzon, was to wonder whether
she would see Jean at the service. And when it was all over,
her grief as a daughter was dominated and, so to speak, eclipsed
by her disappointment at not having caught a glimpse of Mirbel in
the congregation.

Because she was afraid that the thick crêpe that veiled her face
might prevent her from noticing him, she had given me the task
of telling her the moment I caught sight of Jean de Mirbel. So
wholly had I identified my wishes with hers that my own personal feelings counted for nothing in the curiosity with which I
scrutinized the faces of the local shopkeepers and country-folk
who crowded the church. Among all these animal faces, with
their ferrety noses, their foxy or rabbity masks and cow-like expressions, some of the women's eyes looking dead or vacant,
others bright, glittering, bird-like, and utterly stupid, I sought for
the familiar features, the powerful brow beneath its shock of
short curly hair, the eyes, the laughing mouth—but all in vain. No
doubt Jean had been afraid that he might have to pass in front
of my stepmother, but, since it was not customary for the widow
to accompany the coffin to the graveside, I still had hope that he
might pluck up courage and join us.

The morning had promised well, but later a mist had blown
across the face of the feeble sun. Up to that very last moment
when we stood by the open grave, while the trowel was passing
from hand to hand among a crowd of living persons who looked
in the shrouding fog as though they were already half-dead themselves, while skimpy handfuls of earth were falling on the coffin of
that Octave Pian who had perhaps never been my father after
all, I still hoped to see Jean's figure emerge from the ghost-like
figures that surrounded me. More than once Michèle thought she
had seen him, and pressed my arm. For years afterwards we
shared a feeling of shame when we remembered that day. Still,

the very pain it caused us was in itself a proof that we had genuinely loved our father. I no longer feel indignant now at the
thought of that convention which claimed my sister's obedience
in the little cemetery of Larjuzon. She was one of those human
beings whose temperaments are so surely balanced, their hearts
so pure, that their instincts are almost always at one with their
duty, so that their natural inclinations lead them to do precisely
what God expects of them.

In the afternoon my stepmother retired to her room, where we
could hear her pacing up and down until the evening. Contrary
to custom, we none of us appeared at the funeral meal, but the
din reached us upstairs where we had taken refuge. In the absence of any near relation, our guardian, Monsieur Malbec, the
local solicitor, did the honours. He came up to us after coffee, red
in the face and almost merry. We knew that there were clients
waiting for him, and that we should not have to endure his presence for long. If I were writing a novel, I should find it amusing
to sketch in the character of Malbec, who was the sort of man of
whom it is said that "he might have stepped straight out of the
pages of Balzac". But he played no other part in our lives than
that of a man who relieved us of all those responsibilities which
might have served to divert our attention from what was going
on in our hearts and minds. He bored me to extinction. Whenever
I had to visit him in his office to hear him read documents which
I then signed with my initials, I used to tell myself stories in an
effort to alleviate the tedium. During all the period of my youth
I believed (or behaved as though I believed) that people like
him, with their bony skulls, their pince-nez and their whiskers,
middle-aged men of business who looked as though they were
made up for a part, knew nothing of the human affections and
were utter strangers to the emotions of every day.

When Monsieur Malbec had left us, and the last carriages had
driven off, we gave ourselves over to what at that moment seemed
to us no less than sacrilege—to a discussion, in fact, of Mirbel. We
sat there talking of him and smoking, in a room that was separated
only by a partition from the one from which our father's body had
been so lately taken. We realized then that we should have no
difficulty about going over to see Jean at Baluzac. The cemetery,
which we were to visit again next day, lay beyond the village
and directly on the Baluzac road. We could easily make the journey to the presbytery on foot. Brigitte Pian seemed to be in no

state to keep an eye on us, and the death of her father had released Michèle from her promise.

When the next day came, the fog was thicker than ever. If we kept to the woods it was most unlikely that we should meet anybody. At the grave, with its panoply of already faded flowers, Michèle insisted on saying the *De Profundis* twice over. I thought she was never going to finish. Then, with a strong sense that we were abandoning our poor dead father, we began walking so fast that in spite of the mist the sweat began to stand out on my forehead in great drops. Michèle led the way. She was wearing a white beret (the only mourning hat she had was the one she had worn at the funeral), and a short jacket cut close to her waist which, in those days, most people would have thought was rather thick. Her shoulders were too high. Those physical blemishes are still vivid in my memory. But her dumpy little figure radiated strength and an overmastering vitality.

The few houses composing the township of Baluzac seemed stricken with death. They formed no street, and there was nothing that bore any resemblance to a market-square. The presbytery was separated from the church by the graveyard. Beyond it was the new school; opposite, a combination inn and grocery-store, the blacksmith's forge and Voyod's store, which on this particular day was shut. Two-thirds of the abbé Calou's parishioners lived in isolated farms lying some miles outside the hamlet.

The kitchen-garden appeared to be abandoned. "Wait till I've got my breath before you knock," said Michèle. She did not make the gesture she would certainly make to-day, for she owned neither powder nor lipstick. For that matter, she had not even a handbag, but only a pocket in her skirt.

I lifted the knocker. The sound echoed through the house as though it had been an empty sepulcher. Half a minute passed, and then we heard the sound of a chair's being pushed back, followed by the noise of dragging clogs. The door was opened by what might have been a ghost. It was the abbé Calou. He was already much thinner than when I had met him last in the Cours de l'Intendance.

"Ah, my dear young people . . . I was just going to write to you. I ought to have come to the funeral . . . but I didn't dare—because of Madame Pian, you know."

He led the way into the drawing-room and opened the shutters. It was as though an icy cape had fallen about our shoulders.

When he asked us, rather hesitatingly, whether we weren't afraid
of catching cold, I said that, as a matter of fact, we had got very
warm, and perhaps it would be wiser if we went upstairs. He
seemed put out by the suggestion, begged us to forgive the
untidiness we should find there, and then, with a faint shrug,
signed to us to follow him.

I could feel Michèle go tense in anticipation of the longed-for
meeting. Jean would appear, leaning over the banisters. He was,
perhaps, behind the very door that the abbé Calou was even then
in the act of opening—still to an accompaniment of muttered
apologies.

"The bed is not made. Maria is growing old, and I never feel
really up to the mark in the morning. . . ."

What a mess! Books were scattered all over the gray-looking
sheets. On the mantelpiece, in a confusion of papers, stood a plate
with the remains of a meal. The coffeepot was wedged in the
dead ashes of the grate.

The abbé Calou pulled two chairs forward and himself sat down
on the bed.

"I should like to be able to tell you that I share your sorrow,
but for the moment I am incapable of thinking of others. I am the
prisoner of my own misery. Perhaps you know where he is? There
must be rumours going round. I know nothing at all, and it looks
as though I never shall, because it is not very likely that his family will keep me informed of the result of their search—as you
may well imagine! Forgive me for talking like this. . . . Since the
whole wretched business started, I have not exchanged ten words
with a single living soul. . . . The people here turn their backs on
me, or, worse still, laugh at me. . . ."

"What wretched business?" I asked.

But Michèle had understood. "What has happened to him? Nothing serious?"

The abbé Calou kept hold of the hand she had stretched towards him. He repeated that he was the last person in the world
to be able to give her an answer. He was the one person who
must expect to be told nothing. . . . At length he became aware
of our amazement.

"You didn't know he had gone? You weren't told? It'll be a
week ago to-morrow."

We exclaimed with one voice: "Gone? but why?"

The abbé raised his arms and let them fall again. "Why? . . . bore-

dom, of course. . . . Living here with a priest, an old priest. . . .
But the idea would never have occurred to him if someone hadn't
started meddling. . . . No, I can't speak out to you . . . you're both
of you only children. Ah, Michèle, you alone could have . . . you
alone . . ."

I had never seen a man of his age, let alone a priest, cry. His
tears were not those of a grown-up person. His drowned blue eyes
were just like those that his mother must have wiped sixty years
before, on some occasion when he was terribly unhappy, and
there was something child-like in the way his mouth was twisted
awry by grief.

"I thought I had done everything possible. . . . I ought to have
run after you, Michèle, got hold of you by hook or by crook,
brought you here by force. But my judgment was at fault. What
an idiotic arrangement that was of mine that you and I should
exchange letters! Naturally, you couldn't resist the temptation of
slipping a note to Jean into an envelope addressed to me. I ought
to have foreseen that. You probably don't know that, so far as my
part in the affair is concerned, a complaint has been made to the
Archbishop. That dear woman, your stepmother, has lodged
a formal charge against me. Fortunately, Cardinal Lecot is not
so formidable as he looks. I have no doubt that His Eminence
has had a good laugh at my expense. He referred to me as 'Love's
messenger' and quoted some Latin verses. But that was because
he wanted to treat the whole thing as a joke instead of taking it
seriously. The Cardinal is a hard man, and his mockery is terrible,
but he has the heart that usually goes with a fine intelligence. I
realize that he has behaved very well. . . ."

Monsieur Calou hid his face for a moment in his two enormous
hands. Michèle asked him what she ought to do. He lowered his
hands and looked at her for an instant. A smile spread over his
tear-stained face.

"Oh, it's very simple for you, Michèle. So long as you and he are
still alive, all is not lost. Do you know what you mean to him—
really know? But it is different for me. I can suffer: I know that.
One can always suffer for others. . . ." Then he muttered, as
though to himself: "Do I really believe that?" He seemed to have
forgotten our presence. "Yes, I do. What an appalling doctrine it
is that acts count for nothing, that no man can gain merit for himself or for those he loves. All through the centuries Christians have
believed that the humble crosses to which they were nailed on

the right or the left hand of our Lord counted for their own redemption and for the redemption of those they loved. And then
Calvin came and took away that hope. But I have never lost
it. . . . No," he said, "no!"

Michèle and I exchanged glances. We thought he was going out
of his mind, and we were frightened. He had taken from his
pocket a huge purple-checked handkerchief. He wiped his eyes
and made an effort to steady his voice.

"You can write to La Devize, Louis," he said to me. "It is
natural that you should ask the Countess for news of your friend.
You'll have to read between the lines of her reply, of course, for
no one can lie as she can. . . . Perhaps he's back home already.
They can't have got far", he added.

"Then he wasn't alone?" asked Michèle.

The abbé kept his eyes on the fire to which he had just added
a log. I pointed out that one couldn't travel without money, and
that Mirbel was given practically nothing by his family.

"He was always complaining of that. You can't have forgotten,
sir?"

The abbé went on picking red-hot embers from the fire as
though he had not heard my question. We stood there waiting,
while he, obviously frightened of being interrogated, hoped that
we would go. Michèle brought no pressure to bear on him. She
gave one last look round the dirty, untidy room, and then slowly
went downstairs, her hand touching the rail on which Jean's
must so often have rested. The paper on the wall showed damp
patches, the very tiles of the hall floor were wet.

"Please", said the Curé, "write as soon as you hear anything, and
I will do the same."

"I'm not asking you the name of the person he went away with,"
said Michèle suddenly. (I heard later that she had picked up from
Saintis the rumours that were going around about Hortense Voyod
and the odd young fellow who was living up at Monsieur Calou's.)
"Though it's not hard to guess", she added with a laugh.

I remember that laugh very clearly. The Curé had opened the
front door and the mist had drifted in, smelling of smoke. Monsieur Calou began talking very fast, without looking at us, and still
keeping his hand upon the latch.

"What has that got to do with you? It is a matter of no importance, Michèle, because he cares about no one in the world except you. You were his despair. What has it got to do with you",
he repeated, "if another woman took the chance that came her

way simply because you were not on the spot? Have some pity
on me and don't ask questions. . . . You'll hear all you want to
know from the people round. You won't even have to ask them.
It is not for a poor priest to speak of such things. You are a couple
of children. All I am permitted to say, Michèle, is that if Jean is to
be saved, it will be through you. No matter what happens, he will
never forsake you. He has not in any real sense betrayed you. . . .
He was to me as the son of my old age, but I made no attempt to
force his confidence. The office of fatherhood, which I had myself
assumed, put no obligation on him. He is guilty of an offence
against God alone, that God whose presence I so signally failed
to make him feel, of whom he knew no more after all these months
spent under my roof than he did on that first day when the three
of you were quarrelling in the garden: do you remember?"

Yes, I remembered. Young though I was, the past had already
become for me an abyss in which even the most trivial events of
my childhood were transformed into lost delights.

It may have been on this very evening, after we had closed the
door behind us and had plunged into the fog, that Monsieur Calou
wrote the lines that are now lying before me.

*If we want to know in what relation we really stand to God, we
cannot do better than consider our feelings about other people.
This is peculiarly the case when one person above all others has
touched our affections. If he is seen to be the source of all our
happiness and all our pain, if our peace of mind depends on him
alone, then, let it be said at once, we are separated as far from
God as we can be, short of having committed mortal sin. Not that
love of God condemns us to aridity in our human friendships, but
it does lay on us the duty of seeing that our affection for other
human beings shall not be an end in itself, shall not usurp the
place of that utterly complete love which no one can begin to understand who has not felt it. During the retreat I made before I
was ordained, I sacrificed to Thee, O God, all hope of human
fatherhood. I sought to find it again in my feeling for this boy.
How could I hope to overcome in him and conquer those natural
instincts of the young animal, if I found them so attractive? It
is easier to hate the evil in ourselves than in those we love.*

Michèle led the way. Each time I tried to catch up with her she
quickened her pace as though she wanted to be left undisturbed.
She held her head high and gave no sign that what she had just

heard had beaten down her high spirit. All that really mattered to me was that we should get home before our stepmother should have noticed our long absence. This anxiety blotted all other considerations from my mind.

As we crossed the hall on the way to our rooms, Brigitte opened the door of the small drawing-room and called to us. "Wouldn't you like some tea? It will warm you after your long walk."

Michèle replied that she was not hungry, but, faced by the insistence of our stepmother, she felt, I think, that she mustn't seem fearful or anxious to conceal anything. We entered the room, therefore, and found the tea things laid. Brigitte Pian's face was void of the expression that I knew so well when she was girding herself for battle. I was pretty sure, however, that she knew where we had been, and I found it hard to square with her actual appearance of fatigue and defeat the mood of anger that should normally have been hers. She filled our cups and buttered some slices of bread. These she offered first to Michèle, after which she asked us, as though it had been the most natural thing in the world, whether we had seen the abbé Calou. Michèle nodded assent, but the crash of thunder that I fully expected to follow never came.

"In that case", said Brigitte in a sad and sympathetic voice, "I suppose you know . . ."

Michèle, keen to carry the fight into the enemy's camp, interrupted the sentence. We knew all that there was to know, but she would rather not discuss it. . . . As she moved towards the door, my stepmother called her back. "Please stay here a little longer, Michèle."

"If you are going to preach to me, I tell you plainly that I am in no mood . . ."

The note of defiance in the girl's voice seemed to make no impression on Brigitte Pian, who doubtless was pursuing her own train of thought. What was it?

"You need not worry. I haven't the heart to preach to you. I only want you to be fair to me. But I want that very much."

Michèle, her face set in hard lines, was wondering how the attack was going to develop. She raised her cup to her lips and slowly sipped her tea, thus avoiding the necessity of answering Brigitte, and forcing that lady to show her hand.

"You will tell me that it is useless to look for justice to our fellow-men, and that the approval of our own conscience should be sufficient for us. But, like all other human beings, I am weak.

I have no wish to triumph over you, my poor child, but, for my own peace of mind, I want you to admit that I was right in scenting danger for you. You do see that, don't you? This young man has turned out to be even worse than I feared. I knew how to protect you as well as your real mother, if not better. . . ."

We were so used to the fact that Brigitte Pian never spoke aimlessly that our first instinct was always to wonder what lay behind her words. I think she had never been more sincere than she was at that moment. There was nothing to tell us that the question which she had put to Michèle was the expression of an agony of mind which had not left her for a single instant since our father's death. We knew nothing of that. What she wanted was to be reassured. She did not see how Michèle could possibly avoid the necessity of admitting that she had been right.

My sister had no idea of the strength of the blow she was levelling at her enemy when she exclaimed: "You want me to recognize that you were stronger than I was. Well, I do. It was you and you only who separated us. It was you who drove him to desperation. If he is a lost soul, you are the cause of his damnation, and if I . . ."

The sky did not fall. Brigitte Pian remained seated in her chair: or rather, contrary to her usual habit, she lay slumped in it. She scarcely raised her voice.

"Sorrow has unhinged your mind, Michèle. Either that, or you have not been told all. If anyone is the cause of his damnation, it is that Voyod woman."

"A letter from me would have sufficed to turn him from his intention, just one letter. If only I had been able to speak to him, if only you had not put yourself between us with the same merciless obstinacy that has led you to ruin the abbé Calou in the eyes of his Superiors. . . ."

Sobs prevented Michèle from going on. It was the first time that she had ever cried in her struggles with Brigitte. It was as though some instinct prompted by hatred had told her that tears would spoil the older woman's triumph and leave her beaten and bewildered.

"Come now," said Brigitte Pian, "come now." She spoke in the same voice that she had used during the night when I had heard her muttering to herself. "You can hardly deny that the young man has shown himself to be a black sheep, an evil-doer. . . ."

"An evil-doer because at eighteen he has let himself be led away . . . ?" Michèle hesitated to add "by a woman".

"Yes", Brigitte insisted, with the concentrated passion of someone seeking to gain peace of mind. "I mean what I say—an evil-doer. We will leave the woman out of it, if you so wish. The fact remains that this young man of good family has behaved like a ruffian, and that if there was any justice in this world, he would be behind bars at this moment."

Michèle shrugged her shoulders. This kind of talk seemed utterly absurd to her. Its very excess did something to disarm her indignation. She replied that, as everyone knew, Brigitte Pian was quite unable to control herself when she had to deal with a matter of this kind. The prisons would have to be enlarged if all the young men guilty of such crimes were to be locked up.

"It isn't every young man", retorted Brigitte, "who breaks open desks and runs off with his benefactor's savings."

She had flung this remark at my sister with no definite intention, thinking that we knew all the circumstances of Jean's flight. The look of horror on Michèle's face warned her too late of her mistake. She jumped up and hurried to the girl's assistance, but Michèle pushed her away and sought comfort on my shoulder. I was standing close to the wall.

"That's a wicked lie!" She spoke so fast that the words tumbled over one another. "An invention of the Vignottes!"

"You didn't know it, my poor dears?" She fixed on us a long gaze of happy astonishment. Never had she addressed us in tones so quiet, so almost gentle. She felt reassured. We should have to admit that no mother could have acted otherwise.

Evening was deepening into night. Brigitte stood there illuminated only by the flickering flames.

"I should have realized that that wretched abbé wouldn't have the courage to tell you of his pupil's villainy. I am sorry I gave you such a shock, Michèle. But now do you understand? It was my duty to protect you against a criminal. I knew what I was about. The necessary information was given me by the Comte de Mirbel . . . but too late, alas, and for that I ask your forgiveness. My great fault lay in ever letting you associate with that young ne'er-do-well. I should never have regarded the presence of Monsieur Calou as providing a sufficient guarantee. I fear I was wrong, too, in my estimate of him. . . ."

She took our silence for acquiescence and proceeded to yield utterly to her craving for self-abandonment and surrender.

"There are moments in one's life", she went on, "when one fails to see clearly. More than once I have questioned myself, have

felt myself oppressed by doubts. . . . Your father's death had a
greater effect on me than you will ever realize. We are responsible for every one of the souls with which God brings us into contact on our way through life. 'What hast thou done to thy brother?'
That question, put by God to Cain, I asked myself when I looked
at the dead body of the man whose soul had been so suddenly
withdrawn. Sudden death is a fearful warning. . . . Each day I become more aware of all those for whom I shall have to answer.
There may have been times when my judgment was wrong, but
God is my witness that I have always striven for His greater glory
and for the welfare of men's souls. . . . What was that you said,
Michèle?"

My sister shook her head as a sign that she had said nothing,
moved away from the wall, and left the room. I made as though
to follow her, but my stepmother kept me back.

"No, better leave her alone with her thoughts."

Time passed. Brigitte Pian poked the fire, and every now and
again a flame leapt upwards, setting her large face in a warm
glow, and then died down, until nothing but her forehead and the
pale mass of her cheeks was visible in the gathering dusk.

"No", I said suddenly, "it would be better not to leave her
alone."

I went up to Michèle's room and knocked, but there was no reply.
I opened the door, thinking that she was lying in the dark as it
was so often her habit to do. I called to her in a low voice, for I
was frightened of dark rooms. But she was not there. I looked for
her high and low, scouring the house from the kitchen to the
linen cupboard. But no one had seen her. I went out onto the
steps. The cold darkness was lit by an invisible moon. I went
back to the small drawing-room.

"I don't know where Michèle is", I cried; "I have looked for her
everywhere."

"Well, she's probably gone out—into the town, perhaps. What
is there so tragic about that, you little silly?"

My stepmother had risen from her chair. With the tears pouring
down my cheeks, I replied that there was nothing to take Michèle
into the town at this time of night; at which, in a wild sort of
voice, she murmured that these children would drive her mad.
But already she had hurried before me to the steps. Someone was
walking along the path.

"Is that you, Michèle?"

"No, ma'am: it's Saintis."

Saintis, her enemy, had been reinstated, and she could not, with decency, dismiss him until some further time should have elapsed. He was out of breath, and we could hear him panting in the darkness. He told us that Mademoiselle Michèle had borrowed a lamp from him for her bicycle. She had asked him to tell Madame not to wait dinner, as she had something very important to see to.

"Where can she have gone?"

"Gone? To Baluzac, I don't mind betting."

"I suppose it is just as well," said Brigitte Pian when we had returned to the little drawing-room, where a lamp was now burning. "She probably hopes that the abbé Calou will explain everything satisfactorily, will be able to gloss matters over. . . . Still, theft with breaking and entering is theft with breaking and entering: nothing will alter that."

She started to stroke my hair: "What an example for you, my poor boy," she sighed. "At your age you should know nothing of such horrors. But what a lesson, too, Louis! Look at your sister, a good girl if ever there was one . . . yet nothing can keep her from roaming the woods and fields on a winter's night. That is what passion does to human beings—just swallows them up. Promise me that you will be different, that you will never let yourself be changed into a wild beast."

She tried to kiss me, but I turned away my face and went to the other end of the room, where I sat down out of reach of the circle of lamplight.

❧ *XIII* ❧

I SAID nothing that could betray the hatred with which she filled me. But she must have felt its presence there between us as we sat together at dinner, and later still, while we waited for Michéle. It was eleven o'clock before she got back. This time Brigitte called to her in vain. Michèle went straight upstairs without pausing at the drawing-room. I replied in monosyllables to the remarks that my stepmother made as she gave me my candle.

Just as I was bracing myself to stretch my legs beneath the icy sheets, she came into my room. She had on one of the purple

dressing-gowns she liked to wear, and—as usual after she had undressed—her lustreless hair hung in a thick braid.

"It's a cold night: I've brought you a hot-water bottle," she said.
She slipped it into my bed and touched my feet. For the first
time in my experience she kissed me good-night and tucked me
up.

"The poor child didn't dare admit that Monsieur Calou had
finally opened her eyes to what really happened. I think I know
how she must be suffering. We must be gentle with her. She will
realize later that I was right. . . . Don't you think she will?" she
asked, raising the candle above her head the better to see me.

Sheer exhaustion offered me a way of escape. I closed my eyes
and turned my face to the wall, taking refuge in a state that was
half waking, half sleeping, like a swimmer struggling between
conflicting currents.

She sighed. "Asleep already!" she murmured. "How lucky you
are!" and went back to the loneliness of her own room.

I was awakened in the night by the creaking of her floor. I told
myself that she was brooding over her scruples, and the thought
gave me an unworthy sense of pleasure. I did not realize then
the full horror of the torment that they inflict upon themselves,
those servants of God who do not know the true nature of love.

Next day at breakfast, Michèle, looking pale and heavy-eyed,
avoided my questions.

"According to Monsieur Calou it is ridiculous to say that he stole
anything," she told me. "The abbé was in the habit of making small
advances to Jean when he wanted money. This time Jean helped
himself, but he knew that his mother would pay it back at once.
He left a note in the desk, and the abbé knew perfectly well that
he would be reimbursed."

I asked whether it was true that Mirbel had broken open the
lock. My sister was forced to admit that he had, but she was annoyed by the face I pulled, and turned her back on me, refusing
to say any more. The odd thing was that though I regarded such
an act as monstrous, it somehow reawakened my feeling of affection for Mirbel. I could never willingly turn from him or deny
him, and I trembled to think that I was thus indissolubly bound
to a boy who could wallow in crime.

It was only much later, and then in fragments only, that the
details of this adventure were imparted to me, not by Monsieur
Calou but by Michèle herself. Even to-day, the old Countess

sometimes talks of that time when I go to see her, but without the
slightest sign that she finds the memory of it in any way embarrassing. "It would make a good subject for one of your novels", she
says, savouring her words as though they were something good to
eat. "I might have kept it for myself, but you can have it. I'd only
spoil it. It's not really my genre. It has nothing to do with love,
you see. . . ." For her, only fashionable adultery has any right to
the name of love.

The origin of this theft and of this flight which lay so heavily
on Michèle's destiny was to be found in a "good deed" that the
abbé Calou had performed many years earlier during his first few
years at Baluzac. He was suffering at that time from the worst
form of spiritual discomfort to which a priest is subject. He felt
convinced that the great mass of the people with whom he was
brought in contact had no need of him. It wasn't that they cared
nothing for the Kingdom of God: they did not even know that
it existed, had never been stung to awareness by the good news of
the Gospel. For them the Church was merely an organization
which carried out certain pre-arranged rites suitable for special
occasions, using for the purpose a class of men called priests. That
was the most they would admit. What, then, was left for a priest
to do but turn in upon himself and tend in his own heart the
flickering flame that lit his footsteps, and those of a very few
others, until such time as God's intentions for His world should be
manifested with glory?
Such was the abbé's state of mind when, after twelve years
spent in a seminary, he had to give up the Chair he occupied
because of certain charges that had been levelled at his orthodoxy.
Very humbly he had accepted the cure of souls at Baluzac, a
place situated on the border of the heath country, and one of
the most unpopular livings in the whole diocese. Study and prayer
made up the tale of his days. He decided that he would devote
himself entirely to the small flock entrusted to him without looking for any results. On the very first Sunday after his installation
he spoke as simply as he could—such was always his habit—to
about forty faithful parishioners, but without any deliberate attempt to put himself on their level. The subject with which his
sermon dealt was the priest's mission. What he really did was to
meditate out loud, speaking to himself rather than to them. The
next day he found, slipped beneath his door, an anonymous letter

of eight pages. A woman had heard him and had understood. She must be a person of education. She had come to church, she said, out of curiosity, and because she had nothing else to do. She had gone away completely overwhelmed. But she complained that priests had fallen into the error of waiting until the lost sheep came to them. They should imitate their Master who sought them out and carried them home upon His shoulders. She alluded to something shameful that could not be put into words, to a state of despair from which the human soul could not free itself unless God took the first steps towards achieving its release.

That morning the abbé Calou believed that a sign had been vouchsafed to him. He was by temperament inclined (like Pascal) to expect from God perceptible signs, material evidence. This cry which, on the very first day of his new life, had reached him from the wastes of a forgotten countryside, he interpreted as an answer to his prayer for comfort, it is true, as a reply to his questing heart, but also as a gentle reproach. He prepared his sermon for the following Sunday with all his usual care, but, while couching it in general terms, he weighed its every word so that the unknown writer of the letter might hear in it an answer designed for her in particular. As he glanced round the congregation, he saw two brown eyes fixed on him from behind a pillar, and noticed that they were set in a young, fresh face that lacked something of firmness in its contours. Later that same day he discovered that it belonged to a schoolmistress from Vallandraut who came frequently to Baluzac for reasons that his informants would not specify, though they shook their heads a good deal and chuckled. The abbé Calou noted in his diary how fierce a struggle he had had to wage with himself before delivering his sermon, but after that single entry there are no further references to the incident, or only such indirect and obscure hints as would have meaning for no one but himself. This was due to the fact that the schoolmistress had almost at once become his penitent, and that he felt himself bound by the secrecy of the confessional.

I will set down, as discreetly as possible, what I know of the affair. This young and innocent woman had, very early, fallen under the fascination of Hortense Voyod—a type of amazon not wholly unknown, contrary to general opinion, in country districts. There are people who set their toils and are prepared to go hungry for a very long while before any prey lets itself be caught. The patience of vice is infinite. One single victim will content such people, and a brief moment of contact will insure them long years of happy repletion. When at the end of September Monsieur Calou entered on his cure at Baluzac, the apothecary's wife had just completed a different kind of cure at Vichy. Though she was fully aware that her new young friend would be a difficult catch to land, since she was a girl with an excessively scrupulous conscience, she was far from supposing that her influence would be seriously menaced. She could think of no one within a radius of ten miles whose interference she need fear. Consequently, she attached little importance to the letter she received one morning putting an end to the friendship, though it did have the effect of making her hasten her return. No sooner had she got home than she discovered the identity of her adversary. She told herself that it would be mere child's play to get the better of him.

Here, once again, if I am to be faithful to my promise to invent nothing, I cannot describe a struggle about the progress of which I have no precise information. It must have been hard, since the abbé Calou, who never asked favours and hated meddling, managed to get his penitent transferred. The young girl, in spite of the fact that she was sent to another school, was still exposed not only to Madame Voyod's letters, but also to her frequent visits, that lady having recently bought a car, the first to be owned by anyone in Baluzac. But on the very eve of the day that she had chosen for her second trip, the post brought her a short note dated from Marseille. In it the girl announced that she had entered the novitiate of a missionary order, and said farewell to her friend until such time as they should meet in another world.

Although no scene ever took place between the chemist's wife and the abbé, he realized before very long that he had roused in her a degree of hatred which no mere passage of time would serve to allay. The knowledge did not much worry him on his own account, because it seemed impossible that she could get any hold over him, but it did on hers, for he was a man who could well understand the depths of her misery, no matter how shameful its causes might be. He had always had an eye for the unforeseeable repercussions, the mysterious consequences, of our actions when we intervene in the destinies of others, for no matter what good reasons.

His adversary was not slow in opening her attack. At first it was confined to the only field in which she could come to grips with him. Anti-clerical feeling was running high at that time. To-

gether with the schoolmaster of Baluzac and his wife, Hortense
Voyod set up a sort of committee of propaganda, the activities of
which very soon extended to the whole neighbourhood. But in
Baluzac itself her reputation was so bad that the offensive made
very little headway. For the space of two or three years the Curé
seemed to be justified in his belief that he had very little to fear.
For all that, he never felt comfortable when he had to pass the
apothecary's shop, and, if he happened to meet the woman in the
street, it was he who looked away, so violent was the effect upon
him of her cold, implacable glare.

She had waited years for her victim. Her opportunity for revenge was not so long in coming. The abbé had every excuse for
being caught off his guard, since she was known not to be interested in young men, and was not likely to be physically attractive
to them. She often showed herself arrayed in the "bloomers"
which at that time were fashionable among women cyclists. She
sported a low-cut bodice confined by a belt which was adorned
in front by an enormous silver buckle engraved with her monogram. Her hair, arranged "à la Cléo", was parted in the middle,
arranged in two shining bandeaux over her ears, only the lobes
of which were visible, and caught, at the nape of her neck, into
a huge yellow "bun" which rained innumerable pins. Her face
was a mass of freckles which were thickly clustered on her nose
and cheekbones, thinning out above.

The abbé Calou had profited by Jean's convalescence to complete his conquest of him. Or that, at least, was what he thought.
In this, he was the dupe of an illusion from which we all suffer
in spite of the lessons of experience. In dealing with human
beings, no position is ever permanently won in either love or
friendship. Jean de Mirbel, betrayed by his mother and weakened
by illness, was in the mood to feel a shock of passing gratitude
and to surrender before a show of tenderness. But from his very
first day at Baluzac, a hard core of resistance to the priest had
grown up in his mind. It was still there, though Monsieur Calou
did not realize it. The relation of priest to layman is never a
neutral one: he either attracts or repels. Mirbel was always conscious of an instinctive repulsion, a feeling of disgust for the man
who was professionally chaste. Against this instinct he struggled
as hard as he could, but was unable to keep himself from hating
the very smell of a house that had no woman in it. He held it
as a grievance that Monsieur Calou should think it natural for a

young man of his age to subscribe to the same rule as himself, and his brooding rancor was the greater since neither in mind nor in heart was he susceptible to the attractions of piety, purity, and divine love. Those who live by the light of divine love find it hard to understand that the majority of mankind are complete strangers to it. They can form no idea of a state of mind in which it plays no part. The monotony of his solitary life, his losing fight against seeming to be ungrateful to a man who had done so much for him, combined to reawaken in Jean de Mirbel the old slumbering devil. The very affection that Monsieur Calou showed to him played into the enemy's hands, for Jean was by nature just the kind of young man who instinctively sets himself against any display of tenderness. Many and many a time in afterlife I have heard him say: "How I hate being loved!"

As the result of an inward contradiction which he never attempted to resolve, Mirbel resented the fact that the abbé seemed willing to relax in his favour the rigours of a moral and religious rule which he nevertheless hated. The priest shut his eyes to a number of things, and refrained from bothering the boy where the mere letter of the law was concerned. Far from feeling grateful for this latitude, Jean drew strength from the old man's weakness, and began to "run wild". On several occasions he went to the local inn, but he was not naturally sociable and he made no friends there. On the other hand, he was definitely attractive to women, and had had his first "adventure" before the winter was out. The girl's parents complained to the abbé, who intervened, though in rather a tactless way. Like most chaste men he believed that a serious love affair was the best way of protecting a young man from the passing temptations of the flesh. He had no doubts about Jean's loyalty to Michèle, and felt sure that he would never be false to her. Now, however true it may be that a great many young men are capable of remaining faithful to the young women they love, there are plenty of others, and Mirbel was one of them, who think of "being in love" and indulging their senses as two totally different things. They really care for one woman and for one woman only, and it exasperates them to think that the same standard should be applied to the genuine adoration of true love and to the trivial affairs in which the body is all that matters.

This subject was the occasion of the first real quarrel that took

place between the abbé and Mirbel. In the course of it the latter
let himself go with a violence which until that moment he had
kept under strict control. He took advantage of the fact that the
priest did not dream of condemning him on grounds of Christian
morality, but appealed rather to an outworn code of sentiment in
which no one outside the walls of a seminary any longer believed.
Jean went so far as to forbid the abbé to speak of Michèle, adding that he would let no one mention her name in his presence.
The angrier Mirbel became, the less did the abbé press his argument. But Jean felt no gratitude for this consideration, and resented the other's obvious, if unspoken, grief. "He makes it a
point of grievance that I behave to him much too like a complacent father," the abbé noted in his diary that evening. "However little of a Christian a man may be, he wants to be loved in
and for God alone—even though he does not believe in God."

Though Mirbel has never confessed to me precisely what it
was that he said in the heat of anger, I imagine that this sentence
of the abbé Calou's referred to something very cruel that he had
let slip that evening. Jean knew that he had been cruel, and
though part of him was horrified by the realization, he drove
ahead along the same road with a sort of fierce intensity and displayed a needless spitefulness. It was, however, neither out of
malice aforethought, nor with any intention of dealing his benefactor a final blow that he became entangled with the chemist's
wife. It was the schoolteacher and his wife who first took him to
visit Hortense Voyod. On that rainy February day when the
young man whom she had watched for so long from behind her
window blinds crossed the rain-soaked little courtyard wrapped
in his schoolboy's cape and hood and entered the shop, she could
at last heave a sigh of relief, even though her revenge was as yet
far from complete.

Many were the discussions held by the light of an oil lamp
and in the warmth of a roaring stove, with Armagnac loosening
the assembled tongues. Jean would have found it impossible to
say precisely what satisfaction he derived from the presence of
this pallid woman and from the sound of her voice which, for all
its hoarseness, was gentle and quite unmarked by any local accent. While the schoolmaster's anti-clerical passion, when it was
expended on the politics of the moment, had no manner of in-

terest for Mirbel, the mocking sallies of the pharmacist's wife roused an immediate response in him. She spoke a language which he had never heard till then, but which he at once recognized.

On that first evening she insisted that he should come to her shop only after nightfall, and should never enter the door until he was quite certain that no one had seen him. For, said she, the Curé, with whom she had had several passages of arms, would certainly not approve of their friendship; but it would be easy to keep secret. He protested against being involved in his tutor's quarrels. During the next few days they began to realize how deep was the sentiment that bound them.

The ruling passion of this woman (who was without any real education, though she had read a number of modern books both good and bad) was a hatred of—a sense of grievance against— the God whose very existence she denied. The lack of logic in such an attitude did not bother her in the slightest degree. Against an unknown Being in whom she did not believe she levelled the reproaches of a class of creatures for whom there can be no release in this world save in complete destruction.

It is most unlikely that she ever spoke to Mirbel of this private and festering sore. But it so happened that, though there was no particular reason why he should share the special bitterness of a woman twenty years his senior, he did suffer from a wild sense of anger against the Fate that had made him what he was. That he was a Mirbel, the heir to a patrician name, made it all the stranger that he should be animated by so hostile, so stubborn a feeling of resentment against all ordered living, against all constraint where his own happiness was concerned. Hortense Voyod was well aware from what poisoned source her own hatred proceeded, but for no consideration in the world would she have imparted this knowledge to Jean, though she could have done so had she wished. The young man, on the other hand, had no idea why it was that everything in life seemed hateful to him with the exception of one young girl whom he would probably never see again, and a priest whom he detested.

Perhaps Hortense Voyod would have reached her goal less easily had not Jean been an instrument ready to her hand. But the understanding that grew between them from the occasion of their very first meeting, the link that bound them so tightly together, facilitated her manoeuvre. No longer was it necessary for her to feign a sympathy which, in fact, she genuinely felt. The

youth had walked willingly into her spider's parlour and seemed
to take pleasure in the consciousness of his imprisonment. No
trickery on her part had been necessary to attract him thither.

It was the abbé Calou's habit to go into the church each evening with the object of finishing the reading of his breviary before the Holy Sacrament, and he stayed there until dinner-time.
As soon as he was out of the way, Jean used to leave the presbytery by the door that faced away from the main road, and
make his way round the outskirts of the village. It was not necessary to go into the shop at all. He could reach Hortense's house
by jumping over the fence that surrounded the kitchen-garden.

Even had he not wanted to avoid meeting stray customers,
Mirbel would have been careful to keep out of the way of the
chemist, who was a little old man for ever occupied in wrapping
up bottles of medicine as though the lives of all the invalids in
the neighbourhood depended on him. His manners were excessively humble, but his way of laughing and the expression of his
eyes gave them the lie. He looked after his wife's property (that he
should do so formed the essential clause of their secret compact:
he made no claim on her person, but, in return for this concession, had insisted that her property be consigned to his charge).
Consequently he was absent every afternoon, and, on returning
home, never ventured into the back shop when what he called
"the club" was in session.

Scarcely a fortnight passed before Monsieur Calou got wind of
these secret meetings. This time he did not yield to his first impulse, and, when at last he mentioned the subject to Mirbel, did
so without any show of anger, and only after giving much thought
to the problem of how best to deal with the situation. Far from
reproaching the boy, he realized that solitude is a vocation that
can hardly be expected to appeal to youths of eighteen. But he
had good reasons—reasons that he could not mention to Jean—
for holding that Hortense Voyod was a woman bent on his destruction. What he did, therefore, was to make an appeal to his
loyalty. To enter into close relations with such a woman while
he was living under her enemy's roof would be tantamount to
treachery. If Jean felt it impossible to remain at Baluzac without
constant visits to the apothecary's shop, they had better face the
fact, and the abbé would make arrangements for the boy to go
home. But this was what Jean dreaded above all else, since it

would mean that he would be sent to board at some Jesuit college. Moreover, his master's tone in mentioning the subject had touched him. He could not deny that Hortense Voyod wanted to injure the Curé—not that she had ever attacked him in Jean's hearing (he would never have permitted such a thing), but her sentiments were obvious in every word she spoke; so much so, that each time he left the back shop and found himself again in the presbytery dining-room, looking across the steaming tureen at the abbé's child-like gaze, and returning his smile, he felt deeply ashamed. He gave his word that he would discontinue his visits. He told me later that he spoke in perfect good faith and fully meant to keep his promise.

It was about this time that Monsieur Calou arranged for him to have a horse, and stopped me in the street with the proposal that he and Michèle should exchange letters, with what disastrous results I have already explained.

Separated as he was from Michèle, and forbidden to correspond with her, Jean had been suffering from a sense of being exiled even before he made the acquaintance of Hortense Voyod. He felt it still harder to endure his isolation when he was deprived of the distraction provided by the discussions to which he had grown accustomed, and those readings aloud by the schoolmaster of articles by Hervé, Gérault-Richard, and Jaurès. (On these occasions Hortense would toss off her glass like a man, light a cigarette, and hold the company by those bursts of bitter, lively talk which, as Mirbel told me many years later, still remained in his memory as having been curiously exciting.)

The abbé Calou would far rather have faced some active show of resentment by his pupil. How could he deal with this sullen gloom, as of some caged beast?—especially after the Superior of the Sacred Heart had dryly intimated that all correspondence between him and Michèle must cease? Jean no longer occupied his time with reading, but roamed the woods on foot and on horseback until darkness fell. After some weeks he took to paying frequent visits to the schoolmaster. The abbé shut his eyes to all this. He had a pretty shrewd suspicion that the boy found a letter from Hortense Voyod awaiting him each time he went there, and that he left one for her when he said good-night. But nothing had been said about writing. Without these almost daily exchanges, it is probable that their relations would never have taken a passionate turn—that it was the young man's romantic effusions that gave Hortense her great idea. She began to think that certain developments might be possible of which hitherto she had never even dreamed; for Jean was young enough to be her son.

She proceeded with the utmost caution. At first she confined herself to the language of friendship, a sentiment she was adept at using for her own purposes, though quite incapable of feeling in fact. Since her days at boarding-school, where she had remained until she got her diploma, friendship had never been anything for her but an alibi for desire. And now it was her desire for revenge that was at stake. She had no illusions about the kind of feeling she inspired in Mirbel. He had not confided in her, but she knew perfectly well that he was very unhappy, and that his heart belonged to another. But, more clear-sighted than the abbé, she soon realized how strong the animal was in him, and how wholly dominated he was by the blind and irresistible cravings of his senses.

Hortense Voyod had begun by getting a clear picture of this side of his nature. The two or three letters from her which Jean kept, and which he showed me later, were not so much sentimental in tone as carefully composed with the sole object of stirring, without any touch of coarseness, a young imagination condemned to loneliness. One of the few notes left by the abbé on the subject of Hortense shows the extent to which the priest was preoccupied, even obsessed, by the thought of this woman. "It is difficult to account for such knowledge of the human mind in a mere country-bred woman," he wrote. "The explanation is, I suppose, that vice itself has a certain educational effect. It is not given to all of us to look evil in the face. Our petty individual weaknesses, to which we give the name of 'evil', have nothing in common with this violent determination to destroy the soul. . . . The spirit of evil, as the eighteenth century knew it and expressed it in the *Liaisons Dangereuses*, exists, as I know now, actually within a few miles of my presbytery, behind the shutters of an apothecary's shop. . . ."

Spring came early. Jean, though he would have to face his finals before the year was out, continually played truant. Hortense knew that she could contrive a meeting with him as soon as she thought that the right moment had come. All she had to do was to take a walk along the banks of the Ciron. But she was in no hurry and wanted to avoid all unnecessary risk. First of all, she must so arrange matters that the boy was haunted by the thought of her, obsessed by dreams in which she was the central figure. Her plans were beginning to extend further than the mere satisfaction of a desire for vengeance. It was not enough for her to deal the abbé Calou a mortal blow. Ever since she had lost her girl friend she had been seeking a pretext to get rid of her old husband, whose days of usefulness were over. She reckoned that this young Mirbel could not only help her to her revenge, but could serve as a stage in her fight for freedom, provided he was willing to face the scandal. But she was still uncertain what steps to take.

As soon as the first fine weather came, the abbé Calou, as was his custom, made a tour of the district and the outlying farms on his bicycle. He had to round up the children for his catechism classes and visit the sick, especially the old men whom their sons kept hard at work until they dropped down dead. Very often, as they lay helpless in bed, there would be some virago of a daughter-in-law to grudge them the very black bread they mumbled with their toothless gums. Here was to be seen humanity with very little pity for itself and none whatever for others. The general view in such houses was that all priests are sly and lazy. "What's the use of the clergy, anyway? Much better . . ." What it would be much better to do with them was never clear in the speakers' minds, but it had some connection with an idea, so precious at that time to the abbé Calou, of what that stationary cross bearing the figure of the nailed God really meant. The priest, fastened to the same instrument of torment and exposed to the same derision, confronts mankind with an enigma which it makes no effort to solve.

One afternoon towards the end of April, when the Curé got home before dusk, he was met by Maria who had been on the lookout for his return. She told him that Monsieur Voyod the pharmacist had been there for half an hour. She had thought it her duty, she said, to light the fire.

This was the first time that Hortense's husband had crossed the threshold of the presbytery. The abbé, much moved by curiosity, found his visitor seated beside the smoking grate. As the priest entered he rose from his chair. He was wearing his Sunday-best. A narrow black ribbon failed to conceal his shirt stud, and

it would not have been difficult to insert a hand between his
collar and his skinny neck. When he smiled he revealed a mouth
entirely empty.

He apologized for not having come before this to pay his re-
spects to his parish priest. He had feared that he would not be
too well received. Most people, however, knew that he did not
share all his wife's ideas. When his first wife had been alive he
had always gone to church on feast-days, and had sung in the
choir until he was nineteen. He was very anxious that the Curé
should not look on him as an enemy, and hoped that he would be
good enough to give him his custom. It was a nuisance to have
to go into Vallandraut every time one wanted a few lozenges.

All this was spoken glibly, like a lesson learned by heart,
and the abbé could not think what it was that the man really
wanted. He referred once again to the principles expressed by
Madame Voyod, which, he said, he was far from approving.
Things weren't any too easy for him, as the Curé might well
imagine. He had sacrificed much in order to be a father to the
daughter of his old friend Destiou when she was left alone in the
world with no one to look after her property. He fully realized,
he said, that people had imputed interested motives to him . . .
but what advantage had the marriage brought *him*? All the
troubles of ownership without any of the rewards. The ideas of
Madame Voyod had lost him quite a number of customers. She
had been a trial to him from the beginning, and now the cloven
hoof was beginning to show. It wasn't for him to give the Curé
advice, but he couldn't help feeling rather surprised that that
young pupil of his should be allowed to see so much of a woman
who was known to be an enemy of the Church. However that
might be, he, as her husband—though he was more a father to
her than a husband—was getting a trifle worried about the meetings between the two. All Baluzac was talking. He knew that the
boy was just a young scamp, and that at his age such things
weren't very important . . . still . . .

At this point the Curé interrupted him with an assurance that
his pupil would pay no further visits to the shop; but the old man
went on to talk of meetings in the woods, which couldn't do the
young man much good, and which she'd be a great deal better
without, as was shown by the fact that she had taken his remarks
on the subject with a very bad grace. As though he had forgotten
that he had already represented his marriage as an act of disin-

terested devotion on his part, he began to snivel, and to say that
it was very hard that after a lifetime of work for others he should
find himself threatened in his old age with the loss of everything
that he had struggled to build up. When a man has spent years
looking after a property, has got it into good shape, has sown the
waste land, cleared the brush, and fought off encroaching neighbours, it's a bit rough, just when everything is going smoothly, to
find himself threatened with dismissal like a servant.

Monsieur Calou pointed out that all this had nothing to do
with his pupil. The chemist admitted that it was hard to believe
the situation had taken so serious a turn. It was the last thing
that would ever have entered his head because, after all, it was
only fair to Hortense to say that she had never run after men,
and no one could say there'd ever been any reason why she
should . . . (here the old man shot a quick glance at the Curé,
but hastily veiled his eyes behind their inflamed lids).

The abbé had taken up the tongs and was paying very self-
conscious attention to the fire. He said that the chimney was cold,
that they hadn't burned so much as a handful of twigs there all
winter. The smoke was making the visitor cough. He urged the
Curé to give a word of warning to his pupil. . . . Of course there
was nothing in it all . . . but why arouse unnecessary gossip? . . .
Hortense was getting to the difficult age. . . .

The tongs shook in the priest's large hands. He got up. He
had to bend his head in order to see his visitor's face.

"You can be perfectly easy in your mind, Monsieur Voyod.
There shall be no more wandering in the woods—from to-morrow:
I give you my word for that."

His visitor was of the opinion that the Curé was not in the
best of tempers. He said later that he had never seen a man so
beside himself, so capable of giving someone a bad half-hour. He
felt very glad not to be in that young man's skin when he came
in for supper.

As soon as Monsieur Calou was alone he went up to his room,
poured some water into the basin, and bathed his face. Then he
knelt down, but the words got no farther than his lips. Thoughts
swarmed in his brain like dead leaves in a high wind. In his
brother's family there was a saying: "That was during the holidays in 1880, the year when Ernest saw red. . . ." The last of
these terrible fits of temper had delayed his ordination as deacon

by twelve months, and since that time he had always managed, aided by the gift of Grace, to keep his outbursts within bounds.

On this particular evening he knelt at his *prie-dieu* and held his head in his hands. "There is danger . . . you may do him irreparable harm. . . ." But stronger than this appeal to his sense of prudence was an angry longing to take the boy by the scruff of the neck and force him to his knees until he begged for mercy. That done, there should be an end to this business of not taking things seriously. He should be treated as Uncle Adhémar had always hoped he would be. Since he would obey nothing but superior strength, and yield to nothing but fear, the Curé of Baluzac would find some way of breaking his will and making him as obedient as a whipped cur. "Go on praying, give yourself time," went on the tireless inner voice.

Suddenly he heard the well-known footstep on the stairs. He went to the door and opened it.

"Come in here: I've got something to say to you."

And when the other replied, "Later," he remained stern and insistent. "Now, at once."

Jean shrugged his shoulders and started up the second flight. But a hand gripped his collar, he felt the pressure of a knee in the small of his back, and found himself lying on the divan-bed where he had been thrown like a parcel, all among the books and pamphlets.

Staggered, he sat here, conscious of two enormous fists in close proximity to his face. He could do nothing but stammer: "What on earth's up?"

The abbé was breathing hard and wiping his damp brow with the back of his hand. Thank Heaven, he had not given way to violence. For the time being, at least, the worst was over.

His voice was icy but completely under control. He told his pupil that he had been within an ace of getting a sound thrashing. He added that in future he would keep a watchful eye on him until such time as the Mirbel family should see fit to relieve him of his responsibilities. He hoped, he said, that the boy would not compel him to have recourse to physical violence, because he was apt to lose control of himself, and was a hard hitter.

Having delivered himself of this warning, he ordered his pupil to his room, and remarked that supper would be sent up to him.

"All the time he was behaving like a brute," wrote Jean to Hortense Voyod, "the Curé kept his eyes shut. Perhaps he was

praying, though his lips did not move. . . . Priests always manage
to get away with things in that way!"

The abbé kept his word. He never let Mirbel out of his sight
except when duty called him away, and then he left Maria in
charge. No doubt Jean managed to slip away quite often, and
not for a moment did he discontinue his correspondence with
Hortense Voyod. This he managed, thanks to the visits of the
schoolmaster who came to coach him in mathematics. But, for
all that, he was completely dominated by the priest, and was
forced to bow to his inflexible will. Besides, the examination was
approaching and he had to keep his nose to the grindstone, which
meant that he must postpone until later any plans of revolt that
he might have formed. He satisfied the examiners on his written
work, but failed in his orals. He did not return to Baluzac until
September, having spent a month with the Countess at La Devize.
It was the first time that he had met his mother since the terrible
revelation which had come to him at Balauze.

"My Jean has changed," wrote the Countess to the abbé Calou.
"He was always a handful, but he never used to be cynical. Now
all that has changed! I can't utter a word of advice, or even try
to raise the tone of our conversations (hard though I try to do so),
without the little wretch's laughing in my face. I don't want to
question the excellence of your methods, but I hope you won't
mind my saying that they seem to have misfired entirely in the
case of my son."

Almost every day during the vacation Jean got a letter from
the chemist's wife. No sooner had he returned to the presbytery
than her plans began to take shape. In October a fresh cause of
frustration occurred, and he hesitated no longer. The necessity
of making his Retreat had obliged the abbé to be absent for some
days. During all that time Jean was constantly in the company of
Hortense. The abbé found on his return that the boy seemed much
calmer, almost mild indeed, and consequently he somewhat relaxed his watchful attitude. Relations between the two had become merely those between master and pupil. They hardly ever
spoke except about work, and avoided all controversial subjects. The priest was giving himself with renewed confidence to
his little flock. The children were beginning to talk freely to him
and even showed some signs of affection. He failed to notice the
new barrier that had arisen between Jean and himself. Illogical

ing hostile in his attitude to us. At the gate of the cemetery he seemed not to notice the hand I held out to him, and I had to take hold of his. He withdrew it at once. As to my stepmother, she did not dare even to make the gesture, for he bowed his head without giving her a glance or making the slightest movement with his arm.

That evening after dinner, in my room, whither she had followed me, she said that she feared that Monsieur Puybaraud had listened to the promptings of rebellion. It was much to be regretted that she had not been able to have a word with him, for she might have succeeded in softening his hard heart and helping him to achieve a mood of resignation and submission. To this I objected that the enmity he had shown us was no proof that he felt the same way towards God, and I added hypocritically that, since he had been the husband of a saint, my stepmother could ask her intercession for all those particular manifestations of grace of which Monsieur Puybaraud stood in need.

"A saint?" said Brigitte Pian. "A saint?" She looked at me without anger, but with a sort of concentrated gaze that might have been taken for stupidity. For a moment or two she moved about the table, and then withdrew, taking with her, doubtless, an added load of trouble and anxiety upon which to brood during the night.

All through the days that followed Octavia's funeral she made no attempt to see the widower again, though she continued to help him surreptitiously, with the connivance of the Sister. Michèle had gone back to the Sacred Heart, and my stepmother and I resumed our old life of shared solitude. She did everything she could to please me, showing an eagerness in the task that might almost have deserved the name of humility. It was as though her sole hope of succour lay in a young man whose attitude to her was one of frightening correctness.

Following the suggestion made to me by the abbé Calou, I wrote from Larjuzon to the Comtesse de Mirbel asking for news of Jean. I found her answer awaiting me in Bordeaux. Every word of her letter had been carefully weighed, with the sole intention of minimizing the scandal.

I am not at all surprised, my dear young friend, that you should be anxious about Jean, or that you should have been influenced by the ridiculous tittle-tattle that has been going the rounds. He has returned to us here much surprised and considerably disturbed by all the talk there has been about his little escapade. The Curé and the pharmacist are the two persons chiefly responsible. Both are guilty of having stirred up public opinion. For the second of the gentlemen in question there is some show of excuse, but the former has shown a lack of judgment and moderation which is really quite intolerable in one of his cloth, to say nothing of the fact that he claims to be an educator of youth! I said as much when I went to pay back the money he had advanced to my son. It has been the subject of fantastic gossip. I can only hope that if it came to your ears you refused to believe a word. The priest had nothing to say to my charges, and I must admit that my feelings as a mother led me to express myself with what may have been rather excessive warmth.

(Much later I was able to realize how sublime the abbé's silence had been. With a single word he could have crushed the woman who was hurling insults at his head, for she did not then know that her son had spent a whole night shivering beneath the windows of the Balauze hotel, that he had very nearly died as a result of that adventure, and that his mind had been permanently scarred and poisoned by what his eyes had seen on that occasion, and by what his ears had heard.)

The Countess told me, in conclusion, that Jean was to spend the rest of the year in England, and that he would have to be in Bordeaux for a few days before starting on his journey. She hoped that he would be permitted to come and say good-bye to us.

This letter left me with a feeling of embarrassment and uncertainty. Ought I to send it on to the abbé Calou in accordance with my promise? I had to relax my attitude of reserve towards my stepmother in order to ask her advice on the point. As a matter of fact, I anticipated a certain amount of pleasure from watching her reactions. But if I had expected her to rail violently against the Curé of Baluzac, there was a surprise in store for me (as there had often been on previous occasions). She adopted an entirely unexpected attitude. She gave it as her considered view that I should do nothing that might unnecessarily wound a man who had recently been so sorely tried. Since, on the other hand, the document might be useful to him, she advised me to forward it, but with a covering note to the effect that we none of us believed the Countess's allegations. This was the first time, so far as I knew, that my stepmother had ever gone back on a verdict once given, and when I wrote to the abbé Calou I did not hesitate to draw his attention to this extraordinary change in her. I allowed myself to indulge in an expression of irony which he did not at all approve. His answer reached me only a week later. I insert a copy of it here with feelings of respect and admiration. I can truly say that, having read it, I was never quite the same again.

Dear Louis:

I have delayed replying to your letter because it arrived after I had left Baluzac, and was forwarded to me at my brother's house where I shall be for some time to come. I shall not beat about the bush with you. You know too much about what has happened for me to be able to deceive you successfully. I am no longer Curé of Baluzac. I am no longer even permitted to live there. I was told to leave the parish as soon as possible, and to retire into the bosom of my family. The long and the short of it is—I am in disgrace, and circumstances compel me to attach rather more significance to that phrase than it usually bears. The Mirbels and old Voyod have agreed to saddle me with full responsibility for the scandal. But that is not all. The report that Madame Brigitte did me the honour of compiling some months ago and sent to the Vicar-General appears to have anticipated in every detail precisely what did in fact occur. Events have fully justified the weighty and truly remarkable survey which your dear stepmother then prepared of my character and general tendencies. I write this in no spirit of irony, my dear boy, and I will take this opportunity of saying that I did not greatly care for the tone that marked your letter to me. As you know very well, I do not believe in chance, and I do not believe that it is mere chance that all Madame Brigitte's prognostications were borne out by the facts. I will not go so far as to say that her interpretation of the facts or of the motives of others is always very judicious, but she does have a sort of gift for unearthing evil intentions. She would probably be quite genuinely surprised if I told her that my mistake and hers are at bottom identical. They pursue different roads, only to reach the same end. Both of us, she ruled by her reason, I by my feelings, have been inclined to believe that it is our duty to interfere in the destinies of those around us. I do not deny that it is the first duty of the sacred office conferred by priesthood—as, indeed, it is part of the duty of every Christian— to preach the Gospel: but that does not mean that we should try to turn our neighbour into a replica of ourselves, or force him to see with our eyes. Of ourselves we can do nothing. Our concern should be limited to walking before the Divine Grace as the dog goes in front of the invisible hunter. This we can do with greater or less effectiveness in proportion as we are more or less atten- tive and obedient to the Will of our Master, more or less willing to let ourselves be moulded by it, more or less ready to ignore our own. So far as I am concerned, Madame Brigitte has been perfectly justified in her attitude. What she condemns in me is the lack of any sense of proportion, of any genuine power of judg- ment. She points out, with striking truth, that this lack, when found in a priest, and in the highly developed form it has as- sumed in my own case, is apt to produce worse disasters than any low, criminal passion. It led me to interfere rashly, heatedly, and ill-advisedly, in the concerns of others. Naturally, these activ- ities of mine have to some extent served the purposes of Grace, because such is the Love of God that it turns all things to the greater good of those on whom it is lavished. But when it comes to measuring the havoc that accumulates about what we conceive to be our mission, we must give full weight to all those unad- mitted interests, all those secret desires whose existence in our hearts we scarcely realize. That is why we should allow full play to the spirit of compassion.

I am afraid, my dear boy, that all this will seem very obscure to you. We will talk about it again some years from now, should the Father not have seen fit meanwhile to call unto Himself his very useless, nay, his sometimes actively dangerous, servant. For the moment, let me give you the following word of advice in re- gard to Madame Brigitte. You must not sneer at the way her spirit moves nor look on her ordeal as something petty and unim- portant. Up to now she has seen only the edifying aspect of her activities. Suddenly, and without any warning, her eyes have been opened on to a new and horrible view of herself. When Christ makes us see clearly, and we become aware of our actions pressing in upon and surrounding us, we are as much astonished as was the man born blind who, in the Gospel story, saw "men as trees walking". But it is important that Madame Brigitte should under- stand the truth of what I have discovered for myself as a result

*of my present degradation, which is a great deal worse than you
can possibly know. There is no form of calumny that has not
been heaped upon me. People believe of me what they will, both
in the Archbishop's palace and out of it. I can say without fear of
contradiction that now, in my old age, I have lost every scrap of
that honourable reputation I once enjoyed in men's eyes, that, in
my own person, I have allowed outrage to be done upon that Jesus
who has marked me as His own. My family is humiliated and
vexed as a result of the shame I have brought upon it, to say
nothing of the material embarrassment that my constant presence
in this house has caused to its inmates. My youngest nephew has
had to give up his room to me, and share with his brother. I need
hardly say that they are all very kind to me. But my sister-in-law
is just a little too insistent with her questions. What am I going
to do with myself? she asks, and I can answer only that I do
not know, for, truth to tell, I am good for nothing, and can be of
use to none. . . . It would be foolish to deceive myself further.
I stand now in the presence of my God, as naked, as much
stripped of all merit, as utterly defenceless as a man can well be.
Perhaps that is the state in which those of us should be whose
profession it is—if I may so express myself—to be virtuous. It is almost inevitable that the professionally virtuous should hold exaggerated ideas of the importance of their actions, that they should
constitute themselves the judges of their own progress in excellence, that, measuring themselves by the standards of those
around them, they should at times be made slightly giddy by the
spectacle of their own merits. I should like to think that Madame
Brigitte is drawing from her present testing-time an assurance
that her feet are set upon the road to a great discovery.*

Some may think that the abbé Calou, by thus addressing a youth
of seventeen, was merely showing that he had not made much
progress towards bettering his judgment. I did not dare to show
this letter to my stepmother, though she no longer made any
effort to keep her state of mind from me. I lived continuously
now in the intolerable atmosphere created by her condition of
spiritual torment. About this time, an anarchist weekly rag called
The Battle, which flourished on scandal, published a number of
poisonous paragraphs about the "abduction of a pharmacist's
wife". I was amazed when Brigitte Pian asked me to get this scur-
rilous production for her each week. She would never have dared

buy it for herself, nor would she have sent a servant to buy it for her. I could not understand the curious pleasure she seemed to get from reading it, especially after learning at school that Monsieur Puybaraud had been taken on as editorial secretary, and that, rightly or wrongly, the general view was that all the anti-religious muck that it contained came from his pen.

She spent the whole of each Saturday evening reading this paper. I know, for I was always there, and I suspect that she carried her perusal of it far into the night. It was as though she wanted to saturate her mind in the vileness of a man whom she had herself driven (or thought she had) by despair into a state of rebellion and hatred. Children (and adolescents too, for that matter) are not as a rule conscious of the physical changes that take place in the grown-up persons with whom they live. But I did become aware that Brigitte Pian was growing a little bit thinner each day. The amethyst-coloured dressing-gown now hung loosely upon her body, as though the thick, bloated snake of braided hair were indeed feeding on the very substance of her flesh. The oddest thing of all was that after the lapse of a few months, Monsieur Puybaraud not only left the paper and shut himself away in the Trappist monastery of Septfonts for a retreat, but that he stayed there for good and all, and, in the habit of a novice, accomplished that destiny which my stepmother had always urged on him. Once again the views of Brigitte Pian had coincided with those of Providence. . . . But she could not, at the time of which I am speaking, have foreseen such an unhoped-for issue, and if at moments her anxious mind ceased to concern herself with a renegade, it was only because she was obsessed by thoughts of her other victims—of her husband, of Octavia, both of whom might still have been alive (or so she believed) had they not met with Brigitte Pian on their way through life. She thought too of Michèle, of Jean, and of the abbé Calou whom she had denounced.

On one point I am still not clear: whether she could have derived comfort, during her time of crisis, from a spiritual director. I did not know who hers was, and was not even certain that she had one. I have an idea, moreover, that even at the period of her life when she was deriving the most satisfaction from the thought of her progress in virtue, and when there was no reason to suppose that she would one day become a prey to the furies

of scruple, she did not take the sacraments as often as might have
been expected of so convinced a church-goer. The quarrel cen-
tring about the question of "frequent communion", which had
been loosed upon Christendom two and a half centuries before,
was, in my childhood, still very much alive. There are to-day
few Christians, however devout, who have recourse to the Eucharist as often as they might. Forty years ago a spirit of fear and
trembling still ruled the minds of certain persons in their relations
with the Incarnate Love, who, so they had been taught by Jan-
senism to believe, was implacable.

One thing is beyond doubt. All through Lent that year, and the
closer we drew to Easter, Brigitte Pian's worries took on more
and more the character of sheer terror. One evening she came into
my room without knocking. I was already in my bed, reading
Dominique, and the eyes I turned on the intruder were still full
of the imaginary sights from which I had been snatched.

"Aren't you asleep?" she asked in a shy, imploring tone.

She saw from my face that I resented being disturbed. If I
had not been in bed, I should have clasped my head in my
hands, stuck my fingers in my ears, and buried myself in my
book in such a way as to discourage her from persisting in her
interruption. But there beneath the sheets I was, as it were, quite
defenceless.

"I want your advice, Louis. . . . It may seem odd to you that
I should say that, but there are moments when I can no longer
see my way clear before me. Which do you think is worse: to
disobey the Church by not communicating at Easter, or, by obey-
ing, to expose oneself to the risk of receiving the Eucharist in an
improper state of mind? . . . No, don't answer at once: take your
time and give me a considered reply. Remember what Saint Paul
said when he spoke of those who do not fully realize the presence
of our Lord's body. . . ."

I told her that my answer didn't need much thought, and that
there was really no dilemma at all, because the confession of
her sins to a priest would ensure her recovering a state of
Grace. . . .

"That may be true for you, Louis, my dear: true enough for the
heart of a child. Indeed, I am sure it *is!*"

She sat down heavily on the edge of my bed. I was in for a
long visit! I must give up all thoughts of *Dominique*. Instead, I
had to listen to the outpourings of a haggard old woman.

"For that to be true, the sins must in the first place be simple,
easily recognized and defined, capable of being fitted into a formula. But how do you think I could ever make intelligible to a
priest the problems that are tormenting me? How could he understand my relations with your father, with the Puybarauds, with
Monsieur Calou, with Michèle? I have tried three times already. I
have been, in turn, to a Secular, to a Dominican, and to a Jesuit.
All three regarded me as one of those over-scrupulous females
who are the bane of confessors, and against whom they use the
one weapon most calculated to increase the torments of their
pentitents by speaking as though they did not take their self-
accusations seriously. On such occasions one leaves the confessional
convinced that one has not been understood, that one cannot be
pardoned for a sin that has made no real impression on the
priest. . . . Well, that is *my* position", she added suddenly, after
a moment's silence. "The whole problem is to know whether one's
scruples are justified. Surely, the mere fact of suffering as I am suffering *must* mean that my sins are real."

"In such a case", said I priggishly, "scruple is the wrong word.
What you mean is remorse."

"You have put your finger on the sore place, Louis. We try to
comfort ourselves by using pretty words. It is true that I am tormented, not by scruples but by remorse: yes, remorse. You, with
that quickness of mind that poor Monsieur Puybaraud so much
admired, have understood me at once. But I despair of making
myself clear to those inexperienced men who look on sins as so
many easily defined gestures; who entirely fail to grasp the fact
that evil can sometimes poison a whole life, that evil may have
many shapes, may be invisible, incomprehensible, and, consequently, incommunicable—impossible to put into words. . . ."

She stopped speaking. The weight of her body was crushing
me. I could hear her heavy breathing.

"I have an idea", I said. (I now felt as excited as I used to feel
in the old days when Monsieur Puybaraud asked me questions as
though I had been an oracle, and I tried to dazzle him by an
answer that should be at once unexpected and full of wisdom.)
"The only priest who can restore your peace of mind is one who
not only has known you for many years, but is familiar with the
happenings that are causing you so much uneasiness." I warmed
to my task, while she watched me with the same kind of eager
attention that the seriously ill show as soon as the doctor opens

his lips. "The abbé Calou knows everything already. In his last letter to me he described all the details of the trouble from which
you are suffering. Scruple or remorse—the name does not matter.
He will know what is on your mind and, because he knows, will
be in a position to give you absolution."

"The abbé Calou? Do you really think so? Do you think I could
make my confession to him after everything I have done to him?"

"That's just the point: after all you've done *to him.*"

She got up and began to pace about the room. She kept on
groaning that she could never bring herself to do it. . . .

"It will be hard, of course," I said (I was becoming crafty);
"but by so much the more will you acquire merit."

That word "merit" made her raise her head.

"It would be beyond the strength of most people, but you . . ."

She straightened up still more. "After all . . ." she muttered, and
then went on: "I should have to seek him out in the bosom of
his family. But is it certain that he has the right now to hear
confessions?" She addressed the question to herself rather than to
me. "Yes, surely he has, provided it is within the limits of the
diocese."

She started walking up and down again. I yawned noisily and
burrowed down under the sheets.

"Sleepy, aren't you? Lucky you: nothing will keep *you* awake."

She leaned over me, and her cracked lips touched my forehead.

"It *is* a good idea, isn't it?" I asked in a self-satisfied voice.

She made no reply, but stood turning the matter over and over
in her mind. She put out the light, but I lit it again as soon as she
had closed the door. Once more, *Dominique* drew my thoughts
far from the concerns of that hag-ridden woman.

❦ X V ❦

WHEN she left the train that had brought her back from the
abbé Calou, it was still two hours before dinner-time. Instead,
therefore, of taking a cab, she walked back along the gloomy rue
Saint-Jean. It was foggy and she was jostled by the crowd. But
to-day she was indifferent to all that usually she most disliked,

for she carried within her the assurance of pardon. She pursued her way with a light heart and, for the first time, the impulse of gratitude that set her in the presence of God had in it something of a tenderness that was at once humble and very human. Her evil had been taken from her. She no longer suffered, no longer found it difficult to breathe. Occasionally, as a sharp reminder, the prick of her old anxieties returned. Had she confessed everything? Yes, of course she had: and anyhow, he who had listened to her had known it all before.

She let her mind dwell on what had been said in the fireless, whitewashed, almost bare room in which the abbé Calou had received her. He had offered her no words of comfort. Instead, he had made her feel ashamed because she had attached so much importance to her faults, as though she didn't know that it is God's way to turn even our sins to His own purposes. The abbé had begged her to dwell on her own insignificance, and not to substitute for the illusion that she was a person well advanced along the way of perfection, that other, no less vicious, illusion that she was a notable sinner. He had added that she could do much for those to whom she thought she owed reparation; for the dead, naturally, but also for the living. "As, for example," he said, "you can be of great help to me with the Cardinal. . . ." (She realized that he was saying this to help her, from a feeling of charity. . . .) To be taken back into favour was not what he desired, but to be allowed to settle, at his own cost, somewhere between Bastide and Souys, in the poorest, most solitary part of the country he could find, there to take premises where he might be permitted to teach the catechism and to say Mass. Brigitte Pian, walking so light-heartedly along the pavements damp with fog, decided that she would shoulder the expenses of this enterprise. Already she saw in imagination a new parish arising around the abbé Calou.

She had just time to go into the Cathedral before the doors were locked, and remained there for a few minutes, motionless, like someone who has been blessed by a miraculous cure and can find no words of gratitude. Then she set out again and reached her own front door, scarcely conscious of what streets she passed along.

In the hall an unusual smell of tobacco brought her back to earth. Who could it be who dared to smoke in her house? She recognized a voice, Michèle's, mingled with another which she could not identify. Yet, for all that, she knew at once who had penetrated, had dared to penetrate, into her drawing-room. The Countess's letter had hinted that young Mirbel might pay us a visit, but Brigitte had not seriously believed that the young thief would have the effrontery to show himself. But he had come! We had actually received him! There he was, behind this very door, talking freely to Michèle.

Brigitte Pian drew herself up. There, in the hall lit by a single gas-burner in a frosted globe, she became once more her old self, a woman strong in her assurance of Grace, convinced of her right to interfere in the lives of those over whom she had authority. At the same time she heard within herself the low rumblings of that righteous anger which she found it so difficult to resist, which showed itself whenever her orders were flouted and anyone dared to question or evade something she had determined and laid down. With her hand on the latch, she hesitated once more. In spite of her anger, in spite of this blow administered to her newly acquired sense of peace, the deep call of her spirit was still operative. She knew that the people there in her drawing-room felt that she had done them a wrong. On that point, however, her conscience did not reproach her. What else could she have done? She had protected Michèle, who was still a child, and any mother would have done the same. The abbé Calou, however, saw things in a different light. She knew what young Mirbel meant to him, even though he had never once that day mentioned his name in her hearing. But certain words he had spoken came back now into her memory, and doubtless put her in mind of the lost sheep. Each one of us, he had said, has his own peculiar destiny, and it is, perhaps, one of the secrets of that compassionate Justice which watches over us, that there is no universally valid law by which human beings are to be assessed. Every man inherits his own past. For that he is to be pitied, because he carries with him through life a load made up of the sins and merits of his forebears to an extent that it is beyond our power to grasp. He is free to say yes or no when God's love is offered to him, but which of us can claim the right to judge what it is that influences his choice? It was while talking of the Puybarauds that the abbé had said: "We must not interfere blindly between two persons who love one another, even when they do so in sin. The important thing is that we should understand what their being brought together means, for the ways of human beings do not cross by chance. . . ."

As Brigitte Pian listened outside the door she could hear two voices intermingled: that of the young girl, which sounded depressed; the other, virile, uncertain in its register, with occasional rising passages which were muted by distance. No longer annoyed, but still uncertain, she sat down on the wooden chest. That it might not be thought that she was listening at keyholes (though she could not hear what was being said in the drawing-room), she went up to her room a few minutes later, and remained there a long time alone and on her knees in the darkness.

Jean de Mirbel had chosen Thursday for his attempted meeting with Michèle, because he knew that she would be free in the afternoon. It was I whom he asked to see. My first thought was to tell Michèle, and I saw at once that she knew that Jean was there. Her school uniform made her look plain. Her hair, half caught up into a "bun", was tied with a mauve ribbon. Her high shoes gave her ankles a thick appearance. I was not taken in by her assumed air of calmness. It was essential that this visit should not be made an excuse by our stepmother for a show of malevolence, and we agreed that even should Jean ask me to do so, I must not leave them alone together at any time during his visit.

That settled, we went down into the drawing-room. It was not yet four o'clock, but the heavy, fringed lace curtains made the room dark, and the wall-lamp had been lit. A smell of lamp oil hung about the "occasional tables" with their pyrographed tops, and the painted screens. The gilded chairs caught the light. Mirbel was taller than of old and had filled out, but his face was thinner. His hollow cheeks threw into relief the nose that had always been aquiline, though we had thought of it as small. His forehead was more lined than befitted his eighteen years. He was wearing a new ready-made suit, the shoulders of which were too much padded.

The two young people who had fallen in love before the lines of their physical development had become fully determined looked at one another with astonishment. There was what seemed to me a long interval of silence. The poor human insects had to trace backward the stages of their metamorphosis in order to see once more the child whom each had loved in the other. But their eyes had not changed, and it was those, I am sure, that first gave them the clue to their identities.

My boyish jealousy had long ago vanished. I wanted only to get away, to make myself invisible. It was no difficult task, for as soon as they began to speak, they were conscious only of each other. But their conversation dragged. It was as though they did not know what to talk about. Michèle sat down, but Jean remained standing with his back to the window. He had lit a cigarette without asking her whether she minded. From my corner I could not hear them very well, especially Jean, who kept on saying in angry, impatient tones, "But that's not the point . . . that's not of the least importance," to which Michèle replied with an air of mockery: "Really?" I gathered that they were discussing the chemist's wife. Jean, his hands in his pockets and his shoulders hunched, was rocking backwards and forwards on his feet. It was obvious, he said, that she did not want to have anything more to do with him, that she was taking the first excuse that came to hand to send him packing. Not that it wasn't perfectly natural. The only surprising thing was how she had ever come to believe that she cared for him.

Michèle interrupted the flow of his words. She spoke as she used to do in the days of their childhood quarrels. "So *you're* accusing *me!* I must say, I like that: after all, you started it!"

To this, Jean in a fit of exasperation replied: "Why must you harp on that idiotic story? I do wish you'd try to understand that it meant absolutely nothing to me. It was merely my way of smashing things up and breaking loose. I just had to get out of that house . . . because of you, because life had become intolerable. Yes, it was you who were the cause of it all. . . . What about the woman? you say. Well, you'd have laughed if you could have seen us in the hotel at Biarritz. Why, everybody thought I was her son, and she didn't dare say I wasn't. As a matter of fact, she didn't much mind . . . she was laughing at me the whole time . . . but I can't explain. . . ."

And when Michèle struck back with, "I wouldn't try, if I were you!" he assured her that it was the Curé and no one else who had mattered to Madame Voyod from beginning to end of the business. "She kept on talking about him: 'He'll be just about getting home now', she would say. 'He must have been told by this time. What will his first reaction be? D'you think he's capable of crying? Have you ever seen him cry?' Those were the questions she asked me. She wanted to play him a dirty trick, or to revenge herself on him. What for? Oh, I suppose the mere fact that he wears a soutane makes her want to hurt him. . . . However that may be, *I* didn't count for much with her."

Michèle replied that she was quite prepared to believe that the

woman had been laughing at him. But what she could never
forgive was that he had allowed himself to be caught like that.

To this burst of temper Jean replied with a show of tenderness.
It gave the measure of his exhaustion. "What's the good of arguing?" He realized, he said, that everything was over between
them. She didn't know what he had had to stand. There were
things he couldn't tell her. He had trusted her, believed the promise she had made to be faithful to him whatever happened. . . .
But naturally he understood now that she had over-estimated her
strength. A young girl shouldn't get mixed up with a fellow like
Jean de Mirbel. If she did, she ran the risk of being lost for ever.

"You're getting away from the point," insisted Michèle, who kept
on mulishly returning to the subject of the Voyod woman.

Jean groaned: "You don't understand. . . ."

But I, sitting there alone, and more or less outside the arena,
could see clearly into both their minds. Michèle was the victim
of the same sort of evil mood that used to afflict me on their account when I was little more than a child. She could never have
been sure that she had loved this emaciated young man whom
she scarcely recognized, were it not for the fact that he had
caused her so much pain during the last few weeks. And he, indifferent to her jealousy, was calling from the depths of his loneliness: "Take me as I am: I am sick; I am only a boy; take me,
look after me!" But she was deaf to his appeal. She had become a
woman, the kind of woman who cannot see beyond the outrage
done to the craving of her senses, a woman practical and positive.

"I'm really very sorry for you," she said. "To hear you speak, one
would think you were an outlaw . . . you, Jean de Mirbel."

He could find no answer to that, or rather, he could not find
the only words that might have broken down her obstinacy. He
was amazed that she should speak to him of his birth and fortune. . . . How could he make her see what was going on inside
him? that he was repudiating something, longing for something,
and had no idea what it was all about? . . . After a fairly long
silence, he said:

"Tell me, Michèle, why was it that I was always in trouble at
school, always being pointed at? Why did my brute of an uncle
want to break my spirit? . . . As I said before, there are things
you know nothing about."

"What things?" she asked.

He shook his head: not, as I supposed, as a sign that he couldn't answer, but to free himself of an image by which, as he told me later when we had become inseparable, he was obsessed at the time of which I am writing: the picture of a narrow street in Balauze, of nettles growing against the wall of the Cathedral, of the stocky figure of a man at a window, of the white, wraith-like form of a woman who could scarcely find room to slip between his shoulder and the wall.

After another silence, he went on: "I must give you back . . . you know what, surely?" He was thinking of the locket.

She protested: "No, keep it!"

But he had already undone his collar, and was trying to take off the chain. After a bit of fumbling he gave up, sat down, and remained, saying nothing, his head drooped forward.

I did not notice at once that he was crying, but it was to his tears that Michèle at last surrendered. They had moved no nearer to one another. This visible sign of a misery at whose cause she could not guess overcame Michèle's resistance, though she had stood out against everything else. She had not forgotten a single one of her grievances. She would have a whole lifetime in which to brood on them. She would add many others to them, storing up ammunition for future quarrels. But he was crying, and this she found impossible, physically impossible, to bear.

She went close to him and, bending down, wiped away his tears with her diminutive handkerchief. At the same time she laid her hand on his head.

Though I had turned away, I could see what was happening in the mirror. I saw, too, the door into the hall open. It remained open. No one came in. Jean de Mirbel had got up from his chair. Then, Brigitte Pian appeared, carrying a tray loaded with cups and bread-and-butter. I realized that she must have put it down on the chest in order to open the door.

Only her lips smiled, and she looked at us from a pair of sombre eyes.

❧ XVI ❧

SHE served tea with an eagerness of humility very different from the eagerness she had displayed when it was her object to edify us in the old days. Or perhaps I should say that if some concern for our edification was still discernible in her attitude, it made less impression on me than did my feeling, which increased as time went on, that her nature was, as it were, turning back upon itself. People do not change. At my age one can have no illusions on that point: but they do quite often turn back to what they were once and show again those very characteristics they have striven tirelessly, through a whole lifetime, to suppress. This does not mean that they necessarily end by succumbing to what is worst in themselves. God is very often the good temptation to which many human beings in the long run yield.

This was not at once the case with Brigitte Pian, although we were to see her, under the abbè Calou's influence, rid herself in the course of a few weeks of her old tendency to dominate. Clearly, she was seeking the sources of a deep, personal religion. But it was precisely in those things that she was now trying to suppress that she had formerly found that religion, in all that could satisfy her craving to direct others—to rule. She had always been unwilling to take second place to no matter whom in purity of intention or perfection of virtue.

I can see her still, upright in the middle of that hideous room, a cup of tea in each hand. During the few moments in which she imposed the fact of her presence on us, everything that separated Jean from Michèle and from me vanished. We formed a compact block of youth confronted by an aging woman. Three stars that are separated by vast distances of space may seem to be quite close to one another when seen in relation to a fourth, more distant, star.

She looked at us with a sort of hungry concentration. At first I did not understand its full significance.

"We're on top all right now, she'll have to give in!" exclaimed Michèle as soon as our stepmother had left the room. But no, that was not what chiefly emerged from this incident. It is true that Jean was asked, in the most friendly tone possible, to remember us to his mother. Brigitte even went so far as to express a hope that he would let us hear from him when he got to England, which was tantamount to admitting his right to correspond with my sister. This seeming defeat showed its true significance only in the course of the two or three years that elapsed before I went off to Paris. During all that time Jean wrote regularly, several times a week, to Michèle from Cambridge. To say that our stepmother acquiesced in all this is to put the matter too mildly.

Every day she studied the girl's face, trying to read in it whether she had received a letter, and whether it had told of pain or happiness. Not one detail of this love affair, of this interminable succession of storms and stresses, the story of which I must some day tell, was lost on Brigitte Pian.

"She is pleased when I suffer," complained Michèle. But that was not true. Brigitte was not pleased, only interested, passionately concerned.

Another thing that Michèle said was: "Now that she can no longer torment anybody, she has become like those people who find their only sexual satisfaction in watching others make love. . . ." And that I found nearer to the truth. The whole centre of Brigitte Pian's interest in life had shifted. She no longer worked at her old task, adding link by link to the armour of her false perfection. Consequently, she had time now to study others, to observe the strange game they played under the name of love, that game from which, for so long, she had averted her gaze in horror, without attempting to fathom the mysteries the word conceals.

Michéle, so far from being touched by the interest that our stepmother was showing in her, suspected every kind of evil intention, and was careful not to reveal anything that concerned her relations with Jean. But Brigitte interpreted in her own way the girl's fits of ill-temper, and drew her own conclusions from her least sigh, and even from her periods of silence.

Doubtless she was more regular now than she had been in her religious duties, and may even have taken the sacrament more often, for her scruples had at last vanished. But from now on she led two lives. When she was not in church, she spent her time exploring a world which had no connection with the one illuminated by Grace. At the age of fifty she had suddenly discovered the joys of imaginative literature, and I often came on her in my room taking down some book from the shelves. Her method of reading was more like eating—like the greedy eating of a child who stuffs its mouth with food. She had to make up so much time that she had wasted on printed nonsense, the worthlessness of which she was too intelligent not to have realized at the time. I remember the way in which, in the old days, she used to open the regular parcel of "Good Family Reading". She would pick out some volume at random, turn several pages at once, sigh, shrug. Now she showed a similar eagerness in her approach to

Adolphe, Le Lis dans la vallée, Anna Karenina. I indulged her taste for books that dealt in the precise analysis of sentiment. All love-stories appealed to her, provided they did not falsify reality. In just such a way will a man condemned to lead a sedentary life cram himself with tales of travel, but always with a keen eye for the veracity of the writer. She scarcely ever saw the abbé Calou now. The attempt to get permission for him to occupy himself with a "cure of souls" at Souys had come to nothing. Already he was suspected in high places (though quite wrongly) of being responsible for certain venomous comments in *The Battle* on the diocesan administration. He was one of those innocent souls who cannot always resist the temptation to say something amusing, the kind of man who would rather be hanged than miss the chance of some biting rejoinder. Unfortunately for him, the man who had succeeded Cardinal Lecot in the office made illustrious by the Primates of Aquitaine was a cleric of limited intelligence, who therefore became an implacable foe. One of these days I may, perhaps, tell the story of the sainted abbé Calou's road to Calvary. He was already on the point of being suspended, and wore out Brigitte Pian with the tale of his miseries. But it was to talk of herself and not of him that she made the necessary train journey. She always came back from these trips in a disappointed frame of mind. But by next day she had forgotten all about it, and would concentrate her attention once again on Michèle's love affair, or become completely absorbed in some book which she read far into the night.

Not that the pharisee was dead in her. She took pride in the very clarity of mind which enabled her to sit in judgment upon herself and condemn her own conduct. She did not believe that there were many instances of a Christian woman capable at fifty of realizing that her feet had been set on the wrong road. Not that she ever admitted in so many words that she would like never again to meddle in the affairs of her neighbours. Sometimes she would be caught up into a mood of deep nostalgia when she remembered the years gone by. One day it happened that we had just come back from the funeral of my old trustee Maître Malbec. He had been carried from the house of his mistress with his mouth twisted sideways. His affairs were in bad shape, for, unknown to all, he had led a very dissipated life. "All the same", said Brigitte as we were driving home, "he did live." I protested.

Was that what she called living? My stepmother seemed to be embarrassed by my question, and assured me that I had mistaken her meaning. One said of a man that he had lived when he had done things on the grand scale; that was all she had meant to say. I do not doubt for a moment that she was sincere. My studious existence was a matter of surprise to her. "All men are beasts", she said more than once, not in her old, bitter tone, but with a smile. When I settled in Paris to read for a degree in political science, I had to endure endless sessions of acute, subtle questioning whenever I returned to Bordeaux for a short visit. She was convinced that I was leading a life of intrigue and smouldering passion, and she kept up a regular correspondence with the Comtesse de Mirbel of which Jean and I were the constant theme (for, from 1910 on, my old friend had joined me in the capital). Here, too, I must refrain from anticipating the story of these Paris years, though I may tell it later. I will mention one incident only, and that because Brigitte was mixed up in it, and because it illustrated the sudden flowering of the extraordinary change that had come over her.

Very early my mind began to play round the idea of marriage. The thought had obsessed me ever since the days when I was quite a boy, and it still did so at that time of my life when I was better placed than thousands of young men to try my hand at winning happiness. It was due to my fear of losing my way in the chaotic wilderness of my sensibilities. I might well have applied to myself the wise words of Nietzsche which he wrote about the French seventeenth century: "It contained much of wildness, much too of that will to asceticism which was so necessary if it was to remain master in its own house."

One day a friend spoke to me of his cousin, a young woman of wealth, who had spent all her childhood in a world inhabited by writers and painters. He extolled her charms, and I snapped at the hook almost as soon as it was dangled before me. Living as I did in such close communion with God, believing as I did that nothing ever happened to me which did not spring from His direct purpose, and that no one could cross my path without being, in some sense, a delegate of the Infinite, I was prepared to find in this young woman an angel of liberation. *Their eyes all full of light, they walk before me. . . .*

As it turned out, this girl, whom I saw as a sort of combination of Madonna and Muse, hesitated a great deal longer and was far

less easy to capture than I had either expected or wished. She
was anxious not to make up her mind until she had travelled
extensively in Europe. My love was, on the whole, flattered by
the thought of our coming separation and by my knowledge of
her perplexities, which I regarded as a merit in one who lived always in the regions of the sublime.

So taken up was I by this idea of sublimity that I quite failed
to see her as she was: a rich, middle-class young woman who
was in no hurry to bind herself by a definite engagement, who
carefully weighed the pros and cons of the situation, with a wary
eye on me. It was known that I had money, but my family came
from the provinces and was no more than decently respectable.
Did I represent someone who could be relied on? Her parents
belonged to a world of sophisticated Parisians who knew that art
and literature represented no bad investment. . . . Even in those
days they were taking a chance on Matisse. But was I a sound
proposition? They could not make up their minds, were suspicious
of my impatience, and regarded me as, on the whole, a great
blockhead—which I was. They did all they could, therefore, to
keep me hanging on. When I threatened to give up the whole
idea, they redoubled their friendliness. My stepmother had picked
up some disturbing rumours about their medical history, and they
went so far as to beg me to go and see their doctor, whom they
had, so to speak, released for the occasion from his oath of professional secrecy.

That ridiculous, rather sordid errand of mine seems now like a
dream. I have a picture of myself facing, from behind his desk,
the eminent practitioner who waited, icily polite, to answer the
questions I wanted to put to him. The whole business ended in a
final family conclave from which I emerged definitely engaged,
and received from the young woman a rapturous letter. But by
the next day the whole situation had changed, and I found myself
cast off without a word of excuse or explanation. I blamed myself.
The fact was clear to me that, in spite of all the solid proofs of
my worthiness which I could produce, she did not like me. In
view of this check to my hopes, every other encouraging sign went
for nothing. Something about me, I did not know what, had
come between me and the Angelic Being. Was it a sign in me of
the incurable romanticism of youth? The men of my generation
were born with a sense of personal guilt. They imagined that
they were destined for a life of solitude and despair.

I told my stepmother, without going into details, that my engagement had been broken off. I had expected a letter of condolence from her, but what was my surprise to see her arrive in person on my doorstep! She seemed to have taken my misfortune very much to heart. She carried her attitude of pity to excess, and gave me to understand that she feared I might have contemplated some desperate act. Her tactless efforts at cheerfulness bored me. They also had the effect of making me realize that I was considerably less unhappy than I had seemed to be in the first moments of disappointment. I saw that what I was really suffering from was wounded vanity. Brigitte took me back with her to Larjuzon. I felt that she resented the fact that I was being so reasonable. But all through that tropical summer of 1911 the evidence was too plain for her to mistake. Far from being mortally wounded by my disaster in love, I found it a stimulus, and was driven by a wild desire to get what compensation I could from life. That summer I found a wonderful antidote in the prolonged reading of Balzac. An author is neither moral nor immoral in himself. It is our own attitude of mind that decides what his influence on us is to be. In my then state of mind, Balzac put me in love with life, though at the same time he infected my still childish mind with a strong dose of cynicism. I was enchanted by the coldly calculating tricks and subterfuges of his young heroes.

It was about this time that Brigitte began to cut herself adrift from me. I had disturbed the idea of love that she had built up for herself. There was nothing she had come to dislike more in anyone than an absence of passion. She could not bear to think that I had recovered from my disappointment so quickly. She did not dare admit this to me, but I could feel that she suspected me of not belonging to the true race of tormented lovers. I did not then know how far her self-deception had gone.

Michèle spent the summer vacation of 1911 with the Mirbels at La Devize. The only resource, therefore, left to me and my stepmother was reading. Her gloom deepened. Already she had begun to grow slack in the performance of her religious duties. Her talk was more and more concerned with one subject only. Human passion had become an obsession with her. Occasionally she spoke to me of my mother in a tone of hostility that betrayed both admiration and envy. But for the most part she remained silent, lying on the verandah, a faint flush staining the dead white of her face.

I have always had a horror of neurasthenics, and that year I
welcomed the necessity of having to go back to Paris. It was a
way of escape. I still wrote to my stepmother, but our letters
were trivial and colourless. Michèle, who was planning to marry
Jean after he had done his two years of military service, was still
living at the Cours de l'Intendance. In her letters to me she mentioned "something quite unbelievable that has happened to
Brigitte", but waited to tell me what it was until she should come
to Paris, where she was due to stay with the Mirandieuzes.

When at last I heard the details, the whole thing did indeed
seem so unbelievable that I could do nothing at first but shrug my
shoulders. I thought that Michèle was giving rein to her imagination when she told me that my stepmother had fallen in love with
her doctor, a man well on in his sixties. But at Bordeaux I was confronted by evidence that would not be denied. It was not merely a
question of a sick old woman developing a liking for her medical
attendant. No, she had fallen a prey to a fierce, exclusive, and
(what was really odd) a thoroughly happy and reciprocated passion. Not that there was anything "wrong" in their relations. Dr.
Gellis, a fervent Huguenot with a practice that included all the
best Protestant families of the city, was beyond the reach of any
scandal. But, separated from a wife who had dragged his name
in the mud, and plagued by a horde of children, most of whom
were married, embittered, and needy, it had been a matter of delight for him to discover in the evening of his days that he had
become an object of exclusive concern to a woman who was far
stronger-minded and better fitted to face life than he was. He
saw her every day, and took no decisions without first consulting
her. The two lonely old things were perfectly unashamed about
talking of their mutual attachment, and it never seemed to occur
to them that they were making themselves ridiculous. They found
in each other's faces not the signs of old age, but of tenderness.
They lived for one another like two old innocents, blissfully unaware that their irritated relatives were laughing at them, and
that the neighbours were gossiping at their expense.

It was the last year of Jean's military service, and his marriage
was to take place in October. The families exchanged dinners, and
the contract was drawn up. Brigitte Pian had to act to Michèle as
a mother, but did so with a bad grace. Her stepdaughter's passion
no longer interested her. What chiefly worried her was the imprudent promise she had made to divide the family estate during her

lifetime. This was a sacrifice that she had once gladly envisioned
as, in some sort, making up for the wrong she had done the girl.
Brigitte's personal fortune was less than ours. She scarcely had
enough capital left (though she realized it too late) to enable her
to buy a small property adjoining Dr. Gellis's clinic. The Comtesse
de Mirbel expressed it as her view that this "entirely changed the
whole situation. . . ." In her eyes, the loss of half a million francs
only underlined the fact that her son was making a mésalliance.
Brigitte played deaf, pretended not to understand the hints, but
avoided any open warfare and anything that might have disturbed
her strange, deep happiness. This happiness, seen in terms of the
human figure, was a stout gentleman of sixty-odd years, with
short legs. He wore a tight-fitting frock-coat and had a dyed beard
which, taken in conjunction with his austere gestures and bald
head, gave him a certain resemblance to the Chancellor Michel
de l'Hôpital. He talked a great deal and listened to no one except
Brigitte, though she preferred to stay silent so as not to lose a
single word that might drop from the lips of the beloved. Most of
their conversation was concerned with serious subjects, not excluding theology. She showed herself responsive to the logic of Cal-
vinism, though neither gave the least sign of wishing to convert
the other, either because of a mutual tenderness for their respective beliefs, or because they were no longer greatly interested in
the matter of creeds. Age made them conscious of the value of
every fleeting moment. Not a minute must be diverted from the
one essential thing—their love for one another.

From now on Brigitte's life and ours lay apart. I got out of the
habit of dropping in at the Cours de l'Intendance when I visited
Bordeaux. My room had become a pied-à-terre for Dr. Gellis on
those evenings when he took Brigitte to the theatre or to a concert and slept in town. Their love of music was a great bond. The
doctor had no car, but sported one of those ancient broughams
that say "doctor" a mile off. It took a long time to cover the distance between the town and his clinic.

It is not always the case that graybeards fall for young girls, or
aging women for growing youths. It sometimes happens that a
man and a woman who have vainly sought one another through a
long life meet by chance when the shadows begin to fall. When
that happens, their passion takes on a peculiarly intense quality of
isolation. Nothing else seems to matter. There is so little time left!
The world may laugh, but, then, the world knows little of the se-

crets of the heart. When I did pay one of my infrequent visits to the Cours de l'Intendance, Brigitte's attitude to me was one almost of pity. I, not she, was the one who stood in need of sympathy. The old, formidable side of her character still showed at times when she conjured up the memory of my mother or of the Puy-barauds; of all those people whom she no longer needed to envy, who, unlike her, had never known the delights of a love that was truly shared. The sight of that cruel flame flickering beneath the thick eyebrows that almost met across Brigitte's forehead got on my nerves, and I was goaded into dropping allusions to the kind of love that she would never know. I had discovered a chink in the armour of her proud and throned emotion. Passion, I hinted, is but the ghost of itself when it cannot take bodily form. So long as we cannot lose and find ourselves again in the beloved, we merely intoxicate ourselves with words and with the gestures of love, but we can never know whether what we have is the reality.

Brigitte broke in upon my monologue: "You don't know what you're saying, what you're talking about. . . ."

Her face had assumed the same familiar expression of disgust as in the old days whenever the forbidden subject was mentioned in her hearing. I have a feeling of remorse now when I think that I may have spoiled their happiness with these insinuations of mine because, about the time that I was indulging in these bouts of rhetoric, I learned from Michèle of occasional stormy scenes between Philemon and his Baucis. Could it be that Brigitte was conscious of regret? Could it be that she made certain demands upon her lover? One dares not attempt to visualize the squalid little efforts and contortions of those two bodies whose powers had not kept pace with the sentiments that stirred them. When youth suffers (as I was suffering then) it cannot bear the sight of age's placid contentment.

Dr. Gellis had his children and the parents of his grandchildren for ever yapping at his heels. The purchase of the little property adjoining the clinic, which Brigitte concluded on the day before Michèle's marriage, set a match to the powder barrel. One of the pastors of Bordeaux made representations to the doctor, while his family begged Michèle to persuade her stepmother to see some priest in whom she had confidence, and to whose criticism she would listen. This was just about the time that the abbé Calou had been deprived of the right to say Mass. Since, however, he was merely suspended and not excommunicated, his poor, humiliated soutane could be seen among the black dresses of the old women each morning when communion was administered in the small chapel that stands close to the Faculty of Letters. He would go back to his seat followed by the curious or pitying glances of the congregation, and his face was as the face of an angel.

The Gellis family had no time in which to enlist his help. To use one of the cruel and futile sayings of which the Comtesse de Mirbel was so fond—"the whole thing was taken out of their hands". One evening, close to the clinic, a motor-car struck the doctor's brougham a glancing blow. He was killed on the spot. My stepmother saw the news next day in the paper. A number of no doubt highly coloured stories spread through the town to the effect that Brigitte Pian had arrived, haggard and hatless, at the house where the Gellis children were living. It was said that the eldest son had tried to keep her out of the room where the body lay, but that she had thrust him aside, had broken through the barriers erected in her path by the rest of the family, and had thrown herself upon the corpse with never a tear or a cry, and that she had had to be pulled away by main force.

I was living at that time with friends at Cap Martin. I did not feel that so unofficial a case of mourning necessitated my presence. I merely wrote a letter. It was a difficult letter to compose, and it remained unanswered. But Michèle and Jean were away in Algeria on their honeymoon, and the thought of Brigitte haunted me. It was not in my power just then to make the trip to Bordeaux in order to assure myself that my stepmother had not gone out of her mind. I was due back in Paris. I therefore postponed the difficult duty until the beginning of spring.

The servant did not know me, and I was left waiting in the hall. I could hear my stepmother's exclamation: "But of course! Show him in." I was much relieved to find that her voice sounded as usual. She was sitting in her accustomed place by the writing-table, which was no longer, as of old, littered with circulars and invitations to charity sales. She had grown no older in appearance. I noticed, after the first few minutes, that she had gone back to the old way of doing her hair—raised high, puffed out with numberless little curls, and so arranged as to leave her large ears and well-modelled forehead free. A photograph of Dr. Gellis stood on the mantelpiece, shaded by a bunch of lilacs. There was nothing about Madame Brigitte to indicate nervous disturbance or mental unbalance. Her shoulders were covered by a knitted woollen shawl. As I came in, she had just put back on her desk the rosary she had always used when I was a child. She began the conversation by apologizing for not having answered my letter. She made no attempt to deceive me, but said that for several days she had been in a condition of prostration from which she had recovered only with considerable difficulty.

"And now?" I asked.

She looked at me thoughtfully. "If Monsieur Puybaraud were here, he would insist that you were the only person capable of understanding. . . ."

There was calm certainty in her smile. "You see, the real, secret truth is that I have not lost him . . . but there is no one I can tell. Dear Monsieur Gellis was never so close to me as he is now, not even when he was alive. He had already embarked on his mission to me while he was in this world, but we are all of us poor mortal flesh, and our bodies were a barrier. But there is nothing between us now."

She talked at length on this theme, and at first I suspected a trick of sorrow seeking to cheat death of the dear doctor. But at the end of a few days I realized that the sun of human love had not risen too late on the arid destiny of this woman of the Pharisees, that the "whited sepulchre" had been unsealed and stood open at last. Perhaps it still contained a few dried bones, a trace of corruption. Occasionally the formidable eyebrows met in a frown above the smouldering eyes. Some grievance, long mulled over, now and then brought a bitter word to her lips. But "dear Monsieur Gellis" was never far away, was always there at the critical moment to lead Brigitte Pian into the calm ways of God.

An urgent letter from the Comtesse de Mirbel called me to La Devize, where Michèle and Jean were going to return, some considerable time before they were expected. This hurried return of theirs worried me. I set off without delay, and was at once caught up into their drama, the story of which I shall some day tell. I became the satellite of their system, and was whirled about in the constant eddy of strife and reconciliation that made up their existence. I had no leisure in which to think of the old woman I had left in the Cours de l'Intendance, embalmed, as it were, in the posthumous adoration of "dear Monsieur Gellis". It was my

strange destiny to become the go-between for Jean and Michèle—continually warding off the blows that they blindly aimed
at one another—a role especially strange for a young man who
had his own private misery and suffered in a solitude that no one
in the world could break.

The mobilisation of August 2nd, 1914, woke us from our dream.
That thunder-clap disturbed thousands of personal dramas, all of
them much like our own. We struggled up from the depths of our
dark passions, all our saps destroyed, stupefied and dazed by an
appalling disaster which was so infinitely greater than the one
we were inflicting on ourselves. I left Jean and Michèle, who, now
that they were to lose one another, could do themselves no further
hurt, and faced the full extremity of my loneliness when I realized
that there was no one in the world, except Brigitte, to whom I
could even say good-bye.

She looked small now, and had grown thin. She drew me to
her, and her tears surprised me. The name of Dr. Gellis was
never once mentioned between us. She looked after me as a
mother might have done. I found out later that she was seeing
a great deal of Monsieur Calou at this time, and was doing much
to help him. He had been taken back into favour by the diocesan
authorities, but was already near his end.

All the time I was at the Front I was overwhelmed with parcels
and letters and with inquiries about my health and my needs. I
spent my first leave with Madame Brigitte. A few days before it
fell due, Monsieur Calou had died in her arms. She told me about
it quite unemotionally, and without making any attempt to point
a lesson. Monsieur Calou, she said, had certainly not grown less
in spiritual stature, though towards the end he had scarcely been
of this world. He had suffered from agonizing attacks of angina
pectoris—the kind that drive the sufferer to the open window in
a terrifying struggle for air. But as soon as he had recovered his
breath, he would say that he was ready for still greater suffering.
He had on his table a photograph that I had taken long ago in
the kitchen-garden at Baluzac. It showed Jean and Michèle, bare-
footed, their eyes screwed up against the sun, clinging to the same
watering can. Brigitte added that, in spite of the pain he had to
endure, he never gave one a feeling of pity.

When I alluded to past events, she talked of them quite openly.
But I could feel that she had become detached from even the
consciousness of her faults, and that she had decided to lay

everything at the throne of the Great Compassion. In the evening
of her life, Brigitte Pian had come to the knowledge that it is
useless to play the part of a proud servitor eager to impress his
master by a show of readiness to repay his debts to the last
farthing. It had been revealed to her that our Father does not
ask us to give a scrupulous account of what merits we can claim.
She understood at last that it is not our deserts that matter but
our love.